# JESSI

# JESSIE PHILLIPS

## A TALE OF THE PRESENT DAY

*Mrs Fanny Trollope*

NONSUCH

First published 1843


Nonsuch Publishing Limited
The Mill, Brimscombe Port, Stroud, Gloucestershire, GL5 2QG
www.nonsuch-publishing.com

For comments or suggestions, please email the editor of this series at:
classics@tempus-publishing.com

Nonsuch Publishing Ltd is an imprint of Tempus Publishing Group



British Library Cataloguing in Publication Data.
A catalogue record for this book is available from the British Library.

ISBN 1-84588-203-2

Typesetting and origination by Nonsuch Publishing Limited
Printed in Great Britain by Oaklands Book Services Limited

# CONTENTS

# Introduction to the Modern Edition

> For you have the poor with you always, and whenever you wish you may do them good
>
> Mark 14:7

The framers of the Poor Law Amendment Act 1834 doubtless thought that they were doing a 'good thing'. The purpose of the Act was to reform the numerous laws relating to the 'management' of the poor, and in particular the Act for the Relief of the Poor 1601, in order to create a standardised and centralised system, overseen by the three Poor Law Commissioners, based at Somerset House in London. This new system for the relief of poverty would, in theory, ensure fairness in the way such relief was distributed, by imposing the same rules on everyone throughout England and Wales (Scotland and Ireland had different arrangements), but, in practice, it meant that most paupers either had to live in the workhouse, which meant submitting not only to a harsh regime but also to a social stigma, or die outside it.

Under the 'Old Poor Law' (comprising the various acts passed before 1834), provision of relief to the poor was a local matter, to be administered by individual parishes as they saw fit. It was paid for by the poor rate, a tax on local landowners based on the value of their property, and entailed the maintenance of orphans, the elderly and those who were unable to work; the provision of work for those who were able to do it (and placing those who refused it in 'houses of correction'); and the education of orphaned children to a trade. Under the Settlement Act 1662, relief could only be afforded to those who had established residence in the parish, which often led to people being moved from parish to parish by the local authorities to prevent them from becoming eligible and, therefore, a financial burden. Mothers of illegitimate children were required to name the father, who was responsible in law for its maintenance (although this was a responsibility they often contrived to avoid). During the eighteenth century workhouses (as opposed to the poorhouses and almshouses that they succeeded) began to be established, particularly after Knatchbull's Act 1723, which created the concept of the 'workhouse test:' paupers would only receive relief if they came into the workhouse, so that only those who really needed relief would apply for it. Gilbert's Act 1782 allowed parishes to join together to form a 'union,' overseen by a board of guardians, with a common workhouse; able-bodied paupers would not be admitted to the workhouse, but work would be found for them and their wages subsidised by the union.

Neither the rich nor the poor were especially happy with this system and, in 1832, a Royal Commission was established to examine it. It reported in 1834, blaming poverty on the poor rather than on economic or social conditions and recommending the workhouse test be adopted for separating out the 'deserving' and 'undeserving' poor; conditions in workhouses were, in short, to be made as undesirable as possible to prevent anyone other than the truly desperate from seeking relief. The Amendment Act, adopting its recommendations and creating the Poor Law Commission, was passed later the same year. The intention of the Act was to create a uniform system for the relief of poverty, with decisions taken by the Commissioners in London and allowing the local boards of guardians little discretion. Controversially, the so-called 'Bastardy Clause' removed any legal responsibility for an illegitimate child from its father and placed it all upon the mother. The Act met with considerable opposition. *The Times* of 30 April 1834 (a few months before it received the Royal Assent) asserted that it would 'disgrace the statute-book' and some boards of guardians refused to implement the legislation. Charles Dickens' *Oliver Twist* (1837) was written to highlight the suffering of the poor under the 'New Poor Law,' and remains a memorial to its inhumanity. Those paupers who 'passed' the workhouse test found themselves living in cramped and unhygenic conditions—they had to survive on a bare subsistence diet, families were broken up, and the whole system was open to abuse by those who administered it.

The fact that the Poor Law Amendment Act had done little or nothing to improve the condition of the poor, and often made it worse, did not escape the notice of Frances Trollope (1779–1863). Mother of the novelist Anthony Trollope, she began writing in order to support her family and wrote forty-one books in total, both fiction and non-fiction. Her novels addressed social concerns: *Michael Armstrong: Factory Boy* (1840), the first industrial novel to be published in Britain and the first monthly serial to be written by a woman, paints a picure of child labour in an industrialised society, while the evils of slavery are the theme of *Jonathan Jefferson Whitlaw* (1836). *Jessie Phillips*, first published in monthly numbers from 1842–43 and as a novel in 1844, is a blistering attack on the way in which the New Poor Law was oblivious to the individual, and especially how the Bastardy Clause allowed men to father illegitimate children without any regard for the consequences of their actions. The unfairness of a law which allowed a man to seduce a woman, father a child and then if he so wished, deny even having met her—let alone require him to marry her or pay maintenance—is manifest in the treatment Jessie receives following her seduction. Despite her previous popularity and good character, the majority of the citizens of Deepbrook assume that she is entirely responsible for the situation in which she finds herself; while there is no suggestion of rape, Jessie is unlikely to have conceived a child on her own, and yet her seducer is protected by the full majesty of the law. The original intention of the legislators was to prevent women of 'loose morals' from having a child and then claiming that the richest man in the parish was the father, in order to claim money, but the end result was that women like Jessie were left in an impossible situation.

Not only was the Bastardy Clause unpopular, it was also ineffective: illegitimacy became more common after 1834, not less. In 1844 Parliament passed another Poor Law Amendment Act, making illegitimacy a matter for the civil courts rather than the parish authorities, and the Bastardy Act 1845 enabled mothers of illegitimate children to petition petty sessions for an order of affiliation. Perhaps it is no coincidence that such legislation was enacted shortly after the publication of *Jessie Phillips*, a story that describes that unfairness of the Poor Laws in even more stark terms than *Oliver Twist*. These changes were, however, comparatively minor in relation to the defficiencies of the Poor Laws as a whole, and it was not until the National Health Service Act 1948 and the creation of the modern welfare state that the provision of assistance to those in need was properly reformed.

The era when the poor could be effectively imprisoned in workhouses for no greater crime than being poor, and illegitimacy was a stigma that ruined lives, is now long past, in Britain at least. Books like Mrs Trollope's *Jessie Phillips*, however, are an effective reminder of how such unfair measures as the Poor Laws blighted the existence of thousands if not millions of people, and such reminders are important if we are to avoid making the same mistakes again, for

> A nation's greatness is measured by how it treats its weakest members.
>
> Mahatma Ghandi

# I

*London life—"my dear native village"—the parish church—the leading families at Deepbrook—Lady Mary Weyland—Squire Dalton—Lewis Lodge—gentry of the village*

HOW MANY OF US ARE there who, though brought by the irresistible current of circumstances to pass the greater part of our existence in London, still treasure fondly in our memories a whole host of rural recollections, impressed upon us, perhaps, during almost the earliest years of childhood, yet resting with more distinctness on our minds than any of the scenes that have come afterwards! How many a pale artisan may there be at this moment pent into some of the closest little workshops in London, before whose mental eye rises a bright green picture of the village where he was born—greener and brighter, it may be, than ever pastoral poet painted, or the educated imagination of all the great ones of the earth could produce! There is at times a sort of morbid activity in the fancy, created by the fever of privation, which will bring before us, with all the distinctness of a steel engraving, scenes that have been loved and lost for ever. Ask those whose souls sicken under the process that produces this, if they would wish this painful power to wither and perish within them; and though it has wrung their hearts and brought iron tears down cheeks bleached both by sin and suffering, they will still answer—No! This propensity in all men to live through their village days again in memory cheers me with the hope that I may be able to create some interest among them, while recounting an "o'er true story," the scene of which lies in one of the most thoroughly rural districts of England.

The gay-looking, nicely whitewashed, flowery little village of Deepbrook is situated in one of those favoured midland counties where factories are unknown, and where any passing stranger might fancy that enough of rural occupation would be found in the cultivation of the fertile soil, in attendance upon the lowing herds that in springtime peep out from among their abounding pasture as if playing at bo-peep with all who look at them, and in the multitude of profitable offices demanded by at least half-a-dozen good houses scattered round the village. Any stranger, looking at all this, might fancy that if there was a spot of earth where people might hope to live in peace and plenty, it was the beautiful little village of Deepbrook.

And peace and plenty there certainly were in the village; but not quite in every part of it. Perhaps the cases where these precious blessings failed the most, were produced, in the first instance, by these very blessings themselves, or, rather, by the abuse of them. The little village of Deepbrook was too prosperous. There were so many pretty gentlemen's places in the neighbourhood, all kept neat and trim; and so many nice young ladies that wanted a little needlework done, or a little nice washing got up; and so many young gentlemen that, in the vacations of school or college, liked to have a handy lad go fishing, or shooting, or boating, or skating with them, that a little money was easily got, and the young people grew presumptuous upon it. With the thoughtless courage and light-hearted calculations of young men and maidens, they often came to the conclusion that they should find it very easy to maintain a family, and so they married young—too young by at least ten years—losing thereby the happiest portion of existence, and doing all they could towards turning the pleasant village of Deepbrook into a very unpleasant one.

And now, having said enough to give my readers some idea of the place where most of the adventures happened that I am going to relate, I must proceed to give a sketch of some of the people who lived there, in order to make the events which follow more clearly understood.

The parish church should, in every village, be as near to the centre of it as possible,—and so it was at Deepbrook. The few straggling buildings, which seemed as if they had run away from the quiet village green, at one corner of which the holy building stood, to the highroad leading to London, in order to be near the gay world, were the only dwellings in the parish that were not within a mile of its church. These buildings consisted of the two principal inns; a tolerably large brewhouse, which furnished yeast to all the countryside; the substantial dwelling of the wealthy brewer and his five handsome sons; and three or four ugly brick cottages, all in a row, the inhabitants of which by no means bore the best of characters; so that, on the whole, it was pretty generally the opinion of the gentry and commonalty of Deepbrook that this section of the queen's highway did them more good than harm by the attractive influence it exercised; and "High Street," as this said section of the parish was denominated, was considered much in the light of a safety-valve, that tended greatly to insure the safety of the parish.

The centrical little church had very close to it a centrical parsonage, but by no means a little one, for the house was among the best in the parish; and so happily shut in on all sides by a perfect ring-fence of forest-trees, the provident legacy of some long-departed rector, that, by the additional help of its fine garden-shrubs, it was in a state to defy all the winds of heaven and all the eyes of earth; and thus, though close to the church on one side, to the goose-common of the village, where there were no less than three very busy shops, on another, and flanked by one neighbour's grounds here, and by those of another there, the dwelling of the Reverend Edward Rimmington was exactly what that of our English country clergy ought to be—tranquil, gentlemanlike, and comfortable.

To the right of the rectory, were the very pretty house and the very pretty grounds of Lady Mary Weyland, the daughter of an earl and the widow of a baronet, but with a considerably smaller revenue than people gave her credit for, which she made the most of by confining its expenditure solely to her own use and benefit.

To the left was the mansion of Mr. Dalton, *the squire* of the parish *par excellence*, being not only the lord of the manor, but by far the largest landholder in it. If not the most picturesque, his house was by much the largest in the village, which was fortunate for the size of his family, which consisted of no less than ten daughters, with the moderate addition of one son.

As near the mansion of the squire as his little park, or paddock, would permit, was another of the good houses of Deepbrook, occupied by a Mr. Ferdinand Lewis, solicitor, a sensible, respectable personage, who had realised a snug little fortune of 12,000*l.* or 15,000*l.*, and was increasing it yearly, though not quite so much of late as heretofore; for he had two daughters, the pretty Mary and the pretty Lucy Lewis, who had recently returned from an *excellent* school at Clapham, exceedingly well disposed to do credit both to that and to their very indulgent papa, by making, in all ways, what they considered as a thoroughly respectable appearance. This was certainly a very praiseworthy inclination, but likely enough to lead to expense, when vigorously acted upon by very young ladies without a mother, and with a father knowing no more what young ladies ought to spend than his old spaniel.

Next to Lewis Lodge, stood an excellent house with good offices, gardens, and so forth, the property of the solicitor, but the dwelling of Henry Mortimer, Esq., barrister and assistant poor-law commissioner. This gentleman, who had recently been appointed, had fixed his residence at Deepbrook, as one of the most agreeable spots in his district, and where the Union work-house was one of the largest establishments of the kind in the midland districts, comprehending nineteen rather populous parishes, and being, moreover, important as the centre of a rich agricultural neighbourhood, comprehending one or two of the finest estates in the kingdom. The arrival of Mr. Mortimer at Deepbrook gave universal satisfaction. He was amiable, gentlemanlike, possessing various elegant acquirements, and one of the most even, pleasant tempers in the world. He, too, as well as his legal neighbour, was a widower, and, like him, had two very gay ladies making part of his family, namely, his sister and his daughter. The elder of the two, whose age, as she was still very handsome, it is quite useless to mention, was of course his sister. She was a lady blessed with a very brilliantly fair complexion, a good deal of rather Titian-like red hair, a very fine person, and 10,000*l.* Why she was not yet married, nobody seemed able to guess; though her niece, the bright-eyed Agatha, who was the other female embellishment of Mr. Mortimer's household, has been heard to hazard a suggestion on the subject. This young lady is of opinion that her aunt would certainly have been married years ago, had she not been ever, and always, so vehemently bent upon attaining this object, as "absolutely to frighten the people," and drive them away, before they had time to learn any certain facts respecting the nature and extent of her reputed fortune, and "before they had got over her red hair." Mr. Mortimer had also a son, a very fine young man, who had just taken a high degree at Oxford, and was now studying the law in the chambers of one of the first conveyancers in London.

Besides these *leading families* there were one or two more, of less importance; such as a half-pay captain in the navy, of the name of Maxwell, with a wife and daughter. The worthy little curate of Mr. Rimmington and his newly-married little wife; the apothecary and his maiden sister; and an old lady, the widow of a former rector, who lived in a miniature cottage of great beauty, upon an income of 200*l*. a-year.

Of these was the class denominated the gentry of Deepbrook composed. The commonalty can hardly hope for the honour of being enumerated by name, though it is possible that, by and bye, we shall know more about them. And for the nobility, it consisted almost entirely of the magnificent castle of the Duke of Rochdale, which certainly gave an air of dignity to the landscape wherever its lofty and commanding turrets became visible; but the family themselves had of late years been very rarely in the neighbourhood, having passed a considerable portion of every year on the Continent. And even when they did come, the only individual honoured by their personal notice was the venerable Mrs. Buckhurst, the above-mentioned widow of a former rector.

# II

*Breakfast party—family of Mr. Dalton—a young beauty—old maids—the cowslip field—the great dinner—guests invited to it—the ladies—the board of guardians—Mrs. Buckhurst*

"MOST CERTAINLY, MY DEAR: THE arrival of this commissioner is a monstrous advantage, not only to Deepbrook, but to the whole country round," said Mr. Dalton to his wife, as he stood at the bottom of his breakfast-table, cutting slices innumerable from an enormous ham. "I declare positively, that if they had not sent this Mr. Mortimer, or somebody else, holding the same situation, I should most positively have given up my place at the board of guardians. It is the greatest nuisance that a country gentleman can possibly be exposed to, that of being the member of a board with no assistant-commissioner near him."

"I daresay it must, my dear," replied his wife, perseveringly pursuing her occupation of putting sugar into ten breakfast-cups—for her seven eldest daughters and her son were seated round the breakfast-table.

"The girl is a great acquisition, too," said young Dalton, making a sign with one hand to his sister Louisa to give him an egg, and another equally expressive to his sister Georgina to give him a roll. "She has a devilish fine pair of eyes!"

"It would be more civil, my dear Frederic, if you were to say that both the young ladies were an acquisition," observed Mrs. Dalton, who, after resting herself for a moment by putting the palm of her left hand beneath the elbow of her right arm, was pouring cream into all the tea-cups.

"Both the *young* ladies!—both! Well done, Mrs. Dalton!" exclaimed her son, laughing violently. "The red-haired beauty ought to be told of your excessive politeness. I suppose you are looking forward to the time when eight or nine of your own daughters shall have reached the same delectable period of virgin maturity, and you are preparing a sort of *lex-talionis* beatitude for them, by doing to others as you would that others should do unto them. Why do you not all, as many as are here,—and that, unluckily, is just now only seven,—do you not all kneel down and kiss the hem of your mamma's garment, for her prospective kindness towards you?"

"I don't think we *shall* be all old maids, Frederic," said a very pretty nymph of fifteen, looking at him with considerable contempt.

"Don't you, Miss Caroline? I'll bet you five to one, that out of the whole budget there won't be more than two married at the very utmost."

"Well!" replied the young beauty, in no degree alarmed, "and if two are married, I shall be right; for, as I said before, we shall not be *all* old maids!"

"True, most true, you very wise young lady! But on reflection I repent me for having named the possible proportion with so much liberality. For there are no longer ten of you within the reach of chance. Poor sad, sober, silent Ellen has passed the Rubicon; she is doomed—nay, she is more than doomed—the sentence is executed, poor wretch, and Ellen is an old maid already!"

"What! at twenty-three and a half, Frederic? I do think that is rather too bad," said his mother, beginning assiduously to refresh her enormous tea-pot with a good deal more tea from the tea-chest, and a great deal more water from the tea-urn; "I never did hear of a girl's being called an old maid at twenty-three and a half."

"That, madam, is because you never happened to come in the way of such a dull, dismal, doleful maiden as the eldest Miss Dalton. There is a prodigious difference, I beg to assure you, in the facility with which one young lady becomes an old maid, when compared to another. Some of them go on struggling and striving to the very last gasp; and, horrible as it is to watch their sinking agonies, it is certain that their efforts are by no means absolutely useless, and of none effect. Your red-haired friend, for instance, Mrs. Dalton, though she has *now*, despite all her convulsive efforts to avert the doom, reached the point at which no one but your maternal self could blunder—that horrible bourne from which no girl returns, though she has at length reached this, I have no doubt whatever that at three-and-twenty and a half she had still the appearance of being almost young. But, then, you may be very sure that she worked hard for it. But, as for our poor, pale, pitiful Miss Ellen, I really believe that she is such a fool that she does not know the difference between being young and old."

"How should she, Fred?" demanded Miss Henrietta Dalton, aged sixteen and a quarter; "she has never been old yet."

"Speak for yourself, young lady, and give me one of those pigeons," replied her brother. "You are just on the very verge of the acclivity yourself. After seventeen you all, every one of you, some faster, some slower, begin going down hill. But down you do all go after seventeen, depend upon it."

"Did any human being ever hear such nonsense?" said the second Miss Dalton, aged nineteen, for the heir of the family was next in age to his eldest sister; "upon my word, Frederic, you talk quite like a fool."

"And that is true as truth can be, Mary," returned Henrietta, adding in a whisper to her eldest sister who sat beside her, "You don't mind him, Ellen, do you?"

"Not very much, dearest!" replied Ellen, gently kissing the rosy face that was brought close to hers; and as she said it, a smile so sweet lit up her somewhat too delicate cheek, that the beautiful Caroline, who, though she had already thought, perhaps, more of her own face than of any other, was, nevertheless, too much *au fait* of beauty in general, to be brow-beat on the subject even by her clever brother, exclaimed, "It is a capital good joke to be sure, isn't it, Henrietta, to hear Ellen called an old maid? Just look at her now, you stupid fellow! I do think she is prettier than any body I ever saw in my whole life—almost"

"The saving *almost* lets in your charming self, I suppose Miss Caroline," returned the young man, laughing loudly; "you think poor lamentable, lanky, listless Ellen, *beautiful,* because, as I well remember, every body said you were like her, before her woe-begone old face assumed the monumental alabaster hue that it wears now."

"I hope I shan't have a bit more colour than Ellen when I am quite grown up," replied Caroline. "I hate dairy-maid beauty."

"Oh! do you, my dear?" said her brother, leaving the table, and whistling to a dog that lay basking in the sun at a window. "And I hate a death's head upon a May-pole;" and so saying, he left the room, leaving no impression behind him, that he had been at all more rude or disagreeable than usual.

By this time most of the large party had concluded the morning meal, and Ellen and Henrietta were preparing to leave the room together, when Sophia, a fine laughing girl of ten, who was the youngest of the party present, arrested their steps as they were passing through the door by saying,—

"Oh, Ellen! Hetta! do not go to practise till you have asked mamma about the cowslip field. You know you promised us, Ellen,—and about Jessie Phillips, too, you know; because, if she is to carry for us, some of us (do let it be Georgy, and Matty, and me!),—some of us, you know, must run down to the cottage, and ask her mother to let her leave her work. Ask, Ellen, ask Ellen, will you? And remember Bella, Anna, and Clara, too."

The beautiful smile came again, and Ellen nodded and turned back to where her mother still sat, at the head of the breakfast-table. Indeed, it always happened that when a movement was to be made, Mrs. Dalton was ever the last part of the machinery that was put in motion. This might be partly owing to her great size, for she was immoderately fat; but partly, too, it was occasioned by the *vis inertiæ* of mind as well as matter; for this kind-hearted, excellent person, though ever ready to do any thing for the purpose of pleasing other people, knew no way of pleasing herself so effectual as by doing nothing.

"We have a favour to beg of you, dear mamma," said Ellen, looking neither sad, sober, nor silent, dull, dismal, nor doleful, lanky, lamentable, nor listless.

"And what is that, dear?" replied her mother, smiling at her in return.

"It is, that you would let us all, little ones and all, if you please, dearest mother, go into Mr. Rimmington's great meadow to gather cowslips; and that you will let Jessie Phillips be asked to carry them home."

"And then, I suppose, must follow a prodigious tea-drinking in the school-room, and Shepherd must set about making a few bushels of flour into cakes?"

"Yes, if you please, mamma," replied Ellen, laughing.

"And I would say yes, too, my dear, with all my heart, if you would only wait for it till the end of next week. Miss Barton will be at home again then, you know, and I think that would make it a great deal better for you, Ellen. I am sure you will be torn to pieces if they all set off upon such an expedition as this without their governess."

While Mrs. Dalton was still speaking, Sophia whispered to the petitioner, "The cowslips will be all gone!"

"The cowslips will be all gone, mamma," repeated Ellen; "and I do not mind being torn to pieces, now and then."

"That is very good-natured of you, my dear, considering your great age," returned her mother, looking at her very fondly; "and you may settle it all as you will, only take care that Shepherd is told in time."

This was enough; and the same active young arms which had before impeded the exit of Ellen and her musical pupil, now endeavoured to hasten it by pushing them forward towards the door with all their might.

"Stop, Ellen!—stop!" vociferated her father, raising his eyes from the newspaper upon which they had been fixed from the time they had completed his task of cutting half-a-dozen pounds of ham into thin slices. "You must not go, my dear, till you have written a note or two for mamma. Matilda, my love," added the squire, addressing his wife, "we must have this party that I have been talking of invited directly."

"What party, my dear?" returned Mrs. Dalton; "I don't remember."

"No, my dear, you never do remember any thing but your nursery and school-room. I told you before, my dear, and now I tell you again, that I want to have the commissioner, Mr. Mortimer, to dine here, to meet some of the board of guardians, and make him a little acquainted with the neighbourhood. Of course, every body will expect that I shall begin."

"And what day, my dear?" said Mrs. Dalton, hiding a prophetic yawn behind her napkin.

"Let me see. What day is to-day?—Wednesday. Well, then, let it be next Wednesday. That will be the 1st of June, you know."

"Will it, my dear?" returned Mrs. Dalton. "Ring the bell, Sophy; I suppose I had better get Shepherd up-stairs directly, if it's to be a great dinner."

Poor Sophia gave her two sisters a glance that spoke despair. And Ellen, who well knew that if the "great dinner" were brought upon the *tapis*, in its way to the dinner-table, before the cakes were ordered, there would be a very bad chance for the juvenile banquet of the evening, took pity upon her; and, laying her hand upon her father's shoulder, said, "Will it make any great difference, papa, if—if I go and do the errand that mamma gave me first? I shall not be gone five minutes."

"No, no, no, no, my dear Ellen,—no very great difference. Do what your mamma desires, of course, my dear, first, only come back again as soon as you can, because I begin to be very anxious to see how we shall get on when we have got a commissioner close to us. Here is the paper, my dear, you see, full of blunders people are making every where; and we have always managed our parish so capitally well before we had any union at all. So make haste back, Ellen, and I'll have the notes sent out at once." Ellen escaped the very moment her father ceased speaking, and in less time than any one but herself, or Ariel, could have performed the business, had announced the programme of the afternoon's festivities to the nursery-maids, set Mrs. Shepherd to work with her sugar and plums, despatched the desired deputation to the cottage of Jessie Phillips, and again stood beside her father. "Oh! here you are again, my lapwing," said Mr. Dalton, laying down the paper, with which he had again become completely occupied, and telling her to sit down at the little writing-table beside the window, turned, with his accustomed observance, towards his wife, saying, "Well, my dear, and who must we ask to meet him?"

"Why, there must be Lady Mary, I suppose, of course to begin with."

"Why no, my dear, I think not," he replied. "I think, if you have no objection, that we shall not want her, this time."

"Oh! my dear, you know very well that I don't care a single straw about it; only I thought, that if you wished to shew off the neighbourhood a little to these new people, it would be best to have her, because she is the only person of title in the neighbourhood."

"You are quite right, my dear, as you always are," replied her polite husband; "but I don't want to have any ladies at all, if it's all the same to you."

"Oh! I don't care a straw about it, my dear," replied Mrs. Dalton.

"That is just like you, my dear; you are always so good and so kind. Well, then, Ellen, set to work, and write dinner-invitations to Mortimer, Rimmington, Lewis, and Maxwell. We must have them all, because they are all elected guardians, you know, my dear; and for that matter, so is Baxter the brewer, too. I don't know what to do about him. I don't want our prim Lady Mary to make us appear fine, neither do I particularly wish for our burly Mr. Baxter to make us appear vulgar. What do you think I had better do about it, Ellen?" he added, in a half whisper, as was his custom when he asked the advice of his eldest daughter in the presence of her mamma.

"If you wish Mr. Mortimer to meet the guardians, papa, I think you should invite Mr. Baxter, because he is one of them," replied Ellen.

"But you know, my dear, that they have made Deepbrook into one enormous union. Some of the guardians live a dozen miles off; I can't invite them all, Ellen."

"Mr. Baxter lives close by, papa," said Ellen.

Her father smiled, gave her a gentle tap with his large hand upon her delicate cheek, and, nodding to her as he rose to leave the room, said, "Then you must write five notes, my dear,—Mortimer, Rimmington, Lewis, Maxwell, and Baxter."

"Oh! dear me, Mr. Dalton!—you are not going away, Mr. Dalton, are you?" said his wife, with an unusually near approach to being wide awake.

"Not if you want me, my dear, certainly," he replied, laying, however, his hand on the lock of the door.

"I am sure I don't care a single straw about it, my dear," resumed the lady; "but will it not seem very odd if we take no notice of the ladies, after their saying so much, when they returned our call, about hoping to be sociable, you know, and all that?—not that I care a single straw about it."

Mr. Dalton stepped back into the room, and, touching the arm of Ellen, who had just seated herself at the writing-table, whispered, "What do you think, Ellen?—will it be rude?"

"Perhaps you could ask them for the evening, papa, and get some ladies to meet them," said Ellen, drawing forth some note-paper from a portfolio, and preparing a pen.

"I should wish to do exactly as you please, my dear," said the squire, turning round and addressing his wife. "But the party will be rather too mixed, won't it, to ask ladies for the dinner? What say you to inviting the Miss Mortimers for the evening, and getting a good large party of our village belles to meet them?"

"I don't care a single straw about it, Mr. Dalton. But I think that will be better than nothing; only I don't know what to do about Lady Mary—she always likes to come to dinner, you know."

Mr. Dalton looked in the face of Ellen, as if asking for aid, and accordingly she said, "But you know, dear mamma, Mr. Baxter is one of the board of guardians, and I doubt if Lady Mary will like to meet him at dinner."

"Mercy on me! to be sure not!" replied Mrs. Dalton, brought into full life and sensibility by the mention of this alarming incongruity.

"Is it possible, Mr. Dalton, that you are going to ask the brewer to meet Mr. Mortimer the very first time he dines here?"

"The reason is because it *is* the first time, my dear," replied the squire, firmly. "Mr. Mortimer will perfectly understand that he is invited to meet as many of the board of guardians as happen to live in our neighbourhood; but I daresay he won't expect to meet Mr. Baxter the next time he comes."

"Well! I am sure I don't care a straw about it," returned Mrs. Dalton, again relapsing into her habitual state of dormouse quietude.

"So then, upon the whole, my dear, you think it better to ask the ladies in the evening?" said he.

"I am sure I don't—"

"Write to the Miss Mortimers, my dear," said the squire, hastening out of the room in time to escape the "straw," that sometimes almost overwhelmed him, but paused in the doorway to add, "And invite all the ladies, you know, that make up the evening parties, Ellen."

"Oh, dear, how very hot the weather is getting to be sure! I don't know how I shall ever get up-stairs to my own sofa, and I must see Shepherd, you know. Do go and tell her yourself, Ellen, will you?"

"The moment I have finished the notes, dear mamma, I will," replied Ellen, scribbling away as she spoke with great rapidity.

But the next moment, and just as Mrs. Dalton, by a great effort, had got herself under weigh and was in the act of walking round the long breakfast-table in her passage to the door, she was interrupted by the appearance of her father at the window. He tapped, and made her a sign to open it, and upon her doing so, said, addressing his wife, "If you wish, Matilda, my dear, to give these London ladies a notion that we have a gentlewoman in our village, I advise you to get old Mrs. Buckhurst to come in the evening."

"The chief thing, I should think, my dear, would be to get Lady Mary, only I know that she likes best coming to dinner; but, however, I am sure I don't care a—"

"Write to Mrs. Buckhurst, Ellen," said the squire, pulling down the sash from the outside.

"I will call, papa," but papa was gone.

In about five minutes more, Mrs. Dalton contrived to be gone, too, and Ellen was left alone with her pens and her ink, her notes and her old-maidism.

# III

*Frederic Dalton—his dislike of his sister—family details—falling in love—Mrs. Buckhurst—Ellen's walk to the cottage—the conversation—Mr. Mortimer, the new commissioner—the union poor-house—Mrs. Greenhill*

THOUGH FREDERIC DALTON WAS THE very last person in the world whose opinion of his sister Ellen could be safely taken, it is but fair to confess, that not quite all the epithets he had used in speaking of her were misapplied. Ellen was always pale, often silent, and sometimes listless; but she was much besides, which came not within the reach of his philosophy to guess, conceive, or understand. But had it been otherwise, had he possessed sufficient knowledge of human nature to have discerned this, and faculties capable of comprehending the value of it, Ellen would to him have still been an object of dislike rather than of affection.

That a cause existed for this is certain; and it was a cause that, while it left her wholly blameless, shewed him, notwithstanding a great deal of wordy generosity and affected high-mindedness, to be as paltry and poor-spirited a creature as ever existed. The circumstances which led to this were as follow:—When the Squire Dalton, who has just been introduced to our readers, married, at the age of twenty-seven, the beautiful and richly-endowed Matilda Lennox, his father, who possessed a clear landed estate of 4000*l.* a-year, proposed to the guardians of the young lady, that the whole of her own large fortune should be settled upon herself and her younger children, instead of burdening his now clear and unencumbered estate with jointure or settlement of any kind. The proposal was agreed to, and the young couple married. Their first-born child was Ellen, their second Frederic. Contrary to established custom in such cases, the little girl became very decidedly the grandfather's favourite; and though abundance of other little girls succeeded, her pre-eminence in the affection of the old gentleman was never shaken. This partiality, however, did not go the culpable length of leading the old squire to disinherit his grandson; but a year or two before his death (which happened when Ellen was eleven years old), it occurred to him that boys were mortal as well as men, and that if his daughter-in-law persisted in presenting nothing but female descendants to her husband, it might happen, in case the young Frederic died, that his snug little estate would be dismembered, in order to be divided among his numerous grand-daughters,—all of whom, even if their present number of seven were doubled, he considered as sufficiently provided for by the 80,000*l.* settled upon them after the death of their mother. No sooner had this possible evil suggested itself than the old gentleman took means to prevent it, by immediately sending for a lawyer, and causing a settlement of his entire property to be so drawn up, that in case his dearly beloved son Henry died without issue male, the whole of it should vest in the testator's beloved grand-daughter Ellen; and in case of her dying without issue, before her father, it should descend to each of his grand-daughters in the same manner successively. This settlement, though by no means an uncommon one, had something in it which wounded the spirit of the young heir, as soon as he was old enough to understand it. He gloried in being an only SON, instead of one of ten daughters, like his greatly despised sisters; and he fretted under the knowledge that, however improbable, it was just possible, one or other of these contemptible sisters might succeed to his honoured and highly valued place of supremacy. This feeling was sufficiently despicable, but by no means the worst which his grandfather's will created within him. This contempt for his sisters, as he advanced towards manhood, gradually grew into dislike; the one who came next to him in the inheritance being naturally, by much in advance of the others, as an object of aversion, it did not escape him, however, that the hour in which he became the father of a legitimate child, this hateful contingency would cease; and that neither the detested Ellen, nor either of her deeply despised younger sisters, would ever after be able to look with an eye of evil hope upon him, should sickness ever turn his ruddy cheek to pale.

No earthly power could have taught him to believe—what was, however, most completely true—that this *contingent remainder* was no more thought of by the girls than it there had been a hundred male lives in the way of it, or rather no more than if it had never existed at all.

To his jaundiced eye, however, the tone of reprehension which his abominable manners to them occasionally produced, was even construed into deep-rooted jealousy and dislike; and having thus endowed them with detestable qualities, he thought it no sin to hate them accordingly.

The determination to form an early marriage was the secret consolation with which he soothed his spirit under this self-inflicted annoyance; and as neither his father nor his mother had ever yet thought of contradicting him in any thing, it is certain that he might have achieved it with perfect ease, before he had reached the age of twenty-one, even though the object of his choice had been the last woman in the world who would have been the object of theirs; but he was prevented from taking advantage of this, partly because the very ease that he knew attended it robbed the act of all attraction in his eyes, and partly because very dissolute habits of life had already taken such hold upon him as to render the idea of all restraint almost intolerable. But notwithstanding this, the notion of a very speedy marriage was continually before his eyes; and nothing but his determination to get such a sufficient sum of ready money with the happy object of his flattering choice as might supply his secret expenses while his father lived, had prevented his braving all lesser evils, for the sake of rendering that which he most hated to think of impossible. Meanwhile, however, he did not altogether lose his time, but could have told to a fraction the fortune of every marriageable woman, maid or widow, within easy make-love distance of Deepbrook; and as a security against mischance of any kind which might threaten his precious existence, whether arising from casualty or disease, he kept up a species of off-and-on flirtation with very nearly every young woman in the neighbourhood known to be possessed of any tolerably sufficient fortune.

But the perversity of our nature, acknowledged on all sides to exist among our fallen race in a greater or less degree, was so very peculiarly strong in Mr. Frederic Dalton, that he never saw a penniless pretty girl, especially if in the lower ranks of life, without falling violently in love, as he called it, with her; while, on the other hand, every woman possessed of money, let her be as charming as she might, always created in him what he called a matrimonial distaste. Not the less for that, however, did he perseveringly go on making his uncertain love to at least a dozen young ladies at once; and as his person was handsome, and his fortune and future residence (when father, mother, and the ten sisters were disposed of) would be unobjectionable, he was an extremely welcome guest in every drawing-room in the country.

The reader must forgive the length of this digression in favour of the light which it throws on much that is to follow.

Having despatched all her notes, both to the gentlemen and the ladies of Deepbrook, Ellen proposed to keep her promise of carrying an invitation to the venerable Mrs. Buckhurst herself; and having given one moment to the question, which she often asked herself, "Have I forgotten any thing that I promised to do?" and answered it with half a sigh and the murmured words, "No! I have forgotten nothing;" she placed her notes upon the hall-table, ringing the bell beside it, which, by household custom, brought the universal note-carrier to the spot, and proceeded to her room in order to equip herself for her walk.

The pretty, sheltered, unfrequented path which led from Mr. Dalton's mansion to the little cottage of Mrs. Buckhurst, was one of Ellen's best-loved walks; and fondly as she loved her gay young herd of sisters, she often felt that the delicious calmness of the solitary ten minutes which traversing this path allowed her, was among the greatest enjoyments of her existence.

Though not quite so delicate in health as her amiable brother hoped her to be, Ellen was not a very robust young woman. Nature had given her a frame, and a spirit, of great delicacy, which, although nothing at all approaching to *sickness* existed in either to impair the beautiful harmony of the whole, had not been strengthened by the accidents of her early life as much as those who loved her might have desired. The noise, the tumult, the ceaseless unrest, therefore, of a home where she was absolutely worshipped by nine younger sisters was sometimes more than her spirits could stand without a painful degree of fatigue; and this, perhaps, was one reason, among others, why the walk to "the cottage" was so great a favourite with her. That it *was* solitary can only be accounted for by the fact that old Mrs. Buckhurst (who, despite her tiny mansion and her tiny purse, was treated with a good deal more deference throughout the parish than even *the* Lady Mary herself) did not, nor ever had, shewn any inclination to receive morning visits from any of the young-lady parishioners, save and except Ellen Dalton. So that whenever it happened, which of course it did perpetually, that Ellen was met in her progress from her own room to the gate of the lawn, with the questions of, "Oh, where are you going, dearest Ellen?" and "May I go, too?" the answer, "To Mrs. Buckhurst, dear," was always sufficient to secure her being permitted to go alone.

"Welcome! dearest and best!" exclaimed the old lady, as Ellen, with long-established freedom, entered the cottage and the cottage parlour unannounced. And pushing from her the little table reading-desk, which her near-sightedness rendered needful to her, even at seventy, she made way for her young favourite on the sofa whereon she sat, and putting an arm round her, kissing her ivory forehead, as she murmured, almost solemnly, "Bless you!"

"I am come with a message from papa, dear Mrs. Buckhurst," said Ellen, returning the caress by kissing the hand of her old friend; "he wants you very much to come to us next Wednesday evening. He is to have a party of gentlemen at dinner and a party of ladies in the evening; and he very particularly wants you to join them."

"Has he any *particular* reason to think," replied the old lady, with a smile, "that his party of gentlemen will require the presence of an old woman to render the party perfect?"

"I can undertake to say, that one of the gentlemen, namely, my dear good father himself, will think it very imperfect if *you* do not come," replied Ellen; "so let me go home and tell, that he may order the carriage to be here at eight. I do not know if you are aware of it, Mr Buckhurst, but he always chooses to give the order for it himself, that there may be no mistake about the '*very punctual*,' which he never fails to add with such imperative emphasis."

"He is very kind to me," replied the old lady, with a smile of pleasure; "but, dearest Ellen! do not let me come, if it will be *all* noise."

"No, no, it will not be all noise; and though the party will probably be a large one, you are only likely to get your rubber the more peaceably for it. So do come, dearest Mrs. Buckhurst! Your card-table will be in the library, you know," said Ellen, coaxingly.

"Will it? That certainly is a great temptation; and so, dearest, you may say, if you please, that the honoured old cottager will have great pleasure in waiting upon the squire."

"That is dear and kind of you," said Ellen joyfully. "And now, having speeded so well on my errand, I must be gone, for I have my hands full of business to-day. Will you let me gather a handful of your roses, Mrs. Buckhurst, as I go out? I know not how it is that you always manage to have every flower, as its respective season comes round, in full blossom, before other people's buds are visible."

"The statement is, perhaps, a little exaggerated, Ellen; but my flowers *do* blossom early. This little nook is a very warm one, and perfectly sheltered from the biting north and the pinching east also—and—you are welcome, dearest, to as many roses as you can find, only eschew my buds as much as you can."

Ellen rose to go.

"One moment, love," said the old lady, turning the farewell shake of the hand into a means of gentle detention; "stay one moment to tell me who you are to have next Wednesday? An invitation *de si long main*, for our village, announces ceremony. Who are coming to you, Ellen?"

"All the ladies in the parish are invited for the evening," replied Ellen; "and it is very likely they will all come; unless, indeed, Lady Mary Weyland should take offence at not being invited to dinner, and therefore stay away altogether."

"And are all the gentlemen in the parish coming to dinner, Ellen?"

"Yes, Mrs. Buckhurst, and rather more than all. I hope it will not too much shock your aristocratical feelings, but Mr. Baxter, the brewer, is to be one of the party."

"Is he?" replied the old lady, without looking either shocked or surprised; adding, however, "I did not know that he visited at the hall, Ellen."

"I believe he has called upon papa sometimes about magistrate business; but he has never dined with us before. He is invited now because he is one of the board of guardians, that he may meet Mr. Mortimer, the new assistant-commissioner."

"I am not quite certain, Ellen," returned the old lady, smiling, "whether I do not think the new assistant-commissioner a more objectionable personage than the brewer; not that I have any right to say so, I confess, for I have never seen him, and know nothing at all about him, except that he *is* assistant-commissioner."

"Papa says he is a very pleasant, gentlemanlike man, and I hope and trust things may go on better for the poor people, now we have a commissioner so near us, than they have done lately. And in this hope you ought to welcome his arrival among us, my dear Mrs. Buckhurst," replied Ellen.

"Perhaps I ought, my dear," returned the old lady, thoughtfully. "I sometimes fear, Ellen," she resumed, after a moment's pause, "that I am too apt to encourage the propensity of disliking new laws and lamenting old ones, which is attributed to the aged on all occasions. This is so very likely to be the case, from the nature of the human mind, that I have no doubt whatever that it is so, and mean not to combat the application of the observation in my own ease. And yet," she added, "not all the candour I can school myself into expressing, can avail to make me approve the erection of that bare-faced monster of a Union Poor-house, which seems to glare upon us with its hundred eyes from what used to be the prettiest meadow in the parish. I wish I had not seen, the only time I ever ventured near enough to look at it,—I wish, Ellen, I had not seen old Simon Rose, with his grand-daughter, poor soul! and her three little ones, standing before that dreadful Richard Dempster, the governor, looking as if they thought that life and death depended on his will. I have never got the group out of my head since. All the fearful change in the treatment of the poor, which has followed the erection of this prison-like place, *may* be very useful. I am too old to dare express a doubt upon the subject. Old people *are* so prejudiced. But even the new commissioner himself might be inclined to make some allowance for the poor blundering people of the district, if he did but know the

ALL VAGRANTS

contrast between what they see now and what they looked on formerly. We gave a worse name to our house of refuge there, Ellen, than the new folks have given theirs. We called it the workhouse, which bears a sort of threatening in its very name; and it was not, nor was it intended to be, a dwelling to be desired or sought for. But oh! the heavy change! Deepbrook Workhouse was to Deepbrook Union what a free state is to a slave state in America. But this will never do, darling! Go away as fast as you can, for if I begin upon this theme, even you will get weary of listening to me. Let us hope that this gentlemanlike London assistant-commissioner may be a good man, and if he be, he can hardly fail of doing some good among us."

"Amen!" said Ellen, looking almost as meditative as her old friend. "My memory goes not very far back into the history of our poor neighbours, and papa seems inclined to think that the farmers will be better off for the change. But I wish the union poor-house did not look so very like a prison."

"And I, my dear, wish that it *was* not so very like one. But come, Ellen, I do not want to make that dear thoughtful brow of yours look graver than usual. So, no more of this! Give me my shawl, dear, that lies on that chair yonder, and I will go into the garden with you, and look after the safety of my rose-buds myself. You see I am afraid to trust you, Ellen."

"Perhaps you are right, for I have got to assist some half-dozen of my hand-maidens in decorating the school-room for a cowslip-fête this evening; so I am by no means sure of my own discretion."

The old lady took the arm of her young friend, and they passed through the flowery porch of the cottage together; but ere they had advanced three steps beyond it, they were stopped by the approach of a decently dressed, old woman, leading a girl of six years old in one hand, and a little fellow of not more than three in the other. Both the children were cleanly, though poorly, dressed, and the whole group had the appearance of respectability, notwithstanding the very evident poverty of their garments.

"Mrs. Greenhill?" said the old lady, doubtingly, and raising her glass to her eye.

"Yes, ma'am, my name is Greenhill; but it is a good while since I had the honour of seeing you," replied the woman.

"And why is it so long, my old friend?" said Mrs. Buckhurst, kindly. "You know that I am no longer so good a walker as formerly, and that your cottage is almost too far from mine for me to be able to reach it. But you manage your age better than I do; and you know I am always glad to see you. But come in, and sit down; we must not talk standing, for that would not exactly suit either of us. Wait a moment, dear Ellen, will you?" she added, turning to her young friend, "you cannot be in so very great a hurry, for it is quite early yet."

Now, Ellen really was in a very great hurry, being anxious to enchant her little sisters, as she had often done before, by turning their school-room into a bower of bliss for them. But for some reason or other, though there seemed no necessity for it, she lingered, and, after the doubt of a moment, followed the whole party into the parlour, having stood aside to let them pass, while still doubting whether she should take her departure or not: the old woman, as she passed, made her a very respectful courtesy; and then it was that the doubting Ellen turned round and followed her in.

"Sit down, Mrs. Greenhill, and let the little ones sit down, too; there are two little stools for them. And now tell me why it is so long since I have seen you?" said Mrs. Buckhurst, drawing a chair to the corner of the room where the poor woman had placed herself, and sitting down close to her.

"I have had no heart to come, Mrs. Buckhurst," replied the woman, mournfully; "it has always been such a happiness to me to call upon you, and to hear what news you might have received from her Grace and my precious boy, that the visits you were so kind as to permit made almost the greatest happiness of my life: and I always felt sure that you would say something about me to her Grace when you wrote back again, and that in that way my own dear Lord Pemberton would hear of me; but that is all over,—all changed now, madam. It is no longer a glory to me to think that my name should be either spoken or heard by either of them."

"And why so, my poor Greenhill?" said Mrs. Buckhurst, in the gentle voice of sympathy, though she had yet to learn what sorrow had fallen upon her poor neighbour to demand it. "Tell me, I beg of you, what has happened to make you in so melancholy a strain?"

"Ruin, dear lady,—ruin has fallen upon me and mine! Root and branch we are ruined, and never can look up again!"

"Whatever may be the misfortune of which you speak, Mrs. Greenhill, I cannot but think you would have done better to have communicated it before it had brought you so low as you seem to be, now. You know the high value which the Duchess entertains for you, and the affection, as I may truly call it, of your foster-son, and it is therefore unkind to them not to have given them the opportunity of assisting you, if accident has made such assistance necessary."

"Do you not know, madam," said the pale, shattered-looking old woman, in a tone very nearly reproachful, "that the Duke of Rochdale pays me regularly an annuity of twenty pounds a-year, and that my darling nurse-child, the Marquess of Pemberton, always doubles it?"

"I know perfectly well that the Duke had settled a yearly income upon you, Mrs. Greenhill, as a proof of his regard and gratitude for your faithful service, though I did not know that the Marquess had any thing to do with it; but I cannot see why either the one or the other should prevent your coming to visit me, and letting me have the pleasure of informing the family that I had seen you well."

"And it was my pride and my pleasure to believe that you did so, madam, as long as I *was* well; but now I am far, far too miserable and wretched to wish that they should know any thing about me," said the unhappy woman, bursting into tears.

At this moment, Mrs. Buckhurst chanced to turn her eyes towards her young guest, who was standing in the deep recess of the old-fashioned window, and, in fact, almost concealed by the window-curtain; but, nevertheless, the old lady perceived that her cheek was flushed, and that she seemed listening with even painful anxiety to every word that was said.

"Stay here, my good friend, and repose yourself a little, while I go to finish what I was about to do when your arrival stopped me. I will send in refreshment both for you and your children, and will return to you, presently. Come, Ellen, you must wait no longer for your roses; I will speak to Sarah, as we pass the kitchen-door."

Ellen said not a word, but followed the steps of her old friend, pausing when she paused, which she did to order the promised repast, and then they went again together through the porch into the garden.

"I must wish you good-bye, now, Mrs. Buckhurst, without waiting for the roses, for it is really getting quite late, and my sisters are expecting me," said Ellen.

"Dear child!" exclaimed the old lady, mournfully, and looking anxiously in the face of her young friend, Then, tenderly pressing her hand, she added, "Go, then, my dear love; perhaps it is better that you should not stay longer, now. Oh, my Ellen I would things were otherwise!"

Ellen turned away her head without speaking; but she returned the kind pressure of the old lady's hand, and, without again looking at her, took her leave, and passed through the little wicket that led across the quiet fields to her home.

# IV

*The Duke of Rochdale—some account of Tom Greenhill—the new poor examined before the board of guardians—Mr. Huttonworth—Mr. Wilcox—Captain Maxwell—a friend in need—enactments of the bill—decision of the guardians*

THE STORY WHICH GOOD MRS. Buckhurst had to hear upon returning to her parlour was a very sad one, and would have been felt as such by any one of common humanity, but it was peculiarly so to her, for many reasons. In the first place, she knew the person who told it too well to permit her flattering herself that any part of her statement was exaggerated; in the next, she knew that the noble benevolence of the Rochdale family was more in proportion to their rank and station than to their means, which were most inconveniently straitened by the necessity, certainly self-imposed, of clearing for the next generation an estate most wantonly encumbered by the last. It was in vain, as she also knew, that the heir protested against the necessity, or, as he sometimes put it, the propriety, of doing this; the aged Duke who, as one of the consequences of his unprincipled father's conduct, had actually been unable to marry till after his death, which did not happen till he himself was past forty years of age—had suffered too much, from the disproportion between his rank and his income, to endure the idea of leaving his son in the same position; neither could he endure, nor his estimable, high-minded Duchess either, that any of those who were dependent on him should suffer from the process of restitution which he was so perseveringly pursuing; and the consequence was, that he rarely indulged in a residence in England, excepting during the time that Parliament was sitting, or for such occasional visits to his property as were necessary, in order to assure himself that his orders and regulations concerning it were properly carried into effect. Mrs. Buckhurst, who was the only country neighbour with whom the almost banished Duchess had ever formed any intimacy after her marriage, was well acquainted with all these circumstances, and could scarcely have a much less agreeable commission given her, than one which involved the necessity of using her interest with her noble friend, for the purpose of obtaining money from her. This, therefore, made the listening to poor Mrs. Greenhill's story a still greater pain and grief than it would have been, had relief been more easily within reach. Thirdly, and lastly, it was especially painful to the good old lady, because with a heart "open as day to melting charity," an income of 200*l.* per annum rendered any material aid from herself absolutely impossible. The facts of the case which gave rise to the circumstances she had now to hear, were briefly as follow:—

Mrs. Greenhill, who had been the much-esteemed, well-conducted wet-nurse to the young heir at the Castle some seven-and-twenty years before the time of which I am speaking, had returned from her service to her home, with the Duke's annuity of twenty pounds, an income sufficient to assist very essentially in bringing up her family of one son and three daughters. The three daughters had for some years been established in service, at a considerable distance from their home, but the only son, who was her first-born, and the foster-brother of the Marquess of Pemberton, was living with his wife and five children in her house. She had herself been many years a widow, and wished for nothing better than to bestow her whole time and labour, and her annuity to boot (which, during the last ten years, had been doubled by the Marquess), upon this darling son, his wife and children. Young Greenhill was by trade a carpenter, but though an excellent workman, he was, unfortunately, a still more excellent sportsman. He was the best shot in the parish, and the most skilful angler in the county. These accomplishments, together with a particularly handsome person, and the dignity of being the well-to-do Mrs. Greenhill's son and foster-brother to the Marquess of Pemberton, gave him a sort of pre-eminence among the young men of the neighbourhood, which led to most disastrous results. Tom Greenhill was far from being a wicked man; but, though clever in many ways, he was a weak one. Moreover, "he was not without ambition," nor was he without some of the varied "illness" which attends it. He was proud of his skill as a workman, but was not content with exercising it in its merely mechanical shape; he had read books upon architecture, and determined to become a builder. The want of capital for this was really a much greater impediment than any want of skill, for Tom *was* clever; but here his mother's credit helped him on, even more than her annuity, and for several years past, "THOMAS GREENHILL, BUILDER," had taken place of the humbler "THOMAS GREENHILL, CARPENTER," above her door. But most unfortunately, Tom's reputation as a shot and an angler increased still faster than his reputation as a builder; and, though a large yard which he had hired on one side of the common had a very goodly show of timber in it, and though he had entered into more than one speculation for building some very pretty houses "up High Street," he was several hundreds worse than nothing in the world, before his mother had the slightest suspicion that any thing was going wrong. Her annuity, her pigs, and her potato-plat, enabled her to go on with little or no difficulty, though the annual *accouchement* of her good little daughter-in-law was rather a heavy drag upon her. But she observed that Tom always coloured very much whenever she asked him if he could not spare them a little money; and, as she very often saw him setting off to fish or shoot with the young Baxters, and occasionally even with the young squire Dalton himself, looking, as her maternal heart told her, quite as much a gentleman as any of them, she could not bear to plague him, when she was able to go on very tolerably well without his help, especially, too, as she found from his account about the buildings "up High Street," that it would be some time yet before he could expect to receive any return from them.

And thus matters went on for a few years, and then the blow came—the *first* blow. Her son entered her cottage, pale as ashes, with a well-known sheriff's officer behind him, and the business was explained in a few moments. The timber-merchant, who had let the very fine clever young man, with a mother well provided for, have as much timber, on credit, as he chose to order during one whole year, had employed a good deal of steady dunning during the two succeeding ones to get paid for it, but in vain. The two next years the dunning continued, but accompanied with threats so sturdy, that first one speculation, with all the timber, and all the work that had been employed upon it, was disposed of at a ruinous loss, to enable the unfortunate builder to pay something on account; and then, another followed. But now, the fifth year being considerably advanced, without any apparent chance that the large balance was likely to be settled; and Mr. Lawrence, the timber-merchant, knowing by this time a good deal more about the young builder's affairs than he did himself, an arrest was resorted to, as the surest way of getting hold of the mother's assistance first, before any other creditor hit upon the same bright idea. The effect of this upon the perfectly unprepared family of poor Tom may easily be imagined; as may also the means resorted to, in order to release them all from the horrors attending the same, and the thought of a prison for him, even for a few days. His mother's well-known annuity was pledged for five years, with the understanding that the pledge might be redeemed at any time by a ready-money cancelling of the debt. This was bad enough; but this was not all. Where did it ever happen that an arrest in a country village took place, without its being known, at *least* to those any way interested in knowing it? Tom Greenhill had a long bill, too, at the locksmith's, and another at the tailor's. Both these happened to be in particular want of their money, and being also, perhaps, a little jealous of Tom's gentility, did not feel all the repugnance they might otherwise have done, in again employing the same sheriff's officer before the end of the week. But even in this seemingly hopeless extremity, his mother's credit would have sufficed to keep him from being sent to gaol; but the poor soul had now nothing but her personal security to give, and thankfully did she see it accepted, so thankfully as scarcely to be conscious of the predicament in which they all stood. The unfortunate sportsman stood for a while perfectly stunned; and, though he watched with earnest eyes what was going on, it was not till the parties had left the cottage in order to get the proper form drawn up for his poor mother to sign, that the situation in which she was placing herself occurred to him. But then he saw it as plainly before him as if she were at that instant in the act of being dragged to prison for his debts. He threw his arm around her, and pressed his lips to her forehead, and the poor trembling woman thought it was done in gratitude for his release, and pressed him to her heart, in return. In the next moment, he had left the cottage, and overtaking his two creditors as they entered the attorney's door, entered with them, and so clearly explained the utter worthlessness of his mother's security, which he called upon Mr. Lewis, who had so recently been employed upon assuring her annuity to Lawrence, to confirm, that he soon made them understand the uselessness of accepting it; and within an hour or two of this successful display of his eloquence he was safely lodged in the county gaol, there to remain till he could be brought out under the Insolvent Debtor's Act. From this point the downward path of Tom's mother, wife, and children, from comparative ease and comfort to utter destitution, requires not the historian's pen, for it was inevitable, and may only too easily be understood. One by one, every saleable article belonging to any of them was disposed of to purchase daily bread: and then came the next day; and although Squire Dalton was no relentless landlord, it became the duty of his head man, who collected his rents, to give the Widow Greenhill to understand that she could by no means be permitted to occupy one of the best tenements on the estate for nothing, which would, as he observed, be the more out of all common sense, seeing that every body knew she had but to mention the matter to my Lord Duke's steward, in order to have the business properly settled in no time. But Mrs. Greenhill would rather do any thing than mention the matter to my Lord Duke's steward; and she therefore gave up the best tenement, and crept, together with her helpless dependants, into the worst she could find, which consisted of one miserable room, at the very farthest extremity of the parish; its only recommendation being that it was so out of the way that few eyes would be likely to fall upon their misery. Here they had continued to exist for rather more than a month, by means of work obtained in the fields by the wife of the thoughtless prisoner, while his mother managed while she watched over his children, to earn a few pence a-day by mending the garments of neighbours less handy than herself. As the completion of all this misery, the poor wife was drawing near to her sixth confinement, so near indeed that her mother-in-law felt that she must no longer be suffered to pursue her work; and that there was but one resource left them,—they must apply to the parish for relief. Those only who are *well* acquainted with the feelings of our English peasantry before they have been crushed out of all resemblance to themselves by the degradation to which they are reduced, when brought by misfortune under the influence of the present law of the land respecting paupers,—those only who know their minds as well as their persons, their virtues as well as their wants, can be able to understand what were the feelings of Tom Greenhill's mother, when she appeared before the board of guardians of the Deepbrook Union, to ask relief for his starving family. A union so extensive as that of Deepbrook, stretching, as it does, over an extent of many miles, cannot fail of having present at every meeting of the board many members personally strangers to the unhappy applicants who appear before them. And so it happened on this occasion. It chanced, too, that some piece of particularly interesting public news had been circulated amidst the guardians after they had met, and for the most part they were, at the time she entered, deeply engaged in discussing it. But upon her being shown into the room, a particularly active-spirited guardian, but newly appointed, and really liking the employment, addressed her from his place at the bottom of the table round which they were sitting, with the concise question, rather loudly articulated,—

"Who are you?"

"My name, sir, is Margaret Greenhill."

"What do you want?" was the next demand.

"Assistance, sir, for—"

"Yes, yes; you need not go on in that direction, we all know that. Of course, that is the cuckoo cry, from first to last,—'Assistance, sir.' I wish, to my soul, that we could have a little variety, and that some of you would have the exceeding kindness to want something else." To this, Mrs. Greenhill answered nothing. "Where do you come from?" was the next query, and from the same gentle guardian,—a guardian, as it should ever be remembered, of the most unhappy portion of the human race.

"I come from Bushy Lane, sir, in this parish."

"What do you mean by *this* parish? Good Lord! how difficult it is to get a direct answer. What *do* you mean by THIS parish? The parish of the union? Don't you know, foolish body, that there is no less than nineteen parishes in the union?"

"I am of Deepbrook parish, sir."

"Oh! now we get it, at last. You are one of Deepbrook parish, are you? And pray, being myself something of a stranger, may I be so bold as to ask how often you have been here before?"

"Never, sir. This is the first time."

"Oh, Lord; oh, Lord! Of course, *if* you have never been here before, this *must* be the first time. I do believe that you,—all of you think that we country gentlemen have no earthly thing to do but sit here and listen to you. When you have said a thing once, my good woman, for mercy's sake be contented, and don't say it over again the minute after. The business is bore enough of itself, without that. Come, get on, can't you; what do you come for?"

"My son is in prison, sir; and before we can do any thing to get him out, we must get together a little money for expenses, to prove, sir, that he is insolvent."

"Stuff and nonsense, woman! Insolvent, indeed! I should like to know who it is that has been doubting his insolvency? If he is in prison, I take it he has got there upon something a little more substantial than his own credit, or yours either, my good lady. Be so good as to have the exceeding kindness to tell us the truth at once. WHAT IS IT THAT YOU COME HERE FOR? There now. Is that a plain question? And do you think you could have the particular kindness to give us a plain answer?"

This guardian, who had made his fortune in button-making, though now become a *country gentleman*, here took a pinch of snuff, and then offered his gold box to his neighbour, with the air of a man who has said something witty. The gentleman thus favoured took the snuff, and returned the glance with a very intelligent wink of his right eye, though, in truth, he knew not a single word that had passed. Upon which Mr. Huttonworth, the button-maker, laughed a good deal; but, having at length recovered himself, he went on with his examination of "the pauper," no other person, indeed, being at leisure to assist him; which might, perhaps, be owing to the fact, that all the other members present had been longer appointed than himself, and had therefore lost, in a considerable degree, their interest in the business; but as Mr. Otterbury, another of the guardians, frequently observed, while reading or writing letters, one person to examine was as good as a thousand, and indeed better, because it not only prevented people from talking across one another, which was a horrible nuisance to every one either reading or writing, but it prevented a multitude of vexatious disputes about a parcel of trifles that signified not a farthing, between the guardians themselves.

It was Mr. Huttonworth, therefore, who resumed the examination of Mrs. Greenhill, which he did as follows; his first words after he had replaced his snuff in his pocket, being the repetition of his last,—

"*Do* you think you could have the particular kindness to give us a plain answer?"

Mrs. Greenhill trembled from head to foot. It was not from fear, for she felt that she could fall no lower, but she trembled from shame, and faltered out, with eyes fixed upon the ground, that her tears, the conscious starting of which made part of her shame, might not be perceived,—

"I come here for help."

"God bless this lengthy old woman," exclaimed Mr. Huttonworth, with a merry laugh; "if she has not, for the mere pleasure of hearing herself talk, began all over again, only she called it assistance last time, and now she has been clever enough to find out another word, and she calls it help. Come now! there's a darling old soul!—try to get on a bit, will you?"

Mrs. Dempster, the wife of the governor of the Deepbrook Union, who was herself a very gay, merry-tempered woman, always used to say that Mr. Huttonworth was the pleasantest gentleman of the whole board, and that the varmint that came before him wasn't worthy of the pleasure of hearing him. If Mrs. Dempster had happened to be within hearing now, she would, to use a favourite expression of her own, have been "fit to die with laughter," to hear how he went on; while the gloomy-tempered Mrs. Greenhill, on the contrary, flattered herself, as his words and his laugh rang strangely through her ears, that she was not very far from dying from the same cause, though from a different kind of effect.

A strong effort was necessary to prevent her from moving out of the room, for she longed for nothing so much at that moment, as to find herself once more in the fresh air, and alone; but this strong effort was made, for she remembered those at home, and calling all her shattered faculties to her aid, she said, too rapidly to be interrupted, "I am come here, sir, to ask for food for a destitute woman who is just going to lie in, whose husband is in prison, and who has five children to support."

"Shame! shame! shame!" cried the indignant Mr. Huttonworth, all propensity to mirth being for the moment conquered and subdued by his virtuous abhorrence of the profligate maternity, thus openly avowed. "Are you not ashamed,—a woman of decent appearance like you are, to come and ask the active, honest, intelligent, thrifty part of the population to rob themselves and their own children (honestly brought into the world, with the consciousness that there was power to maintain them),—are you not ashamed, old woman, to come here to take their money out of their pockets, in order to feed this litter of brats, that you know in your own heart and conscience ought never to have been born at all? Get along!—stand back, do! You must wait a little, if you please, till I have had time to recover myself." Then leaning across the table to address a gentleman who sat opposite, and whose attention had been called from some papers he was examining, by the vehement tone in which the last words were spoken, he said, "You are a clergyman, Mr. Wilcox, and doubtless, sir, you would tell me, and very properly, too, that it is a sin for a Christian man to get into a passion. I know it, sir, I confess it, and I am truly ashamed of myself; which fair and frank acknowledgment I hope you will accept in the way of apology and atonement. But if there is one thing upon God's earth that I cannot listen to with patience, it is the hearing of a parcel of children being born when there is nothing to give them to eat. Now just observe, sir,—I beg your pardon, Mr. Wilcox, for interrupting you, when, maybe, you are attending to something that concerns yourself—but do, just for one moment, observe the difference between these creatures who have the audacity to claim a maintenance as their right, and the people of our class who have got the misfortune of being obliged to pay it. Just, I say, observe the difference. There's my own daughter, with a fortune down of 15,000*l*.—that girl, sir, has been engaged to be married nearly a twelvemonth, and there they are waiting, she and the excellent young man that is engaged to her, till he gets a living that he has been promised by his uncle, Sir William Wise. That's what I call an example, Mr. Wilcox. *We* are expected to be prudent, and provident, and thoughtful, and careful, and all the rest of it, while these creatures that burden the earth with themselves and their filthy rags must go and marry forsooth, and then send politely to tell us that they have five babies and another coming, and will be much obliged if we will provide breakfast, dinner, and supper,—lodging, furniture, firing, and clothing, for them all, as well as for their dear excellent papa and mamma, because they don't happen to have a single penny of their own. Isn't this monstrous, Mr. Wilcox?"

"It is a tremendous evil, sir," replied Mr. Wilcox, very tranquilly; "but I believe it to be the inevitable consequence of the enormous wealth we possess as a nation, and which, of course, must produce such prodigious incentives to industry, as must often lead to a false estimate of the value of individual labour—a fund often calculated upon as certain by the labourer himself, but which, by the nature of things, must, of all funds, be the most uncertain. The question, I think, sir, lies in a nutshell. If by our excessive luxury in requiring the perfection of every thing that labour can produce, we teach the operative classes to believe that by the incessant use of all their faculties in our service, they *can* make money enough to maintain a family, the excessive increase of population, of which you so justly complain, will, of course, be the result; and as the power of continuing incessant labour is, to say the least of it, exceedingly uncertain, I conceive it follows that large masses of destitute persons must, of necessity, be thrown upon the country for support. I really see no cure for it. For I do not think it would answer, as a national measure, to let all operatives, whom accident, sickness, or their own over-productiveness in filling the magazines of their employers, have thrown out of work,—I do not think it would answer to let all such persons perish, even though they have been rash enough to marry and surround themselves with children. And I am even doubtful, sir, whether your argument, respecting the laudable discretion of your daughter and her affianced husband, would be considered by the labouring poor as a case exactly in point. But may I suggest to you the advantage of dismissing, in some way or other, the aged person with whom you have been speaking? I perceive that many others are in waiting outside the door, and business is impeded by her detention. I regret excessively the impossibility of my being useful here. My living is exactly seven miles off, and if the union were *there*, I certainly might be occasionally of some service, for I am, I am glad to say, personally acquainted with every individual in my parish, and therefore might be able, now and then, to be useful by reason of my familiarity with their different characters and modes of life. But here I know nobody; and, as it rarely happens, I believe, that many of the parishioners of Hortonthorpe apply for assistance here, I feel that I am occupying a place which might be better filled: but, nevertheless, if you are fatigued, sir, by your exertions, I am willing to find out what this person wishes us to do for her."

"By no means, Mr; Wilcox. I will by no means trouble you to finish what I have begun. Besides, I know that you have been engaged with your papers during the whole time that my examination of her has been carried on, and it would be only time lost to begin again."

"Just as you please, sir," returned Mr. Wilcox, resuming the examination of his papers; "but I believe I am quite aware of most of what has passed between you."

To this last observation Mr. Huttonworth did not think it necessary to pay any attention, but raising his voice so as to be heard at a much greater distance from him than where Mrs. Greenhill stood, he said, "Come forward, you most audacious of beggars! don't stand staring at us all as if we were so many wild beasts, but tell us at once whether it is your intention to favour us with your company during the whole of the day."

"I shall be glad to go directly, sir," replied Mrs. Greenhill, "if you will be pleased to give me an order for some sort of relief for my starving grandchildren. I am a stranger, sir, to almost all the gentlemen I see here; but there is one yonder—Captain Maxwell—who knows me."

"Oh! He does, does he! Now then, perhaps, we shall catch a glimpse of light, at last, as to the nature of your right to establish a claim upon other folks' property. Beg pardon, Captain Maxwell; but be so good—will you?—as just to turn your eyes this way. Here is a respectable lady here who boasts the honour of your acquaintance, and we should be vastly obliged to you if you would he so good as to tell us what you know about her."

Thus called upon, Captain Maxwell bent forward, and by doing so obtained a full view of the unhappy petitioner. "Mrs. Greenhill?" said he. "Sure it can't be Mrs. Greenhill—Is it?"

"Yes, sir, I am Mrs. Greenhill," said the poor woman, faintly.

"I am very sorry to see you here, Mrs. Greenhill; but it can't be by way of asking for any thing, neither. That's quite impossible; but it may be for somebody else, perhaps?"

"Yes, sir; it is for my five grandchildren and their destitute mother," she replied.

"Dear me! You don't say so. I am very sorry, indeed. But I should have thought, I must say, that you might have done something yourself to help them, instead of coming here. All I know, gentlemen, of this good lady is, that she has a very handsome pension from his Grace the Duke of Rochdale, and that she has always borne a most excellent character in the parish for respectability in every way; and I should almost as soon have expected to see my Lord Duke himself here to ask assistance as to see her."

"There it is, you see," exclaimed Mr. Huttonworth, with indignation, "from first to last, from the best to the worst, it is all the same. If one of them does but tumble down, and hurt the tip of his estimable toe, off they set for the board—husbands and wives, fathers and mothers, uncles and aunts—off they all come to the unfortunate hoard, and, in heart-breaking strains of the most profound misery, implore our honours to be so merciful as to let them live for a few weeks in idleness; all they want being paid for out of our freehold property. Freehold, indeed! I bought my estate as freehold; but it was little better than a cheat to call it so. A better term, a great deal, would be beggar-hold property. We all hold our property, as it seems to me, for the use of the beggars, and have only got just exactly what they please to leave us. And now, then, Madam Greenhill, by what this gentleman, whose testimony you called for, says of you, I really think that the best thing you can do is to tramp home again to the lane that you talk of, and spend a little of my Lord Duke's annuity in helping your grandchildren yourself: and so I beg to wish you a very good morning."

"I have no longer my annuity," urged Mrs. Greenhill, in a voice that shewed her courage and strength were sinking fast; "I have pledged it for the debts of my son."

"A very pretty story, indeed! Pray, gentlemen, what do you say to this? Here is an old vagabond, who has been handsomely pensioned by a nobleman for some service or other, God knows what; and for some cause or other, God knows what about that too, she makes away with it, and then comes bothering us. Do please, Mr. Deputy Chairman, to send her off, will you? For to my request that she would be pleased to take her leave she pays not the slightest attention."

"Stay a moment, Mr. Huttonworth, if you please," said Mr. Dalton, who, in the absence of Mr. Rimmington, the clergyman of the parish, had been requested to act as chairman. "Stop one moment, if you please. I am sorry to say that I was listening to my friend Mr. Lewis here, upon a little point of business that he wanted to speak about, and I did not perceive who it was you had got there. I know Mrs. Greenhill perfectly well, and I know, too, that her son has been unfortunate; but it is no fault of hers, gentlemen, as I take upon myself to assure you. I am sorry, to my heart, to see her come here for assistance, but I am quite sure she would not come if she could help it, and I am, therefore, decidedly of opinion that she must not be sent away without relief."

This strong support renewed in some degree the courage of the unfortunate woman, and prevented her from obeying the mandate she had received to depart. It brought her also other assistance; for Mr. Lewis, the attorney, who had transacted the business for giving security upon her annuity, seconded Mr. Dalton's testimony in her favour, and declared, that as she *had* thought fit to apply to them, she ought not to be dismissed without a hearing.

This, of course, led to the rescuing her from the fangs of the pleasant and facetious Mr. Huttonworth; her story was again asked for, and listened to with very businesslike patience, and though more than one prudent head was shaken at hearing of the number requiring relief, it was agreed, with tolerable unanimity, that it should be accorded and she was told that, though a person provided for as she herself was, ought not to be considered as a pauper, or relieved as such, that the wife of her son, together with his children, might *come into the house.*

The spirits of Mrs. Greenhill, which had been greatly cheered by the interest expressed for her by Mr. Dalton, sank again into a state of the most miserable despondence as she listened to this tremendous sentence. She was too kind-hearted a neighbour not to know from the report of the poor around her what coming into the house meant. She knew that the little creatures she so tenderly loved would be in one part of the building, and their broken-hearted mother in another; she knew, also, that she should not be permitted herself to see either the mother or the children and, unable to endure the idea of carrying home to them this dreaded doom, she ventured to implore, instead of it, the very smallest aid that could enable them to exist, declaring herself still able and willing to contribute in some degree to their support, and particularly during the approaching confinement of her daughter-in-law, to have it in her power to save the union trouble, by attending to her, without throwing the charge of doing it upon them. So ably did she plead, that the members of the board who knew her, and were therefore able to judge in a great degree of the value, to the poor woman who was to be relieved, of the services thus earnestly offered, every one of them espoused her cause,—excepting, indeed, the lawyer, who, though by no means a hard-hearted man, felt it due to his consistency as a professional one, not to sanction any departure from the letter of the act, which it was their office to administer. But, with the exception of Mr. Wilcox, who seemed to think that he had no right to interfere, there was not one of the many strange gentlemen from a distance, who formed the great majority of the board, but what had some strong word to say against what she pleaded. As for Mr. Huttonworth, he declared that if the paupers were permitted to come and dictate to the board, not only their will, respecting their final determination to get something (to which, it must ever be remembered, they had not the slightest natural right), but also precisely the manner of it, however much that manner might be, in the very teeth of the law they were bound to administer, if the paupers, he said, were permitted to do this, he would immediately resign his place at the board. "Not," he added, standing up, that the important words might be heard to the most distant part of the room,—"not that I have any wish to escape from the duties which, in my opinion, every country gentleman is bound to fulfil; not for that reason would I resign, though, of course, the doing so would be an immense relief; but I would resign, if I found it impossible properly to perform those duties. Nay, I will do more, gentlemen,—I will not only resign, but I will strongly recommend it to the Secretary of State for the Home Department, that no pauper shall ever be permitted to appear before a board, any members of which were likely to know them personally. It is that, gentlemen, that does all the mischief. Such it is now, at this present meeting, gentlemen. Who is it amongst us that flinches from doing their duty? Who is it that suffers themselves to be talked over by a canting old crone, that cares no more for the laws of the land than I do for the buzzing of that fly yonder? Who is it, I ask you, of all the gentlemen here present, who would be ready and willing to let that old woman have exactly her own way, if the rest of us did not stand forward to prevent it? Why, just exactly the people that know her, to be sure. It is as plain as a pike-staff. It is influence, gentlemen,—local influence. You—all of you—the gentlemen of Deepbrook I mean—you, all of you, more or less, seem to care about her, and to value her, and to want to cosset her, just as if she was part and parcel of yourselves. Now, is there any thing, I would ask these very same gentlemen,—is there any thing in such feelings suitable to the strictly carrying into effect a strict law? I say it is impossible that the bill can work as it ought to work, as long as local acquaintance and neighbourly feelings have any opportunity of interfering. And that, gentlemen, is what I shall consider it as my duty to represent to the Right Honourable the Secretary of State for the Home Department, if I find that you act in such a manner as to render my doing so necessary. I would beg to know, sir," said the eloquent orator in conclusion, and specially addressing himself to the gentleman immediately opposite to him, whose eye he observed to be fixed upon him,— "I would beg to know, Mr. Wilcox, if you find any possibility of dissenting from a single word I have said?"

"Decidedly not, sir," replied Mr. Wilcox. "My opinion has ever been, that stern as some of the enactments of this bill appear, the severity of them, upon which you seem to lay so much stress, would in a very great measure disappear, were the centralisation part of it abrogated. If every parish had a receptacle, however humble, for its own poor, with no guardians but those who dwelt within its limits, and no commissioner to settle their doubts and difficulties, excepting the clergyman and the nearest magistrate, nothing at all like what has just past among us would be likely to recur."

The voice of Mr. Wilcox was low-toned, and did not make itself heard either by the deputy-chairman or the gentlemen near him, and therefore neither did nor could affect their decision, which, from respect to the opinions of the majority of the meeting, was very soon declared to be against affording Mrs. Greenhill's family any out-door relief. "They may all come into the house," was the final resolution of the board, and having received it, the old woman left the room, and returned to her home.

It was this decision of the guardians of Deepbrook Union which so far subdued the spirit of Mrs. Greenhill as to induce her to present herself and her fallen fortunes before the friend of the Duchess of Rochdale. She had passed the night which succeeded her visit to the Union in meditating upon the comparative suffering that would arise from seeing poor Jane and her children "go into the house," and applying to the Rochdale family for assistance. Had the question related to herself alone, she would not have hesitated for a moment, as no misery, at least in perspective, could be so horrible to her as the idea of abusing the generous kindness of her patrons; but the penalty for indulging this feeling would not be paid by herself, but by her grandchildren and their miserable mother, and before this all other feelings yielded. The whole of this miserable story was recorded to Mrs. Buckhurst, before the old acquaintance parted; but this was only owing to the kindness of one heart, and the fulness of the other, for it was in no way necessary to the performance of Mrs. Greenhill's errand; which was but to learn whether there was any truth in the report that "the family" were expected immediately at Rochdale Castle. Mrs. Buckhurst, in answer to this inquiry, told her that she fully expected their arrival in a month; and with this information the unhappy nurse departed, doubting whether she was most glad or sorry to hear that she should have no letter to write, but have to tell her terrible story instead.

# V

*Ellen's return home—conversation respecting Jessie Phillips—her arrival—her beauty and accomplishments—Jessie a universal favourite—accident to her mother—Frederic Dalton's interview with the village belle—a conversation touching Mrs. Greenhill—situation of her son—a stratagem—first love*

A LITTLE OF THE LISTLESSNESS which Mr. Frederic Dalton attributed to his eldest sister seemed to be creeping over her as she pursued her walk across the fields from Mrs. Buckhurst's cottage to her home; and on reaching it, she certainly did hesitate for half a moment or so, whether she should not yield to the strong temptation of retiring to her own room, securing her door, and remaining alone for one dear precious hour, instead of entering at once upon the bustling business of preparing for the children's fête; but the recollection of the expectant group that she knew were waiting for her, chased all such selfish notions, and bestowing no more time upon her retreat than was absolutely necessary for disencumbering herself from her bonnet and shawl, she hastened down stairs again, crossed the large hall, ran through the long passage that traversed one entire wing of the building, and presented herself in the retreat sacred to noise and learning at the end of it, without giving herself time to think, of the headache that she knew full well was about to be her portion. But no one who had looked at her in the midst of the delighted throng that crowded round her the moment that she entered the door, could have believed that any thing of heaviness was at her heart, or that she was less likely to enjoy what was going forward than the rest of them. "Here she comes!—Here she comes!" was the chorus with which she was received, and, from that moment, till many hours after, no one that had observed Ellen would have been at all likely to discover that she had headache, heartache, or any other ailment whatever; nothing was seen but

> "Jest and youthful jollity,
> Quips, and cranks, and wanton wiles,
> Nods and becks, and wreathed smiles."

At length the moment for departure drew near, but no Jessie Phillips was visible. "Now is it not abominable," demanded Caroline, "keeping us all waiting in this manner? If it were only the children, of course, it would not signify so much. But Jessie knows that we are *all* going—and I really do think it is too bad."

"And so it is, a great deal too bad," joined in Matilda. "I took care to tell her that all the great ones were to be of the party; and I do think it is treating us all as if we were so many little charity children."

"The fact is, that you have spoilt her among you," observed Mary. "Nothing can be done without Jessie, now; of course, she has found that out, and therefore chooses to indulge herself with a few airs. I heartily hope this sort of impertinence will be a lesson to you, girls, and that you will take the first opportunity of making her understand that you can do very well without her."

"But, Mary, we cannot do very well without her," cried Sophia, eagerly. "I would not give a penny for the cowslip-picking if Jessie Phillips was not there to carry for us; would you, Georgina?"

"I don't know about that, if she behaves in this way," replied Georgina, gravely. "I should be sorry to judge her unfairly. But I do think it is very wrong, when she knows there are so many of us, all longing to be off, to keep us waiting in this *very* disagreeable manner. I certainly think that if the servants could any of them find us a basket that would do as well as Jessie's, we should be quite right to set off directly, without waiting another moment for her. Indeed, I should not be at all surprised if it turned out that she had forgotten it altogether. What do you think about it, Ellen?"

"Why, Georgy, I think there are about five thousand, five hundred, and fifty-five reasons more likely to have either delayed or prevented her coming, than her forgetting that she had engaged to do so."

"Well! really, Ellen, I do not see how it is possible for a poor cottager's daughter, like Jessie, to have such a prodigious number of interruptions," observed Caroline. "How can she have five thousand, five hundred, and fifty-five reasons for not coming to walk with the children, if she remembers that she promised to do so?"

"I don't think I said that she had,—did I?" said Ellen, smiling. "We must remember that one reason may be quite sufficient; suppose poor Jessie should have fallen down and broken her leg?"

"Nonsense, Ellen! as if Jessie Phillips was likely to stumble and tumble, like a tottering old body of fourscore!" said Matilda.

At this moment, a gentle knock was heard at the door of the school-room, and, when the clamorous "Come in!" which followed, had caused it to open, such a figure was seen timidly waiting for a little further encouragement to enter as might have disarmed even more violent anger than the Miss Daltons had been expressing against the tardy Jessie. "Better late than never, Jessie!" exclaimed Henrietta, gaily: "we began to fancy that something very terrible had happened to you—or else that you had forgotten us."

"And that would have been the most terrible of all, Miss Henrietta, if indeed it could have been any way possible," said Jessie, "but that, ladies, you must all know, could never have been!"

"What was it made you so late, Jessie?" said Ellen, kindly. "Sit down, my poor girl! you look as if you had run the whole way."

Lord Byron calls beauty a "fatal gift," but the gift, like all others from the same divine hand, is a very good gift, if not turned into mischief by the agency of sin and folly. How can that gift be called otherwise than good which causes every eye to look kindly, and every heart to feel disposed to love and cherish it! Such was the beauty of Jessie Phillips. It is true, indeed, that she was a most expert needlewoman, and from the construction of a nightcap to the embroidery of a lady's collar, few Englishwomen could surpass her. It is true, also, that when she quitted the village-school, she read infinitely better than any girl she left in it, and that at church her sweet voice might be distinguished in the Psalms amidst those of all the singing part of the congregation. But no one of these accomplishments, nor all of them put together, could have gone so far towards winning all hearts, as did her lovely, gentle, innocent face, and her light, flexile, active figure. It certainly did seem as if it were impossible for any one to look at Jessie Phillips and not to love her. The school-mistress, from the first hour of this pretty creature's pupilage to the last, had never been able to look at her without a smile of kindness; and this, instead of generating jealousy in her school-fellows as might, perhaps, reasonably enough have been expected, seemed only to act upon them as an example, as irresistible in its influence as that of the famous prize piper immortalised in the annals of "Anster Fair." They would, one and all, do any thing to please Jessie, any thing to shew that they loved her and liked her "better than any body in the whole world, except mother."

At the various houses in the neighbourhood into which the skilful needle of Jessie had introduced her, it was still the same thing,—the ladies made a pet of her, and the servants forgave it. As to the male part of the population, it is hardly necessary to say that they did not escape the influence of a fascination in which a lovely face and form had so much to do; and, in fact, with one or two elsewhere enamoured exceptions, there was not a man in the whole neighbourhood, gentle or simple, old or young, who did not think, and for the most part venture to declare, that Jessie Phillips was the most beautiful girl in the country! Had a degree of admiration, equally unqualified, been expressed by any one individual, the effect would, however, have been infinitely greater upon the feelings of its object; but coming as it did promiscuously from all sides, it produced wonderfully little influence upon her mind. She had lived, if the expression may be used, in an atmosphere of admiration, to which she was too much accustomed to be able to feel any particular influence from it. As to the Daltons, from her having been admitted into the nursery for at least two days in every week during the last five or six years—in short, ever since she left school—for the purpose of assisting in the never-ceasing manufacture of frocks, she had become, according to her invariable custom, the especial favourite of the whole establishment, nurses and all. The only dissentient voice ever raised to stem this tide of popularity was that of Miss Barton, the governess, who very conscientiously did believe, that unless the girl had been a *very* sly girl indeed, she could not thus have bewitched them all, and *therefore* she really disliked her. Moreover, the sort of familiarity which this frequent intercourse and strong liking produced between her pupils and the pretty villager did not accord with Miss Barton's ideas of propriety, and occasioned a good deal of checking and reprimanding, whenever it happened, as in the present instance, that by way of a great treat to the children Jessie Phillips was permitted to join in their sports; which checkings and reprimandings, of course, added very greatly to the value of every moment that the favourite could find leisure to bestow upon them, and made the prospect of this cowslip-gathering superlatively delightful from the freedom from restraint which the absence of the governess afforded.

Jessie's apology, therefore, was listened to by ears which were by no means disposed to be deaf to its reasonable sufficiency. Her mother (the only parent she had left) had fallen down stairs and sprained her ankle, just as Jessie had made herself ready to come out, and she had stayed, first to bathe the injured limb in vinegar, and then to get a neighbour to come in, and see that she had "got her tea comfortable and wanted for nothing."

A severer set of judges might, in truth, have been satisfied with this apology, even without the gentle pleading accent in which it was delivered, and considerably before Jessie had concluded her statement, every trace of being angry with her had vanished, and more than one voice was heard to exclaim that it was very good of her to come at all.

The two upper nursery-maids and the three younger children were now summoned, and the joyous troop set forth, the elder girls getting as close to Ellen as they could manage to do, and the younger ones crowding in like manner round Jessie, the possession of one of her hands being very strenuously struggled for among them.

There are some fair faces to which every thing approaching to haste, heat, fatigue, or disorder, is exceedingly injurious, destroying altogether, it may be, the soft harmony and delicate repose of the features. But it was not so in the case of Jessie Phillips. Beautiful as were her features and complexion, her loveliness did not depend on the undisturbed perfection of either for its principal charm. On the contrary, it was the extraordinary variety of expression which her countenance possessed that produced the powerful attraction which all seemed to feel, but which few or none understood. On reaching the stile by which the numerous party were to pass into the field, Jessie for a moment drew back, and stood apart a little, as if to recover more fully her presence of mind and composure after the hurry, agitation and alarm, which she had been enduring for the last hour. And Ellen, as she looked at her thus, her hand pressed upon her heart, in hopes to impede its too vehement movement, her beautiful lips parted, as if to facilitate her breathing, and her lustrous eyes, one moment hid by the "fringed curtain" that dropped over them, and anxiously raised the next, to see if she were wanted, Ellen thought, as she looked at her, that she had never in her life seen any thing so perfectly beautiful.

The nursery-maids had just completed the process of handing over the younger children, from one to the other, across the stile, and the elder ones were in the act of following, when young Dalton leaped into the road, over a gate exactly opposite to that of the field they were about to enter.

Had the group consisted of his sisters only, he would, beyond all doubt, have passed on, probably without ever condescending to notice them even by a nod; but his quick eye failed not to perceive that the beauty, *par excellence*, of Deepbrook, was with them. Whereupon he immediately became most fraternally observant, and, with the exception of Ellen, gave the tips of his fingers in succession to all who had not yet passed, in order to give himself the opportunity of offering his hand to their beautiful companion also. Some rustic beauties would have been confused and confounded by such an honour, and others, probably, would have shyly declined it, but not so Jessie Phillips,—with a quietness of demeanor better calculated to check a presumptuous young gentleman than all the shyness in the world, Jessie accepted his offered assistance, and skilfully, but very soberly, passing over the stile, placed herself beside the upper nursery-maid, and offered to carry the little girl she had in her arms.

This was not exactly the first time Mr. Frederic Dalton had found opportunity to discover the surpassing beauty of this village belle; but like most other gentlemen of his own principles and pursuits, he had discernment enough to discover also, that Jessie Phillips was not a girl to be pleased with the idle language of gallantry, or the unceremonious expression of admiration, which he knew perfectly well must be vastly less precious to her than to any girl of any rank to whom it was less familiar. He treated her, therefore, with greatly more reserve, and infinitely less apparent attention than any other damsel in the neighbourhood whom he thought attractive enough to be noticed at all. But Frederic Dalton was extremely handsome, and though possessed of fewer qualities deserving affection than the generality of his fellow-creatures, his manners, excepting to his sisters, were both bland and animated; and had Jessie Phillips *not* thought him the handsomest young gentleman she had ever seen, she would have been in the minority of one among all the young females, gentle and simple, in the parish of Deepbrook. Jessie Phillips, however, was much too well conducted a girl to permit this opinion concerning his striking pre-eminence in all external good gifts to affect, in the slightest degree, her manner towards him. It made her neither more reserved nor more familiar, nor did it produce any one of these infinitely varied shades of mannerism which indicate latent coquetry, and which are as well understood by such accomplished gentlemen as Mr. Frederic Dalton as the points in a Hebrew page to a rabbi. It was probably to this clear perception on his part, that Jessie owed her exemption from those attentions which he lavished upon pretty nearly all the humble fair ones of the district within reach of a morning ride, but which were, however, less known and less guessed at than the gallantries of any other individual of his class. This arose chiefly from the undeviating prudence which prevented his ever having a confidant of any age, sex, or condition; and he had, moreover, various modes of convincing the young damsels themselves, that the very slightest indiscretion on their parts would, to a certainty, prevent their ever having the honour and happiness of seeing him again.

As the pre-eminent personal advantages of Frederic Dalton did not produce the same paralysing effect on his vanity as a similar sort of pre-eminence did on that of Jessie Phillips, this very strict concealment of all the adventures which tended to prove its power would probably not have been presevered in so resolutely, had not the idea of a speedy marriage been ever present to his mind,—an idea which rather increased than diminished every day he lived, though ever looked at with a reluctant eye as a measure of necessity. His rural gallantries, therefore, had hitherto been entirely confined to such adventures as required no such attentions as were likely to render them conspicuous, and the *Beauty of Deepbrook* had hitherto escaped from any more decided marks of his admiration than such as were afforded by his looking pretty steadily into the window of her mother's cottage, at which, when not pursuing her vocation at the houses of the neighbouring gentry, she usually sat at work, and the placing himself at church in such a position in the family pew as commanded a tolerably good view of her face.

The present occasion, however, appeared, for some reason or other, too favourable to be resisted. Perhaps he had never before thought Jessie so very lovely as he did then; perhaps he considered the presence of his ten sisters and the two nursery-maids a sufficient protection against all possible scandal; but whatever the cause, he did now what he had never done in the whole course of his life, that is to say, he joined the youthful party in their sports, and assumed the air of the most playful and good-humoured grown-up brother in the world. With the exception of Ellen, who was now really suffering severely from headache, the whole party, nurses, children, and all, were soon scattered over the flowery field, and Jessie's basket was often called for in more directions than one. Obedience to these numerous calls rendered more exertion necessary than could he used without visible fatigue on the part of the basket-carrier; whereupon, young Dalton offered to be her substitute, an offer which she thankfully accepted, and having done so, placed herself on the grass beside the youngest little girl, who seemed perfectly satisfied to sit still, and pluck up as many herbs of all kinds as grew within her reach. This arrangement was convenient to all parties; for it enabled the nurse to devote her attention to the more excursive gambols of the other children, and it gave Mr. Frederic an opportunity of shewing a great deal of playful kindness to the baby, to look at Jessie a great deal, and to talk to her a little. Till he had made her smile at him by some of these playful sallies, he had, perhaps, no idea how very beautiful she was; and it is probable that he permitted the discovery to escape him in some manner that the young sempstress thought more direct than respectful, for, upon his turning towards the little Charlotte, in order to sustain the by-play that he felt to be necessary, Jessie sprang lightly from the ground, and crossed a corner of the field to the spot where Ellen had found a shady seat for herself upon a fallen tree.

"Are you tired, Miss Ellen?" said Jessie. "You look very pale."

"Yes, Jessie," replied Ellen, "I am rather tired; and so I think are you too—though you look more flushed than pale. Sit down by me, Jessie; there is room for us both on this log."

Jessie gladly obeyed, and after a moment's silence Ellen said, "Do you know any thing of Mrs. Greenhill, Jessie, mother of Tom Greenhill, I mean, the carpenter?"

"Oh! dear yes, miss," replied the girl, "I know her very well, indeed. She used, before her troubles, poor dear woman! to be mother's best neighbour and kindest friend."

"She seems to be in a very melancholy condition now, poor woman," rejoined Ellen. "What are the circumstances that have happened to her?—I think I remember hearing that her son was not going on well with his business—he was too much of a sportsman, I believe, at least so papa said, but I always thought that Mrs. Greenhill herself was taken care of by—by the family with whom she lived as a nurse."

"And so she was, miss, nobly taken care of, both by my lord the Duke, and my lord the Marquess too, and it is by no fault of hers that their generosity is no longer of any use to her."

"How do you mean, Jessie? If the generosity of the family is continued to her, what is there can prevent its being of use to her?" demanded Ellen.

"She has pledged her annuity to pay her son's heavy debt to the timber-merchant," replied Jessie.

"Poor woman! that is sad, indeed! But can they—none of them—do any thing to get a little money to help her on with, after she has made such a terrible sacrifice? Her son was, I know, an excellent workman and unless he is very wicked indeed, he certainly will not go on shooting and fishing now," said Ellen.

"No, miss I that I am sure he wouldn't," replied Jessie, "for Tom Greenhill is not a wicked man. He has always been a good son and a good husband;

though I believe he has been rather over fond of his gun. But he can't work now, Miss Ellen, let him wish it ever so much, because he is in prison."

"In prison? Has he got into debt again then, since his mother made such a sacrifice for him?" asked Ellen.

"Oh no! Miss Ellen," was the reply. "Only the annuity went to the first claimant, and there were other debts that came in after. So, for these, he was obliged to go to prison, till the debtor's law can set him free again. And while he lies in gaol, his poor wife and his excellent mother are absolutely starving; and, poor souls they could not pay the squire his rent any longer, and are gone into a sad dirty little shed of a place in Bushy Lane. It almost broke my heart when I went first to see them there."

"Do you mean my father when you say the squire, Jessie? I do not think it was at all like my father to turn honest poor people out, because they had fallen into misfortune," observed Miss Dalton, doubtingly.

"So I said, miss, the moment that I heard it," replied Jessie, eagerly. "But Mrs. Greenhill answered she had nothing to complain of about that. It was not your papa, you know, Miss Ellen, but the steward, who is obliged to do his duty to one as well as to another, without shewing favour more to Mrs. Greenhill than to any one else; and that was what she said herself."

"I do not understand why such severity should be necessary any where," said Ellen.

"Mrs. Greenhill said that she had no severity to complain of," repeated Jessie. "For that she went out quite of her own accord, when she found that it was quite impossible for her to pay the rent."

"I wish you would describe to me exactly the place where she is gone to live, Jessie. I should like to call upon her," said Ellen.

Jessie Phillips again named Bushy Lane, and then described the part of it in which the miserable cottage might be found in which the poor woman had taken refuge.

While this conversation had been going on, Mr. Frederic Dalton, who had been left sitting upon the grass beside his little sister, felt as thoroughly thrown out and embarrassed by the strangeness of his situation, as a man-of-war's man might do if left sitting before an embroidery-frame with a needle and thread between his fingers. For a moment or two he felt unmitigated anger against Jessie, not so much for leaving him perhaps, as for the refuge she had chosen; till a moment's recollection suggested that the little sempstress could not know *how* impossible it was that he should follow her thither; nor guess that, if she were ten times more beautiful than he had just hinted he thought her, such close vicinity to his sister Ellen was enough to keep him at a distance for ever. When he had so far recovered himself as to remember this, he thought that there was some thing of coquetry in the manœuvre; and taking up the child about as handily as a man-monkey might have done, he conveyed it into the safe vicinity of its especial attendant, and then selecting one from among a group of young ones, whom he deemed both old and young enough to do his bidding featly, he told her that she would lose half her flowers if she did not get Jessie Phillips to carry the basket; adding, "Go, you little thing, and make her come back again to help you."

One or two of the children, whose frocks were already over full of the fragrant toy, welcomed this proposal very joyfully; and Sophia exclaimed, "Why, Bella! what fools we are! Didn't Jessie come here on purpose to do it?" And thereupon a whole deputation scampered off, leaving a heap of cowslips on the ground, and their amiable brother close beside, as it should seem to guard them.

Jessie, who thus reminded, immediately became conscious that sitting beside dear Miss Ellen, and talking to her, was not the purpose for which she was invited, instantly jumped up, and yielding herself unresistingly to the guidance of the half-a-dozen little hands which seized upon her, she was led amidst gambols and shoutings to the spot where destruction awaited her. Pretty, innocent, young creature! it was like leading a lamb to be sacrificed amidst the garlanded decorations of a heathen festival.

The sports of that evening went on to their close in a manner more than usually delightful to the young partakers in them. For, where Frederic Dalton had an object before him, he had skill that seemed inspired by his Satanic master to obtain it. And, while the children, for the first time in their lives, thought brother Frederic the nicest fellow in the world, the elder ones saw nothing in his whole demeanour beyond a sudden and capricious fit of high spirits and good-humour and the only observation spoken between them on the subject was from Caroline to Mary.

"What a pity it is, Mary," she said, "that Frederic is not always as pleasant as he is this evening! How soon we should get to love him, if he were!"

"Yes, I dare say we should," was the reply; and here all commentary upon it stopped. The young man left the party as they entered the house, wisely remembering that as he had not made his appearance in the school-room for the last dozen years or so, his doing it now might excite an inconvenient degree of observation. He therefore retreated to dress for dinner; his four eldest sisters doing so, likewise, as soon as they had seen the rest of the party seated at their banquet of cakes and tea, under the superintendance of poor Jessie; who, when left to the unobservant eyes of her little companions, performed the laborious task she had undertaken, with vacant smiles, and with thoughts wandering back to the soft accents of gentle kindness, which for the first time had stolen into her ear, from the only man whom her eye had bewitched her heart into thinking charming.

Ellen only, of all those who were present when the village beauty was beguiled into thus taking her first downward step—Ellen only, when she was quietly alone in her own room, remembered the strangely novel circumstance of Frederic's having joined himself to their party, and the possible motive for it flashed painfully across her mind, But the mind of an innocent young woman, and such Ellen most truly was, despite her three-and-twenty years, is not a favourable soil for bringing such thoughts to maturity; and the next minute it was dismissed, with a feeling of displeasure against herself for having ever conceived it.

This was fortunate for Frederic; for, excepting the first slight imprudence which had given birth to Ellen's short-lived thought, nothing else of the kind could for many a day after have been laid to his charge. He never was seen to look again into the cottage window of Jessie's mother; nor did his eyes ever wander towards her from his place in the family pew at church.

# VI

*Ellen's visit to Nurse Greenhill—she wins her heart and her confidence by showing that she is still respected—the good nurse's reason for not applying for relief to her former benefactors*

BY THE AID OF A little care and dexterity, Ellen continued to escape on the following morning from all her sisters, old and young, and following the instructions given her by Jessie, found herself, after a pleasant walk of half an hour's length, before the habitation of Mrs. Greenhill. That it was so, she learned by inquiry of a woman whom she encountered near the door; and glad would she then have been to find either that Jessie had blundered in her description of the road, or she herself in finding it, rather than have been assured that so vile-looking a hovel was the abode of the worthy and highly valued Mrs. Greenhill. There used to be many, and there still are some, villages in England, where the resident gentry have familiar personal acquaintance with every poor family in the parish, excepting where notorious ill conduct of any kind may render it objectionable. This happy state of things had existed *in perfection* in the parish of Deepbrook, till within the last few years, and did still exist there at the time of which I am speaking, with the exception of the residents of "High Street," and of the unfortunate families whom the sudden and awful change in the poor laws had driven to become inhabitants of "the Union." This terrible abode seemed in the parish of Deepbrook to have the faculty of obliterating from the minds of all without, the remembrance, even of the names, and the existence, of those within it. This was not the result either of praise-worthy, or blame-worthy, pride, in the more fortunate, but was one of the inevitable consequences of being absorbed into what might be truly called the common sewer of misery; which served as a drain for the helpless wretchedness of nineteen parishes, and which was so dammed up on every side, as carefully to prevent all intermixture, either for good or for evil, with the happy denizens of earth and air, whose fate had not yet engulphed them in it. With these exceptions, the poor families of Deepbrook were still, for the most part personally known to the rich ones; and Mrs. Greenhill, though a short time before not strictly belonging to either class, was most certainly unknown to none. Her neatness, her activity, her universal kindness, and even the grand-mother petting that she delighted to bestow upon "Tom's little ones," were all matters of village notoriety; and her name was rarely mentioned without some epithet indicating affection or esteem being annexed to it. Nor was Miss Dalton an exception to this. She knew a great deal about Mrs. Greenhill, and not only had a very high opinion of, but a very considerable degree of affection for her; though some accidental circumstances, not exactly relevant to the present portion of our narrative, had prevented Ellen from cultivating much personal intercourse with the good woman. The heavy misfortunes which now appeared to have fallen upon her, however, seemed at once to remove every impediment to their better acquaintance, and the hope that, by her agency, some easy arrangement might be made for restoring her to her former residence, made her eager to set about cultivating the intended intimacy immediately.

Ellen, before she entered the wretched-looking dwelling, looked up, and reconnoitred it with a sigh. She had known it in better days; for it was one of the very small, but umwhile decent tenements, which, before the sweeping operations of the new act, had been the home of labourers; no longer, perhaps, in the full vigour of their strength, yet still able, by the aid of a weekly shilling or two, from the parish, to maintain existence; and still as capable of enjoying the sweet unfettered air of heaven, "the pomp of groves, and garniture of fields," as the highest potentate in the land. She remembered that an old woman who had lived there, before starvation had goaded her to take refuge in the Union poor-house, had been celebrated for having in her tiny garden (containing a space of about twelve feet by ten) the finest plot of anemones in the country; and she recalled the proud air with which the contented old soul was used to present the brightest tinted and the largest flowers to herself, as being an especial favourite. But since this old woman's departure, the place had fallen almost wholly into ruin; and the *lodging,* which Mrs. Greenhill and her son's family now occupied, was in fact the only sleeping-room of the miserably poor tenants who had taken it in its present deplorable condition, at little more than a nominal rent, and who were glad to repose their bones on the earthen floor of the lower room, for the purpose of receiving Mrs. Greenhill's shilling a-week, to assist in keeping them out of "the house" as long as possible.

Ellen tapped at the door, but her summons receiving no answer, she opened it, and found three children squatted on the floor, safely enough at play, as it seemed, for there was no fire on the hearth, and scarcely any movable object within their reach.

"Where is Mrs. Greenhill, little boy?" said Ellen addressing the eldest of the group, who appearing about five years old, she thought might be capable of giving her an answer. And so in effect it proved, though he replied not in words, he pointed to a broken stair-case, and having climbed to the top of it, she found that the answer thus given was correct; for, in the chamber to which the stairs led, she found the emaciated, sick-looking wife of Tom Greenhill, endeavouring to patch into decency the garments of her eldest child; while he, and four lesser ones, occupied the floor at her feet. The greatly changed grandmother of the once-petted group was seated in a chair at the little window, busily employed upon work, the payment for which was to furnish their next meal.

Ellen Dalton was exceedingly shocked at the aspect of the whole scene; though for reasons hinted at above, she had not been in the habit of entering the dwelling of Mrs. Greenhill, she was perfectly familiar with its comfortable and neat appearance; she knew, also, the nature of the service in which she had passed many years of her life, and was quite aware how ill it was calculated to prepare her for the hardships of her present situation. Many thoughts connected with this good woman, and with other persons also perhaps, came upon Ellen's mind, and tears started to her eyes.

"Sit still—pray sit still," said she, addressing herself first to one, and then to the other Mrs. Greenhill, who both rose up to offer the chair

J Leech

they sat on for her accommodation. "Let me sit here," she added, placing herself on the side of the bed; "this makes a very good seat."

The elder Mrs. Greenhill, who, in spite of Ellen's entreaty that she would "sit still," did not replace herself, blushed deeply as she stood thus displayed in all her wretchedness before the almost stranger young lady, and Ellen felt in an instant that she had been thoughtless in thus intruding upon her. It had, in truth, never occurred to her as possible that Mrs. Greenhill could be reduced thus suddenly to a situation of such very abject misery, and the contrast between her present dwelling and that she had been used to admire for its neatness as her former one, made her feel how painful must be the eye of one so nearly unknown, and yet so well acquainted with her previous condition. But it was now too late to retreat, and rallying her spirits as well as she was able, she said,—

"I hope, Mrs. Greenhill, that you will excuse my breaking in upon you, but I really wish to speak to you upon business, and I knew not how otherwise to obtain an opportunity."

There was a mixture of respect in the manner with which this was spoken, which, more perhaps than even its kindness touched the poor woman's heart, and sinking down into the chair she had quitted, she burst into tears. Ellen, with very delicate perception, understood far better than most others would have done the feelings which caused this burst of emotion, and, stepping quickly towards her, she took her kindly by the hand, saying, "Whatever may have been the unfortunate accidents, Mrs. Greenhill, which have placed you for a time in a situation so far unlike all to which you have been accustomed, you have at least the satisfaction of knowing the temporary personal inconvenience to yourself and your family is all you have to fear. This is bad enough, and must be remedied as quickly as possible; but you, I am sure, would feel it a much greater evil did any one consider your high respectability in the slightest degree affected by it. This, however; as you well know, is not the case; and your friends, therefore, may confidently look to your good sense as a support under a misfortune which cannot be lasting."

"You are right, Miss Dalton," replied the gratified old woman, again rising from her chair, but in a manner that shewed her to be cheered and strengthened by this address; "my best support is, indeed, in the hope to which you have so kindly pointed. I would rather lose life than esteem, Miss Dalton; and when," she added, large tears rolling down her cheeks as she spoke,—"when my heart sinks within me under the fear of this, I will remember your words, and your looks, and your manner, and shall feel that I have not lost every thing."

It was impossible that the conversation could have opened in any manner so well calculated to place Ellen on the footing on which she desired to stand with the excellent person before her. The tact which made her at once perceive at what point her sorrows hurt her most, enabled her to lead the much-comforted poor woman to lay before her the whole circumstances of her situation. To Ellen's offer, however, of negotiating her return to her former residence without any fear of being again disturbed in it, she gave a decided, though very grateful negative, alleging as one reason for the refusal the utter impossibility of recovering possession of the furniture which had been seized. Ellen then led the conversation to the future, frankly desiring the poor woman to tell her what she meant to do, that she might be able, if possible, to assist her in it. Had the young lady began the conversation with this question the proud old nurse would certainly have told her in return that she had not yet decided; but now her heart was opened, and without a shadow of reserve she told Ellen all she had done and suffered in the hope of obtaining aid from the parish till her son could be restored to liberty under the Insolvent Act, and be enabled to support his family by his labour. It was with all the eloquence of honest indignation that Mrs. Greenhill described to her the reception she had met before the board of guardians, nor were graphic touches wanting to bring the whole scene before the eyes of her earnest listener. Ellen's cheeks glowed and tears started to her eyes, but for a minute or two after the narrative was closed she spoke not a word. Many thoughts and feelings were busy within her, to which she could not give utterance. Her father was a member of that board, and her heart sickened as she remembered how often she had heard him say, that the being so gave him no power to avert any single hardship its enactments brought upon his poor neighbours. She remembered too, that it was with all the sensitive freshness of feeling which untried suffering brings with it, that this poor woman had stood to he browbeaten, insulted, and vilified, by one who knew her not, and who, therefore, like nearly all the other persons present, neither was nor could be acquainted with her well-earned claims to respect, notwithstanding the misfortunes that had fallen upon her. Neither could Ellen Dalton forget that the object of all this unmerited severity possessed the esteem, nay the affection of some of the highest and noblest in the land.

Throughout all the conversation that had hitherto passed between them, Miss Dalton had carefully avoided making any allusion to Mrs. Greenhill's noble patrons, but now she felt as if it were doing them injustice to pass them over thus, even in appearance, and she said,—

"Do you not fear, Mrs. Greenhill, that the Duchess of Rochdale will think you treat her unkindly by keeping all this a secret from her?"

Either from the dread of being considered as giving unnecessary advice, or from some other cause, Ellen blushed deeply as she said this, and the pale face of the old woman seemed to reflect the glow, for she, too, coloured, and for a moment cast down her eyes, as if embarrassed how to answer. But that moment sufficed to decide her as to the line of conduct she should pursue. Her daughter-in-law had managed to convey herself and her children to the room below, so that the good nurse and her young visitor were *tête-à-tête,* and this certainly assisted in producing the result to which her meditations brought her.

"The Duchess of Rochdale would, I am quite sure, Miss Dalton, blame me very much, if I scrupled at this moment to ask the advice of a person who seems so well capable to give it as you do. And I could almost think that you were sent to me in mercy, my dear young lady, at a time when every earthly hope seemed to fail, on purpose that I might do so. I do feel that the noble family I have served (generously as they have already requited my services),—I do feel, Miss Dalton, that they might think I misdoubted their goodness more than I ought to do, did they know into what distress I am fallen; and but for one single reason I would have long ago conquered all dislike to apply for more, where so much has been already given. But for one reason, the Duchess of Rochdale, and the good Duke too, and my dear Lord Pemberton, should have known all. Now this one reason is what I would not lightly mention to any body, and I never have done so, but you cannot counsel me, Miss Dalton, unless you know all. One reason why the noble family I had the honour to serve have ever been so very kind to me, is that they think I saved the life of Lord Pemberton, when he was given over in convulsions, by putting him, of my own judgment, into a hot bath. It was a lucky fit of courage that seemed to seize upon me when I did it, but I am far from thinking it deserves all that they have said and done for it. However, whether it was so or not, they have always been pleased to say that it was I who saved the dear child's life; and when it was settled that they were to go abroad, and that I was to leave them, her Grace told me of the Duke's noble intention of settling twenty pounds a-year upon me for my life; and then she added, 'We all of us think, my good Greenhill, that you have well deserved a handsomer independence than this from us, but the Duke *cannot afford it.* We should not leave England, Nurse Greenhill, if we could afford to live in it.' Now after this, Miss Dalton, and after the dear young lord's doubling the pension, as he has done for many years past, can you wonder that I do not like to apply to the family for more money? Indeed, ma'am, I should dislike to do it much less, if I did not feel so very certain that, whether convenient or not, as much money would be sent as we should want to set us right again; and that, Miss Dalton, would not be less than some hundreds of pounds."

Ellen assured her that she entered very fully into her feelings, and that she could not but approve them; and then, suddenly rising, she added, again colouring deeply, "Do not communicate your situation to them for a few days to come—perhaps —" and here she stopped.

"There is no chance of my doing so for a longer time than that, Miss Dalton; and God knows I would gladly put it off for ever! But the family will be at the Castle in about a month, and then—"

"And then you will be guided by circumstances?" said Ellen.

"Of course, Miss Dalton. But I fear that every thing must be known to them then."

"There are many things may happen in a month, Mrs. Greenhill," said Ellen, cheerfully. "And now I must leave you. But you will let me come and call upon you again?—and you must not be offended if I leave this behind me;" and so saying, she laid two sovereigns upon the table and immediately descended the stairs.

# VII

*Squire Dalton's dinner to the board of guardians, and the new assistant commissioner—Mr. Mortimer's mode of avoiding discussions on business—the great convenience of oranges at a dessert*

On the day fixed for Mr. Dalton's dinner-party, that gentleman gave notice at the breakfast-table that having in the course of his yesterday's ride met Mr. Wilcox, the clergyman of Hortonthorpe, he had asked him to join the party, adding, with his usual politeness to his wife, "I hope, my dear, this will not put your table out? But altogether the party will not be a very large one." Mrs. Dalton's answer was as usual, that she did not care a straw,—but that she was afraid they should have a monstrous large party of girls in the evening.

"It can't be helped, my dear," was the very reasonable reply of her husband; who added in a whisper to his eldest daughter, "People who have ten of their own, Nelly, cannot very fairly complain of their neighbours."

"I am afraid not, papa," was the smiling reply. "But we may at least hope, you know, that as Mr. Mortimer is rather a youngish widower, the Deepbrook young ladies may be kind enough to account him a beau; and then your Mr. Wilcox is a bachelor, and that will help us. I only hope Frederic will be in high feather, for when he sets about what I have heard you call his circular flirting, he is a whole host in himself."

"Yes; and you will have him in the drawing-room long before the rest of us. For if we get into poor-law discussion, he will soon get tired of us, I suspect."

Mrs. Dalton's dinners were always very good dinners, and on the present occasion every thing was exactly as it ought to be. The four eldest Miss Daltons, all looking very pretty and elegant, dined at table, and thereby prevented the appearance of its being a mere gentlemen's party. It very soon became evident that Mr. Mortimer, the assistant poor-law commissioner, was one of the most agreeable men that the neighbourhood of Deepbrook had ever possessed; and his appearing so on this occasion was a strong proof of his power to support the character so universally accorded to him, for the two principal gentlemen at the Dalton dinner-parties always laboured under a very great disadvantage. The leading Mrs. Dalton into any thing in the least degree deserving the name of conversation was a task that no man, in perfect possession of misunderstanding, ever attempted twice; yet for a stranger to give it up during his first visit in time to recover the opportunities lost while making it, could scarcely be considered as a feat possible to be achieved without risking his character both for the mysterious grace called *savoir faire,* and the home-bred grace called civility. But Mr. Mortimer shewed what our old play-wrights denominate "his town breeding," with great skilfulness upon this occasion, for he neither permitted the wet-blanket peculiarities of Mrs. Dalton to affect his brilliance, nor yet did give either her or any one else cause to accuse him of any deficiency of observance towards her. After the experiment of one single sentence, addressed to her in the *sotto voce* tone of next-neighbour table-talk, he felt as completely acquainted with the extent of her powers in that line, as if he had sacrificed the dining hours of a whole week to making the experiment. But should he, for that, rudely present her during the remainder of the repast a *profil perdu* instead of a full face, radiant with smiles and gaiety? However justly, according to dinner-table morality, she might deserve the punishment, Mr. Mortimer felt, as he had often done under similar circumstances before, that there would be something very harsh in inflicting it, and harshness made no part of his character; for though lively, animated, and often witty in his conversation, he was exceedingly good-humoured, and rarely permitted his gay spirits to find what sustained them, either in quizzing or neglecting those about him. Instead, therefore, of turning from the lady of the house, and taking his chance of finding something a little less dull on the other side of him, Mr. Mortimer only changed the tone at which he had pitched his voice, and the clever things which might have been for the lady's benefit alone, had she been Lady N. or Mrs. S., immediately became the property of the whole table, while, from time to time, as the gay smile his sallies elicited went round, he failed not to turn full upon Mrs. Dalton his own face, radiant with white teeth and good-humour, till being obliged, of course, to smile upon him in return, she became convinced not only that he was very agreeable, but that she was herself very agreeable too, and that altogether they had never managed a dinner-party better.

Meanwhile Mr. Dalton forgot not the object he had in view by bringing the present party together, and in spite of the miscellaneous chit-chat which Mr. Mortimer continued so cleverly to circulate round the table, he managed to set Mr. Lewis talking upon county business, quarter-sessions, and the objectionable tone of the county newspaper. In this Mr. Rimmington and Captain Maxwell soon joined; and although Mr. Wilcox pertinaciously persisted in talking to Ellen, and all that Frederic Dalton contributed to the conversation consisted in sporting remarks addressed to Mr. Baxter, he had the satisfaction of finding that, by degrees, the light and lively phrases of Mr. Mortimer appeared to retreat, as it were, and give way before the more important matters of the regular county talk, which he himself did his best, and he did it ably, to establish round him; so that he flattered himself, that when Mrs. Dalton and her fair daughters left the room, he should be able to bring forward the subjects that he particularly wished to discuss with their important new neighbour.

Amusing as Mrs. Dalton found it to be made to smile so very pleasantly without having the trouble of finding out what it was about, she did not forget the troublesome way of coming early, to which many of the *beau monde* of Deepbrook were addicted, and she therefore made a signal to her daughters, not very long after the cloth was removed, which caused them all to rise at the same instant, and demurely follow her out of the room.

Mr. Dalton then took his place at the head of the table, and the gentlemen who sat near him at the bottom of it closed ranks with those above. With the exception of his son, there was no one present who did not share in his anxiety to find out something of the views and feelings of their new neighbour, concerning many things of great importance to the well-being and well-doing of the neighbourhood, in which he was likely to have such great and important influence. They were all of them fully convinced already, that Mr. Mortimer was an extremely gentlemanlike, agreeable man, and this was of no small importance in a country village like Deepbrook, where the gentry lived on very sociable terms, and liked dining together frequently; so that there was not a single person at the table who did not feel disposed to propitiate his good opinion and good will. Mr. Baxter, indeed, though daily becoming a more important personage, from various purchases of lands recently made in the neighbourhood, was as yet only in a sort of transition state between the tradesman and the country gentleman. One of his sons had been sent to college, which had already considerably assisted the gentility of the family; and this, together with his conscious wealth, made the brewer feel that he, too, had an interest in establishing a personal acquaintance with the assistant-commissioner. Nevertheless, and to their honour be it spoken, there was so much thorough genuine, old-fashioned English feeling amongst them, that, greatly as they were pleased with the man, and well as they were disposed to profit by the social qualities which he seemed so eminently to possess, there was scarcely one of Mr. Dalton's guests who did not feel more anxious to find out in how great a degree he was likely to be useful in his character of assistant poor-law commissioner, than agreeable in that of a new neighbour.

It was, therefore, without any restraint from the fear of *boring* so lively a companion, that Mr. Dalton opened upon the subject that was next his heart, by saying, "We are happy, Mr. Mortimer, in having this opportunity of making personal acquaintance with a gentleman whom we all consider as holding a very important situation among us. You will find, not only at Deepbrook, but pretty generally throughout your district, I hope, that there is still a sprinkling of the true English country gentleman breed left, who for the most part *know* their poor neighbours, and take such a degree of interest in their welfare as will make you, sir," he added, smiling, "a very important personage."

Though none of the company received this speech with a positive "Hear! hear!" there was not wanting a very intelligible sort of murmur that did as well, and which, graduating from Captain Maxwell's perfectly audible "Very true!" to Mr. Rimmington's gently whispered "Yes, indeed!" left no doubt that the host had spoken very correctly the sense of the company.

"You do me great honour, gentlemen," replied Mr. Mortimer, bowing round, with an expression of countenance the most amiable. "Believe me, there is nothing I wish for more than to be with you and of you. I fell among you completely as a stranger, and your extending to me thus the right hand of good fellowship, makes me feel my extreme good fortune in the chance that has sent me here?"

"It is altogether a pleasant county to live in," observed Mr. Wilcox. "Is this your first acquaintance with the neighbourhood, Mr. Mortimer?"

"Indeed it is," answered the London barrister; "and I am perfectly delighted with it. The roads are so excellent! And I think I never saw timber more beautifully scattered in my life."

"Ye-es," replied Mr. Wilcox, with a slight and, perhaps, not unintentional affectation of tone and manner; "we live in a perfect bower. What part of the island are you most familiar with? The more boldly picturesque, perhaps?"

"Alas! no," returned Mr. Mortimer. "There is no profession, Mr. Wilcox, that of necessity centralises so completely as that of the law. We poor barristers cannot, in truth, be said to know any thing of our own country, except its capital. You all know what assizes and sessions are, and how very little of rural beauty we get by attending them. The long vacation, indeed, gives us an opportunity of looking about us a little; but, like birds long debarred the use of wings, we all fly as far as we can when they are restored to us. I always go abroad in the long vacation."

"That is perfectly natural. I understand the feeling completely," replied Mr. Wilcox. "So that, in fact, I presume lawyers in general are the most uncountrified class in the community."

"Perhaps they are," returned Mr. Mortimer, modestly, and slightly bowing, as having received a compliment. "But, depend upon it, we have our share of awkward tricks amongst us—professional, perhaps, though not rustic."

"It is rather a large union that you will find brought together here, Mr. Mortimer," said the master of the house, pushing the claret towards his stranger guest. "It will take you a good while to get acquainted with our habits and ways, so as to understand the questions as to right and wrong that will be likely to come before you."

"Of course, Mr. Dalton—of course. But I fortunately have a very intelligent young man as a clerk, and I expect to find him to be of great use to me."

"Your clerk, sir," said Captain Maxwell, pushing the bottle, "cannot be expected to do much in the way of a pilot, unless he happens to be acquainted with the chart."

"Captain Maxwell, I presume," said Mr. Mortimer, smiling and bowing to him by way of reply.

"You have found me out by my lingo," returned the captain, good-humouredly "I shall never quite lose it, that's certain, though peace were to last, and I stay on shore for another score of years or more. But, nevertheless, Mr. Mortimer, my anchor has been so long down here, that I may well call the place my home; and I know a thing or two about it, though I am no landsman. By your description, our profession is a good deal the reverse of yours. We don't centralise at all (except, perhaps, a little towards the Admiralty), and we have a tolerable knack of finding out the natures of all the creatures,—flesh, fowl, or fish,—that come across us."

"It is an excellent species of intelligence," said Mr. Mortimer, by way of reply, for Captain Maxwell's speech was evidently addressed to him; but the reply was uttered in a manner that was not intended to make it appear as if he had seen any particular meaning in the words.

"You have not, then, been much accustomed to live among the rural poor, sir?" said Mr. Rimmington, fixing his mild but searching eyes on the face of the barrister.

The rector of Deepbrook was an admirable preacher; but on ordinary occasions he was no very copious speaker, and it was, perhaps, for this reason, that, whenever he joined in conversation among persons who knew him well, a more than common degree of attention was given to what he said; and, indeed, there were few who, if about to speak themselves, did not, like Mr. Dalton on the present occasion, check their purpose, rather than interrupt him. Mr. Mortimer, however, who was not to the manner born, and who saw nothing in the elderly gentleman who addressed him but a respectable-looking black suit, grey hair, and somewhat quizzical white cravat, while his words certainly did not appear to him to have any very important meaning, merely bowed, and smiling a sort of acquiescence to the remark, addressed young Dalton, who sat opposite to him, with an inquiry respecting the quality of the trout found in the stream which gave the village its name.

Frederic was entering upon a somewhat minute dissertation in reply, when his father cut him short, by saying, "Come, come, Frederic, you must not frighten Mr. Mortimer by making him fancy that our talk, if not 'of oxen,' is ever of fish. You and Mr. Baxter have already proclaimed that we have the finest trout stream in the county, and I and my less sporting friends here," looking towards the two clergymen, "are more anxious to hear Mr. Mortimer's opinion respecting the new arrangements we are proposing to make at our union, than any more of your knowing critique upon the fins of our trout." Then, decisively addressing the newly arrived commissioner on the subject which at that moment was occupying all the thinking heads in the parish, he said, "We shall want a little of your assistance, Mr. Commissioner, before the next meeting of our board; for the truth is, we are at issue upon a point of considerable importance to some of our poor neighbours." Mr. Lewis, the solicitor, who, of all the gentlemen present, was the only one, except the brewer, who differed from the squire on the point to which they all knew he alluded, settled himself in his chair, drew one corner of it nearer the table, perched himself upon that, and then pushing aside the finger-glass that stood before him, seemed preparing himself for combat. Mr. Mortimer began very slowly and carefully to peel an orange; and the rest of the party, with the exception, perhaps, of young Dalton, appeared ready to give great attention to what was to follow.

"The gentlemen of our Deepbrook board of guardians, Mr. Mortimer," began the squire, "are a good deal at variance,—not personally, observe, nothing can be more sociable and friendly than we are together, for the most part, when we get away from the board,—but at the board, Mr. Commissioner, we cannot quite agree as to the degree of power left in our hands by the gentlemen of Somerset House as to the management of the rates and the relief of our own poor. Of course we have all of us got the act, and have read it, and tried to understand it as well as we could; but our good Mr. Lewis here generally tells us that we don't understand it at all, and that what seems to several of us, and especially to Mr. Rimmington, our valued chairman, to be the clear and direct line of our duty, is in flat contradiction to the statute."

This was said with an air of smiling good-humour that appeared intended to lead the party to discussion, but not with sufficient gravity to give an appearance of business to it. The two clergymen and Captain Maxwell took the attitude of listeners, but Mr. Baxter, bending forward so as to meet the eye of Mr. Lewis, said, "I believe, sir, I may range myself on your side. I have no notion, for my part, of taking an act of parliament and reading it just as if it was for amusement, and then turning round and saying to one's neighbours, 'Oh, yes, to be sure I have read the act, and now, gentlemen, if you please, we will do what we think best for the poor people.' That will never do—never, as long as the world lasts. Will it, Mr. Lewis?"

As the brewer withdrew his eyes from the person he had addressed, he suffered them to rest for a moment on as much of Mr. Mortimer's face as was visible; but that gentleman was still too much occupied in preparing his orange, either to look up, or even, as it seemed, to hear what was passing.

"Yes, sir," returned Mr. Lewis, "that is a good deal my way of viewing the thing. However, we have now the satisfaction of knowing that no more time will be lost among us in idle discussion. When people are within reach of authority, Mr. Baxter, they have no occasion to discuss." And having thus spoken, the solicitor followed the example of the brewer, in endeavouring to discover from the countenance of the commissioner how his speech had pleased him. But he, too, was defeated by the bending position of the head, which seemed to be still required for the preparation of the orange.

Mr. Rimmington's eyes were also turned towards Mr. Mortimer; and if the expression of his own countenance might be trusted, the orange operation offered no impediment to his understanding that of the commissioner. After the steady gaze of a moment, he withdrew his eyes, and then he, too, took an orange to peel.

Mr. Wilcox, the keen, quick glance of whose coal-black eye was in striking contrast to the mild, deliberate, contemplative speculation of Mr. Rimmington's pale blue one, could hardly have been perceived to have looked at all in the same direction. Yet he, too, seemed to have seen quite enough to satisfy his curiosity, for it was impossible for any man to appear more perfectly indifferent to what was going on than he did. The worthy squire however, was not so easily contented, and civilly pushing the sugar towards Mr. Mortimer, in the hope, perhaps, of making him raise his eyes, he said,—

"You see, sir; that you will not have quite a sinecure among us, and that you must prepare for the trouble as well as the dignity of passing judgment."

Mr. Mortimer did raise his eyes, and took the sugar with a smile of the most amiable politeness. "Thank you, very much," said he; "we shall pass judgment on one point, at least, in perfect unison, Mr. Dalton. Be it Midsummer or be it Christmas, the sugar-cane should always make half the orange;" and as he said this, it was impossible not to perceive that Mr. Mortimer had as fine a set of teeth as ever embellished the mouth of a gentleman of five-and-forty.

Squire Dalton looked puzzled—Mr. Wilcox smiled—Mr. Rimmington sighed—and Captain Maxwell frowned. The brewer, being rather a slow man, looked as if he were taking time to consider what he should say next; but the quicker-witted Mr. Lewis appeared to understand the state of the case perfectly; and, pulling a dish of preserved fruit towards him with considerable eagerness, he helped himself to it largely, asked young Dalton for the biscuits, observed, with a nod to the squire, that he should "stick to the sherry," and in short, indicated very distinctly that he thought, at that moment, there was nothing so much to the purpose as making himself comfortable

Very complete silence ensued for about a minute and a half; which is rather more than enough at a dinner-table to make it obvious that conversation flags. Mr. Lewis was the man to revive it, which he did by saying, with the air of a person communicating intelligence which he was rather proud to possess,—

"The Duke of Rochdale and his family are to be at the Castle in a week or two."

"Indeed!" exclaimed Mr. Mortimer, looking up with sudden animation. "I understood that they had quite given it up as a residence."

"Oh, dear no!—by no means, sir!" returned Mr. Lewis. "They have been a good deal abroad for several years past, but Pemberton is perfectly kept up, and whenever they remain in England after the parliamentary season is over, they come here."

"I am exceedingly glad to hear it," replied the barrister. "My son was very much acquainted with Lord Pemberton both at Eton and Oxford, and will be quite delighted to meet him again."

"Well, sir, he will have an opportunity," rejoined the solicitor, "for the young Marquess will most certainly be here."

"You seem to do every thing at Deepbrook too much in London style," said Mr. Mortimer, dipping his fingers in water and hastily drying them on his napkin, "to sit in the old country fashion a thousand hours after dinner, and I shall therefore take the liberty of escaping to the ladies. I think I have just descried my carriage sweeping round to your drive, Mr. Dalton, and I must be the first, if I can, to announce to my damsels this good news from the Castle." So saying, the assistant-commissioner rose and glided out of the room before the astonished Squire Dalton could think of any fitting form of words by which to prevent his exit.

Captain Maxwell screwed up his mouth and produced a long low whistle.

"Devilish queer—isn't it?" said the squire, raising his eyebrows. "What do you think of it, Rimmington?"

"I think, my good friend," replied the rector, "that our assistant-commissioner does not particularly wish to be drawn into discussion upon the subject of his commission."

"I am not sure that I think the worse of him for that, Mr. Rimmington," said his brother clergyman, rousing himself from the apparent apathy into which he had seemed to have sunk. "Mr. Mortimer has the air and manner of a person of good ability and common sense; and if this be so, he knows, as well as you and I do, that the less he says upon the subject the better."

"Then you are in absolute despair as to any good resulting from his coming," said Captain Maxwell.

"No, no; I do not mean to say any such thing, I assure you," replied Mr. Wilcox; "but I have long been of opinion that all the good that can be hoped for from any right-thinking men employed to carry the enactments of this stupendous law into effect, must arise from his silently and conscientiously doing all he can to evade it."

"That is rather a new way of being conscientious, isn't it, Mr. Wilcox? said the solicitor laughing.

"Certainly not so new as the occasion which calls for it, Mr. Lewis," he replied. "If all that has been done towards rendering the labouring poor of England helpless, hopeless, destitute, and desperate, was *intended* by the framers of the New Poor-Law, they would stand before us in colours that it would be libellous to assign them. We are, therefore, bound not only by Christian charity, but by social discretion, to nourish a belief in their having so far blundered in their most difficult task as to have done much which they had no intention of doing. For my own part, I am perfectly convinced that this is the case, and that by far the best and wisest mode of assisting the legislation in saving the country from the absolute and inevitable destruction that must have ensued from the continuance of the old law, is by NOT following to the letter the enactments of the new one."

"But why the d—l," vociferated Captain Maxwell, "should they not repeal a law so infernally bad as to make it, according to your own account, the duty of every Christian man to break it as often as possible?"

"I have not exactly said that I do not wish it to be repealed," returned Mr. Wilcox, smiling; "but I think it much better, while it continues to exist, to endeavour rather to modify it in practice than to rail against it in theory."

"My dear good reverend sir, that is just what I call jesuitical," said Captain Maxwell.

"Do you?" returned Mr. Wilcox, relapsing a little into a tone of apathy.

"What you say, sir," said Mr. Lewis, addressing the rector of Hortonthorpe, "would be all vastly well, perhaps, if the legislators whom you so charitably wish to defend from blame, by declaring that they did not know what they were about, had not expressed their wishes and intentions so very clearly on the subject; and you must excuse me, therefore, if I differ with you altogether about Mr. Mortimer's reason for taking himself off when he found that we were getting a little to business. I should rather suspect that a man so likely to rise as I judge Mr. Mortimer to be, would hardly have taken the situation, good as it is, if he had not got his eye upon other loaves and fishes. There is Somerset House, you know, straight before him, and I should like to know how any man can hope to rise by pretending not to understand words as plain as those of my Lord Brougham, when he talked roundly of the *good effect of a rigid abstinence in administering relief* and of the necessity of *a vigorous system of central authority*. That's pretty plain, and no mistake, or I don't understand words; and how they can safely be got over by an assistant poor-law commissioner, who hopes either to stay where he is or to get on a little farther, I don't exactly see."

"I doubt if the authority you have just quoted be absolutely beyond appeal," muttered Mr. Wilcox, playing with his wine-glass. "However, that is not any part of the question we are considering. Though I should never, perhaps, have thought of calling the old law, which can, I think, only be stigmatised as a most dangerous instance of UNCALCULATING charity,—though I should never, I say, have termed it, like Lord Brougham does, 'the accursed statute of Elizabeth,' yet still it is impossible for any thinking man to deny that it was framed without any mixture of that sort of prophetic science which, in our days, has taught us to perceive that if persevered in, it must, of necessity, have utterly overwhelmed and destroyed the country. This being allowed, it pretty evidently follows that some strong legislative measure was necessary to save us, and short-sighted, indeed, must be the eye that does not perceive also the enormous difficulty of the task. The *inevitable* inconvenience, not to say suffering, certain to fall on the objects of the new law, and the fearful responsibility attached to the framers of it, might have daunted the courage of a Hercules; and strongly as I have been, and ever shall be, opposed to the political notions of the party who brought it in, I cannot but consider the country as greatly indebted to the boldness which first breasted the difficulties of this necessary enterprise. But noble as is this quality of courage, it is not the only one required in a lawgiver, and when unchecked by the holy restraints of true philosophy and moral justice, it is apt to degenerate into a reckless indifference to results, which converts it into a scourge instead of a blessing."

"Yes, sir, by Jove! Much such courage as what is shewn by a bull-dog when he worries a lamb to death," said Captain Maxwell, vehemently.

"But God bless my soul, captain, don't you perceive, even upon the shewing of Mr. Wilcox, whom nobody ever suspected, I believe, of being over and above friendly to the bill, nor to the framers of it, that something must have been done to save us from perdition? Then what good is there to make an outcry about what can't possibly be avoided?" demanded Mr. Lewis, looking angry.

"Come, come, Lewis," said Mr. Dalton, pacifically, "we seem to have failed in our object of getting a little information out of our new commissioner; but that is no reason that we should set about quarrelling with our old friends. Perhaps, after all, Wilcox is right, and our best course may be to pad this pinching law a little where it wrings us the most, and wait patiently, for a time at least, to see what they will do for us at head-quarters."

"Pray, Dalton, do you mean Somerset House by your head-quarters?" said Captain Maxwell.

"No, indeed, my good friend, I do not," replied the squire. "That is certainly the very last tribunal I should think of looking to for relief. I really look upon that unfortunate trio as being, notwithstanding their comfortable salaries, the three most uncomfortably situated gentlemen that I know. In no single instance can any good result, arising from this awful bill, be considered as emanating from them, while all that is most mischievous and most galling in it does come to us direct from their hands. Their commission seems framed as if on purpose that it should appear to be so."

"I am almost inclined to think, Mr. Dalton, that you might very safely go a step farther," said Mr. Rimmington, "and say not only that their commission has been framed to appear, but to be the source of by far the greater portion of the mischief arising from this *awful* bill, as you most justly call it. Take from the bill the hateful Frenchified principle of centralisation, in its administration, and all its bitterest,—all its most *unconstitutional* faults disappear at once, and nothing would remain to complain of but what English patience on one hand, and English good sense on the other, might be able to remedy. The cruel part of the business is the having cut the tie that, throughout the whole country, bound the rich and the poor together by interests that were reciprocal, and which could not be loosened on either side without injury to both. What is the connexion between them now?"

"Why, that pleasant gentleman who was just now peeling his orange with us is the connexion," said Captain Maxwell.

"Exactly so," returned Mr. Wilcox, bowing to him; "and being a very smooth-polished, non-conducting sort of a substance, we have nothing to do but to interpose him between ourselves and any poor people that may happen to be starving near us, in order to prevent our feeling the slightest inconvenience from their vicinity. Depend upon it, our best chance of escaping the mischief he is empowered to do us is by soothing him into the belief that his nice little revenue is a pension, and not a salary, and that he had much better employ himself in fishing for trout than in teaching the local guardians of the poor how to perform a duty of which they know much, and of which he knows nothing. Let us hope the best from his placid and gentlemanlike exterior,—let us hope that he will let us alone."

While this conversation was going on, the heads of Mr. Lewis and Mr. Baxter gradually drew nearer and nearer to each other, till at length they were close enough for their respective owners to mutter sundry observations to each other without being overheard by the rest of the company; and it is pretty certain that the opinions thus uttered were not in unison with any of those that had been spoken aloud. The causes which influenced these two individuals in thus differing from their neighbours were by no means the same, though the result was so far similar as to make them agree in thinking that what they had just heard spoken by their companions was wrong and improper. "Very wrong, sir," were Mr. Lewis's words,—"very wrong and improper, indeed."

Yet their difference from each other was pretty nearly as great as that of both from the rest of the party. Mr. Lewis was a sound, well-informed, and genuine lawyer, in whose eyes an act of parliament was of more authority than all the philosophy in the world. He was really a clear-headed and perfectly honourable man; but upon all points where a direct and positive law was established, he saw no more room for argument, or variety of opinion, than upon a question whether white was black, or black white. With this unaffected reverence for the omnipotence of the laws, it was almost a matter of course that the makers of them, for the time being, should be reverenced also; and Mr. Lewis had therefore been often accused of vacillation in politics, whereas the fact literally was, that he had no politics at all. When Whigs and Tories were in and out of power with more than common velocity of movement, Mr. Lewis felt embarrassed; not from any fear of appearing inconsistent—no such idea ever entered his head, but merely from a slight imperfection in memory, which occasionally rendered a moment of recollection necessary, before he could pronounce, with his usual firmness of opinion, that any individual on whose conduct the conversation turned was "most perfectly wrong" or "most perfectly right."

Far different was the case of Mr. Baxter. He was, heart and soul, a thorough-going Radical. Daniel O'Connell was his "great Apollo;" and the passing of the Reform Bill a commencement of the millennium. In most cases, perhaps, men were more important in his eyes than measures; but in the case of the new Poor Law it was otherwise. Like ALL advocates for unlimited popular emancipation from restraint of all kinds, he doted with a feeling of fanatic fondness upon the exercise of power in his own person; and though a rich and thrifty tradesman, he loved the profits of his business less than the power it gave him over his numerous workmen. And as for the new Poor Law, had he been a sentimentalist in his ways, he never would have laid himself upon his bed without having "the act" placed next his heart. The indignation with which he rejected the idea that the poor man had any rights upon the resources of the country was so vehement, that many thought it was likely, if often discussed in his presence, to cause his death by apoplexy; so fearfully had every vein been seen to swell when he spoke upon it. Both these gentlemen, therefore, found great cause for displeasure in the manner in which the subject under discussion had been treated; and as Mr. Baxter, both at dinner and after it, had been quietly drinking a good deal of wine, it was perhaps fortunate that the squire broke up the sitting, and proposed adjourning to the drawing-room, which he did, by saying, "Nobody seems inclined to take more wine;" which observation, by the way, might certainly have been easily interpreted into his having declared that Mr. Baxter was nobody.

But as pretty nearly all the ladies in the parish of Deepbrook were assembled on this occasion in Mr. Dalton's drawing-room, we must, in compliment to them, begin a new chapter before we enter it.

# VIII

*Brilliant assemblage of young ladies in Mr. Dalton's drawing-room—general love-making—graceful antiquity—maternal anxiety—metropolitan pertinacity of purpose*

THE FEARS OF MRS. DALTON respecting the preponderance of young ladies at her party seemed to be fully justified; for when the gentlemen from the dinner-table entered the drawing-room, it appeared to be wholly occupied by various specimens of this prettiest part of creation; while the only gentlemen they found there were the two Mr. Mortimers, father and son (the latter having unexpectedly arrived in time to accompany his aunt and sister on this visit), and Mr. Johnson, the apothecary. The apothecary was, of course, deeply engaged in conversation with Mrs. Dalton. What lady, having ten daughters, and two or three of them almost babies, could miss such an opportunity of seeking a little medical information about freckles, pimples, and growing too fast? The commissioner and his gentlemanlike-looking son stood apart, in earnest conversation with each other, and therefore were not so useful as they might have been, in counteracting the extremely feminine appearance of the party.

Nobody, however, but the mistress of the house and the young ladies themselves could have found any inclination to complain of this, for the groups which presented themselves on the opening of the door were very gay-looking and pretty. As no consideration ever induced Mrs. Dalton to permit any of her daughters, of whom she was very justly proud, to remain out of sight when she received company, the ten young ladies, varying in age from Ellen's terrible twenty-three to little Charlotte's rolly-polly three, were here, there, and every where, throughout the room.

In addition to this domestic sprinkling of muslin, lace, and ribands, there were first, the two Miss Mortimers, aunt and niece, newly arrived from London, and giving evident testimony, by their extremely elegant dress, that they well deserved all the earnest attention which the other young ladies see inclined to bestow on them. Miss Maxwell, the only daughter and only child of the worthy captain of that name, who has already been introduced to the reader, may come next in order. This young lady was a small, neatly-made little personage, with little of positive beauty, perhaps, but with quite charm enough to deserve and receive from most people the epithets of "very sweet, nice, little creature." Frederic Dalton had taken considerable pains to ascertain the amount of her probable fortune, but had found so many difficulties in his way, that he determined to go no farther in preparing her for the immediate acceptance of his hand, in case the sudden death of her father might shew reasons why he should offer it, than a mere slight hint, repeated about once in every three or four weeks, of his thinking her by far the loveliest creature in existence. This, however, was quite sufficient to answer his purpose. Martha Maxwell was an odd girl, and was one instance among many, that strong ability and natural shrewdness cannot avail to guard the heart of a woman from the fascination of fancying herself beloved by one whose external qualifications please her fancy, even where no single symptom exists likely to satisfy her judgment on the subject. Miss Maxwell knew that her own fortune would be but moderate, while that of Mr. Dalton's heir would be large, and believed that the opposition likely to arise on the part of Frederic's father, on this account, was the only obstacle which prevented the young man's openly addressing her. She sometimes feared, indeed, that there must he some feebleness of character, which rendered him more the slave of his father's will than he ought to be, and was, perhaps, less *perfectly* in love with him in consequence, but, nevertheless, in thinking of marriage, Frederic Dalton was the only man who had ever presented himself to her fancy.

The two Miss Lewises, the acknowledged heiresses of all the thousands, and thousands-worth, which the well-to-do solicitor of Deepbrook had accumulated, were both of them really very pretty girls, and both of them quite sure, each in her own individual little heart, that there was but one girl in the world for whom Frederic Dalton really cared a farthing, and that this happiest of created females was herself. Nevertheless, there was a good deal of sisterly confidential repeating, between them, of the tender things said by the young man to each of them; but this did him no sort of harm with the other, both being persuaded that he did nothing but what he thought necessary for keeping himself upon the best and most intimate terms with the family; and fully persuaded that whatever he might say, he had never pressed her sister's hand as he had pressed hers, or breathed such eloquent sighs in her ear, or—in short, Mary was sure that poor dear Lucy was making a monstrous fool of herself, and Lucy was equally certain that poor dear Mary would find out in the end which of them it was that Frederic Dalton was really in love with.

It is quite in defiance of etiquette that I have thus given to the junior part of the population of Deepbrook precedence of the seniors, especially as no less a personage than Lady Mary Weyland was one of the latter. But really it is difficult, even in imagination to enter the drawing-room of Mr. Dalton, without thinking at the first glance that young ladies "possess it wholly." Let me atone for this by respectfully presenting to my readers, without further delay, the Lady Mary Weyland, daughter to the Earl of Crompton, and widow of Sir Stephen Weyland, Bart. Her ladyship was at this time near upon sixty years old, of an extremely lean constitution of body, and with a superiority above the common height, for which she daily returned thanks, never permitting her rather stumpy abigail, or any other female of altitude inferior to her own, to cross her path without exclaiming, "Thank God! I am not short!" Whether her thanksgivings for personal advantages extended to her face, I have never happened to hear; but if they did, it should not be reckoned amongst her moral demerits as a sin of vanity, but rather set on the other side of the account, as proof of such a disposition to be "thankful for small mercies," as must ever be considered as commendable. Her ladyship had seated herself, as was her wont, on first entering Mrs. Dalton's drawing-room, at the upper end of the apartment, in one of those elegant inventions for lounging gracefully, which are among the glories of modern art. A footstool was before it, and her prodigious length of limb, charmingly defined by the lights and shades of her amber satin dress, enchanted her eye as she looked down upon them. At precisely the most distant part of the room sat Mrs. Buckhurst, her appearance being only remarkable by her very white hair, the nice simplicity of her black dress, and the air of ladylike tranquillity which seemed equally to pervade her countenance, her person, and her manners. By her side was seated her friend Ellen, and they made in their distant corner a group apart. One other group completed the party. This consisted of Mrs. Maxwell, a very lively little lady of fifty, and of Miss Johnson, the maiden sister of the apothecary, who sat together in very friendly vicinity, conversing with considerable interest on the dress and appearance of the two Miss Mortimers, now seen for the first time within the precincts of a Deepbrook drawing-room.

Nothing less irresistible than the having a few quiet moments' talk with Mr. Johnson, just at a time too when no single individual in the house could furnish an excuse for sending for him,—nothing less than this could have detained Mrs. Dalton from the side of Lady Mary, a post which she rarely failed to occupy for the first ten minutes of every visit made by that noble lady to the mansion. Beyond this, the strength of poor dear Mrs. Dalton could not go; for Lady Mary talked without ceasing, and never of any thing that did not relate in some way or other to her own greatness; so that Mrs. Dalton, who, excepting when talking to Mr. Johnson, greatly preferred dozing to any conversation whatever, found it impossible to keep her eyes open for a longer period.

For a short time, her ladyship seemed to have no objection to the dignified isolation of her position, and made herself, as she was fully aware, "a perfect picture to look at," both as to attitude and the arrangement of her rich drapery; but having performed this *tableau* for the benefit of the company as long as she thought necessary, she raised her voice to a pitch very sufficiently audible, and said, "Miss Johnson! come here, if you please, I want to speak to you."

"I beg your pardon, Mrs. Maxwell," said the delighted spinster, rising hastily; "but I must go, if you please?"

"Go? To be sure you must," said Mrs. Maxwell, laughing behind her little fan; "run along, Miss Johnson, as fast as ever you can trot."

And the worthy Miss Johnson did run, and having reached the side of her ladyship, stood there, without any attempt to reseat herself, till she had answered nearly as many questions as might have sufficed (numerically) for a Cambridge examination. And now the party from the dinner-table entered the room, and distributed themselves about it according to their various propensities and inclinations. Mr. Dalton made his usual ceremonious bow exactly in front of Lady Mary's chair, and having hoped that he had the honour of seeing her ladyship well, he nodded with friendly familiarity to Miss Johnson, and right and left, as he proceeded, to every body else, till he made his way to the corner in which his old friend Mrs. Buckhurst had ensconced herself.

"I must have that chair, Ellen," said he, tapping his eldest daughter on the shoulder; "and you must go, like a good girl, and be civil to those two new young ladies. Upon my word, I hardly know which is the aunt and which is the niece. Oh! I see! Yes, yes! the lesser lady is really young, and the taller one only looks so."

Ellen obeyed, though not without a little, gentle, quite inaudible sigh, and began to circulate among her younger guests.

Mr. Wilcox, who knew personally all the ladies, excepting the new arrivals, went everywhere where they were not; and when Ellen asked if she should present him, he replied, "Not just now, thank you; it will be time enough by and by, you know."

Mr. Baxter and Mr. Lewis came in together; and the former, not being apparently very intimately acquainted with the rest of the company, seemed inclined to maintain his position at the elbow of the latter, an affinity which the popular solicitor did not particularly approve; and as the best way of escaping from it, he did but give a friendly nod, smile, bow, or word, to every individual as he passed, and winning his way to Mrs. Buckhurst, proposed that they should make up their rubber directly.

"But what can *I* do, Lewis?" said the squire, doubtingly, who, being always one of the old lady's whist-party, did not much relish the idea of giving up his place. "How can I manage about Mr. Mortimer? Who is it that he is talking to? Where did that young man come from? I don't know him."

"That is his son," said Mrs. Buckhurst, looking at him for a moment through her glass, "and I have seldom seen a more pleasing-looking person. The *prejudices* that you reproach me with, neighbour Dalton, will hardly stand before that young man's charming countenance."

"I am delighted to hear it," returned the squire, laughing; "if you lose your heart to the son, my dear lady, you will soon take the father into favour."

"I don't know," replied the old lady, sighing very nearly as a younger one might have done, when talked to about her heart; "I'll do as well as I can; but you ought to remember how old I am, neighbour Dalton, and not expect too much of me."

"No, no; I will be content with very little," he replied. "And I'll tell you how we will begin. We will leave Captain Maxwell to flirt with the young ladies or play casino with her ladyship, and invite Mr. Mortimer to play whist with us."

"Surely it is Mr. Mortimer that should play casino with her ladyship," said Mrs. Buckhurst, beseechingly. But Mr. Dalton was already moving off, and holding up his finger as he retreated, in order to remind her of her promised good behaviour.

Half-way across the room he met Mr. Mortimer, advancing with his son, in order to present him; and, after a few words of cordial welcome to the young man, Mr. Dalton proposed a rubber of whist to his father. The manner in which the proposal was accepted shewed that it was welcome, and this displayed another excellent material for good neighbourhood in the agreeable barrister. The business, therefore, was soon arranged, and the table, according to promise, placed in the library, where, with no annoyance from the thoughtless chattering of uninitiated lookers-on, the old lady played, what she was obliged to confess was, "a very pleasant rubber indeed." Fortunately, however, for the immediate establishment of Mr. Mortimer's general popularity, the departure of Mrs. Buckhurst was always as attentively arranged as to its punctuality as her arrival; and he was therefore released in time to be introduced to all the ladies, young and old, to say something amiable and appropriate to each, and to leave the impression upon the whole party that he was decidedly the most gentlemanlike, animated, and agreeable person that they had ever had the good fortune to meet. Nor was this in the least degree the result of any effort on his part, to conciliate good opinion by appearing any thing that he was not. Mr. Mortimer really was amiable, animated, gentlemanlike, and agreeable, and too well disposed to be on pleasant and friendly terms with all his neighbours not to receive their overtures cordially.

At the first appearance of Henry Mortimer, as he entered with his sister and aunt, it was really as much as the young ladies could do to suppress an exclamation expressive of their agreeable surprise and admiration. He was, indeed, extremely prepossessing in appearance; though whether equally so with their old acquaintance Frederic Dalton, nothing but individual taste could determine; for they were as little alike as any two handsome young men could be,—the young squire being rather of a florid complexion, with large blue eyes, and a very beautiful profusion of rich clustering curls of dark chestnut hair; while the young lawyer had peculiarly black hair and eyes, with a complexion at once dark and pale, and which certainly required the relief afforded by his handsome mouth and teeth, to make it forgotten or forgiven. Both the young men were tall and well made, but in carriage and general demeanour young Mortimer had very decidedly the advantage. Neither this advantage, however, nor any other he might happen to possess, could long suffice to make him an object of *first-rate* attention in a circle where so many fair bosoms were fluttering, more perhaps than they had ever fluttered before, from the admirably managed secret love-making of young Dalton. The system of "circular flirtation," of which his father had spoken, was, on this occasion, managed with peculiar skill, and it would have been nearly, if not altogether, impossible for any individual there to have approached the truth, had they set themselves to guess in what manner he addressed the several young ladies who were present. That he did address them all in succession was evident; but as this was, of course, a duty imposed upon him by being at home, it created no particular observation, even from those most interested in all he said and did.

On being presented to the two strangers, or rather to the younger of them, he took care that his large wide-open eyes should express unbounded admiration, mixed with something of astonishment, which seemed to say that he certainly never had expected to see any thing so superlatively lovely as what he then beheld. There was much skill in this. Had he talked much, it is possible that his total ignorance of the scenes which the pretty Agatha had just quitted might have made her recur to the conversation when it was over with less of partial approval, than he was pretty sure he could inspire while it lasted. But his *look,*—his most speaking and most eloquent look, might be commented upon till they met again, without the slightest chance of its being severely criticised, at least, if Miss Agatha Mortimer at all resembled what he considered to be the usual run of young ladies possessed of eyes that could see. He did not, however, trust altogether to this one startled and expressive look. On the contrary, he approached her frequently, appeared to listen with much more than common attention whenever she spoke in his hearing, and finally left upon her mind exactly the impression he intended, namely, that he was an exceedingly handsome, but rather eccentric young man, and had something in his manners *remarkably interesting*. Then she was sure that he was excessively clever, but thought it would take some time to make him quite out. In short, he managed so well that (a little by the help, perhaps, of his heirship to the Dalton property) she returned to her new home, with her head, if not her heart, as full of the young gentleman as he could well desire.

As to his long-established loves, Miss Maxwell, and the two Misses Lewis, he, as usual, felt not the slightest embarrassment as to any of them. The drawing-room was quite large enough for him to manage exceedingly well with them all. To Miss Maxwell he only said, with one steady look of his marvellous eyes, "Are not these new people a horrid bore? I wonder if I shall ever be at liberty to say and to do what I like!" and then turned away, leaving her almost as perfectly satisfied as if he had made the long-expected declaration of his love. In the ear of the eldest Miss Lewis he breathed a profound sigh, and pronounced the name of "Mary!" in which she had never rejoiced so much as at that happy moment. This was all, except merely general conversation, that passed between them that evening—but it was enough. Nor was the pretty Lucy at all less satisfied. While handing a volume of engravings for her inspection, he continued to press her hand so tenderly, that nothing short of seeing him at the altar with another woman could have shaken her belief that she should one day or other find herself standing there with him in the very act of saying "I will."

In this manner the ingenious young squire contrived to profit in all directions, by hours, which, to one less skilful, might have been found extremely dangerous to his wish of being considered by each of his pretty neighbours as her especial adorer. Nor did his spirits flag for a moment under the ceaseless attention necessary to effect this. Never, perhaps, had he been equally successful in making the eyes and the voice, the looks and the words, the alternate vivacity and plaintiveness of one man, do the work of many, as upon this occasion. His obvious success, indeed, acted as a stimulant, and thus every labour of love which he performed only gave him fresh courage to proceed. Had he not battled resolutely, however, against the one genuine feeling which really lay at the bottom of his heart, while thus displaying by turns so many that were fictitious, he might not have succeeded so well. He found no difficulty in gliding from Mary to Lucy, from Lucy to Martha, from Martha to Agatha, and then back again; but now and then he did feel some little impediment to the smoothness of his progress and the perfect satisfaction of its result, from remembering, in spite of all his efforts to prevent it, the face and form of Jessie Phillips.

It must not be supposed, however, because the pretty youthful Agatha alone is mentioned as being added to the list of Mr. Frederic Mortimer's conquests, that Miss Mortimer, her aunt, was not still *une belle à pretention*. Nothing could be more utterly fallacious than such a supposition. This lady was not only still *à pretention*, but her pretensions were very generally allowed to be exceedingly well founded, and not a few among the male acquaintance of the family considered the established and acknowledged beauty of the aunt as more than an equivalent for the more youthful prettiness of the niece. Nor is it at all probable that, on the present occasion, she would have suffered judgment to go by default in favour of her young relative, had not the almost repulsive manners of the still handsome, though not quite young, Mr. Wilcox, so piqued her into a determination of making him talk to her, as effectually to prevent her bringing herself before the eyes of the young squire.

The quick eye of this lady had caught the refusal of Mr. Wilcox to be introduced to her, though it had not been within reach of her ear, and there was considerable skill discernible in the means which she employed to render this refusal of none effect. Most of the young people, with Frederic Dalton at their head, and Miss Johnson in the midst of them as a chaperon, had placed themselves at a large table in the middle of the room, to play a round game. Miss Mortimer declined joining this party, for she perceived that Mr. Wilcox had moved as far as possible from the spot where it was forming, and very decisively placed himself on an unoccupied sofa at the upper end of the apartment. Ellen, also, declined playing, and seated herself near the elegant stranger, determined to be as hospitably polite as possible, though dreading, at her heart, a long young-lady sort of gossip for the rest of the evening. But it was not thus that Miss Mortimer intended to profit by her first introduction to a Deepbrook drawing-room. Having answered Ellen's advances to conversation with smiling vivacity, she raised her glass to her eye for the purpose of reconnoitring the company.

"Oh! what a pretty party you have here, Miss Dalton!" she exclaimed; "it is long since I have seen so many white frocks and gay ribands. How many of these are your sisters?"

Ellen answered with a smile, "That five of the young things in white, round the card-table, were Daltons."

"Imagine! what a contrast is your destiny to mine! I am an only daughter, and my brother, old enough, as you may perceive, to be my father, was the only other child of my parents! The worst of this, my dear Miss Dalton, is, that it gives one, through life, all the wilfulness of a petted child,—as, by the way, I have the greatest possible inclination to prove to you this moment. Do you see that solitary gentleman yonder?—Mr. Wilcox, I think, is his name. I know perfectly well that he wishes to avoid being introduced to us, and precisely for that very reason, I do most particularly wish to be introduced to him. Do not look so exceedingly astonished; when you know me better, you will perceive that I am the most whimsical creature in existence, and, what is worse, that I invariably do whatever this whimsical propensity prompts me to desire. Therefore, my dear Miss Dalton, I must insist upon your accompanying me forthwith to yonder sofa. *Allons!*"

Miss Mortimer rose as she spoke, and seizing Ellen's hand, gently, but firmly, almost constrained her to rise from her chair. Having so far succeeded in her purpose, she passed her arm through that of Miss Dalton, and led her in the direction she wished, the acquiescence on Ellen's part being nearly involuntary, as she could only have opposed the will of her new acquaintance by a positive exertion of physical strength, to which she certainly had no inclination to have recourse. As they moved onward, however, Ellen ventured a gentle remonstrance,—

"I am sorry to tell you, Miss Mortimer," she said, "that I am hardly sufficiently acquainted with Mr. Wilcox, myself, to venture upon seizing him thus by storm."

"Indeed!" replied her new acquaintance; "but never mind that. If you will only give me the favour of your company, you shall see the sort of style in which I manage such matters."

By the time this was said, they were already close to the gentleman who was to be either quizzed or propitiated, as he might be found to deserve, by the adventurous fair one, who was determined that he should not altogether escape her. Ellen felt a good deal alarmed by the resolute tone of her companion, and the more so, because all she had yet heard or seen of Mr. Wilcox led her to dislike the idea of being made, in his eyes, a party to so very lively a proceeding. But she was agreeably surprised on reaching the chimney-piece, beside which the threatened sofa was placed, to find that Miss Mortimer's first device for attracting attention was the modest one of looking at the French time-piece which ornamented the chimney.

"Yes, indeed, I am right," said she, examining it on all sides with great attention; "this is precisely the duplicate of one my brother had in his London drawing-room. It is quite a pleasure to look at it, for it was one of the pretty things I never expected to see again."

Miss Dalton not being well skilled in the innocent art of "making believe," to which her clever companion had thought proper to have recourse, said nothing; but her presence was, nevertheless, by no means useless, for Mr. Wilcox immediately rose upon her approaching him, and made some observation which naturally led to conversation. This was all Miss Mortimer wanted. After silently listening for a minute or two to what he said and to what Ellen answered, she addressed him with the prettiest air of ladylike shyness imaginable, and said,—"Am I wrong in believing that it is Mr. Wilcox of Hortonthorpe, to whom I have the pleasure of speaking?"

The gentleman bowed, and Ellen then hastened to name the parties to each other in the usual style of introduction. "I have the pleasure, Mr. Wilcox, of being acquainted with a lady who knows you, or rather who did know you before she was married,—Mrs. Smith —Mrs. John Smith. She told me that Hortonthorpe was at no great distance from Deepbrook, and charged me to take the earliest opportunity of making your acquaintance. I hope you will forgive me for having so punctually obeyed her."

"Of course I am greatly flattered," replied Mr. Wilcox, a little stiffly. "May I inquire," he added, "the maiden name of the lady who is so kind as to remember me?"

"Upon my honour, Mr. Wilcox, it is more than I can tell you. I have known her for three years past, at the very least, but never once remember to have heard her maiden name. But do you not know her as Mrs. John Smith?"

"I know two or three Mrs. Smiths," replied Mr. Wilcox, smiling; "and I think it is exceeding likely that the name of John may belong to the husbands of some of them. But I fear this is scarcely enough to identify an individual."

"Most true!" replied Miss Mortimer, laughing; "but I do entreat you to believe that my friend that is, and your friend that was, has more individuality than her unfortunate name, and that she really is a very charming person."

Miss Mortimer had lived long enough in the world, and knew enough of society, both in town and country, not to be quite aware that Mr. Wilcox was a sort of neighbour whose acquaintance was exceedingly well worth cultivating; and having the power of exhibiting as many aspects as a cameleon, she continued, in the course of the next half-hour, to make him feel a good deal ashamed of the precipitate prejudice which had made him decline an introduction to so very agreeable a person. When she perceived that he had reached this point, which she did pretty nearly at the same moment that he was aware of it himself, she said, with a flattering vivacity of manner, which she well knew how to wear becomingly, "Mr. Wilcox, you must let me introduce you to my brother." His answer was such as to render her immediately rising to put her purpose into effect only exceedingly amiable, and nothing could be better on all sides than the manner in which this introduction was performed and received. Far from being annoyed by having her rubber thus disturbed, Mrs. Buckhurst was much pleased by the incident, for her own prejudices against Mr. Mortimer, or rather against the poor-law commissioner, were so rapidly melting away, that she was well satisfied to find those she suspected to have existed in like manner in the mind of her especial favourite, Mr. Wilcox, were inciting away too. In short, notwithstanding the disappointment of the gentlemen at the escape of Mr. Mortimer from their after-dinner discussion, the result of the visit altogether was to leave, with the great majority of the party, a very favourable impression in his favour.

# IX

*Some account of Mr. Frederic Dalton's notions concerning himself—accident favours his solitary meeting with Jessie—how Jessie felt towards him—his mode of reasoning with her—its effect upon her mind*

HOW MANY TIMES FREDERIC DALTON contrived to see Jessie Phillips in the course of the following week I know not, but by the end of it he had made up his mind as to the line of conduct he should pursue towards her. With all his faults, he was not unmindful of the recondite wisdom wrapped up in pithy proverbs, and he now recalled to mind that which says, "So men are born with a silver spoon in their mouths." He remembered this now, as he had often done before, and his application of it also, was as heretofore murmured in these words, "And I am one of them." No Eastern stickler for the power of destiny was ever firmer in faith on this subject than was Frederic Dalton. As for the next world, he confessed to his fishing and shooting crony, Dick Baxter, who was just about as estimable an individual as himself, that he knew nothing about it; and boasting that he never did, nor ever would, pretend to more knowledge than he had, he declared that he made a point of never turning his thoughts that way at all. But, on the other hand, he was equally free, as he said, to confess, that he thought he had about as clear notions of the present and visible world, which men actually have before their eyes, as any one in it; and this knowledge led him to perceive that he *was* one of the silver-spoon born gentlemen. Why else, out of eleven children, was he destined to possess the broad lands of his father? Why else did every woman he looked at fall in love with him? Why else was he always able to do whatever he said he would do? And, in short, the result of all his lightest sallies and his gravest meditations brought him to the same result, namely, that he might indulge himself safely, and with assured impunity, in the gratification of all the wishes and inclinations which destiny, that is to say, his peculiar and individual destiny, suggested to him. In the case of Jessie Phillips, this principle of action was roused into more than ordinary activity by the consciousness that there were some rather strong objections to his pursuing the course his inclination pointed out. In his estimation, the strongest and most obvious of these was the possible obstacle which any discovery of a little *affaire de cœur* with her, might oppose to his views upon any other fair one, whom the ever-dreaded necessity of defeating his sister's chance of succeeding him might make him suddenly desirous to wed. But the arguments which he brought to obviate this were twofold. First, the improbability that *any thing* could ultimately influence a young lady to refuse him, if he actually and *bonâ fide* offered her his hand; and, secondly, the obvious fact that he should always have it in his power to marry Jessie herself at a moment's warning, if untoward circumstances should render so desperate an act necessary. Of this, however, he had little fear. The terror that formerly kept so many libertines of all classes in check was no longer before him, the legislature having, in its collective wisdom, deemed it "discreetest, best," that the male part of the population should be guarded, protected, sheltered, and insured from all the pains and penalties arising from the crime he meditated. "No, no," thought Mr. Frederic Dalton, "thanks to our noble law-givers, there is no more swearing away a gentleman's incognito now. It is just one of my little bits of good luck that this blessed law should be passed precisely when it was likely to be most beneficial to me."

As to all secondary objections, such as the destruction of the pretty creature who was the object of his passionate admiration, he dismissed them all with a gay smile; and the moral reflection that it was "the little lady's business to take care of herself." Thus armed at all points, and *firm as fate* in the assurance that no mischief could reach himself from indulging in his inclination for Jessie Phillips' society, he strolled across the fields in the twilight of a Sabbath evening to her mother's cottage. Here again, as he already well knew, his good star had been at work for him, for Jessie's mother had never recovered from the effects of the accident which had befallen her on the night of time cowslip-picking; and having once or twice attempted to use her foot and come down stairs, she had suffered so much that she made up her mind to endure the confinement of a few weeks up stairs. She was still far from being an old woman, and being very nearly as industrious as her daughter, continued to add considerably to the joint purse by plaiting straw. This occupation required by long practice very little light, and she was therefore able to pursue it in the dark little chamber which served as a bed-room to herself and her daughter. Unfortunately, the delicate work of Jessie could not be performed under the same disadvantage, and it was this which enabled the "lucky" young squire to find such repeated opportunities of conversing with the poor girl alone. On the Sunday evening, indeed, the reason which caused him to find Jessie by herself in the lower room of the cottage was different; her mother had fallen asleep, and Jessie, who had been sitting with her, and reading to her, during three or four hours of heat and want of air, gladly stole out of the room for the purpose of seeking a fresher atmosphere below. Though it was Sunday evening, Jessie had not taken her usual Sabbath walk into the hazel copse, where all the lads and lasses of the parish were wont to congregate after the evening service was over. She had lost all relish for the jocund laughter and gay gossip of such a rendezvous. Pretty, gentle, kind-hearted Jessie, the admired of every eye, the beloved of many hearts, and the envied of not a few, was no longer the cheerful girl she had been. Jessie was in love—deeply, devotedly, passionately in love; and since falling into this condition, one solitary, dear half-hour passed in a corner of the neat little room which "served her for parlour, and kitchen, and all," with the sweet air blowing upon her through the open door, over the clustering blossoms of the finest honeysuckle in the parish,—one quiet half-hour so spent was dearer now to Jessie than all the joyous welcomings with which her appearance was sure to be greeted in the hazel copse. That the expression of her sweet features at such moments was that of melancholy is most certain; but it was a tender, soft and soothing melancholy, neither gloomy nor desponding; nay, there were times at which a charming smile dimpled for an instant round her lovely mouth; and though in looking at her it would have been a very dull eye that should have failed to guess that her thoughts were with an absent one, dearly, clearly loved, no one, while so reading her love, would have deemed it hopeless. Nor was it hopeless. Jessie in her very soul believed that every word breathed in her ear by Frederic Dalton was true as honour, faith, and affection, could make it. He said he loved her. And why should she doubt it? She knew full well—though, hitherto, the happy little creature had cared not much about it—that almost every one that looked at loved her. Then why should she doubt the love of Frederic Dalton? And for his honour, it would have been easier for her to doubt the brightness of the noonday sun than to have entertained a thought against it.

It was thus wrapped, and lapped, and blind-folded, and infatuated by her own passionate fancies, that the heartless young scoundrel squire found her on the Sunday evening above mentioned. He entered with the sly, noiseless movement of a cat, and any other than Jessie might have read mischief in his eye. But, instead of seeing this, she thought, as she gazed upon him, that there was something almost super-human in the beauty of his aspect. The absence of clownish awkwardness appeared in her eyes like almost god-like grace, and the soft accents of his voice fell on her ear like music! Where passion exists, let it be of what nature it will, every thing becomes fuel to it; and it mattered little, perhaps, how Frederic Dalton looked or spoke at that moment. She loved him, and she looked at and listened to him with as little chance of passing a sane judgment upon any thing he said or did, as if she had been in the delirium of a fever. Vain as he was—and few men are so vain as Frederic Dalton—he guessed not the strength of the passion he had inspired. How should he? He was as incapable of feeling such self-forgetting devotion himself, as of mounting to the "sphery chime" from whence he seemed to her to have but just descended.

"Sweet Jessie!" he murmured as he passed her threshold, in the low tone in which he always addressed her, and which was modulated with equal skill for the purpose of penetrating to her heart and *not* penetrating to the room above. "Sweet Jessie!—How like a lovely wild rose dost thou look at this moment, breathing perfume to the lonely air of heaven!" One of poor Jessie's misfortunes was the having, very literally, been "made poetical."

It is necessary to have met with a mind in a state similar to that of this unfortunate girl, in order to comprehend it. She had read verses of all sorts, whenever they had come in her way, with a degree of ignorant enjoyment (if such a phrase can be allowed) that had more, perhaps, of sense than of intellect in it. It was to her like harmony enjoyed, in utter unconsciousness of the science that produced it; but had this wild flower of intellect been cultivated, the case would have been different. There was no intellectual deficiency in Jessie Phillips; but the awakening process of education being wanting, the finer faculties slept, or looked out but vaguely and dreamily through the mist of ignorance. Frederic Dalton, however, had spied out this fanciful propensity in the poor girl, and turned it to great account; for not only did he take care to supply her with love-rhymes unnumbered, but failed not to assure her that not merely in person, but in mind, she was totally unfit for the station in which the chance of birth had placed her, and scrupled not—the villain!—to declare that the accident which had made him acquainted with her had, doubtless, been ordained by Heaven to atone for her having been misplaced among the lowly-born daughters of the earth. To all of which poor Jessie listened with the most undoubting belief. She knew that in many things she thought and felt in a manner greatly unlike the young companions who were of equal station with herself; and accepted, without a shadow of doubt as to its correctness, the theory by which her beloved explained this difference, and the remedy by which the incongruity might be set right.

He perceived that this mode of addressing her seemed more effective in silencing the scruples which common sense suggested respecting their clandestine intercourse than any other; and for this reason he took care that, if the gods had made her poetical, he would make himself so.

In reply to the words stated above, Jessie only smiled; but her eyes told him, if her lips did not, how greatly she rejoiced that he was come.

"My lovely girl will not speak to her Frederic?" he continued, as he closed the door, sat down by her, and took her willing hand. "My Jessie has no word of welcome for the man who is willing to sacrifice every thing for her sake?"

"Ought I then to welcome you?" returned Jessie with a sigh. "Would it not be like welcoming you to destruction?"

"Destruction! Can Jessie love, and call any sacrifice destruction that love dictates? Ah, dearest! did you love as I do, you would feel that what to others might appear like degradation, must to me be glory. But my Jessie loves not after this fashion. She cannot comprehend the intensity of affection which makes station valueless, and the opinion of the world as worthless as the buzzing of a fly, when put in competition with the possession of what we adore. Such love is all too great for Jessie's comprehension. She knows not what it means."

"Oh, say not so!" she replied, with trembling fervour. "Could we change places, Frederic—for Frederic you will have me call you—could we change places, you should quickly see that poor Jessie does know how to love, though she hardly knows how to let the man she adores ruin himself for her sake. It is that thought, beloved Frederic! that spoils all. Without it I should be at this moment the very happiest girl that ever lived."

"Then be the happiest, my most charming Jessie," replied the young man, with a passionate caress; "for nothing but the most wilful folly on both sides can make the love from whence I hope to derive the happiness of my whole life a source of ruin to me. I have already explained to you, dearest, the nature of the settlement under which I am to inherit my father's large landed property. Should I marry without his consent before I am thirty, I forfeit every acre of it; and then the estate is to be cut up among my sisters and a great number of cousins, some of them very unworthy people; so that I should think it very wrong, independently of my own interest, were I so to act, as to place my dear and honoured father's property in their hands. It is this, my Jessie, that must prevent my marrying now; but, thank Heaven! there is no obstacle of any kind to prevent my making my best beloved my wife after the interval of a few short years."

"Then for these few short years Jessie must live on hope," she replied with a soft, and almost inaudible sigh. And then followed a discussion upon the best and least miserable manner in which this interval could be passed; and, for a good while they could not agree upon this point, Jessie being of opinion that it would be best for them both that they should be separated, which, she said, could easily be arranged, by her persuading her mother to change her residence to a village in the next county where a sister of hers was living, and "very well to do." But to this scheme Frederic Dalton vehemently opposed himself, and at length succeeded in convincing her that his life would, in all human probability, be the sacrifice if she persevered in a project so full of cold-hearted barbarity.

"I shall die, Jessie," he said; "I shall die! I know the nature of my own mind perfectly! Such misery would sap the very springs of life; and with blasted youth, and a heart broken by the hard cruelty of my soul's idol, I should sink into an early tomb, another victim on the fatal shrine of unrequited love!"

Poor Jessie! She—

> "—believed him true,
> And she was blest in so believing."

But "the story is extant, and written in very choice" language of many lands—so it need not be repeated here.

# X

*Ellen's interview with her father—Mrs. Greenhill's second visit to the Union poor-house—Lawyer Lewis makes some very acute remarks on Mr. Mortimer—the assistant commissioner speaks out at last—splendid eloquence on the part of Mr. Huttonworth the button-maker—Mrs. Greenhill gets an insight into the domestic arrangements of the work-house*

FROM THE HOUR THAT ELLEN Dalton paid her visit to the two Mrs Greenhills in their miserable cabin, she could not get the idea of what she had seen and heard there out of her head. Personally she knew less of the Greenhill family than of almost any other in Deepbrook; but by character she at least knew one of them well, and for this one (the kind-hearted widow) she felt more than common interest. There were, moreover, other circumstances connected with her, and with the distress which pressed upon her, which were pretty nearly as interesting to Ellen as to the good woman herself; and these so worked upon her mind, that it might almost be said she thought of nothing else. Nor was it merely in idle, though anxious speculation, that she meditated upon the subject. From the day on which she met Mrs. Greenhill at the house of Mrs. Buckhurst to that of her visit to Bushy Lane, she had been meditating on a scheme for her relief; and this scheme would have been executed immediately had it not been for some little embarrassment which she felt would attend its being put in action. This feeling produced delay, but could not turn her from her project; and at length, having armed herself with as much composure of manner as she could muster, she sought her father in his library, and plunged into the business at once, by saying, "Papa, are you at leisure? I wish to speak to you for a few minutes, if you are."

"I am always at leisure to hear you, my Ellen," he replied affectionately; "but you almost frighten me, dear, you look so very grave. What is the matter, Ellen? Tell me at once, my love."

"Nothing, dearest papa,—nothing is the matter," she replied in a manner well calculated to reassure him; for the words were spoken with a smile, and with no very distinctly visible trepidation. "If I look grave," she added, "it is only because I am very much in earnest in what I wish to say to you. The 500*l*., papa, that mamma's old aunt left me last year—it is quite at my own disposal, is it not?"

"Certainly, Ellen," he replied, looking a little surprised. "What do you want to do with it?"

"I want to use it immediately, papa, or at least the greater part of it, I believe; and I want you to have the kindness to tell me what I can to do in order to get at it."

"It is very easily got at, Ellen," he replied ; "but is the use to which you intend to put it a secret, my dear child?"

"Not to you, papa," she answered, in a tone that was intended to be very gay and easy; "but to *every* body else it is, and you must promise not to betray me."

"Let your secret be what it may, I will promise to keep it safely, Ellen; but I confess I am a little impatient to hear it."

"Well then, papa, I will tell you instantly." And then, but with a great deal more difficulty as to her articulation than her companion perceived, Ellen proceeded to explain herself, "My secret is, papa, that I wish immediately—that is to say with the least possible delay—to get into my hands as much money as will suffice to pay Tom Greenhill's still remaining debts, and to re-establish him and his family in the cottage they inhabited before he was sent to prison."

The handsome countenance of the squire underwent a very perceptible change as he listened to these words; and not only were his features contracted into something exceedingly like a frown, but he coloured violently. For a moment he was silent, however, and when he did speak, it was only to ejaculate the name of "Ellen!" The composure which his daughter had struggled to maintain now forsook her; she first blushed violently, and almost immediately turned as violently pale.

"Is it possible, father," she exclaimed indignantly, "that you can mistake my motives?"

"I am afraid not, Ellen," was his reply. "I do not think it *is* possible that I should mistake your motives."

"But you do, father—you do, or you could not speak to me thus."

"Why, Ellen! my poor, dear, unhappy child, how can I, how could any body acquainted with the circumstances, fail to perceive for whose sake it is that you do this? Can you, even to your own heart, affect to believe that it is for the love of old Dame Greenhill or any of her race?"

"I have no wish," replied Ellen, in some degree recovering herself, "I have no wish whatever, father, to delude either you or myself in this matter, or to affect any greater degree of interest in Mrs. Greenhill than I really feel. Her situation is a peculiarly painful one, and would, I think, under any circumstances, have excited in me a very strong desire to help her; but certainly," she added, another deep blush rushing over her fair face, "I should never have thought of taking aunt Ryland's legacy out of the funds for the purpose of relieving her had she never nursed the Marquess of Pemberton."

On hearing these words, her father looked at her with some surprise, but this was immediately exchanged for an expression of affection and confidence.

"Dearest Ellen!" he said, "forgive me! I ought by this time to know you too well to suppose that you could be conscious of any feeling which you might not, to me at least, most freely avow. Would to Heaven, my dearest love, that the sentiment which you have so often told me, and which I so truly believe, is become too essentially part of yourself to be ever changed or forgotten—I would to Heaven, Ellen, that it were felt for one who had the power of returning it! But as it is, my poor girl, would it not be wiser to do nothing that may betray it, either to him or any one else?"

"I knows it all too well, father," she replied, composedly, "to learn any thing new on the subject, by finding that I had made this sacrifice for the sake of saving his nurse from the poor-house. It is not, therefore, from any feeling of reserve that I should care about his knowing it. Nevertheless, my dear father, I do not intend that he shall ever know it, because, as you are well aware, there are circumstances which would render it inconvenient, nay, perhaps difficult, for him to repay me; and, therefore, if I did not quite believe that what I am going to do could be concealed from him, I would not do it at all, even though I so very well know what he would suffer upon learning that old Margaret Greenhill was in the poor-house. But he will never know it, dear father. Trust to my management about that, will you?"

"Ellen!" replied Mr. Dalton, looking at her with great fondness, "there is nothing in the world that I would not trust to your right thinking and your right feeling. The father who has been the chosen and selected confidant of his daughter, throughout such a history as yours, dear girl, is not likely to be tormented by any doubts or fears concerning her conduct. I have none such, believe me. But, my dear child, I would wish, for many reasons, that this poor woman should avoid what you, and herself too, I suppose, so greatly dread for her, by some other means."

"And so do I, too, papa," replied Ellen, frankly. "Shew me any other way, and you shall see that I will adopt it readily."

"At any rate, then, my dear, I will try what can be done in my capacity of guardian. Our new commissioner appears exceedingly good-natured and amiable, though neither knowing nor caring, as I suspect, much about the business on which he is employed; but I think, in a case of such peculiar hardship as this seems to be, I shall find no difficulty in obtaining his sanction to giving a little help to these poor people, without dragging them all into the house. She is to appear before us again next Monday. Will you wait, my love, to see the result of this?"

"Most certainly I will," she replied; adding, with her own peculiar smile, "I have, at least, not blundered much in the confidant I have chosen."

The important Monday arrived; and once again the greatly altered widow Greenhill, looking pale and emaciated, and with a spirit pretty well broken to the endurance of any thing and every thing that could befall her, set off to implore the board of guardians of the Deepbrook union to afford the family of her son a little temporary relief till, by taking advantage of the Insolvent Debtors' act, he should be released from prison, and in a situation to assist by his labour in supporting them. His unhappy little wife had added another burden to the parish since her poor mother-in-law's first application for relief; and it was not without hope, that the difficulty of moving her at present might induce the guardians to relax, for a week or two, in their decision, that they must come into the house, if they persevered in demanding parochial assistance. That such assistance must in some way or other be obtained, or that the family must actually perish from want, was certain, as the old woman's earnings had been completely put an end to for some days past, by the needful attendance upon the lying-in woman and her six children. She now, therefore, set forth with the bitter conviction, that if she failed in obtaining such aid as might support life in the hovel that now sheltered them, it must at all hazards be immediately sought within the dreaded walls of the poor-house.

As she approached the building, a group met her eye whose jocund, well-fed air might be supposed likely to afford her some comfort; for the good living so unmistakably conspicuous in their appearance proceeded from the identical kitchen to which she looked as the worst that could befall her in her search for food for the starving little throng she had left at home. This group, which was stationed at the door of the court-yard, and within the shadow of the lofty wall which surrounded it, consisted of Mr. Richard Dempster, the governor; his plump and laughter-loving wife, Dolly; and Growler, the huge mastiff dog, who was the especial darling of both, and stood them, as both the husband and wife were frequently accustomed to say, in the stead of children, most excellently well.

In bygone days Dolly Dempster had been accustomed to look upon Mrs. Greenhill as a "darnation stiff old gentlewoman, too proud by half;" and, perhaps, Mrs. Greenhill had been accustomed to look upon Dolly as rather too blunt, bluff, and jovial in her manners, to make a very desirable companion. There was, therefore, no great intimacy between them, although, when there was more equality of condition in their respective circumstances, they had been acquainted.

"And who may this skinny, bony body be?" said the governor's lady as Mrs. Greenhill approached the gate. "Just look at Growler, Dick, do," she continued, as the darling dog advanced a step in front of her, and standing with his two front feet firmly set, and his tail erect, seemed disposed to dispute the entrance. "Just look at him!" and she laughed aloud. "I know the woman now, well enough,—'tis fine Madam Greenhill, that's fine Master Tom's mother; and if that blessed beast don't know that she's come mumping, and has not a copper in her pocket to help herself, never believe me again. There never was such a beast as that on God's earth before. Talk of Christians? Why, the biggest half of 'em is no more to be compared in straight forward common sense to Growler than double X to small beer. I'll wager just whatever you like, Dick, that if that 'dentical same woman had comed here six months ago, the beast would have bided as quiet and still upon his bit of straw there as if he had been fast asleep. God bless his sweet nose!" she added, bending over him to caress the honoured feature. "It serves un as well as a pair of money scales does a Christian, and better too, for he knows the weight and walley of all that comes to shop, without taking any more trouble than just one little sniff."

"Down, Growler!" gently ejaculated Mr. Dempster, affectionately caressing him at the same time. "Thou be'st a jewel of a dog, and that's a fact. Soh! mistress," he added, "you'll be after bothering the board again, I suppose, by just asking 'em to do the very exact thing what they've determined they won't never do. That's the way with ye all, and much good it does ye, don't it? A set of everlasting grumblers as you are! I do sometimes wonder, in my own heart, that you ben't all ashamed of yourselves. It is something unaccountable and unheard of, to be sure, to see one bundle of rags after another coming up here, to bully and bother all the first and foremost gentlemen for miles and miles round, as if they knowed or cared a potato-paring about any one of ye."

"Are the gentlemen of the board sitting, sir?" inquired Mrs. Greenhill, taking hold of the railing that enclosed a plot of potatoes.

"Oh, my eye! madam's going to tumble!" exclaimed Mrs. Dempster. "Dick! look about you, man! Can't we get a chair? or can't we carry her in handy-dandy, in this fashion?" And she crossed her hands over each other, to indicate the mode of conveyance she proposed.

"I should be proud and happy," replied the governor, catching his lady's merry vein, and shewing his large teeth, from ear to car, by a broad grin, "only as she have been used, you know, to ride about with my lady Duchess in a coach, it may be doubtful, I'm thinking, whether she'd altogether like this t'other mode of riding."

"Will you please, sir, to tell me whether the board is sitting?" reiterated the pale, trembling old woman.

"Yes, Mistress Greenhill, they be, as sure as you is standing," he replied.

"Then, please, sir, let me go in," she said.

"Yes, madam, I will," said he, with a low bow; "and then they'll be pleased to let you go out again, and so we shall all be pleased together, you know;" and so saying he pushed open the door behind him to let her pass; his wife laughing till she was obliged to hold her sides the while, and exclaiming, as soon as she had recovered her breath, "You are first-rate, Dick, in a dry joke, and let them deny it as dare."

Mrs. Greenhill passed on to the well-remembered room, where the gentlemen forming the board of guardians were assembled. Several other "bags of rags," as Mr. Dempster facetiously denominated those unhappily driven to claim the assistance which the law has provided for the several of these broken-down, destitute, suffering creatures, were waiting round the door of the room; and poor Greenhill trembled as she looked at them, for she doubted if her strength would last through the long standing that would be necessary while their business was despatched. But here fortune favoured her, for no sooner had the door opened, near which she had placed herself, than the eye of Mr. Rimmington caught sight of her, and instantly perceiving that she was in no condition to wait, he desired the man who attended at the door to send in the Widow Greenhill immediately.

She was thankful, and she was cheered by this lucky accident, and determined to take courage, and explain, to the very best of her power, the peculiar circumstances of her son, which rendered it so highly probable that he would soon be able to maintain his family by his labour, and, therefore, that their coming into the house would be far too short a time to render such a step necessary or advisable.

Thus armed, poor soul, she stood before the powerful phalanx which was to decide the important question, with more steadiness of aspect than she had yet exhibited; that is to say, she did not tremble quite so much, nor were her cheeks and lips so utterly colourless.

"Isn't it curious, Mr. Lewis," said the barley-brewer of Deepbrook to the solicitor, next to whom he generally contrived to place himself, "isn't it curious, now, to watch how these creters get bolder and more audacious every time they come before us? Do you remember, sir, how this one pretended to totter and tumble about the other day, for all the world as if she hadn't either strength or courage to stand upright, and just look at her now, that's all."

Mr. Lewis shook his head, and then nodded it half-a-dozen times, to testify his perfect concurrence; but he was not at leisure to reply in words, being very earnestly attending to a conversation between Mr. Mortimer, who was seated at no great distance from him, and Mr. Dalton, not only because these two gentlemen were the most important persons there, but because it was his especial wish and object at the present moment to make himself acquainted with all the views and opinions of the new commissioner, that so he might be enabled to render himself both agreeable and useful to him in his new capacity. This system being by far the most promising within his reach for making his name known to the dictators of Somerset House, some one of whose numerous appointments he privately hoped might be obtained by means of his ever appearing to the eyes of their assistant as the most accomplished man of business in the whole country; but his hopes of learning any thing respecting that gentleman's ideas respecting any one of the knotty points connected with his commission, were not very likely to be gratified by the act of listening to the conversation in which he was at present engaged; for, after catching the words "absolutely necessary," and "no doing without it," which seemed to promise well, he at length discovered that the subject under discussion was not the new Poor Law, nor the Union Poor-house, but the prodigious superiority of one particular sort of bait over every other, for one particular sort of fishing. Lawyers are said to he pretty generally exempt from the weakness of feeling which produces blushing, but our Mr. Lewis coloured as he made this discovery. He was vexed to think how very earnestly he had been watching to catch what was so greatly unlike that which he wished to find; and then, having withdrawn his eyes and his ears from the two gentlemen who had so absorbed his attention, and set himself to the mending a pen, he began meditating upon the singular fact that never, in any of the various interviews with Mr. Mortimer, with which good luck and his own skilful manœuvring had favoured him, had he ever heard him utter a single word respecting the delicate and difficult business in which he was engaged.

"I suspect I have been altogether mistaken in him," thought Mr. Lewis; "he is deep, very deep, and much too wise to carry his heart, or his brains either, upon his sleeve, for daws to peck at, or for his neighbours to scan. But I must unravel and unriddle him; and so I will too, let him be as tangled and as subtle as he may."

Having made this resolution, Mr. Lewis assumed a look considerably more careless than usual, and turning to his neighbour, the brewer, said, "That's Tom Greenhill's mother that you were noticing, Baxter; and, upon my soul, she looks as dignified as the Duchess herself. I suppose she took lessons while she was nursing the heir."

The usual ready laugh rattled in the throat of the jocund democrat, who never was so merry when a pauper was the subject of the jest

"Let's have her Grace forward, Lewis," said he; "I remember her when, upon my soul, she seemed to fancy it rather a condescension to speak to me. It's capital good fun, to be sure, to see her stand there with her threadbare old things put on with as many pins, and as much nicety, as if she had been dressing for court, and she looking all the time so very considerably more than half starved. If there is one thing that I hate and abominate more than another, it is the sight of pride and poverty mixed up together. I'd fifty times rather give my vote for helping such a one as that," he continued, indicating a slovenly self-neglected figure, whose garments seemed to be secured by a solitary skewer; "she looks as if she'd be humble, and thankful, don't she? If I'd my way, I'd shew that we saw a difference between 'em. Will you support me, Lewis?"

But Mr. Lewis, though at that moment a very goodly-sized tin box stood in his office, inscribed with the words "Joseph Baxter, Esq." was quite determined not to let any species of partiality appear before the eyes of the "deep" Mr. Mortimer; and he therefore whispered in his good friend's ear, that it would be better not to let any particular feeling (except general respect for the act) to appear in any thing they said or did, till they had fully ascertained that of the commissioner.

"*My* going with the commissioner must depend altogether upon what sort of a chap he turns out," replied Baxter; "and as to my likes and dislikes, Master Lewis, I neither mean to change 'em or hide 'em for all the boards or all the commissioners in Christendom!"

"You are a fine fellow, Baxter," returned the popular Mr. Lewis, with an approving nod, "but I never like to quarrel with a man before I know him."

While this was passing on one side of the table, Mr. Rimmington was gently interrogating Mrs. Greenhill on the other; and having heard all she had to say in support of her petition for aid, for a few weeks, during the detention or her son, without placing the family in the poorhouse, he bade her retire, while he brought the question before the board, advising her, however, not to leave the place till she had learned their decision. With grateful blessings for his kindness she withdrew, and the good clergyman, with that *douceur qui fait plus que violence*, begged the attention of the gentlemen present for one moment upon the case of the poor woman who had just left the room.

"I have known her well," he said, "during the whole course of my ten years' ministry, and can venture to assure you all, from that knowledge, that you may believe implicitly what she tells you. The deplorable inconvenience that would arise to her from her being obliged to bring her family into the house, will, I hope, induce the board to deviate a little from their usual practice in her favour, and lead them to make her such an allowance at her own dwelling as may enable the family to exist till the Insolvent Debtor's act shall have released her son from prison."

The voices of Mr. Dalton, Capt. Maxwell, and Mr. Wilcox, were immediately raised in support of this proposition. The two first declaring that they knew the poor woman well, and could fully confirm Mr. Rimmington's testimony in her favour; and Mr. Wilcox, observing that though she was personally a stranger to him, her statement evidently proved, backed as it was by her excellent character, that there would be very gross injustice, as well as very great impolicy, in treating her as a common pauper.

"Of course, sir," observed Mr. Huttonworth, the retired button-maker, addressing the reverend chairman,—"of course, sir, we all, and you amongst the rest, speak under authority, having the advantage of this gentleman's presence" (pointing to Mr. Mortimer); "but as free discussion, that greatest of privileges to a free people, is permitted to us, I must beg to observe, that I have never before happened, since I came into possession of my estate, to hear such doctrine as to parish help as that which it has seemed expedient to you, sir, to lay down. Now please to observe, gentlemen, here comes a woman, telling us that she wants our money, and must have it, but that it must not be given her according to the law, made and provided for the protection and fostering of the lazy, idle, dissolute portion of the community to which she belongs, but she must have it in her own way, and no other,—that way, observe, being in the very teeth of an act of parliament! Now this is going it pretty strong, you'll think, perhaps. But what is *that* to what follows? Here's a gentleman who is the parson of the parish, I take it, and chairman of the board into the bargain, and he coolly tells us that we had better let the good woman have her way, because it will be very *inconvenient* to her if she has not. Now, if this doctrine is to be held to, I should like to be told what sort of condition the parliament is put into? Much good, isn't it, for them to make laws? If this isn't downright rebellion in a quiet way, I am pretty greatly mistaken. And then, gentlemen, just please to observe the arguments from the other gentlemen who have thought fit to follow on the same side. Two of these gentlemen say, in so many words, that the woman is an old crony of theirs, and for that reason they particularly wish to favour her; while another, with equal sincerity, scruples not to avow, that he wishes to favour her too, on account of their good opinion of her. The rate-payers of the Union may be thankful that they happen to have a commissioner among them who has the power, and we will flatter ourselves the will likewise, to put a stop to such illegal proceedings; and if we find ourselves disappointed here, I, for one, shall vote for publicly burning the act of parliament by the hands of the overseers and church-wardens of the parish in which this make-believe of a union is established!"

Having delivered this speech, Mr. Huttonworth wiped his mouth with his hand, and looked round the table as if to challenge an answer to what he very evidently considered to be unanswerable. It seemed as if the rest of the party were of the same opinion, for no voice was raised in reply, though more than one individual spoke to the person next him, but not loud enough to be heard by others.

"You seem, sir, to have the good luck of knowing how to silence opposition," said Mr. Baxter, after looking about him, and seeming to enjoy the silence for a minute or two, "and I can't but say that I am happy to find that we have got among us such a stickler as you are for what is lawful and right; so now, I think, since it is plain that nobody is able to oppose the reasonableness of your arguments, Mr. Huttonworth, I will propose that the audacious pauper who has just left the room shall be recalled, in order to be told that we neither will or can do more, or other for her, than for any one else, and that she and her family is either to come into the house, or let us hear no more about her from this time forth for evermore."

Instead of making any reply to all this, either by addressing the board generally, or Messrs. Huttonworth and Baxter in particular, Mr. Dalton at once appealed to the assistant commissioner saying, in a voice that was, however, audible to the whole room, "Though you do not know this poor woman, Mr. Commissioner, quite as well as her neighbours of long standing do, I conceive that you have heard fully enough to enable you to judge of her very peculiar case, and therefore, without arguing the point any farther, I think, our best course will be to take your judgment upon it. Do you think, sir, that under all the circumstances, it will be expedient to give to this woman an order that herself, her daughter-in-law, and her six grand-children, shall come into the house?"

Mr. Mortimer, the amiable expression of whose very gentlemanlike features formed a strong contrast, by their bland indifference to the interest, the eager and anxious humanity, and the hard brutality painted on the countenances of many round him, paused for a moment before he replied; and that moment was to himself a very embarrassing one. It would have been difficult for the awfully powerful triumvirate of Somerset House to have chosen a delegate more perfectly well disposed to do what was right, proper, and fitting, or to render more implicit obedience on all occasions to the enactments of the law under which he held his appointment than was Mr. Mortimer. He was possessed, too, of so really excellent and amiable a temper, that it seemed impossible any roughness or difficulty should arise between him and the various boards of guardians who were to act under his authority. In short, he might truly be said to be the *beau idéal* of an assistant poor-law commissioner. Nevertheless, he felt himself greatly embarrassed upon this appeal from Mr. Dalton. The common sense part of the question was, of course, as obvious to him as it must have been to every one else who chose to look at it on that side; but he had already perceived, notwithstanding his earnest endeavours to keep himself clear of all cabal, and from every species of local or individual interest in any question brought before him,—notwithstanding this, and all his pre-determined diplomatic officiality of non-intercourse (professionally speaking) with any of those for whose use and benefit he was sent to interpret and enforce the new law,—notwithstanding all this, he had already discovered that he was surrounded by conflicting opinions, feelings, and interests. This discovery, however, only served to strengthen him in his determination of being impenetrable to all attacks upon his individual feelings, or even upon his individual judgment, and to cling to the letter of the act, in order to save himself from the interminable difficulties that must inevitably multiply around him should he attempt to modify his decisions according to circumstances. After a short struggle, therefore, against dictates of common sense and common humanity, he replied to Mr Dalton's appeal by saying,—

"I believe, my good sir, that the circumstances of the case must not beguile us into losing sight of the principle of the act. If this family, for whom you are so amiably interested, receive parish pay at home, it will be hardly consistent with justice that we should refuse it to the next applicant who may chance to prefer this mode of relief to a residence in the house."

Mr. Lewis, who had been closely watching the effect of Mr. Dalton's interference, no sooner heard these words than he had the inexpressible relief of perceiving that his own path was plain before him, and that, too, in the direction wherein it would be the most convenient and the most consistent for him to tread. Mr. Lewis was neither cruel nor unjust in the abstract; but he was a man of business, and would no more think of being turned aside from a straightforward conformity with an act of parliament, by any destruction or misery that it might be the means of producing to the poor of the parish, than an industrious sawyer would from dividing a block of wood, because a nest of animalcula lay in the path of his saw. Nor was the reply of Mr. Mortimer agreeable to him only because it accorded with his own ideas of what was right, he perceived in a moment that he should in all reasonable probability have it in his power to be useful. He not only knew the act by rote, that was a matter of course; but he had carefully read, and commented upon at length, every page of every report from the select committee on the Poor Law Amendment Act, with the whole body of the evidence produced before them. And these commentaries of the industrious lawyer not only furnished a clear compendium of the most important evidence, but what was greatly more to the purpose, it furnished also a very neat sort of bird's eye view of the *leanings* of the honourable committee themselves. Thus furnished with a sort of secret fund of authority, the lawyer of Deepbrook felt that he was likely to become a person of some importance in the estimation of a gentleman who expressed himself with so much commissioner-like propriety as Mr. Mortimer; *provided always*, that his good gifts, both natural and acquired, were properly made known to that personage. With a view, therefore, of making them so, Mr. Lewis, in a tone of voice more earnest than loud, and rather as an ejaculation than as addressing an observation to any particular person, said, "Admirable! admirable! a more perfect definition of our duty was never uttered, and I trust in Heaven we shall now go on straightforward as we ought to do."

These words were not lost on Mr. Mortimer, and were really very consolatory to him, but excepting by a very slight glance of the eye he took no notice of them; neither did the gallant half-pay captain on the other side of the table; for having taken an ample pinch of snuff upon hearing the speech of the commissioner, he only allowed himself time to close his box, and replace it in his pocket, before he replied to it by saying, "By your good leave, Mr. Commissioner, I must just take the liberty of observing that this new law, with all its startling and terrible clauses, comes to us with the assurance that all the abuses incident to the former system of parish relief were to be remedied by it,—that what was necessary to be done for the relief of the destitute was to be done, and nothing more; and above all things, that most especial care was to be taken that the rates collected for the purposes of necessary relief should not be wantonly expended. Now, I shall be very grateful if you will shew me how the admission of eight human beings into the poorhouse, to be wholly and entirely provided for at the expense of the parish, and that for a period unlimited, can be a less burden upon us than giving the aid of a few shillings a-week for a short time, in compliance with the wishes of our chairman."

"The LAW sir,—the LAW," cried Mr. Lewis, eagerly, "it is the law, sir, as set before us in the late act of the united Parliament that must regulate our conduct in this matter as well as in all others, and unless we make this the only rule of right, you may depend upon it we shall go on blundering to the end of time, squabbling with one another, and doing nothing but mischief every time we meet. This is exactly one of the occasions upon which we shall feel the immense and incalculable advantage of having an assistant Commissioner within easy reach of us. And I trust we shall hear no more of worthy Mrs. Greenhill and her troublesome progeny, till we are told how they behave themselves in the house,"

"Send the woman Greenhill in," vociferated Mr. Huttonworth to a man who was stationed at the door, "and in the name of common sense let us have done with her. If I don't greatly mistake, and I'm not thought to be much of a blunderer, that woman is a pestilent, factious, plausible, mischievous old hussy, who is determined upon giving us all the trouble that she can—I'd stake my life upon it, I would, upon my soul."

"I have only known her about ten years," said Mr. Rimmington, gently; "perhaps you, sir, may have known her longer?"

"That is not the question, Mr. Chairman," replied the button-maker; "and so the assistant-commissioner will tell you, if you will ask him, I fancy. What is the use of centralization, which is becoming our blessing and our boast, you know, and what's the use of it, if we administer the law according to our local knowledge of individuals instead of according to the act?" This was said with a triumphant air, and concluded with a very jocular laugh, that was echoed lustily by Mr. Baxter. "I should not have thought," continued the button-maker, addressing Mr. Rimmington, "that a learned gentleman like you, sir, had any need of being told what this centralization means; however, as I have studied the subject a good deal, I have no objection to telling you that it means just this, that in the administration of parochial relief, there is to be no difference made between man and man, or between woman and woman. The relief is to come, sir, just like the sun and the rain, upon the good and upon the bad, all alike. No difference, no preference, no good character, no bad character, to make any change or alteration whatever. And all this capital scheme of equal claims is to be made sure by the gentle commissioners and assistants settling the whole matter, and preventing the country gentry and the farmers from having any thing to do with it from their own judgment. And if this don't prove a cure for partiality, and all the rest of the old countrified notions about character, I don't know what will. As if a rogue didn't eat as much as an honest man! And if we are bound to feed one, arn't we bound to feed t'other? I take it, Mr. Commissioner, that you won't find much to gainsay or contradict in my interpretation."

Mr. Mortimer, to whom these last words were addressed, with a smirking bow slightly bent his head in reply, but said nothing.

While all this was passing, the object of the discussion, who had been dismissed while it was going on, was seated in a small square room in a distant part of the building, awaiting a summons from the board for her return to receive the announcement of their decision. The walls of the room into which she was shewn were whitewashed, and it was evident, from their spotless condition, that the operation had been very recently performed. Its one window looked out upon a small interior court, the principal, and, indeed, nearly the only object in which was a pump, with a cistern under it, where all the inmates of the establishment, old and young, male and female, performed their ablutions. Round the walls of this small chamber, and firmly fixed to them, were wooden benches, as narrow as it was well possible for an adult human being to sit upon. On these benches of little ease were seated, when Mrs. Greenhill entered the room, seven or eight aged females,—the youngest among

them must have been considerably passed sixty, and one or two of the oldest appeared to touch the very last stage of human life. These last took no notice whatever of her approach, but the rest looked sharply up, and fixed their eyes upon her eagerly. Mrs. Greenhill bent her head in salutation to them all, and then placed herself at the end of the bench that was the least occupied.

"Why, sure that's Dame Greenhill," said one of the women, looking at her with a pitying glance. "You bean't come to bide here, I hope? I han't forgot how you doctored my grandchild in the croup, and I'd be sorry to have you keep company with us here."

"I can't answer you yet, Betty Thomas," replied Mrs. Greenhill, "for I am waiting for the answer to that question myself. But why do you all sit here, doing nothing, Betty? I won't pretend to say that I wish to come in, but if I am obliged to do it I don't mean to pass my time in idleness."

"Don't you, Madam Dainty?" said a savagely cross-looking crone, who, being from the most distant parish in the Union, neither knew, nor was known by, Mrs. Greenhill. "If you get in here, I take it that you'll find you haven't much choice."

"About most things I shouldn't expect to have a choice," she replied; "but I don't suppose I should be stopped from working if I wished to do it."

"Yes, but you would, though," answered the other.

"Nay, I can't quite believe that," said the good woman, with a melancholy smile. "It is called the workhouse, you know, and sure they wouldn't try to prevent people from employing themselves."

"Much you know about the matter, don't you?" was the rejoinder. "If you stay in the house, I tell you that you can't work—unless you choose to beat stinking hemp—or if you work, you can't stay in the house. That's the law and the gospel here, mistress, whether you like it or lump it."

Mrs. Greenhill, who was not much in a humour for discussion, said nothing in reply to this; but the woman who had first addressed her, and who thought, perhaps, that something like an accusation of idleness had been made against herself, addressed her again, saying, "What she speaks, Mrs. Greenhill, is only a deal too true. They won't let us weed in the garden, which, God knows, I should think was like being in Paradise compared to sitting here day after day, from morning to night; they won't let us weed the garden, nor take a turn at watering the plants, because they have got hands enough, they says, and to spare, that can do it stronger and better. Nor they won't let us help in the house for the same reason; they like the younger ones better. And all this, you see, goes to prove that she speaks the truth, poor sour old soul, about not working in the house; and then, as to not staying in the house if you do work, that means that if any poor body can get something to do that they could be paid for, and have got eyes left to see how to do it, they'd be handed out in no time, to get their own living, without a single blessed penny to help them, though, may be, they mightn't be able, at the very best, to turn above twopence or threepence a-day,—and I know what that is, for I've tried it, and twice I've been nigh to death's door with starving myself, for the sake of keeping out of this sorrowful den. But hunger will conquer any spirit."

At this moment the door of the room opened again, and a huge, tall girl appeared at it, who looked in upon them all, and burst into a fit of laughter. Though her size, her stature, and the hard, coarse aspect of her features, might have belonged to years considerably more advanced, her dress was that of a girl of fourteen or fifteen, and there was something strangely incongruous in the disparity between her harsh features and her girlish attire. The wiry black hair upon her large head was shorn as closely as that of a charity boy; her dark stuff frock was short and scanty, and the leading outline of her singular figure was formed by an ample garment of coarse linen, made in the form of a child's pinafore. One of the old women made a faint attempt to smile in reply to her laugh, and at the same time beckoned her forward with her finger.

"A pretty pass we are come to, ain't we?" said another of the sad circle, addressing herself to Mrs. Greenhill. "It seems a blessing to see even idiot Sally open the door and look in upon us. Why should human creatures in their senses, and that never did harm to man, woman, or child, be cooped up here, and made to sit all of a row in this dismal little den of a hole, while God's blessed sun is shining over their heads? I wish I could change places with idiot Sally, and then I shouldn't sit, day after day, as I do now, puzzling my poor old head to guess why God lets it be so."

The idiot girl, who was one of those harmless, imbecile unfortunates of which almost every parish can shew a specimen, obeyed the invitation to enter, but instead of approaching the woman who gave it, she walked straight up to Mrs. Greenhill, who knew her well, and seizing her hand, shook it with a vehemence that was far from being agreeable. But poor Sally was a privileged person, and those of much harsher temperament than the widow Greenhill were wont to receive her rough greetings rather with cordiality than resentment. Nay, so universal was the indulgence with which she was treated, that it extended even to the iron discipline of the poor-house. Not even Dick Dempster, or his wife either, were exempt from the species of superstitions respect which her condition appeared to inspire. They never abused her, they never beat her, they never mulct her of a meal, by way of keeping her in order, as they called it, when exercising this power upon others. Nay, they even suffered her, without let or hindrance, to wander out of the house wherever she liked, and spend the hours of daylight how and where she pleased,—a privilege freely permitted by the guardians and sanctioned by the parish doctor. For Sally was not only perfectly harmless, but so well known to be so by the whole neighbourhood, that nobody felt any dislike to meeting her. Nor was her harmlessness her only merit; she had various good qualities, which, though probably more the result of habit than of moral feeling, were not without their value. Every body knew that Sally always spoke the truth; and there was nobody in the parish who, if they wanted to ascertain a fact about which she knew any thing, but would have taken her testimony in preference to all others. She was, too, very tenderly fond of little children, and so careful of the safety of any one who chanced to be near her, that nothing but the uncertainty of purpose, which would often lead her suddenly to change her place and wander away for miles, till the hour of rest or the calls of hunger brought her back again, nothing but this inconvenient uncertainty would have prevented her being able to get her bread by nursing.

Rough as her greeting was, Mrs. Greenhill received it kindly, saying, "It is a great while, Sally, since I saw you. Where have you been wandering that I don't see you in the village? Little Jane often says, 'Where's Sally?'"

The idiot shook her head, and, after a moment's pause, replied, "I don't like Jane, nor any of them now."

"What! because they are become poor, Sally? You shouldn't say that," returned Mrs. Greenhill.

"I don't like 'em," persisted Sally, shaking her head. "The place don't look happy. I like the lambs and the fields a deal better."

The woman who had beckoned Sally in, laughed, though in no very amiable spirit. "Catch Sally saying a civil thing or a false one," said she. "You have been a grand lady in your day, Mrs. Greenhill, and maybe Sally liked you better then than she does now. And if so be that is the case, you'll just get that much out of her, and no more."

"I have no right to expect a poor thing like her to have the feeling for me that another might," replied poor Greenhill.

"And who is the t'other, pray?" demanded the woman, with a sneer. "Is it the gentry sitting out yonder? The guardians, as they call themselves? Blessed guardians, arn't they? Don't they guard us nicely here now?—don't they? D'ye think I would not sooner be guarded by silly Sally? Why, the poor wench, when she saw us looking sad and sorrowful, would just open them these cursed gates outside, the very first thing she did, and she'd say to us, 'Off with you, old women! Go, and take a peep of the sunshine, and when you're too hungry to bide out any longer, then come back again, and not a minute afore!'—'cause Sally knows right well that the dirtiest bit of common highroad, with the air blowing and the sun shining over it, is Paradise to these here dismal walls, with nothing but stone and mortar, and miserable faces to look at."

These words, though spoken in that tone of unkindly grumbling which creates no sympathy, nevertheless made a deep and very sad impression upon the heart of the poor woman whose fate was now in the balance, as to whether she, and those she loved, were to be doomed to the prison-like precincts of "*the house*," or to be aided by the donation of a morsel of bread without the loss of liberty. While silently meditating on this alternative, one of the officials of the establishment opened the door, and bluffly told her that she was called up to appear again before the guardians.

# XI

*Mrs. Greenhill receives judgement from the board of guardians, and Squire Dalton sets to work in consequence—he makes his report to Ellen—another visit to the cottage*

On re-entering the room where the arbiters of her fate were sitting, Mrs. Greenhill might have seen traces of somewhat rough discussion on more than one countenance, had she been in a condition to study them. But, in truth, she saw nothing but the face of Mr. Rimmington, on which her eyes immediately fixed themselves; and whereon she read, not exactly strange matters, for the doom she saw there had already been again and again foretold by her fears; but still, as it was all she most dreaded, it shook her whole frame, almost as violently as if it had not been anticipated.

"I am sorry to tell you, Mrs. Greenhill," said he, "that the board have decided it to be impossible to grant you any out-door relief. If your circumstances are such as to render the assistance of the Union necessary, you must obtain it by coming into the house. If you consent to do this, an order shall be made out accordingly."

For a moment the unhappy woman remembered only the scene she had just left, and the melancholy imprisonment that threatened the dear children, whose gambols had so often been her delight, and she felt as if she were only waiting for breath to say that she would try to work harder still, rather than rob them of the blessings of fine air to breathe, and green sod to roll upon; but ere she felt sufficient courage to say it, the image of their eager hungry eyes fixed upon her as she entered (alas, empty-handed!) amongst them, recurred to her, and seizing upon the back of a chair to steady herself, she said, "Thank you, sir. If you please."

The eyes of Mr. Dalton were fixed upon her as she spoke, and the agony her features betrayed almost reconciled him to the somewhat imprudent act which he was quite sure his Ellen would claim his promise to permit, as soon as he should report to her what had passed.

Nor was he in any degree mistaken in supposing that her eagerness to achieve her object would now admit of no longer delay. He would gladly, for many reasons, have avoided the business altogether, but after the conditional consent he had given, this was impossible; and, such being the case, he yielded to his wish of making the relief to be afforded as prompt and as complete as might be, both for the purpose of gratifying his darling, and of healing the misery he had witnessed. Ere he reached his own gates, therefore, he had already done much towards the performance of the good work. His first care was to see his bailiff, and in his interview with him he did all he could towards remedying the most objectionable part of the transaction. No man living ever placed less undue value upon money than Squire Dalton; and the fact of Ellen's expending her little legacy in the manner she proposed was a matter of absolutely no consequence in his eyes, compared to the evil of having her interference in the affairs of Mrs. Greenhill reported at the Castle. He did his admirable girl the justice to believe that she would wish to avoid this, fully as much as he did himself, and feared not to trust to her discretion in managing the business with Mrs. Greenhill; but how to restore her to her former habitation as his tenant, without his own interference becoming known, was the difficulty. While meditating on this really knotty point, he rode onwards at the very slowest pace that his stout hackney could be made to walk, and the time thus gained sufficed to settle his plan of operations. "I need tell him no falsehoods about the matter," thought the worthy gentleman; "a little very innocent mystification is all that will be necessary."

"Ralph, I am come to you upon a secret embassy," said the squire, as he entered the cottage of his old servant, "and you must be a very discreet fellow, and ask me no questions, and then, you know, according to the pithy old proverb, I shall tell you no lies. You know all the sad story about the Greenhills. Their cottage is not taken yet, is it?"

"Why, no, sir," replied Ralph, "I can't say as it's taken. But there's no less than three that's pretty eager to get it; and I have promised neither of them as yet, because I wanted to know a little bit more about the character of the one as bids the highest."

"Oh—well, that's all very right, Ralph; and now you must just tell them all that it is not to be disposed of, for the old tenant's coming back again."

"The old tenant? What! Mrs. Greenhill, sir? Sure, sir, begging your pardon, you must be mistaken," replied Ralph "for I am amost as sure as I can be of any thing, that the whole family, bag and baggage, are all going into the workhouse."

"It is always wisest to be sure of nothing, Ralph," replied his master, smiling; "and yet I will give you leave to be sure of what I am going to tell you, and that is, that a good friend of old Mrs. Greenhill's has given me to understand that she shall take it as a great favour if I will let the poor woman go back to her old cottage, and I have promised that I will, Ralph."

The bailiff rubbed his chin, and looked intelligent. "That must be the Duchess, sir. It is easy enough to guess that riddle, whether you are pleased to tell it or not. And I don't much wonder that her Grace shouldn't wish to have it talked of, for it's no great credit to be for ever going on helping to uphold such extravagance as Tom Greenhill's. However, that's no business of mine, any way. But I hope you'll get your rent paid, your honour."

"I have no doubt of it, Ralph,—not the least in the world, so you need not be uneasy on that score. Only you must please to remember, that though you have said it was the Duchess by whose desire I have undertaken to manage the widow Greenhill's return to her old quarters, I have not said a single word to confirm your suspicions."

"No need, sir," replied the man, laughing; "the thing speaks for itself, as we say. However, my lady duchess, nor you neither, sir, have got no reason to be afraid of my tongue. I shan't say nothing to nobody. Let every man have his own guess about it, and that you know, sir, will be neither your fault nor mine."

This delicate part of the business got through, Mr. Dalton returned home, and immediately summoned Ellen to a conference in his library.

"Well, papa, how have they treated her?" were her first words.

"Why, by no means like wise men, in my opinion," he replied; "and I am obliged to confess, Ellen, that, do what I will to prevent it, my allegiance to the new law is so often shaken by the want of wisdom in its administration, that I am terribly afraid I shall turn round before it is long, and confess that the amendment wants sadly to be amended. But this is not what you are listening for, with your dear earnest eyes, and you are a good girl not to tell me so. But I can reward you, Ellen. I have shewn more prompt obedience to your commands than you could well expect, young lady, considering that I do not altogether consider your scheme a prudent one. I have already settled with Ralph that your *protegé* is to return immediately to her own dwelling; and, what is better still, he has not the very slightest suspicion that either you or I have any thing to do with the matter."

"I cannot thank you half enough, my dear father," she replied, "and I feel so very happy about it, that Frederic must, I think, leave off calling me an old maid for a little while, I shall be looking so gay and so young. But you must go on, my dear, dear father," continued Ellen, earnestly; "I must have the money I spoke to you about, or the business cannot prosper."

"I know that quite well, my dear child," replied Mr. Dalton, "and you shall have as much money as you please. But this very interesting-looking old woman, Ellen, told us that she felt quite confident that they should be able to maintain themselves again when her son got out of prison; and, therefore, if you will take my advice, you will not, for a thousand good reasons, do more than is necessary. Were I you, Ellen, I would not attempt to restore them to the unincumbered possession of the old woman's annuity. I don't believe Tom Greenhill is at all a bad man; but I have no doubt that it was his leaning too much upon this independence, which caused his neglect of business, and all the misery that has followed."

"What sort of a creature should I be, if I refused to obey implicitly every suggestion of yours, my dear, kind, considerate father?" said Ellen, while a tear, which the tender caress he gave her seemed to say he understood well, started to her eye. "We must get back as much of her furniture as we can," she resumed. "I believe it is none of it sold, but pawned at that wicked-looking shop in the High Street. I will ask her what she will require for this, and give it to her; and afterwards she shall have only a few shillings a-week to help out what she gets by her work, till her son is at liberty."

"Very well, Ellen, that is exactly what I think you had better do; and here is fifty pounds for you to begin with," returned her father. "I need not caution you, dearest," he added, after the pause of a moment, "to be very careful to make it a point of honour with her, not to let either your name, or mine, be mentioned in the business."

Ellen's fair face became of a very bright carnation as she answered, "Trust me, father!"

It was never without so little difficulty and good management, that Ellen Dalton could continue to walk out *alone* in any direction, save that which led to the abode of Mrs. Buckhurst. But, nevertheless, she did now and then contrive to escape from the loved and loving throng, who would never willingly have lost sight of her. She waited, on the following morning, for the arrival of the dancing-master, whose lesson almost always assembled the whole of the school-room party in the dining-room; and, having heard his kit in full action, she walked forth by a path that avoided the windows of that room, and took her solitary way to the melancholy abode of the Greenhills.

She was shocked at observing the altered aspect of the poor widow. All strength, all effort, every trace of animation and interest in what she was about, had vanished from her countenance. She was languidly, and almost negligently, holding a child, almost like a bundle, under one arm, while, with the other hand, she was cutting the fragment of a loaf which lay on a table into very small pieces, while the five elder children stood round it with eagerly expectant looks.

The sight of Ellen caused something like a slight frown to cross her face and though her lips moved, as if uttering some word of salutation, no sound proceeded from them. "You are busy, Mrs. Greenhill," said Ellen, "and I am sorry to interrupt you. But I must speak to you for one minute."

"Yes, ma'am," replied Mrs. Greenhill, making an effort to speak civilly; "I *am* very busy,—too busy, ma'am, for any thing, if you'll please to excuse me for saying so;" and as she spake, she put the morsels of bread she had cut into the eager hands of the children.

"That is but a poor meal for them, my good friend," said Ellen, taking a few shillings from her purse.

"It is the last bite of bread that I am likely to give them," replied the miserable woman, while tears stole down her haggard cheeks. "Their next meal will be at the work-house."

"The two biggest children are old enough to run to the baker's for a loaf, are they not?" said Ellen, holding up a shilling before their eyes.

"Yes, yes," said the boy and girl at the same moment; "we always goes for granny." She put the money into the hands of the eldest, and they were both out of sight in a moment.

"Now, Mrs. Greenhill," said Ellen, with a degree of authority that was intended to rouse her from the miserable state of mind into which she appeared to have fallen, "I must really get you to listen to me. For I have a promise to demand of you; and if you do not attend to what I am saying, and to your own words also in reply to it, the promise will not be worth having, for, of course, it will mean nothing."

The poor woman stared at her with a surprised and puzzled look, and replied, "I think, ma'am, there must be some mistake. You are Miss Dalton, I think, ain't you, ma'am? And I am quite sure that no young lady like you can have any thing to say to me. I know you are a very kind and good young lady; but I hope you'll excuse me, miss, I can't talk to any body now. I am no longer one of those that ladies like you ought to talk to; and please to forgive me, ma'am, but I am very, very busy."

As she spake, the tears ran from her eyes upon the child in her arms, who, having devoured the morsel she had given it, was wimpering for more, and she tried to soothe and quiet it by pressing it to her bosom.

"Mrs. Greenhill," said Ellen, almost sternly, "you must not give way to such low spirits. If you will promise me never to tell any one, that is, never to mention my name or that of my father as having assisted you, I, on my side, will promise that you shall not be driven to do what you appear so greatly to dread,—you shall not go into the work-house, Mrs. Greenhill."

The poor woman looked at her for a moment so wildly as almost to frighten her. The deadly paleness of her cheeks was changed into a deep glow, and, gently laying the child she held in her arms upon the floor, she approached Ellen with a good deal of agitation in her manner, and said, "Dear, dear young lady, tell me what you mean at once!"

"My good Mrs. Greenhill," replied Ellen, deeply touched by the vehement and evidently uncontrollable agitation that she witnessed, "I mean exactly what I have said to you. My father and I will undertake to keep you and your family out of the work-house, if you will promise not to tell any one that we have had any thing to do with preventing your going there."

"I do promise," replied Mrs. Greenhill, with her eyes earnestly fixed on the face of her visitor, as if not yet quite certain of her meaning.

"Now then," resumed Ellen, cheerfully, "we can come to particulars. My father thinks, Mrs. Greenhill, that the board dealt harshly with you, and unwisely also. He thinks that if you are restored to your former abode, and that your son finds you there on his release from prison, he will be more likely than he has ever yet been to maintain his family by his labour. Every body says he is an excellent workman; and if he will give up shooting and fishing, and be steady, I dare say you will all do as well as ever. Now then, the first thing to think about is getting back your furniture. I think you said, when I was here last, that you had been obliged to pawn it?"

"My furniture?" repeated Mrs. Greenhill, again looking as if her faculties were bewildered, and as if she did not fully comprehend the words which were spoken to her.

Ellen laid her hand kindly on the poor woman's arm, and said, with a very soothing smile, "Yes, your furniture, my good friend. My father would be doing you little kindness in putting you back in your old dwelling, if we did not take care that you should have your furniture put back there too."

"But how can I believe in such happiness, Miss Ellen?" said the astonished woman. "And what can I ever have done to deserve such kindness?"

It was now Ellen's turn to look confused and embarrassed. For a minute or two her cheeks were crimson, and apparently seized with a fit of anxiety for the safety of the child who had been laid on the floor, she snatched it up, and began playing with it very assiduously, giving it a little gold locket, which was suspended to her neck, to handle, which obliged her, of course, to hold down her head a good deal. But Ellen Dalton was too much accustomed to command her feelings, to give way to them long; and, quickly recovering her composure, she placed the child in the arms of its grandmother, saying, "I shall feel very happy to see them all back again, poor little things, in their old quarters, and you must get ready to remove, Mrs. Greenhill, as soon as ever your daughter-in-law is sufficiently recovered." Ellen drew out her purse as she spake, and placing one half of the sum she had received from her father on the little table, added, "This is five-and-twenty pounds, Mrs. Greenhill. Will that be sufficient to take your furniture out of pawn?"

Again an expression of astonishment, that almost equalled her pleasure, was visible on the countenance of Mrs. Greenhill, so visible, indeed, that Ellen again coloured violently, from the consciousness that what she was doing was in truth quite as much calculated to create surprise as gratitude. She wished the scene over and her errand done; but ever and always, more considerate for others than for herself, she took care, before leaving the cottage, to make the thrice-happy widow understand that although her father did not mean to guarantee to her the annuity she had sacrificed to the debts of her son, she would receive from him such regular weekly assistance as would enable them, with the assistance of their own work, to go on till the debts were paid, and her income restored to her. Ellen's eye dropped before the look of almost adoring gratitude with which Mrs. Greenhill regarded her as she said this, and she turned to go. But, while her hand still rested on the latch, he felt so strong a desire to ask one question that she could not resist it; and, with her eyes fixed upon the way she was about to go, instead of upon the face of her she addressed, she said, "When I met you at Mrs. Buckhurst's, you were talking of informing the noble lady with whom you formerly lived of the misfortunes that had happened to you. Have you done so, Mrs. Greenhill?"

"No, Miss Dalton, I am thankful to say, I have not. After thinking about it, day and night for above a week, I made up my mind at last that

I would suffer all things rather than do it. Oh! Miss Ellen you cannot understand, it is quite impossible you should, what reasons there are why I should no further burden their generous kindness; I know the heart of my dear young lord, and that he would have never rested till every thing was straight again with me. And that's just the reason why I would not tell him. And my noble lady, too, would have been all goodness; but I would rather have died, Miss Ellen, than have told her of all poor Tom's folly and wild extravagance. And now; thanks be to God, and to you, she need never know it, nor my dear, precious foster-child, either." Having received this extremely satisfactory answer, Ellen, with renewed courage, turned back for a moment, and entered into some minor particulars respecting the removal of the family, and then, her heart lightened of a good deal of uneasiness, and warmed by seeing the sedate look of happiness which was now rapidly taking place of Mrs. Greenhill's painful agitation, she once more bade her adieu, and departed.

# XII

*A pair of village graces—a few rather profound observations, tending to prove that love leads to much sisterly affection towards sisters—innocent manœuvrings—a visit to Jessie Phillips, who receives her company with much dignity—the ladies think they understand all about it; nevertheless, two out of three are at fault—an apparition*

ELLEN HAD NOT QUITE TRAVERSED half the distance between Bushy Lane and her own home, when she met two of the very smartest young ladies that ever stepped along the heathy precincts of a village common. The two Miss Lewises, dressed exactly alike, in delicate white muslin, with twin decorations of pale blue, arranged with an immensity of taste and skill, had just set off upon their daily walk with the enlivening hope of meeting somebody to look at them, and not quite despairing that the somebody might be Frederic Dalton himself. Never did rival sisters, or rivals of any kind, go on together so peaceably and well as pretty Mary and Lucy Lewis. This was certainly partly owing to their being good-tempered girls, but more still to the admirable skill and management of the object of their mutual adoration. During this morning's walk, as during all other walks, they had talked of nothing but him, and his beauty, and their chance of meeting him; each in her heart a good deal pitying the other for being silly enough to fancy that the meeting him could signify one single farthing to her.

Every body who knows any thing about young ladies who are in love must be aware that at all times when the dear object of the passion is not to be got at, the next best thing is to get hold of his sister. Oh! there are so many nice little words and phrases, which may be dropped, that if the sister should repeat, might make him hit upon so many amiable inferences about them, in so many different ways! It is so easy to say things to a sister, that they could just die rather than say to the brother himself. And then it is so very nice to catch the family laugh and the family look! Not to mention the inestimable advantage of cultivating a close family friendship. In short, there was but one of the grown-up Miss Daltons that had not good reason to believe that both Mary and Lucy Lewis perfectly doated upon them.

No sooner had these young ladies espied the figure of Ellen Dalton approaching them, than they both, as if set in action by one common spring, darted forward, each at the same instant making a movement to quit the arm of the other, and each, with the accuracy of a soldier upon parade, wheeling round at the proper moment, so as to flank their intended sister-in-law, each of them affectionately seizing upon an arm, which they respectively pressed against their loving sides.

"Darling Ellen!" exclaimed one, "what a pleasure!"

"My dearest girl!" murmured the other, "this is a delight!"

Ellen was too much accustomed to the fond affection of the Miss Lewises to be much moved by it, in any way, but she felt very glad on meeting them now, that she had not chanced to meet them before; and being, too, considerably relieved and comforted by the manner in which she had accomplished what she wished, her gentle endurance of their sisterly love was more smilingly demonstrated than usual, and her two pretty supporters became fonder of her than ever in return.

"Only think of your being all alone, darling Ellen!" said Mary; "and you one of such a large family, too."

"This is dancing day," replied Ellen; "and I am the only one too old to practise."

"But your brother is not learning dancing, Ellen, is he?" said Lucy, with another hug of the arm, that was perhaps involuntary.

"Oh, no!" replied Ellen, "he is not learning dancing."

"Heaven knows that there is no need he should," remarked Mary. "But for goodness sake do not tell him that I said so."

"Mercy on me, Mary! you need not alarm yourself by supposing that Ellen would repeat any such nonsense; and much her brother would care, to be sure, if she did," said Lucy, with a little laugh, suddenly adding in the most indifferent manner in the world, "Where is he gone to-day, Ellen, that beautiful brother of yours? He is so like you, love, that though I never do, by any chance, think a man handsome, I positively *do* think him beautiful. What is he doing with himself this morning?"

"I really do not know where he is," replied Ellen, quietly.

"How I do envy you having such a brother!" exclaimed Mary. "Are you aware of your own happiness, my dearest friend? Is it not the most delightful thing in the world to have such a companion?"

"I often wish I had more brothers," replied Ellen, rather evasively.

"Dear me!" cried Lucy, with energy, "I am sure that if I had him, I should not wish to have any one else. But don't tell him that I said so—or—he would only quiz me, perhaps, because I have got no brother at all. Pray don't tell him what I said."

Ellen had been so much accustomed during the last year and a half to receive similar injunctions from the Miss Lewises, that she rarely did more than give a little nod in return for them. No answer she could have hit upon, however, would have pleased them so well, for both the enamoured sisters soothed themselves with the belief that Ellen fully intended to repeat every word, and was too honest and honourable to pledge any positive promise to the contrary. It was probably this conviction that made them proceed so perseveringly in confiding their flattering opinions to her concerning her brother's various graces and perfections; but as some of these out-pourings now came in the form of questions that demanded reply, she grew weary, and on arriving at a point where the road divided, she made a pretty decided effort to disengage her arms, saying, "I must wish you good morning now, for I want to inquire for Mrs. Phillips, and I will not take you over so many stiles, and so much out of your way."

Her pretty companions paused, though they still held her greatly beloved arm fast; but they both felt that the path which Ellen proposed to follow was very much out of the way,—not so much out of their way indeed, but out of the way of other people.

"Oh! I should not mind the stiles the least bit in the world," said Lucy, at length. "Your brother says I spring over the stiles like a fairy, and I'm sure I should think nothing out of the way that kept me with you, darling; but I will tell you honestly, Ellen, I have got something very particular, and a little bit of a secret too, that I want to say to your brother. You must not tell him, mind, for the whole world, that I confessed as much to you,—no, not for your life, Ellen. But I *do* want to see him, just for half a minute, and I really wish you would tell me exactly which way you think he is gone?"

"I would tell you with the greatest willingness, Lucy, if I knew, but I really do not," replied Ellen. "He went out of the room, as he always does, immediately after breakfast, and I did not hear him mention to any one what he was going to do this morning."

"Well, then, I am sure it is nonsense giving up walking with you, with so little chance of meeting him, if we go another way," said Mary Lewis, renewing her tenure of Ellen's arm by making her grasp of it rather tighter. "You may go, and try your chance elsewhere, if you like it, Lucy, but I shall stay with dear, darling Ellen. Besides, I want to speak to Jessie Phillips about my cambric pocket-handkerchiefs that I gave her to hem: she has kept them a most unreasonably long time."

"You may depend upon it, Mary, you don't love darling Ellen one bit better than I do," returned Lucy, in like manner clinging to her on the other side. "Besides, I, too, want to scold Jessie Phillips about something she has had to do for me for these hundred years past."

The party accordingly proceeded across two or three small enclosures to the dwelling of Jessie. Though the weather was bright and warm, the door was closed, and Mary Lewis exclaimed, "Oh! Jessie is gone out to work, I am quite sure, for she never sits with the door shut."

"Jessie does not go out to work now that her mother is so ill," said Ellen, knocking. "She refused to come to our house on Saturday, because she could not leave her."

After an interval sufficiently long to make the lively Miss Lewises declare that it was no good to wait any longer, the door was at length opened by Jessie herself, but looking so ill that the two sisters exclaimed together, "Good gracious, Jessie! what's the matter with you?" while the gentler Ellen took her hand, and led her back into the house, and placed her in a chair, for she felt her tremble so violently that she thought she would fall. "Is your mother worse, Jessie?" she said, kindly. At the moment that the beautiful cottager had first met the eyes of her three visitors, her lips and cheeks were so extremely pale, as naturally to suggest the idea that she must be ill, but before Ellen Dalton had ceased speaking, her whole face and bosom were in a glow; and whether ill or not, she so far conquered the trepidation which appeared to have seized upon her, that rising from the chair in which she seemed to have seated herself unconsciously, she replied with even more than her usual pretty sedateness, "No, thank you, Miss Dalton, my mother is still suffering, but I do not think her worse than she has been; indeed, I rather hoped today that she was better."

"What in the world made you turn so deadly pale, Jessie, when you first saw us?" inquired Lucy, with considerable curiosity.

"Your knock startled me, Miss Lewis," replied Jessie, with a sort of forced composure that almost appeared like an assumption of dignity.

"Mercy on me!" resumed the young lady, "you must be monstrously nervous, Jessie?"

"I believe I am very easily startled," replied the fair sempstress, turning her beautiful eyes upon the ground, but still speaking with very ladylike sedateness.

"You should get the better of that, my good girl, as soon as you can," said Mary Lewis, laughing; "for it must be horridly inconvenient when you are stitching away as fast as your needle can go, if you turn as white as a sheet, and tremble all over every time you hear a knock at the door."

"I am not quite so bad as that, Miss Lewis," replied Jessie, with a faint smile; "but I believe I was thinking of something else when your knock came."

"Oh, dear yes; I dare say you were not thinking of us," said Lucy; "for I am sure that if you had not forgotten us most abominably altogether, you would not have kept us waiting so long for our things."

"I am sorry, ladies," replied Jessie, rather with politeness than mere civility,—"I am very sorry if you have been put to any inconvenience by the delay. It has been really unavoidable."

"On account of your mother, I suppose?" said Mary, good humouredly. "Well, never mind, we don't mean really to scold you, because everybody knows that you are a very good girl, only you must not get into a way of keeping people's things so very long, you know." Jessie bent her head, with a very graceful air that seemed to say, "I stand reproved, but do not very greatly care about it."

Ellen, whose eye had at first been fixed upon her from an affectionate feeling of interest, and from really fearing she was ill, remained so from different feelings. She could not in any way comprehend the altered manner of her young favourite. In speaking to her indeed, though there was something more than usually grave in her manner, it was with her usual gentle and grateful-toned humility; but to her companions there was evidently an assumption of something that might have been called dignity, if the word could, without absurdity, have been applied to the little sempstress. The Miss Lewises, though with much less observant eyes than their darling Ellen possessed, seemed puzzled by the girl's manner; but after looking at her for a moment or two, to find out what she meant, Miss Lucy's self-consequence suggested that the poor little soul was frightened by the idea of having offended them, and said, very condescendingly,

"You need not be unhappy about it, Jessie, we shall both forgive you if you don't do so any more."

Again Jessie threw her eyes down, but there was a pretty furtive smile about her beautiful mouth that Ellen could not help thinking was very saucy. However, as she loved Jessie a great deal better than she did the Miss Lewises, she did not feel very angry, but smiled too.

At this moment the latch of the door was raised without the ceremony of any previous knock, and the poor idiot girl entered. Notwithstanding all her nervousness, Jessie appeared not to be at all alarmed by this abruptness, but, on the contrary, received the poor creature with a friendly salutation, and immediately proceeded to pluck a handful of honey-suckles for her, which she accepted with a broad grin, but with an air that seemed to indicate that the nosegay was a daily offering, as in truth it was.

"How d'ye do, Sally?" was pronounced by all the three young ladies, nearly at the same moment, for the idiot girl had decidedly the largest speaking acquaintance in the parish, nobody ever passing her without some salutation or other. But Mary Lewis, on the present occasion, seemed inclined to push the conversation further than the ordinary "how d'ye do?" for she added,

"And where have you been, Sally? and who have you seen?"

Now this question was not quite so idle as it might seem to be, considering the person to whom it was addressed; for Mary Lewis perfectly well knew that she might expect a rational answer: and, indeed, silly Sally's habit of noticing every body and every thing she saw, joined to the invariable fidelity of her replies to every question relative to whatever objects her eyes fell upon, rendered her not unfrequently rather a valuable person to meet, for she would prate of the whereabouts of every man, woman, and child she encountered with the utmost matter-of-fact accuracy. To the question of Miss Lewis she now replied,—

"Sally has been to the High Street and back again; and Sally has been to the wood where the white lilly bells grow, but her couldn't find one; and Sally has been to the baker, and he gave her a cake; and then her walked by the back lane, along by Butcher's Close, for Jessie Phillips to give her a nosegay."

"And who did you meet in the way, Sally?" inquired Mary.

"Sally met Dicky Smith just close to the milestone, up High Street, and he'd got a mug in his hand. And Sally met Becky Roberts under the big tree on the Common, and her had got Susan More's baby in her arms, and her let Sally kiss it and hug it. And then Sally met three cows and a donkey that was upon the high road, before her turned into the lane. And then, close by here, her met the finest thing of all, and that was the young—"

"Look here, Sally,—look here!" cried Jessie Phillips, suddenly seizing upon her arm, and directing her attention to the honey-suckle that hung its rich festoons across the door. "Did you ever see any thing so beautiful as that!"

The suddenness of this action brought the eyes of the whole party upon her, and neither of the young ladies failed to observe the vivid blush that died the cheeks of Jessie at that moment; neither did they fail to come to one and the same conclusion, namely, that the "*young*" somebody or other, who, in the estimation of Sally, was "*the finest thing of all,*" could be nothing less than a smart young man, and probably one of the innumerable adorers of the village beauty. Mary and Lucy Lewis laughed, but Ellen looked at the agitation of her young favourite with great concern. She knew, or at least she believed that hitherto the lovely Jessie had lived fancy free, having heard that she had refused a multitude of better offers than she could ever reasonably have expected to receive. But now Ellen at once, and with a sympathising sigh, felt certain that this heart-whole condition was gone for ever from her pretty favourite, and she would have been about as likely to laugh had she seen the lawn that covered her bosom on fire.

"Pretty creature! Heaven grant that happiness, and not misery, may grow out of it!" prayed Ellen, while her lighter-spirited young companions began to rally the poor girl on the agitation which had betrayed her.

"Why, Jessie! what a silly girl you are, to be sure, to let out every thing, as you do, without saying a, word!" said the eldest Miss Lewis, fixing her eyes upon her most unmercifully.

"I would not have such a trick of turning red and pale, as you have, for all the world," observed Lucy; "not, however," she added, rather pointedly, "that any such '*fine things*' as silly Sally was talking about could ever be found shut up at Lewis Lodge."

This attack appeared to act upon Jessie Phillips as the most effective restorative that could have been applied to her tremors and agitation. She suddenly turned from the door-way, to which she had had recourse, in order to conceal her conscious face from her visitors, and, looking first at one Miss Lewis, and then at the other, she said,—

"You are still very young, ladies, and for this reason no one, who though equally young, may, perhaps, be more considerate than yourselves, ought to resent seriously what you say in jest. Dearest Miss Dalton!" she added, turning to Ellen, while tears started to her eyes, "I would that I had this moment the power of proving to you how deeply I value the good opinion which your manner to me shews. Perhaps the time may come when I may be able to do so, and there is no happiness,—no, none in the whole world, that I should value more dearly than that."

Though there was certainly something of mystery in all this, Ellen, and her companions also, at once comprehended that, whoever had been at the cottage before they entered it, Jessie felt rather proud than ashamed of the visit; and, in fact, they all began to suspect that Jessie Phillips was going to make some very great match, but that for the present there were reasons, probably some opposition from the young man's family, which prevented its being acknowledged publicly. And if Jessie Phillips herself had explained the state of the ease, she could not have done it more accurately. She did believe, without the slightest mixture of doubt, that she was going to make a very great match, but that there were, for the present, family reasons, on the young man's side, for its not being acknowledged publicly.

After the interval of a moment, the three young ladies each extended a hand to the beautiful cottager, uttering, with proper reserve, but very friendly smiles, their wishes for her future happiness.

Jessie courtesied and blushed, but looked up into their faces with a pretty air of innocent hopefulness, that fully confirmed their sanguine anticipations for her.

"I don't suppose, Jessie, that you wish for any more work now, do you?" said Miss Lewis, archly.

"Oh, yes, indeed, miss!" replied Jessie, with a smile; "I wish to get needlework quite as much as ever. And you shall not wait for it so long again, Miss Mary. But poor mother takes up a great deal of my time, as well as other things."

"Oh, never mind!" replied both the girls at once, with that ready good-nature which is sure to spring in young hearts when their sympathies are touched. "You shall have all we have got to do—sha'n't she, Mary?" added the youngest; "and we won't plague you about making haste, either."

The three young ladies then took leave of Jessie, and departed.

"Let us go home by the pretty shady back lane," said Lucy Lewis. Her companions made no objection, and the trio proceeded in that direction.

"Who is that?" said Mary, pointing to the figure of a man that flashed, as it were, before their eyes, as he sprang from the path by which they were advancing over a gate on one side of it that led into a copse, among the thick underwood of which he was immediately concealed.

"Good gracious! I do believe it was Frederic Dalton!" cried Lucy.

"Nonsense!" responded her, sister. "I will bet sixpence that it was Jessie Phillips's lover, and that he is hiding himself till he sees us fairly out of the way."

Ellen Dalton said nothing; but she, too, had seen the retreating figure for an instant, and, very greatly to her own discomfort, she agreed in opinion with both the sisters.

# XIII

*A mystery satisfactorily explained without any explanation at all—how to write invitations advantageously—successful manœuvrings—happy confidence*

WHERE THERE ARE STRONG MOTIVES to urge forward such a business as that of restoring Mrs. Greenhill to her former habitation, an agent whose heart is as much in it as was that of Ellen, an operative assistant as warmly sympathetic as her father, and pecuniary means *à discrétion*, delays are few and performances prompt. The good woman was accordingly restored to all the comforts of her former home, with a degree of celerity that appeared to her, when the whole business of the transit was completed, as having been more like the work of a conjurer than any thing else. The happiness of the whole family need not be dwelt upon, as it is sufficiently easy to imagine it; but when the worthy mother of the race began, after the happy re-arranging of all their old familiar household tidinesses, to have leisure to look about her, and to listen to and answer all the congratulations and interrogations of her neighbours, she felt a good deal of embarrassment in replying to the oft-repeated question, "How did it all come about?" The promise of secrecy demanded by Ellen, and given by her without scruple or hesitation in the moment of suffering, now became a source of very considerable inconvenience to her; for folks did stare not a little when they perceived the whole Greenhill family restored to all their former comforts, though that clever fellow Tom was still in prison, and not a word said as to where all the money came from. At length, however, one of those acute bodies who would rather invent a cause for all they see than submit to confess they know nothing about it, began to hint that people were unaccountably stupid not to perceive at once that it was the Duchess who had done it all. "Nobody who knew any thing about her Grace," observed this reasoning quidnunc, "could believe for a moment that she would let her old favourite, Margaret Greenhill, go into the workhouse; but it was likely enough, too, that she might not choose to have all she did for her talked about, as nobody could deny but what their extravagance deserved a downfall, and the Duchess, maybe, might think she would only get laughed at by the neighbours for setting them all up on their legs again." There was quite enough of probability in this suggestion for it to gain ground, especially as no one was found to contradict it. Even Mrs. Greenhill herself, when the general surmise was mentioned to her, only smiled and shook her head by way of denial, but spoke not a single word, either to check or confirm the report.

The circumstances attending this sudden restoration of Mrs. Greenhill to her well-known home were too remarkable not to get into the stream of village gossip, which found its way every where; and Mrs. Buckhurst was neither the least delighted with the news, nor the last to hear of it. Even without the conjectural explanation by which it was accompanied, Mrs. Buckhurst would probably have come to the conclusion that it was her kind-hearted friend, the Duchess of Rochdale, who had relieved the poor woman; and she sighed to think how likely it was, notwithstanding the fine-sounding rent roll of the Duke, that this additional act of generosity to an estimable old servant was not performed without pecuniary inconvenience to herself. It was not, therefore, from any wish to obtain further information on this point that the good lady sent a request to her old acquaintance that she would come to call upon her, but solely because, having herself been rather longer than usual without hearing from the Duchess, she hoped to gather from the good woman, who must so recently have been in communication with her, some tidings of the family; not to mention that she anticipated with sincere pleasure the seeing her much-esteemed neighbour in a happier state of mind than at their last meeting. Mrs. Greenhill obeyed the summons within a very few hours after she received it, and the meeting was as pleasant a one on both sides as might have been expected from the contrast it offered to the last. But when, the congratulations being over on one side, and the expressions of thankful happiness on the other, Mrs. Buckhurst said, "And now, Greenhill, do tell me something about the Duchess; it is a long time since I heard from her," the answer she received was by no means satisfactory.

"I do not know any thing particular about her Grace," said the old woman, colouring, as she anticipated the questions that were likely to follow.

"How can that be, my good Greenhill?" returned Mrs. Buckhurst. "All that has happened could hardly have come to pass without her having written to you. At any rate, you must know where they are."

"Indeed, madam, I do not," was the reply.

"Why are you so mysterious with me, Greenhill?" said Mrs. Buckhurst, laughing. "You cannot suppose that I blame you for having done at last what I myself advised you to do long ago? You cannot seriously wish me to feel any doubt as to the quarter from whence the necessary funds came which have restored you and your family to comfort?"

"I shall be very grateful to you, Madam Buckhurst," said the greatly embarrassed Mrs. Greenhill, "if you will be so kind as not to ask me any questions about it. And, indeed, I am sure you will not when I inform you that I have promised not to tell from whence the assistance came."

"You are quite right, Greenhill. I will not say another word on the subject," returned Mrs. Buckhurst, perfectly satisfied that she understood the whole affair, and by no means surprised that the Duchess, who she well knew was often obliged by dire necessity to abstain from being as liberal as she wished, should desire that this new proof of her partial munificence to her old servant should not be talked about. And thus the interview ended, which Mrs. Greenhill had felt would be the most dangerous to the secrecy she had promised, without in any degree endangering the *incognito* of her benefactress.

While these events were going on amidst the humbler part of the population of Deepbrook, its aristocracy were profiting by the unusually hospitable movement excited by the arrival of the new commissioner and his very agreeable family. It would, indeed, be difficult to conceive any addition to a country neighbourhood more calculated to be universally welcome. Mr. Mortimer himself was not only one of the most amiable-tempered men alive, but possessed a vast deal of that elegant and producible sort of information which renders a man valuable even in

London, but absolutely invaluable in the country. He was, indeed, "good at need" in every way, being an excellent whist-player, a good average chess-player, touching the violincello with considerable taste and skill, by way of accompaniment, and possessing a good bass voice, with which he was ever ready to assist any vocal performance that was going on, from a quartet of Handel to a chorus of Dibdin. His manners were bland and gentlemanlike, his person pleasing, and his character irreproachable; the worst thing, perhaps, that had ever been said against him being, that he was not fond of his profession. If the truth on this latter point had been broadly spoken, this moderate phrase might have been changed for one much stronger, and he might fairly have been said to detest it. Nevertheless, he had had resolution to endure all the mortification and *ennui* of small and fluctuating practice for many years; but glad at heart was he, notwithstanding his regret at leaving London, when his appointment to the situation of assistant poor-law commissioner permitted him, with a safe conscience, to throw aside his wig and gown for ever. His family, also, though not all of them quite so richly endowed with agreeable talents as himself, were a great acquisition to Deepbrook, the ladies, both aunt and niece, being well-looking, well-dressed, and well-bred, and his son being all this, and a great deal more that was excellent, besides.

Such being the value of the new comers, it was no wonder that the whole neighbourhood experienced a simultaneous fever of hospitality, and that parties of all sorts and denominations were most perseveringly arranged to entertain them. It was not often that Lady Mary Weyland thought it necessary to return the more substantial invitations of her untitled neighbours by any thing but a sort of ostentatious tea-drinking and sandwich-nibbling; the deficiency of more appetising comestibles, and more generous draughts, being supplied by sundry articles of old-fashioned plate, the prodigiously showy liveries of her two serving-men, and the privilege acquired by all her guests of boasting to their various correspondents that they had been at a fête given by a "Lady Mary." But after meeting Mr. Mortimer and his family at dinner at every house in the parish that she condescended to enter in the character of a guest, she at length made up her mind to give a dinner to them herself, a good deal to the surprise of her old cook, house-keeper, and Abigail (the venerable domestic being to this extent a pluralist), and greatly to the delight of her upper serving-man, who, having been transplanted at the period of her ladyship's marriage from the place of under-footman in her noble father's household to that of upper-every-thing in that of his daughter, knew no joy greater than lording it at the sideboard over all the more rustic domestics borrowed from her guests on such occasions as the present.

Having screwed her courage to this undertaking, her ladyship wisely determined that neither the extravagance nor the trouble should be incurred for nothing.

"They shall see, at least," thought she, "that I am the first person in the neighbourhood, and all the rest of the good folks who have ever taken the liberty of asking me to dinner shall find out, if they have common sense enough to make the discovery, that as it is quite impossible for people in my station of life to do things in the same style as people in theirs, it would be a most inconceivable absurdity were I to repay such dinners as they give by such dinners as mine."

In short, Lady Mary Weyland was determined to give the Mortimers a very handsome dinner indeed, and, in order to achieve this object in the best manner possible, she took the trouble of adding a little postscript to every note of invitation which she sent out, that to the strangers being alone excepted. The formula of invitation was the same to all; but to the Dalton note was added, "If the grape-house should chance to have more fruit than is necessary for Mr. Dalton's immediate use, Lady Mary will be greatly obliged by a bunch or two—her own garden being unfortunately at this moment without fruit of any kind."

The Lewis *envoi* had a still more flattering conclusion, "Should Mr. Lewis chance to have a bottle or two to spare of the same champagne that Lady Mary has repeatedly tasted at his house, her ladyship would be exceedingly obliged by his sending them, as unfortunately she has discovered that several bricks have fallen upon the champagne bin in her cellar, leaving, as she greatly fears, not a single bottle unbroken."

To the Maxwell note were appended the following words, "Will Mrs. Maxwell kindly bestow a couple of her peculiarly white chickens on Lady Mary Weyland upon this occasion? Lady Mary having in vain endeavoured to procure some of the same admirable breed elsewhere."

To Mr. Rimmington there was a hint of the extreme difficulty of finding early strawberries; and to Mr. Wilcox, to whom, as a rich bachelor rector of good connexions, she was always pre-eminently civil, condescending even to remind him pretty frequently, that, by the marriage of his sister to one of her nephews, they were rather nearly allied, she wrote the following extremely important epistle:—

> "My dear Mr. Wilcox,
>
> "I hope you will give me the pleasure of your company at dinner on Wednesday, 7th July (a fortnight from yesterday, you know), at six o'clock, to meet Mr. Mortimer and his family, together with several other of my worthy neighbours, who, though not so highly connected as some of us, my good sir, are, nevertheless, very estimable people, to whom I hold it to be a matter of Christian duty, as I am sure you do likewise, to extend such patronage and support as I have it in my power to bestow. And now, my dear sir, I am going to ask a favour of you, which I am sure you will receive as it is meant, and will consider as a compliment paid to the very near connexion existing between our families. I have no means just at present of obtaining venison from my brother's park, and as one nearly allied to my Lord Crompton by marriage, I am certain that you will feel all the awkwardness of his sister's giving a dinner at this season of which venison makes no part. Will you then, dear Mr. Wilcox, for both our sakes, exert the privilege which I well know (from Mrs. Buckhurst) the Duke left with you, of telling his Grace's keeper when you wished for a haunch? Your doing this will convince me that I have not judged amiss in believing that you acknowledge with pleasure the alliance which permits me to subscribe myself, with
>
> "The highest consideration,
>
> "Your affectionate relative,
>
> "Mary Plantagenet Weyland."

As it luckily happened that a splendid haunch was hanging in the larder of Mr. Wilcox (without his having used *his privilege* to obtain it), at the moment her affectionate letter reached him, Lady Mary had the satisfaction of finding when Wednesday, the 7th July, arrived, that not one of the requests which she had condescended to make had failed to produce the desired result. The whole of the invited party arrived, and all that she had asked for arrived too.

Though her ladyship piqued herself on having the largest dining-room in the parish, except those at the Castle and the squire's, she carefully avoided the *mauvais ton* of over-filling it, excepting, therefore, in the ease of the two Miss Mortimers, all the young ladies, together with the youthful curate and his wife, were invited for the evening, a regulation which restricted her party to the number of fourteen, her august self included; and by the aid of as much dexterous manœuvring on the part of her old servants as on her own, together with all their ancient Crompton Abbey recollections brought into full play, the entertainment went off, as she assured her two domestic counsellors on the following morning, exactly as it ought to have done.

Whether all her ladyship's guests were as well satisfied as her ladyship, may be doubted. Mr. Wilcox had the fatiguing task of carving his own venison. Captain Maxwell was unfortunately placed next Mrs. Dalton, which he considered to be a much worse job than going aloft in a storm. The scarcity of ladies placed Mr. Lewis next Mr. Wilcox, whom he disliked more than any gentleman of his acquaintance. The agreeable Mr. Mortimer was seated between the fatiguing Lady Mary and the ultra sharp-witted Mrs. Maxwell, and young Mortimer had to school his London and Oxford comprehension into such a degree of new intelligence as might enable him to comprehend the very sensible, but very local conversation of Mr. Dalton.

As to the younger Dalton, the all-accomplished and too-charming Frederic, his conduct during the whole day was a *tour de force*, the perfect success of which was well calculated to increase, if increasing it were possible, his proud consciousness of ability to do whatever he liked, not only with impunity, but with a degree of success that turned difficulties into triumphs, and obstacles into aids. Every thing indeed, on this occasion, seemed to conspire in order to exhibit him to himself in all his glory. Not only had he the two Miss Mortimers to manage during the dinner, both of whom he knew were already distractedly in love with him, and both of whom he was determined to keep in the same condition, but the two Miss Lewises and Miss Maxwell were to arrive in the evening, with each of whom he was on terms, and fully intended to keep so, which would have rendered his making her an offer of marriage precisely the occurrence that she, at once most ardently desired and most confidently expected. Nor was this all, though, to say the truth, this would for the present have sufficed to satisfy him; but it so chanced that Lady Mary's usual well-dressed and very aristocratic-looking serving-woman, Mrs. Monckton, being on this occasion head-cook, her ladyship had thought it necessary to supply her place as holder of shawls, and repairer of pins to the ladies (several of whom traversed the short distance from their dwellings on foot) by the neat-handed Jessie Phillips.

When this summons was sent her, Jessie was beside the bed of her still suffering mother; but Mrs. Monckton, who felt conscious of her importance as lady's-maid and housekeeper to the only lady of title in the village (for, of course, nobody ever thought of reckoning the Castle for part of the village), had no notion of being kept waiting till the girl chose to come down to her, and therefore marched up to the sick room without ceremony.

Ere her message, however, was well delivered, Jessie replied that it was quite impossible she could leave her mother, whereupon the poor sufferer herself interfered, desiring the messenger to convey to her lady Jessie's humble duty, and that she would take care to be at her ladyship's house "exact to the time." The factotum, who had abundance of business on her hands, waited for no more, and descended the stairs with the same resolute step with which she had mounted them, though poor Jessie's gentle voice in vain sought to follow her with assurances that she did not think it would be possible for her to come at all.

"Hush! hush! Jessie! do be quiet!" said her mother, holding her firmly by the hand, to prevent her following the messenger. "Betty Dawson will come and see after me; and this is no time, Jessie, to neglect making friends. Think, my darling, how you'd be in the world without friends if any thing was to happen to me!"

Jessie longed to tranquillise her mother by uttering one little sentence,—one little sentence that should make her understand how little likely she was ever to require the help of any such friends as Lady Mary; but she was sworn to secrecy, and turning away her head to hide a gentle smile, she meekly set herself to do what her mother required, so as to enable her punctually to keep the engagement that had been made for her.

# XIV

*An unlucky accident and dangerous rencontre—admirable arrangements of Mr. Jones, the Lady Mary's butler—admirable demeanour of her ladyship in all things, save in making the conversation a little too particular*

IT SO HAPPENED THAT THE carriage which brought Mr. Dalton, his wife, and son, to Lady Mary's dinner was closely followed to the door by that of Mr. Mortimer, conveying himself, his sister, his daughter, and his son.

Young Dalton, in springing from the equipage, perceived at a glance whose it was that followed, and, standing back while his father and mother passed on, was ready to receive the Miss Mortimers as they descended. Now, it was only the younger of these ladies that he had felt, on first making their acquaintance, to be in any degree worthy of his particular notice. The other, though really a very handsome woman still, he had abused as old, chiefly in the hope of plaguing his sister Ellen, and neglected as ugly, chiefly because he did not deem it advisable to put her upon the list of those whom it was his object to hold in readiness to accept him; for never did he for a moment forget that the time might come when he might deem it necessary to conclude a rapid matrimonial arrangement, to secure himself from the hateful idea that he might pass away to make room for his detested sister, "no child of his succeeding." But there had been something in the unrestrained admiration of the elder Miss Mortimer which he had found perfectly irresistible, and, no longer designated as a "hideous old maid," she now came in for a very satisfactory share of that promiscuous, but most skilful gallantry, by which he contrived to enchant all and offend none. After assiduously handing out the fair young Agatha, who, being seated next the door of the carriage, received his first attentions, he let her pass on after her father and brother, while he performed the same office to her aunt. It was nearly impossible for any young lady more cordially to admire a young gentleman than Miss Agatha Mortimer admired Mr. Frederic Dalton; but it *was* possible to betray that admiration more coquettishly, and in this the handsome aunt very greatly surpassed the pretty niece; the consequence of which was, that, although the younger lady really enjoyed the inestimable advantage of being on the list from which the incomparable Frederic intended some day or other to select a wife, and that the elder one did not, it was the latter who occupied the gentleman's attention most, and received the least timid proofs of his devotion. In thus indulging his vanity, the young man knew that he run no risk with his younger adorers; well aware that, let him go what lengths he would, he could in a moment set all right again with any of them, by merely muttering in their youthful ears the mystic words "*old maid*." While under twenty, a girl not only thinks that every woman five years above it has passed her bloom, but feels her own youth to be such a tower of strength against rivalship, that she laughs at all the artillery which riper beauty, or riper talent either, can bring against it. No one knew all this better than Frederic Dalton, and in the case of Miss Mortimer this knowledge permitted him to enlarge his love-making amusements very agreeably.

Amongst many other good points, Miss Mortimer had an extremely pretty foot; and as she stepped out of the carriage upon the present occasion, this pretty foot slipped on one side, and there appeared to be most imminent danger of her falling forward upon her handsome nose. Frederic Dalton gallantly saved her, however, from this catastrophe, and, when he had placed her on the ground, said, "Upon my soul, Miss Mortimer, you ought always to have a pair of clogs ready to put on when you get out of your carriage."

"Clogs?" she replied; "what can you mean, you cruel creature?"

"Why, I mean, Miss Mortimer, that your feet are positively too small to trust to: I wish to heaven you would let me have a cast taken from one of them! By Jupiter, I would have it modelled in gold, and wear it,—natural size, observe,—at my watch-chain!"

"How can you run on, talking such abominable nonsense," she replied, "while I am suffering so? I have positively sprained my ankle—I have, indeed," she continued, leaning heavily on his arm as she spoke.

Under these circumstances, it was, of course, absolutely necessary that Frederic Dalton should continue to support her till she could be placed in a chair; and he accordingly accompanied her into the little parlour, fitted up for the nonce as a lady's robing-room, where Agatha was already engaged arranging her ringlets, and where Jessie Phillips stood, unequalled in loveliness, but turning so deadly pale upon seeing him enter (regarding with an air of tender solicitude the lady on his arm), that, upon raising his eyes to her face, he felt persuaded that she was about to fall to the ground in a fainting fit. As much power of loving as the young gentleman possessed (which, in truth, was not much) was certainly at that moment in as full action as it ever had been for the frail fair creature before him, and for the space of about two seconds he felt disposed to stretch forth his arms to support her; but a second thought suggested a better mode of saving her from the effect of her over-wrought feelings; he looked at her steadily, and frowned. The result proved his wisdom. Poor Jessie had never before met his eye without receiving from it all the passionate tenderness that it had power to express; and the contrast was quite as effectual in rousing her spirits as a glass of cold water could have been. She gave one short gasp, unobserved by all but him, and then furtively supporting herself by the back of the chair that had received Miss Mortimer, she contrived to articulate an inquiry if the lady had hurt herself.

"Indeed, I am afraid so!" replied Frederic, assiduously bending over her, and ingeniously manœuvring, as he did so, to insinuate his hand under a shawl that hung over the chair, and to give a very eloquently tender pressure to the hand of Jessie, which lay concealed under it; "what can we do for her?"

"Do for me?" cried the lively lady, jumping up, and very nearly displacing, as she did so, the protecting shawl. "Do for me? You have very nearly done for me already by your extraordinary manner of helping me out of the carriage. But I believe, nevertheless, that I shall survive, and even reach the drawing-room, if you will give me your arm in a quiet rational manner, and without playing any more tricks."

On hearing this, Dalton started forward from his station behind her chair, and bending himself down, so that she might have the support of his arm in rising, said, "I will assist you to reach the drawing-room, Miss Mortimer, because, if I do *not,* I suppose it will not be correct for me to have the honour of conducting Miss Agatha; but the very moment I get you there, I mean to commence a quarrel with you that shall be eternal!"

These words were accompanied with the tenderest possible pressure of the arm that had coquettishly entwined itself with his, while precisely at the same moment he exchanged a glance with Agatha, his share of which expressed as broad a degree of quizzing towards her aunt as he thought it decorous to exhibit; and then, just as they were leaving the room, the young man turned his head, and, safely unseen by both the ladies, contrived to give a look at Jessie, which ended by raising his fine eyes to heaven as if fervently calling upon the angelic host to witness the intensity and eternity of his passion for her!

Frederic Dalton knew, when he set out, that he should have a good deal of business on his hands before the day was over; he had remembered this as he stood before his glass, giving the last triumphant brush to his glossy hair, and he smiled at himself softly and sportively, as he was wont to do upon all the ladies in succession, as they submitted themselves, one after another, to the magnetism of his eyes. And then he laughed outright, exclaiming half aloud, "Poor little fools!—Yet, upon my soul, I don't see how they can help it, either."

But, when making his calculations, upon this occasion, of the business that lay before him, he certainly did not anticipate that an interview with his lovely victim was to make a part of it; and for an instant the sight of her sweet sad face had given him a slight pang, made up in about equal proportions of fright, pity, and love; but from this he recovered, almost before one could say "it was," and for the rest of the day no thought of Jessie interfered of sufficient weight to check the airy gaiety of his spirits for a moment.

When Lady Mary Weyland did permit herself to be wrought upon by her vanity to transgress the laws prescribed by her economy, she enjoyed the display which it led to exceedingly. Strongly convinced that no person, not nobly born, could, by possibility, acquire elegance of manner in equal perfection with those who were, she keenly relished the opportunity which receiving company afforded her of displaying to advantage all those nameless graces of demeanour which she was conscious of possessing. Her standards of perfection in this respect were, of course, to be sought among her early associates; and, her memory not being over-charged with any great variety of matters, she retained in all their pristine freshness the recollection of the ways and manners of Crompton Abbey, before its stately owner had been forced to bend a little before that powerful flood of Continental innovation which has released English drawing-rooms from so much ungraceful stiffness. Lady Mary, however, had wholly escaped this contagion, and nothing could be more perfect in its way than the reception which she now gave to the rather miscellaneous party she had invited. Her ancient serving-man, and the village youth who filled the twofold office of gardener and footman, were both habited in full dress livery suits, the black and yellow lace on which, at the least two inches wide, was boldly mitred into points, round collar, pocket-holes, and waistcoat flaps, till it formed such an armour of splendour as might well defend them from the ordinary familiarity of the neighbouring domestics, who were condescendingly informed, on arriving with their respective masters, that they might "stay to wait." The side-board was made to seem very massively resplendent by the Caleb Balderston-like skill of the venerable Mr. Jones, her ladyship's butler; and, as every successive servant that arrived was desired to stand in line between the hall steps and the drawing-room door, while Mr. Jones and his broad-shouldered deputy, with their blazing liveries, made the very most of themselves as they pronounced aloud the names of all comers at the two extremities, the general effect was really every thing that the high-born hostess herself could desire.

Fortunately for the feelings of the invited, her ladyship's graciousness increased in exact proportion to the state which the occasion permitted her to put on. When her powerful love of a rubber and a good dinner induced her to convey herself in her pony chaise from house to house throughout the village whenever a kitchen chimney sent forth a broader column of smoke than usual, she was rather apt to settle accounts between her pride and her condescension by putting on a good deal of *hauteur* in receiving the hospitalities offered to her; but on this occasion her pride displayed itself by a more amiable species of dignity, and she was made up of bows, and smiles, and all sorts of graciousness and affability.

When the important moment of placing herself at the head of her table arrived, she gave a glance over the well-covered board, and was satisfied. And, in truth, her old servants, who had pretty nearly as much Crompton Abbey pride as herself, had made the very best and the very most of the privilege accorded by their lady mistress to do what they could amongst the farmers round in the way of ducks and pigeons, and eels and trout, and those sort of trifles, which, of course, cost them next to nothing; but which, if she set about buying, would run up bills a great deal higher than she should like to pay. There is certainly still remaining in England, notwithstanding all our long intimacy with the Continent, a very mysterious affection for titles. It would be vain to deny that the begging cajoleries of her ladyship's domestics would have been probably much less successful had her ladyship not been her ladyship, and had the phrase ran, "Missis will be so pleased," instead of "My lady will be so pleased." As it was, however, the result was an excellent dinner, and there was considerable tact and cleverness in the way in which Lady Mary exchanged a glance, first with one contributor and then with another, with a flattering air of *sous-endendu* intelligence, that, while it perfectly satisfied the person to whom it was addressed, left the rest of the company most judiciously in the dark.

Up to this point it was quite impossible that any degree of talent on her part could have improved the reception thus given to the new commissioner; but it may, perhaps, be fairly doubted whether a little more general knowledge of the world might not have led her ladyship to permit the conversation to flow on in the desultory course which it had followed during the dinner, instead of paying him the questionable compliment of turning it upon the subject of his arrival among them, and the nature of the commission which had brought him.

When Mr. Mortimer first found himself in the society of his new neighbours, not at the guardians' board, but at the dinner-table, he carefully and successively manœuvred, as we have seen, to avoid being led into any discussion on the subject, and made his escape to the ladies as speedily as possible. But on the present occasion there were no ladies to escape to; and, moreover, he had no longer the same nervous averseness to the subject which he had felt when sitting down with a party of gentlemen, to whose character, temper, and opinions, he was a perfect stranger. This was the case no longer. Mr. Mortimer was by this time as well acquainted with the feelings and opinions of his neighbours on the subject of the bill as if he had heard every syllable that either of them had ever said upon it, from the day it was first canvassed among them to the present hour.

Mr. Mortimer was too much a man of the world, and of much too sound a judgment, to permit any of the Deepbrook variations of opinion on this subject to affect in the very slightest degree his feelings towards the individuals who held them. If he found those who were hostile to the bill agreeable and estimable men, they continued in his opinion as agreeable and estimable after he had discovered their hostility as before; nor did the most cordial approval of the act, and all the consequences which had followed it, in the slightest degree propitiate his good liking. The subject was one to which, previous to his appointment, he had given very little attention. Essentially, from his youth upwards, a London man, his statistics were London statistics, his experience London experience.

Few men could have spoken better, or judged with more clear-headed, practical good sense, on the new system of police than Mr. Mortimer. He was old enough to remember the abuses and absurdities of the old mode of protecting the metropolis, and young enough to comprehend all the advantages of the new one. He was tolerably well acquainted, too, with the comparative excellence of the different charitable institutions, and liberally and conscientiously supported those which he judged to be most serviceable to the poor; but, like most other denizens of the metropolis, he did not estimate the importance of the rural population at its just value; or rather its value was not a subject to which he had been led to pay attention. The stream of wealth for ever flowing into London, fed as it was by the ceaseless industry of the three kingdoms, was to him, as to all other Englishmen, a source of patriotic pride; but of the actual or comparative condition of those who contributed to it he knew infinitely less, notwithstanding his various and widely extended intellectual knowledge, than any fair average specimen of a country gentleman, who, besides living in the midst of industry, as every Englishman must do, has that sort of personal acquaintance with its agents which all the resident rural gentry must have, and which the resident city gentry must be without.

This is a species of ignorance, however, with which no genuine Londoner can be fairly reproached. How is such a one to become personally intimate and familiar with any portion of the industrious poor, except his own domestic servants, who are a class as much essentially apart as the bishops or judges? He may pretty well guess at their wants, indeed, *en grand*, inasmuch as food, clothing, and shelter, are needful to all; but as to the enormous importance to their moral as well as to their physical existence, of every regulation, however seemingly trifling, which touches upon their humble rights and old-time privileges, he knows no more than his lady's lapdog. And so it was, OF COURSE, with Mr. Mortimer. He had accepted, with the conscientious eagerness of an affectionate father, an appointment which, he trusted, would enable him, together with his moderate patrimony, to permit his children to continue in the enjoyment of the comforts and advantages to which they had hitherto been accustomed, and which his declining business had lately given him reason to fear must be restricted. Who can blame him for this? Who can reproach him with any dereliction of principle, though he did undertake duties upon the judicious discharge of which depended the well-being of hundreds, while in utter ignorance of what those duties were? He had received his instructions with that honest intention of abiding by them, which every honourable man ought to feel when accepting an office for which he is to be paid, upon condition of performing the duties annexed to it. In short, it was impossible for any public servant to come to the execution of his trust with a mind more free from prejudice, and a spirit more willing to do what was right, than Mr. Mortimer. After stating this, it is melancholy to be obliged to confess, that either of the silly Miss Lewises, had they been called upon to decide how relief should be administered in any individual case in the parish of Deepbrook, would have been more likely to decide judiciously than our accomplished commissioner.

But though Mr. Mortimer had already, with all the innocence of a child unborn, committed one or two sad blunders; though, in one case, he had decided that a drunken young rogue, who had *just* married a female, about as estimable as himself, by whom he had three children, should receive four loaves of bread at his quarters, "up at High Street" (where he carried on a snug little trade as a receiver of stolen goods), because he had broken his arm (in a drunken squabble); and though he had enforced the legal necessity of coming into the house upon a widow woman, who had maintained herself and three children by working like a horse at any labour that was proposed to her, because he did not happen to know that she stuttered dreadfully, and could not pronounce the word "yes," which would have been the satisfactory answer to a question he had very attentively put to her when inquiring the reason of her present want of help; though these, and some few other accidents of the same kind, had already occurred, Mr. Mortimer, strong in the consciousness of upright intentions, and totally unconscious of the mischief he had been doing, in no degree shared the embarrassment of one or two of the gentlemen present, when Lady Mary pompously entered upon the subject of his commission, and the peculiar happiness of the neighbourhood in having him appointed "to watch over the wants of the poor and the interests of the rich."

"You are very kind," replied Mr. Mortimer, smiling; "I shall be only too happy if I can continue to merit the continuation of such kind feelings."

"Continue to merit!" muttered Captain Maxwell to himself, as he recollected the miserable countenance of Nanny Briggs at the moment he had been silenced in his pleadings for a little temporary out-door relief for her, till a bill at the baker's was paid off, which had been run up during a long illness.

"May I have the pleasure of taking wine with you, Captain Maxwell?" said the unconscious commissioner, just as this bit of private grumbling had passed through the heart of the kind-hearted veteran.

"It isn't his fault," thought the captain, with a smiling nod of assent. "It is not with him we ought to quarrel, but with the fools that sent him."

"How thankful we ought to be, particularly such of us as are connected with the landed interest," resumed Lady Mary, "that the provisional and hereditary legislature have at length relieved the country from the tremendous burdens under which it was sinking during the existence of the old poor-law, Mr. Mortimer! It must, I am sure, be delightful to you to become an agent in so excellent a work!"

Mr. Mortimer bowed and smiled, and employed himself very assiduously in carving some chickens which were set before him.

"I, who have still in my ears the lamentations of the half-ruined land-owners of my native county, cannot fail to experience extreme satisfaction at the prospect of peace, plenty, and happiness, which this recent most invaluable enactment is likely to produce," again resumed the indefatigable lady at the head of the table, determined to make her flattering reception of Mr. Mortimer as perfect as possible; "I suppose, Mr. Dalton," she added, facetiously, "we shall soon hear of your raising your rents, notwithstanding we all know that you are no griping landlord."

"Your ladyship is very obliging," replied Mr. Dalton, dryly, "but I cannot say I anticipate at present any increase of landed revenue from the operations of the new poor-law."

"God forbid you should!" said Mrs. Buckhurst, earnestly; "it would be very terrible to think that a measure which has brought increase of suffering to many a needy, hard-working man, should bring superfluous wealth to the idle rich."

Lady Mary drew herself up, and looked offended; Mr. Lewis ventured to utter a faint whistle, but, speedily recollecting himself, stopped short, and said, laughingly,—

"This is quite new, Mrs. Buckhurst. I never expected that I should live to see you turn Radical."

"Live a little longer, Mr. Lewis," replied the old lady, returning his smile, "and you may chance to see the very stanchest old Tories among us turn Chartist. The peace of the country may be tolerably safe, perhaps, from us at present, and I pledge you the honour of a gentlewoman, that, to the best of my knowledge and belief, I have not a single pike, or even pike-head, in my possession; indeed, I think I may, for a good while to come, abstain from acts of overt violence, on account of the temperament of my household; for Molly, who is very nearly threescore, has never yet mustered physical courage enough to kill a mouse; and I know that, with all the pains I can take, it will require a good while to work her up to any active pitch of valour; but I would recommend no man to judge of the danger of rash legislation by estimating the mischief that an old woman may do."

"I beg your pardon, Mrs. Buckhurst, for expressing my sentiments so plainly; but, certainly, I never was so astonished in my whole life as at hearing what sounds so very like treason and rebellion fall from your lips," said Lady Mary, looking most unfeignedly shocked. "I solemnly assure you, ma'am, that till this very moment I firmly believed you to be a Conservative; and I cannot help saying, that I imagine the Duchess thinks so too."

As her ladyship pronounced these words, which she did in the freezing tone of subdued indignation, she gave a circular glance round the table, which seemed to challenge the sympathy of the company in her dismay. Mr. Rimmington and Mr. Wilcox both looked as if greatly inclined to laugh; Mr. Dalton seemed surprised, Captain Maxwell delighted, Mr. Lewis amused, and Mr. Mortimer puzzled; while young Dalton whispered, in a tone which was intended to be audible to his two fair neighbours, and to nobody else,—

"Capital! isn't it? We shall have the two old ladies pulling caps in a minute."

Nobody else, however, spoke for a few seconds, and then Captain Maxwell broke the silence by saying,—

"And what principles do you assign to me, Lady Mary? Am I Radical or Conservative, in your estimation?"

"Oh, my dear sir," replied her ladyship, in a tone that was almost affectionate, "I doubt if there is any body living bold enough to doubt *your* principles. Thank God! on that point there can be no delusion. We all know that Captain Maxwell has fought and bled for his king and country, and I, for one, should think it a sort of treason to doubt his loyalty."

"I thank you, madam," replied the veteran. "I believe, as times go, my loyalty may be considered as pretty tolerably stanch; but yet, saving Mr. Mortimer's presence and your ladyship's, I suspect that upon this point I am quite as much a Radical and a traitor as Mrs. Buckhurst."

"I feel very grateful to you, Captain Maxwell," said Mr. Mortimer, good-humouredly, "for not treating me as the incarnation of the law under which I hold the appointment which brings me here. I assure you, I should feel this appointment an intolerable burden, if you did."

"We should pay you a very bad compliment, sir, if we thought you likely to take umbrage at a discussion upon the poor-laws, even though some among us may not consider them as the most perfect code that ever was formed," replied Captain Maxwell, with an air of professional frankness that well became him, adding, after a pause of a moment, and with a very courteous bow, "And moreover, Mr. Mortimer, this bad compliment would, if I mistake not, be very ill deserved."

"I really think it would," replied the amiable commissioner, returning his bow with a nod and a smile of cordial good-will. "I fairly confess that I think the law is an exceedingly good law, and that I hope and trust I may do good by endeavouring to act up to the spirit of it; but this opinion has not with me the slightest tendency to make the free examination of the question disagreeable. On the contrary, I am of opinion, that it is always good to find an opportunity of giving reason for the faith that is in us; and I give you my honour that I would rather be deaf and dumb this moment than shrink either from speaking my own opinion, or listening to that of others."

There was in Mr. Mortimer's manner of saying this so much evident *bon foi* and sincerity, that no single individual present, who appeared to listen to him, except Lady Mary, felt the slightest doubt but that he would rather like discussion on the subject than not; but the lady hostess herself was in a perfect agony. A sudden recollection of the cautious politeness of her noble brother shot across her brain, and gave her such a thrill of shame and regret at having alluded to the vocation of her stranger guest, and thereby bringing upon him so much intolerable impertinence, that she at once resolved to put a stop to it by the authority which she felt vested in her, both as lady of the feast and daughter of the Earl of Crompton. Having come to this determination, she drew herself up to a considerably greater height than the generality of ladies can obtain when sitting, and, while the gentlemen of her party were beginning to look particularly comfortable and at their ease with their agreeable new acquaintance, she thus addressed them:—

"I trust you will excuse the liberty I take, gentlemen, in interfering with the subject of your discourse; but you must forgive me for saying, that my notions of good breeding and hospitality (received, as I must take the liberty of observing, in the halls of my noble ancestors), render the tendency to personality, which I now observe, indescribably painful to me, and I therefore request that you will do me the favour of changing the subject of conversation immediately."

This manifesto was received with considerably more good nature than it deserved. The gentlemen bowed in return for the solemn circular bow she bestowed upon them, as she concluded her speech, and then began drinking wine together, and gossiping about the roads, and the rain, and the corn, and the covies, and such "small deer," till her ladyship had recovered her composure. By the time this happy recovery was effected, the dinner was over, and the cloths withdrawn. Then followed the valedictory glass of wine to each lady, a signal bow first addressed to Mrs. Dalton, and then circulated among the rest, and then the party separated; the luckless ladies to endure the dignity of Lady Mary till they were reunited, and the happier gentlemen to enjoy their release from it.

As soon as the movement at the dinner-table, which follows this separation, had been made, bringing Mr. Wilcox to the top of it, and the rest of the gentlemen into the chairs next him on either side, he gave the health of Lady Mary Weyland, with a very decorous half-smile, which was immediately drunk by all present, with a degree of good-humoured readiness which seemed slightly to indicate the pleasure they received from having reached the moment when it was proper to pay her this compliment. Mr. Dalton, who, by the recent movement, was now placed next Mr. Mortimer, addressed him with an air of great cordiality, and, in a tone that was intended to be audible to the whole party, said,—

"Thank God, Mortimer, that you are not of the same mind as her ladyship respecting the style in which your commissionership is to be treated among us. Free discussion, and a sincerely cordial co-operation between the commissioners appointed by the crown and the resident country gentlemen, is, in my opinion, exactly all that is wanted to make the new law an exceedingly good law; and I rejoice heartily to perceive that we have every reason to hope for this under your sway."

"I hope and trust we shall go on well together," replied Mr. Mortimer, with equal cordiality of manner; "and as for the inconceivable folly (begging her ladyship's pardon,) of fancying that my business here involves some occult mystery which it is not safe to allude to in my presence, I can only thank the gods that it does not seem epidemic. *Entre nous,*" he continued, laughing, "I am sadly afraid that Lady Mary, notwithstanding her loyalty, takes a very sinister view herself of the powers that have been assigned to me. Does not the agitation she displayed when she feared that the veil which covers my proceedings was shaken, and about to be lifted, look very much as if she thought that there was something a little Star-Chamberish, or in the good old secret tribunal style, in the mysterious authority I bring with me?"

"And so she does!" shouted Captain Maxwell, laughing heartily; "and be quite sure, Mr. Mortimer, that she likes you all the better for it. Her confidence in her own principles, and the delightful consciousness which she bears about her—that power and privilege, crowns and coronets, pedigrees and rent-rolls, are all too holy in her eyes to permit the possibility of her ever falling under your suspicion herself, makes her gaze on your grand-inquisitor sort of greatness with admiration, unmixed with fear. I would bet fifty to one that she thinks herself the only person in the parish who has absolutely *no* cause to shrink before your inquiring eye; and the power invested in you appears, to her noble mind, considerably more sublime than any other she ever heard of, because she feels it to be more new and incomprehensible."

This sally was received with very general laughter, and more than one voice was raised to declare the captain understood the character of her ladyship completely. "But it is not Lady Mary only," said Mr. Dalton, as soon as the laugh had subsided; "it is by no means Lady Mary only who feels awe-struck by the commission and the commissioner, solely because their powers are new. I for one am quite ready to confess that I am in the same condition. I have sometimes been immensely annoyed since the new act came into operation by the novelty of its enactments; and I often think, after the feeling has subsided, that we shall find it, perhaps, all very right and proper, when we are a little more used to it."

"The one broad reason which ought to make men of all parties contemplate the new law with as much indulgence as they can," said Mr. Wilcox, "is the notorious fact that the old law *could not* have continued in force many years longer, without positive destruction to the country; and as the changing it must obviously have been a business of enormous difficulty, it follows, beyond all contradiction, that the legislature undertaking the task ought not to have this difficulty increased by factious opposition; or even by a demand for unmixed good in the place of almost unmixed evil. All this is obvious; and yet, with the admission of all this, there are some points on which every conscientious man, who knows enough of the subject to be aware of them, will think it his duty to pause before he silently permits them to be melted down into the general mass of English law, without entering his protest against it."

"What you say, sir, is just what I should have expected to hear from a gentleman who has always given us reason to think at the board that he was no great friend to this new law," said Mr. Lewis; "nor, if I may take the liberty of saying it, to reform in general," he added this with something approaching to a wink of intelligence directed towards young Dalton, who, in addition to his other claims to superior intelligence and talent, professed himself a thorough Radical reformer. This attack on the politics of Mr. Wilcox was followed by a minute or two of general silence, and it appeared as if that gentleman did not think fit to reply to it; but at length he said,—

"I was not aware, sir, that I had ever been guilty of the indiscretion of introducing political discussion of any kind, when attending the board where I have had the honour of meeting you."

"Oh! dear no, sir, by no means; I did not at all mean to insinuate any thing of the kind. But as to the bill itself, I must confess, gentlemen, that it often strikes me as an odd sort of particular misfortune attending it, that every body, lawyer or no lawyer, always seems to suppose that upon this subject, if upon no other on God's earth, they have, every man-John of them, as good a right to reason and cavil, and reject and decide, as the Lord Chancellor himself in his own court. Now it strikes me, gentlemen, that law is law, and that such a knowledge of jurisprudence as can only be acquired by devoting the best part of life to the study is necessary to understanding it, in this branch as well as in all others. But no; every man his own lawyer seems to be the general notion in this particular case, and thus a code, which is of necessity one of the most complex and difficult ever framed, is, in equal defiance of common usage and common sense, pulled to pieces by men, women, and children, who one and all seem to think that they have an undoubted right to sit in judgment upon it."

"Your observation is perfectly just, Mr. Lewis; and I can easily understand the weight it must carry in the estimation of gentlemen of your profession," said Mr. Rimmington, fixing his earnest eyes on the keen, wide-awake looking features of the lawyer. "It is perfectly true that we do all of us enter upon the discussion of this great national measure with vast audacity; I plead guilty to this accusation, not only in my own name, but in the name of all those who feel as I feel. But the fact is, that though we have very decidedly the fear of the law before our eyes, we have the fear of the Gospel also. The law, if I understand it rightly, Mr. Lewis, seems to assume as a principle that the poor, who, as we are told, we have always with us, have no natural RIGHT to assistance from the rich. Now this, I take it, is the point upon which a vast number of us who have never studied jurisprudence hitch. Not, I believe, that there are many who would undertake to dispute this terrible dictum by any arguments suggested by a process of abstract reasoning, but a good many of us think that the doctrine of the Gospel is at variance with it."

"Of course, sir, now that you have got upon your own ground, I cannot presume to follow you," said Mr. Lewis, filling his glass, and seeming to think that his promised silence was in this case the most eloquent answer it was possible to give. He could not help adding, however, "That's all we ask on our side, Mr. Rimmington. Let those learned in the Gospel stick to the Gospel; and those learned in the law stick to the law."

"I should be sorry to think that they must of necessity be divided," said Mr. Rimmington.

"Not a bit of it—not a bit of it," cried Captain Maxwell, with such a hearty accent of affirmation as shewed he was very honestly in earnest. "I am neither lawyer nor priest, but I know just enough of both callings to be certain that they were meant to dove-tail into one another, as neat as my nail. We shall never do any good, Lewis, to the poor, or the rich either, if we set off with that notion. It is more likely, I think, to lead us right a-head towards the truth if we say that first and foremost what we have got to remember is, that the Gospel tells us we *are* to take care of the poor; and next, that it is but wise and fitting, and like good prudent citizens, that we should set about making laws to put us into the best way of doing it."

"Your definition could not, in my opinion, be easily improved, sir," said Mr. Wilcox; "but though it tells us in what direction we are to set out, it does not exactly shew us how we are to get on. That *best way*, Captain Maxwell, is by no means easy to hit upon. For my own part I feel quite certain that the mistakes from which we are now suffering will be remedied as soon as their importance becomes clearly evident to those who have the power of amending, as well as of making laws. By far the greatest difficulty we have to contend with arises from the discrepancies between abstract reasonings and practical experience. It sounds so very well, for instance, to talk of the uniformity of the new system. I was caught by the phrase myself, in the first instance, and thought that if a uniform system of parochial relief could be established, accurately proportioned to the necessity of the paupers, and independent of the brief authority of parish officers, it would be the finest thing in the world for the country, and equally beneficial to the payers and the receivers of rates."

"All moonshine, Mr. Wilcox"" exclaimed Captain Maxwell, somewhat vehemently "The blessed uniformity they talk of is in its very essence precisely in the style of the Procrustes legislation. Bad and good, tall and short, all's one to the gigantic machine at Somerset House; and the only relief from a tyranny considerably worse than either stretching a man's legs, or chopping them off, is only prevented by this same uniformity that they insist upon, being morally impossible in execution. Yet even this relief from the vain and impotent theory is paid for by the poor helpless victims, by their being incessantly subjected to experiments for the performance of what is impossible."

"You cannot be more aware of the futility of this attempted uniformity than I am, Captain Maxwell," resumed the rector of Hortonthorpe; "but I believe it has still great influence with those who practically know nothing about the matter. It sounds so well. It seems to be a principle so just, so enlarged in the views it teaches, that it really requires a good deal of courage to controvert it; and to attempt proving by mere homely, every-day experience that its application is either totally impossible, or else much worse."

"Precisely," said Mr. Rimmington, in the quiet voice that always made every body within reach of it turn round to listen to him. "Our thanks are very often due to the impracticability of some of the regulations. You see, Mr. Mortimer, that the candid manner in which you have invited discussion is not lost upon us, and the liberty of speech which has followed is the best proof possible that we have all felt full assurance of your sincerity."

"And your feeling that assurance," replied Mr. Mortimer, "is, I do assure you, the most welcome compliment you could pay me. But I confess I have heard much that has surprised me. I had no idea that the law under which I am to act was so greatly disapproved by the higher classes. Of course I am aware that the poor people in general are opposed to it, but, as I have been always assured, very unreasonably."

"Before that judgment is definitively received," replied Mr. Rimmington, "we should take some pains to inquire into its soundness. No man can be more fully convinced than I am, Mr. Mortimer, of the enormous, the almost incalculable importance, of preventing all those who are permitted to claim parochial relief from considering the doing so as an agreeable release from toil. Were such a feeling permitted to take root among the labouring classes of England, no thinking man can doubt for an instant that the result would be the utter destruction of what we call, with very just pride, the national character. As far back as history can give us any hints on the subject, it is perfectly evident that the *people* of England, as distinguished from her hereditary aristocracy, have shewn themselves to be a race unequalled on the face of the earth for steadfast industry; and the basest traitor that ever lived never sought to do his country such fatal wrong as that man would do who should so legislate as to paralyse in the very least degree this noblest source of independence."

"This consideration," interrupted Mr. Mortimer, with some vivacity, "is precisely what I have heard put forward by the framers and advocates of this new measure, as the very key-stone upon which the system has been erected."

"I most sincerely believe it," replied Mr. Rimmington. "I am very far, I assure you, Mr. Mortimer, from being one of those who are inclined to suspect the individuals who undertook the absolutely necessary, but almost desperately difficult measure of reforming the poor-laws, of having gone to the work with any evil intentions whatever; on the contrary, I consider the country as infinitely and eternally indebted to them. It is not the having founded their law upon the broad principle of not permitting parochial relief to become a bonus to idleness, it is not this which has caused so large a portion of both poor and rich to raise their voices in condemnation of it. No man, let him belong to what class he may, could venture to deny the vital necessity of this principle to the well-being of the country; and it is painful to think that, this first and most important foundation being so excellent, the superstructure raised upon it should be weakened by defects which all who conscientiously examine it in operation must perceive, and which unhappily ranges apparently on the right side many factious voices which have hitherto been only heard from the wrong."

"Do not think that the question is meant to express doubts as to the correctness of your statement," said Mr. Mortimer, leaning forward, and addressing Mr. Rimmington with much earnestness; "but kindly remember, my dear sir, how greatly the chances are against my knowing as well as you do how this new measure works. What is it, Mr. Rimmington, which renders what you allow to be excellent in principle so much otherwise in practice?"

"It would be unpardonable," replied Mr. Rimmington, with his own benevolent smile, "if so much candour on your part, Mr. Mortimer, should not be answered with equal candour on mine. The *bad working* we complain of arises, as I believe, solely from the adoption of that pernicious modern system of CENTRALIZATION, which has already converted Paris into France, and which, if persevered in, will very speedily convert London into England. How much France may have lost by this, I will not pretend to decide, but I should not have the same scruples if asked to declare what I thought it would do for England. If steadily and boldly persevered in for about a quarter of a century, it will melt the whole nation down into two classes, namely, the highly educated, artificial, over-refined Londoner, and the laborious, but ignorant, brutal and half-savage boor. By this process, London will become more vast, more opulent, more predominating over all other cities of the earth, than it is at present; but England, old England, merry England, free England, will be no more."

"True as the gospel, Rimmington," exclaimed Captain Maxwell; "but you must particularise a little, my good friend, or you will not give our worthy commissioner as plain an answer as he has a right to expect to his plain question."

Mr. Rimmington looked a little embarrassed; he *had* answered Mr. Mortimer's question as to what it was which rendered a measure excellent in principle pernicious in practice, but did not feel disposed to *paint* the explanation by saying that it would be better for the country if county justices had retained their former position of referees, and if no commissioners from London were employed to decide upon difficult questions, of which it was morally impossible they could know the merits; but thus pressed, he resumed, with a deprecating sort of smile,—

"Mr. Mortimer, if I do not greatly mistake the feelings of my neighbours, we are, one and all, exceedingly well disposed to believe ourselves pre-eminently fortunate in having you amongst us. The law of the land has ordained that the very intricate and important branch of statistics connected with the moral peculiarities of our rural population shall be confided, for the most part, to persons possessed of the least possible degree of previous information on the subject; such being the fact—and it is a fact which we have none of us any power to alter—we ought most unfeignedly to rejoice that we have you, instead of a less indulgent judge, to decide upon points of vital importance to the well-doing of the poor people among whom we all of us pass our lives, but concerning whom it is quite impossible that you can know any thing. Permit me to propose your health, with the assurance of very sincere welcome, which I am quite sure will be most cordially echoed by every one present."

Mr. Mortimer, though certainly a good deal surprised that any such knowledge should be expected from him as that in which he was declared to be deficient, was too wise and too amiable a man to express the feeling, or to permit it to influence, in the slightest degree, the gracious cordiality with which he expressed his gratitude for the friendly warmth with which the rector's toast was received, and only added to the *neat and appropriate* expression of his thanks an assurance, worded with mingled dignity and gentleness, that he should be most happy to obtain from his better-informed neighbours any knowledge that might enable him to be conscientiously useful in the discharge of the duties which had been confided to him.

Mr. Wilcox, then, by way of changing the subject, which he thought had been dwelt upon as long as politeness to the strangers warranted, mentioned the information which had reached him as he rode from Hortonthorpe, that the Duke of Rochdale and his family were arrived at the Castle; which piece of news was received with the more interest from being quite unexpected. But before the why and the wherefore could be half discussed, Lady Mary's magnificent serving-man entered to announce that coffee was served in the drawing-room.

# XV

*Difficulties to overcome, but without bringing great enjoyment to the conqueror—an unlucky discovery*

ALL THE BELLES OF DEEPBROOK, together with Mr. Daly, the curate, and his girlish wife, were assembled in her ladyship's drawing-room before the gentlemen from the dining-table entered it. Four Miss Daltons, two Miss Lewises, one Miss Maxwell, and the blooming young bride in the midst, made so pretty a group, and what, perhaps, was more provoking still, a group so exceedingly well dressed into the bargain, that Miss Mortimer was almost feeling herself, and her London milliner to boot, in danger of being rivalled, if not eclipsed; and both herself and her niece Agatha experienced a degree of anxiety, more pungent than agreeable, to see in what direction the captivating Frederic Dalton would move when he should first enter the room. Nothing could be a greater proof of the position which this young gentleman held among the young ladies of Deepbrook, than the fact, that there was not one of them, except three of his own sisters, who either knew or cared how the elegant-looking Henry Mortimer disposed of himself, while every eye and every heart were on the alert to ascertain what chance there was for each respective owner of the said hearts and eyes that the young squire would approach them. Few, very few, of any age, rank or nation, could be found so capable of managing safely the multiplicity of tender affairs which now demanded his attention as was our village swain Frederic Dalton.

He knew, as well as the pretty creatures themselves did, exactly what was passing in each fair bosom; he knew that it was the *first word* which would be the most eagerly watched, the most eagerly wished for, and the most dangerous, and he, therefore, without even using his eyes sufficiently to be accused of giving a first look, walked straight up to Mrs. Daly, who, in the pretty habiliments of a newly made wife, stood like Venus surrounded by her nymphs, and whose position, both as a married woman and a bride, rendered this first notice not only proper, but absolutely *de régneur* in a young man so perfectly *comme il faut* as himself. And what was to be done next? Was the outstretched hand, denoting the familiar intimacy of village friendship, to be offered to the fair one who stood nearest? Had the elder Miss Mortimer been one of those to whom he was at this moment to pay his compliments, the business would have been easy, for he would have saluted her first, as being the eldest, and, this order of salutation once established, there would no longer have been any wish among the pretty troop for any particularly early mark of his attention. But he had already paid his compliments to Miss Mortimer, in every possible way in which compliments could he paid by a gentleman to a lady in a room full of company; some other device, therefore, was necessary, and, while still making his pretty speeches to the bride, his thoughts were intent upon the difficult question. Chance, however, favoured him, and put a speedy end to his uncertainty. A little movement among the fair troop, who were all standing very close together near him, gave him an excellent opportunity for turning himself suddenly round, which he did, as if startled by having been touched by some one, and, with both hands hastily extended, and with a smile of universal friendliness, which none could fail to share, yet none appropriate, he seemed to take the first hands he could reach, and, to give the hurried movement the more effect, actually permitted that of his sister Henrietta to be among the number.

"How impossible it is for any man to speak to one in such a crowd!" was the internal exclamation of Miss Maxwell and of both the Miss Lewises, and they all began to sidle off in different directions, to place themselves where it *might* be possible for a person to speak to one, if they happened to wish it. But the Rubicon was passed for the skilful Frederic. That fearful phrase, "You always *do* speak to" somebody or other "first," being well avoided, all that followed was easy, and the more so, because it was an understood thing among all the young ladies, that "there was nothing in the world Frederic Dalton hated so much as bringing people's eyes upon one, and it was such a comfort!" And then, he understood so admirably well the *multum in parvo* system, by which a man, learned in love, knows how to make every thing tell; that is to say, to the particular eyes and ears for which each particular bit of intelligence is intended. Nay, better still, Frederic Dalton, not seldom, made one sigh do for two young ladies at once; for, if placed by accident at equal distance between them, and having prepared the way, first in one direction and then in the other, by a suitable glance, the sigh which followed was, as a matter of course, appropriated by each.

Whenever Lady Mary Weyland gave a party, the routine of the evening entertainments was as strictly regulated, and as perfectly well known to her guests, as the ceremonies of a court were in the good old times that are gone. There was ever one whist-table, one quadrille ditto, and a round game for the young people. This round game, whether at Lady Mary's or elsewhere, was another of those epochs of youthful female agitation at Deepbrook, which, like the earliest word bestowed at meeting, possessed a power that, although not exactly that of life and death, might fairly be said to decide the happiness or misery of many fair individuals for an hour or two. Who would Frederic Dalton sit by? It is true that the young man knew well how to make design look like accident, and how to look in the eyes of two or three for pity under the unavoidable infliction of being placed at a distance from them; but this, though it brought the consolation of a moment, could do no more. It could not heal the anguish of seeing the triumphant joy that danced in those four other eyes which sparkled to the left and right of the conquering hero. All this would have probably been very delightful to the young gentleman himself, if he had not known all that was to come next so perfectly well. But although the vital hope of his existence hung upon his hopes of being married, and that the so managing matters as to render his being able to achieve this at almost any given moment was the primary object of all he did and all he said, it is certain that his gay spirits did occasionally wax weary at the eternal repetition of the same scenes; and though his projects and his plans were too precious to permit his ever relaxing in his persevering manœuvres for long together, he did sometimes enjoy an idle day exceedingly.

Exactly when it might have been most easy to have found two or three young ladies whispering in sacred confidence to their own hearts such phrases as "Poor dear Frederic Dalton! I know where he would like to be now, instead of scampering over hill and dale with those horrid Baxters! But he is *so* right. I would not have him alter any one single thing that he used to do for the whole world!" Just when it would have been easy to have found such thoughts as these (were any thoughts to be found by those who seek for them), young Dalton was enjoying probably the very highest degree of gratification which his rural residence could give him. But the sort of gratification enjoyed by the absence of the fair creatures, who each and every of them believed that he knew no joy save in her presence, was not always, nor of late often, tasted in the society of the "horrid Baxters." In fact, Frederic Dalton was at this time as thoroughly in love with Jessie Phillips as it was possible for him to be with any woman; and if it ever chanced to him to address the words of truth to any of the fair creatures whose affection it was his object to win, it was when he said to her, as they sat together within the shelter of her lonely dwelling, "What a devilish deal happier I am, Jessie, when sitting close to you in this darling little hole of a room, than when I am stuck down in the midst of all the smirking misses of Deepbrook!" This *was* most strictly the truth; and it happened, rather unluckily, perhaps, that this truth flashed across his mind just as he saw the young ladies fluttering and fidgeting, preparatory to settling themselves round Lady Mary's great card-table, and perceived, as clearly as he perceived the table itself, all the little tricks that were being put in action by the five young ladies concerned, in order to ensure for themselves the felicity which, alas! could only be enjoyed by two.

He was delighted, of course, to perceive that every thing had hitherto gone well, and that his somewhat broad flirtation with the elder Miss Mortimer had been satisfactorily atoned for, in the opinion of his younger worshippers, by the judicious use he had made of the words spinster, aunt, and old maid, skilfully administered to their respective ears. Nevertheless, he was tired, and the thoughts of Jessie's changing cheek, and the timidly tender glance he had caught from her soft eyes, as he left the room that contained her, came so powerfully over him, that he suddenly determined to escape, even at the risk of having to select his own place when he came back again. But it not unfrequently happens that "*homme propose et femme dispose*," and so it was now. Miss Mortimer was very nearly as much aware of the manœuvring of the young ladies as Frederic Dalton himself, and with the strength of nerve with which ladies of thirty sometimes equalise matters between themselves and their younger neighbours, she playfully passed her arm under that of the highly favoured young gentleman, and said, with a degree of easy gaiety that was equally criticised and envied, "Mr. Dalton, observe! I mean to drag you as a prisoner chained to my chariot-wheels, even to the card-table; for I should be loath to disobey her ladyship's commands, but must perforce do so, though the penalty were the loss of her favour for ever, if you consent not to sit at my right hand and befriend me, for never yet did I encounter the perils of a round game without a *preux chevalier* to stand my friend." To this appeal there was but one possible answer, and the treacherous Frederic, tenderly pressing the arm he would gladly have had severed from its fair shoulder, and cast into the sea, so that he might thereby recover the freedom of which it had robbed him, gave up all hope of a five minutes' *tête-à-tête* with Jessie, and sat himself down to the card-table. Of the adventures which befell him there, little need be said, because they may without much difficulty be imagined. Now and then he cheated a little for Miss Mortimer, and occasionally performed a similar feat of dexterity for Miss Maxwell, who had quietly managed to slip into a chair on the other side of him. This lasted till Mr. Mortimer's carriage was announced, which, as that gentleman never suffered his horses to wait, was followed by the prompt departure of his family. Frederic, of course, attended them to the door, and, of course, to the cloak-room, in their way to it; and there again he found poor Jessie, looking pale and weary, but, to his great satisfaction, still alone. With affectionate solicitude, he implored the Miss Mortimers not to hazard catching cold by lingering in the hall; and having at length seen their equipage drive off, he flew back into the house, and muttering something about having lost his gloves as he passed a servant at the hall-door, turned into the room that concealed the lovely and lonely Jessie, and shut the door as he entered.

Her beautiful eyes were full of tears as she raised them to look at him, and she was deadly pale; but even so, looking as she did like a fair flower, bruised and broken, he had never felt, perhaps, so much aware of her surpassing beauty as at that moment, when he had just quitted a set of what every body declared to be exceedingly pretty girls, in all the becoming flutter of drawing-room gaiety and of drawing-room dress.

"What ails my beauty?" cried the young man, unceremoniously approaching her, and throwing his libertine arm round her waist. "These tears, Jessie," and he kissed them away as he spoke, "should be shed for my sufferings in company, and not for your own in loneliness. You know not, dearest, what I have suffered this night!—so distant, and yet so near to you!"

"Ah! Mr. Dalton!" she replied, submitting, as it seemed, rather meekly than willingly to his caresses, "I am sure you think what you say, or you would not say it. But, alas! you could not think so, if you knew, or could by possibility guess, what it is to sit for long hours silently and sadly alone! The one only being that the heart clings to within reach of your voice, yet knowing, and feeling with horrible certainty, that you must die, and perish rather than make that voice heard! I do believe you love me, Frederic," she added, resting her head upon his shoulder, and looking up in his face, poor victim! as if her destroyer were a guardian angel,—"I do believe you love me; but is it possible that I should not, in my silence and sorrow during all the long hours of this dreadful day, remember all the beauty and the elegance that was surrounding you? And do not I know,—does not every one know,—that there is not one of these you have left who would even wish to speak a single word to any other, if *you* would only look at and listen to them? Is it possible that I can sit thinking, thinking, thinking, and forget all this, Frederic?"

"You would be cured in half a moment of all such nonsensical thoughts, my angel, if you could but watch me a little, and see how I repay smiles with yawns," replied the young man, drawing her more closely to him, and imprinting a kiss upon her lips.

It was exactly at this moment that the door of the room in which they stood was opened, and a troop of ladies, with Ellen Dalton at their head, entered it. The silken slippers had glided too noiselessly towards

J Leech

the door to give any signal of their approach; but Ellen's hand upon the lock was just in time, so far, to give the lovers' notice, as to prevent any eye *but her own* from perceiving their situation; but most unhappily for her, poor girl, she saw it, and, hastily starting back, closed the door again, exclaiming, "Oh, my scarf! I have left my scarf in the drawing-room."

The *étourderie* of shutting them all out, because she had forgotten her scarf, caused a general laugh; and when the hand of Miss Maxwell reopened the door, she only perceived Jessie busily engaged in arranging shawls and cloaks at one side of the room, and Mr. Dalton assiduously seeking for his hat at the other.

"Mortimer must have taken my hat," he exclaimed, turning suddenly round as the party entered.

It was quite enough, at any time, that Frederic Dalton should speak, in order for every one of the Deepbrook young ladies to attend to him, and to nothing else; so there was immediately a clamour raised among them, expressive of their sympathy; and, under cover of this, Jessie stood up before them with very little outward symptom of the deadly faintness at her heart.

After the noisy interval of a few minutes, the party were all dispersed. "I shall walk home," said Frederic, as the carriage of his father, which happened to be the last, drove off. There was nothing extraordinary in this, inasmuch as there was no room for him; but poor Ellen saw him return into the house, and again felt all the misery, all the terror, of her recent discovery. The misery was chiefly for the hapless Jessie; the terror was for herself. Had Frederic seen her? She knew him, all too well; and she trembled to think this *possible*, even while believing that she had escaped unseen. She was right; Frederic had not seen her, but the hapless Jessie had, and when Frederic re-entered the room for one short moment, the only words he uttered were, "Who opened the door?"

"Ellen!" was the agitated reply. And so they parted.

# XVI

*Night thoughts, which begin in darkness, but end in light*

THE EFFECT OF THIS DISCOVERY on Jessie Phillips was terrible. In one short moment—literally, "in the twinkling of an eye"—had fallen from the envied condition of the most esteemed and respected girl in the parish into what, in her very heart of hearts, she felt to be, or to have the appearance of being, precisely the reverse! No sooner had the door closed upon Frederic Dalton, after the question and answer recorded in the last chapter, than the unhappy girl, feeling utterly incapable of replying with composure to the kind words she was sure to receive from the Maxwell family, who still remained, waiting for the conclusion of the captain's rubber, seized upon her bonnet and shawl, and rushed out of the house.

The night was dark and rainy, and poor Jessie's thin wrapper was but a poor protection against the falling shower; but of this she was perfectly unconscious; and as for the darkness, it was, perhaps, the only circumstance which she could at that moment have felt to be a luxury. "Nobody can see me now," she muttered, as she crept along under the deep black shade of the avenue: "Oh, would to God that nobody could ever see me more!" On reaching her home, her wet and dripping condition was another blessing to her, for it gave the friendly neighbour who was still sitting by her mother's bed-side an object whereupon to exercise all her attention, without leaving any to spare for the examination of the almost haggard countenance of the poor creature herself.

"Why, now then, to be sure, there never was such a bit of ill luck, Jessie," exclaimed the good woman, taking off the bonnet and shawl from the pale shivering girl. "Such a neat pretty bonnet as it was, to be sure, and the riband is neither more nor less than downright spoilt and ruined. But Lord bless my soul, girl, how thee dost shake!" continued the woman, laying her hands upon the two shoulders of the poor trembler. "God send you may not have got the ague, child! Get to bed, Jessie—get to bed. Poor mother's fast asleep, and as warm as a toast, I warrant, and you'll be warm too, in a jiffy, girl, if you'll make haste and lie down by her."

"Go now, then, go now. God bless you! I thank you. Go now!" cried Jessie, who longed for nothing so much as to be alone; but her good neighbour, seeing nothing in this eagerness to send her away but gratitude for her having already stayed so long, tortured her for a while longer by earnestly assuring her that she did not mind staying at all. At length, however, she departed; and the miserable girl, having secured the door of the house, sat herself down in the lower room, for the sake of shedding, unchecked and unseen, the bitter tears which she had hitherto restrained. But even this sad indulgence was not allowed her long, for she heard the feeble voice of her mother calling to her from the room above, whereupon, once more checking her tears with an effort that almost choked her, she obeyed the unwelcome summons, and placing her candle as far from the bed as possible, hung over her mother, and gave her the accustomed kiss that ever followed their being separated for an hour or two.

"I thought I heard you weeping, my Jessie—I think it was that woke me," said the poor sufferer, raising herself in the bed, and endeavouring to look into the face of her child.

"Oh, you dreamed it, mother," replied Jessie, with a caress which enabled her to conceal that altered face. "Lay down again, there's a darling mother, and I'll come to bed in half a minute," she added, withdrawing herself from the arms that were fondly thrown round her.

"Do, dearest, do!" was the unsuspicious reply. "You are as cold as a stone, Jessie."

"Because it has been raining, mother," said Jessie; "but the bed will warm me, and I am so very, very sleepy!"

"Poor little soul! Then I won't say another word to you, my darling!" And the fond mother kept her word, and her wretched daughter seemed to profit by her forbearance, for she presently lay as in the stillness of profound sleep. The mother inwardly breathed a fervent "God bless her!" and was soon in the enjoyment of the repose that the hopeless Jessie feigned. And then followed a long, long interval of such sleepless misery as can only be known by those who contemplate in the future a species and degree of suffering hitherto unknown, and a thousand times more terrible for that reason. Nothing is so utterly subduing to the spirit as the state in which an unknown, though certain suffering is before us—

> "When forward, though we cannot see,
> We guess, and fear!"

What was to become of her? What was to become of her poor helpless mother? Jessie knew well, and had often felt her young heart swell with honest pride as she remembered it, that the good will, the esteem, nay the respect of her rich neighbours, obtained by her ceaseless industry and uniform good conduct, was a sort of fund that she might reckon upon with confidence, as promising her the continued employment which would ensure to her disabled mother sustenance and comfort. But where was all this now? Instead of good will, she must look for reprobation, and for indignation, and contempt, in the place of respect and esteem. Unhappy creature! She buried her face under the bed-clothes to stifle the groan that burst from her bosom, as the thought of the altered looks she might expect from her young customers rushed through her brain. Yet, in the midst of all this anticipated degradation she fondly flattered herself that she was not in reality degraded; for truly did the deluded girl believe that the vows she had exchanged with Frederic Dalton were as sacred in his eyes as in her own, and that she was in spirit and in truth his wedded wife, although the ceremony which was to proclaim their union to the world was delayed till it could take place without injury to the interests of her betrothed husband. But, till this unlucky evening, their connexion had been so carefully and so successfully concealed, that she might almost have been said to consider it as impossible that it should be discovered, as long as it was her idolised Frederic's wish that it should remain unknown. The first hours of this dismal night were thus passed by Jessie in painting to herself every possible species of insult, degradation, and misery, all of which she felt certain would come upon her, yet none of which she fancied she deserved. An imagination thus gloomily employed generally goes on in its prophetic painting, from bad to worse, till it reaches an acme of misery at which it must of necessity stop, from the absolute impossibility of going any farther. And so it was with Jessie. Having imaged her mother dead with grief, herself driven with insult and obloquy from door to door, and her beloved kept, by some strange concatenation of circumstances, in utter ignorance of her condition, till it was too late to save her; having imagined all this, with the crowning catastrophe of her own death from hunger, and that of her lover from despair, she suddenly stopped short in her forebodings, and, after the stillness of a moment, she mentally exclaimed, "But why need all this be? What is the loss of fortune compared to such frightful horror as this? Fool that I am to fancy that he who loves me so fondly, so tenderly, so devotedly, would suffer me to perish, rather than forestall the period of our marriage! Oh, forgive me, Frederic, my own noble Frederic! forgive the thought—forgive the vile suspicion! To-morrow I will tell him all—ALL! He knows not yet all the dear claims I have upon his noble heart." And then, with a feverish anxiety as to the time and manner of the communication she had to make, and the entreaty, nay, the demand for their immediate marriage, with which she meant to follow it, as destructive of repose as her previous agony had been, she lay till morning without enjoying, for a single instant, the healing balm of sleep.

Nevertheless, having once made up her mind to tell her devoted lover, her adoring Frederic, that all considerations of pecuniary interest must give way at once, not only for his sake, and her own, but for that of an unborn treasure more precious than either; having once made up her mind that this must and should be done, her bosom now fluttered more from the anticipation of quickly coming happiness (more quickly coming than she had hitherto ventured to hope for) than from doubt or dread of any kind; and, but for the fear of Ellen's "altered eye," she would, strange to say, have felt happier on that morning than she had done for many weeks. But even of this evil hope whispered that it might not be always so. The marriage which must now immediately take place would, of course, be managed with every possible attention to secrecy so that the precise moment of its occurrence could not be known; and then, when Ellen saw her favourite Jessie the beloved wife of her brother, and the mother of his precious heir, would it be possible that she should remember with unforgiving harshness the scene in Lady Mary's robing-room? The bright beams of the early morning poured through the little casement, and the cheerful chirping of the birds burst upon her ear, as she asked herself this question. Who has not felt the inspiring influence of a bright morning after the heavy silent gloom of a sleepless night? Poor Jessie felt it; and all the sinful weakness of her immeasurable love forgotten, she answered it with the sweet self-flattery of hope: "Oh no! Ellen, the ever-kind and gentle Ellen would not long look coldly on the wife her brother loved—and such a brother!"

Most certain is it that Jessie Phillips was innocent and pure when her unlucky beauty first attracted the notice of Frederic Dalton. But it is a strange blunder that confounds innocence with virtue. When the poet, the English poet of Paradise, says—

"And if virtue feeble were,
Heaven itself would stoop to her."

he speaks not of that lovely, but unsubstantial quality called innocence, but of the self-sustaining principle of which the Red-cross knight says—

"Virtue gives herself light through darkness for to wade."

Of this poor Jessie Phillips knew very little, or she could not have thus looked forward to an almost unclouded future. Yet let her not be harshly judged. The process by which innocence is strengthened into virtue had, in her case, as in ten thousand others, never been applied; and the result was what common sense might tell us was likely enough to follow from the deficiency,—a deficiency, by the way, which is *felt* more generally than it is *understood,* and which will continue to be so felt, with all its hateful consequences, till our theories of popular education are improved.

But, be this as it may, the unfortunate Jessie Phillips rose on the morning after the first shadow of suspicion had fallen upon her (and of which too she was perfectly aware) with a spirit strangely buoyant with renovated hope, and only wondering that she could ever have made herself "so *very* miserable about it." Let it not be thought, however, that the poor girl was become indifferent to the blessing of an unsullied name. So far was this from being the case that, contradictory as it may appear, she would rather have lain down again on her humble pillow, there to breathe her last sigh, than live to meet the obloquy which she well knew must fall upon her, were not all danger of it to be avoided by her appearing at once, the wife of Frederic Dalton. But such was her perfect and entire confidence in him, that the idea of his refusing to ratify the promise so repeatedly and so solemnly given, when she should demand its performance, never entered her head for a single moment. She feared he might be vexed by the necessity for hastening the ceremony, which he had told her it would be advantageous to delay as long as possible, and this fear might have annoyed her but for one dear precious thought. "When he said that last," she murmured to herself unheard by all, "when he said that last, he knew not his poor Jessie was in the way to present him with AN HEIR!"

# XVII

*More night thoughts and the result of them—the wavering magnet of Deepbrook appears fixed at last—and the reasons for it*

JESSIE PHILLIPS WAS NOT THE only person whose rest was disturbed, during the night which succeeded Lady Mary Weyland's party, by meditating on the scene which had occurred in the shawl department at its conclusion. If Frederic Dalton and his sister Ellen did not lay awake through the whole live-long night as she did, they closed not their eyes till a painful hour or two had been passed in meditation on the probable consequences of the incident which had made known a secret that had hitherto been so very carefully hid. As for the hero of the adventure himself, he was one of the very last young gentlemen in the world who would have given the business a second thought, if the destruction of the poor girl's character had been the only danger to be feared from it. He was certainly fond of Jessie, and actually believed himself, that he was passionately in love with her; but as for being reduced by this passion to such a degree of fatuity as to conceive for an instant that her life or death, her well-being in this world or the next, or any other imaginable contingency respecting her, could be reasonably put in competition with any thing, however trifling, that specially and individually concerned himself, no such idea ever entered his head for a single instant. But he was annoyed by what had occurred, for reasons with which poor little Jessie had nothing to do. He had little or no doubt that his sister Ellen detested him as heartily as he detested her; and, with this persuasion actively alive within him, he could not doubt that what she had witnessed would be repeated by her with all possible exaggeration, and precisely in the quarters where it would be most likely to do him injury. Nay, so excited did he become while meditating on the mischief that might possibly ensue, that he contrived, ere he fell asleep, to work himself up into a belief that Ellen was aware how absolutely determined he was that she should never profit by being placed next in succession to him, and that the most obvious and natural use for her to make of the discovery at Lady Mary's would be to make it known to every marriageable woman within his reach. He uttered a frightful malediction upon her innocent head as this idea occurred to him, and at length closed his eyes under the soothing influence of a resolution suddenly taken, but likely enough in his present state of mind to be steadfastly kept.

As to poor Ellen herself, her share in the business was already painful enough, though she was far from guessing all the misery it threatened. The very high opinion she had hitherto entertained of Jessie Phillips now seemed to turn against her, and she felt, naturally enough perhaps, that little as she had actually discovered which could strictly be called criminal, it was sufficient to forfeit a larger portion of esteem than it would have cost one who had been previously less honoured for good conduct. As to her brother's share in the adventure, it was quite impossible that she could be equally surprised at it; for earnestly as she would have wished to keep herself in the dark on the subject, it was totally impossible that she could have lived thus long in the belief that harshness to his sisters was his only fault. But, had her worthless brother known her a little better, he would have been spared the annoyance of believing that his character was likely to be injured in the public estimation by Ellen's becoming acquainted with his delinquencies. If half her hours of wakefulness were given to lamentation for the falling away of her beautiful favourite, the other half was divided into meditations on the best mode of making her poor mother aware that her much-admired discretion was not sufficient to keep her from danger without the aid of maternal watchfulness, and on the most effectual manner of preventing the attention of others from being called to the fact by the almost inevitable alteration of her own manner towards her.

While revolving all these matters in her heart, she suddenly remembered the scene which she had witnessed in the cottage of Jessie on the day she had entered it with the two Miss Lewises. She remembered the words of the idiot girl, the vehement agitation of Jessie, and the figure which they had seen as they retreated from the house. The slightest ray of light can make many things visible, which without it may remain concealed from every eye. The more she thought of what had then passed, the more she became convinced that it was indeed Frederic whom they had then seen; and that it was Frederic, and no other, who had been paying Jessie the visit which had caused her such violent emotion.

No sooner did she feel convinced of this, than the project which had occurred to her of visiting the mother of Jessie, mounting to her sick chamber, and whispering a caution against so very young a girl being permitted to sit alone in the room below, was abandoned. She could not endure the idea of running the risk of again disturbing her worthless brother there, and *her* eyes closed upon the resolution of sending to the unfortunate girl herself a request that she would come to her. Could she contrive to make her feel the tremendous risk she was running by receiving the insulting attentions of Frederic, she thought that even now it might not be too late to save her.

Of the three steadfast purposes thus decided upon at night, there was not one abandoned in the morning, despite the proverb which predicts a different result to the resolutions so formed.

Poor Jessie, who awoke with a flushed cheek and fevered head, though, perhaps, the most eager to perform the promise she had made to herself, being the least of a free agent, was the last to obtain the interview upon which she had fixed her hopes; while Frederic, who, on the contrary, had the least difficulty to encounter, was, as might be expected, the first who put his scheme into action. What this scheme was will be seen in the sequel. No sooner was the family breakfast ended, and the party that had partaken it dispersed, than young Dalton strolled into the village, and twisting about a little through an orchard, and across a farm-yard, to avoid the danger of passing before Mr. Lewis's house, he presented himself beneath the pretty rustic porch of Captain Maxwell. Now Frederic Dalton knew perfectly well that the worthy captain never failed to repair to the little reading-room of the village library every morning of his life; for there he was sure to find a paper of the day before, left there by mail during the night (for the said library was the post-office also), and the being the first to open this daily paper was an object sufficiently important to make the breakfast of Captain Maxwell a very punctual one. The young man had also, somehow or other, acquired the information that Mrs. Maxwell was as constant in her daily visit to her larder, her dairy, and sundry other domestic departments of the household, as the captain to the reading-room, and it was therefore with the most perfect assurance of finding the young lady of the family disengaged that he now approached her dwelling. *Why* it was that this very important visit was made to Miss Maxwell, in preference to either of the other young ladies who would have been equally well pleased to receive it, would take more time to explain at full length than it is necessary to give to it. Most certainly it was not because he liked her better. He considered Lucy Lewis as infinitely better looking, and Agatha Mortimer a hundred times more elegant. But there was a businesslike way of doing every thing in Martha Maxwell which gave him a sort of confidence in her bringing matters rapidly to a conclusion, which at the present moment was his especial object; and this it was which probably led to his turning his steps in this direction in preference to any other.

It may, perhaps, appear strange that a young gentleman, in the position of Mr. Frederic Dalton, conscious of great personal attraction, and secure as entail could make him of so good an estate as few of the first county families would disdain to ally themselves with—it may appear strange that an individual, thus favoured alike by Nature and Fortune, should feel any doubt as to the certainty of his being, at any time, able to obtain a fair hand in marriage, even though his affair with Jessie Phillips *were* unfortunately to be made public. To explain this mystery fully would require a more ample and accurate memoir of the early life and adventures of the said Mr. Frederic Dalton than it would be at all necessary, or at all agreeable, to give. His dissolute habits had been of that worst kind which often remain unguessed at and unknown by reason of their very vileness and degradation. The only individual who really knew young Dalton thoroughly was Dick Baxter, because he alone of all his friends and acquaintance was bad enough to be his companion and associate in a multitude of adventures which, if generally known, would certainly have closed the doors of every tolerably respectable family man against him.

Of this he was himself perfectly aware, and, till he committed the great imprudence of yielding to his inclination for poor Jessie, his native parish and his father's house had never been made the theatre of his libertine exploits. Nevertheless, had the destruction of Jessie Phillips been a solitary sin, his confidence in his own powers, and in the influence he had already obtained in more than one fair bosom, might have given him courage to brave its disclosure; but he felt pretty sure that if this affair got wind before he had secured a wife, the blaze of reprobation which it would occasion would be likely enough to communicate to much that had hitherto remained concealed, and that the train once kindled, he might find himself pointed at from one end of the country to the other as a libertine, with whom no respectable family would connect itself. It was this fear or rather this conviction, which now decided him to delay no longer, but at once to secure himself from the terror which harassed him beyond all else, namely, that of seeing Ellen likely to take his place, or of only being thought likely, even for an hour, of taking it.

# XVIII

*A little feminine agitation, followed by a good deal of feminine cleverness*

THE ANSWERS WHICH FREDERIC DALTON received to his various questions from the servant who opened Captain Maxwell's door to him were in all respects precisely what he wished: "Master is out." "Missis is busy." "Miss is in the breakfast-parlour." To the breakfast-parlour, therefore, he repaired, and found, as he expected, the fair one he sought, "*sans papa, sans maman*," and apparently quite at leisure to hear any thing that it might be his wish to say.

Martha Maxwell was by no means the most violently enamoured of Mr. Frederic Dalton's fair adorers; but she fidgeted a little, and coloured a good deal, on perceiving that he sat down beside her on the sofa with the air of one who had some particular object in coming there. Nor did he leave her long in doubt as to what that object might be.

"The finding you alone, dearest Martha," he began, "is a blessing which I receive as an atonement for all the misery I have been suffering this morning. Oh, Martha! you little think what a tremendous scene I have gone through!"

"What scene, Mr. Dalton?" returned the young lady, a good deal agitated. "You really terrify me!"

"Compose yourself, my dearest Martha!" said the young man, taking her hand with an air of the most soothing gentleness; "compose yourself, and prepare to hear me speak with my lips what my eyes must have told you a thousand times already;—I love you, Martha! But you have long known this; and may I not say, dearest, that you have not so received that knowledge as to leave me utterly without hope?"

"Surely, Mr. Dalton, this avowal is very sudden," returned Miss Maxwell, looking and feeling very genuinely surprised.

"Gracious Heaven! Have I then been mistaken?" he exclaimed, in the most impassioned tone imaginable. "Have I fancied myself understood, while, in fact, you have been ignorant of all that has been passing in my soul! Alas! alas! how dreadfully have I deceived myself! Martha! your manner, your words, your accents, distract me!"

Martha Maxwell was much too straightforward a person to wish to deceive any one, and she immediately put a stop to the young man's lamentations by saying, with as much composure as she could muster, "No, Mr. Frederic Dalton, I do not believe you have been deceiving yourself,—that is, not entirely. I hardly know exactly what I ought to say, but I did not mean to deny that I have sometimes thought you—you were partial to me."

"Partial to you! Good Heaven, what a phrase! Say, rather, that you know I adore you! But what you do not know, my beloved girl,—what it is absolutely impossible that you should know, is the torture and torment in which I have lived, because I have for months felt certain that my father had views for me destructive of all my dearest hopes. This day—this dreadful day, has proved that I was right. I was closeted with him, my dearest Martha, for a horrible hour, before the family assembled to breakfast, in order that I might be told of the prodigious happiness that was in store for me in the possession of the only daughter and heiress of one of his oldest friends! Guess what were my feelings! I knew not what to do nor what to say. If I declared at once my love for you, I doubted not that my father, in the humour he then was, would utter a positive command that I never should enter your father's house again. Oh, it was dreadful! Can you not imagine my sufferings?"

"You have then left him in the belief that you intend to obey his will?" said the young lady, looking a little pale.

"Good Heaven, no! How can you believe me such a wretch? No! But I did not name you, my beloved Martha! I only told him that my affections were already engaged, and that it was impossible I could ever comply with his wishes."

"And what said he?" demanded the anxious girl, her varying complexion shewing plainly enough how deep was the interest she took in the question.

"He said," replied Dalton, "what has been a thousand times said before by old men, to torture the hearts of young ones. He said that it would be his duty to prove to me that he could be as steady in doing what was right as I in doing what was wrong. That he knew the charming person he had chosen was, in every respect, calculated to do me honour and to make me happy, and that he would never give his consent to my marrying any other."

"And why do you come to tell me all this, Mr. Dalton?" replied the young lady, in a tone of very matter-of-fact common sense. "I will not deny, that had you asked me to marry you, with the consent of your father and the approbation of all your family, I should have listened to the avowal of your affection with pleasure; but as it is, I cannot but say that I wish you had never named the subject to me at all; and, certainly, I hope that you never will recur to it again. You have my best wishes for your happiness, and I must now beg of you to go away, as I should like, if you please, to go to my own room before mamma comes in."

It would he difficult to describe the rage and disappointment which took possession of young Dalton as he listened to these reasonable words. He had not only felt well assured that every young lady in the parish was in love with him, which to a certain degree was unquestionably true, but, to this moment, he had firmly believed also that the passions he had inspired were, in every instance, as vehement as that of the unhappy Jessie Phillips, and that not one among them all could have retained sufficient command of herself, upon hearing him confess his love, to enable her to speak as Martha Maxwell had now done. His purpose was to have wrought upon her feelings, by means of his own vehement love and the difficulties which attended it, so as to induce her to promise that if nothing else could be done she would elope with him, trusting to the affection of the parents, on both sides, for forgiveness, when the deed was done. But now he began, with equal astonishment and indignation, to doubt if his influence with the too-much-honoured fair one would suffice to obtain any promise of the kind; nevertheless, he was quite sure, and perhaps he was right, that Martha Maxwell was a good deal in love with him, though not quite so *distractedly* its he had imagined, and, after one short moment of reflection, he determined upon not putting himself under the awkward necessity of making another visit of precisely the same kind, without first making a vigorous effort to obtain what he wanted from this. When she rose, therefore, to leave the room, extending her hand as she did so to bid him farewell, he seized the hand, and held it in a very passionate grasp, so as effectually to prevent her escaping, and then poured forth a rhapsody of love, which it was difficult, not to say impossible, for any young lady to listen to with indifference, especially when her own heart had very decidedly received "a hit from Cupid's bolt," through the eyes of him who uttered it. Martha Maxwell certainly did not listen to Frederic Dalton with indifference; on the contrary for a minute or two she actually trembled from head to foot, and tears, a very unusual circumstance with her, for she was by no means a sentimental person, started to her eyes, as she listened to his touching picture of the misery he should endure if torn from *her,* the only woman he had ever loved, in order to become the husband of one whom of necessity he must ever abhor as the cause of the separation!

"The thought is dreadful!" he exclaimed, assaulting his forehead with his clenched fist. "It is more than I can bear! Consent to elope with me, and put my happiness beyond the reach of fate, or—" and again he attacked his forehead, "I will release myself from life by my own hand!"

What word or what look, what action or what accent, it was which, during the course of this concluding rant, fell upon the ear or eye of Martha Maxwell as something that outraged the modesty of nature, I know not, but most certain is it that something did. The gush of passionate feeling which seemed threatening to overwhelm her suddenly stopped, and she looked at him with an earnestness that had more of scrutiny than love in it. Of this, however, he was in no degree conscious, but, perceiving that she fixed her good-looking intelligent black eyes upon him more earnestly than she had ever done before, he thought he had conquered, and began again with redoubled energy,—"You are silent, my lovely Martha! Ah! let me interpret that gentle silence into consent to my wishes! Be mine, promise,—swear to he mine! Swear to me, my beloved, that you will accompany me to Scotland as soon as I have arranged every thing for our departure.—Speak, thy sweet love! say, will you promise this? My life hangs on your reply."

Martha Maxwell was a very odd girl, though nobody guessed it. Her father, indeed, now and then fancied that there was something in her a little out of the common way, but whenever he attempted to find out what it might be she defeated him, often turning out very particularly stupid on his hands just when he fancied she had betrayed something like great acuteness.

If her own father, who was by no means a dull man, could not make her out, it was not very likely that Mr. Frederic Dalton should, and accordingly he blundered now most egregiously.

"Let me reflect a little, Mr. Dalton, before I answer you," said Martha Maxwell, suddenly fixing her eyes upon the ground, from whence she did not again remove them.

"And how long is this torture of suspense to endure?" he cried, perfectly satisfied that, having brought her to capitulate, he should have every thing his own way. "Say,—tell me, dearest! You cannot have the barbarity to keep me long."

"No!" she replied, without for an instant raising her eyes to his face, "I will not keep you long in uncertainty. But what you ask is too important to be decided upon without reflection; may I communicate your proposal to my father?"

"Good Heavens! No!" he replied, with considerably less of tenderness than haste; "that would be to plunge me into all the difficulties I wish to avoid."

"Well then," she returned mildly, but with looks still fixed upon the carpet, "I will only consult my own heart, and will tell you the answer it dictates the day after to-morrow."

"You are a tyrant!" he said, kissing her hand with an air which spoke pretty plainly his confidence in the gentle feelings which were to plead for him, "but I must submit. At this same hour, beloved Martha, I will repeat my visit on the day you have named. Farewell! farewell!"

These words were accompanied by a profusion of kisses on the passive hand he still held, the ardour of which might have fluttered some young hearts (as conscious of the seductive powers of the performer as was that of Martha) into forgetfulness of the bold and fearless confidence with which this advice was uttered. But it was otherwise with Miss Martha Maxwell. She bent her head to him repeating the word, "Farewell!" and then suddenly added,—

"Hark! my mother!" upon which he darted off, leaving her in possession of the much-desired comforts of solitude and meditation.

# XIX

*A terrible moment—a strong effort—how to bully young ladies of high and low degree*

AT AN EARLY HOUR OF that same morning, Ellen Dalton had despatched the maid that waited upon herself, and some half-dozen of her sisters, to desire Jessie Phillips to come to her immediately. On receiving this message, which was given and delivered in precisely the same words which had been used a hundred times before when she had been summoned to some job of needlework at the squire's, Jessie Phillips started, and coloured as if either some great insult had been offered, or some great terror fallen upon her. The servant, who was an old acquaintance, looked at her with astonishment; she looked at her too, poor creature! with suspicion. With the tender watchfulness of love, which shrinks from causing anxiety, or pain, or peril to the dear centre of every thought, word, and deed, Jessie had cautiously concealed her situation even from Frederic, while there was no possible degree of inconvenience or suffering which she would not have endured rather than have permitted it to become visible to any other. Hitherto the care and caution with which she had dressed herself had prevented any single observation being made upon her altered appearance, but, at the entrance of the Miss Daltons' attendant, she was totally unprepared in every way to sustain the character of the gay, the happy, the fawn-like Jessie Phillips, with any tolerable chance of success. The full consciousness of this immediately came upon her, and she felt she must immediately decide between two lines of conduct which both lay open before her. She must either fall prostrate to the earth at once, before the eyes of all who had ever known her, or she must turn instantly and stand at bay, trusting to the assistance of her lover to sustain her through this hour of trial, and to bring her to shelter, safety, and honour at last. For one terrible moment her bodily weakness became such as to render it probable that the struggle would be decided by this means alone. But ever in the midst of this agony there was a movement of hope at her heart that enabled her to rally, and instantly to reply with equal composure and decision that she would wait upon Miss Dalton immediately.

Without exchanging another word with her old acquaintance, Sophia departed, and "chewed the cud" of a good many fancies before she reached the squire's mansion.

"Jessie Phillips says she'll come directly, Miss Ellen," said the hand-maiden. "She looks dreadfully ill, poor creature! and Heaven knows I would be the last to throw a stone at her if she has got into trouble; but if ever my eyes saw a young girl look—look as she ought not to look, Miss Ellen, it is Jessie Phillips."

Ellen coloured violently, and said, in a somewhat harsher tone than was usual with her, "I do not know what you are talking about, Sophia, but I am very busy, and I wish you would leave me to myself."

The waiting-maid knew her place better than to say any more, and retreated, thinking to herself that it was sometimes a good thing to be a favourite.

Before Ellen had found half time enough to arrange her troubled thoughts, and decide upon what she should say to Jessie under this new aspect of affairs, the unhappy girl was announced. Instead of entering, however, as Ellen expected, trembling and ready to sink before her, she came into the room, closed the door behind her, and advanced towards the chair in which Miss Dalton was seated, with infinitely less timidity instead of more, than was usual to her.

"You sent for me, Miss Dalton," she began, "and I am very glad to come to you. After what passed last night, I could wish for nothing so much as to see you and explain every thing."

"Explain!" repeated Ellen, mournfully shaking her head.

"Yes, Miss Ellen, there is much—very much to be explained before I can hope that you will look at me as you used to do. Nay, I well know that there is much to be excused and forgiven—so much indeed, that I will not venture to be my own advocate. There is one who will plead my cause better than I can plead it myself; and to whom, I well know, it will be a pleasure as well as a duty to place me before you in the light in which I ought to stand. Miss Dalton, I entreat you to let me see your brother immediately, and in your presence."

"You ask what it is not possible for me to grant," replied Ellen, in considerable agitation. "If you seek an interview with my brother, be very sure that he will not approve my being present at it."

"Miss Dalton!" said Jessie, with solemn earnestness, "I conjure you, by all you hold most precious upon earth and in heaven, not to refuse me this indulgence. To you it can bring no evil, and it may save me from a situation ten thousand times worse than death!"

There was something so inexpressibly touching in the pale beauty of the youthful face that was bent upon her in supplication, that Ellen for a moment forgot her displeasure and the afflicting cause of it, and answered in the kind accents of for days, "What is it, Jessie, that you wish me to do for you?"

"I wish you, Miss Dalton, to request the presence of your brother in this room."

"Be very sure, Jessie," reiterated Ellen, "that if I send such a message to him he will decline to come; and were it otherwise, did I believe that he would obey my summons, I confess that I should not think it wise to send it. His presence at this moment could do neither of us any good."

"Let not all the years of condescending kindness with which you have honoured me end by your refusing me so small a boon as this!" said Jessie!

"Will you let Sophia tell him, Miss Dalton, that there is a person in the east parlour who wishes to speak to him? But, say it, if you please, without mentioning my name."

There was a sort of dignity and composure in the manner with which Jessie said this which for the first time suggested to the startled Ellen the idea that her brother had, perhaps, already been guilty of the wild imprudence of making her his wife. This thought caused the bright carnation of sudden agitation to dye her cheeks, and for a moment she remained without answering a word.

"Will you do this, Miss Dalton?" reiterated Jessie, in the same steady tone.

"Yes, Jessie, I will," replied the young lady, deciding, in her own mind, that for all their sakes such a doubt as had now suggested itself ought to be explained as speedily as possible. "Yes, I will send for my brother; I will send the message in the words you suggest, and it is possible he may come." She then rang the bell. It was Sophia who answered it, and to whom she gave the message, adding, "Remember, Sophia, that I do not wish you to tell my brother who is here, nor that you should mention my name in any way. Do you know where to find Mr. Frederic?"

"I have this moment seen him come in, Miss Ellen," replied the girl. "I think he is in the hall still."

"Then hasten back to him, Sophia," said her young mistress, "and take care to give the message cautiously."

Sophia, who was dying with curiosity to know what all this strange mystery meant, determined that the young squire should not refuse the invitation from any fault of hers, justly thinking that, if he accepted it, it would be strange if, with a very quick ear outside the door, she should fail of catching some slight hint of what was going on within it; and accordingly, she managed so well, that Frederic Dalton, unconscious of the snare that was laid for him, walked boldly and unhesitatingly into the little parlour, where he met a reception as unexpected as disagreeable. The figure of Jessie was the only one he at first perceived, that of his sister being concealed by a large cabinet of minerals near the door, and he advanced into the middle of the room without being aware that she was in it, exclaiming brutally enough, "What the devil brings you here, Jessie? And what could put it into your silly head to be so mad as to send for me?"

"No choice was left me, Frederic!" said the wretched girl, struggling to maintain the air of calm confidence which she thought befitting her situation. "Your sister"—and by a movement of the head she indicated the place where Ellen stood —"your sister sent for me, and I feel that she has a right to know, as well as the rest of your family, Mr. Dalton, the terms on which we stand together."

The rage of the violent young man on hearing these words was again such as to defy all description. He turned towards his sister, with teeth clenched and eyes glowing, "I understand it all!" he exclaimed. "Contemptible plotter! Delicate young lady! You saw me kiss a pretty girl in a corner, sweet Miss Ellen, and you thought you should like to find out all about it, and ruin her and shame me! It is worthy of you, Ellen Dalton. Do I not know you?" Ellen, all innocent as she was, trembled before him; he saw it, and went on, "Nay, I am not in the very least degree surprised,—it is precisely what I should have expected of you, Miss Ellen. But it is just possible, my very delicate-minded sister, that you may find yourself thrown out and disappointed. Did you ever happen to hear of a mountain bringing forth a mouse?"

Ellen listened to all this with mingled shame and indignation; but Jessie heard it with hope that increased with every word. Already she had heard enough to bring instant conviction to her mind that the gentle Miss Ellen, whom for years she had almost idolised, was exactly the reverse of all she had supposed her to be; and not only did she lament that she had condescended to obey her haughty summons, but deeply regretted that she had paid her the undeserved compliment of making her the first confidante of her brother's engagement with herself. Perhaps it was this coarse-minded, evil-spirited sister, who had thus long prevented the generous Frederic from performing the promise he had so solemnly made? Perhaps it was Ellen, whose ill offices he feared, and whose opposition, for her sake, he had dreaded to encounter? Yet still there was something doubtful in his eye that made her tremble, and she waited for the next words he should speak as if more than life hung upon them. Ellen, meanwhile, strongly felt that it was no scene for her, and turned to leave the room, but in this it seemed that her brother intended to forestall her, for having muttered the words, "Contemptible old maid!" he suddenly moved towards the door. This movement at once roused the deluded Jessie to the necessity of instantly coming to the point, and (unworthy as Miss Dalton might be) of making her at once understand in what light she was herself for the future to be considered by the Dalton family. "No, Frederic!" she exclaimed, suddenly placing herself between him and the door; "No! whatever you may think of your sister's conduct, dearest Frederic, it has become your bounden duty now to defend mine. Tell her at once, Frederic Dalton,—tell her, without either subterfuge or delay, what and who I am."

"What and who you are, my pretty dear!" exclaimed Frederic, with a loud laugh; "upon my soul, I don't think I know any thing upon that point that my precious sister does not know already; not, however, that I have the slightest objection to state fully and fairly all I think of you, and that is, that you are a devilish nice girl, and a very good girl into the bargain, ten thousand better than she is in every way. And, moreover, for her particular satisfaction, and for yours too, my pretty lass, I am quite ready to add, that if Lady Mary's good wine made me frisky, and led me to take the prodigious liberty of giving you a kiss, it was no fault of yours, my dear, and I am ready and willing to repeat this to all the old maids in the parish, if you wish it. You have nothing to do, but to say so, and I'm off in a minute."

How was this artful speech to be answered by the astonished, the bewildered Jessie? Where was now all the strength derived from the dignified position which she fancied awaited her? Was this jest? Was it earnest? Was it only a continuation of his former policy? Or was it the announcement of a degree of treacherous perfidy, which must crush her under the feet of all men, lower—a thousand fathoms lower—than the grave? While she pondered upon these tremendous questions, and gazed with widely distended eyes on the face of him who seemed to stand before her like the incarnate image of the destroying angel, Dalton, whose progress towards the door her shrinking figure still impeded, bowed to her with a laughing air of mock humility, and then, playfully clapping his hands as we do to children whom we mean to frighten into running away, he said, "Pretty Jessie, I must positively kiss you again if you do not decamp. If you were alone, my pretty lass, I should not, perhaps, be in such a hurry, but, being by no means very partial to the company in which I have the honour to find you, I must beg to intimate that I insist, young woman, upon your detaining me no longer."

Jessie Phillips had no courage left to resist this. Had she understood him more clearly, she would have felt less bewildered, and perhaps more decided; but now every thing seemed wrapped in doubt and mystery; and, fearful of doing mischief to what she still believed was the common cause of Frederic and herself, she stood back to let him pass.

"Thank you, kindly, my pretty maid," he said, gaily kissing his hand as he passed her. "I hope the sweet saint with whom I leave you will not quite lecture you to death!" These words were said as he passed through the door, and Ellen and Jessie were again alone together.

Had it not been for some things that had been uttered by Jessie herself, this strange scene would have produced a very favourable effect in her behalf on the mind of Ellen. It would have seemed to her that her worthless and unprincipled brother had taken advantage of the familiar terms to which Jessie had been admitted by his family, and that she had received the insult of an unwarranted caress from him, when he had been excited, as he had himself suggested, by having taken more wine than ordinary. This might have happened with little or no impropriety on the part of Jessie. But how was Ellen to account for the young woman's having addressed him as Frederic, dear Frederic? A single word, the utterance of a name, seemed but slight authority upon which to withdraw from her the respect and esteem which years of good conduct had produced. Nevertheless, the effect of it was as strong as it was involuntary. The sound of her brother's name, so pronounced, seemed to ring in her ears. If she had made an effort to conquer this impression, it would have been in vain; but she could not even attempt it, and she felt justified in withdrawing herself from the attempt she had meditated for the protection of her former favourite, by deciding that she was either too innocent to want her assistance, or too guilty to benefit by it. With these feelings she turned towards the unhappy girl, and gravely said, "You may go, Jessie; I have no longer any inclination to lecture you, as I meant to have done, on the danger and impropriety of suffering any gentleman to take a liberty with you. Your eyes must be sufficiently opened to this by the levity of Mr. Frederic Dalton's conduct. I have no more to say on the subject."

Jessie was aware that, at this moment, there was nothing which she could say in reply which could avail her; but she felt an indignant consciousness of injustice done her, though she could hardly, at this moment, accuse Ellen of being a party to it; nevertheless, it caused her to bend her beautiful head with more of pride than sorrow as she obeyed the young lady's wish and left the room.

At the door of this room, or rather ensconced at the entrance of a dark passage which led from the hall to the offices, the arm of the trembling Jessie was seized by some one whom, for an instant, she did not recognise, for her eyes were full of tears. But in the next the voice of Frederic Dalton sounded in her ears. Not, however, as heretofore, in tones bland and seductive as the breath of love, but hoarse, harsh, and hollow,—

"Is it your purpose, mad woman, as you are, to drive me mad too? A little more, a very little more imprudence will suffice to do it, girl! Go but one inch farther towards betraying me, and, by the heaven above us, I swear that I will shoot myself before your eyes!"

"No! no! no! May that pitiful Heaven grant my prayer," she murmured in reply, "and permit me to die before yours!" And as she spoke she sunk on the floor at his feet.

His resolution was instantly taken. He knew the locale; at three yards distance from where he stood an outward door opened upon a court surrounded by wood-house, dog-kennel, and other offices, and which led by another door to a path used only by the gardener, and which wandered away through the shrubberies towards the park, or paddock, that surrounded the house. The catching up in his arms the senseless Jessie, and carrying her into this paddock, by the route above described, was the work of a moment. But, short as was the time, it was sufficient to enable Dalton entirely to recover his presence of mind. Had he met any stragglers in this little-frequented path, he would have told them that he was bearing the poor girl away from the insults of his sister Ellen, which had first thrown her into hysterics, and then caused her to faint away. But if more fortunate, and that he met nobody, his part would be easier still. He *was* more fortunate; he met no one in his progress; and by the time he had reached the little gate which opened upon the paddock Jessie Phillips had recovered her senses. He placed her on the grass, with her back resting against the shrubbery fence, and then stood before her and thus addressed her,—

"Jessie Phillips, you have very nearly destroyed me, and yourself, too. My presence of mind has, I trust, saved us both. I think not that your fine friend, Miss Ellen, will be in haste to interfere again in your affairs. By your mad conduct you have, of course, banished yourself from the house.

But this matters little. It may in some degree increase your difficulties, but not one-thousandth part so much as you deserve. I had arranged every thing; you have disarranged it all. Whether all my efforts will now prevent destruction from falling on you, I know not. All may yet, perhaps, depend upon your own future conduct. Of course, I must not see you. It may be months, perhaps, before I can venture to come near you again. That is one effect of your disobedience to my instructions, to my fond entreaties! Whether, indeed, I shall ever see you again, must depend entirely upon yourself. The slightest effort on your part either to see or hold communication with me of any kind will instantly cause me to leave the kingdom. And in that case, trust me, I will bring home a wife whose good name shall not have been destroyed by her own hot-headed imprudence, before I have sheltered her by my own. *You hear me, Jessie*, and, as a friend, I counsel you to believe and to remember my words. Make no effort to write to me, unless you would wish to have it said, by all the parish, that Jessie Phillips was trying to win the smiles of the young squire, but that he turned a deaf ear to her, as she deserved; for, be very sure, I will send back any letter you may write to me unopened. All this you have brought upon yourself. Beware how you go now!" As he pronounced the last words, he sprung over the fence, against which he had rested, and following another turn in the walk was out of sight in a moment.

The young man was quite right. The wretched girl had heard every word he had said, but with nerves too shaken, and strength too much exhausted, to interrupt him; nor was it till he was out of sight, and absolutely beyond her reach, that she remembered how utterly impossible he had now made it for her to communicate to him the important secret upon which she fancied (poor soul!) that so much depended. This was her first and foremost grief; *not* the fatal fact itself; *not* the appalling certainty that she was about to give birth to a poor little being, who had no right to call any man father! It was not *this* that pressed upon her heart with the heavy weight of despair; but it was the unspeakable misery of not being able to communicate the tidings to the hard, cold, corrupted heart of Frederic Dalton. Having dwelt on this idea till her reason seemed to waver under the suffering it occasioned, she suddenly recalled his altered looks and words during the past meeting, and then, strange to say, for the first time, with any thing like distinctness, a doubt suddenly shot through her heart as to the possibility that any thing she had done could have caused him to speak so harshly, if his love for her still continued as great as ever? It was after enduring the pang which this thought produced, for about half a minute, that also, for the first time on that memorable day, she felt herself to blame. "I have been angry with his sister," she said, "and no great wonder. If it is a sin, it is a very natural one. But dare I have doubts of him?—of him, my own dear, matchless Frederic? Well might he reproach me! I have deserved it all, and ten times more, if it were possible, for daring to fancy that my noble-hearted Frederic could be wrong!" Whether this pertinacious belief in one who had already proved himself so utterly base was quite genuine, or wilfully clung to by a mind that seemed already struggling with madness, it is impossible to say; but certain it is, that instead of permitting herself to meditate on her own miserable condition, she beguiled herself, as she sat on the spot where he had left her, welcoming the chill October wind that blew in her fevered face, with imagining scene after scene in which every thing was to be explained to his honour and her glory. And what was it that roused her at last from this worse than fool's paradise? Was it the sudden consciousness of her real situation? No; it was the thought that she might be seen loitering about the premises, and so incur the killing disgrace with which her lover had threatened her.

"They may say, if they see me, that I am here to look for him, to wait for him," she murmured, as she hastily rose and made her way through the long matted grass towards the road. "But I never waited for him—no, never! It is he who has waited and watched for me. Nobody shall ever say that I waited and watched for him;" and the dread of exciting a suspicion so mortifying lent her all the strength she wanted to reach her home.

Poor Jessie! this excessive dread of forfeiting, not her *honour*, but her *renown,*—her too, too fondly valued village renown, as the most beautiful, the most admired, and by far the most respected girl in the parish, furnishes the key to all her deepest and strongest feelings. There was something better than mere vanity in it, for the being accounted, as she ever was, the loveliest girl in the whole neighbourhood, would not have satisfied her, unless she had believed herself the most popular and the most respected also. It was this, poor little girl! which had prevented her ever seeing any thing very extraordinary or improbable in the young squire's being ready to sacrifice every thing for her sake; and it was this which soothed her into the belief that it was impossible he could ever cease to love her. But ere she reached her mother's bedside some of the terrible realities of her condition pressed upon her mind, together with the conviction that he who alone could rescue her from them could not, might not, would not be called to her aid! Alas! was not poor Sally, the village idiot, a thousand times less pitiable than the village beauty?

# XX

*Ellen Dalton receives a visit from another of her brother's loves—the conversation that ensues between them—much mutual confidence is displayed, but it is not quite perfect on both sides*

THE DAY FOLLOWING THIS SCENE at the manor-house, Ellen Dalton was again sitting alone before her drawing-desk in the little east parlour, when another young female visitor who had inquired for her was shewn into it. This was no other than Martha Maxwell, who took the privilege, allowed by long-established intimacy, to pay a visit to her especial favourite, among her beloved's sisters, at a much earlier hour than usual. As an excuse for this, she produced some marvellous piece of dexterity in the way of cross-stitch, for the welfare of which some instruction from Ellen was absolutely necessary.

"Thank you, Ellen! Thank you!" said Martha. "Now I understand it perfectly; and I shall go on twelve knots an hour, as papa says: but you must let me stay here till I have just got round this corner, for that is the difficulty. Cannot you go on drawing, Ellen, while I work?"

"Oh! yes!" was the ready reply. "Pray do not hurry yourself, dear Martha, from any anxiety about my drawing. It is no very sublime composition. Only a portrait of the children's darling 'Tiny,' and a cabbage-stalk."

"Well then, I will indulge myself with a few minutes' stitchery and gossip, which papa says supplies the want of grog and a cigar to the ladies," replied Miss Maxwell, placing herself advantageously, so as to have an uninterrupted view of the face of her fair friend. "And talking of gossip, Ellen," she continued, "I want you to tell me if the news I have heard be true about your brother?"

"What news?" returned Ellen, colouring violently.

"About your father's having fixed upon a young lady of fashion and fortune, whom he insists upon your brother's marrying directly. I assure you, my dear, I have heard, upon what seemed very good authority, that your brother was breaking his heart about it, and that your father was treating him with most extraordinary harshness and cruelty. It is really very shocking."

"And you believe this, Martha Maxwell?" said Ellen, looking up from her drawing, and fixing her eyes on the face of her companion.

"Nay, Ellen, do not look at me so sternly," returned Martha, laughing. "Upon my word I have not invented what I tell you; and it is because I know you always speak the truth that I repeat it to you, as I wish much to know whether I may believe it or not."

"Believe not one single word of it, Martha," replied Miss Dalton, earnestly, "for it is utterly false from beginning to end."

Martha Maxwell performed three or four cross-stitches in silence, and then suddenly raising her eyes again, and fixing them on the face of her friend, she said, "How can you be so very certain of this, Ellen? What should you say if I tell you that it was your brother himself who informed me of it?"

"I should say," replied Ellen, her delicate cheek again mantling with a blush, "that for some reason or other"—then suddenly seeming to change her purpose, she added, as she resumed her employment, and in a different and lighter tone, "I should say that he was jesting with you."

It was now Miss Maxwell's turn to blush, which she did violently, her eyebrows at the same time contracting themselves into a frown, which Ellen, however, saw not, and which, if she had, she could not have interpreted. For several minutes they both remained silent, and both young hearts were swelling with indignation, though not quite in the same degree. Ellen was indignant at her worthless brother's having, either in jest or earnest, dared to accuse her father of interested motives, of which she well knew him to be incapable, and of harshness and cruelty, which were about as foreign to his nature as to that of a dove; and she was indignant, too, that so gross a falsehood as the whole statement contained should have been uttered to Martha Maxwell, for whom she had a very sincere esteem: and Martha Maxwell deserved this esteem, for she was true, unaffected, and possessed a species of practical good sense, which prevented her, even though she *was* in love, like all the other young ladies of Deepbrook, from being guilty of the silly tricks by which her fair companions in the tender passion endeavoured to advance their respective claims; but the indignation of Martha was of a very different quality. Ellen's estimate of her character was perfectly just as far as it went. She *was* sincere, sensible, and unaffected; but these, though perhaps the most obvious in the social intercourse of Deepbrook, were not her only qualities. She not only, like Ellen, disdained falsehood, and disliked those who were guilty of it, but she hated them. She hated, too, sternly and deeply, the treachery that could trifle with affection; and there might be, perhaps, something vindictive in the feeling which swelled in her bosom, as she believed herself to have been the object of this treachery. She remained silent as these emotions arose, and, as it were, settled themselves in her mind; but this over, it took her not long to determine that she would not blunder by suffering any thing like doubt to remain on her mind. She perfectly well understood and appreciated the sterling character of Ellen, and promptly decided upon telling her what had passed. The most painful part of this communication consisted in having to confess that she loved Frederic Dalton well enough to have listened to his professions of answering love. But Martha had made up her mind to endure it and, moreover, she had the solace of being able very honestly to declare that, even in the midst of his most impassioned pleadings, she had detected something forced and suspicious, and had therefore given him the reply which was to keep him in suspense till the morrow. Having finished her narrative, which she had given as simply and shortly as possible, she said,—

"Now, dear Ellen, you know every thing, excepting that (which you may probably guess) I have not, nor ever have had, the slightest intention of entering your family in secret, or against the wishes of your father. Have I not, after this communication, some claim on you for all the light you can throw upon this most mysterious proposal? I have told you that I will not marry your brother clandestinely; but I have not told you that my peace of mind for the rest of life may not hang upon the correctness of the opinion I may be now enabled to form of him. Have I not some claim on your sincerity?"

"You have, Miss Maxwell," replied Ellen, from whose complexion this appeal had chased all the angry roses, "I should be unworthy of the confidence you have reposed in me, if I refused to give you every information in my power. My brother and I are not on confidential terms; we never *have* been; and I have therefore as little power as inclination to offer any opinion of what his real feelings towards you may be. I have seen him pay you attention; I have soon him do the same to both the Miss Lewises; and during the whole of this summer I have seen him, at least, equally devoted to both the Miss Mortimers, sometimes to one, and sometimes to the other, as opportunity offered. Farther than this, I can only say, that I should not have been surprised at hearing that he had proposed to either one of these ladies, or to yourself either, my dear Martha. But why it should be done in so strange a manner,—why he should propose an elopement,—or why he should have told so strangely false a history of my father's conduct to him, I know not."

"Thank you, dear Ellen! thank you!"' replied the young lady but the words were uttered musingly, and as if her mind were occupied on some point that had not yet been discussed between them.

"You have told me all, Ellen? " she said, at length. "I cannot believe at this moment that you would hide any thing from me."

"Indeed I would not," replied Ellen, again changing colour. "I would hide nothing that I thought it could do good to mention. And yet," she instantly added, "perhaps I am wrong to make any reservation. A circumstance, which I dare say my brother would treat as a light jest, has occurred; but if I tell you of it, Martha, remember it is in confidence, and that it is to be repeated to no one. If it be as trifling as he certainly endeavoured to make it appear to me, it may, indeed, be nothing, and in that case it would be cruelly harsh to remember it to the poor girl's injury."

Ellen then repeated succinctly what she had witnessed at Lady Mary's, and also the scene which passed with Jessie.

"Again I thank you, Ellen," said Miss Maxwell, rising to depart; "I will *not* abuse your confidence. I have only one question more," she added, as she employed herself in folding up her work, "Is it supposed among you that your brother is likely to marry early or that he is not?"

"That is, indeed, a difficult question to answer," replied Ellen, laughing "but as I have told you so much, under the firm belief that you deserve my confidence, I will confess to you that this identical question is a constant source of debate amongst us all. My brother is perfectly independent of my father; I mean that the entail of the property is such that, let him marry whom he would, my father could not alter the disposition of any part of it. Of this we have all of us heard Frederic boast, as long as we can remember any thing; and this boast has often been accompanied by a sort of threat that he would startle us all some day. But my younger sisters, with whom he talks much more familiarly than to me, tell me, that when he is in high spirits, and running on to them about his conquests, and all that sort of nonsense, he never fails to declare that he would a great deal rather go to be hanged than to be married, and that nothing would drive him into the 'hated noose' but seeing in his looking-glass that his beauty was on the wane—always concluding, foolish boy! with repeating, that Miss Ellen had better not encourage any hopes on that score, for that he should always take care to have a wife ready. Of course you know, Martha, because every body does, that our names are all mentioned in the entail. But poor Frederic need not fancy that we, any of us, either expect or wish to profit by it."

"Oh! yes, dear Ellen, I know all that, because, as you say, every body knows it. God bless you, dear! I leave you to guess my answer to Mr. Frederic."

# XXI

*The Duke of Rochdale's family arrive at Pemberton Castle—a conversation between the Duchess and Mrs. Buckhurst, which partly betrays a secret—another between the noble family and Mrs. Greenhill, which completes the disclosure—a note, and its effect*

IT WAS RATHER HARD UPON Ellen Dalton that, having for various weighty reasons made up her mind to be contented under the shelter of a tranquil spirit, instead of looking for the more vivid enjoyments which youth, beauty, well-developed talent, and a conscience void of offence, might have led her to hope for—it was certainly hard upon her, that with so moderate an object for her hopes and wishes, she should so completely fail of attaining it.

The scene with Jessie had not only agitated her very painfully at the moment, but had left her exceedingly unhappy; and that which followed on the day after with Miss Maxwell, though less embarrassing while it lasted, had also left an impression on her mind of a nature effectually to destroy that peaceful state of spirits which she was so anxious to obtain. The poor girl had been hardly aware herself what her real opinion of her brother was till those scenes had occurred. She had never embodied that opinion in words, she had never accurately defined it, even in thought; but a multitude of passing circumstances, having various shades of moral delinquency, had for years been leaving their dark impressions on her mind, which now, by an involuntary act of memory, came forward as testimony against him, and caused her to interpret what had now come before her with more severity than a harsher spirit would have done if blunted with less knowledge of his character. Her mother's habitual dreaminess and indifference of temper placed her almost beyond the reach of any great mental suffering, but Ellen dreaded the effect which any public exposure of Frederic would have upon her father. Though rarely, very rarely indeed, had any word passed between them on the subject, Mr. Dalton's most familiar companion and friend (and such was Ellen to her father) could not be ignorant of the low estimate which his son had by degrees contrived to establish of himself in his mind. But hitherto the young man had never exposed himself at Deepbrook by any very flagrant act of dishonour or libertinism. His far from creditable association with Dick Baxter was, by common consent, allowed to pass current, as the natural result of the atrocious young brewer's superior sportsmanship; and for the rest, as the young squire stood high in favour with all the ladies in the parish, the gentlemen for the most part judged him with indulgence, and received him with apparent cordiality. But all this could not last; Ellen felt it could not now last much longer, and the thought of what was to follow, with its probable effect on her father, made her more unhappy than she had ever thought her brother could render her. All this was bad enough, but it was not all which at this time threatened her tranquillity; another circumstance occurred, concerning which, moreover, she could not wholly acquit herself from blame, and which seemed likely to awake many painful emotions which it was the great study of her life to set at rest.

The Rochdale family had arrived at the Castle. Ellen Dalton of course knew this, for had not the Deepbrook bells rung incessantly for at least eight hours after their arrival? This very naturally made her head ache, but, when the noise ceased, she did all she could to make her headache cease too. In fact, the arrival of the Rochdale family could hardly be likely to affect her in any way,—they did not visit, nor was there any probability of their meeting. But though this was the case with the Daltons, it was not so with all the inhabitants of Deepbrook. Mr. Rimmington always welcomed their return with joy, and mourned their departure as one of the very worst things that could happen to his parish; Mrs. Buckhurst ever hailed their angel-like visits as the greatest happiness that could befall her; and good nurse Greenhill pretty well forgot, as long as they remained at the Castle, that she was not so young, and could not walk quite so well, as she had done five years before.

The ivy-covered cottage of Mrs. Buckhurst was, as usual, the first dwelling before which the Duchess's plain green chariot was seen to stop; and beautifully cordial was the meeting between the two old friends, although, among all the various sources of human sympathy, they had nothing to draw them together save long-tried conviction of each other's talents and each other's worth. Immediate arrangements were, of course, made for the old lady's passing a few days at the Castle, and when this was settled the noble visitor said she must not indulge herself long on this occasion, as she had left the Duke at one farm, and Pemberton at another, and had promised not to leave either long before she returned for them. "For we have brought no horses to the Castle," she added; "my neighing steeds that you hear at your door are your old acquaintances that have won the range of the park as a reward for their long service. But then, dear friend, every thing is going well with us. I never hoped to see my noble husband—he is nobler, my dear Mrs. Buckhurst, than any strawberry-leaves could make him—I never hoped to see him so nearly free as he is now. Five more years, old friend, five more years of equal constancy and courage will bring him back to his dearly beloved castle as he ought to come to it. All this is Pemberton's doing. Was there ever such a son as that?"

"Not often, dear Duchess, not very often, I fear," replied the old lady with a melancholy smile.

"Ah, I see what you are thinking of!" exclaimed the Duchess, the happy expression of her fine countenance suddenly changed to a look of sadness. "I know you think that I have treated him harshly. But he is happy, Mrs. Buckhurst, I am quite sure that he is happy. His father's improving health, his father's improving peace of mind, leave no room, no time, for selfish boyish regards. I am quite sure he is happy, Mrs. Buckhurst."

"I trust he is happy," replied the old lady; "I am sure he has much to make him so; and first in the list of blessings I must put his own approving heart. I greatly doubt, all things considered, if any young man ever made so great a sacrifice as Lord Pemberton."

"I understand you again—I understand you perfectly," returned the Duchess, a slight frown passing across her brow. "But you know we long ago dismissed this subject for ever. It was not kind of you to allude to it."

"Was it I, Duchess?"

"I do not know—perhaps not. Dearest Mrs. Buckhurst! you will know it is no selfish feeling that makes me wish so cautiously to avoid it,—you well know it is my terror lest the Duke should ever, by any possible or impossible chance, discover how dearly the resolute economy of his life has cost his son. The only way to avoid this is never, never, never, to allude to it! Is it not? Do I not say truth?"

"Perhaps it is, dear Duchess," replied the old lady, with a sigh. "But there is another reason still—it is painful."

"Well, then, the carriage shall come for you on Tuesday," said the Duchess, after the silence of a moment. "You must come before luncheon. Shall we say twelve?" This was agreed to, and the noble lady rose to take her leave; but ere she reached the door she stopped, and said, "By the by, I forgot to ask you about Greenhill. What in the world was it you meant in your last letter about the dear Duke's generous kindness to her? That the dear Duke is the most generous and the most kind person in the whole world I have no doubt, but, nevertheless, I know nothing just now about any particular kindness to Greenhill."

"I should believe you had forgotten it," replied Mrs. Buckhurst, smiling, "only I do not think you are at all likely to forget all the suffering she endured before she applied to you, and which of course she stated."

"Suffering! Has my poor dear Greenhill been suffering? She never let me know it,—she never applied to me at all," said the Duchess.

"Then I must have misunderstood her," replied Mrs. Buckhurst. "Perhaps," she added, "it was Lord Pemberton. But it was so large a sum that I thought you had probably counselled together about it."

"I am totally in the dark," said her grace. "Of what large sum do you speak?"

"I think she said it was three or four hundred pounds," replied the old lady.

"Nonsense! my dear friend, I thought you understood the state of the ducal exchequer better than to fancy that we could either of us have indulged our fondness for good nurse Greenhill to that amount. I do really suspect that you have been dreaming."

"It is very strange," said Mrs. Buckhurst. "I cannot recall Greenhill's precise words, but she certainly left me with the persuasion that they had been relieved from all their troubles by you."

"I cannot understand it," was the reply; "but I shall have seen our good nurse before Tuesday, and by that time shall be, I doubt not, *au fait* of the whole mystery."

In driving through the village the Duchess of Rochdale stopped, as she had very often done before, at the cottage of the Greenhills, and seeing it wear in every respect the same aspect of neatness and comfort, which it had always done, she had nearly forgotten the mysterious allusion of Mrs. Buckhurst, till her old servant, having satisfactorily answered all her Grace's inquiries about the welfare of all her progeny, drew nearer to the window of the carriage, and whispered, "Though to nobody else in the whole world, your Grace, I must tell *you* that I know who it was that helped us when we were about to perish, and may God reward you! It is only He who can."

"Greenhill," said the Duchess, "you must come up to the Castle to-morrow. I want to speak to you, but I have no time now."

On rejoining the Duke and her son, the first theme started between them was the history of Tom Greenhill's imprudence and its terrible result. Lord Pemberton had been deeply touched by a description of the state in which the family had been living after they had been turned from their house, by the harshness of the board of guardians to his poor nurse, by Tom's imprisonment, and various other details. "But the most singular part of the business," continued the young man, "is they are now all living again *in statu quo*, exactly as they were when we saw them last, and yet I am assured that, only a few weeks ago, poor Greenhill had been obliged to make over her little annuity to one of Tom's creditors—and with all this nobody is able to say who helped them."

"Greenhill herself says, that it is *we* who have done it," said the Duchess. "I, for one, however, positively declare I know nothing about it; if you do, gentlemen," she added, "you have been very successful in keeping your secret." Both father and son united their voices in disclaiming all participation in this good deed, and, after wasting a few more conjectures on the riddle, they agreed to adjourn the subject till the morrow.

The family party had not left the breakfast-table on the following morning when their old servant sent up her name. She was instantly admitted, and made to sit down amongst them, as she had often done before. "And now, nurse Greenhill," said the Duke, after the first salutations were over, "you must explain to us the history we have heard about you. Is it true that Tom has been in prison?"

"But too true, your Grace," was the reply, "and most certainly he would have been there still, but for the kindness of your Grace and my Lord."

"By means of the annuity, you mean, nurse?"

"Alas! no, your Grace," she replied, colouring deeply, "that ought to have done it, sure enough; but that was gone too, your Grace, and it was the noble donation which came after it that set all right."

"The cloud thickens instead of dispersing," said the Duke laughing, "upon my word, nurse, you must explain this a little more intelligibly. Who was it, in one word, from whom you received the money of which you speak?" For the interval of a moment poor Greenhill gazed with eyes and mouth wide open at the noble questioner, and then exclaimed in great agitation, "If your Grace does not know already, I have been guilty of a great crime."

"What can she mean?" cried Lord Pemberton hastily; "upon my word, this is confusion worse confounded.'"

"Come, come, my good Margaret," said the Duchess gravely, "you are not acting with your usual good sense in this matter. Why should you try to puzzle us thus?"

"I will be very, very much obliged if you will not ask me," said the poor woman, in most genuine distress. "I see plainly now that I have been quite mistaken, and in my blundering I have broke the solemn promise that I made to—to the kindest friend that poor creature ever had."

"At any rate, it is quite evident, nurse Greenhill, that this kind friend of yours has thought proper to make use of our names," said the Duke, "and I shall not be pleased if you refuse to tell me who it is that has taken this liberty."

"Nobody, my Lord Duke, nobody," eagerly exclaimed the frightened Mrs. Greenhill, "neither the squire nor Miss Ellen ever named any name at all as now I well remember; all they said was that I was to promise never to tell who had helped me, and for that very reason it was that I felt sure it was your Grace or my Lord."

What it was she had now said to displease her noble patrons, poor Greenhill could not guess, but certain she was that something was wrong, for the air of gay good-humour which, despite the puzzling mystification of her replies, had reigned in every eye, now suddenly vanished. The Duchess became red, her son became pale, and the Duke knit his brows and looked uncomfortable.

"Never mind, nurse, it is of no consequence," said the Duchess, recovering herself; "you need not fear we shall repeat what you have accidentally said, so there is no harm done. Go now, and visit your old friends in Price's room. They will be very glad to see you."

The poor woman received her dismissal joyfully, hoped she had done no great harm, and felt tolerably easy, because she thought it was impossible. Lord Pemberton left the room immediately afterwards, the Duchess took a book, and the Duke a newspaper, and not a word more was said among them about nurse Greenhill or her munificent friends.

About three o'clock in the afternoon of that day Ellen Dalton received the following note from Mrs. Buckhurst:—

"Come to me immediately, my dear Ellen, if you can contrive to do so alone."

This might have been a startling invitation from any one else, but from Mrs. Buckhurst it was not so. Ellen knew that she enjoyed the privilege of being the only young lady in the parish freely admitted to share the retirement of Mrs. Buckhurst, and it was enough that she should mention to her sisters that she was going to the cottage, in order to prevent their proposing to go with her.

She found her old friend flushed and feverish, and her first idea very naturally was, that she had been taken ill, and ought to be in bed with the doctor beside her; an opinion which the young lady very freely expressed, accompanied with sundry reproaches for not taking sufficient care of herself.

"No, Ellen, no; that is not it, my child," said the old lady, "but all my troubles are come back upon me, Ellen. I never meant, my poor girl, to pronounce his name to you again, yet now I have promised to do it; and, perhaps, I am something worse than an old fool for my pains. Lord Pemberton has been here, Ellen, and, while protesting that nothing on earth should ever induce him to occasion you another pang, implored me so earnestly to give you this note, that I consented to do it. How, indeed, could I refuse him, when he pleaded the tremendous sacrifice he had made as proof that he might be trusted?" Mrs. Buckhurst then put the note which she held into the passive hand of the statue-like Ellen, who really scarcely looked sufficiently alive to open it. Somehow or other, she contrived to manage it, however, and read the following lines:—

> "I have, as you already know, pledged my honour to my mother, Ellen, that I would never again, without her consent, petition for your love. The keeping this promise has robbed my life of every enjoyment, save that of believing that I was performing my duty to a devoted mother, who was suffering no common sorrow, and from no common cause. But this promise involves not the necessity of my fearing to thank you for an act of kindness to my poor nurse. Do not blame poor Greenhill, Ellen. It was accident which led to our knowing who it was that relieved her from a situation which it would have wrung my heart to see her in—and from which it would but have been easy for me to release her. I thank you, Ellen! and I break no promise in relieving my heart by saying so.
>
> "PEMBERTON."

There was nothing in this note to excite any violent emotion, yet, nevertheless, it sufficed to send poor Ellen Dalton to her room precisely in the state of mind which the efforts of a whole year of very resolute exertion had been endeavouring to subdue.

# XXII

*Two old ladies are very near quarrelling, but think better of it—a love scene upon a new plan*

Mrs. Buckhurst, though she had been reduced into the difficult and seemingly equivocal situation of being confidant in a very thorny love affair, to both mother and son, was no traitress. Fortunately for her, both parties knew this, and nothing was ever communicated to her by either which it was intended to conceal from the other. In fact, she was rather the medium by which much passed between the different parties in this melancholy little romance than a receiver of secrets from any. It was, therefore, without either doubt or compunction that the old lady, when she arrived at the Castle on the following Tuesday according to appointment, took advantage of her first *tête-à-tête* with the Duchess of Rochdale to relate what had passed respecting the note. She certainly did not expect, however, that the circumstance would have produced the effect it did upon her noble friend. Instead of seeing in it, as she did herself, a most satisfactory proof (had any such been wanting) that Lord Pemberton and Ellen Dalton were precisely on the terms on which she had wished to place them, she fell into a state of the most violent agitation, actually shook from head to foot, and turned so pale that poor old Mrs. Buckhurst was very seriously alarmed.

"Good Heaven! Dearest lady!" she exclaimed, "what can I have said to affect you thus? Do you blame me for giving Lord Pemberton's letter to Miss Dalton? Was it not settled between us, long ago, that Lord Pemberton's conduct had purchased freedom from all restraint? Have you not yourself desired that I would never refuse to do any thing he requested of me in this unhappy business?"

"Yes, yes, yes, again, and again, and again!," replied the Duchess, vehemently; "no motive, not even the welfare of his father, should ever induce me to control Pemberton's actions, either by force or fraud. He has nobly deserved his freedom, and he shall have it, come what will. But if at last!—Dear old friend! I fear, I fear, the disappointment would be more than I could bear! I have struggled against so much, Mrs. Buckhurst!—I feel as if I had no more courage left."

"If such disappointment as you seem to fear really awaited your Grace," replied Mrs. Buckhurst, "I could hardly wonder if you were to feel overwhelmed by it; but I see no reason whatever for fearing this."

"No reason! what can any renewed intercourse between these two unfortunate young people lead to but renewed affection?" said the Duchess.

"My dear Duchess," returned the old lady, rather impatiently, "do not let us go over all the old ground again. Their mutual affection has never ceased, nor remitted for a single instant; nor is it very likely that it should, since every act, and every feeling which has led by mutual consent to their separation, has on both sides been of a nature to endear them to each other." The Duchess winced at this, and for a moment her fine features were in a glow; but in the next she was paler than before. "It is not the first time I have stated this very certain fact to your Grace," pursued Mrs. Buckhurst; "and it follows that you can have no rational hope of keeping them asunder by any change in their sentiments. But the same high principle which has regulated their conduct hitherto will, as I fully believe, continue to actuate it still."

"And yet he writes to her!" said the Duchess.

"If he wrote to her once a-week or once a-day," returned Mrs. Buckhurst, "I should still feel it impossible to believe that either of them were likely to forfeit their pledged word."

"You cannot have more confidence in my son than I have, Mrs. Buckhurst," said her Grace, a little reproachfully; "but, though you share this feeling, you cannot share that which renders the possibility of disappointment in this matter so agonising."

"Perhaps not to its full extent," replied the old lady; "but it is not there, Duchess, that the chief difference between us lies. *I* know Ellen Dalton, *you* do not."

At this moment the Duke of Rochdale entered, and the conversation took another turn. Perhaps the last words uttered by Mrs. Buckhurst on the subject thus abandoned made the more impression because they were not followed by any other.

There is, perhaps, nothing in all the complicated machinery of nature so marvellous as the varieties that may be traced in the immortal part of mortal man. To class these varieties would require a catalogue nearly as numerous as the species, and to analyse them thoroughly, an eye little short of divine. Martha Maxwell, with very little in appearance that might distinguish her from a multitude of other tolerably well-looking, tolerably well-taught, and tolerably sharp-witted young females, had, nevertheless, a talent so very peculiarly her own, that very few, if any other, under circumstances not more favourable to its development than those in which she was placed, ever possessed it in equal perfection. This gift consisted of a shrewdness of observation into character, which, like that of a practised fortune-telling gipsy, often seemed to give her something wonderfully like a power of divination. If this power had been somewhat less acute, and perhaps somewhat less minute also, it would have made much more *show* as a talent, for her observations might then have had the effect of brilliant hits and lively sallies. But Martha Maxwell had a shy sort of consciousness that the process by which she looked into the hearts and souls of her fellow-creatures was not such as the generality could understand or appreciate, and this made her keep her speculations pretty much to herself. There was a degree of Denner-like distinctness in the wrinkles and warts of her portraits that looked a little as if she had used a moral microscope to assist her; and though not without some secret pride in her skill, she felt no inclination to make a public exhibition of it.

Such a faculty as this was extremely likely to keep its possessor from falling in love; but if it did so happen that the insidious urchin crept into the heart in spite of it, there could be little doubt but that he would take his revenge for former discomfitures, by keeping in durance vile the faculty that had resisted him. And so it proved in the case of Martha Maxwell. The striking personal beauty of Frederic Dalton, and the skilful cunning with which he had led her to believe, that let him flirt with whom he would, she was the only woman he really loved, had together made wild work in her heart, and for many months her art had been as completely lost, as far, at least, as he was concerned, as if she had burnt her books, and thrown her wand into the sea. It seemed a perverse accident in the history of one, usually so very sharp-sighted, that, having believed the protestations of the captivating Frederic when there was no shadow of truth in what he uttered, she should begin to suspect his sincerity, precisely at the moment when he was for the first time in earnest in suing to her to be his wife. But so it was. Just as he was vehemently exerting all his eloquence to express the eager wish that he most truly felt, to hear her promise him her hand with as little delay as possible—just at that very moment, the thought crossed her odd little head that he was feigning. Her resolution was taken instantly, but nevertheless with more coolness of judgment than could fairly have been expected under the circumstances. She determined not to decide upon a question of such vast importance to her happiness without surer evidence than the instinct (as she sometimes called it) of her own opinion, a resolution the more readily taken, because she felt pretty sure that the power of obtaining such evidence was within her reach. One result of the analysing process to which she submitted her friends and acquaintance was the having satisfied herself that Ellen Dalton was incapable of uttering an untruth, and to Ellen Dalton she resolved to apply, for the purpose of obtaining a little external light, to assist her own internal resources; for although on ordinary occasions Martha Maxwell was apt enough to trust her own judgment, which, to say truth, very rarely deceived her, she felt that, on the present occasion, there was something so misty and mysterious in the circumstances in which she found herself, that a little matter-of-fact information might be extremely useful.

The result of Miss Maxwell's visit to Ellen has been already detailed; and the result of that result shall be told hereafter. In the meantime the young squire arrived punctually at the hour appointed to receive the answer which was to make him, as he declared, the most happy or the most miserable of men; such, of course, being the formula used on this as on all similar occasions. But so very sure did Frederic Dalton feel that the only answer it was possible he could receive must be in the affirmative, that, like many other mortals, he had begun to doubt the value of this assured success, and to think he had been somewhat over-hasty in offering to sacrifice his precious freedom, in order to avoid a danger that might perhaps be avoided without it. He felt pretty tolerably confident that his taunts and innuendos would silence his sister Ellen; and the passive obedience promised by Jessie in the few words which she had uttered before he left her almost satisfied him that he had nothing more to fear at present from her imprudence.

When, therefore, Martha Maxwell, instead of falling in a fit of consenting silence into his arms, replied to his demand for the sentence that was to decide his fate by a gentle request that he would not be too vehement, he felt very much as if he had received a reprieve. It did not appear, however, as the conversation proceeded, that the young lady had the slightest intention of refusing him. On the contrary, she very explicitly declared herself to be devotedly attached to him, and that the prospect of their future union was as precious in her eyes as it was in his. "Nevertheless," she added, with a very amiable mixture of tenderness and discretion, "it appears to me, Mr. Dalton, that by an immediate elopement you will he running into danger instead of avoiding it."

"How so, my charming Martha?" said he, with an air of deference which very clearly shewed that her slightest word would be attended to with all the devoted obedience it deserved.

"Because," she replied, "your instantly marrying me, when your father has just commanded you to marry some one else, cannot fail of bringing upon us both the utmost violence of his displeasure; whereas, if by solemnly engaging ourselves to each other we put it out of your power to obey him, we shall not only gain time, which may enable you to reason him out of his cruel purpose, but, in case that purpose continues, your refusal to comply with it will then be an act of faith to me, instead of disobedience to him."

"What an admirable creature you are!" he exclaimed, in an accent which at once convinced her that her answer was a great relief to him; "happy,—thrice happy the man who may look forward to possessing such a counsellor for life!"

"And happy,—thrice happy the woman," she returned, "who may look forward to be ruled by a spirit so open to truth! Here, dear friend," she continued, drawing from her open writing-desk a sheet of note paper on which a few lines were neatly written, "just sign your name to this, and your refusal to marry any other woman can never bring down the reproach of disobedience upon you."

Dalton took the paper, and read what was written on it, which was a brief and succinct promise of marriage.

"I would sign this," he cried, "with the greatest pleasure in the world, did I not feel that if it were ever brought forward it would subject us both to the imputation of not having had faith in each other. I cannot bear this, dearest Martha!"

"How truly do our hearts sympathise, dear Frederic!" she replied. "If you will read that paper again you will perceive that I have carefully avoided the possibility of an insinuation so unmerited and so painful. You will perceive that my name does not appear, nor is it needful. You have but to sign this, in order to prove, by shewing it, that you are no longer free. But I trust we shall laugh together at this idle precaution, ere long; its present use is, that should your father press you immediately upon this threatened marriage, which has so violently alarmed your nerves, you may instantly silence him, by saying that you have already bound yourself by a written promise. This will answer the purpose quite as well as the elopement you talked of, and without any of its inconveniences."

"And you, Martha, you must give me a similar promise," said he, while the slightest possible shade of suspicion crossed his brow.

"Of course, dear Frederic, I cannot have the slightest objection to doing so," she replied carelessly, "and will certainly do it, if it be your wish; but you must he aware that it cannot be necessary to your object."

"It is necessary to my heart!" he replied in a tone of impassioned energy.

"I will give it to you instantly," replied the young lady with a gentle smile, adding, as she presented him with one pen, whilst she took another herself, "you sign your name to that, Frederic, while I write the same form over again here, and then I too will sign."

The young man obeyed, while his fair companion set about copying the words from the paper that lay before him.

"Let us make no mistake," said she, gaily; "I must copy it exactly, word for word." And so saying, she drew the paper to which he had affixed his name towards her, following with a finger of one hand the words written there, while she carefully copied them on the second paper with the other. She was within a word of having finished her duplicate, when she suddenly started, exclaiming, in, a hurried whisper,—"For Heaven's sake, just open the door, and see if that is my mother! If it is, you must lead her back to the drawing-room, and say you have a message from Ellen, or your mother, or any thing. Only take her away!"

This alarm seemed to startle the lover quite as much as it did his mistress, and he flew to the door without losing an instant, quite determined that the person he expected to see on the other side of it should not pass him. The passage upon which the breakfast-parlour opened was not a very light one, and the young squire very prudently stepped forward a few paces, that there might be no farther danger of a surprise. But he had the pleasure of finding that the anxious ear of his betrothed had deceived her; for neither Mrs. Maxwell, nor any one else, was near. Having fully satisfied himself on this point, he returned, but to his infinite surprise found the breakfast-room untenanted, the glass door to the garden standing open, and nothing left on the table or writing-desk but blank paper.

"What a silly fool to get into such a fuss for nothing!" muttered Frederic, as he too walked through the open glass door into the garden. He knew the premises too well to feel in any doubt as to which way to turn, and accordingly soon found himself before another glass door, which opened into the drawing-room. And here he discovered the runaway, her colour a little heightened, and with some traces of hurry and confusion on her countenance.

"Mercy on us! Where do you come from, Mr. Frederic?" cried Mrs. Maxwell, who was standing at the window, with her arm round her daughter's waist.

"Dear mamma, do sit down," said the young lady, with great appearance of anxiety. "You will certainly catch cold if you run about in the garden with these thin shoes."

"Not such a silly fool neither!" thought the young man, who immediately concluded that Mrs. Maxwell had actually made her appearance at a very critical moment at the garden-door of the breakfast-room. He could, however, find no possible opportunity for asking any questions concerning the fate of the papers, but reasonably flattered himself that the mother of his lady-love had made no untoward discoveries, because she said nothing, and looked nothing, in the least degree, out of the common routine of accustomed civility. He stayed a good while, however, in the hope of getting a confidential word from Martha; but in vain. It was quite evident that she was exceedingly afraid of her mother; so at length he took his leave, with the comfortable conviction that every thing had turned out according to his usual good luck, for that he had a bride affianced, and nevertheless was still a single man. As to the accident which had prevented his receiving from the hands of the young lady the paper which he had seen her write, it never occurred to him that it could be of any importance whatever. He perfectly understood that she was anxious to keep the matter secret, and admired the dexterity with which she had avoided discovery. Having therefore found, or made, an opportunity to give her one parting look of intelligence behind her mother's shoulder, he departed, more perfectly convinced than ever that he was one of the happy mortals with whom every thing prospers.

# XXIII

*Jessie's meditations while sitting at work—she waits upon the Miss Lewises with the result of her labours—their reception of her—Frederic Dalton flirts with Miss Mortimer, and forgets all his vexations*

THE STATE OF MIND IN which Jessie Phillips returned to her home was terrible enough, but it would have been more terrible still had she been in such a state as to enable her quietly and rationally to comprehend her real situation; but she was, in fact, incapable of doing this. The short and perilous period of her existence which had passed since she ceased to be a child, and to bound all her hopes and wishes to the being accounted the cleverest scholar and the best-beloved girl in the village-school, had been, from first to last, a season of ceaseless and ever-increasing delusion. The admiration of her beauty, which had caused every eye to look upon her as none other of her class was looked upon, was the primal cause of this; and the poetical and half-understood studies in which she subsequently indulged completed it. Even the good-natured notice of the ladies who employed her made up, as it was, partly from the good opinion produced by her industry and modest demeanour, and partly by the gratification of looking at her, which all seemed to share, contributed to confirm her belief that she was not as other girls of her position, but marked out by nature and Providence as a *Pamela* sort of exception. Terrible, therefore, as her actual position now was, nothing which she had as yet suffered had come home to her heart and understanding in the naked shape of truth. She still fancied herself a heroine, still looked forward, almost without a shadow of doubt, to being some day the mistress of the Manor-house, the adored wife of its master, and the respected mother of his children. She hoped and believed that all her sufferings—and they were really frightful—were for the present only, and that, if she endured them with patience and courage, and with implicit obedience to the rules and regulations laid down for her by Frederic, every thing would be well in the end. She struggled vehemently, therefore, to conquer every external symptom of agitation, battled with every thought, as it rose, that pointed to the threatened suspension of intercourse with her future husband, and determined resolutely to keep her own secret and his till the necessity of doing so should cease. To her poor failing mother's half-fretful inquiry of what Miss Ellen wanted, and why she had detained her so long, she answered slightly, that it was nothing of very great consequence, and that they had been interrupted, which made her stay longer. This did very well for the moment, and during the whole of that day and the next Jessie worked hard to finish a set of shirts for Mr. Lewis, that had been rather longer on hand than they ought to be; but Jessie was beginning to fear that money might run short. Hitherto she had not only had more work offered to her, both at home and abroad, than she could possibly get through, but her skill and unwearying industry had made her employment seem light; and though it was now nearly four months since her mother had been able to add a single shilling to their funds, she had still found that, if her own health did not fail, she should be able to manage very well. But of late her health had been less good, and her spirits less buoyant. Her work would often fall upon her lap, while her imagination seemed to gain all the activity which her fingers lost, and she would sometimes sit for half an hour together without doing a stitch, while painting to herself, with the most scrupulous accuracy, all that it would be necessary for her to do and to say when she should be Mrs. Dalton. But now again her newly formed resolution not to be wanting to herself, and in no way to increase the difficulties through which it was necessary to pass before she could arrive at the promised goal of all her hopes and wishes, gave an impulse to her needle which speedily brought her long job to a conclusion.

The work was completed before twelve o'clock on the day but one following her interview with Ellen, and having, with her wonted attention, prepared her mother's little dinner, and seen her eat it, her feverish and shaking hands arranged her own dress with cautious carefulness, and she set off for the dwelling of Mr. Lewis, with a basket containing her work. Without any questions asked, she was shewn, as usual, into the drawing-room, where the two young ladies were employed, one in practising a song at the pianoforte, and the other in preparing some article of dress. Both ceased their occupations as soon as Jessie entered, and the younger turned herself round from the instrument, apparently to look at her, while the elder received the basket from the hands of the pale sempstress, but for a minute or two not a word was spoken by either. There was something in this very painfully unlike the manner in which poor Jessie used to be received by the good-humoured sisters, and she fancied that the delay of the work had offended them.

"I am very sorry, Miss Lewis," she said, "that I should have kept your papa waiting. I hope it was no inconvenience?"

"No! not any inconvenience at all," replied Mary Lewis. "Have you brought the bill with you?" she inquired, in a dry tone, that shot like an ice-bolt through the heart of Jessie.

It was lucky for her that no words were necessary in reply, for she could hardly have spoken had her life depended on her doing so. She drew forth from her pocket the little paper, on which she had written down the account of the work she had done since their last settling, and laid it silently on the table before Miss Lewis. The young lady in like manner silently took it up, and, after casting a glance over it, drew forth her purse, and laid the sum of one pound five shillings and sixpence on the table. She then took a pen from an inkstand which stood near, and presented it to Jessie, at the same time placing the little bill before her, and saying,—

"I wish you to write '*received*' upon it, if you please."

Jessie was rather proud of her handwriting, and not without reason, for she had contrived to make it greatly superior to that of any person of her own class in the parish; but now her hand shook so violently as scarcely to permit her forming any characters at all. But on this no observation was made; the young lady seemed perfectly satisfied with the acquittance, such as it was, and nodded her head in token of dismissal.

Jessie felt as if she must have fallen; but it was only for a moment. The recollection that she was the affianced wife of Mr. Frederic Dalton renewed and sustained her courage. She stretched out her hand to the back of a chair which stood near, to support the limbs which she sighed to think had so much less strength than her mind, and then said, meekly, but by no means very humbly,—

"If you have any work to be done, Miss Lewis, I shall be very happy to undertake it."

"I have no work whatever to be done: we have neither of us any thing," replied Miss Lewis, repeating her nod, and at the same time resuming her occupation; while Lucy, who had never before failed to honour her pretty favourite with a little village gossip, whenever an opportunity occurred, uttered not a word, and, perceiving that her sister thought it time that the interview should end, turned herself round again in her chair, and resumed her practice of "*We met, 'twas in a crowd*."

A cold perspiration broke out from every pore of the miserable Jessie. She now felt that her condition was more than suspected,—that it was known,—and that all that was now left for her was to hide herself from every eye till the blessed moment should arrive when she should be able to prove to all the world that she was not the degraded creature they had believed her to be. But with all this reliance upon the future, she would not have stood for another moment in the presence of those two young ladies, if a hundred golden sovereigns had been offered to her as a reward for doing so.

It required all the courage that the unfortunate girl's most foolish faith in her most faithless lover could inspire to enable her to bear up against this first "mark of the world's scorn" that had, as yet, been pointed at her, except, perhaps, the glances of Miss Dalton's maid, and those had escaped her notice. But now the case was plain; the Miss Lewises either knew, or guessed, all that had occurred, save and except the solemn promise upon which she rested as upon a rock of adamant, and which, in her silly heart, poor child! she believed to have power not only to embellish all her future years with wealth and honour, but also to wipe out and obliterate for ever all that the envious world might conceive to be disgraceful in her past conduct. This fluctuation between what she felt to be the very lowest depth of misery and degradation, and what she anticipated as the highest perfection of happiness and splendour, which her lonely musings caused her to undergo, at times almost drove her mad, and probably would have done so quite, had not the daily and hourly necessity of attending upon her sinking mother with assumed composure, and even cheerfulness, kept the vehemence of her imagination in salutary subjection. It might be, too, that the dread of losing that devoted mother which now, for the first time, a newly summoned medical attendant told her was but too probable, assisted in withdrawing her thoughts from herself, and thus, for the moment, became a salutary sorrow. The new apothecary stated that he had little doubt but that she had received some internal injury at the time of her fall, for so only could he account for the gradual wasting away of flesh and strength, which every passing day rendered more visible. But this fresh sorrow, though it might have saved her reason, wrung her heart, as poor Jessie, her bloom all flown, her bright eye dimmed, and her light bounding step changed for a movement precisely the reverse, was an object that might have created pity in an ogre. But Frederic Dalton, "*le désiré*," was not such an ogre as that. He pitied nobody in the world but himself, whom, with the most perfect sincerity, he considered to be a very singularly ill-treated young gentleman, inasmuch as his detestable sister Ellen had driven him into doing what he began to think was an exceedingly foolish thing, by frightening him out of his wits about that tiresome Jessie: she certainly was, with her simplicity, her love, and the pertinacity of her confidence in the inconceivable absurdity that he meant to marry her, altogether the most troublesome girl that ever a man of fashion had to do with.

It was thus the young man's thoughts ran on, whenever he gave himself time to think at all; but, in truth, this was but seldom, for, after transacting the little precautionary affair that has been related above with the fair mother, he became more than ever occupied with the elder Miss Mortimer, throwing the little Agatha into despair thereby, and often tempting the two Miss Lewises to wring their hair instead of curling it.

By degrees, however, he very nearly forgot both Ellen's impertinent behaviour, its troublesome cause, and its dangerous result, for of Jessie he neither saw nor heard any thing; and he comfortably made up his mind to believe that the foolish girl had at last found out that it would be wisest to make the best of a bad matter, as others had done before her, to obey his orders, and keep silent, and to trust to chance for the rest.

As to Martha, she had caught, she said, a violent cold, which obliged her to refuse all sorts of invitations; and as she was always in her own room when he called, she never, of course, had any opportunity of giving him the promise he had asked for, in return for the one she had received. But Frederic Dalton was in no degree annoyed at this. He knew that Miss Martha could not bring an action against him for breach of promise (in case he changed his mind on the subject) without Captain Maxwell's being privy to the transaction; and the sharp youth felt a very comfortable conviction that his old acquaintance would disapprove such a proceeding exceedingly. With the young lady herself it was impossible he could have any difficulty, for he could always plead as a cause for breaking off the affair her own failure in returning the pledge he had given. And thus, in the course of a month after Lady Mary Wayland's party, the awkward catastrophe of the cloak-room was very nearly forgotten by the hero of it, and every thing seemed going on, as far as he was concerned, precisely as if the vexatious *contretemps* had never occurred.

# XXIV

*Jessie loses her mother, and rehearses in silence and solitude all the circumstances of her own situation—the catalogue shakes her philosophy*

"I FEAR, MY POOR GIRL, that your mother is worse than you think her," said the kind-hearted apothecary to Jessie, after having patiently watched beside her dying mother's bed for nearly an hour; "she is quite insensible. I cannot raise her pulse, and in the state she is now in I will not undertake to answer for her life through the night."

This dreadful sentence was as unexpected to poor Jessie as it was terrible. When her mother's accident first occurred, neither herself nor any of her neighbours had the least idea that the injury was any thing beyond an ordinary strain, which a few days' rest would suffice to cure. When this cure was delayed so much beyond the expected tune as to make Jessie think it right to procure advice, a certain Mr. Hatherly had been sent for. This person was the parish doctor, having obtained the situation by demanding a less sum for his services than any other practitioner would accept. This election was a recent one, and Mr. Hatherly was very little known, as yet, in the neighbourhood. Jessie, however, who had heard it said that his charges were moderate, thought, naturally enough, poor girl, that he was the properest person she could apply to, and accordingly she sent to him. His prescription consisted in sending what he called "his bottle," with the contents of which the injured limb was to be constantly bathed; which was done for several weeks with the most assiduous attention, but no amendment followed. At length, the restlessness and fever, which evidently increased rather than diminished, had reduced the poor woman to a state of weakness which suggested the idea that the sprain could not have been the only injury received, and

Mr. Johnson, the very able practitioner who resided in the village, was applied to. This gentleman would have been the parish doctor, had his conscience permitted him to offer himself for the situation at a sum less than half what he knew would be required for necessary drugs. He at once pronounced the case to be hopeless, the spine having been injured in a manner that left no chance of recovery.

The condition of Jessie when this was announced to her may be easily conceived; it acted like that last ounce which, as the proverb says, breaks the horse's back. Despite the occasionally shadowy glance, which in her most reasonable moments she caught of the host of sorrows that were gradually closing around her, she had, up to this moment, lived in a sort of waking dream, throughout which much more of delusion than of truth might have been traced as the cause of her enduring fortitude. But now she sunk at once. Whatever evils might await her she suddenly felt must be borne alone, and penniless. From the moment young Dalton had left her on the grass, to recover, as she might, from her faintness, she had neither seen nor heard of him; but it was only now that she felt this neglect must be intended as a signal of final desertion—it was only now that she saw the abyss into which she had fallen. It was with much less of sorrow, than of envy, that she gazed on her dying mother, and deeply in her heart of hearts did she wish that she was breathing her last sigh instead. Long were the dark hours of that dismal night, and the morning dawned before any very perceptible change took place in the dying woman; but then, just when there was light enough for the two friendly creatures who had joined themselves to Jessie in the task of watching her bedside, just when there was light enough for them to examine, without the aid of the waving rushlight, the form that the sunken features had assumed, they knew that all was over.

"It is better it should be so, since hope there was none," said one of the watchers, while the other, laying her hand upon the arm of Jessie, led her away, and with gentle force made her sit down in a chair by the little window, which she opened to let in upon her the fresh morning breeze; and then she looked in the poor girl's face, and thought in her heart that she had never, through all the troubles of her own long life, looked upon any thing so very sad before.

"She mustn't bide here, Sally," she said to the woman who was busying herself in straightening the limbs of the deceased. "She mustn't bide here, 'twould be the death of her, poor young thing, and she with no other bed to lay her aching head upon but THAT"

"Poor lamb!" responded Sally. "But where on earth can we take her to, Mrs. Martin? Neither you nor I, Heaven knows, have a place to put her in."

"There be places, enough, Sally, I'll answer for it, where she would be welcome as the day, and the squire's above all, where they have always been so uncommon partial to her. There isn't one in the house, from the highest to the lowest, I'll be bound for 'em, but would be happy and glad to do a kind turn to poor Jessie. Don't you think they would, dear?" she added, looking kindly in the tortured mourner's face: "I will go up, right at once, Jessie, to ask for leave, if you will but speak the word. Shall I, Jessie? Shall I go up, dear, to Squire Dalton's, to ask leave for you to come there for a night or two?"

It was only when the proposition was thus directly addressed to her that Jessie fully comprehended what they were talking about; but the instant she became aware of it, her face, which had before been little less ghastly than that of the corpse she had been gazing upon, suddenly became crimson, the fast flowing tears disappeared, and seemed to return to their source, and her filial sorrow gave place to feelings more bitter still. She did not speak, she had no breath left to do so, but, vehemently rushing back to the bed from which she had been removed, she threw herself upon it beside her mother, and, after an interval of frightful silence, sobbed out the words, "Here! Here! It is here I will stay till they have buried her! And then—it will be time enough then, to tell you where I mean to go."

"She is thinking about her relations, Sally," said Mrs. Martin, "them, you know, as we have heard her poor mother talk about, as being so well to do, up the country; it is to them she'll be after going, no doubt, and very proper and natural she should. But what can we do for her till then? Her poor dear young head will never stand it, if she is to be left here, day and night, with the dead body."

The kind-hearted souls then set their heads together as to how they could manage between them so as to avoid this; and many were the schemes canvassed to enable them to watch over Jessie without quite giving up what they had to do elsewhere.

Jessie was not fainting, she heard all they said, and, satisfied that the proposal of applying for charitable aid at the manor-house was given up, she yielded to the entreaties which followed, that she would rise from the ghostly pillow on which she lay, and permit those who were ready to serve her in all they could to perform those last offices for her poor mother which she was in no condition to perform herself.

The paroxysm of terrible agony which the name of Dalton had caused her being passed, Jessie resigned herself to all the misery that pressed round her with an uncomplaining submission and gentleness that few could have witnessed unmoved. The two homely beings who were with her had no refinement of feeling beyond what will always be found in the heart of a woman where no vice has entered to smother or pervert her natural tenderness. They both gazed at the pale young face which lifted itself at their bidding from beside that of her dead mother, and then exchanged a glance together; and more heart-felt pity never beamed from human eyes than that glance expressed.

"Jessie must go down, and light the fire for us," said Mrs. Martin, "and then she will be able to get us a cup of tea. We have had a long watch, Jessie dear, and you'll do that much for us, won't you?"

"I'll try," said Jessie, turning towards the door.

"You must go down with her, Mrs. Martin," said the equally thoughtful Sally, "and just open the window-shutter for her, and see that she has got the matches and a bit of wood ready; and then come up again to me."

All this was done, and not all the philosophy in the world could have devised any thing more likely to rouse the energy, yet calm the spirits, of the poor sufferer, than thus leading her to perform her wonted morning task; and well satisfied was the widow Martin, when she saw her engaged in it, that she might leave her safely and return up-stairs. But alas! not all the kindly sympathy that filled the widow's heart could enable her to guess the agony that was secretly throbbing in that of Jessie. To no human being had the wretched girl ever mentioned the falling away of her customers; but certain it was, that one by one, with no reason assigned, they had all seemed to have forgotten her, as completely as if no intercourse between them had ever existed. All had forsaken her, save one. Miss Maxwell, though still declaring herself too much afraid of the night air to join in any of the Deepbrook parties, still ventured out in the early mornings, and made very frequent calls at Jessie's cottage before any eyes polite were open to look at her. These quiet visits were rarely made without bringing to the forsaken sempstress some trifling job of work to do, or some little assistance to her dwindling housekeeping; and often did the young lady kindly sit down to chat with her about her mother's condition or the work she had brought. Martha Maxwell, in short, was the last of all her lady customers, and the last of all her lady friends; and the few shillings she had thus earned was all the money that Jessie had received since her last interview with the Miss Lewises. Yet even this frightfully near approach to utter destitution had never, till now, made itself fully felt by the wretched girl. The great question which every morning had brought had not been as to where she should get money, but whether she should see HIM. But now every thing seemed to pass before her eyes together, with all the vivid distinctness of truth. Her mother lay dead in the room above, and must be buried by the parish, for two shillings was all she possessed in the world. She felt horribly certain that her own condition could not be concealed much longer, and yet, that she would a thousand times rather die than disclose it. Her rent was more than due, she owed five shillings to the baker, and thrice that sum to the "village shops." And all this was first remembered together in the same hour that she had first felt deliberately convinced that her worshipped Dalton was a villain—that he had deceived and forsaken her!

# XXV

*Jessie Phillips very ardently desires to be left alone, and at length obtains her wish—during the meditation which follows she hits upon a remedy for all her sorrows in the world, not quite new, but very effectual—the arrival of a visitor interrupts her*

NO SOONER WAS JESSIE LEFT alone in the little sitting-room which had been the scene of so many blissful moments and so many suffering hours, than she gave herself up to an unchecked burst of weeping which, after the restraint she had been enduring, seemed like a positive luxury!

"Oh, if I could but be alone!" she whispered, "unseen, unlooked at, unexamined by any human eye! If I could but live, and die alone, I could bear it all! Even though I knew that he is a villain, and that I am his helpless and degraded victim, I could bear it all, so I were sure that no eye could see, no finger point at me! Could I but be alone,—certainly, surely alone, for only one single hour, I could think, and think, and think, till at last I should find some way out of this horrid labyrinth! Good, kind souls! Oh, how must my heart be hardened, to make me feel their presence so painful, that it should seem the worst misery of all! Good, kind souls! I will give them breakfast and then drive them from me,—I must, and I will be alone!"

With this morbid longing for solitude before her, the unhappy girl set in earnest to perform the task allotted her, and the fire was well lighted, the tea-kettle singing upon it, the cups and saucers carefully ranged upon the board, and every morsel of food that the house contained placed there likewise, when the two good women, their mournful task performed, came down-stairs.

"There's a good girl! isn't she, Sally?" said the widow Martin, looking very complacently at the preparations that had been made for them. "You may believe a true friend's word when I tell you that there is nothing will do you one half so much good, Jessie, as just forcing yourself to do the things that you know ought to be done. I do believe that it has been contrived so on purpose, out of God's own pity for us."

"God bless you, Mrs. Martin! You are very kind to me, and Sally Rice, too. God bless you both!" said poor Jessie. "It is all very true what you say about doing what ought to be done; and the first thing necessary is for me to think, quietly and steadily, and think I must. And for that reason I shall beg of you both to leave me quite alone, which just at present will be the very kindest thing you can do. It is the only way for me to get my mind composed and my head clear, for now it feels sadly confused and unsettled."

"I won't contradict you, my dear girl," replied Mrs. Martin; "for it is plain to see that you are wishing and willing to do what is proper and right. But it seems to me a sad, dismal plan to leave you here all by your own self, Jessie. Doesn't it, Sally?"

"Dismal!" repeated the other woman, with a shudder; "I should expect she would just go mad; and that is what will happen to her, you may depend upon it, if we let her give way to any such fancy as that. The thing to do her real good would be to send for our pious minister, and let her have the comfort of listening to him a bit."

"Sure enough you are right there," replied the other; "and sore troubled was I last evening, I promise you, that we did not know the great peril of she that is gone till it was too late for her to listen to the voice of man. Let me step over to Mr. Rimmington, dear Jessie, shall I?"

The certain knowledge that a thunderbolt was about to burst upon the roof that covered her would have been a thousand times less terrible to the wretched girl than the idea of meeting the gentle eye of Mr. Rimmington fixed upon her, or of being questioned by his friendly voice. With a steadfastness of purpose that in some degree resembled the wilfulness of insanity, and with a species of cunning that resembled it more nearly still, Jessie meekly replied, that if they would grant her the solitude she so greatly needed for a few hours, she would prepare herself to do every thing they wished, but that, unless she were first indulged in that one wish, she could not consent to see any body.

Though these words were uttered very gently, they had in their accent something that convinced both the good women it would be better to let her have her own way; and, having taken the refreshment they needed, they again returned to the chamber of death, drew the little clean white curtain over the open casement, lifted the napkin that covered the face of the dead that they might once more look at the familiar features which had so often greeted them kindly, but which now lay so chillingly fixed in unmeaning tranquillity; then looked round the little room, to see that all things were in that decent order which the mysterious respect of the living for the dead requires, and finally returned to the room below, where Jessie, in compliance with their advice, had employed herself, as usual, in setting every thing in order, and giving to the humble dwelling its accustomed aspect of excelling neatness.

"Do you still keep in the same mind, Jessie?" said Mrs. Martin. "Do you still wish us to go away?"

"I can bide with you an hour or two longer, dear Jessie," said Mrs. Rice, looking pitifully in her face, and wiping away the tears that the last sight of her old friend had cost her.

Jessie kissed them both, but only answered "Go! go!" and then, as if fearing that she had spoken harshly, she kissed them again; after which, without saying another word, she went to the door, drew back the bolts, and stood with it open in her hand, with a look of piteous entreaty, which they no longer attempted to withstand. With streaming eyes and aching hearts they left the cottage, the door of which was immediately closed behind them, and Jessie at last felt that she was indeed alone.

The consciousness of this was, for the first few moments, a positive pleasure, but it was not a pleasure likely to last long, and when it was passed it would not have been easy to find any human being more utterly or more hopelessly wretched than Jessie Phillips.

She sat before the fading embers of her little fire, her arms resting upon the table, and her throbbing forehead supported upon them. Now, indeed, she had all the leisure for thinking that she had so passionately desired; and the wild and desperate thoughts that rushed, like demons jostling each other, through her brain, seemed to threaten the madness that her neighbour had predicted for her. And, in truth, a stronger intellect might have been shaken by what she had endured and was enduring. Long uncertainty, hope perpetually disappointed, the ceaseless terror of discovery, and the spectre-like glimpses of the truth, which from time to time had haunted her, had worn into her very soul, and paralysed that beautiful elasticity of spirits which naturally belonged to her age. Such was the history of the last four months, and the present hour seemed to contain the bitterness of the whole, for hope was no longer fluttering and fitful, but utterly extinct; and so conscious, indeed, did she now feel of her past infatuation, that she seemed eager to take refuge in despair, in order to convince herself that she saw every thing as it really was, and that nothing worse lay lurking behind.

Is it wonderful that at such a moment the desperate idea of the "end all here," which has tempted so many miserable wretches to release themselves from the sufferings they themselves have made, should suggest itself to her? Softly and insidiously did it steal upon her, as if the foul fiend that sent it knew that it was thus temptation must now assail her. She remembered on a sudden, and as if, as it seemed to her, by inspiration, a lovely and remote nook beside the bright capricious stream that danced in mazy gambols through the village. It was a tiny meadow, surrounded on all sides by willow-trees, save where the brook watered the narrow outlet which sloped towards it into eternal verdure. Often and often had Jessie taken refuge there, when a Sunday evening nutting party had proved too boisterous for her taste; and she now recalled the cool, calm aspect of the water at that spot, where a deeper bottom than it found elsewhere hushed its noisy gambols, for the distance of a few yards, into a level smoothness, that seemed the very emblem of rest.

"If I could but lay myself down on that dark bed!" thought Jessie, "how gently, gently, should I sink, till all was over!" The thought brought no terror with it; she was not enough herself for any reasonable fears, either of earth or heaven to mix in her reverie, and gradually was the idea, thus conceived, settling itself into a resolution to steal at nightfall to the well-known spot, when a hand, applied to the latch of the cottage door, made her start as violently as if the intruder had caught her in the perpetration of the desperate deed instead of the meditation on it. Almost before this first nervous movement had passed away, and left her in trembling expectation of being summoned by some voice she knew, the idea that it might be Frederic Dalton himself occurred to her, and with a movement that was positively involuntary she sprang to the door, withdrew the bolts, and opened it, when instead of Frederic Dalton she beheld Miss Martha Maxwell.

The young lady stood silently gazing at her for a moment. "Poor dear Jessie!" she then said, "how sadly I have disappointed you! You expected to see a very different person, my poor girl, did you not?"

Utterly confounded at these words, and unable to reply to them, Jessie retreated from the door into the cottage in silence, and Miss Maxwell followed her.

Either thoughtless of what she was about, or actually unable to stand, Jessie replaced herself in the chair she had before occupied, and, covering her face with her hands, burst into tears.

"No wonder that you weep, my poor girl," said Martha, kindly; "I have heard of your sad loss, Jessie, and am come to know if there be any thing that I can do to help or comfort you."

It is often more difficult to bear unexpected kindness with composure than unexpected harshness. Jessie had just made up her mind to believe herself utterly forsaken by all her lady friends, and considered as no longer worthy to stand in their presence; and though Miss Maxwell's occasional visits ought to have made an exception, the conscious Jessie always expected that each of these visits would be the last, and that it had only been made because the young lady *had not yet heard the report*. As she listened to the friendly words now addressed to her therefore, the unexpectedness of the blessing quite overpowered her, and she sobbed aloud, utterly in capable of restraining herself.

Miss Maxwell drew forward a chair, and, sitting down beside her, took her hand. After waiting for a moment, till this hysteric emotion had subsided, she said very gravely, but very kindly too, "Jessie Phillips, I wish I could persuade you to open your heart to me fully and completely. I am aware that you have a natural and a heavy cause of sorrow in the loss of your mother, but I am quite sure, my poor girl, that this is not your only source of grief. Without knowing exactly how matters stand between you and Mr. Frederic Dalton, it is impossible I can be of any real service to you; but if you would trust me entirely, it is possible I might be."

Jessie did not shrink on hearing, for the first time in her life, this fatal name mentioned to her, as one in which it was possible she could have any interest, for it was far otherwise that Ellen had alluded to him; but the wild and startled glance of her beautiful eyes answered the same purpose, for it made Martha understand that she had touched upon a string that vibrated through her whole frame.

"You look terrified at my naming Mr. Frederic Dalton to you, Jessie. Conquer this feeling at once and for ever, or I cannot serve you. But if you will do this—if you can have sufficient strength of mind to do it, and to remember that, in such a situation as yours, it would be madness to suffer any feeling of repugnance to prevent your doing what it is only *possible* may be useful to you, I really believe that things may turn out better for you than you have any reason to expect, and better, perhaps, Jessie, than you deserve."

It was not contumacy that kept Jessie silent after this most unexpected appeal, but she trembled from head to foot so violently as to be entirely incapable of speaking. Miss Maxwell saw this, and, drawing a bottle of salts from her pocket, put it into the poor culprit's hand, saying, "Smell this, Jessie, it will revive you. I will leave you for a minute or two, both to give you time to recover yourself, and also to consider whether in your present circumstances it may not be wisest for you to accept unconditionally the assistance I offer."

Martha then left the cottage, and, having closed its door, sat down in the porch before it, which was still sweet with straggling clematis, though no longer so neatly trimmed as in the happier days of summer. Having remained there for about ten or fifteen minutes, she re-entered, and found Jessie standing, as if expecting her.

"Well, Jessie," she said, "how have you decided?"

"I have decided upon telling you every thing I know myself," was her reply, "even though I should die with shame as I utter it. But you have said you would be my friend, Miss Maxwell, and that is more than I ever hoped to hear from any one like you again."

It is not necessary to follow Jessie through her painful narrative. She did tell all; and if the part of her story which she dwelt longest upon was that which related to the solemn promises of marriage she had received who is there can blame her for it?

"It is *all* exactly as I thought it was," said Martha, when the story was ended, and the pale speaker sat gazing in her face as if she could have read her future fate there. "It is neither better nor worse, Jessie, than I expected. You have been basely treated, and the sad fact that your own imprudence has helped the mischief will not make you suffer the less for it. That this unworthy young man means to desert you, there can be no doubt, and, such being the case, you must be aware that great difficulties lie in the way of your obtaining any thing like justice; nevertheless, I am not without hopes some thing may be done. But this, Jessie, is no time to talk about it, you have other sorrows now to think of, nor would I have broken in upon you at such an hour as this did I not believe it probable that you would be in want of money, for I know that of late you have not had much work to do. And I thought, likewise, my poor girl, that all your sorrows together would be almost more than you would have strength to bear, especially if you have no one near you sufficiently acquainted with all the circumstances of your situation to permit your speaking of it openly. Am I right, Jessie, in supposing this to be the case?"

"Alas, yes!" replied the greatly puzzled object of this very soothing but very mysterious visit; "from the falling off in my work, I have guessed, of course, Miss Maxwell, that the ladies who used to be so kind to me had heard or observed something that made them think me no longer worthy of their esteem. And they were right, Miss Maxwell, very—very right! I have lost their esteem, and I have lost my own, too. It seems as if I had all along been blinded or dreaming, for my understanding seems to have been entirely darkened or taken away from me. I looked upon myself as Mr. Frederic's wife, Miss Maxwell, and have been deluded enough to think the ladies cruelly unjust to me, because they seemed to believe I had done what ought to forfeit their good opinion. But now every thing appears changed to me! I see the whole as it really is, and, considering all the tender love and goodness of my poor mother that is gone, I cannot but think I am quite as bad for going wrong as that hard-hearted young gentlemen for tempting me to do it."

These words were uttered amidst a shower of such bitterly repentant tears, that had Miss Maxwell felt harshly disposed towards the poor culprit (which she certainly did not), her heart must perforce have melted at the sight. As it was, the eccentric, and, in some sort, whimsical young lady, although in general by no means given to the melting mood, now wept for company, and confessed to herself that, notwithstanding the grievous fault of poor Jessie, she had never in her whole life pitied any one so heartily. Perhaps Martha remembered at that moment that she too, with all her acute perspicuity, had once loved the pitiful villain who had wrought the ruin she now looked upon; but as she gazed at the poor broken lily before her, and remembered with what pretty graceful liveliness its fragile glory had shone but a few short months before, the tears on her cheeks seemed suddenly dried up by the indignant blush that glowed upon them, and deeply in her very heart of hearts did she resolve that at least some part of the punishment inevitable upon the fault committed should fall upon the most guilty head. Having made herself this promise, and derived very considerable consolation from it, she set about the almost vain attempt of soothing her pale and trembling companion. The tears Martha had shed, however, had in truth soothed poor Jessie far more than any words she could utter, for it had proved that she was not too deeply scorned to be pitied; and beyond that she was at present incapable of receiving consolation.

Miss Maxwell marked the expression of the fixed eye, which, though it gazed upon, hardly seemed to behold her; and, suddenly stopping short in the sort of vague distant sketching of possible atonement by which she was endeavouring to cheer her, she said, "I see, my poor girl, that these distant possibilities avail nothing,—at this moment you are mourning the loss of your poor mother, Jessie, is it not so?"

"No, Miss Maxwell, no!" exclaimed Jessie, eagerly; "I do not mourn for her. I was thinking of her,—dear, dear soul,—I was thinking of her, but I cannot mourn for her death. She is gone without knowing the sin and the shame of her only child. I thank God that, in His great mercy, He has spared this agony to her, and to me the anguish of seeing it! Oh! I am thankful, very thankful, that she is gone!"

Again the unwonted tears came to the eyes of Martha, for it was, indeed, a melancholy sight to see the look of hopeless misery impressed upon the lovely features of the unhappy girl. But Miss Maxwell was not a person to yield to any emotion so much worse than useless.

"I shall see you again, Jessie, after the funeral," she said, "and these five sovereigns will be enough, I dare say, to prevent the expenses. of it from adding to your anxiety. Meanwhile, you must promise me not to fancy things worse than they are. You have been very weak, and Mr. Frederic Dalton has been very wicked; nevertheless, without wishing to raise your spirits by false hopes, I do believe that better days may be in store for you. God bless you! Farewell!"

"Stay one moment, Miss Maxwell,—only one moment!" exclaimed Jessie, as her munificent visitor was moving towards the door. "Yet I know not," she continued, "why I should ask you to stay, for I cannot, it is quite impossible that I should be able to speak my thanks to you … Miss Maxwell! When you came in, the only hope I had was that I might be able to find some means of destroying myself without danger of interruption; but now,—I know not what it is I hope, yet I feel something at my heart that seems to struggle against my misery. May God reward you for your generous kindness, whether there is really hope for me or not!"

"At any rate, Jessie Phillips, it shall not be my fault if justice be not done you," said the affianced bride of the young squire, again moving towards the door. "Good-bye; take care of your health, and get some friendly neighbour to sit with you; it is too dismal for you to be left quite alone."

With these words Miss Maxwell passed through the cottage door, leaving its fair but frail inhabitant with more of renovated hope fluttering at her heart than any one who knew her condition before she entered it could have believed possible. Whether Miss Maxwell was consummately wise and perfectly right in making this visit, or rather in saying all the comforting words she did in the course of it, is another affair. It is extremely possible that many very sensible persons may think this doubtful.

# XXVI

*A tête-à-tête conversation between the affianced lovers—the Young Squire pays Jessie a visit—so does Miss Maxwell—Jessie is greatly benefited in mind by both*

Within a hundred yards of Jessie Phillips' door, Miss Maxwell encountered the individual whom, perhaps, beyond all others, she least wished to meet; although it is undeniably certain that, not only at this moment, but for many weeks past, he had occupied a very large portion of her thoughts. In short, just before she turned the corner where the village highroad crossed the bottom of the lane in which Jessie's cottage stood, Mr. Frederic Dalton stood before her. She certainly blushed as violently as she could have done had she been as much in love with him as he fancied her to be, nor was there in his demeanour any symptom of indifference; on the contrary, he, too, coloured a good deal; but, though somewhat embarrassed, he looked exceedingly handsome, and the young lady, as she looked up in his face, while returning his salutation, inwardly soliloquised,

"I was a prodigious fool for being in love with him; but, if I could ever forgive my eyes for rebelling against my judgment, it must be here."

"How very fortunate!" exclaimed the young man, with every appearance of satisfaction. "How are you? You have no idea how anxious I have been about you! I hope you know how often I have called to inquire for you?"

"Oh, yes!" replied Martha, smiling, "I do, indeed."

"And why did you never let me see you?" he said, with rather a tender sort of reproachfulness, as he walked on beside her.

"I assure you I have hardly seen any body," she replied.

"Then have you been really so very ill?" said he.

"Some people, you know, are more easily alarmed about themselves than others," she answered; "and, perhaps, after all, the symptoms may not have been really dangerous; but, I declare to you, the idea of going out, particularly in an evening, was quite too much for me."

"You will easily imagine, dearest Martha," he resumed, "that I must have been dreadfully anxious during this interval. Our position, relatively to each other, is not quite fair, my dearest Martha. I must beg that you will either give me the written promise which I ought to have had so long ago, or else that you will return that which you received from me."

"Perfectly right and reasonable!" she replied. "For myself, perhaps, I might be willing to do either, but I should greatly prefer following your wishes rather than my own. Which do you decide upon, Mr. Frederic Dalton? Shall I give you your own promise back, or shall I give you mine instead?"

Miss Maxwell again looked smilingly up in his face as she asked this question; and if he had possessed a little more of her peculiar acuteness, or a little less of his own peculiar vanity, it is probable that he might have seen something a little puzzling in the expression of that smile; as it was, however, he saw nothing but tender devotion, and instantly determined to profit by the choice she offered, which he felt convinced he could do, by the aid of his own exquisite skill in such sort of manœuvring, without exciting the slightest suspicion in her breast.

"Dear, generous girl!" he exclaimed, with an accent of passionate admiration. "You bid me decide, my dearest Martha, and I delight in thinking that this noble confidence on your part enables me to prove to you that I am not less generous than yourself. You shall return to me that most unnecessary pledge, my dear girl! Not for the world would I lead you to believe, by demanding your written promise in return, that I have less confidence in you than you have in me. And, as to my father, I have every reason to believe that, for some reason or other, he has abandoned the scheme which so alarmed me, and that there will be no need of my pleading this written promise to him."

"How delighted you must be at this release from persecution!" cried Martha, gaily. "We shall now have no more difficulties to contend with.

Are we not the most fortunate creatures in the world? This news is positively enchanting!"

"We are, indeed, most singularly fortunate," said he; "and I am sure I feel at the very bottom of my heart that it is almost impossible we can be sufficiently thankful! My father has entirely ceased to name this hateful marriage to me, and I am convinced, by the general kindness of his manner, that he is sorry for what has passed."

"Good, excellent man!" returned Miss Maxwell. "Depend upon it, Frederic, that when I am your wife," she added, very fondly, "I shall perfectly doat upon him! But I shall like to remind him, now and then, of his being so violently determined that you should marry another,—it will be so very droll, won't it?"

"Excessively!" replied the young squire, with a grimace not intended for the eyes of his betrothed.

"And you, dearest Frederic, I trust you, too, feel dutifully and affectionately disposed towards my dear and honoured parents?" said the exemplary Martha.

"Beyond what I have the power to describe!" he replied, with fervour. "But tell me, my enchanting girl, do you happen to have that foolish morsel of paper about you? I absolutely long to destroy such a detestable symbol of doubt!"

"Oh, dear! I am so sorry!" she replied, with great simplicity; "but I never do carry it about me when I go out walking."

"When may I call upon you to receive it, my dear girl?" said he.

"You may call any day, and every day," she answered; adding, with a bewitching shake of the head, "Ah, Frederic, you know that only too well."

"And when I do come next, my sweetest Martha, may I be quite sure of receiving this most ridiculous document, of which I really do feel most heartily ashamed, as I feel it is positively a disgrace to us both?"

"Nay, Frederic," she meekly replied, "you speak too strongly now. I cannot think that our motives are altogether disgraceful."

"Oh! no, my love; of course I do not exactly mean that. But, at any rate, it is idle and useless, and therefore it ought to be destroyed. Will you give it to me if I call to-morrow?" he said, with the air of a person a good deal in earnest.

"Assuredly!" she answered. "You have only to ask and to have, Frederic! Nevertheless, we must neither of us forget, if you please, that it is still necessary to be cautious about mamma. You have no idea how dreadfully suspicious she is! Depend upon it, that if she got the slightest notion into her head that there was something going on that we wished to conceal, she would never rest day or night till she had found it out. And I can't say that I should like to have her know any thing about it; for, in the first place, she would be sure to publish the whole story, by way of a capital joke, from one end of the parish to the other. And then my father would get hold of it, and he would begin storming, like the sea in a hurricane, till you had explained to him all about it. And I dare say it would be very disagreeable to you to do that now, as yours seems inclined to behave so remarkably well. And then, those Miss Mortimers, that you quiz so, would find it out. In short, I own, I should not like to have that paper seen by any one."

"Seen!" exclaimed the startled young man, "good Heaven, no! not for the universe, my dear angel! But surely you will be able to contrive some mode of giving it to me without letting your mother see you do it, or your father either."

"That may not perhaps be quite so easy as you think for," replied Martha, shaking her head. "However, you may depend upon my managing it in the way I think best. But now I must really drive you away, my dearest Frederic, painful as I know it is to both our hearts to be separated. But it won't do, you know, for us to be seen walking *tête-à-tête* in this way, till you have found courage to open your whole heart to your now indulgent father, to which there seems now, thank Heaven, no objection whatever."

Another charming smile accompanied this speech, but, without waiting to see the effect of it upon her lover, the young lady suddenly tripped across to a shop celebrated for the sale of gingerbread, to which she thought that, in the present state of affairs, it was not very likely her adorer would follow her.

In this conjecture Miss Maxwell was quite right; but her sagacity did not suffice to suggest to her the way he was about to go. Having doubled, very needlessly, more than once, for no eye was looking at him, he at length found himself once more at Jessie's door. He was on his way thither when Miss Maxwell met him for, having just heard of the death of the poor girl's mother, he had made up his mind, after very brief consideration of the subject, that the kindest thing he could do would be to make her understand, at once, that she must take herself off at least for the next few months, he being a good deal better acquainted with all the circumstances of her situation than he had hitherto thought it necessary to mention.

Jessie was sitting, when the door opened, exactly on the spot she had occupied during her conversation with Miss Maxwell, and, though looking miserably ill, had less, perhaps, the look of abject wretchedness than he expected to find. She started, and half rose from her chair as he entered; but she spoke not, and, quietly reseating herself, seemed prepared to await with meekness and submission whatever he might be pleased to say.

"I am sorry to hear of your loss, my dear Jessie," said he, "I had no idea your mother was in any danger."

There was nothing very particular in these words; but it is often in the power of intense anxiety to give an acuteness of perception, when listening to a voice from which we expect our doom, that will catch the latent thoughts and feelings from the speaker much more rapidly than they are uttered. Miss Maxwell had never explained herself as to the grounds on which she had founded her hopes of the happier days for Jessie of which she had spoken; but ere the young squire had completed the short speech above quoted the heart of Jessie whispered, "it is not on his honour, his humanity, or his love for me, that she reckons for the atonement she talks of. Miss Maxwell could not be so deceived in him."

Jessie bent her head in reply to his words, and tears fell on her hands, which were clasped before her, but she said nothing.

"I am sorry to see you so much out of spirits, my dear girl," he resumed, "though, to be sure, I cannot much wonder at it. As to my not having been to look after you before, of course I need not tell you that it has been altogether owing to your excessively silly visit to my confounded old maid of a sister. I am sure I don't know what you could expect, excepting exactly what you got. However, it is no good to talk any more about that; I suppose you must be aware that you have put it totally, and for ever, out of my power to perform my promise of marrying you? You cannot have forgotten that it was only a conditional promise, and your conduct at the house of my father has rendered the performance of it impossible. All I can do for you, however, I am still willing to do. The time has been, Jessie Phillips, when I considered you as much richer than myself, for my father does not allow me enough for my expenses, and, till quite lately, I know you have made more than you wanted to spend. But now, I suspect, the case is altered. All the spinsters in Deepbrook, with my odious sister Ellen at their head, have got a notion, I fancy, that all is not right with you, Jessie, and I should not wonder if you never get another stitch of work to do for any of them. I shall give you this ten-pound bank-note, Jessie, which will be more than enough, I hope, to take you up the country to the relations you talked of going to when you talked of running away from me; and as things have turned out, I am sure I wished you had, for both our sakes."

Mr. Frederic Dalton, as he spoke, laid down a ten-pound bank-note upon the table, and then ceased, and looked at Jessie, as if he expected she would thank him for it.

It was rather more than a minute before Jessie spoke at all, but at last, after a little tremor, and a struggle more strong than outwardly perceptible, to rally her failing strength, she said, "Mr. Dalton, I have no need of your money; take it up again, if you please, and leave me. The body of my mother is lying above our heads, and the soul that has left it is above us too,—perhaps it may still be conscious of what is passing near the clay that was its earthly dwelling. Let no more words, from you to me, or from me to you, disturb it. Go, sir! go!"

Frederic Dalton was comforted in his very heart and soul at being thus roughly dismissed. It saved him all he dreaded.

"Oh! yes, I'll go, never fear; you shall be troubled no more with me, I promise you. From first to last you have behaved most abominably to me!" And, so saying, he flung out of the cottage, banging the door rudely after him.

* * * * *

Jessie Phillips fell upon her knees, and prayed for strength and forgiveness.

* * * * *

The humble funeral of the happily released Mrs. Phillips took place before the end of the week, and on the following day Martha, true to her purpose, repeated her visit to the orphan. She found her quite alone, and busily employed in putting an old bonnet into "decent mourning." Jessie looked dreadfully ill; but her manner was more collected and composed than at Martha's last visit, and she welcomed her entrance almost with a smile.

"It is kind—oh, very kind, Miss Maxwell," she said, "not to turn away from me after all I have told you, and it seems to give you a power over me that it is comfort to think of. Where, or what I should now have been, if you had not come to me, Miss Maxwell, I dare not think of. But you have given me courage to look at what I am, and, terrible as my condition is, I will try to endure it patiently. I am doomed to suffer, but I have deserved it, and I will endeavour to bear it as I ought to do."

"I rejoice to hear you speak so, Jessie," returned the young lady, "for it is only by the help of present patience and resignation, on your part, that I can hope eventually to be of service to you. My own means are not large, Jessie, and for many reasons, some of which, I dare say, you may be able to guess, I am unwilling to apply to my father and mother about you. I am, therefore, a good deal puzzled as to what it will be best to do for you, till—till—after your baby is born, Jessie."

Both the young women coloured violently as these words were spoken, and both were silent for a minute or two, during which time poor Martha felt almost doubtful whether she were doing wrong by thus interfering in so miserable a business; but when she raised her eyes, and looked at the piteous wreck before her, every thing like doubtful motives, or faintness of purpose, disappeared, and were forgotten, and she thought only and wholly of the wrongs and the sufferings of the frail creature who seemed to have no earthly support but herself. She longed to speak to her again—to speak more kindly than ever, to soothe, to comfort, and, more than all, essentially to assist her. But the difficulty of this kept her silent; for though she had been thinking almost incessantly on the subject since her last visit she was still as far as ever from having at all made up her mind as to what she ought to advise. The project she had conceived, almost at the moment she had first heard Ellen Dalton's statement respecting her interview with Jessie, she still firmly adhered to, and felt little doubt that, if it failed to compel the young squire to fulfil the treacherous promises he had freely made to the unhappy girl, it would at least enable her to extort from him the only atonement that would be left, namely, a sufficiently ample provision to enable her to withdraw herself from the scene of her disgrace, without having to endure any pecuniary difficulties, in addition to the sorrow and repentance that must inevitably be her lot. But this project had, of necessity, too much of agitating uncertainty about it to be safely communicated to her for whose benefit it was conceived in her present condition; and poor Martha in vain sat meditating on all possible expedients, for the interval, without finding any at once with in reach of her own scanty powers of assistance and the comfort of poor Jessie.

Greatly was she relieved, therefore, when Jessie herself took the leading oar, which she did with all possible submissiveness of manner, but at the same time speaking with a quiet sedateness, which plainly shewed that what she said was said advisedly, and that it was the ripened result of much previous meditation.

"I have been thinking, Miss Maxwell," she began, "that the way to benefit by your exceeding kindness, which is so much greater than I deserve as to bring burning blushes to my cheeks every time I think of it,—I have, I say, been thinking that the way for it to do me most good is not by dragging on my painful life under your eyes, in need of every thing, and with no means whatever to help myself,—a burden upon you, so great as to make me more and more hateful to myself every day I live, while the very act of seeing me, as you do now, will soon be counted a sin, and a disgrace against you; for all these reasons, Miss Maxwell, I have, if you please, made up my mind to hide myself, for the present time, from all eyes, and from yours among the rest, my dear young lady; but go where I will, your kindness will go too,—I shall remember that, though you knew all, you still shewed tender pity for me, and wept instead of reproaching me."

The large tears which had been very quietly coursing each other down her cheeks from the moment she began to speak, now came so plentifully that she was obliged to stop, and then Martha said,—"And where is it you propose to go, my poor girl?"

Jessie wiped her eyes—nay, she ceased weeping, and replied with Perfect composure, "To the workhouse, Miss Maxwell."

"The workhouse, Jessie?—impossible! Surely you cannot be in earnest?" exclaimed Martha.

"Oh, quite in earnest, Miss Maxwell, and if you will think of it for a minute or two, my dear young lady, I do believe that you will approve it," said Jessie.

"Never!" cried Martha, vehemently; "I am very sure you do not know what you are talking about. I have heard enough from my father, who is one of the guardians, to be very sure that you could not bear the terrible discomfort of that melancholy abode."

"Ah! Miss Maxwell," cried Jessie, "you forget how impossible it is for any house or home, however cheerful, to be otherwise than melancholy to me. The brightest sunshine in the world could not cheer me now!"

There was truth in this, but, nevertheless, it did not tend to reconcile Martha to the scheme, and she argued the point for some time very earnestly with her poor *protégée;* but although Jessie listened to every word she said with the deepest respect, she adhered steadfastly to her purpose—nay, she found so much to say in support of the wisdom of seeking such a shelter at the present moment, that Miss Maxwell, whose ultimate hope was to withdraw her entirely from the neighbourhood, at length consented that, for the present, at least, she might make the experiment, as she was greatly in earnest in her wish to do it, but on condition that, if she found herself worse off than she expected, she should immediately let her know it.

Jessie seemed greatly relieved by this consent, and exerted herself with more energy than any one who looked at her would have thought at that moment she possessed to convince her most friendly visitor that she should be better off than she imagined.

"There is one point, Miss Maxwell," said she, "on which I fear that you would think it bold that I should touch, but you are so very kind, that I think, perhaps, you may be glad to know that my heart is quieter, in one way, than I ever thought it would be again. You already know that I have been destroyed by believing that Mr. Frederic Dalton considered me as his wife, and you know too, partly, what my misery was when I first began to doubt his truth,—all that misery is over now, Miss Maxwell."

"Indeed!" said Martha, an expression of very sincere sorrow passing across her features; for well she knew, that if any thing had happened to revive poor Jessie's hope, it would be to increase her final disappointment.

Jessie looked at her with a melancholy smile.

"You do not quite understand me, Miss Maxwell," said she, "it is not that my hopes have been revived, but that they have changed their object. I now hope, by the pitying mercy of God, to live in penitence, and such peace as it can bring me, but I would not be the wife of Mr. Frederic Dalton if doing so would make me a crowned queen!"

# XXVII

*Some very profound reasoning, which goes to confirm the old adage, that "where there is a will there is a way"—Jessie Phillips shews great energy of purpose, but it ends by her falling into a swoon*

THOUGH THERE MAY BE LESS of ripened experience and practical wisdom in the results of a newly conceived principle of action than in those of long-tried truth and steadiness, there is more of zeal and vigorous energy of purpose. Had Jessie Phillips been led to present herself before the Board of Guardians before Frederic Dalton's last visit to her, it is by no means improbable that she would have sunk under the effort, and that either her life or her reason might have been very fearfully shaken by the attempt. But when, in one single tremendous moment, the whole fabric of her adoring love was overturned as by the blasting stroke of a thunderbolt,—when all the gentle confiding tenderness of her young heart was suddenly turned to the bitterest contempt, by her lover's displaying exactly the reverse of every quality with which her bewitched fancy had invested him,—it was not weakness that trembled through every fibre of her frame, but indignation. She then KNEW that in her heart and soul she was immeasurably his superior, though, had he murdered her with his own hand before he had thus excited her contempt, she would have died loving him. As it was, however, the words she had spoken to Martha Maxwell were strictly true. Jessie, with all her misery upon her, would not have married Frederic Dalton, could he, when making her his wife, have made her the sovereign of the world also.

This violent revulsion of feeling had, beyond doubt, too much of passion in it to be greatly beneficial to the unhappy girl, as a means of restoring her to any humble consciousness of her fault, and to that state of Christian penitence which forms the only passage from sin and sorrow to faith and hope; but it lent her energy, for the time, to endure any thing and every thing that could place her beyond his reach, and, better still, beyond the possibility of his supposing that she looked to the offer of any further insulting gratuities from him as a means of support.

Armed with this new-born strength, Jessie Phillips put together such decent necessaries as she thought she might retain without attracting attention by any undesired superiority of appearance, and walked forth, as she hoped for the last time, from the door she had so often opened, with all the ecstasy of joy, to admit the destruction that had overwhelmed her.

Her first welcome, as she awakened the heavy sound of the great bell which hangs suspended over the outer gate of the Deepbrook Union Poorhouse, was the loud bark of Mr. Richard Dempster's mastiff from within. But Jessie's spirit was engaged in too desperate an enterprise to be checked by such a Cerberus, and she wisely remembered that when the door should be opened it would be by Mr. Dempster himself, and not by his dog; so she scarcely felt any movement of terror at the sound.

When the external walls of a Union Poorhouse are as lofty as those of Deepbrook, it is customary to have some means of reconnoitring from within what order of person it is who stands without, when this harsh bell, and its still sterner echo, Growler, give notice of an arrival. This prudent look-out is doubly useful, as it gives Mr. Dempster, or his lady, or both, as the case may be, an opportunity of displaying their dutiful zeal in more ways than one; first, by the alacrity with which the summons is obeyed when coming from dignitaries who have an official right to enter; and, secondly, by the deliberate slowness with which those are admitted whose coming will probably tend to increase the expenses, which it is the bounden duty of Mr. Governor Dempster and his lady to reduce as much as possible.

The eye which first caught this occult glance of poor Jessie was that of Mrs. Dempster, and the eye was puzzled.

"I don't know what sort of a body we have got now," she said to her husband, who, as usual, was lounging on a bench at no great distance, with his darling Growler between his knees. "It is a woman, and therefore she can't have any real right to come here upon any business but her own; and she don't look a bit like one of the tatter-demalions who troop up with a 'Please, ma'am, may I speak a word to the Board?'"

"Well, then, let her in, at any rate, for she must be something new, and I, for one, should like a little variety of all things. And so will Growler too. Faith, wife, 'twill be fun if the dog should be at fault, and not know whether he ought to bark or wag his tail."

The buxom dame shook her sides at this clever notion, and lost no time in returning to the door with Growler, invited by a slight movement of the head, at her heels. The massive but by no means rusty key turned easily in the large hand applied to it, and Jessie Phillips became visible at once to Mr. Dempster, Mrs. Dempster, and their dog Growler. The effect of her appearance upon those three distinguished individuals was very different. Mr. Dempster stared at her,—Mrs. Dempster laughed at her,—and Growler, after making his own intelligent inquiries, in his usual way, remained perfectly silent, but without giving any indication of intending to bite instead of bark.

"Well, now, to be sure, you are a trim figure of a lass to come up here. May I be so bold as to ask your business, miss?" said Mrs. Dempster, casting a glance of less cordiality than usual on her husband, who, to say truth, had never taken his eyes off Jessie from the moment she became visible.

"My business is with the Board," replied Jessie, composedly.

"Oh, I dare say it is, miss,—I haven't the least bit of a doubt of that," replied the Governor's lady, "only I thought that maybe you mightn't think it altogether too much of a liberty if I axed ye what you might happen to have to say to them. However, Miss—But, mercy on me!—I beg your pardon, Jessie Phillips, a score of times! As sure as I stand here, I had no more notion of who you was than the man in the moon!—Dick, you fool! what for do you stand glowering there? As if you never saw a decent-dressed young woman before, in all your born days. Off with you into the house, do! Be sure the Board will be asking for somebody or something by this time."

To do him justice, there were but few things that stout Dick Dempster was afraid of,—but his wife was one of them; and whistling the dog to follow him, he entered the house according to order, leaving Mrs. Dempster and Jessie Phillips *tête-à-tête.*

"For goodness sake tell me what you are come here for, my dear?" said the former, recovering her brilliant good-humour as soon as the eyes of her very thoughtless husband had removed themselves from the face of Jessie. "I can't and won't believe," she added, "that such a clever girl as you are with your needle, and so in favour with all the ladies, should come to look for any thing here, for it is long, Jessie, you know, since you had time to do any work for such as me."

"I am come to ask for assistance, Mrs. Dempster," said Jessie.

"Well!—to be sure, now, that is the very last thing I should have expected!—and you always so particular well to do. Howsomever, I suppose 'twill be something about the funeral expenses of your mother; but that will be too late now, my dear. You should have come before she was put in the earth, Jessie, if really and truly you had not got enough to do it; for though we keep ourselves pretty strict, as we ought to do, in the article of refusing, we most times gives way when a dead body is lying above-ground. Many of the gentlemen are rather particular in that respect, which is natural enough, seeing that we have got more than one person among us."

"I have already paid for my mother's funeral," replied Jessie, with a slight convulsion about the mouth, but without shedding a tear.

"You don't say so?" returned the puzzled Mrs. Dempster. "Then what in the name of wonder can have brought you here?"

"Great poverty, ma'am," replied Jessie, slightly colouring, "and the consciousness that I am no longer able to maintain myself."

"No longer able to maintain yourself, my girl! That's a good one, to be sure,—and you with such a business as you have got! You don't mean to look in my face, and say that you made your mother maintain you as long as she was alive, and that you spent all your own earnings in finery, and dressing yourself up to look like a lady? You won't have the audaciousness to tell me that, will you?"

"No, ma'am; I always helped to find every thing we wanted as long as my health was good: but now my health is gone, and my custom is gone after it."

"A mighty queer story!" muttered the mistress of the establishment, casting a scowling and suspicious glance at the new applicant. "We shall see what the Board will say to it, Miss Jessie. Goodness forgive me! but I do begin to suspect that all is not gold that glitters; if wrong, I beg your pardon, miss. But in with you, Miss Jessie Phillips. You've held your head high enough, there is nobody will deny that. I never heard any body say that you thought small beer of yourself; but, if I bean't mistaken,—only *if*—observe, you see I say *if*,—but, if I bean't mistaken, you'll be just after giving all the girls in the parish a good lesson not to think too much of themselves."

To this speech Jessie made no reply, not even by a sigh, but followed the speaker, who moved on before her into the interior of the establishment.

Being rather eager to gratify her curiosity both as to the manner in which this unexpected petitioner would present herself, and that in which the application would be received, Mrs. Dempster lost no time in making it known, at the door of the room where the Guardians were sitting, that there was a female applying for leave to enter the house.

Though determined, with a steadfastness of resolution that almost seemed unnatural, to endure with firmness every thing that could happen to her, Jessie felt a sharp pang of disappointment at being told that she was to wait till the business at that moment before the Board should be despatched. Despite the assurances which she constantly repeated to herself, that, after all she had suffered, there was *nothing* that she could now consider as a very serious evil, Jessie *was* sorely disappointed at finding that the tremendous moment of presenting herself as a pauper before the Deepbrook Board of Guardians was postponed. Most literally had she screwed her courage to the sticking-place, and perfectly satisfactory had been her conviction that she should *not* fail; but now she feared, for one short moment, at least, that this postponement would be fatal to her, and that all her resolute purposes would be frustrated by the delay. But she did herself injustice by misdoubting thus her own constancy; the feeling that sustained it was too strong to give way before so trifling a check.

The business at that moment before the Board of Guardians was of a nature deeply interesting to the poor people belonging to the Deepbrook

Union, though the length of time which the discussion endured caused more than one anxious individual to wish that it had been shorter.

The apothecary who had some months before obtained the situation of medical attendant to the Union, in consequence of having very considerably underbid every other person who had applied for it, had been found twice within the last ten days in a state of complete intoxication at the village inn. In both cases the disgraceful discovery was made in consequence of his having been sought after in all haste to attend two pauper women by whom his professional assistance was very urgently required. In the first case he arrived too late—the birth was over, and the child dead; in the second he was assisted in reaching the spot where he was wanted, and got there in time to administer a strong dose of laudanum, which happily, however, produced not any fatal effect; but the singularity of the prescription, under the circumstances, and the cause to which it was naturally attributed, produced a degree of sensation throughout the neighbourhood, which led to a proposal among the Board of Guardians that he should be dismissed. It was the discussion upon this proposal which now occupied the Board; but as it as not a discussion upon principles, but merely a trial of numerical strength between a party of the jovial apothecary's personal friends, among the farmers, and such members of the Board as were not under this influence, it could be neither profitable nor interesting to enter among them, in order to observe how the matter went. It is enough to say that very considerable exertions having been made among the friendly faction, in order to muster strongly, the proposal for the dismissal of this dangerous Galen was negatived by a large majority, though not without a stout though ineffectual struggle on the part of the reverend chairman, and the party who thought with him. At this scene Mr. Mortimer was not present, having been suddenly summoned to a distant part of the district, or it is probable the result would have been different.

While this was passing in "the great room," Jessie obtained leave to seat herself in an obscure corner of the court, where there was a bench, sometimes used to support a washing-tub, and where she was perhaps more out of the way of being questioned, and talked to, than she could have been any where else. There was a sort of nervous vibration in her spirits, poor girl! between a strongly self-sustaining confidence in her own courage and power of endurance, and a lurking terror lest something might be done or said that should overset her, and render her unfit or unable to execute her resolute purpose. She shrunk, therefore, from all intercourse with the pauper inmates of the place, lest they might recount to her greater horrors concerning it than she had ever heard before. Not that she feared the endurance of any of the hardships they might have to recount; on the contrary, she was positively eager to enter upon the trial to which she had condemned herself, all her fear being lest the energy of her spirit should in any degree be weakened before it began. Perhaps she was right; perhaps, if she had watched, as poor Greenhill had done, during a similar interval of delay, the dim-eyed sadness and the stagnant dull despair of those with whom she was about to live, her courage might have given way, and she might have dwindled into the state she most deprecated, namely, that of hopeless, helpless self-abandonment.

But, as it happened, she was exposed to no danger of this kind; for the place she had chosen, being frequently one of busy occupation, was interdicted to the miserably idle inmates of the place, who would have been more happy than the principles of "THE BILL" could permit had they been suffered to roam freely to a spot where human voices might have been heard discussing themes so interesting as soap lathers, rincing-tubs, and drying-lines. Such license would very clearly have approached to the degree of indulgence stigmatised by the philosophical statisticians of the day as a "bonus for the encouragement of depravity." So it was in perfect solitude that Jessie passed the interval till she was summoned to appear before the Board; and the result of this quiet hour of meditation was rather elevation than depression of spirit, for such was the composure of countenance, and sedateness of step, with which she entered the awe-inspiring room, that, considering what she had been and what she was, it might have puzzled any one to interpret its meaning, who had never witnessed and watched the effect of such an undercurrent of subdued feeling as that which now influenced her.

Yet not even Mr. Huttonworth himself, with all his partiality for dirt and degradation in those who presented themselves for parochial relief, could have interpreted any thing in Jessie's manner, nor even in her perfectly neat appearance, to the species of presumption which his soul abhorred; for the sedate stillness of her look and manner, joined to the pale beauty of her marble features, was more likely to suggest the idea of a being rising supernaturally from the tomb than of one of those audacious beggars who venture unblushingly to declare that they would rather not be forced to take refuge in it.

Every eye (and in consequence of the previous business there were many persons present)—every eye was fixed upon her; but, contrary to what was usually the case among the many busy individuals there assembled, none seemed anxious to undertake the customary task of examining her, relative to the business which brought her there. It was indeed a wonderful effort that enabled her to stand before them, as she did, firm, perfectly collected, and without visible tremor in any limb or fibre. It is true the fluttering pulse throbbed, stopped, and throbbed again; but of this she was not even conscious herself, and still less did any one else suspect how doubtfully her heart beat, as if uncertain whether she should live or die. It was, however, Jessie herself who at length brought this silent examination to a close by raising her eyes to those of the reverend chairman, with a look that seemed to beseech his attention to her case. Mr. Rimmington appeared to understand this appeal, and immediately answered it by saying, "What is it brings you here, my good girl?"

"The hope that you will be pleased to let me come into the house," was the reply.

"Is it possible, Jessie Phillips, that you can wish to do so?" said Mr. Rimmington, with something like severity of manner; "you are considered by the whole parish as perfectly capable of maintaining yourself; and the loss of your helpless mother, my poor girl, must surely make it rather more than less easy for you to do so, for you must have more time for work and fewer calls upon your earnings. Think better of it, Jessie Phillips; this must be some fit of low spirits, I am sure. It is quite impossible we can listen to your request. I am certain that the Board will not permit your coining in here to live in idleness when you are so perfectly well able to maintain yourself."

"I have been able to maintain myself and my mother too, sir," replied Jessie, "and I did it with good-will and thankfulness,—but now my health is gone; I have not a shilling in the world, and I must perish if I am refused a shelter here."

"This is very strange," said Mr. Rimmington, turning to Mr. Dalton, who sat next to him; "you know this girl perfectly well, Mr. Dalton, as well as myself, and I am sure you must think with me that she is no object for parochial relief."

"Assuredly I am very greatly surprised at her asking for it," returned the squire; "nevertheless I think, from all I hear of her, that if she says she is in want, we may believe her."

"Why surely you must have property, Jessie Phillips?" resumed Mr. Rimmington. "Your mother rented a cottage of Mr. Baxter, I think, but the furniture was hers, was it not? And if so, it must now be yours, I suppose."

"Yes, sir," replied Jessie; "and but for that I should be sadly in debt; but there are three shops where we owed money that have agreed to take what there is between them in the way of payment."

"How long, then, have you been unable to work, my poor girl? You certainly look greatly out of health," said the kind-hearted rector, his manner becoming more gentle as he remarked the melancholy contraction of her youthful brow. This question, simple as it was, seemed to shake her firmness more than any thing which had preceded it, but again she roused herself, and was about to answer, when the worthy Mr. Dalton, in the most friendly accents possible, said to her, "How long is it, Jessie, since you went cowslip-picking with my young ones?"

When the squire had first spoken in reply to Mr. Rimmington's appeal, Jessie began, for the first time since she had entered the room, to tremble from the fear that her courage might fail; she had, however, carefully avoided looking at him, and told herself, again and again, that his being there, and having the power of repeating to his family all that passed, was a reason, ten thousand times stronger than any other, for her shewing no sign of weakness; but now, that he had directly addressed her, now that he had asked her a question which, in that moment of agony, seemed to convey an intimation to her guilty heart that he knew all, the crisis of her fate appeared to be arrived; she turned her large lustreless eyes upon him as if about to reply, but in the next moment the eyes closed, and the unhappy girl fell prostrate upon the floor.

# XXVIII

*Jessie is received into the workhouse, and makes several new acquaintances, and listens to much edifying conversation*

MANY PAUPERS MIGHT HAVE FAINTED, perhaps, before the presence of a board of guardians without creating so great a sensation as that produced by the fall of Jessie Phillips. In speculating upon human nature, there is no need to make it out to be worse than it really is; and there is, methinks, some disposition to do this when we attribute such a feeling as was produced among the majority of the persons present, by the sudden illness of poor Jessie, to such an influence from her beauty, as a good man might blush to feel. There unquestionably is a tenderness of pity excited in most hearts, whether old or young, male or female, by the sight of youth and beauty in a state of suffering that is more likely to have had its origin in the providential mercy of Heaven than in the corrupt sinfulness of earth, and the eager manner in which almost every one present rose up, and hastened towards the spot where she lay, did them honour. Those nearest to her, however, did what was at once most likely to restore tranquillity to the honourable Board, and animation to the seemingly lifeless object of their care. Jessie was speedily carried out of the room, and laid upon a bed, with earnest injunctions from the venerable chairman himself to the bustling Mrs. Dempster that she should be treated with all possible care and kindness.

This fainting, though the terrible moment which preceded it brought a pang like that of death to the bosom of Jessie, spared her all further trouble as to the matter of her immediate admission to the workhouse. Being still perfectly unable to rise from the bed on which she had been laid, she was, when the Board separated, left under the care of Dempster and his wife, as a matter of course, with orders that she should be kindly treated, and that medical attendance should be afforded her, if she appeared to require it.

This order was subsequently confirmed, after due inquiry had been made respecting the disposition of the few articles of furniture which her mother had possessed. These inquiries left no doubt as to the correctness of the facts which Jessie had stated, and her deathlike swoon, together with her excessive paleness, being received in proof of failing health, all opposition to her admission to the house, at least for the present, was withdrawn, and "the pride of the village" established as the most desolate, though least complaining inmate of the union workhouse.

The scenes which followed the slow recovery of her senses were terrible enough, in many ways, but they did not come upon her unexpectedly; and, though the sort of stern tranquillity into which she had forced her spirits could not be considered as the result of a perfectly natural and seasonable state of mind, it nevertheless gave her strength of some sort, and enabled her to maintain such an aspect of uncomplaining resignation, as saved her from much of the sharp, scolding discipline which Mrs. Dempster thought it beneficial to adopt with most of the new inmates committed to her charge.

But there was one initiatory process which nothing could enable her to escape, and which probably nothing could have enabled her to endure so perfectly without a murmur or a sigh, but the idea so strongly fixed upon her mind, that the more she suffered the nearer should she be to having expiated her fault, and consequently the nearer to such a state as might justify Miss Maxwell in again extending to her the inestimable blessing of her personal kindness.

This most painful initiatory process was the having her own garments taken away, and the strictly regulated dress of the Union given her in its stead. In the pain produced by this, there was no mixture whatever of wounded vanity; nay, even when told that her luxuriant chesnut tresses must be cut off, the loss of so much beauty produced not a single pang. No, it was not vanity that was wounded, it was a deeper, a better, and a holier feeling. It was the degradation which she shared in common with the felon inmates of a gaol, that caused her spirits to sink, and almost die within her. An involuntary, but irrepressible sentiment of indignation swelled her heart as she thought how many miserable human beings were exposed to this degradation, who were guiltless of any crime, save poverty. "For me, for me," she inwardly exclaimed, "it comes in the shape of punishment, and it is welcome. But, alas! for the honest pride of those who are innocent! Why must the worn-out labourer, who has toiled till nature denies him strength to toil again, why must he wear the hateful livery of crime, and close his eyes with no greater symptoms of sympathy, or respect around him, than are bestowed on a convicted thief?"

It is scarcely necessary to say that poor Jessie's secret speedily became known to Mrs. Dempster, and afterwards, with as little delay as possible, to every one of her companions. Had these companions been all of the same decent, sober class as the poor neighbours with whom she had been accustomed to associate, dreadful as would have been her feelings under this inevitable disclosore, she would have endured them, as she did the wretched diet, the crowded chamber, and the comfortless bed, as a necessary part of her awarded punishment. But among the recklessly mingled beings with whom she was now associated there were many grossly vicious, and the gibes and jestings which she had to endure from these produced a species of torture that she would willingly have died to escape. By degrees, however, the novelty of the sport she thus afforded this "worser part" of the miserable community wore off, and she was suffered to sit amidst the oldest and most infirm of the helpless beings whom hunger had driven to mingle together in that dismal prison, with little interruption from the levity of the more profligate part of them. This was so great a relief that even the sour, moody melancholy of those poor old women appeared precious to her as a protection, and more than one among them declared it was "a blessed Godsend to have one in their company who was not worn too low with sorrow and suffering to have any patience or pity left in her heart."

Dismal and dreary, oh! frightfully dismal and dreary was the daily routine of that last refuge of helplessness and want; and, not withstanding her resolute patience, poor Jessie in truth felt it more keenly than her companions, though they bemoaned themselves without ceasing, and she never uttered a complaint. But the poor girl had loved all the sights and sounds of nature with more of fervour and devotedness than the generality of her companions, and the change she had made, therefore, was greatly more severe. No one, perhaps, sympathised with her so sincerely in her longings for fresh air and green fields as Silly Sally. There may be a luxury in idiotism (as we are told there is in madness) which none but idiots know, and the vivid enjoyment of the blessings which nature freely bestows upon all living things may form a part of it. "Poor Jessie Phillips!" said the idiot girl, on seeing the new comer standing before a window that looked out upon the high wall which surrounded the court; "poor Jessie Phillips! Her's thinking of her pretty honeysuckle that her saw every day, and all day long, afore her comed here. Ask missus for leave to take a run with Sally. Do, Jessie, will y'?" Jessie shook her head. "Her won't?" said the girl, with a loud laugh. "Then her's a worse fool than Sally. See else! Look at me, Jessie! I'll bring thee a nosegay, see if I don't!" and so saying, she strode away, and stationed herself in waiting at the outer door till it should chance to be opened; for, if Sally was not of sufficient importance to be restrained from wandering here, there, and every where, like the birds, who were her especial darlings, neither was she worthy, in the estimation of the magisterial Richard, of having a door opened expressly for her use and benefit. Let the weather, however, be what it would, Sally might daily be seen, as soon as her breakfast of gruel was swallowed, standing bolt upright, her hands behind her, her back supported by the wall, at the distance of a few inches from the door-post, and her roving eye watching eagerly for the approach of the hand that was to set her at liberty. The full possession of the profoundest wisdom could not have taught the poor natural to catch the opportunity more skilfully when it arrived, for she would slip sideways through the very least available aperture, and bound away across the common beyond with the frolicsome enjoyment of a Newfoundland puppy, before the sober eyes of those who looked after her from within were fully aware that she was gone.

"And isn't it sin and wickedness, now," said a woman, addressing Jessie, while watching this envied escapade on tiptoe from a small square window, the lower half of which was protected from the too-captivating view without by wooden blinds, sloping outwards,—"isn't it sin and wickedness, young woman, to see a poor natural like that set up above us all, as if she was a queen, and we was her slaves? Think what I'd give for such a run as she'll be after getting through the fields?"

The woman who said this was still in the prime of life, but having entirely lost the use of both her arms by a tremendous scald, and being unmarried, without either father or mother to help her, she was one of the few who not only entered the workhouse from absolute destitution, but who did it cheerfully and thankfully, well knowing its shelter must, in her case at least, be the greatest blessing she could hope for. But this cheerful spirit had been sorely tried during the three long years that she had been its inmate. Never, to do her justice, had she been heard to utter a murmur at the very scanty and most unsavoury nourishment which the rule of the house accorded. Never had she been known to remark that the garments which covered her were ill-suited for comfort, either in heat or cold; never had she seemed conscious that her bed differed in nothing from the floor, save that it was less smooth and even; neither did the absence of all occupation suggest any idea of discontent, for Nanny Smith had no hands to work with, and had never been taught to read. But there was one privation which seemed to enter her very soul, the patient submission to which was beyond her philosophy, and the restless discontent that was its consequence preyed without ceasing upon the health both of her mind and body. She was perishing for want of air and exercise. The occupation of this unhappy creature, from the age of ten, or somewhat earlier, to that of thirty-seven, had been one of ceaseless out-of-door activity as servant-of-all-work in a small farm. Cows, pigs, and chickens, were her daily care; it was a sort of rest to her when she had crocks and pans to scour, and a hard day's washing was a chatty holyday. Sober, honest, cheerful, and industrious to perfection, her terrible misfortune brought her all the sympathy that poor folks, labouring for their living, could bestow. They could not maintain her, but they pitied, and they loved her; and cheerily did her good mistress point out, during the long suffering through which she nursed her, "that there was much to be thankful for still, for one so cheerful as Nanny, for her eyes, and her hearing, and her speech, were spared, and that would go far to keep her from being melancholy, though her poor hands were gone." But, alas! of what avail are eyes, hearing, and speech, to the inmate of a union workhouse? For several months after poor Nanny's admission to her living grave, her former mistress, and two or three other worthy souls who had known her through the whole of her innocent and hard-working life, perseveringly visited the door of the Union, beseeching admission to poor Nanny, whom they hoped to cheer by a little out-of-door news, or, at any rate, to comfort, by proving that she was not forgotten by them. But beyond the door they never penetrated, being uniformly told that it was contrary to the regulations laid down by the commissioners to permit any of the paupers to receive visitors. "What was law for one was," as Mrs. Dempster incontrovertibly observed, "law for another; and a pretty life they should lead, if all the women in the house, good, bad, and indifferent, or the men either, for that matter, were permitted to see all the rag, tag, and bobtail idletons that come to look after them, and to spy and to speer about every thing that was going on in the house." When convinced that it was useless to attempt comforting the poor cripple by seeking to see her at the workhouse, her old master, a man of unimpeachable character in all ways, and, moreover, a regular rate-payer of above thirty years standing, waited upon the Board of Guardians to petition leave for Nanny Smith, his old servant, to come out, once now and then, of a Sunday evening, to his house, in the hope that it might cheer her under her heavy affliction.

It would have done good to the hearts of the political economists and philosophical statesmen, who have of late worked themselves into such a fever of admiration at the national benefits arising from a central board, and the "uniform" administration of the law, which was its consequence, could they have witnessed the noble burst of indignation with which this proposal of farmer Mitchell was met by Mr. Lewis and Mr. Huttonworth. The reasons given by these two gentlemen for their irate refusal of this request were different, but both of them in strict conformity with the principles promulgated at Somerset House. Mr. Lewis knit his brows as he looked fixedly in the startled farmer's face, and said, "The bill, my good man, the bill, which, Heaven be praised! is now become the law of the land, is point blank in opposition to your request; and this, I trust, will be sufficient to prevent such a decent, respectable person as you are, from ever expressing such a wish again."

Mr. Huttonworth exclaimed, with equal earnestness and considerably more violence, "A pretty pass we should be come to, old man, if we hadn't the power of sending you about your business in the style that your errand deserves. I know nothing about you, thank God nor about your dear friend the pauper either,—the girl, I mean, that you are so anxious to befriend and befavour. But this I know, my old fellow, and it is quite time that you should begin to know it too, the country gentlemen of England, in their capacity of guardians of the poor, don't come galloping seven miles across the country for the sake of giving leave and license for such unprincipled partiality in discipline as that which you have the face to propose. By Jove, if I give your dear friend leave to come and go, at pleasure, I'll insist upon all the rest of the ragamuffins having the same. Uniformity is the keystone of the whole law; and I'd as soon forge, break open a house, or cut a man's throat, as give my vote for any such barefaced partiality."

But these by-gone details relative to poor Nanny are taking us from Jessie, whom it is our present business to attend to. In reply to the repining observation which the poor cripple had addressed to her, she said, soothingly, though with a heavy sigh,— "No, no! Poor Sally is not meant to be set up above us. After all, we ought rather to pity than to envy her."

"Pity!" harshly exclaimed the once kind-tempered woman; "she an object of pity? I tell you, girl, that you know not what you are talking about. *You* have not sat, and stood, and sat again, gazing on these horrid walls, for six-and-thirty dreadful months, and three hateful days over! You have got the look and the smell of the fields fresh in your mind as yet. Ay, and I'll be bound for it, you can still shut up your eyes for a minute, and fancy that you feel the cool soft grass under your feet. And maybe, if you try for it, you may call back like the pretty chirruping of the happy birds. I could do so for months and months; but I can't do it now! It's all gone, gone for ever! Oh! what would I give for only one such walk in the fields as Silly Sally is let to have every day!"

"Give! You give! You pauper you? I should jist like to know what it is you have got to give," croaked a sour-looking, little old woman, who was kneeling down upon the stone floor, in order to vary her position from sitting upon a bench about nine inches wide, and placed too high against the wall to admit easily of her touching the ground with her feet. "Will you be pleased to tell us what it is you have got to give them as have the power to say yes, or no, to you?"

It was a bitter laugh, that rung round the bare walls, and sounded strangely hollow, as it repaid this witty sally; but the melancholy cripple replied, with more earnestness than anger, "I'd just offer 'em half my life, if they'd let me walk for one hour of every day in the fields, for the other half."

"And you are a 'cute woman for that," mumbled another haggard old soul, who was twisting her stiff fingers about by way of occupation. "A piece of your life is just the thing they'd like best. If we would but all die off a little faster, they'd be ready to do a'most any thing to please us."

Jessie shuddered. But Jessie had yet a good deal to learn before she fully comprehended the nature of a union workhouse. We must now, however, leave her for awhile, for the purpose of looking a little after the fortunes of one whose destiny was strongly blended with hers. When we return to her, we shall probably find that the excellent opportunity she will have enjoyed of obtaining this knowledge will not have been altogether thrown away; and the gentle reader, in his easy chair, shall be permitted to profit by her experience.

# XXIX

*An interview between a village damsel and a great lady*

IT CHANCED ONE MORNING THAT Ellen Dalton, having heard that her old friend Mrs. Buckhurst was indisposed, determined upon taking one of her rare solitary walks to her cottage, in order to inquire for her; but it chanced, also, that instead of achieving this immediately after breakfast, as she intended, a score of services, at the very least, were demanded of her by father, mother, and sisters, the performing which rendered it impossible to leave the house before luncheon was announced. This was exceedingly inconvenient, because it occasionally happened that persons visited Mrs. Buckhurst whom Ellen did not desire to meet; and as these persons were not in the habit of calling early it was highly advantageous to get her own visit over as soon as possible. But Ellen could not refuse her father, would not refuse her mother, and rarely refused her sisters, any thing; neither did she like to let the day pass without inquiring for the venerable invalid; so, trusting to chance, which she reasonably thought considerably in her favour, and intending to watch for certain indications which were likely to announce the arrival of those whom she wished to avoid, she ventured forth, and took her wonted path to the cottage. It was quite evident that no wheels had drawn up to the little gate since the early shower which had washed out all traces of the goings and comings of the day before, and Ellen, therefore, made her *entrée* boldly. But not only did she find the little parlour free from the presence of those she wished to avoid, but also without that of the dearly loved friend by whom she had hoped to be welcomed. Ellen's intimacy at the cottage, however, reached even to the kitchen, and thither she now went to learn tidings of the old lady. There she found the minister plenipotentiary of the establishment busily engaged in the preparation of chicken-broth, who, the moment she saw the young lady, exclaimed, "Oh! bless you, Miss Ellen! I am glad to see you are come, for my poor missis have been looking out for you all day. I don't believe there is any body, except just the Duchess perhaps, that she loves as well as she does you, Miss Ellen."

"And how is she, Molly? and why is she not in the parlour?" demanded Miss Dalton.

"Why, she is not right, Miss Ellen, nor haven't been for these three or four days. But now, thank God! she's getting a nice nap; but I could not make her lie down till I had promised that if you come I would keep you till she woke up."

"Most certainly I will not go till I have seen her," replied Ellen. "I shall find plenty of books in the parlour, and there I will stay till you call me."

And to the parlour Ellen returned, and found, as she expected, plenty of books, but probably did not set about reading any one of them with as unbroken attention as she might have done, had not the name of "Pemberton" been inscribed on the title-page of nearly all.

But nothing could be farther from Ellen Dalton's wishes or intentions than to spend her time there, or any where, in meditating on the name of Pemberton; she exerted herself, therefore, to break the spell, and succeeded so well, that she was already deeply engaged in following the noble but vain struggles of "Edwin the Fair," when the parlour door was gently opened, and a lady entered, who, though a stranger to Ellen in the conventional sense of the word, she instantly knew to be the Duchess of Rochdale.

There was a great deal of quiet self-possession in the character and in the manner of Ellen Dalton; but now, for a moment, she lost it, and her quickly varying colour, and the agitated manner in which she rose from her seat and stood trembling, with her eyes fixed upon the ground, proved that the meeting was as little desired as expected. But this vehemence of emotion did not last long, or, at least, did not last long uncombated; she recovered herself sufficiently to look up, and to say, as she prepared to leave the room, without any appearance of strong emotion, "Permit me, madam, to send Mrs. Buckhurst's servant to you."

"Stay, Miss Dalton," said the Duchess, who, to say the truth, appeared little less agitated than Ellen herself. "This meeting is an unhoped-for gratification to me. I have wished for it more earnestly than you can easily believe, and yet it was what I dared not ask for. Do not, therefore, leave me, I entreat you. Sit down by me, Ellen Dalton, and let me speak to you as a friend, though I may not speak to you as a mother."

Where could her Grace of Rochdale have found words likely more effectually to shake the firmness of poor Ellen than these? Had she spoken sternly, or even coldly, or had she proudly turned from her without speaking at all, however painful the remembrance of it might have been afterwards, it would for the moment have roused the energy of her character instead of its softness, and prevented the starting of the tell-tale tears, to have stopped which she would almost have given one of the beautiful eyes that shed them. To articulate a single word was totally beyond her power; but she obeyed the command she had received, which, gently as it was uttered, carried with it an intimation that could not be thus pronounced without awakening sufferings which she had vainly hoped were lulled and hushed for ever. Nothing that she could have said, however, could have had half the eloquence of that "mute silence." The Duchess looked at her for several minutes with an earnestness which Ellen seemed rather to feel upon her blushing cheek than to see, for she raised not her eyes to the face of the devoted wife and mother, who, while ready to sacrifice every thing for the interest of her son, scrupled not, as it seemed, to crush the only being who had any real power of contributing to his happiness.

The silence, which, awfully long as it appeared to Ellen, she dreaded to have broken, was at length ended by the Duchess, saying, "My son has thanked you for the munificence which saved my poor Greenhill from the workhouse, Miss Dalton, but you must permit me, both in the Duke's name and my own, to thank you likewise. We must all of us ever feel grateful to you for it."

Ellen's heart swelled within her bosom painfully. To be thanked thus for a deed, which she never would have performed could she have anticipated its being known to those who now seemed to appropriate the favour to themselves, produced a greater feeling of mortification than all the grave reasonings which had heretofore been officially conveyed to her by Mrs. Buckhurst, in order to prove that the attachment, which was dearer to her than life, had been withdrawn, in obedience to mandates too sacred to be uttered in vain. To this she had listened infinitely more in sorrow than in anger; but now the case was different. She fancied that the thanks thus ostentatiously offered were meant to shew that the family were aware the service was intended to be rendered to themselves; and this was a thought almost too painful to bear with what she felt to be a necessary degree of external composure. She made no reply to the words of the Duchess, and, involuntarily perhaps, turned her head, so as to leave as little of her face visible as possible. "May I ask you one question, Miss Dalton?" said the Duchess, after another interval of silence. Ellen bowed; but it was coldly and slightly. "Will you tell me whether the obstinate resistance of Greenhill to name her benefactor was in obedience to any order of yours?"

Startled out of her dignified yet respectful reserve by this sudden question, which touched directly upon the point at which she felt herself the most deeply wounded, Ellen turned suddenly round, and fixing her soft, earnest eyes upon the Duchess, while a bright blush dyed her cheeks, replied, in an accent that certainly implied reproach, "Does your Grace doubt it?"

"Certainly not, if our belief that it was so be confirmed by you, Miss Dalton. But will you go a step farther, and tell me why it was that you laid so heavy, so difficult a task upon the poor woman? I assure you that she very nearly got herself into a scrape with her old master by the pertinacity with which she endeavoured to obey you to the letter. Why were you so averse to her stating who it was that had befriended her?"

"Because I wished to avoid the possibility of receiving such thanks as have followed the avowal of it," replied Ellen, with something a little approaching to asperity.

"Have I then offended you, Miss Dalton, by thus availing myself of the accident that has brought us together?" said the Duchess.

"No, madam, no! I am honoured—doubtless I ought to be gratified; but—" And Ellen stopped short, as if afraid to trust herself with any genuine expression of her feelings.

"But you are offended," said the Duchess.

"I would willingly be spared the rudeness of saying so, madam," returned Ellen. "But it may be perhaps ruder still to refuse an answer when pressed for it. Yet an answer can only be conveyed by my taking the liberty of asking a question in return. Have I not reason to think that this unlooked-for honour has been accorded me for the purpose of discovering whether the assistance afforded to our poor neighbour, by my father and myself, was the result of humanity; or of a wish, on his part and mine, to propitiate the favour of your noble house?"

"You wrong me, Ellen Dalton! you wrong me!" exclaimed the Duchess, colouring in her turn, and with so much genuine sincerity that the heart of Ellen reproached her for the bitterness she had both felt and expressed. "You wrong me cruelly in thinking so. The sincerity and the vehemence of Greenhill's wish to keep your secret convinced me that you had been equally in earnest in enjoining it; and you must forgive me if I confess that I longed to hear a confirmation of this from yourself. Mrs. Buckhurst has more than once told me that I did not know you, meaning, of course, that I did not do you justice in still retaining fears lest the unchanging affection of poor Pemberton should finally induce you to alter the line of conduct you have hitherto so nobly preserved. I have wished to know you, I have wished to do you justice, Miss Dalton, and allow me to say that it is now only that I can do justice to my unhappy son, for it is now only that the sacrifice he has made to his father has been fully appreciated by me." The Duchess rose, tears were in her eyes, and her whole aspect was nervous and agitated in no common degree. "I cannot stay to see my old friend now," she said, "I am not fit for it. Tell her I have called, my dear, but was unable to wait for her to see me. Farewell, Ellen Dalton! I little thought that the sight of you would cost me all I now feel. But, beautiful as you are," continued the weeping Duchess, looking mournfully in her face, "I can well fancy that you have been more beautiful still, and would be so again, if you were happy. It is a cruel destiny that rests upon us all! Poor Pemberton! I think I must not tell him that I have seen you; and yet, though cruel, would it not be kind to tell him, as frankly as you have told me, that the feelings which once existed between you had no influence in what you did for Greenhill?"

"It were better not to name the subject to him, madam," returned Ellen, "but, above all, not to make the statement you now mention, for not only would it be impossible for him to believe it, but it would be essentially untrue."

"How?" exclaimed the Duchess, the expression of her countenance changing from tenderness to surprise and vexation; "have I misunderstood you, Miss Dalton?"

"I would greatly wish to prevent your Grace's doing so," said Ellen gravely, and with much more composure of manner than was evinced by her companion, "and I will do myself some violence rather than be the cause of what I so much desire to avoid. Most truly did I wish and intend that the assistance rendered to Mrs. Greenhill should never be traced to me; and had I not been disappointed in this there would have been no need of my disclaiming, as I have just done, any intention of propitiating your Grace's good opinion by it. But this has nothing to do with other secret feelings that may have been at work within me. Into these no human eye has any right to penetrate, nor do I propose breathing such to any human ear. Your Grace is aware that I have long ago been made to understand what was required of me; I have obeyed, strictly and faithfully, the injunction thus conveyed, and so will I continue to do. This must suffice, for I can pledge myself for nothing more."

Having spoken these words, Ellen, who seemed from a starting tear to be in danger of losing her composure of manner as she concluded them, somewhat abruptly broke from the presence of the Duchess, and took refuge through a well-known garden-door at the back of the house, which led into a little copse, across which she found her way without much difficulty, and happily gained her home; nay, even she longed for the shelter of her own room without encountering any of the various interruptions she dreaded.

# XXX

*A retrospect*

POOR MRS. BUCKHURST WAS NOT fated to profit by the visits of either of her favourite friends on the important morning, the events of which have been recorded in the last chapter; for no sooner had the Duchess watched Ellen, as she passed her with the hurried steps of agitation to the door, than she rung the bell for the old lady's factotum, and, leaving word that she would call again on the morrow, hastened to her carriage, and drove home. She, too, sought the solitude of her own apartment, and never before, perhaps, in the course of her often anxious life, had she so strongly felt the necessity of examining her own heart, her own motives, and her own judgment, as she did then.

Never had there been a more undeviating course of principle and of conduct than that of the Duchess of Rochdale, from the time that her husband had succeeded to the encumbered estates of his father up to the present day. Never had there been a shadow of concealment between them; the Duke stated to her plainly and clearly the position of his affairs, and declared his resolution, if she would assist him in the effort, of nursing his rickety estate till he had restored it to such a state as might secure to their almost worshipped son the affluence of which he had himself been so cruelly deprived.

Far from opposing this purpose, almost desperate, as it appeared, the high-minded Duchess of Rochdale declared herself able and willing to second him in every plan he could propose for such an object, let the privations attending it be what they might. But of these privations it was her earnest wish to bear the largest share herself. The joys of a splendid mansion in London, of a gorgeous equipage, and large establishment, she was fully capable of resigning without a single feeling of regret, as far as she was herself concerned; but when the needful severity of the system of economy which was to achieve the darling object of both rendered it necessary for the Duke to make any sacrifice that seemed to interfere with the dignity demanded by his station, she suffered bitterly, and would certainly, if she alone had been consulted on such occasions, have preferred losing ground a little in the difficult upward path they were treading to seeing her husband exposed to what she thought must wound his feelings. But in such matters no choice was left her. The Duke's earnest desire to accomplish the difficult task he had set himself to perform seemed to increase as he approached its termination; and his noble companion became convinced that the only effectual mode of ensuring his happiness was by assisting in this, not only by every means she perfectly approved, but by every means in her power.

It was just as she had at last reluctantly decided upon withdrawing all opposition to the over-rapid achievement of this object that Lord Pemberton, the idolised object of it, came to the Castle for the purpose of shooting over his father's property near Deepbrook, and of settling some accounts with the steward, which a severe fit of the gout prevented the Duke's coming to manage in person. The young Marquis had neither wish nor intention to mix in the society which the surrounding neighbourhood might have afforded him; for, notwithstanding the tender care with which both his parents sought to guard him from feeling the pressure of the restraint under which they lived, the young man was perfectly well acquainted with the state of his father's affairs; and though heartily wishing that a partial clearing of incumbrances would have satisfied him, and that he had power to convince him that he could himself be well contented to pass through life with about half the income which it was the good Duke's will to recover for him, he too sensibly felt for whose sake all these efforts were made not to yield himself systematically to the family habit of withdrawing greatly from society when in England. He therefore was, in fact, personally unknown to nearly all the country families round the castle, and, with the exception of Mrs. Buckhurst and Mr. Wilcox, had no intention of seeing any one during the sylvan month he proposed to enjoy there.

But it matters little what the projects of man may be; the great and leading features of his destiny will ever be found to depend upon accidents with which his wishes, his will, his intentions, and his resolutions, have little or nothing to do. Lord Pemberton was quite aware that his devoted father, in common with a multitude of other devoted fathers, cherished a project in his heart for the union of his heir with the richly endowed daughter of some noble house. This favourite hope had been the more freely mentioned to the object of it, because as yet no individual fair one had been selected; and the young man therefore had listened to it with the sort of smiling indifference with which such allusions are generally received, as long as they retain the vague uncertainty of general instead of particular recommendation. Nevertheless, it would have been difficult, perhaps, to name half-a-dozen men in England, of any rank or station whatever, who would have submitted with more reluctance to the having a wife chosen for him, or worse still, who would have found more difficulty in teaching his heart to follow his arithmetic, had the selection been left to himself. But as yet there had been no need of protesting seriously against any thing of the kind, for nothing of the kind had ever been directly proposed to him. The Duke of Rochdale, to whom the purpose of leaving his estates unincumbered to his son had long been the principal object of existence, had in his own mind decided upon going steadily on in the process of paying off incumbrances to a certain point, which his often-repeated calculations led him to hope would be attained by the time his son reached the age of twenty-eight; that the young man should then be informed that the period was arrived at which it would be desirable for him to select such a wife as would at the same time be likely to secure his happiness by her moral, intellectual, and personal advantages, while her fortune might realise the natural and reasonable hopes of his family for his forming such a connexion as would prevent their again crippling the estate by giving him an establishment adequate to his rank; which must infallibly be the case if he married without attending to this vitally important consideration. Nothing could sound better, or more conscientious, or more reasonable, than the worthy Duke's thoughts and opinions on this subject, even in his most confidential communications with the wife of his bosom; nevertheless, the real fact was, though he was at the greatest possible distance from being aware of it, that his heart was wholly and solely fixed upon getting the very highest price he could for his reversionary strawberry-leaves; and thus, like all other human beings who suffer themselves to get astride upon one particular hobby, he gallopped away without looking either to the right or to the left, and certainly was in great danger of doing considerable mischief by the way. In all this, the Duchess was to him the most perfectly devoted wife that it was possible for a woman to be,—more so, indeed, a thousand times than if she had fully sympathised in all his views, for then his hobby would have been her hobby, and they might both have gone on galloping together, leaving it difficult to say which would have been first to cry, "Hold, enough!" But his hobby was *not* her hobby. It was his happiness, his peace of mind, his release from the gnawing anxiety which had for so many years destroyed the enjoyment of his life, which was the most passionate wish of her heart; and next after this came the well-being, the happiness, of her son. But never, had she been the sole guardian of it, would she have thought of a wealthy wife as one of the means by which it might have been secured.

But to return to Lord Pemberton. This young man was an excellent son, and quite aware of the more than common debt of gratitude which he owed to both his parents for the sacrifices they were constantly making for his interest, though Heaven knows, poor youth! he would have been more deeply thankful still had their estimate of a sufficiently large, unincumbered rent-roll been more in unison with his own. But at twenty-four years and a half, he had not yet to learn that any hope of this kind would be about as reasonable as a longing to possess the moon; so, to the very best of his power, he aided the family politics, indulging in no expenses that he could with propriety avoid, and at the same time making them feel that he was conscious of no privations. On the important subject of marriage, however, his thoughts were still his own, for never, though the subject had been very often alluded to, had he uttered a single serious word concerning it. Not the less serious, however, were his thoughts upon the subject; and he, too, had made up his mind upon it as well as his noble father. His determination not to put himself and his coronet up for sale was as firmly fixed as that of the

Duke, that the crowning act of his long-sustained and exemplary good management should be the acquisition of some one of the largest female fortunes in England for his son. But, on the other hand, the young man was equally determined never to crush the hopes so long cherished by the indulgence of his own affections, if unhappily they should ever be engaged by one out of the small permitted class. And thus, while the father was eternally meditating on numberless descendants who were all to be restored to the pristine glory of their race by his wisdom, the son was deliberately cherishing a determination that he should never have any descendants at all.

Hitherto his sage resolve never to fall in love had been easily kept, for the taste of Lord Pemberton was at once simple and fastidious, and amidst the very many lovely women he had known abroad he had never yet seen one whom he could have been tempted to make his wife. But the time was rapidly approaching when the lightness of heart, which had hitherto enabled him to enjoy life, despite many circumstances in the manner of it which were not exactly to his taste, was to be lost to him for ever! Not, indeed, that happiness was of necessity lost to him by the adventures which befell him during his month at the Castle, but the gay indifference which rendered one mode of existence very nearly as good as another was never destined to be his again.

The young man's first, and very nearly his only visit in the country, was to the cottage of Mrs. Buckhurst. He was the bearer of a packet of new books for her from his mother, and on the day but one after his arrival he carried them to her with his own hands.

His venerable friend was not alone when he entered; beside her on the sofa, with a volume in her hand, from which she had been reading aloud, sat Ellen Dalton, not then, as we have seen her since, exposed to the lively sallies of her brother's satire, for having attained, unmarried, the age of twenty-three years and a half, but blooming with the delicate freshness of twenty, before sorrow had faded the wild-rose tincture of her cheek, or any deep feeling of any kind had given to the gentle eye that look of thoughtfulness which teaches us to know at a single glance that the first rush of young hilarity is past. The Duchess was quite right when she said, that lovely as Ellen now was, she had been lovelier still.

She was so when the doomed young Marquis first saw her sitting beside old Mrs. Buckhurst on the sofa. But the head of Lord Pemberton was not accustomed to run upon thoughts of falling in love; no such idea occurred to him now; and though the words, "Oh! what a pretty creature!" might be said to have passed through his mind, no feeling was suggested by them that at all interfered with the very affectionate greeting passing between him and the very oldest friend he could remember.

"How kind this is of you, my dear boy!" exclaimed the delighted old lady, pressing his hand between both hers; "and your dear mother! has she quite recovered the sad attack she wrote me word of?"

An old lady between seventy and eighty years of age is very likely to know a great variety of people whom her young friends have never heard of, and Ellen thought that the most obliging thing she could do would be to go on reading her book to herself, while the handsome young sportsman (for Lord Pemberton was *en habit de chasse*) and the old lady discussed together the various distant acquaintance of whom she knew nothing. But Mrs. Buckhurst had no inclination to leave her beautiful favourite thus in the back-ground, and the young people were introduced to each other. But little conversation, however, passed between them, for Mrs. Buckhurst had, in truth, a great many questions to ask, which the young man answered with good-humoured and affectionate loquacity, and his visit had already been a long one before it occurred to him that the squire's fair daughter (who was perfectly well known to him by name) would have cause to think him a very churlish neighbour if he exchanged not a single word with her after being introduced. He accordingly addressed to her a civil inquiry after the health of her family, and as to the *statu quo* of sundry of the village aristocracy, whose names he happened to remember. To all this Ellen answered without blushing, or faltering, or losing one atom of the gentle sedateness of her beautiful features, although the querist *was* the oft-talked-of young heir of the Castle. "I wish," thought Lord Pemberton, as he idly shouldered his gun, and took his solitary walk homewards, "I wish we were not obliged so completely to give up England. If that lovely, graceful creature be a fair specimen of a country squire's daughter, the *elégantes* of every court in Europe might take a lesson from them." But this was all; Lord Pemberton ate a very reasonably good dinner, and slept soundly; so, indisputably, he was not in love. But unfortunately, for the *sans souci* of the squire's daughter, and the Duke's son, their first was not their last meeting.

Well has it been said that to be forewarned is to be forearmed. Had Lord Pemberton been told, that upon arriving at Deepbrook, he should discover one of the village young ladies to be exactly every thing which he had heretofore rejoiced to find that other (not eligible) young ladies were not—had he been assured that under the shelter of a little straw bonnet, and with no richer decoration than a very plain muslin frock, he should find the only woman upon whose head he would ever wish to place his coronet—had all this been clearly revealed to him, he would most certainly have struggled hard to keep out of the danger. But, as it was, he never struggled at all; and the fact of his having fixed his affections for ever, and for ever, upon one whom he dared not hope to marry, came upon him as unexpectedly as if the operation had been performed at once by a *coup de fusil*.

It would be bootless to follow this unfortunate attachment through all the lingering stages of ill-founded hope and bitter disappointment, or to relate how unreasonably, despite all his knowledge of his father's purposes and steadfast resolution, the unhappy young man had been led to believe it possible that, when he confessed how irrevocably his affections were engaged, the purposes might be abandoned, and the resolution give way. The melancholy affair concluded at last by a very solemn promise being given by both the young people that the health of the poor tortured Duke's mind and body should never be again put in peril by any mention of their union. This tremendous promise had been granted to the entreaties of the Duchess, who had, on her knees, implored her distracted son to spare her the agony of seeing his father die of a broken heart. It is but justice to the Duke, however, to mention, that although this terrible sacrifice was made for his sake, he was not himself a party to the heart-breaking process by which it had been obtained. The Duchess, in her unbounded devotion, had spared him this, and had never for a moment repeated the part she had taken, for the purpose of securing his tranquillity, till she had seen and conversed with Ellen Dalton.

# XXXI

*Some strong opinions uttered by Captain Maxwell in the presence of his daughter, the effect of which proves that in these days old gentlemen should be cautious in talking politics before young ladies—Miss Martha Maxwell is obliged to consult a lawyer*

NOTWITHSTANDING THE LONG RETROSPECT WHICH has kept us during the preceding chapter from Jessie, the subject must be returned to again hereafter, as being connected with her story, although it seems not to have any immediate influence on her destiny. Neither, though we have quitted Ellen, can we immediately return to look after my hapless heroine, till we have watched the efforts made in her favour by the most zealous friend that fate had left her. Martha Maxwell had, indeed, not forgotten Jessie, nor did she yet despair of obtaining for her the atonement which had been suggested to her thoughts during the first violent burst of indignation which her full discovery of young Dalton's treachery had excited. The intelligent reader will probably long ago have guessed at what was passing in the eccentric young lady's mind when she so skilfully contrived to obtain a promise of marriage from him, without the disagreeable reciprocity of giving him one in return. This project still continued to hold the first place in her thoughts; although the many hours of reflection which she had given to it had certainly suggested various difficulties as to bringing her plot to a successful conclusion, which had not occurred to her inexperienced queer little head, when she first so boldly conceived it. How to find out the degree in which the promise signed by Dalton might be made to terrify him into making a liberal provision for the child and its deluded mother was the great difficulty. It would be doing great injustice to that portion of her intellect which most nearly approached to common sense, were it supposed that she had ever contemplated the possibility of getting Frederic to marry Jessie, because he had signed a promise of marriage intended for herself. Martha Maxwell knew better than that; she knew better, indeed, than to desire it. Reasons enough there most certainly were for her feeling the deepest indignation at the young man's perfidy, which had been shewn with equal baseness, both by the marriage he had sought, and that which he had perjured himself to avoid; yet she had no wish that her friend Ellen, or the worthy squire either, should have the terrible task assigned them of receiving into the family a girl who, however greatly to be pitied for the delusions practised against her, had disgraced herself by the culpable weakness with which she had yielded to them. What she did wish was to terrify young Dalton into providing for her.

Notwithstanding Captain Maxwell's very tender love for his young daughter, his care and watchfulness did not reach the refinement of keeping from her ears various village anecdotes which had been canvassed with a good deal of warmth by the worthy veteran in the common sitting-room, and all of which had tended to inspire his kind-hearted daughter with a profound abhorrence for that very tremendous specimen of modern legislation which, while charily sheltering the seducer from every annoyance or inconvenience of any kind in his licentious amours, throws with unmitigated vengeance the whole burden of retribution on the frail creature seduced. Often had Martha listened to the indignant eloquence of her father (for on that theme the blunt veteran could be really eloquent) as he pointed out to all whom he thought likely to listen to him the impolitic as well as hateful cruelty of this *most uneven-handed* legislation. The severest penalty that had ever been exacted by the law, so unhappily repealed, was to oblige a man to make that woman his wife whom he had made the mother of his child, and thus to sanctify by the laws of man the tie already sanctified by nature. Yet even this enactment, as the clever-headed old sailor observed—even this enactment, with all its healthful severity, might be avoided, only too easily, by the payment of a small portion of the libertine father's wages. But how did the law stand now? The frail creature, who had no defence against her own love, and that of its dear object strong enough to combat the hope that she should become his wife, is doomed, when that hope, justified

"By all the vows that ever lover spoke,"

fails her, to become answerable in the eye of the law for all the consequences of the mutual sin!

"Setting aside the obvious and horrible injustice of thus making one responsible for a fault committed by both, let us look," he would say, "at the wisdom, justice, and humanity of the choice which has selected the woman as the sacrifice. Did any man ever commit this offence, being beguiled thereto by the promise of the woman to marry him? Did any man, having committed it, find himself excluded thereby from the possibility of earning by his labour the same wages that he had earned before? But how is it with the wretched woman? Alas, poor wretch! she is the victim of her lover, the victim of the virtuous abhorrence of her fault in those who once employed her, but will employ her no more—the victim of the short-sighted policy of her country, which, while hoping (vainly) to save a few yearly shillings from the poor-rates, has decreed that a weak woman (that is to say a weak *poor* woman) who has committed this sin shall atone for it by being trampled in the dust, imprisoned in a workhouse with her wretched offspring till driven from it to seek food for both by labour, that the most respectable part of her own sex refuse her upon principle! What is the obvious refuge of such a wretch as this? What, but the hiding herself among a class who know not shame, and cannot, as she approaches, drop the awful veil which divides the woman protected by law from her who is its branded victim? And how fares it the while with the privileged seducer? Why, he, being of the sex which make the laws, is so snugly sheltered by them that there is no earthly reason whatsoever why he should not go on in the course he has begun, and thank the gods that he is not a woman."

Such notions as these, pretty frequently repeated in the hearing of Martha, had gone far towards making her think that if in days of yore every English maid and matron felt it her duty to testify her abhorrence of the offence from which they vaunted themselves more free than the females of any other nation on the globe, the violent change which had taken place in the law of the land called loudly for a corresponding change in them. It was no longer reprobation, but mercy that was called for towards the erring creatures whom this new-born tyranny had selected as the helpless scape-goats of the whole community; a feeling this, by the way, which however just, holy, and natural, may prove in the end of very doubtful advantage to the female morality of England.

How is it possible that, with the Bible before us, we can forget those words both of mercy and rebuke, "He that is without sin among you let him first cast a stone at her?" Do these words never occur to the legislators who framed the new poor-law? Let us hope not, for it is better to disobey from oblivion than defiance.

No such oblivion, however, rested on the sense of Martha Maxwell. She had read the Bible, she had listened to her father, and knew, almost as well as poor Jessie herself, the whole history of Frederic Dalton's conduct towards her. She contrived also pretty accurately to guess by what sort of reasoning the young gentleman had persuaded himself that what the law held to be blameless no individual had any right to condemn, and how comfortably he had convinced himself, by the admirable *lex talionis* species of morality, so popular with his class, that there could be no harm in doing that which did him no harm in return.

These reasonings and guesses, joined to what required no guessing at all, namely, his abominable conduct towards herself, did certainly create altogether a very strong desire to punish him and to assist Jessie. It was for this she had obtained his written promise, and for this that she continued to torment him by innumerable tricks, and seemingly playful caprices, in order to evade his remonstrances, which gradually increased in vehemence, upon her unjust detention of a document which, by their contract, she had no right to retain unless she gave him another to the same effect. This sort of struggle went on for many weeks, greatly to her amusement, and equally to his annoyance, for, as he dared not for his own sake betray the secret which existed between them, he had no means whatever of bringing her to reason upon the subject. He had, indeed, of late been led to suspect that she would care much less were it actually made public than he should; and this idea kept him more in order than any other could have done, till at length, irritated past endurance by the sort of smile with which she received the most peremptory demand he had ever yet ventured to make, he had the great impudence to revenge it by saying, "It is very well, Miss Maxwell. I see you are determined to provoke me in this matter beyond my endurance. I shall trouble you with no more applications. The next demand for that paper, so basely obtained, will be made to you by Mr. Lewis."

This was a knavish speech, but one by no means likely to sleep in the ear of Martha Maxwell. It was spoken at the very moment that the young man ought to have been wishing her good night upon leaving her mother's drawing-room after a small evening party, and Martha retired to her pillow with it fresh in her thoughts, and did not close her eyes in sleep till she had taken hem resolution as to the manner in which she should heed the threat she had received.

It was now the latter end of December, and among those who had arrived to partake of the Christmas festivities at Deepbrook was the young barrister, Henry Mortimer, between whom and Martha Maxwell there had arisen a sort of friendly intimacy, wonderfully little like any ordinary kind of flirtation, but which nevertheless led to their dancing together oftener, and talking together more, than either of them did with any other of the little society. The sort of quizzing which was inevitably seen to follow upon this appeared to be a matter of perfect indifference to them both, and that it was so, no sooner became generally evident, than the quizzing, of course, ceased, and the friends talked and walked together as much as they liked without any body's thinking it worth their while to notice it. In this state of things it was natural enough that Martha Maxwell, when consulting her pillow upon the alarming threat of Frederic Dalton, should remember that her friend Mortimer was a lawyer as well as Mr. Lewis, and might be both able and willing to help her in the rather difficult business she had in hand. But to obtain this assistance it was necessary to tell him a strange story, some parts of which, perhaps, she rather disliked to dwell upon; but Martha very speedily conquered all such idle feelings, and finding, or making, an early opportunity for the conversation she sought, she lost no time in preparing the mind of her auditor by any elaborate preface, but, having resolved to speak plainly, immediately set about doing so.

"I wish you to give me some legal advice, Henry Mortimer; will you do it?"

"Willingly, Martha Maxwell," he replied, laughing, "if your questions be not too profound and puzzling."

"I will make them as plain as I can," she replied, colouring slightly. "You know Mr. Frederic Dalton?"

"Yes, Miss Maxwell, I know him," replied the young lawyer, rather dryly; "I know him as much as I wish to do!"

"That is unfortunate, Mr. Mortimer," she rejoined, "because I suspect that I am going to make you know him better. Do not blame me," she added, again colouring more deeply than before, "if I am forced to speak more plainly to you than any girl would wish to do; but I cannot help it."

She then narrated, as shortly and cleverly as it was well possible to do, not the history of Mr. Frederic Dalton and Jessie Phillips, but her own history, including her former conviction of the young gentleman's attachment to herself, his profession of love, and subsequent proposal of elopement. Then followed her sudden suspicion of his sincerity, her visit to Ellen, and her consequent determination to beguile him into giving her such a written promise of marriage as might enable her to compel him to make some sort of atonement to the unhappy girl he had destroyed. She drew the paper from her pocket-book, as she concluded this statement, and placed it in the hand of Henry Mortimer.

"This is a promise," said the young lawyer, after he had examined it, "made to no one, and therefore clearly not available to any one."

"I quite know that," returned Martha, endeavouring to conceal a smile; "but *he* does not, and I think, if you will tell me how to do it, I may frighten him into believing that, if he does not provide for this poor deluded girl, his conduct will be made public by her claiming the promises he has a thousand times made her, and exhibiting this paper as a proof of it."

"You have loved this man, Miss Maxwell," said Henry Mortimer, gravely, "and you have devised this scheme to revenge his having treated you with insincerity."

"No, sir, no! You do me vile injustice if you can really think for a single instant that such are my motives," replied Martha, with vehement indignation. "You fancied that you knew Frederic Dalton, and you fancied that you knew me. You are equally mistaken in both suppositions. And I, too, fancied that I knew you, but I doubt it now,—I very greatly doubt it."

"Say not so, Martha Maxwell, but listen to me calmly," replied the young man, gently. "Perhaps I have only accused you, because I wished to hear your vindication. It is impossible not to perceive that your very conduct in this matter lays you open to the construction that I have put upon it; but I am much more likely to admit that this construction is utterly false than that I should perform the duty of a friend if I failed to make you perceive the thoughtless levity of your conduct."

"Thank Heaven!" cried Martha, bursting into tears as she spoke; "thank Heaven! I have not been deceived in you. How like the lightning flash from heaven is a word of truth when uttered bravely, brightly, fearlessly! That you are right in your judgment, Henry Mortimer, I feel as strongly as you do yourself; and yet you have blundered, young gentleman, in your interpretation of my motives."

"I suspect, Martha, that I might with great propriety repeat your exclamation, and thank Heaven that I was not deceived in you," said young Mortimer, in a tone that perfectly satisfied the comforted culprit that she had not lost her friend, by the free confession of what she now truly felt to have been very thoughtless conduct, to say the least of it; but, this somewhat rough opening of their consultation over, the subject of it was discussed between them fully, calmly, and reasonably; and before the conversation ended the young lawyer became so deeply interested in the business, and so perfectly awakened to the fact that the motives of poor Jessie's rash young champion deserved more sympathy than condemnation, that his parting words promised her his most cordial assistance in endeavouring to draw some good from the Quixotic effort she had made to obtain justice.

# XXXII

*Jessie makes some discoveries respecting the workhouse which appear to have escaped the observation of English law-givers—some practical observations from the inmates—the blessings of an uniform law impartially administered*

WHILE MARTHA MAXWELL AND HER new ally proceed in their difficult business of converting to practical utility a piece of madcap folly, we will return to look at Jessie's condition in the workhouse. Many terrible weeks had now passed over her since, with the overstrained resolution to *endure,* which arose partly from remorse, and partly from despair, she had entered its walls, determined that nothing should force a murmur from her lips, or a rebellious groan from her heart. As far as her moral condition was concerned, nothing would have been more salutary than the last interview with her cold-blooded, unprincipled lover. Till then she knew him not. Till then the wild visions concerning both his character and her own, which had equally been her ruin, still held their place in her mind, though robbed of their beguiling brightness by sufferings, which as yet, however, had only convinced her "that the course of true love never did run smooth," and by no means that her silly ignorance had transformed a designing libertine into an angel of light, and a poor little village sempstress into a heroine. But all this folly was cured at once and for ever by the expression of the villain's eye, and the tone of his voice, as he offered her the gratuity which was intended to atone for the injury he had done. Had this sudden cure of all her illusions been less complete, it might have been more fatal, for then some touch of softness, some lingering tenderness of regret, might have mixed with it, leaving her with the killing canker of disappointed love at her heart, which, while it lasts, is often felt to be a heavier woe than many which have less of fancy in them. But no such softening emotions were left to relax the firmness of courage with which the abashed and penitent Jessie determined to endure the consequences of her fault. It might be truly said that she deserved to suffer, for so only could she be fitted in her own judgment for the forgiveness which she still ventured to hope the mercy of Heaven might accord to her penitence and patience. But all this referred to her own sufferings, her own hardships and privations, and her own endurance of all the discomfort which she anticipated from such charity as she expected to meet at the Union workhouse.

But the imagination of Jessie had shewn itself more skilful and alert in finding noble qualities with which to endow her lover than in figuring to herself how far her utter helplessness and destitution may be pushed below the ordinary level of human misery, where the engine employed for the purpose is *a Central Board*, whose action is deemed perfect, when its tremendous engine is in full activity, while those who are at work at the screw waste not their labour and strength in looking out to watch what its effect may be on all the objects to which its power extends.

The first unexpected misery which sufficed to shake her courage was the finding herself shut up with, and constantly surrounded by, some of the vilest and most thoroughly abandoned women that the lowest degradation of vice could produce. One of the nineteen parishes which formed the Deepbrook union was on the coast, and included in its population many of that wretched class of females which a seaport town is sure to produce. When sickness, accident, or age, drove any of these miserable creatures to such extremity of want as to leave them no resource but the parish, they were immediately consigned to the Union workhouse; and deeply would many of those whose vote and interest have aided the arrangement which makes this necessary, very deeply and profoundly would they be shocked, could they be made aware of the tremendous mischief which such Union produces. Jessie had made up her mind to believe that she should herself be the most unhappy individual there, but never had it occurred to her that the fellowship to which she was so freely consigning herself was not only that of paupers, but of prostitutes. Nor could she be greatly blamed for this want of foresight. Older and more experienced persons than Jessie might have failed, while meditating upon the miseries of a rural workhouse, to have anticipated such companionship as making part of them. And strange indeed it is, and not over easy of belief to those who take not the trouble of inquiring into facts, that virtuous Englishwomen, against whom rests no shadow of suspicion as to the respectability of their conduct as wives and mothers, should be liable to such association, only because sickness or misfortune have deprived them of the power of finding food and shelter by their labour. Any one who will give time and trouble for the inquiry may still find in every village of England honest, virtuous, hard-working females, who, in case their power of labour fails, have no resource but the workhouse against certain death by starvation, but who are as morally undeserving of having such association forced upon them as the noblest and most justly honoured matron in the land. IF THIS BE TRUE, let every Christian in the country ask himself if "further amendment" be not wanted.

The discovery that she was consigned to the companionship of such associates was indeed terrible to Jessie in every way. She thought less of the fault she had herself committed, and of the patient submission with which it was her duty to bear its consequences, than of the hard injustice which forced her, in her desolate poverty, to listen to the light jestings of hardened sin, instead of the solemn yet healing meditations of her own conscience. Vainly did she strive to withdraw herself from the destruction with which their hateful language seemed to surround her; they had but to guess at the feelings which made her turn from them in order to make them find the pursuing her with their conversation the very best amusement they could enjoy. It was in vain that she repeated to herself, "I have deserved it all;" the Magdalen humility by which she strove to reconcile herself to offended Heaven was no longer genuine and sincere. She did not deserve the degradation to which she was now exposed, and she knew it.

That such feelings are, have been, and will be, found to exist beneath the loathed roof of a Union workhouse, will be doubted only by those who have never examined into their interior at all, or have so distorted their moral vision, by looking at the whole theory and practice of the arrangement as a great national measure required for the welfare of the country, as positively to have no power of perception left for the minor details, and all the fearful mass of suffering they exhibit. As to the half, or quarter of a dozen, instances where a wealthy, aristocratic neighbourhood is prevented from being too thickly populated by the wide-spreading domain which surrounds each residence, they cannot in common honesty be quoted (as they often are), as instances of the excellent effects of the new poor-law. They want no poor-law at all, and have no more to do with the question than the arrangements of my Lady ★ ★ ★ ★ 's almshouse, with those of the stys erected for such as work in the cotton-mills of this rich and prosperous country.

It is very difficult to touch on any of the most mischievous points of this ill-digested law without being led to dwell upon them till the thread of the story is dropped and almost forgotten; but this will be considered as excusable by all who take a real interest in the subject, and for the rest,—their disapprobation must be patiently endured.

Paler and thinner grew the cheek of the poor penitent as the miserable weeks passed over her; and in some sort it was better for her that it should be so, for, as her health and strength faded away, her beauty faded too, and there was more than one among those who delighted to torment her who certainly loved her not the better for her beauty. Two wretched creatures, who a few short years before had been perhaps almost as lovely as herself, but who now, like miserable wrecks, had nothing left of all their gorgeous beauty save what might just suffice to warn all who beheld them to avoid the rocks upon which they had perished—two wretched creatures, from the seaport above-mentioned, had made Jessie the principal object of their attention from the moment she was (charitably!) permitted to enter the common abode of the female paupers. It was certainly with no kindly feelings that they contemplated her. Notwithstanding the grievous fault she had committed, there was in her whole aspect a something of shyness and of decent modesty which was as irksome to their sight as gold that can never be recovered to the impotently longing gaze of the spendthrift who had wantonly cast it from him. Her "misfortune," of course, became a favourite theme of gossip, and, of course, also continued, to be so the longer because the partner of her guilt was unknown. This was the point on which the girls from Shipport-town best loved to torment her. "That's a darnation bad job, isn't it, miss, that not letting a young lady make lawful oath?" said the elder of the two, following Jessie to the very farthest and darkest corner of the gloomy room. In this corner she had often sought shelter from their ribald talk by placing herself between two suffering and soured old souls. who, from being destitute of exactly every thing which their miserable infirmities required, never spoke but to utter some snarling complaint, which it was more easy to forgive in theory than to endure in practice. Here she thought that none would choose to follow her; but she was mistaken. Caroline Watts had a tongue that two months of workhouse gruel had not sufficed to silence; she was hungry and she was miserable, but still she could talk, although such of her present companions as had listened to her when she first arrived declared that she would not go on much longer so, for that nobody did, and that it was easy to see that her "gab" was neither so glib nor so strong as at first. "Never you mind her, Jessie, she'll be dumb-foundered at last, you'll see," said the crippled woman who had watched the effect of the board and lodging of the workhouse upon many a new-comer since her own arrival there. "She won't have strength to last on that way much longer."

This was an unfortunate observation, for the headstrong Caroline only snapped her fingers in defiance, exclaiming, with a frightful laugh, "Hold your false tongue, you nasty cripple! It isn't for such an ugly creature as you to guess what a sight of starving it takes to break the spirit of a real Shipport-town beauty!" And again she attacked Jessie with a multitude of tormenting questions and conjectures respecting the man whose perfidy, as she justly enough conjectured, had sent her there. On this point, indeed, it was not likely that such a one as Caroline Watts should be mistaken. Most certain is it that, on all subjects which concern the earthly existence of man, "experience can attain to something like prophetic strain," and it is highly probable that if such an actor, and looker-on, as this wretched girl could (without corrupting their imagination) turn forth to the innocent the hard and heartless PRINCIPLE upon which the destruction of those once as innocent as themselves was effected, the warning would produce a deeper effect than all the brightest examples in the world.

But the terrible lore of Caroline was not now offered in a way to profit her hearers—the old were shocked and disgusted, while the young, though appalled, were contaminated. To whichever class the reader may belong, the language of the reprobate shall not be recorded to offend him; yet was there one observation made by this same Caroline which had enough of truth and practical wisdom to redeem it from oblivion. "They pretend to think," said she, with a bitter sneer, "that they will save some of their precious parish money by making a poor girl's bad luck too hard for her to bear, and that they shall keep her, that way, from bringing babies to them (kind tender creters!) to be nursed. But they are fools for their pains, and so they will find, whether they are honest enough to say so or no. In the old times, when a boy and a girl wasn't too bad, and too miserable, to be past caring for any thing, both the one and the other had something they were afraid of, that, in two cases out of three, maybe, kept 'em out of mischief. But now our precious gentlefolks have been clever enough to find out that by leaving one to suffer for both, and letting the t'other go free, they have made the girl's share too bad to bear, and so they shall get quit of the paying, either by the poor wench killing herself or her child, or both. A nice charity scheme, isn't it? And don't ye think now that God A'mighty must be unaccountable pleased with them for their goodness? But for all that, miss, they'll find themselves the wrong side the post with their cleverness; if they do not, my name's not Carry. I know, if they don't, that a girl's more like to go wrong, when a man has got no particular reason himself for wishing to go right, than when the thoughts of having the two shillings a-week to pay was before his eyes, as well as the plague of a bad name, and a baby, before hers." And then again she fell to teasing her for the name of "the rogue," alleging, in excuse for her curiosity, that there might be mischief to him in sending the story of his shabby, skulking cowardice over the country, "and that would be vengeance."

But to all this Jessie rarely replied, save by a gentle shake of the head; and often, while placed on the high, hard, narrow slip of wood which surrounded the walls, while her aching limbs sustained her with difficulty in a sitting position, she would close her eyes, and feign to be asleep, in order to escape the necessity of appearing to listen when she was thus spoken to.

Had these wretched girls, or any females at all resembling them, been her only companions, her heart would probably have speedily grown callous to the misery of all around her, and her feelings, with a sort of hardened apathy, would have become concentrated upon her own sufferings, with less of sensibility than selfishness. But from this she was saved by the tender, gentle, womanly pity, inspired by the eloquent, though almost silent, sorrow of one heart-broken individual amidst the throng. This poor woman had entered the workhouse about a week after Jessie; she was from one of the distant parishes of the wide union, and therefore a stranger to all the Deepbrook inmates. Her story had nothing very extraordinary in it, and may be briefly told. Within a month of her entry into the workhouse, herself and her husband had rented a comfortable decent tenement, and the were held in peculiarly high respect by their neighbours, from the respectable regularity of their lives, their tidy habits, and their ceaseless industry. They had not been guilty of that most deplorable imprudence, an early marriage, but both remained in the service of the farmer, with whom the husband continued to work till he could work no more, long enough to save from their moderate rural wages sufficient money to furnish their cottage decently, and to set them off with a sow and a litter of pigs. They had one child, a sturdy, hopeful little fellow, who was a wonderfully light impediment to a little fine washing, by which his notable mother contrived to add to their cottage comforts; and, in short, they were an admirable specimen of what English labourers used to be. The cause of the dreadful change in their condition was one that no prudence on their part could have foreseen or averted. Their dwelling was at no great distance from that of the village baker, whose too well-dried premises caught fire one windy night, and were not only burnt to the very foundation in less than an hour, but sent forth on the blast materials of destruction sufficient to insure a similar fate to three or four cottages which stood near. William White's was one of them; and so complete was its consumption, that his wife, their precious child, and a small quantity of wearing apparel, was all he could save from the flames. Nor was this effected without very grievous injury to both the poor man and the child. The whole family were profoundly asleep when the fire seized their dwelling, nor did the smothering smoke awake them till the roof had caught fire, and the first intimation of danger came not till every hope of escape seemed almost desperate. It is needless to describe the minute particulars of all the dangers they passed through; it is enough to say that the poor man had been miserably burnt, but not dangerously, and that the child also had received a painful injury on one of its arms. But every thing, furniture, clothes, pigs,—nay, even the little crops in their diminutive garden, were lost, gone, and destroyed for ever. Had poor White's cottage stood alone, or had he been the only one in the service of his worthy master who had suffered by the conflagration, it is probable that he, his wife, and child, would all have found shelter at the farmer's house; but as matters stood this was impossible. No less than four other labourers employed on the extensive farm were burnt out of their dwellings on that unhappy night, and therefore the assistance that could be afforded was equally divided among all. It was speedily evident that the only resource of White, who, though in no danger of death, was utterly incapable of labour, must be the workhouse, unless they could prevail upon the board of guardians to break through the rule, so strictly adhered to at Deepbrook, of refusing out-door relief to any. So many instances had recently occurred there in which this question had been canvassed, and so successfully had the letter of the law been pleaded against the joint eloquence of humanity and common sense, that little hope was entertained by the guardians of White's immediate neighbourhood that any relaxation would be permitted in his favour. There was, indeed, one case, and that too of recent date, in which this regulation (equally wise when discreetly adhered to, as absurd when persevered in, with no discretion at all)—there was one case in which, greatly to the surprise of most people, this ordinarily strict regulation was dispensed with, and it was this which gave the neighbours of poor White the courage to ask for equal indulgence for him. But this was one of the many instances in which those who chose to use their eyes might see that the boasted uniformity of the law was much more easily traced in its cruelty than its justice. The drunken fellow in the High Street at Deepbrook, who obtained this indulgence when he broke his limb in a scuffle, had one or two bullying friends at the board, and among them was Mr. Baxter, who, by some means or other, contrived to convince

Mr. Lewis that he would be acting unwisely if he did not give him a helping hand on this occasion; and a helping hand he did give him, by quietly hinting to Mr. Mortimer that this was just a fitting opportunity to prove that, steady as they were in their adherence to the letter of the admirable law to which they were going to owe such an immense increase of national prosperity, they were still willing to mitigate the sternness of its justice whenever a proper occasion occurred. The gentle-tempered Mr. Mortimer was only too happy to find an opportunity of shewing that he had no sort of individual partiality for severity of any kind, and being as utterly a stranger to the character of the man thus favoured, as if he had newly descended from the moon, his fiat at once sanctioned the order: but this occurrence, though naturally enough it had created a hope of success in the friends of William White, was in effect exceedingly against him, for, on the one hand, Mr. Lewis and his co-sticklers for "the law," shrunk from the idea of confounding the late exception with the general rule, while, on the other hand, Mr. Dalton, Captain Maxwell, and. others, who thought with them on the subject, and who had been recently defeated on sundry occasions when they had struggled hard to obtain temporary out-door relief for individuals with whose circumstances and character they were well acquainted, were by no means disposed to accord greater indulgence to objects unknown to them than had been granted to those for whom they felt interested. So the petition of William White was rejected, and himself, his wife, and suffering child, admitted into the house.

# XXXIII

*Cases in which the laws of nature and of God are made to give way before the wise and admirable regulations of "The Bill"—a rather favourite specimen of eloquence from a female magnate—an old wife's blundering interpretation of the marriage ceremony—religious consolation*

It was the condition of this poor man's wife which preserved the heart of Jessie Phillips from sinking into the last dark abyss of selfish misery. Susan White, among many other merits, had that most "excellent quality in woman," a gentle temper, a quality which, like its first-born offspring, Mercy, "blesseth him that gives and him that takes;" and this truth was proved in the tiny cottage of William and Susan White as satisfactorily as it ever could have been in the most important theatre that the world ever furnished. But gentle hearts, having more of heaven than of earth in them, are but ill fitted to endure the buffetings of this nether world, and often seem to pay a penalty in the hour when suffering comes upon those they love, for the happiness they have been permitted to confer in better days. But alas! for poor Susan White, her present misery arose not only from knowing that all she most dearly loved were in pain and misery, but that she was not near to soothe and comfort them. The lacerated father and child were, of course, lodged in the hospital, and the still more suffering mother and wife was, of course, also forbidden to approach either of the different chambers where they lay. Poor Susan, practically speaking, knew as little about the new poor-law as the majority of those whose voices had created it; and it was for many hours difficult to make her comprehend that the law of the land, while extending its munificence to the destitute, prohibited the approach of the faithful wedded wife to the mattress of

J Leech

her suffering husband, and of the doting mother to the pillow of her wailing child.

"To-morrow then, or the day after?" sobbed the agonised mother; "may I see them to-morrow? For the love of God, let me see my poor crippled husband! If you are a woman, let me see my child!"

This prayer was addressed to Mrs. Dempster, who, for some cause or other, had entered among the female paupers a few hours after the admission of Susan White. At first she seemed inclined to return no answer at all, except, indeed, the sort of merry grin with which she habitually received all remonstrances from her pauper subjects; but just as she reached the door, she turned, and said,—"Listen to me, Mrs. New-come, and if you are a wise woman you will remember what I say. We must have no noisy maundering here. Mind that. There's a many governess, ladies, if all is true as I hear tell, what don't allow of the least bit of talk at all going on among the paupers, and she pokes the very first what speaks into the cage, to teach 'em the way to be silent. But my worstest of enimies can't say as I ever did any sich cruelty as that; I knows the vally that a woman's tongue is to her, and I don't want to keep 'em, beggars as they be, so contrary to natur as that. So, when I aint by to be pestered by it, I never says a word about their talking; but then, you must please to observe, they must never let me hear 'em, either in the walls or out of 'em. And that is just what you'll be wise to remember, 'cause you see we've got our cage as well as other folks. So don't aggravate me, that's all."

And with these words she departed, leaving the unhappy woman standing in the middle of the room, with every eye fixed upon her, and not a few lips curling into a hard smile at the "set-down" she had got. Had these same women, who now seemed positively to feel relief from having the tedium of their imprisonment varied by this scene, witnessed an equal degree of suffering while under the humanising influences of heaven's sweet unfettered air, and with the consciousness that they stand as free under its glorious vault as the happy herds that lowed around, or the gay birds that soared above them, they would not thus have found a solace in a fellow-creature's misery. But the glowing furnace does not more surely harden the pottery that is placed within it than does the unnatural condition of a union workhouse harden the hearts of those exposed to it.

"What's the use of sobbing and howling?" said one "I haven't set eyes upon my husband for almost a year, and yet there he is, I suppose, somewhere or other, within a few yards of me. And I don't expect ever to get sight of um again," she continued, while the trembling of her lip and voice shewed that she was not wholly turned to stone; "for both together, work as we will, we can't earn above half a crown a week in the luckiest of times, and that wouldn't find us in clothing, lodging, firing, and food; and not one single sixpence would they give to help us out of doors. So here we be for life, old Thomas on one side the house, and I on t'other; and yet we have stood side by side together, loving and kind enough, for above forty years, since Parson Buckhurst told us that we were man and wife, and that no man was to put us asunder. But that's all changed now, and they tell us it's just their bounden duty to do it, which seems odd too, considering the book that the parson read it out of."

There was little consolation in this for poor White; indeed, she could hardly be said to hear it, for, though she ceased to sob while the old woman addressed her, she put her hands before her eyes, as if to shut out every object, that she might turn in spirit towards those whom her very soul yearned to watch over and console.

There was something in this deep and quiet sorrow that went to the heart of Jessie. She felt herself, both from the length of time she had been among the miserable and degraded crew, and also from the consciousness of what brought her there, unworthy to address the wretched, but not dishonoured, wife and mother who stood before her; but she fixed her languid, yet still beautiful, eyes upon her, with such a look of gentleness and pity, that the poor woman, as she caught the glance, instinctively moved towards the place where she was sitting, and quietly sat down beside her, but without either of them speaking a word. This was enough, however, in that dismal desert, which seemed barren of all human sympathy, to establish a sort of acquaintance between them, which, despite Jessie's conscious shyness, and poor Susan's aching heart, was not long before it manifested itself in words.

"Do I crowd you, young woman?" demanded Susan, in a whisper.

"Oh no!" answered Jessie, in the same tone; "I only wish I could make the bench more comfortable for you."

This was again quite enough to establish between them a more kind and friendly feeling than existed between any other individuals there. Yes, this feeling decidedly existed, and each would willingly, nay, gladly, have done for the other any service within the reach of their miserable condition. But, alas! poor souls, the power both of giving and receiving comfort seemed palsied within them; and they felt it, even as they gazed in each other's pale spiritless face, and inwardly murmured, "Poor soul! she cannot be so very wretched as I!"

But by degrees the human feeling warmed, and they began in a low voice to talk together, for there was enough of sympathy between their hearts for each to feel that, if she spoke at all, it was the other only that she wished should hear her. But, oh! how great was now the advantage of the innocent woman over her that had sinned! It was something like a solace for Susan to speak of her husband and her child, and to consult the young stranger, who had been longer in that terrible prison than herself, as to what hope there might be of her being permitted to see them. But how could any solace arise to Jessie from talking of her situation? Alas! the more the words and manner of her new acquaintance impressed her with a favourable idea of her character, the more did she shrink from exposing her own unworthiness. But she was spared the task of being her own historian, for her gibing, jeering, tormentors of Shipport took care that all they knew and all they guessed concerning her should receive as much publicity as they could give it; and pitiable was the agony with which Jessie Phillips hid her face in her hands, while she knew that the ears of the virtuous wife beside her were receiving the knowledge of her shame. Excepting during the terrible moments in which she had stood before the "altered eyes" of the Miss Lewises, she had never suffered so keenly from the degradation consequent upon her fault; and the punishment thus endured went far deeper into her soul than any which the mere bodily hardships of the workhouse had brought. The drooping head, the averted eye, the stifled groan of the unhappy girl, were rather instinctively, than by reflection, received as a mitigation of her fault by the gentle-spirited Susan White; and there was so true a touch of pity in the sound of her voice, when she again spoke to poor Jessie, that it soothed, though it could not console her; and, sadly unequal as were their claims to respect, there existed between them from that time forth, as long as they remained together, the sort of kindly feeling which accompanies pity when deeply and sincerely felt by hearts not hardened by a too busy commerce with the world. By tacit consent they kept side by side in their melancholy idleness, and every word voluntarily uttered by either was addressed to the other. Both were benefited by this intercourse, but Susan White incomparably the most, for when Jessie talked to her of the speedy recovery of her husband and her child, and the return to welcome labour, and the sweet free air of heaven, Susan felt that it might be so—that it *was* possible, and that she ought to take patience, and would do so. But what could she say to her poor companion in return? Alas! nothing—nothing that could open before her a vista of recovered happiness. She saw this, and felt that she was the least miserable of the two; and the tender pity with which the visible anguish of her drooping companion inspired her increased tenfold. She saw, too, that her hour of trial was approaching, and that there was no strength of spirit left to support her under it.

"Jessie!" she said to her one day, when watching that self-abandonment of look and attitude which shews that hope is dead, "Jessie, my poor girl, nothing would do thee so much good as opening thy poor heart to some kind and holy minister. I have been here four days, but I haven't seen any clergyman yet. Perhaps their visits are only to the sick?"

"To-morrow is Sunday," replied Jessie, "and then there will be one come to read prayers."

"Then after service speak to him, Jessie. Don't be afraid because he is a gentleman. If he is like him as both christened and married me, he knows he is God's servant, and that it is his duty to comfort the sick and sorrowful."

"And it would be a comfort to be spoken to by such an one," replied Jessie, with a sigh, while her thoughts reverted to the almost parental kindness of Mr. Rimmington; "but it would not be so easy to manage as you seem to think for, Mrs. White. The gentleman that reads prayers to the paupers in the workhouse never stays a minute here after they are over."

"And that may be more because nobody seems to want him to stay," replied the good woman, "than because he is not willing to do so. Clergymen have got a deal to do, Jessie, and oftentimes more than ignorant poor people think for. But, perhaps, you feel shy, my poor girl, and I would be glad and proud to help you to such comfort as that. So I'll speak to the gentleman myself, Jessie, and, maybe, I may be able to say a word to him about my dear husband too."

The morrow came, and with it the reverend divine who had been engaged by the board of guardians of the Deepbrook Union to read prayers to the paupers in the workhouse every Sunday morning. For this he received from the parish funds twenty-five pounds sterling per annum, and, as he resided at the distance of seven miles from the workhouse, there were only a few of the board who considered him as overpaid. This gentleman resided in a large parish, of which he was curate; but, as he had a wife and six children, he thankfully accepted the above-mentioned twenty-five pounds, and probably would not have refused half the sum had it been offered him. A well-intentioned, worthy man was this Reverend Mr. Simms, and truly it was no fault of his if he had more to do professionally and domestically than the 168 hours of the week allowed time for. At any rate, no man could accuse him of ever wasting an hour in idleness, or spending it in amusement. Four of his six children were old enough to require teaching, and he taught them. About a dozen children, upon an average, were christened every week in his parish, and he christened them. Somewhat more than half that number required to be buried, and he buried them. A proper proportion of couples desired to be married weekly, and he married them. Sick folks demanded to be prayed with, and he prayed with them. Moreover, his bishop would have been highly displeased if he had omitted to read prayers on every Saint's day; so that, upon the whole, he was a good deal occupied; and as the shuffling pony which he kept upon the common near his parsonage had to convey him from the Deepbrook Union, after he had read prayers there, in time to begin reading them again in his own church, before the clock struck twelve, he was not in the habit of spending much time in the workhouse after he put off his surplice, although he never failed to get into it a little before nine. But fortunately, though Mr. Simms' pony trotted slowly, the reverend gentleman himself got over the ground with great rapidity, being one of the most rapid readers in England. But of all these particulars Mrs. White, worthy soul! of course knew nothing, and she placed herself in the cold dark room, converted for the nonce into a chapel, with the comfortable consciousness, not only that she was going to say her prayers, but also that she was about to do a good and pious action, for she was determined not to let the clergyman leave it till she had told him how greatly one amongst them required the spiritual consolation which it was in his power only to give.

Mr. Simms had not quite recovered his breath when he got into the deal inclosure, which served him as a desk; but not for this did he pause, or linger, for stop, emphasis, or accent, for the hundredth part of a second, from the first word of the holy office to the last. For his pony was that day decidedly rather more lame than usual; and the dread of infringing the canonical hours, by not beginning the service in his church in time, haunted him like a spectre, and drove him on from verse to verse, and from prayer to prayer, with a degree of velocity which certainly tended not a little to puzzle and confound the slow capacities of his poor hearers. In one respect, however, he had a very considerable advantage over the generality of clergymen who are obliged (by any cause) to get through the service as rapidly as possible, for, having no one to officiate as clerk, and finding that the waiting for the slow enunciation of the very quickest of his congregation would take more time than he could possibly spare, the Psalms were got through by his reading every other verse without the loss of a moment between—an accidental advantage this, for which the reverend gentleman felt very piously thankful.

Susan White was a very humble-minded poor woman, and, not finding herself able to follow the service through this rapid delivery of it, heaved a gentle sigh to think what an ignorant poor soul she was. This humility, however, did not cause her to shrink from her resolution of getting the minister to say a few words of comfort to poor Jessie Phillips; and, being in some degree instinctively aware that the reverend gentleman's movements were likely to be rapid, she kept her eye upon him throughout the whole of the valedictory blessing, the words of which were too familiar to be mistaken, even from the lips of Mr. Simms, and, darting forward the very instant he had pronounced it, she contrived to reach him before the second arm was emancipated from the sleeve of the surplice, the operation having, fortunately, been a little impeded by the hitching of a button at the waist in the cuff of his coat. So placing herself before him, therefore, as to render his escape by the narrow interval between the forms pretty nearly impossible, she made him a low courtesy, and said, "I ask your pardon, sir, but there is a young woman in the house who is sadly in want of a little comforting talk with a minister. Will you be pleased, sir, to come along with me only just for a quarter of an hour or so?"

"A quarter of an hour!" exclaimed Mr. Simms, positively trembling with haste, eagerness, and alarm, "a quarter of an hour, good woman,—you know not what you ask! Go away, good woman, go away! Mercy on me, how you stand staring! Do you mean to make me push you over the forms that I may get away? Get along, do! It must be a quarter past ten if it's a minute! Get away, do!" And, so saying, the greatly irritated gentleman did push her a little on one side, and then made his escape, with as much nervous trepidation as if he had been a thief with the constable behind him.

Courteous reader, be just and reasonable as well as courteous, and say, if you be a rate-payer, where the blame lies. Is it in Mr. Simms, who, with unremitting labour in what ought to be the first of all professions, can, with such desperate difficulty, maintain his family, as to make him accept your pitiful stipend, though forced to earn it in the way described? Or, is it with you, and those whom you permit to assess and distribute your contributions, and who eagerly accept the services of those whose price can most easily be beaten down, though it is notoriously impossible that they can accept the terms you offer, *and live*, unless they, in some degree, limit the time they give, in the same proportion as you have limited their reward?

But it is thus, as if you look carefully round you will find, once and again, that the miserable wretches who have a million times more need of spiritual comfort than their happier fellow-creatures are defrauded of it. If it, indeed, be necessary to make the pauper a prisoner, care should at least be taken that the light which enables the sufferers of earth to see the blessed perspective of a happier state of existence should not be excluded from his dungeon.

# XXXIV

*The story returns to Ellen—she relates to her father the circumstances of her interview with the Duchess—a very pleasant family merry-making interrupted by the arrival of a letter—great confusion occasioned thereby*

WE MUST NOW GIVE A backward glance to Ellen, for, despite her earnest aspirations for such a state of indifference as might enable her to endure with philosophy the touch of either joy or woe, she seemed doomed to learn, that in this wish, as in some former ones, a more powerful will than her own directed her destiny; and no condition could be much more removed from indifference than that which followed her little-desired interview with the Duchess of Rochdale.

There were but two human beings in the world to whom Ellen would have wished to communicate this strange interview, namely, her father and Lord Pemberton. To the latter, however, had the wish been multiplied ten-thousand fold, she would not have done it; but to her sympathising, her indulgent, her approving father, she hastened the moment she returned to the house, though, with all her eagerness, she would probably have been too considerate to enter his presence so abruptly had she been aware of the flushed and agitated expression of her countenance.

"My dearest child, what is the matter with you? What has happened, Ellen?" demanded the startled squire.

"Nothing, papa—that is, nothing that need alarm you," replied Ellen, vainly endeavouring to look tranquil, rational, and composed. "I am sure I am very foolish if I look frightened, for I certainly have had nothing to frighten me. I have only seen the Duchess, papa."

Mr. Dalton looked vexed, and sighed involuntarily. "My dear girl!" he said, "I am sure you did not mean it, Ellen, but you have deceived both yourself and me. I would not have believed, my dear, that the sight of the Duchess, or the Duke either, could have thus moved you. Oh, Ellen! Where is the tranquil philosophy on which we have both prided ourselves?"

"In my heart, I hope, dear father!" replied Ellen, though the tears that started to her eyes as she spoke made her words sound exceedingly like an empty boast. "I have been discomposed and somewhat agitated by what has passed, but—"

"Passed!" exclaimed Mr. Dalton, with great vehemence; "you don't mean that you have been conversing with her? Good Heaven! how unfortunate! I would not have had you exposed to this for the world. Tell me, Ellen, at once—was she rude to you?"

"Rude? Oh no! papa; not rude, certainly. But, though I really believe she intended to be civil, she made me, somehow or other, speak rather rudely, or, at least, rather bluntly to her. I can hardly explain *what* it was that I felt. I trust it was not anger, I trust it was not pride, but—"

"Never mind, my Ellen," said the squire, again interrupting her; "better a thousand times that it should have been either, than that she should have suspected you of any wish or intention to please her."

"You may set your heart at ease, dear father, on that point," returned Ellen, with a melancholy smile; "there was not the very slightest danger of it."

And then, by degrees, Ellen endeavoured to repeat all that had really passed, while the good squire, on his side, cross-examined her as to looks, accents, and attitudes; but, though she answered him with all possible fidelity, the result was any thing rather than a clear understanding, on his part, as to what the noble lady's feelings towards his exemplary daughter either were or had been.

Not to have entered into this conversation with her father was impossible; but when, at length, it was concluded by the dinner-bell, which sent her to dress, Ellen essayed, with all the power she had, to drive the subject from her thoughts; and in the evening, when she found it impossible either to read or to talk, she proposed to her mother that the children should all come into the drawing-room and dance to her playing. Mrs. Dalton, who was never so well pleased as when she could find an excuse for calling together and reviewing her children, consented with a delighted smile, and Ellen sat down, and pursued her self-imposed task unshrinkingly, amidst the incessant repetitions of "Not quite so fast, Ellen,"—"A little quicker, if you please, dear Ellen," "Just please to play that over again," &c. &c. &c. for about two hours. At the end of that time, Mr. Dalton, who had taken refuge in his library, interrupted the revels by entering the drawing-room, and walking up to the pale musician with a somewhat peremptory request that she would leave off playing and come with him. There was something in the tone of his voice which startled her, though she would have been exceedingly puzzled if obliged to say why. But, on looking up in his face for explanation, the puzzle became worse still, for never had she seen him wear the same sort of look before. It was not jocund, it was not sad, neither was it angry,—far from it. On the contrary, indeed, there was a sort of condescending gentleness, such as he might have worn when giving alms to a beggar who stood greatly in awe of him. In short, well as Ellen thought she knew her father, she was now completely at fault, and, having answered the plaintive remonstrances of a dozen young eyes by beckoning Henrietta to take her place at the instrument, she rose without saying a word, and followed him out of the room.

The squire stalked before her across the ample hall, in very ghost-like fashion, neither speaking a syllable, nor even turning his head to look at her. When they were both fairly within the door, which he held open to receive her, he closed and bolted it, and then, throwing his arms around her, he pressed her to his bosom with a vehemence of emotion which almost frightened her.

"My dearest father!" she exclaimed, "what is it you have got to tell me? Something, I'm sure, that you think will overpower me. Is it something terrible? Has any thing dreadful happened to HIM?"

"Nothing dreadful has happened to him, my Ellen; but it is terrible, or something very near it, for such a stout-hearted old fellow as myself to discover that, on the very point where I most prided myself, even in moral dignity and strength of mind, I have no more firmness than a love-sick girl, nor half so much perhaps as one who, if not love-sick, has loved well. Sit down, my love, sit down, and don't despise me, if you can help it."

Ellen obeyed, but without uttering a word in reply. She felt that something strange had occurred, and felt too, throughout her whole frame that, whatever it might be, it came from the quarter from whence no breath, however slight, could reach her without fearfully shaking the tranquillity she so earnestly sought to preserve.

Her father looked at her anxiously; he felt that to prolong these moments of suspense was cruelty, and yet he so greatly feared the effect of sudden emotion upon a young heart, which had already been tried so severely, that it was literally in trembling that he put the following letter into her hand.

Ellen, too, trembled; for, though the writing was unknown to her, some species of instinct that it would be difficult to define convinced her, almost beyond the reach of doubt, that it was from the Duke of Rochdale. For a moment there was a mist before her eyes—she could not clearly see the characters—but it passed, and she read as follows:—

> "Sir,
>
> "It is a mortifying thing for a man who has, during many years of life, been enduring many sacrifices with a tolerable degree of philosophy, because he believed himself to be doing what was right, suddenly to discover that he had, on the contrary, been doing what was very wrong. Such, Mr. Dalton, is my case; and I trust that this avowal will tend to soften any severity with which you may have hitherto been disposed to judge me. I may spare myself the painful task of entering at length upon all that has passed between your daughter and my son, for, as Lord Pemberton assures me, nothing has been concealed from you. But you must permit me to explain to you, as briefly as possible, my own conduct in the business. In order to do this, it is necessary that I should expose my family affairs in a manner that I have never done before to any one save my wife, but I feel no fear that this confidence will be less safe with you than with her."
>
> [Here followed a statement of the deplorable incumbrances with which his father's extravagance had burdened the

Rochdale property (the detail of which it is unnecessary to give), and the letter then proceeded as follows.]

"I need not point out to you that the strict, I might say, the severe economy, which I was called upon to practise in order to clear the demands made by many creditors on the already crippled property of my family, was more painful in my station than it might have been to one of inferior rank. In truth, my whole life has been a struggle; and the first wish of my heart has been to save my son from passing his days in the same manner. I have nothing with which to reproach myself on the side of the well-ordered and well-sustained economy by which I have sought to clear my property; I have had faithful agents, both in and out of my family, to assist me; and the painful task has proceeded without a single backward step. That during the whole of this time my mind has been very earnestly fixed upon the hope of a wealthy marriage for my son, I will not deny. It was the only means (except that of self-denial which has been practised by us all as far as the demands of our station would permit) by which it was possible to expedite the process by which I was labouring to emancipate my son from the painful trammels which had shackled me. You will therefore conceive, Mr. Dalton, that his confession of an attachment to your daughter was a severe blow to me. I fear that I suffered my admirable wife to perceive how strongly the disappointment of my hopes affected me more openly than I ought to have done.—She had an interview with her son, the particulars of which I never learned till this day. The Duchess knew, by what passed at this interview, both the professed attachment and the bitter sorrow of her son, but for my sake she endured this bitter knowledge without wavering, and without suffering any such portion of it to reach me as would have made my self-imposed task the harder. I only learned, and learned from her (for with my son I never entered on the subject), that the young people had both pledged themselves to give up their engagement, unless it was sanctioned by the parents on both sides. With this I was fully satisfied, and have been living ever since under the comfortable delusion that Pemberton saw the necessity of the arrangement, and submitted to it accordingly, without any greater sacrifice of happiness than a few months' change of place and scene might suffice to cure. That poor Pemberton's mother knew better is certain; but, however I may lament the concealment which has produced so much greater a degree of suffering than any motive would have induced me to inflict, I at least cannot blame her, for all she has suffered herself and has caused others to suffer has been produced solely by her wish to save me. But this day has ended a very pernicious state of delusion for both of us. My dear wife has ceased to think that it was her duty to keep me in the dark, and I have at length obtained such a knowledge of facts as will, I trust, enable me to atone for the unhappiness of which I have been the cause. The Duchess of Rochdale has seen and conversed with your daughter, Mr. Dalton; and the consequence has been a frank and noble avowal of the rashness which led her to judge and decide upon a question while ignorant of what was most essential to it. It was to me she first avowed this, together with all she had done and suffered in order to keep me ignorant of the tenacity with which Lord Pemberton adhered to his attachment, while consenting to forego the hope of possessing the object of it. It was to me, too, that she first confessed the conviction, to which the interview of this morning gave rise, that the man who had once loved Miss Dalton would never consent to be the husband of any other woman. The result of this conversation with her was an interview with my son, of which it is not necessary that I should give the particulars, inasmuch as my chief object in now addressing you is to request your permission for his waiting upon yourself and your daughter, to communicate the result of it. I will not affect to fear that such a woman as your daughter will refuse to receive the addresses of my son, because he submitted to the restraint imposed by his father. May God bless them both! They have deserved to be happy, and I trust they will be so. It would be doing neither of them justice to suppose that the restricted income to which they must submit for the next four or five years would interfere with this. After all that my son has suffered, I could not condemn him to another night of anxiety; and have therefore yielded to his earnest entreaties not to suffer any delay on my part to add to the mischief which has been already done by the want of a perfectly clear understanding between your family and mine. Lord Pemberton's groom will convey this letter to the manor-house; but I should wish your daughter to know that his master will be waiting at the distance of some half-dozen paces to receive your answer to it.

"I remain, Sir,

"Your obedient Servant,

"ROCHDALE."

How did Ellen bear it? But little has been said concerning her love for Lord Pemberton; nevertheless, there was that at her heart to which not even the magic strength of poetry has ever been able to do full justice, though many a fluttering little heart, beside Ellen's, may have felt it. However, she did not faint on learning this sudden change from despair to happiness; she only rose gently from her seat, and, passing the little table that stood between them, dropped on her knees before her father, and in that attitude silently breathed her thanks to Heaven for the change. Certainly her tears flowed the while; and it was best perhaps that it should be so, for, without this natural and most blessed relief, it is probable that not even the hard-learned philosophy of Ellen would have sufficed to preserve her from sinking under emotions so violent. It would be hardly fair, perhaps, to look under the squire's eyelids, as they fell over the eyes that looked fondly down upon his daughter; but, if we did, it is likely enough that we should find on this occasion, as heretofore, that there was "most excellent sympathy" between them. That it was a moment, however, of very exquisite happiness to both, nobody can doubt; nevertheless Ellen, from not being used perhaps to this sort of thing, very speedily took means to interrupt it, for, even while the lips of the squire were still pressed upon her forehead she started away from him, exclaiming, "Papa! Lord Pemberton!"

"Bless my soul!" exclaimed the happy father, in his turn, "I had forgotten that part of the business altogether, Ellen. Fancy him pacing up and down the drive all this time!" and, without waiting for any further hints or instructions, or even for his hat, the squire rushed out of the library, across the hall, and through the portico, in search of his future son-in-law.

# XXXV

*Ellen Dalton is rather astonished at finding herself happy—other people are puzzled as well as herself*

ELLEN MEANWHILE SEATED HERSELF IN a chair as far from the fire as possible, for her cheeks were burning, though her hands and feet were as cold as marble. How utterly impossible would it be to follow the thoughts which began careering through the head, lately so very reasonable!—how infinitely beyond the power of words to describe the emotions which throbbed, and thrilled, and swelled, and fluttered, in the little heart! It was considerably more than a year since they had seen each other. Poor Ellen had lost much of her bloom in that interval, and she knew it. Now was it, and for the first time, that the ribald observations of her brother brought a pang to her heart as she remembered them. In some degree she knew that he was right; could she be sure that he was not more so than she suspected?—could she be sure that Lord Pemberton might not think so, too? This may, perhaps, appear to the high-minded and sublime as a trait of very pitiful vanity, but, nevertheless, there may be some honest hearts in fair bosoms who may have courage enough to confess that the feeling, although weak, was natural, and to these I must trust her defence. It was, however, but for a moment or so that any such thoughts possessed her, and in the next a multitude of delicious recollections, all tending to prove how little such considerations were likely to influence her lover, succeeded, and for a bright brief interval she was conscious, notwithstanding thc vehement agitation which still shook her frame, of feeling perfectly happy. But the poor girl was not permitted to enjoy the unwonted sensation long, for very speedily after all doubts and fears were comfortably merged in the sober certainty of soon, oh! very soon, beholding the beloved one whom she had so vainly struggled to forget; an impetuous hand was heard to seize the lock, and before she could be quite sure whether the bounding of her heart would choke her or not, the door opened, and in bounced three of her sisters.

"Now this is too bad, Ellen," exclaimed the eldest of the three. "It was all very well to stay away as long as papa wanted you, but Frederic is just come in, and says he met him going out, so that you can only stay away now out of naughty laziness. But now you must come, for mamma has sent us to fetch you." And with this the three messengers seized vehemently upon her, two of them securing her hands, and the third grasping a portion of her muslin dress in a style that would evidently have made resistance very dangerous.

What was the trembling Duchess elect to do in this domestic dilemma? The question was entirely one of expediency; right or wrong, pleasant or unpleasant, had nothing to do with it. To get rid of the children would, she knew, be impossible; and she had therefore only to decide on the comparative advantage of being found at that moment by Lord Pemberton, engaged in a violent game of romps, or of not being found by him at all. Half an instant decided it; she preferred the latter, and quietly saying, "Don't tear my frock, Rose," she yielded herself to their will, and in the next moment found herself in the drawing-room, surrounded by seven of her sisters, her mother, and her brother.

"It is very foolish of you to stay away so, Ellen, when you yourself had asked for all the children to come down," said Mrs Dalton, looking a little vexed. "You should have told your papa at once how you were all engaged, and I am quite sure he would not have wished to keep you away."

"The governor had nothing to do with it, ma'am," said young Dalton, from his favourite position on the hearth-rug; "it was all the amiable old lady's own sweetness of temper, which kept her steadfastly in one place because she happened to know that she was particularly wanted in another. And, by the way, I wish you would ask her, ma'am," continued the young man, passing his fingers through his beautiful hair, as he stood before the large mirror over the chimney-piece,—"I wish you would have the kindness to ask her what she has been saying or doing to put the old gentleman in such a horrible rage? I thought positively that he would have knocked me down as I passed him at the front door. I never saw him in such a way in my life. I really think she must have been shewing herself off under her true colours."

"What was the matter, Ellen, dear?" said her mother, rising sufficiently from her customary attitude to look her daughter in the face. "Good gracious me, Ellen! What is it all about? You are as red as the geranium in your bosom, and I do believe that you have been crying."

"There is nothing at all the matter, mamma?" said Ellen, with an involuntary but very happy smile. "And now, dears, begin dancing again, there's darlings;" and Ellen endeavoured to make her way to the pianoforte.

"Just see how she is sniggering at the idea of having put the poor old gentleman in a passion. The older she grows the worse she is, you'll all, find it out, one of these days, as well as I. Upon my soul I would not mind her being so confounded ugly if she had not such a devil of a temper," said Mr. Frederic Dalton.

At this moment the bell of the house door rang rather violently, as if pulled by a hasty and impatient hand.

"Who the devil can this be?" said the young gentleman, striding towards the door of the room as he spoke.

"Don't go, Frederic! I am quite sure it is my father come back!" exclaimed poor Ellen, not knowing what to say, or what to do.

"Well, Mrs. Ellen Dalton! and if it is, why should I be afraid of meeting him, I wonder?"

"Don't go, Frederic," said Mrs. Dalton, who hated nothing so much as the rare occurrence of hearing her son reprimanded by his father. "I am quite sure that Ellen has some meaning for what she says..

"Perhaps he means to speak to you about that odious young Baxter. Pray, pray, stay where you are, and don't let us have any quarrelling."

While this was passing, the saucy Mary had employed herself by gently opening the drawing-room door, and peeping out; which manœuvre having been performed with equal caution and success, she closed the door, and tripping back into the middle of the room clapped her hands, exclaiming, "Papa is not going to quarrel with any body, but he has brought back the most beautiful young man in the world with him!"

"What stuff you are talking, child!" said her brother, sharply ringing the bell. "Beautiful young man, indeed! I do wonder, mother, that you can let a woman of Ellen's age, who is up to every thing, and afraid of nothing, talk as freely as I am sure she does to the young ones. Who was that, pray?" he added, addressing the servant who at that moment answered the bell. "Who was it came in just now with my father?"

"My Lord Pemberton, Sir," replied the man.

"Who?" vociferated Mr. Frederic Dalton.

"The Marquis of Pemberton, Sir," repeated the servant.

"What the devil brings him here?" exclaimed the young squire as soon as the footman had retired. "Can you guess, ma'am, what should make him call, and at this time of night too?" he added, addressing his mother.

"Good gracious, Frederic, no! How should I?"

"Most likely he is coming to look after me," resumed the young man. "Miss Mortimer told me that every body said it was a shame we were not acquainted, because we were the only two young men at all in the same class; except, of course, young Mortimer."

"But if he did want to make your acquaintance, Frederic," observed Henrietta, "it surely would not be done in this way. Certainly it is very odd. Isn't it, Ellen?" It must be observed, strange as it may seem, that no single individual of the Dalton family had the slightest idea of Lord Pemberton's attachment to Ellen except her father. The little parlour at Mrs. Buckhurst's had been the scene of some few transcendently happy, but of many more transcendently miserable meetings between the lovers, but Lord Pemberton had never entered the manor-house till this evening.

When Henrietta addressed the question above stated to her sister, she turned round her head to look at her, and, very naturally astonished at the vivid carnation which dyed her cheeks, exclaimed with a gay laugh, "Why, Ellen! What can make you blush so very beautifully? Surely not a visit from the high and mighty Marquis of Pemberton? Of the whole race, excepting perhaps papa himself, you are the very last I should have thought likely to be moved in spirit by the honour and glory of such an event. What are you thinking about?"

"Of Lord Pemberton," replied Ellen, with a smile that cannot possibly be described, for it was as if all the youth and gaiety that for the last two years, or near it, had been shut up within her, in a sort of death-like trance, were now suddenly awakened, and looking out at her eyes.

"Yes, I dare say you are, you antediluvian spinster," cried Frederic. "Ladies of your age are vastly apt to waste a good many of their precious thoughts on young gentlemen of his. But they get nothing, poor dears, but Irish reciprocity—the thinking is all on one side."

At this moment the door was again opened by Mr. Dalton, who, pausing for an instant to ascertain in what part of the large room Ellen might be found, walked up to her, and, placing her trembling arm under his own, led her away without uttering a word.

Shall we follow the father and daughter to the library? Or shall we remain with the mother, and the rest of her progeny in the drawing-room? The last, decidedly, and that for two reasons. First, the scene that followed in the library would require more skill to describe; and, secondly, it would be more easy to imagine, without any description at all. We will remain, therefore, with Mrs. Dalton, and by so doing shall have an opportunity of observing the effect produced by the pantomimic performance of the squire.

The general astonishment was so great, that not a single word was spoken for several seconds; a much longer space of time, be it observed, than was at all likely to occur under ordinary circumstances among any seven of the Miss Daltons, without taking either the mother or brother into the account. This really awful pause was at length broken by Caroline, who, gravely walking up to the side of her mother, said, in a tone of mingled astonishment and curiosity, "Mamma, can you tell why papa led away sister Ellen in that manner?"

"Tell, child! How on earth can I, or any body else, be able to guess what it means? Your papa and Ellen are always having secrets together—every body knows that; and I am sure, for my part, I don't care a single straw about it. But certainly this is something out of the common way. Do you suppose, Frederic, that Lord Pemberton is there still?"

"There!—what! in the library for Miss Ellen to do the honours to him? No, to be sure, ma'am, that is quite out of the question. I suppose Lord

Pemberton stepped in for half a moment to ask some county question or other, and the moment he was gone the governor rushed in here, as you saw, to look for his darling, that he might tell her all about it. It is quite in his usual way, I think. I really see nothing in it to astonish any one."

"No, Frederic, it is not in his usual way," said Caroline, with great solemnity. "Mamma! I have got a thought come into my head. Will you tell me if you believe it is possible, only just possible, mind, that Lord Pemberton has fallen in love with sister Ellen, and is come to tell papa so?"

"Nonsense, child!" replied Mrs. Dalton, colouring violently, as she fixed her eyes upon her, and seemed falling into a reverie.

"No, ma'am, it is not nonsense, it is a great deal worse than nonsense," ejaculated the young squire, in a tone of vehement indignation. "This is the sort of stuff the children get into their heads by being permitted to be so much with their precious sister Ellen. If you will take my advice, ma'am, you will please to send Miss Caroline to bed, just as a lesson to teach her that it is perfectly disgusting for girls of her age to be for ever talking about love and lovers, upon all possible occasions, however disgustingly absurd."

"In love with Ellen?" said Mrs. Dalton, removing her eyes from the face of Caroline, to fix them on that of her son. "What can have put that into the child's head?"

"I have told you, ma'am," replied the young gentleman, with every appearance of being very angry—"It is Ellen, who has put it into her head. You may depend upon it that you will find out, some day, that I have not formed my opinion of her from nothing."

Mrs. Dalton, however, was in a dream, from which neither the anger of her son, nor the valuable opinions he was delivering, could awaken her.

The girls, meanwhile, were divided into groups. The three eldest stood whispering together near the pianoforte, the three youngest were endeavouring to atone to themselves for the loss of their dance by hiding and peeping out at each other from behind the curtains, and the inspired Caroline still stood before her mother, apparently in as deep a reverie as herself. How long the young squire, who still stood frowning upon the hearth-rug, would have continued to endure the "abominable bore" of this strange suspense, it is not easy to guess; he certainly was beginning to think that he should like to push all the detestable children out of the room when the door once again opened, and for the third time Mr. Dalton entered.

There was a most provokingly serene air of composure upon his countenance, which seemed as effectually to baffle the inquiring eyes that were instantly fixed upon him, as if he had worn a mask. And, though he immediately spoke, neither his words, nor the tone of his voice, gave the slightest reason to hope that he intended to occupy himself by gratifying their curiosity.

"Henrietta, my dear," said he, very mildly, "I fear I must trouble you to lend me your writing-desk. I want to write a letter directly, and you are such a tidy girl that I am sure you have every thing ready."

A very acute observer might perhaps have suspected, from the furtive sort of glance that Mr. Dalton directed towards his wife, his son, and his elder daughters, that he had some little notion in his head of the real state and condition of their minds as to what was going on in the library. That is to say, that he thought they might be rather curious as to the reasons for his not writing his letter there; but he knew not that they were aware how it was occupied.

Henrietta, having uttered a cheerful "Oh, yes, papa!" left the room, and Mrs. Dalton, having by that time roused herself sufficiently to speak, said, "Do come here, Mr. Dalton, will you? I want you to tell me—"

But before she could finish the sentence the impatient young man on the hearth-rug exclaimed, "Pray, sir, is Lord Pemberton still here?"

"Lord Pemberton?" repeated his father, raising his hand to his chin, perhaps to conceal a smile that he could not restrain. "Who can have told you that Lord Pemberton was here?"

"It was William, sir. Pray, may I ask if his lordship is shut up in the library with my sister Ellen?"

"Yes, Frederic, he is." replied the squire, demurely.

"What for, Mr. Dalton? What for? Oh, goodness! what can it all mean?" exclaimed his wife, effectually roused by this startling intelligence from her usual state of apathy. "Mr. Dalton, you will be the death of me if you do not tell me instantly."

"God forbid, my dear!" he replied, in the gentlest possible accents, as he took her hand, and then pressed his lips upon her still fair forehead. "I should never contemplate the idea of your dying without extreme sorrow, but just at present I do assure you that it would be peculiarly inconvenient to me."

"Why, Mr. Dalton? Why would it be peculiarly inconvenient to you?" returned the lady, with most unusual impetuosity. "I am quite sure," she added, in an accent which seemed to threaten a sudden flood of tears, "I am quite sure, Mr. Dalton, that you have got some thing in your head, and that you are trying to make a fool of me!"

"On the contrary, my dear; I am only trying not to frighten you out of your wits by the news I have got to tell. Frederic," he added, turning towards his son, "I have more than once heard you express some anxious doubts and fears respecting your eldest sister's chance of finding an establishment in marriage—nay, I think I have heard you remark that she was already to he considered as a confirmed old maid. Let me have the pleasure, while announcing my good news to your mother and sisters, of removing this painful idea from your mind for ever. Dear wife, your eldest daughter will, ere long, be Marchioness of Pemberton."

Were I to say that Mrs. Dalton uttered a scream, it would scarcely be an exaggeration, so vehement was the "Oh!" with which she prefaced the "Gracious, mercy on me! are you in earnest?" by which she replied to her husband's speech. As to Mr. Frederic, his fine teeth were set so closely together, that they might well be said to grind each other, and it was only across this beautiful ivory barrier that the single word he uttered was breathed.. It was therefore inaudible, and it may be very fairly said that the deep d—n, which his heart spoke, returned to it. As to the clamorous exclamations of the younger branches of the family, the whisperings, the smiles, and all the pretty sisterly wonder and delight which such news was likely to produce, it may all be very easily imagined. Mr. Dalton, however, who really had to write a letter to the Duke, and, having generously yielded his library to others, was obliged to occupy the drawing-room himself, soon became conscious that in its present state it was exceedingly ill calculated for the production of an epistle which he certainly wished to have nothing absurd in it, and he felt that, as long as he was within reach of such happy mutterings as now buzzed around him, he was in great danger of not achieving this. He therefore thus addressed them all, seniors and juniors *en masse*, "My dear girls, I would not stop your beloved tongues for the universe, but I have got a letter to write to your sister Ellen's august father-in-law that is to be, and if you stay here I shall be sure to write, 'Caroline says this,' and 'Charlotte says that,' which I am sure you will agree with me would he very objectionable. So get along all of you into the school-room, order lights, bread and butter and tea, in any quantities you please, and sit all night, if you will, talking over this wonder of wonders. Only don't utter a chorus of thanksgivings aloud as you pass the library door, because perhaps Ellen might not like it.

The superlatively happy troop lost no time in making an elaborate reply to this harangue, but, uttering an universal "Thank you, papa!" moved off towards the door, which they reached just as Henrietta and her desk entered it; and then good Mrs. Dalton indulged herself by slowly uttering these solemn words, "Henrietta, my dear, I wish myself to have the pleasure of informing you that your beloved sister Ellen is about to become Marchioness of Pemberton, and will, by the blessing of God, some day be the Duchess of Rochdale!"

# XXXVI

*A very clever girl finds herself obliged to confess that she has made a mistake—but her confessor is not so severe upon her as she deserves*

TWO OR THREE DAYS, VERY anxious ones to Martha Maxwell, passed over, after her interview with Henry Mortimer, without her hearing from him on the subject of Frederic Dalton's promise of marriage, but at the end of that time he contrived, as cleverly as the hero of that document had done himself, to find the young lady alone and disengaged, and then the subject was resumed between them with the most confiding and friendly unreserve on both sides.

"I grieve, dear, kind-hearted friend," said the young lawyer, "to have nothing to report that can leave you with the slightest ground for hope that the curious document of which you have got possession can avail you for the service of your poor client. Such a transfer as you propose to make of it is quite impracticable."

Perhaps Martha discerned the least possible inclination to smile about the mouth of her counsellor as he said this. She coloured a little, shook her head, and said, "I am sure you are quizzing me, Mr. Mortimer." This, however, he stoutly denied, and indeed with such genuine sincerity that she permitted herself to be satisfied, and the consultation went on. "The transfer is impracticable!" she repeated musingly, "Truly I believe it, Mr. Mortimer; and, though I do not pique myself upon being a very accomplished lawyer, I do not remember that I ever felt, or expressed a hope, that any legal use could be made of it. But we quarrelled, you know, when we talked of it before, so perhaps you did not quite understand me."

"I deny the quarrel," he replied; "however, I am quite ready, being a particularly courteous and amiable judge, to hear you again."

"Well, then, hear, and listen, not only with your ears, Mr. Judge, but with your understanding. I never, as I tell you, believed it likely that this most absurd paper could give me any legal power over my incomparable lover, but I think now, as I ever have done, that if properly managed it may give all we want and wish for as an instrument by which to work upon his fears. I have an infinity of faith, Mr. Henry Mortimer, in the young gentleman's ignorance, and I have little doubt that, if poor Jessie Phillips could make him understand that this paper was in her possession, and that it was her purpose to bring it against him in a court of justice, he would immediately give her such a sum of money for the precious document as might enable her to release herself from her present sad abode (don't take my calling the workhouse *sad* as a personal affront, Mr. Mortimer) and enable her to leave the neighbourhood that has been so fatal to her. Cannot you believe that all this might be done?"

"You have, as you say, Miss Maxwell, an infinity of faith in the young gentleman's ignorance," replied young Mortimer, "and I have an infinity of faith in his rascality. I do not believe this unhappy affair would ever have occurred if he had not known himself to be safe under the existing law (I might have taken *this* as personal, if *you* had said it); but depend upon it that on such points his ignorance is not so great as you suppose. Your poor Jessie has put it out of her own power to expose him in any way without exposing herself also, and that, as you must be aware, much more fatally for herself than for him. I would venture a prophecy, Miss Maxwell, that not one single solitary sixpence would be squeezed out of the young squire in this way."

"Well, then," said Martha, colouring, "in that case I must try another, for I stand, in some sort, pledged to the unhappy girl that the world should be made to do her justice. Do you not think that at least it might be easy to frighten him by making him believe that I intended myself to use this inestimable promise?"

"To frighten him into paying a sum of money, Miss Maxwell?" returned the young barrister, colouring pretty considerably in his turn.

"Not exactly for my own use and benefit," replied Martha, laughing.

"And how do you propose to make him aware of that?" returned Henry Mortimer. "No, no, Miss Maxwell, believe me, no real friend of yours could suffer you to enter upon any such negotiation with him if he had power to prevent it."

"Then what *can* I do for her, Mr. Mortimer?" said poor Martha, piteously, while tears started to her eyes. "Alas! how very thoughtlessly, how very ill I have acted!"

"Thoughtlessly, if you will, Miss Maxwell," replied the young man, eagerly, "but, most assuredly, not *ill.* For you have acted from motives of the gentlest charity on one side and a very righteous feeling of indignation on the other. Nor do I think the matter quite desperate yet. Should you have any objection to letting him know that you have confided the business to me, both as a friend and a lawyer? I confess that I think it is very likely that I might be able to bring him to reason."

"And *I* confess, Mr. Henry Mortimer, that I think it very likely *your* friends might object as much to this mode of proceeding as *mine* might do at the other; at any rate, I assure you that I should not approve it at all. Let the matter rest for the present," she added with a sigh. "For I see not that any good can be done by talking of it."

"Will you then consent to send back this promise to the worthless giver of it?"

"Oh! yes, very willingly. But must I do it without at all hinting to him the motives for which I took it?"

"Why, I confess there is something disagreeable," said young Mortimer, after a pause, "in suffering him to suppose that the time has ever been when you wished to receive his precious hand as your legal property."

"It is intolerable!" exclaimed Martha, vehemently.

"Well, then, suppose you simply state the truth, and then conclude by telling him that you now return the paper because you think, upon mature reflection, that it will be best to trust the future fate of your poor *protégée* to his own honour and generosity."

"So it shall be then," returned Martha, sighing; and I thank you heartily, kind friend, for giving me what I truly believe, after all my egregious folly, to be the best advice possible under the deplorable circumstances!" And so they parted.

# XXXVII

*Susan White is puzzled in mind respecting the clergyman—but, fearing the case is hopeless, takes upon herself to advise Jessie, and proposes a strong measure to her*

It was with a strange, and almost comic mixture of feelings, that the excellent Mrs. White at length followed the last of the pauper congregation out of the (so called) chapel, and sought out her young acquaintance, in order to inform her of the ill success of her enterprise. The good woman had conceived much real affection for the wretched Jessie, although she contemplated her fault with the feelings of a well-ordered, virtuous mind. But, while fully aware that her frailty had forfeited one of the very strongest claims to esteem that woman can plead, she could not help thinking there was still a great deal in the character of Jessie that might lead her to turn out well, notwithstanding all that was passed, provided, at least, that she could be removed from the fearfully contaminating vice and degradation by which she was now surrounded, before all the better feelings of her heart were rooted up and destroyed for ever. Susan White had the greatest possible confidence in the utility of listening to the advice of a clergyman on all points of moral difficulty, having herself profited thereby, notwithstanding the straightforward and peaceable course of her own existence; and it was this which had made her so anxious that her erring young friend should have the benefit of the reverend chaplain's counsel under her present dreadful circumstances Her disappointment, therefore, was of the most serious and reasonable kind possible: but there was joined to it the most whimsical puzzle imaginable as to its cause. That any clergyman of the Church of England should be forced to perform his holy work, precisely upon the same principle that a mail-coachman performs his, never entered her head. If it had, the whole scene which had occurred in front of the deal desk would have been perfectly intelligible; but, not having this clue to the mystery, every species of *non causa pro causa* suggested itself.

"It was all of no use, Jessie, dear," she said, as soon as she had succeeded in getting her young friend into a quiet corner. "I have done my very best, but all for nothing."

"The clergyman then refused to speak to me, Mrs. White?" said Jessie, mournfully. "Alas! he knows that I am no longer worthy of such respect as that would shew!"

"No, Jessie, that was'nt it at all, for he never knew a single word about what has happened to you."

"I thought that you meant to prepare him for speaking to me by telling him every thing?" said Jessie.

"God love your innocent heart, my dear; it was altogether impossible. I can't help thinking, Jessie, that he must have been taken ill."

"Indeed," said the poor girl. "Well, to be sure, that was unlucky! For though I had never dared to think of such a thing till you mentioned it, Mrs. White, I can't say I have ever had it out of my head since. Now then I suppose I must wait for a better chance next Sunday?"

"A better chance, Jessie! It is natural enough that you should say that because of what I said about his being ill, and it is true, too, that it was very much like being taken ill; and yet I don't think somehow, at the bottom of my heart, that he ever will be better, poor gentleman, that is, better as to hearing what one has got to say. I hope it is no sin to have such a thought about clergymen, but when I remember the whole of it, and his terror and fright like when I spoke to him of stopping a bit, I can't, for the life of me, help thinking that maybe he is not just that right in his poor head that his well-wishers would desire. And if that be so, Jessie, it is we that ought to pray for him who has doubtless often prayed for us."

"What! do you think he is out of his mind, Mrs. White? And he sent to pray for so many miserable creatures who have so greatly need of prayer? Oh no! that is impossible. You startled him, Mrs. White, by asking him to take any notice of such an one as me."

To remove this terrible idea, which seemed to be taking gloomy and fixed possession of the poor girl's mind, Mrs. White entered into a very minute and graphic description of what had passed; and in detailing all the particulars, in order to prove that no possible opportunity had been afforded her for entering into any such narration as poor Jessie feared might have revolted him, she suddenly, and from a movement is unexpected to herself as to Jessie, burst into a laugh. She instantly checked it, however, exclaiming, with very serious self-reproach, "Oh dear! But that's very bad of me to laugh at such a thing, and in such a place, too, Jessie, and at such a time. But I hope I shall be forgiven, for, truth to say, I could not help it."

Being, however, "quite at the bottom of her heart," as she said, very perfectly convinced that it would be no good to wait for the chaplain's opinion on the matter, Mrs. White took upon herself to be Jessie's adviser, for want, as she modestly remarked, of a better. Having found out, by dint of most respectful, submissive, and persevering questioning, that her boy was a great deal better, and her husband almost well, she began to feel for herself the delightful assurance that, though they had neither house nor home to cover them, they should soon turn their steps away from the Union workhouse, for, once again able to labour, she well knew that her good husband would fearlessly take her by the hand, and lead her and her boy back again to the blessings of unfettered light and air, the joyful sight of nature, and the glorious privilege of knowing that no prison walls surrounded them. She, therefore, determined to lose no more time in opening her heart to Jessie upon what she thought it her duty to do, for, with all her genuine humility as to her own incompetency to give advice, she strongly felt that she was more likely to look at things clearly, and so make the best of them, than a poor broken hearted young thing like Jessie, whose very heart and soul had been too much crushed by sorrow to leave her in a condition to judge for herself. In order to render herself, however, as competent to the task as might be, she got Jessie to relate to her all the circumstances of the case, and charged her, above all things, not to exaggerate in stating how far, how distinctly, and how positively, the young squire had promised her marriage.

On this point Jessie was able to answer her with equal truth and perspicuity, for, among

"All the oaths that ever man hath broke,"

although

"In number more than ever woman spoke,"

none had ever been uttered with more daring effrontery, or pledged with more solemn asseverations, than those by which Frederic Dalton had promised to make Jessie Phillips his wife. Repeatedly had he told her that he rejoiced, nay, gloried in the independence which her industry procured her, as it would prevent even their own secret hearts from feeling that his wife had ever submitted to the degradation of having been kept by him. "No, Jessie!" he would say, with affected sublimity of sentiment, the absurdity of which she was totally incapable of judging—"no, Jessie, I doubt if my family pride would ever have permitted me to get over *that.* But, thank Heaven, this trial will be spared me! Never, as you well know, dearest, have you been indebted to me for any thing, save for the purest and most devoted love that ever warmed the head of man!"

This, and a great deal more stuff, in the same vein, did Jessie repeat to her new friend, amidst repentant tears and blushes that now glowed almost as much from the consciousness of folly as of guilt.

"And at the last, then," said Mrs. White; "when this wicked farce of promised marriage was pretty well over, the young gentleman offered you a present of ten pounds?"

Jessie bent her head in token of assent, but articulated, as soon as the fast-flowing tears would let her, "And that it was that opened my blinded eyes at once! And that it was which put it into my bewildered thoughts to come here. Oh! I remembered at that dreadful moment all he said to me about my independence. I knew that I could be independent no longer. No choice was left me but between the workhouse and his alms. Was I wrong in choosing the workhouse?"

"No, Jessie, no," replied the good woman, eagerly. "And, dreadful as it is, I could find it in my heart to be thankful that here you have been, for the very thought of coming here shews that you would not live by the wages of sin. But, Jessie, it is a far different thing to live as the mistress of a young rake like Mr. Dalton, and to make him pay for the bringing up of his child. When your child is born, Jessie, your heart will tell you that nothing whatever, whether it is hate, or whether it is love, can compare with the duty of doing the best you can for it. And the best you can do for it is, *not* the letting it be taken away from you and brought up among the misery and wickedness that you see here."

"And how can I prevent it?" said the wretched girl, bursting afresh into tears.

"By taking enough of good honest courage to face the villain, and to tell him that you will expose him amongst high and low if he does not at once secure your poor child what will be enough to keep it from starving, *out* of the workhouse."

"It will be worse than death to me to see him," said Jessie, after remaining silent for a minute or two, and then speaking with difficulty, and shivering from head to foot from the cold horror that crept over her.

"I can believe it, Jessie, I can easily believe it," returned her kind-hearted adviser, while tears came to her eyes. "But if you once come to see it as I do, my poor girl, you will feel altogether different about it, for then you must feel that it is your duty. I have heard you say, Jessie, that nothing you can suffer was worse than you deserve; and, though I am far from thinking that like, I was glad to hear you speak so, because it was a sign of true sorrow and repentance for your fault which all Christians know is the only road to forgiveness. But there is a difference between your case and that of your child; and I can't but think that it is as much your duty to guard its innocent life from suffering by your sin as it is for you yourself to submit patiently to all such suffering."

"And I think so, too, Mrs. White," returned Jessie, with sudden energy; "and I will bless you, to the longest day I have got to live, for rousing me out of the wicked thinking only of myself in which you found me. But how is it to be done, Mrs. White? They won't let me go out from here, you know, unless it is for good and all. If I go out, I must stay out; and, bad and dreadful as it is to bide here, it would be worse still to have no roof at all to shelter me."

"True, Jessie, true; we must manage better than that, though it is not easy to see how," returned her adviser. "I'd offer to go to him myself, as soon as I get out, only that it is easy enough to guess what would be the end of that. He'd just deny the whole of it, as the new law justifies, and upholds him in doing, and so it would he a folly to think of it. No, Jessie, the only way will be for you to slip out, and in again, without saying any thing about it. And then see the villain, see him face to face, and don't think about yourself, my dear, when the trying moment comes, but think of the poor unborn innocent, that must begin and end its days in misery, if you don't manage to make its sinful father maintain it. I would not have you go at all, Jessie, unless you think that you have strength and courage to go through with it."

"And I do think it, Mrs. White, now that I hear you proving so very plainly that it is my duty. And better would it be by far that I should die at once in the struggle than live to give being within these horrid walls to a wretched little creature whose only prospect would be to die here too. Only tell me how I am to get out, and I will try it, let it end how it may," said Jessie.

"You are a good girl yet, Jessie, notwithstanding the dreadful mischief you have fallen into," returned her pitying adviser. "And as for contriving to get you out, you must just let me have a little time to think about it."

# XXXVIII

*Miss Martha Maxwell writes a letter to Mr. Frederic Dalton which causes very violent emotions; but these subside, and the young gentleman replies to it in a very temperate and sensible manner*

THE RESULT OF MR. HENRY Mortimer's advice to Miss Maxwell was the following letter to Frederic Dalton, which, together with his promise of marriage inclosed in it, she forwarded to him by a safe hand; and he had the good fortune of receiving and reading it when no one was near to watch the emotions it produced.

> "I herewith inclose you, Mr. Frederic Dalton, the promise of marriage which you were imprudent enough to give me some months since; and as a friend to your family in general, and to your excellent sister Ellen in particular, I advise you never again to bestow a similar document upon any one. I cannot doubt but that you have been pretty nearly as much puzzled as vexed by the manner in which I have retained this promise, for, although I do not think that, upon the whole, you have shewn yourself particularly sharp-witted, I still give you credit for sufficient acuteness to have discovered, at no very recent date, that I was not sufficiently enamoured of your perfections to have any wish or intention of becoming your wife. As I wish not to be generous by halves, I will, therefore, at the same time that I restore to you the paper which you have been so long struggling to recover, relieve you from all further trouble of guessing what the motive could have been which induced me both to obtain and to keep it. In

the short interval between your proposal of an elopement to me, and my requesting this promise of marriage from you, I had become acquainted (no matter how) with a full, true, and particular account of your infamous conduct towards Jessie Phillips; and also, upon unquestionable authority, with the fact, that the whole history of the paternal persecution, which you were pleased to assign to me as the reason of your abrupt declaration, was false from beginning to end. Strange, and almost incredible as it may appear to you, this double discovery sufficed to cure me, and very effectually I do assure you, of the tender passion for which you so flatteringly gave me credit when you were induced to give me the paper which I now return. The one day which elapsed between your making your declaration and giving me this paper was not only sufficient to permit my obtaining the two valuable anecdotes concerning you which I have mentioned above, but also to afford me time to decide upon my own line of conduct in consequence. Perhaps, if this time had been longer, I might have decided differently. I do not exactly mean that any more mature consideration would have induced me to have accepted your obliging proposal for an elopement, but I think it possible, if I had meditated upon the subject a little longer, I might have hit upon some better plan for effecting the objects I had in view. These objects, Mr. Frederic, were, first, to punish you for your audacious attempt to make me marry you as a matter of convenience to yourself—and that, too, by means of uttering the most atrocious falsehoods against your excellent father; and, secondly, to place you so far at my mercy as might enable me to enforce something like justice to the unhappy girl you had destroyed. I almost flatter thyself, indeed, that I might honestly reverse the order in which I have stated these motives; I *trust* that the deepest feeling within me was pity for the unhappy Jessie. Be this as it may, however, I do not scruple to confess that I have retained the paper which you have so often demanded chiefly for the satisfaction of watching your various emotions when asking for it. But I begin to think that it is time this idle sport should end. Before I conclude this letter, however, I must address to you a few words of very serious admonition and advice. At present, or, at any rate, up to the time of reading this communication from me, you have believed that your conduct towards Jessie Phillips was unknown, and under this belief you have suffered to hide both her own shame and your villany within the dismal walls of the Union workhouse. I conjure you, Mr. Frederic Dalton, to let this be so no longer. I conjure you, for her sake and your own, to withdraw her from this miserable abode, and place her in some distant county where, by a little assistance from you, she may be enabled once again to support herself by her needle in decency and comfort. I will not threaten you, Mr. Frederic Dalton, with becoming your accuser before the eyes of the Deepbrook neighbourhood. For rather would I hope that this quiet remonstrance may produce the effect I wish, without exposing further either the poor girl or you. Nay, instead of threatening, I will make you a promise; I hereby pledge you my word that I will not make public the information of which accident has made me the mistress for a whole month from the date of this letter. When that interval shall have elapsed, I shall take measures to ascertain whether Jessie Phillips be still in the workhouse; and I sincerely hope, for the sake of many, that I shall find she is not.

"MARTHA MAXWELL."

Having finished this epistle, Martha remained with it open before her for a minute or two before she could decide whether she should or should not shew it to Henry Mortimer before she sent it; but at length she decided she should not. This was not because she thought he would disapprove it, but because she was conscious of having given way, in some degree, to a sort of contemptuous irony, to which she did not think it fair to make him a party, although her conscience gave her no trouble on the subject, as far as she alone was concerned. She determined, however, to copy it, as the shewing it to her confidant after it was sent could involve him in no responsibility respecting its contents. Having done this, she made up the packet and despatched it.

It reached its destination, as stated above, not only safely, but when the person to whom it was addressed was alone. The first characters which caught his eye as he opened the envelope were those of the well-remembered promise, written by the hand of Miss Maxwell, but signed by his own. It was hardly possible for him to have received any document with more pleasure than he received this; for, not withstanding his threats to Martha of intending to apply for legal assistance in order to recover it, he was quite as little disposed to try the experiment as she could be to let him. In fact, the publicity of this adventure, or of any part of it, was about the last thing in the world that he would have desired. Such, indeed, had been his feelings concerning it from the very first; and this wish to keep it secret had increased, instead of diminishing, with every day that had passed over him. But his aversion to the idea of having the whole story published, commented upon, and all the feelings it was likely to produce put in action against him, had hitherto been as nothing, a mere languid and half-indifferent preference for one contingency instead of another, when compared to the state of his mind at the time Miss Maxwell's letter was delivered to him.

In order to explain this, it will be necessary to describe the effect produced on the said Frederic Dalton by the startling change which had taken place in the prospects of his eldest sister. The one word of exclamation which he uttered when the fact of her approaching marriage with Lord Pemberton was announced by his father has been already recorded, and may fairly be taken as evidence of the state of mind into which the intelligence threw him. His first emotion was that of malicious vexation, and his first impulse led him to withdraw himself as speedily as might be from the sight of the happiness which beamed on every countenance, and in which he was so very little disposed to share. This impulse led him at once to seek the retirement of his own room, and could he, while passing the door of the library in his way to the stairs, have conveniently blown the two supremely happy persons within through the ceiling, and so upwards through the roof, till they were in a fair way of being annihilated, he would probably have done it. But, not having this power, he passed onward in no very amiable or enviable state of mind. Having reached his room, stirred the fire with a sort of savagely cross look and movement, as if he hoped he was giving it pain, and thrown himself into a remarkably comfortable arm-chair which stood immediately before it, he fell into a reverie. How long it took to change the idle poutings of impotent ill-humour into a more agreeable state of mind, I know not, but the well-stirred fire was still burning brightly, when he began to mutter inwardly to himself these words:—"Yes, I hate her; and I suppose I always shall hate her, for somehow or other it is in my nature to do it, and I can't help it. But it is not like me either to quarrel with what every other young fellow in the kingdom would make such a good thing of, as having Pemberton for a brother-in-law, and, by and by, having a duchess close to my own place by way of sister. If she has children, I must be uncle to all the young lords and ladies, and there's something in that to a fellow who knows how to turn every thing to account like me." Such thoughts, once generated, began to grow apace; and as his meditations continued they increased, not only in strength but in number. By degrees a multitude of visions, all of exceeding brightness, and himself the hero of each, began to rise before him. Rank and fashion, grace and splendour, the love of titled ladies, and the envy of ugly lords, all wove themselves together into a romance, the *dénouement* of which was his marrying a certain lady, Isabella Montgomery, a niece of the Duchess of Rochdale, of whom mention had been made in his hearing as one of the fairest and most richly endowed among the reigning stars of the day.

"A pretty fool should I be, shouldn't I?" he again began muttering, but this time with a very pleasant smile. "A pretty fool should I make of myself if I spoiled such a scheme as that just because I took a fancy that Miss Ellen used to cast a sheep's eye at my estate! not but what I was right too in fancying that she was plotting and planning something, and she has plotted and planned to some purpose, I must say that for her. Devilish well done,—devilish well managed, from first to last. And, if that's the sort of game she likes to play, who knows but she may lend me a helping hand, if I can but come round her a little, and there's few things I can't do. It's in the family I fancy."

And then the young man got up, took his candle in his hand, and walked across the room to his looking-glass. He certainly was very handsome; and it happened now, as it had often done before, that as he gazed, his lips parted into a most becoming smile, the effect, perhaps, both of the satisfaction which he felt in contemplating what was before him and the wish to make it more charming still by the display of his beautiful teeth.

It was just at this moment, just as he felt how irresistible such a face and figure must be when animated with an ardent desire to please, that the recollection both of Martha Maxwell and of Jessie Phillips flashed across him. Not, indeed, that they were in any degree connected together in his mind, but it was, at the same moment, that he felt how tremendously the disclosure of his adventures with either would tend to destroy all the brilliant hopes to which the approaching marriage of his sister had given birth. It would be difficult to describe the mixture of fear and rage into which these thoughts plunged him. He actually tossed his arms about, first assailed by the one and then tormented by the other, with a degree of impotent violence which might have made the presence of either fair one a matter of considerable personal danger to herself. At length, however, he contrived to master these disagreeable and very useless emotions by repeating, again and again, "Nonsense! They cannot, they dare not, betray me! What could either of them get by it? Nothing on earth but shame and exposure for their own share; and that will keep them quiet, if nothing else can, and to that I must trust."

It was on the morning which followed this evening, so important for the family of Dalton, that the letter of Miss Maxwell was put into his hands. For a few moments after he had perused it he was in a state of ungovernable rage, which, had he been some thirty years older, might have brought on a fit of apoplexy. He clenched his fists, he ground his teeth, he stamped with his feet, he tore the letter and its enclosure into a hundred fragments, and only recovered his self-possession by the vehement exertion with which he calmed himself sufficiently to utter a horrible oath, by which he bound himself to be revenged on both the women whose united endeavours seemed linked together to destroy him.

This paroxysm of violence, however, did not last very long, for it was less natural to his character than the more deliberate process by which he had hitherto contrived to find out, on most occasions, the best way of getting out of a scrape without having recourse to any violent measures whatever. The first thing he did, after recovering his composure, was to collect and burn every fragment of Martha's letter, and its precious inclosure, and the next to write the following answer to it:—

"My dear Miss Maxwell,

"I have too often, in common with all your other neighbours, enjoyed the pleasure of a good laugh from your witty mystifications to be either very much surprised, or at all offended, by your now selecting my humble self as the subject of a jest; and, though I cannot as yet exactly comprehend what you mean, I am willing to wait till the point of the joke shall be revealed. We are all aware that some thing a little more tender than a common flirtation is going on between a certain young lady, who shall be nameless, and a certain young gentleman, who, for the present, shall be nameless also. But as this latter individual is not an acquaintance of very long standing, and as his visits to our rural shades are only occasional, it is possible that his joining in any of our little village pleasantries might be dangerous, inasmuch as this accomplished stranger, not being thoroughly acquainted with all the persons of our Deepbrook society, might get into a scrape with some of them before he was aware of it. Your excellent understanding, my dear Miss Maxwell, will, I am sure, enable you to understand and receive this friendly hint as I wish you to do. As to the pretty little girl called Jessie Phillips, whose name figures so mysteriously in your lively and truly comic letter, I really know nothing about her. Once, indeed, as I well remember, I was guilty of the indiscretion of giving her a kiss, at which frolic my sister Ellen was present.

> My excuse was, and is, that I had taken too much wine; and I confess I doubt if Ellen, with all her good qualities, which no one can more love and admire than I do,—I doubt, I say, if my sister Ellen, if she really has mentioned this circumstance to you, can plead any cause equally satisfactory for doing so. And now, my dear Miss Martha, let me assure you that I feel, as every man in the world would, I am sure, delighted by having received a letter from you, and have not lost, as you will perceive, a moment in answering it. Let this induce you to repeat the favour whenever you have a few minutes of leisure to bestow on yours,
>
> "Faithfully and gratefully,
>
> "FREDERIC DALTON."

"Now let her shew *that* from one end of the parish to the other," thought the well-satisfied young squire, as he concluded a second and very careful reading of this epistle. "I strongly suspect that there may be others, and her enchanting self among them, who would feel more repugnance to having it seen than I should." As to Miss Maxwell's letter to him, the young man had no uneasiness whatever from any fear of her making it public. He doubted greatly if she would even have the imprudence to keep a copy of it; and as he had seen the original, together with its important inclosure, converted to the very finest dust into which post paper can resolve itself by the assistance of fire, he felt hardly a single qualm left of that paroxysm of terror into which the first perusal of the packet had thrown him. As to Jessie, indeed, the case was somewhat different. But even on this point his habitual confidence in himself and his good fortune did not desert him. His angry feelings having been soothed into positive good humour by the act of writing the excessively clever and exquisitely impertinent letter which lay before him, he was rapidly recovering that happy frame of mind which leads such specimens of humanity as himself to make (as he called it) the best of every thing: that is to say, he determined to snap his fingers at all the gossip which could by possibility be got up between two such young ladies as Ellen and Martha, respecting his love adventures with a miserable little pauper, shut up in the workhouse. "Stuff and nonsense!" he muttered half aloud. "As if it did not happen every day in the year? What's that blessed clause in the new law for, I wonder, if a man is to be frightened out of his wits by such a matter as this?" And then, having sent off his letter, he refreshed himself by a solitary walk on the sunny side of the garden wall, while he meditated on the most likely method of getting properly introduced to the Lady Isabella Montgomery.

# XXXIX

*A plot in which the idiot girl takes a distinguished part—a medical accident—Jessie leaves the workhouse in search of Frederic Dalton*

THE EVENTS RECORDED IN THE last chapter took place during the last day or two of Susan White's residence in the workhouse. At length the happy moment was come for her deliverance, for her excellent English-hearted husband no sooner felt himself restored to health and the use of his limbs than he determined to trust to them for the support of his family, notwithstanding all the difficulty of beginning the world anew at the age of forty. But not all the joy of being restored to her husband and her boy made Susan forget her promise to poor Jessie. She had undertaken to think about the manner of her getting out; and she had done so to such good purpose that the wretched girl had only to follow exactly the instructions she received in order to achieve the object proposed. Mrs. White had not failed to remark the very steadfast feeling of affection which Silly Sally constantly manifested towards Jessie. Whether it were that her gentleness and her drooping sorrow touched the poor idiot's heart, or that the memory of former kindness on the part of the once gay and happy sempstress, had created a lasting feeling of gratitude that baffled even her folly to obliterate, certain it is that Sally never did look at Jessie Phillips without exhibiting a greater approach to meaning on her vacant features than they had ever displayed before. She would follow her about, during the few hours that she remained in the common den, as a faithful dog may often be seen to follow at the heels of his master, pausing when she paused, and moving on when she moved on. The only very obvious superiority that the idiot had over the dog was the gift of speech, for whereas the dog could only wag its tail,

Sally could repeat again and again the words, "I love you, Jessie Phillips, I love you."

It was the observing this which suggested to Mrs. White the contrivance by which the temporary absence of Jessie from the work house was, at length, very easily effected. Having contrived to take the idiot girl apart while she was herself permitted to breathe the air of the court-yard, she began talking to her of what she always seemed to understand better than any thing else, namely, the pleasure of walking in the green fields, and then she spoke of Jessie Phillips, and of her longing to see those green fields once more.

"Then let her go out with Sally to-morrow," said the girl.

"Nay, Sally," replied Mrs. White, "that can't be, for nobody is let to go out but you."

The good woman then went on gently and quietly, till she made Sally comprehend that the only plan would be for her to stand loitering about close to Jessie when the women were out taking air in the court, and to lend her the great pinafore she always wore (to keep the workhouse garments from being spoiled by her awkward mode of feeding herself), together with the comical relic of an enormous black chip bonnet, which she was permitted to put on whenever the fancy took her, and, thus disguised, to let Jessie take her chance of slipping out, in the same way that she so constantly did herself. When, at length, the girl fully comprehended the scheme, she was in ecstasies of delight; and Mrs. White began to fear that the project would be rendered abortive by the eagerness of the agent she was obliged to employ. But Sally seemed to understand her perfectly when she said, "You will be found out, Sally, if you laugh and talk that fashion; and then all will be spoilt, and Jessie will never see the green fields again." This quieted her in a moment, and she nodded her head, and walked away with such an air of sedate demureness, that Mrs. White felt persuaded she would not fail in the performance of the part allotted to her. Could the exit be thus effected, the return would, of course, be easier still, as, even if discovered at the moment, no great harm could come of it beyond a rebuke; and, even if discovered in going out, the whole might be passed over as merely a jest of Silly Sally's, whose harmless vagaries were always treated as a matter of pleasantry by the laughter-loving couple who presided over the Deepbrook Union.

But, well as the plan was arranged, no experiment to prove either its success or failure was attempted for some time after it was projected, for Jessie fell sick, and was unable to leave her wretched pallet for many days. The women about her thought that her hour of trial was come, and the doctor was summoned to attend her; but, fortunately for Jessie, perhaps, he was so completely intoxicated, that, though Dick Dempster contrived to make him reach the room, amidst shouts of laughter from his wife and himself also, he fell prostrate as soon as the governor's supporting arms were withdrawn; but, being an especial favourite with both the governor and his wife, he was permitted to lay where he had fallen, in the enjoyment of a very particularly sound sleep, till long after the sun rose on the following morning. During this interval, the fever from which Jessie was suffering abated; it had probably been caused by the tremendous pressure upon her nerves, occasioned by the interview she was anticipating with Dalton. For some hours she had been delirious; and the frightful pains in her head, which accompanied this attack, seemed to threaten a continued loss of reason. But soon after the apothecary fell asleep on the floor she also fell asleep in her bed; and the orders given, that "nobody was to disturb the doctor," caused the over-full room to be so much more tranquil than usual, that her healing sleep lasted also to the morning. When, however, she learned, on waking, that the strange figure which still lay snoring near her bed was the doctor, who was come to look after her and her child, she immediately rose and made her way down stairs with the rest. Here she was, of course, exposed to scoldings from Mrs. Dempster for "*making believe,*" and ridicule and ribaldry without end from some of her companions. Short as had been the interval during which she had been out of the way of this, its effect upon her seemed more terrible than ever; and heartily did she pray for strength to make the attempt she contemplated. Poor Jessie! her pride, indeed, was gone now; for, instead of dreading worse than death the idea of asking, or even receiving, pecuniary assistance from Dalton, all her hope now hung upon it. But for three days after leaving her bed she felt that her strength was not equal to the enterprise; the prudence and patience, however, with which she postponed the undertaking was the surest proof of the strength of purpose which enabled her at last to achieve it.

For another two days after she fancied that she had recovered sufficient strength for the walk she meditated, it rained hard, and Jessie had still to endure that hardest of all trials, uncertainty and suspense. At last, however, the February sun rose brightly, and the very birds began to sing, as if they had forgotten that March was to frown upon them for thirty-one nights and days before they were to be greeted by the smiles of April. Even the poor prisoners of the workhouse rejoiced that the rain had ceased, and eagerly profited by the permission given to turn out into the court for half an hour, and enjoy all the liberty that its area of one acre could bestow.

"Will her go into the fields this gay day?" said the idiot girl, whispering into the ear of Jessie.

"Yes, Sally, yes!" was the reply; and, cunningly pretending to be playfully plaguing her friend Jessie, the idiot contrived to push her back behind a water-tub, and invested her, as slyly and as cleverly, with the bonnet and pinafore, as if she had been in the very fullest possession of her understanding.

"Now, Jessie!" she exclaimed, as a group of paupers, who were come up for orders, were waking their way out of the house where the board of guardians were sitting, "Now her scramble away to the door, and that 'ill do. Nobody shall see t'other Sally."

Jessie obeyed, passing behind a cartful of potatoes and a huge pump that favoured her purpose. No eye was directed towards her; and in another moment she had passed through the door, and found herself at liberty to turn which way she would in the fields.

Suffering in body, tortured in mind, trembling as she looked forward, shuddering as she looked back, Jessie Phillips was in no condition to enjoy her recovered freedom; yet even so the influence of the free air was felt, though unconsciously, and she walked hastily forward, with less danger of falling as she went than she expected. Had her condition, however, been less desperate, and the tumult of her spirits less violent, it would have been totally beyond her power to go through with the task she had set herself; for by nature she was both gentle and timid, and as unfitted for the performance of the business she was upon as it was well possible to be. But at that moment, though she knew where she was going, and where she had been, and could have answered any question put to her very rationally, Jessie could scarcely be said to be in her tight mind. Her pulse gave nearly a hundred throbs in a minute; and her fixed purpose of finding Frederic Dalton, and demanding from him a provision for her child, much more resembled the dominating idea of a maniac, such as often leads through all opposing difficulties to a successful attempt at self-destruction than to the steady resolution of a rational being. But this mattered not; on she went, always in the right direction, and unchecked and unchallenged by any. She encountered, indeed, but few, for, though the day was fine, the paths were still wet, and none of those accustomed to wander through them for pleasure were as yet abroad. Had it been otherwise, indeed, it is doubtful if she would have attracted any troublesome degree of notice, for the well-known pinafore, the unique black chip bonnet, drawn forward over the face, and the workhouse dress, which was rarely seen abroad, except on Silly Sally, would probably have prevented a second glance being directed towards her from any one, for her incessant wanderings made her too familiar an object to attract attention.

Jessie knew the young squire's habits well; she knew that he was wont, after breakfast, to visit the stables, and after this to lounge up to the village "reading-room," where he not only got a glimpse at the newspaper, but was pretty certain of meeting his friend Dick Baxter, from whom he was rarely separated for twenty-four hours together.

It was, therefore, to the door leading from the stable-yard into the lane that opened at no great distance upon the high road that Jessie Phillips directed her steps, and, having reached it, she sat herself down upon one of the low posts to which the gates were fastened when the carriage went out in that direction, and there determined to remain, if necessary, till nightfall.

# XL

*Brotherly affection kindly received—the young Squire meets an old favourite rather unexpectedly—an interesting conversation ensues, which does not end amicably*

THE INTERVAL WHICH HAD ELAPSED since Frederic Dalton despatched his letter to Miss Maxwell had only served to confirm him in all the purposes and intentions which he had formed when writing it. He had the audacity, at the very first meeting with his sister Ellen, after the announcement of her engagement, to commence his operations for converting himself from the most insolent and detestable brother that ever existed into something precisely the reverse. There was so little effort made to conceal the fact, that this remarkable change in his sentiments was produced by the equally remarkable change in her situation, that there was no possibility of bringing the charge of hypocrisy against him; and the happy Ellen felt too well disposed to be pleased with every body to quarrel with her contemptible brother because he thought it best to cease quarrelling with her. She, perhaps, smiled a little aside at the sudden metamorphosis; but, far from ejecting this newly proffered brotherly affection, she only hailed it the more gratefully, as another benefit arising from the generous and devoted attachment of her noble lover.

All, therefore, was going well with him in that quarter; and, for about the thousandth time in his life, Frederic Dalton felt persuaded, that whatever he chose to do *that* he could do, and that he had only to form a plan in order to succeed in it. As to Miss Maxwell, and any possible annoyance he could receive from her, he would have altogether forgotten it, in his present state of delightful excitement, had it not been for a sort of gnawing longing for vengeance against her, and the "false-hearted

Jessie," for first daring to throw off the chains of the fascination which he had condescended to throw over them, and then joining together in a plot to bully and torment him. Had he, indeed, conceived it possible that either of them could dare to peep forth from their obscurity and the secrecy in which the pride of the one and the shame of the other must in common prudence keep them concealed, this longing to be revenged on both would not have remained so quietly waiting an opportunity to shew itself when it might be done with impunity; but, as several days had elapsed without his hearing a word more from Martha, though he was pretty sure that his letter must have stung her to the quick, he reposed in the most perfect security, and thought of nothing but the Lady Isabella Montgomery, and the Thursday of the following week, which was the day fixed for the Duke and Duchess of Rochdale and Lord Pemberton to dine at the manor-house. The only stranger invited to join this strictly family party was Mrs. Buckhurst; and the handsome Frederic looked forward with the most delightful exhilaration of spirits to this opportunity of exhibiting himself without a rival to the eyes of his venerated new relations. Whistling from a superabundance of pleasant thoughts rather than from any want of them, the young man stepped forth from the stable-yard into the lane as nearly as possible at the hour when he was expected, and the first object that met his eye was the back of a female figure, in the dress of a work house pauper, but wearing on her head the unmistakable bonnet of Silly Sally.

"What do you come hanging about here for, you dirty idiot, you?" cried the brutal young man, stepping forward probably in the intention of assisting her removal from the seat in no very gentle manner; but ere he could reach her the figure started up, with a movement so sudden as to cause the unfastened bonnet to fall to the ground, and, turning towards him, presented to his startled eyes the wan features of Jessie Phillips.

So great was the change in her appearance, since he had seen her last, that for one wild moment of indescribable terror and dismay the guilt-struck young man fancied that he beheld a vision from the world of shadows; but, of course, the thought was gone "ere he could say it was," and fixing upon her a glance in which neither love nor pity had the slightest share, he exclaimed, "What in the devil's name brings you here? What do you hope or expect from daring to shew yourself before my father's gate in this condition? Speak, girl, this instant! Is it Miss Maxwell who has dared to send you here? By — she shall pay for it!"

"No, Frederic Dalton, no!" returned the pale girl, fixing her large and almost unnaturally lustrous eyes upon him. "It is the welfare of your child that has sent me here. For my own sake gladly would I never have seen you more, but for my child, for your child, Frederic Dalton, I demand support."

"Demand?" returned the villain, with a sneer. "Where did you get your law from, Jessie Phillips? There's a sovereign for you," and he chucked the coin he named to her feet, "Go back to the workhouse and tell them to spend that in caudle. I offered you more once, but I never will again, you may depend upon it. You are a bad, good-for-nothing girl as ever lived, false at heart, and most hatefully ungrateful. Do you think I don't know all the villanous lies you told Miss Maxwell about me? You think she kept your secret, perhaps? Likely enough, for I believe you are as silly as you are wicked, and I am too kind to you by half speaking to you as gently as I do now, for you deserve to be horsewhipped for having gone and told such tales. If you had behaved only decently well, I should have been only too kind to you, but you have deserved all the sorrow that has come upon you and ten times more. So off with you this instant, or it shall be worse for you."

Jessie felt as if she was rather strengthened than overpowered by this brutality, and, still fixing her eyes upon him, she said "Frederic Dalton, will you maintain your child?"

The natural gentleness of the girl seemed suddenly changed into courage capable of enduring any thing. He looked at her for a moment with astonishment, and then the conviction flashed upon him that she was *acting under orders*. The steadfast and desperate spirit which shot from her beautiful eyes was not, could not be, her own. He remembered the timid softness of her character, which had robbed even her virtue of its strength, and then thought of the bold manœuverings of Martha Maxwell to attain the object she had in view, and not a doubt remained on his mind that it was Martha who had sent her to him.

John Leech

Not all the dignified reserve of Mr Dalton senior, nor Ellen's earnest wish to keep her approaching marriage a secret from her gossiping neighbours as long as possible, had sufficed to prevent the wonderful news of her approaching marriage from spreading through the whole parish. It could hardly have been reasonably expected, indeed, that Mrs. Dalton could have given orders to her confidential housekeeper for the dinner at which the family at the castle were to make their first appearance in form at the manor-house, without some little hints escaping her enough to set the household into a ferment of expectation, which was likely enough to spread to butcher and baker, to master and man, till no single ear in Deepbrook had escaped the hearing something about it. Besides, to say the truth, the young squire himself saw no good reason why such particularly interesting intelligence should not be communicated to their particular friends, and he had therefore taken upon himself the pleasant office of mentioning at the Mortimers', the Lewises', the Dalys', the Johnsons', &c. that his dear little sister Ellen was in a fair way of becoming a marchioness, and, in process of time, a duchess.

To a man so wrapped up and enveloped in self as Frederic Dalton, such a sudden and unexpected accession of consequence, as this connexion could not fail to give, was productive of an effect upon his spirits and feelings that resembled intoxication. A perfectly new state of existence seemed opening before him. Visions of peers and peeresses, of places and pensions, of stars and garters, of crowns and sceptres, seemed to float around him. Accustomed upon all occasions to consider himself as the principal person in whatever was going on, he now felt that, although accident had made Ellen the instrument by which this pleasant movement in advance of all the county squirearchy had been caused, it was himself who would be chiefly benefited by it; and, while he sneered at Lord Pemberton's want of taste in selecting so undistinguished a beauty, he hugged himself in the belief that it was only another instance of his uncommon good luck, that turned every thing, even such a whey-faced girl as Ellen, into the means of pleasure and advancement.

Such being his state of mind, and such his consciousness of the brightness of the future which was opening before him, it is not difficult to guess the sort of emotion to which the sight of Jessie, and the belief that Miss Maxwell had sent her, gave rise. All the possible consequences of the discovery likely to ensue rose before him like palpable pictures. All his greatness, all his fashion, all his pre-eminence, were seen crumbling into ashes before the blasting eyes of the miserable object before him, while a phantom of Martha Maxwell appeared peeping over her shoulder, shewing its white teeth from ear to ear, in delighted laughter, while its head nodded and its finger pointed to himself.

Jessie saw him turn pale and tremble. "Well may you tremble, now," she exclaimed,— "well may you look almost as pale as I shall do to-morrow, perhaps, for you shall rue the day you saw me—you shall rue the lies you spoke, and the vows you swore! At a day, not long ago, I think I would have crept into a hole that a dog would have turned from, so I might have hid my shame and its wretched fruit. But that wickedness passed away from me, and then I thought that I would bear all, even the looking once more upon you, so I could save my child from want and wickedness. But that is all gone together now; I care not for my shame—I care only for my child, though it has such a wretch as you are for its father, and I will not die without telling the whole world what you are. This, this I will do, Frederic Dalton," she added wildly, "though it shall be with the last breath I draw. Not swear the child to you, villain? who says I sha'nt? who can prevent me? God give me but strength to reach the lawyer's door, and your infamy shall make more noise than Jessie's shame."

As he listened to the failing, faltering voice that uttered these last words, Dalton longed in his savage heart that he had the power to stop its feeble accents for ever; and so desperate was the rage and hatred which burned within him, that his glaring eyes looked here and there, as if seeking to discover if he was sufficiently safe from human eyes to murder her. Whether any such horrible idea really arose within him with sufficient distinctness to be called a purpose, it is impossible to say; but it is certain that he laid no hands upon her, save for the purpose of withdrawing her from the conspicuous place she occupied to a sheltered nook close by, but concealed from the sight of any one, going or coming through the gates, by a thick holly-bush. Jessie had fainted; and a new idea had suggested itself to the young squire, he left her, safe enough upon the turf, and quietly walked away.

# XLI

*The lawyer of Deepbrook receives two visitors on business—he gives them both important legal information, which proves exceedingly satisfactory to one, but not quite equally so to the other*

MR. FREDERIC DALTON RE-ENTERED THE gates of his father's stable-yard, gave one or two directions, in his usual tone of voice, to the groom as he passed back to the house, entered the library for a moment, spoke a few gay and laughing words to his father about Ellen, and then started off, and made the best of his way to the house and the office of his excellent friend Mr. Lewis.

Few elderly lawyers and youthful squires could be on better or more familiar terms together than Mr. Lewis and Mr. Frederic Dalton. The time had been, perhaps, when the fond father of the fair sisters of Lewis Lodge thought it by no means impossible that one or the other of them might at some future period figure in the dignified capacity of "lady of the manor;" and perhaps it was this vague, but very pleasant idea, which first led to the peculiarly kind and friendly manners of the old gentleman to the young one. As the young gentleman liked both the champagne and the daughters of the old gentleman exceedingly well, it naturally followed that his manners in return were uniformly cordial and agreeable, so that it was quite impossible that any two persons in their respective situations could be better friends. Of late, indeed, the hope of having a daughter lady of the manor had somewhat faded, particularly since the arrival of the two charming Miss Mortimers; but nevertheless Mr. Lewis still was, and still hoped to be, confidential man of business at the manor-house, and had never for a moment suffered his civility to relax, even when the eldest Miss Mortimer had set all her young neighbours at defiance, and displayed herself for weeks together as the reigning belle of Deepbrook. Nor was it likely that the astounding news of Ellen's approaching marriage should in any degree chill the lawyer's friendship for her brother; so far from it, indeed, that the moment the young man made his appearance in the office the lawyer sprang from his writing-table. Mr. Lewis was too gentlemanlike a person to sit at a desk. And, though the said table was covered with law papers, red tape, and books bound in rough brown leather, he cordially stretched out both his hands to his visitor, and exclaimed, "My dear Dalton, I am glad to see you."

"How are you, Lewis? I'm glad you are alone. I've got a queer story to tell you," said the young squire.

"Have you? I will listen to it, you may depend upon it, even if the lord-chancellor were waiting for me. But first, my dear fellow, I must say one word to you about this delightful connexion with the Rochdales. I wish you joy with all my heart, Dalton. Nothing on earth could be so fortunate for you, Fred. It is exactly the sort of thing, with your handsome unencumbered estate, to make you one of the first men in the county."

"Why, yes, Lewis," replied the young man, "I am quite aware that it is an advantageous connexion. It is just the sort of thing that gives a man the power of helping on a friend now and then. We all know the value of a good word in the right place. But we will talk of all that another time, Lewis; I have got something to tell you now that will make you stare, I'm sure, and you really must listen to me attentively, and give me your advice about it."

The lawyer most cordially protested that Frederic might command him freely and securely in any way he wished.

"Well, then, Lewis," resumed young Dalton, "what do you say to my having the very unexpected honour of receiving a visit from a young hussy this morning, and a pauper, too, by heavens! who threatened in good set terms to swear a child to me, if I did not immediately give her a sum of money?"

"What do I say to it my dear fellow? Thank the gods, Dalton, the saying in such cases now is not very difficult. If you feel any repugnance yourself to instructing the young lady in the law of the land, just send her to me."

Frederic Dalton was within a breath of saying that the girl had herself threatened to pay "the lawyer" a visit, but recollected that the case would have a better aspect, if her appearance before him, should she indeed have strength and courage to fulfil her threat, were seemingly the result of his will instead of her own. He, therefore, replied, "Thanks Lewis! I shall very greatly prefer it, I assure you; for, upon my honour, I should be afraid to trust my own temper in the business. For, please to observe, my good friend, that though I by no means pretend to be better than my neighbours, I plead altogether not guilty in this affair, and, therefore, as you will perceive, the girl's conduct is atrocious. I won't detain you two minutes, Lewis; but, for the sake of justice and fair play, I must explain to you the accident which put it into the creature's head to fix upon me, of all the men in the parish, to make this attack upon. It is now—"

"I beg your pardon for interrupting you, Fred., and will listen to any anecdotes you may have to tell me most willingly, for no man tells an anecdote better, but I should be no lawyer, my dear friend, if I could hear you speak of this business as if you were not aware that, whether the girl's charge be true or false, it makes no sort of difference to you. Is it possible, Dalton, that you are ignorant of this most important clause in the new act?"

The young man laughed heartily at this question; but at length composing his muscles, he replied, "No, no, Lewis, not quite so bad as that either. I never boasted of being a particularly deep lawyer, but, as far as that goes, I am up to the mystery, and I rather suspect, my good friend, that you would find it tolerably difficult to discover in any part of the three kingdoms a young fellow who was not. I do not, therefore, apply to you to get me legally out of a scrape into which, legally, I never fell, or, in fact, could fall, but merely to do just the sort of thing you have now offered, namely, to point out the best way of letting the saucy minx understand, that she is not likely, either legally or illegally, to frighten me into giving her money; and above all, to make her understand that if she intends to bully me, by running about the parish repeating a story of her own invention, in the hope that I will bribe her to hold her tongue, she is likely to be sent to prison for her pains."

"Clearly," returned Mr. Lewis. "It is exactly what will happen, as I will give her plainly to understand if you will send her to me."

"She will not refuse to come, depend upon it. She will fancy, perhaps, that I shall employ you as an agent to give her hush-money. But just let me tell you, Lewis, how the business began. The girl has taken, I am afraid, to a thoroughly depraved course of life, for she is quite a dreadful object now; but I remember her, about a year ago or so, an exceedingly pretty-looking girl and as modest, if you please, as possible. I dare say you remember Lady Mary's famous dinner-party, when we were all collected to meet the Mortimers? Well, this damsel was on that occasion hired by her attentive ladyship to take care of the ladies' cloaks and shawls, and it so happened, that having left my hat in the room where she was stationed, I found her alone, and looking devilish pretty, when I went to seek for it. Whereupon, Mr. Lewis, saving your presence, I was indiscreet enough to give her a kiss, being led to commit such folly more by Lady Mary's wine, perhaps, than the maiden's beauty. As ill luck would have it, however, my sister Ellen (dear creature!) came into the room immediately after me, and actually caught me in the fact. The girl gave herself a vast many dignified airs, and had the impertinence to go up to my sister a few days afterwards and make a formal complaint. Ellen was, of course, excessively shocked and annoyed; and I suspect that it was seeing this which first put it into the girl's head to do me this very unexpected honour. But just observe, Lewis, how completely the dates exculpate me, if nothing else did. I daresay you could turn to some memorandum or other which could prove to you, if you happen to forget it, that it is something between four and five months since the day we met at Lady Mary's; and when you come to see this audacious girl, yon will perceive what sort of a character she had to boast of at that time. There certainly never was a more impudent attempt."

"And it is exactly to render such attempts utterly harmless and abortive, Dalton, that the admirable clause has been inacted, against which so many blundering criticisms have been directed. But the wicked or the witless may maunder against it as they will, here we have it, safe and sound" (laying his hand upon the act, which made part of the furniture of his table), "and as completely the law of the land as that which awards hanging for murder. So, as to the date, you see, it matters nothing. We have nothing to do with facts now in cases of this sort, the law is comprehensive enough to do without them."

"Well, then, now I'm off," cried the young man gaily, "for I promised to ride with Pemberton this morning;" and, exchanging a friendly nod, the lawyer and his client parted.

As the riding with Lord Pemberton was merely a freak of inventive fancy, suggested by an affectionate inclination to pronounce his name, young Dalton had leisure to dodge about the vicinage of the lawyer's premises for half an hour or so, in order to ascertain whether the wretched Jessie kept her word. Nor did he watch in vain. Just as he began to think that it might be as well to return to the place where he had left her, in order to see whether she was dead or alive, he perceived her strange-looking figure, half ghostly, half grotesque, slowly, but decisively approaching the lawyer's door. He just paused long enough to see her enter it, and then wandered away, to enjoy a little pleasant chit-chat with the Mortimers about "the Rochdales."

Mr. Lewis, like every body else in the village, knew Jessie Phillips perfectly well by sight; but when she now dragged her aching limbs into his presence, he had not the slightest notion that it was the much admired village beauty who stood before him. Her beautiful hair cut close to her head, her soft and blooming cheek pale and dreadfully emaciated, the pretty neatness of her dress changed into a garb of sordid wretchedness, and, to complete the whole, the large bonnet of Silly Sally, drawn so low upon her head that it rested on her shoulders, rendered the disguise complete.

The last time she had stood beneath the roof of Mr. Lewis was in the presence of his daughters, and she had then felt so very wretched that she would almost have defied fate to make her more so. But what was that moment when compared to the present? The door of the room was closed upon her, and she stood face to face with the lawyer; but her breath seemed gone, and she spoke not.

"What do you want with me, girl?" said the tender father, the obliging neighbour, the good-tempered man, in a voice of genuine indignation, and that honest feeling of aversion to fraud and duplicity, which a lawyer can feel as well as another man when nothing particular mixes with the business in question to prevent it. "What do you come here for?" he reiterated.

"To ask," replied Jessie, with a desperate effort, "if there is any help for me?" and then, feeling that she had not explained her meaning, she added, with another gasp, "I come to know if the truth told plainly and boldly before all the world may not make a rich man take care of his own child when the mother is dead?" Still this was not what she intended—what she wished to say; but her senses were partially disturbed, and she seemed to have lost the power of expressing in words the thoughts and the facts which she wished to communicate. But this mattered little as to the success of her application to Mr. Lewis. His mind had been made up, both legally and morally, as to the answer she was to receive before she had uttered a word; there was nothing in her manner or appearance to make him alter it, nor is it very likely that even had she been ten times more able than she was to do her own story justice, he would have listened to her with sufficient patience to comprehend it. As it was, he cut the matter short, by thus addressing her.

"Young woman, you talk of speaking boldly before all the world, and I am a good deal afraid that it is likely enough you are capable of doing it. But that is not the question, so we will say no more about it. You have said something about making a rich man take care of his child. Now, this is a point on which I consider it a very important duty to speak clearly and intelligibly to every body ignorant enough not to understand it already. It does seem pretty nearly impossible, to be sure, that, after all the pains taken by the government to make the law as plain as plain can be, that any body should *really* misunderstand it. However, whether the ignorance is make-believe or not makes no difference in my readiness to speak out upon the subject, and I, therefore, tell you, my girl, that you may stand all day swearing that one man or another man is the father of your child, and no more notice will be taken of it than if you whistled. If it turns out, indeed, that you can't manage to maintain it yourself, and that it is actually and *bonâ fide* thrown upon the rate-payers, why then *they* may look about them, if they like it, and if they can prove, without any help of yours, mind you, that this one or that one is the father, why then, by bringing forward their proof, they may make him just pay the workhouse charges, and no more. But *you*, and the like of you, have no more to do with it than the man in the moon."

"And who is it, then, can prove that the child is HIS?" said Jessie, trembling with eagerness, and overlooking in her nervous agony of impatience to learn how her miserable offspring might be benefited, that it was the parish and not the child whose interest was to be protected by this ludicrously useless proviso.

"That's no business of yours, young woman. If you can't maintain yourself, it will be born in the workhouse; and if you can't maintain your child, why then it will be bred in the workhouse. Let the father be a king or a cobbler it will not make the slightest difference, so you need not trouble yourself to say any thing about that. The law has taken care of them, and such as you too, in that respect, at any rate, for it won't let you tell lies, you see, however much you may desire it."

Jessie listened to him with all her faculties upon the stretch, and the intensity of her purpose seemed for the time to steady the wavering thoughts which had so recently rolled so wildly through her head, as to make her believe, poor soul, that she was about to lose her senses. But not all her attention, nor yet the perfect sanity of her mind at the moment, could enable her to comprehend the meaning of what was said to her. Jessie knew well enough, as every body else did, that the new law had ordained many severe enactments against women in her unhappy situation, but so far from complaining of this, she had often, in the silence of the night, prayed with penitent humility that the knowledge of all the anguish which would follow the fault, might save others from committing it, and never had she murmured at the portion of retribution allotted to her. But Mr. Lewis's exposition had opened to her a perfectly new view of the case. It was not only then to punish the offending woman, but to spare the pocket of the fondly protected man, that this new regulation was established. She heard it declared, that all men so circumstanced, whether, as Mr. Lewis comprehensively expressed it, they were kings or cobblers, were proclaimed by the law of the land to be henceforward, and for ever, clear from all blame and all shame. Any atonement to the "gentle fool" who had condemned herself to pretty nearly every imaginable species of suffering, for believing that the man she loved might smile, and not be a villain, having being rendered as nearly impossible as very careful legislation could make it.

"No! it can't mean that," said she, unconsciously answering her own thoughts, rather than the lawyer's word; "Mr. Frederic Dalton—"

"Get along with you, girl!" cried the indignant attorney, positively shuddering at her presumption, in thus contumaciously naming an individual in defiance of the law. "How dare you come to me, of all men living, in the hope of having your impudent way in the very teeth of the statute? You had better be off, I promise you; for if you stay here much longer, defying queen, lords and commons, in this style, I shall lose my temper; I know I shall. So get you gone, do, and never let me set eyes on you again."

The raised voice and the frowning brow of the gentleman, as he spoke these words, destroyed completely all that was left of Jessie's firmness; she started away with a feeling of terror, such as she might have experienced if an angry bull-dog had been let loose upon her, and making her way out, she hardly knew how, she found herself in the village street, with such sudden consciousness of bodily agony, that all mental suffering was suspended for the moment, and she was conscious of nothing, but the belief that her death was rapidly approaching. She supported herself for a few moments against a post that flanked the footpath. Her head reeled, and her strength seemed rapidly failing. But the bodily anguish passed away, and then the full consciousness of her situation returned. She looked desperately round for some shelter—some covert into which she could creep and die; she looked round, and every object that met her eyes was familiar, and yet strange—familiar, even as the dear features of her lost mother to her, in the former condition, but fearfully strange, and, as it were, incongruous, in her present one. And then came the horrible terror lest the eye of some for friend might rest upon and recognise her. She stepped forward wildly, without knowing whither she intended to go, then stopped again, and tried to think, but all seemed confusion and perplexity; the only distinct idea left was the wish to hide herself; and then the idea of the workhouse came, and she longed, oh! ardently longed to be there. But the distance seemed to magnify itself in her imagination to a degree that made the wish to get there as wild as if she wished to reach the moon—for another pang had seized her; but again it passed, and then she remembered a lonely shed at a few paces only down the green lane, at the entrance of which she stood, and thither she directed her feeble steps. This lane was a favourite walk in dry weather, but the recent rains had made it wet and muddy, and the unhappy girl passed along it to the building she sought, without having endured the agony of perceiving any eye fixed upon her.

# XLII

*The governor's lady gets angry, and affronts Silly Sally—the natural does not like it, and takes herself off—she meets with sundry strange adventures, but behaves very rationally on the whole*

THE DELIGHT OF SILLY SALLY, as she watched from behind a water-tub the success of her favourite's stratagem, was excessive. Till the door had closed behind Jessie, she had remained perfectly mute and as still as a mouse; but no sooner did she lose sight of her than she began clapping her hands and laughing vehemently. As the poor idiot, besides being perfectly harmless, was almost invariably good-humoured, and ready, to the very utmost extent of her power, to obey the behests of Dick Dempster and his lady, she was, for the most part, treated with considerable indulgence by them both; but now her noisy and prolonged laughter proved too much for the nerves of the governor's helpmate, and having, once and again, vainly admonished her by an uplifted finger, and a very imperative command, to be quiet, she at length lost her temper, and gave the poor natural a tolerably sharp box on the ear.

Had Silly Sally been more accustomed to this sort of chastisement, she would probably have been less affronted by it, but now she did not approve it at all. She uttered not a single syllable, however, either of complaint or remonstrance; and, as far as rendering her quiet went, the measure was perfectly successful, for Sally instantly ceased laughing, and, clasping her hands together under her pinafore, she remained as still as a post. But in her heart the poor girl was as angry as she could be at any thing; and all the wit she had was immediately centred upon one project, namely, that of contriving to let a second Silly Sally slip through the outer door without drawing official observation upon the escape of the first. All the quiet cunning which may so often be traced in brains so constituted was now put in practice by the girl, in order to compass this object; but several hours wore away before she could effect it. At length, however, Dempster, who had been standing near the door when Jessie passed out, left his post, and, the door being opened shortly afterwards by one who had license to go and to come, Sally, in her usual way, slipped out after him, without attracting the observation of any one.

"Now, then, her's out!" she exclaimed, with a joyous hound, as she scampered forward towards the village; and perhaps, if she could be said to think at all, she did think then that it would be some time before she came back again. For some time she continued to amuse herself in the fields by a variety of gambols, rather more childish and frolicsome than usual, for at that moment she certainly felt, as keenly as if she had been wiser, that it was pleasanter to jump about outside the walls than to have her ears boxed within them.

But after this had lasted for some time poor Sally began to feel hungry; nevertheless, she turned not back, but, on the contrary, only walked more steadily forward towards a small farm at a considerable distance from the workhouse, where she had more than once helped the good wife, at harvest time, by playing with the little ones, and where in return she had often got a more savoury meal than her usual quarters afforded.

But now Sally arrived too late for the farm-house dinner-time; which unwelcome fact was announced to her by the mistress of the mansion, who hospitably added, however, "You must come earlier, Sally, another time."

But this, which might have satisfied her tolerably well on other occasions, did not do so now, for she continued to loiter about the door; and at last, though by no means an habitual beggar, she ventured to whisper, "Sally's very hungry." The good-natured woman received the hint very kindly, saying, "Is she, poor soul?—wait a minute, then;" and after an absence that even hungry Sally did not think long she brought out and put into her hands wherewithal to furnish more than one substantial meal. On all such occasions, Sally's thanks were invariably rendered by a broad grin; having performed which, with its accompanying nod, she turned away, as usual, in search of some pleasant spot wherein to enjoy the only gratification that she shared in perfect equality with her fellow-creatures—a species of equality, by the way, more satisfactory to the idiot than flattering to the intellectual superiority of some other folks.

The weather throughout the whole morning had been bright and beautiful, but now the wintry wind began to blow again, accompanied by sleet and rain. Sally, however, knew a great deal better than to make her dinner-parlour of any spot to which such disagreeable companions would be admitted; and, having looked round her for half a minute, darted off for a well-known and often-enjoyed place of shelter, where many a similar meal, bestowed in a similar manner, had been devoured. This favourite retreat of the by no means unhappy idiot was a shed erected by sufferance upon the waste, by an humble carrier possessed of a large donkey and a little fish-cart, but who, not having space enough beside his dwelling for their accommodation, had been quietly permitted to erect this shed. It was here that Jessie had taken refuge and it was here that her faithful friend and ally found her, within three hours after she had entered it.

The corner in which the miserable Jessie lay was dark, but not sufficiently so to prevent Sally's immediately spying her out and knowing her. Setting down her bacon and bread on the window-sill, she knelt down beside her, and called her by her name, but, receiving no answer, came to the conclusion that she was fast asleep, and was in the act of quietly withdrawing herself, when she was startled by the feeble cry of a new-born babe. This was responded to on the part of Sally by a cry of joy. She speedily found the little being whose voice had so delighted her, and immediately set to work to swathe and bandage the child in the most careful and tender manner, and in very perfect imitation of all that she had heretofore seen performed upon similar occasions. Many, indeed, were the poor bodies who had joyfully accepted the "half-reasoning" services of Sally in occasionally nursing and dressing their babies; and it was impossible that the most accomplished nurse that ever lived could exceed her in fondness or in care.

Nothing but her inveterate love of roving need have prevented her from nursing babies all the days of her life; but as the good women of Deepbrook did not relish the idea of having their little ones sometimes carried away to the distance of a dozen miles, and sometimes borne through a briskly running stream, with no better bridge under them than Sally's arms, no one had ever thought proper to engage her services, except occasionally, and when there was little or no risk of her eloping with her little charge.

Notwithstanding her moon-struck brain, Sally shewed considerable ingenuity in arranging garments for her newly found treasure. The pinafore which had assisted the escape of Jessie being carefully withdrawn from the person of the unconscious mother, Sally very dexterously tore it into strips, with which she carefully enveloped the infant, using a corner of it to cover its head, with a degree of ingenuity that would have done credit to the adroitness of a Red Indian squaw. In all this she was very conveniently aided by her teeth, without which, indeed, her curiously constructed baby-wardrobe could never have been brought to such perfection. Having completed this business greatly to her own satisfaction, she rewarded herself by hugging and kissing the baby, and cooing and chirruping to it for several minutes. But then it began to cry again, and the embarrassed girl began to look around with considerable uneasiness for any species of food, which she was too good and experienced a nurse not to know was the panacea always found the most successful in stopping such wailings. She thought of her bread and bacon, but shook her head very disconsolately as she did so. "Her must get milk, and her will too, for poor little Jessie!" This resolution was hardly taken before it was acted on. The daylight was already fading fast, but before starting she contrived to satisfy herself that the bundle of dry hay which was under the head of poor Jessie would make her very comfortable by way of a pillow till she came back, and, having collected all the loose litter she could find, she laid it gently upon her motionless favourite, in order to keep her warm, and then sallied forth upon her errand, not forgetting, however, to carry her provender with her, which she contrived to eat with great enjoyment as she trudged along, without its interfering in the least degree with the tenderest care for her little charge, which soon lay fast asleep upon her bosom.

The rustic habitations at which Silly Sally was in the habit of calling, in the certainty of being always kindly received, and often comfortably fed, were numerous, for every body seemed to feel that she was an object of compassion, and, moreover, that she was made happy at so little trouble or cost, that it was impossible to be kind and charitable in any quarter where it would answer better.

Among these numerous friendly resorts, there was one large dairy farm, which was an especial favourite; for not only was she sure of getting there what she dearly loved, namely, an unstinted draught of milk, but many a proof of good-will beside, for there were a parcel of good-natured children, several of whom were old enough to take great delight in making Silly Sally laugh and jump for joy by their little gifts. Fortunately, perhaps, for the perpetuity of the kind reception she met there, this farm was nearly at the most distant point of all her haunts, and, as Sally knew how to measure and calculate time and distance better by far than many of her wiser neighbours, she often gave up the project of going there, because she had not got out of the workhouse in time to make her sure of being able to get back again early enough to escape a scolding. But Sally had no intention whatever of returning to the workhouse at present; for she had not only been affronted by Mrs. Dempster's box on the ear, but had her hands much too full of the business she best liked to think of any thing of the kind: so off she set for Farmer Smithson's, and walking, as she always did, at a good steady pace, contrived to present herself at the kitchen door just as the family were sitting down to their eight o'clock supper.

"Why, mother! here's Silly Sally!" exclaimed a girl of ten or eleven years old, who was the first to perceive her.

"Why, Sally, my girl, what brings you here at this time of night?" said Mrs. Smithson. "How will you ever get back to the workhouse to-night? It is very naughty, Sally, to be out so late, and you'll get trimmed for it, I know."

"Her won't," replied Sally, stoutly. "But see here, missus! Her will give a drop of warm milk to the baby?"

"Mercy on us! Here's a new-born child!" cried Mrs. Smithson. "Where on earth did you get this, Sally?"

"From the mother on't," replied Sally, very quietly.

"But why did you bring it away so far?" demanded the good woman. "I am sure the mother could never tell you to take it out at night after this fashion."

"There was nothing for it to eat," replied Sally, in her most steady and rational manner. "Please, missus, give it a drop of warm milk." The kindly mother of many children was not likely to refuse such a petition as this. A little warm milk was put into the infant's mouth, and Sally's provisional clothing considerably improved by the addition of some warmer garments. The infant again dropped asleep in the arms of its loving nurse, who was strictly interrogated as to the manner in which she had come by it. But there was nothing in the girl's manner to create alarm; and, as every body knew that Silly Sally was often employed as a nurse by many poor people in the neighbourhood, the whole family came to the conclusion that the babe's mother was probably some poor creature who had sent her out with it to beg, and that Sally's certainty of being kindly received at Highland's had tempted her to come thus far afield for the help which was evidently much wanted. The night being cold and stormy, the kind-hearted Smithsons thought the best thing they could do would be to shelter both baby and nurse till the morning, which they contrived to do, very greatly to the delight of Silly Sally, who felt and looked prouder and happier than she had ever done in her whole life before, when permitted to sit down before the kitchen fire, and rock "hers baby" to sleep without interruption.

On the following morning the sun shone again, and then the idiot set off on her return, with a jug of gruel in one hand, the baby supported by the other arm, and a bundle fastened round her, containing not only sundry fragments of wholesome food, but sundry contributions from the charity of the family, such as it was likely enough the mother of the baby must be in want of.

# XLIII

*Jessie Phillips is visited in the donkey-shed by Will Reynolds and his wife—they account for the absence of her child in the most natural manner possible, and after some few doubts and difficulties they decide upon sending her back to the workhouse—her reception there*

IT MIGHT BE ABOUT THREE or four hours after Silly Sally had set off from the carrier's donkey-shed, with the new-born baby of Jessie in her arms, that the owner of the little building, together with the live and dead stock that were its usual occupants, arrived, as usual, the day's labour being ended, in order to put it to its accustomed use. The man carried a horn lantern, and a small bundle of better provender than donkeys are usually favoured with; but the Deepbrook fish-cart was a profitable concern, and its owner knew the value of his beast.

Though the eyes of Will Reynolds were not of the youngest, nor his lantern of the brightest, he had not entered the shed two minutes before he discovered Jessie, and, holding the light close to her face, he perceived that, though perfectly motionless, she was neither dead nor asleep. The old man spoke to her kindly; and she fixed her languid eyes upon him with a look that spoke such suffering and such weakness that he got frightened, and fancied that his premises were about to become the scene of the last act of a tragedy. Fastening his beast to a ring, well enough placed to secure the hapless Jessie from his heels, he hurried back to his dwelling, and summoned his faithful wife to assist him in developing the mystery.

"For the love of God, Mary, come with me to the shed!" he exclaimed, the instant his head was inside the door. "There's a dying woman lying there, if I ever seed one, and I shall never get her face out of my mind the longest day I have to live if we don't do the best we can for her. Come along, wife, and bring some water and a small drop of gin with you." Startled by the appalling summons, the woman started up, but for a moment stood staring at her husband, without appearing to have any inclination to obey him.

"Come along, Mary—come along," he reiterated. "Why, it ain't like you, wife, to be so slow at helping a fellow-creature."

"Dying, Will!" cried the woman, with a look of dismay. "Did not we better send for the doctor?"

"And let her be dead before he comes? We shall get into trouble in this world and the next if we do any such a thing. Come, give me the gin; if you haven't the courage to look upon a creature like that, I must manage the job myself." Thus admonished, the woman obeyed his orders with all promptitude, and though really "scared," and looking as pale as a ghost herself, she followed her husband to the shed. Nothing, however, could be farther either from indifference or unkindness than the manner in which the good woman addressed the poor object that lay stretched on the floor of the building.

"Poor creature!" she exclaimed, kneeling down beside her. "And she all alone, too! Poor soul! poor soul! But what on earth have she done with her child? Will Reynolds, there has been mischief done here as sure as you are a living man! Give me the cup, Will; a spoonful or two of water, and half a one of gin. We must make her speak, I promise you, or we *shall* get into trouble sure enough."

The cup was put to the lips of Jessie, and she eagerly swallowed its contents. "Now, then, you can speak," said Mrs. Reynolds, putting her arm gently under Jessie's head, and raising her up. "Now, my poor soul, you will be able to tell us what brought you here at such a time as this. Come, say the word, then; what is your name? And where is your child?"

Jessie looked at her earnestly, and with a puzzled air, as if vainly endeavouring to understand what she said. It was evident, however, that what she had taken had greatly revived her, for her complexion was already less ghastly, and her eyes had a greater look of life in them. "You can speak now if you will try for it, my friend," repeated Mrs. Reynolds. "Tell us where your baby is?"

"I don't know," replied Jessie, distinctly, but at the same time looking about her wildly, and as if greatly terrified.

"Do you hear that, Will Reynolds?" said the woman, withdrawing her arm; "and do you see the terror of her? Oh, me! oh, me! that ever I should have come to this! And shan't I have to be brought up and examined, Will, just for all the world as if I was a good-for-nothing hussy myself? You should have known better, William Reynolds, than to have fetched me out to get into such a job as this. What's the good of marrying a man old enough to be one's father if he can't take better care of one than that comes to?"

William Reynolds received this rebuke without hearing a word of it. The very darkest suspicions against the unhappy Jessie had taken possession of his mind; he felt not the shadow of a doubt that she had given birth to a child, destroyed, and concealed it. The distinct manner in which she had spoken the words "*I don't know*," when questioned respecting it, were perfectly conclusive in his judgment, for they proved both that she knew what was passing about her, and was determined to conceal what it would be dangerous to tell. His indignation against the supposed culprit was very great, but his embarrassment as to what to do with her still greater. To shelter her, even as she was then sheltered, and to watch over, attend, and feed her would, he firmly believed, render him guilty in the eye of the law as an accomplice, and might likely enough expose him and his wife Mary to imprisonment and trial at the very least, if not to hanging in the horrible infanticide's company. But what was he to do with her? Could he go five miles to get a warrant, and send her off ten more to gaol at that time of night? Could he set his Mary to watch that she did not crawl away and escape if he *did* go to the justice? Or must they both keep guard till morning to prevent the success of an experiment which, according to his judgment, she was so very sure to make?

These thoughts were all working and fretting in his brain, poor man, together with so helpless a consciousness of not knowing what he ought to do in the case, that his wife's words sounded in his ears as hollow and unmeaning as the notes of a drum. His eyes, however, during this time were fixed upon Jessie, and when he saw her eyes again close, and the same death-like paleness return to her features, a fresh cause of terror suggested itself; he fancied, what indeed seemed but too probable, that she was at the point of death, which idea very greatly increased his agitation and dismay, from the position in which such an event would place him and his wife, they having been the last persons who had seen this mysterious person alive. It was with infinite satisfaction, therefore, that he heard his wife exclaim, "Why, William, she is a workhouse body! I know the dress right well. In God's name, carry her back right away to the Union, and then, let what will happen, it is their business and not ours!"

"Well thought on, Mary! That's the cleverest word as have come into your head for many a day. Give her a drop more of the mixture, wife. 'Twas wonderful to see how it brought her round. I will just harness the beast to the cart again, and will have her to her proper quarters in no time. When you have given her the gin, just pick up all the soft stuff you can find, to lay under her, poor wretch! Don't let us have the killing of her to answer for, whatever may come to her afterwards. It is fitting the law should take its course, but there is no need to be hard-hearted for all that."

In pursuance of this plan, Jessie was speedily laid upon a tolerably soft bit of litter in the fishmonger's cart, and in this manner conveyed to the workhouse.

Will Reynolds pretty well knew that ten o'clock at night was by no means a very regular hour for the transacting business at the Union workhouse; but he knew, also, that it was far better to encounter a few rough words from Governor Dempster than run the risk of what might happen if his uninvited guest remained all night in the shed. It was with a resolute spirit, therefore, that he pulled the handle of the hoarse-voiced bell, till the unwonted summons was heard from one end of the building to the other. Whether pleased or not at being thus unexpectedly disturbed, the governor did not linger on his road to the outer gate, and, perhaps, felt almost as much curiosity as displeasure at a disturbance so very unusual, for the house was a regular house, whatever else it might be.

"Who, in the devil's name, have we got here?" said he, in no very silvery accents, and holding high the lantern he carried in order to throw its light upon the cart and its occupants. "*William Reynolds, Fishmonger, Deepbrook*," he read aloud from the board conspicuously attached to the vehicle. "And William Reynolds it is, sure enough," he added, lowering the light till it flashed full upon the well-known features of the driver. "And pray, Mr. William Reynolds, what sort of fish may it be that you are after bringing us at this time of night? I won't promise to take it in, mind I tell you that."

"But you must, if you please, Mr. Dempster," replied Reynolds; "at any rate what I have brought that I must leave, but whether inside the gates, or, outside of 'em, that of course will be for you to decide."

"Then outside that will be, as sure as you are born, Master Reynolds, unless you happen to have an order from some one as have got a right to give it; and that isn't your own self, as I've a notion, neighbour."

"I don't pretend to have any right in the matter," replied the fishmonger, "except just downright necessity, and I think you'll get into trouble, Mr. Governor, if you don't yield to it as well as I. It is for no pleasure, I can tell you, either to my beast or myself, that I have come up here after a long day's work; but what must be must be, and you'll find out that as well as I, maybe, if you will but just listen. This young woman here has been in the workhouse, and belongs to it still, as may be seen by the things she has got on, though how she got out with them I can't say. But the principal matter is, Mr. Dempster, that there have a child been born, and I am sadly afraid made away with. And now please to say how we can be justified in leaving the mother of it to get off out of the way of law and justice, as she will be sure to do if you refuse the taking her in."

During this explanation, Mr. Richard Dempster had possessed himself of the fact that the wretched woman in the cart was no other than the identical Jessie Phillips, whose privately absconding from the workhouse had been discovered not many hours before. Under any other circumstances, he would most assuredly have refused her re-admission without a fresh order from the board; but the very strong suspicion of infanticide under which she now lay induced him to think that the fishmonger might be right, and that it would cause less trouble to receive than to refuse her.

On being conveyed into the house, the miserable girl looked round her for a moment, as if to ascertain where she was, but then closed her eyes again with such evident feebleness that both the men were frightened; and, having laid her on a bed, Dempster lost no time in calling up his wife, who was already fast asleep, and making her acquainted with the facts, as far as he knew them himself, he charged her, in the names of law and justice, to take good care of that wench, if she never troubled herself about another to the end of her days. "Trust me for that, Dick Dempster," was the reply; "she'll ask nothing better now, maybe, than just to lay there and die, and so cheat the hangman, horrid monster as she is; but that she shan't do if care and watching can keep her alive." In pursuance of this resolution, poor Jessie was fed and watched during the night, and the apothecary summoned to attend her on the following morning. As the summons was an early one, this professional personage was found tolerably sober, and having heard the circumstances of the case, as far as the Dempsters were capable of telling him, before he reached his patient he fully participated their determination that she should not escape the punishment of her crime by dying beforehand from want of care. Greatly did the wretched girl stand in need of the attention she now received; and it was so far effectual, that the utter prostration of strength which had seem to threaten her life, speedily disappeared, and she became perfectly restored to her consciousness and her senses.

"Now, then," said Mrs. Dempster to her husband and the apothecary, as they walked off together from the room in which she lay, for the purpose of holding a consultation as to what was to be done next; "now, then, I think it be our duty to begin asking her a few questions; and you, Dick, ought to have your ink and paper ready, didn't he, sir?"

"Why, yes, upon my honour," replied the apothecary; "I think it is quite time that we should take care to have something straightforward to answer when we are called upon to give particulars. It will never do, I promise you, for us to have nothing more to tell than that we gave her plenty of gruel."

"Come along, then," returned the governor, "there's paper, pens, and ink, in here; you two go on, if you please, and I'll follow with 'em in a minute."

And in a minute the three witnesses began to prepare themselves for the business they anticipated by placing themselves in a row on that side of the bed towards which the face of Jessie was turned. Her eyes were closed, but there was a catching nervous movement in the hand which lay on the coverlid, which the impatient Mrs. Dempster declared was a sign that she could not possibly be asleep, and accordingly she herself began the purposed investigation as follows:—

"I say, Jessie Phillips, it is no good to keep shutting up your eyes that way; you ar'nt no more asleep than I am, so you may just look up, if you please, and answer straightforward to all the questions as we shall think proper to ask. First or last, you must do it, my girl, take my word for that; so you had better do as you are bid at once."

Thus effectually roused, poor Jessie opened her lack-lustre eyes, and fixed them on the face of Mrs. Dempster.

"Now then be pleased to answer me," resumed the governor's lady, with dignity. "At what time was it as you made your escape from this house?"

"Yesterday morning," replied Jessie, faintly.

"Ay, ay, we know that well enough," returned the matron, knitting her brows; "but what o'clock was it?"

"I don't know," murmured Jessie.

"And how did you manage it, girl, so that no single soul saw you set off?"

"I put Sally's bonnet on," said Jessie.

"That must be a lie, for Sally's gone, too."

Jessie said nothing.

"And where's your child, you bad one?" said the stately governor himself, after a short pause.

"My child!" cried Jessie, suddenly starting up; "Have you found it? Tell me where it is! For the love of God, tell me!—I know nothing—nothing—nothing." And with clasped hands and haggard eyes she looked wildly and eagerly from face to face of the group that stood beside her, as if something dearer than life hung upon their answer.

"Do you hear that?" said Mr. Dempster, shaking his head. "*Have we found it,* indeed?" and he carefully inscribed the question on the paper he held.

"And where did you see Silly Sally last?" said Mrs. Dempster. "To think of your hooking the poor natural into the job! You are a deep one, ain't ye?"

"Sally was willing," said Jessie, without having the slightest idea of what their questions aimed at.

"Did any body ever hear the like of that?" exclaimed the indignant Mrs. Dempster. "Think of her cunning!—trying to throw it all upon a poor natural, that haven't got wit to defend herself! But that won't do her no good when the time comes, for where's the fool that can't see through it, I wonder?"

"Pretty tolerable bad, that, I must say," said the apothecary, shrugging his shoulders. "But you are right, Mrs. Dempster, it will do her no good."

"God forbid it should, sir," said the matron, casting up her eyes. "And now be pleased to tell us where you last saw Silly Sally."

"Here," replied Jessie.

"Oh! here, was it? Isn't she first-rate, and for one so young, too? And where is poor Silly Sally, now, you false friend?" continued Mrs. Dempster, renewing her examination.

"Here, ma'am, isn't she?" said Jessie, looking weak, weary, and sad enough, but without being at all conscious that any danger threatened her.

"Here?" reiterated the matron. "Here, indeed! And pray do you mean to say that you gave her your child to bring here along with her?"

"My child!" exclaimed the poor girl, her pale cheek flushing into crimson for a moment. "For the love of mercy, let me see it!"

"Do you think, sir," said Mrs. Dempster, in a sort of whisper, to the apothecary, "that she has got any notion of pretending to be out of her mind? It is very much the fashion, you know, sir, now."

"Impossible to say, Mrs. Dempster," he replied, in the same tone; "but it is likely enough she may." Then raising his voice, so that Jessie might be sure to hear him, he said, "Don't play any more fool's tricks with us, my girl, but tell us, if you please, at once, whereabouts it was that your child was born?"

"I don't know," said Jessie, bursting into tears.

"You don't know?" repeated the apothecary, shaking his head. "This won't do, my girl," he added, with a look of severity which was perfectly unintelligible to the poor sufferer; but, seeing her again become deadly pale, he judged it prudent to suspend the examination for the present, and telling his bewildered patient to keep quiet now, and go to sleep, he beckoned the Dempsters out of the room, and, closing the door, ordered that care should be taken not to let any person go into the room to question or disturb her.

"And what do you think of the case, doctor?" said Mr. Dempster, solemnly, as they proceeded along the passage.

"What part of the case do you mean, Dick?" returned the apothecary, laughing. "Is your question legal or medical?"

"Legal, sir,—legal. I want to know if you think there is the very slightest chance that she will escape hanging?"

"Not the slightest, Dick; no more than that you and I shall escape dying when our time comes."

"I think, doctor, you must be pleased to sign your name to what I have written down. It will be but regular and proper, sir, as I take it."

The doctor immediately complied with this request, and then took his leave, advising the governor, however, before he departed, to give notice of the affair to the nearest justice of peace without any further loss of time.

# XLIV

*Miss Maxwell visits the Union workhouse, and hears the news—the Captain pays a visit there, but obtains very little information, and that little he dislikes much, but misunderstands more—the assistance of a magistrate is called in, who speedily places Jessie in safe quarters*

ABOVE A WEEK HAD NOW elapsed since Martha Maxwell had despatched her letter to the young squire, and, though his very audacious answer to it seemed to defy all the efforts she might attempt to make in favour of Jessie, she still thought it probable that consideration might dictate to him the wisdom of giving the unhappy girl the means of withdrawing herself from the Deepbrook workhouse, as a measure of precaution, at least, if not of justice and humanity. In order to ascertain whether this had been done, she turned her steps towards the Union on the very morning that the unfortunate object of her interest had re-entered its walls. It was the governor himself who answered her summons to the gate, and who replied to her inquiry, as to whether Jessie Phillips was still in the house, by saying, "Yes, Miss Maxwell, sure enough the cretur is still here, worse luck for the honest folks as have got to tend her, but we look that she will be removed to the county gaol as soon as the doctor says that it may be done safely."

"To gaol?" exclaimed Miss Maxwell, changing colour; "Jessie Phillips sent to gaol, Mr. Dempster? What can you mean?"

"Just what I say, miss," he replied: "To gaol she must go, and to the gallows afterwards, if I don't very greatly mistake. The girl have made away with her baby, Miss Maxwell, and that's the cause why she is to be sent to gaol."

Inexpressibly shocked at this fearful intelligence, and feeling herself in some sort guilty from having suffered her uncertainty as to what she could, and what she ought to do, to prevent her for so long a time from doing or attempting any thing, Martha returned home in a state of great agitation. As to believing it possible that the young and gentle-spirited Jessie Phillips could have committed murder, and that upon her own child, it appeared to her so wholly out of the question that she could hardly be said to have bestowed a single thought on the contingency. Martha's scrutinising faculties had not been idle during her intercourse with Jessie; and her conviction on this point amounted, as far as her own opinion was concerned, to something very little short of certainty. But, if this dreadful charge had been indeed brought against her former favourite, her own opinion, as she well knew, could avail nothing towards proving her innocent. With a countenance sufficiently expressive of the painful emotion from which she was suffering, Martha returned home, and entered the morning sitting-room, where she found both her father and mother. Her terrible tale was soon told, and, though neither of them was in her confidence as to the private history of her ill-used *protégée,* they listened with that sort of belief in her judgment, which they knew it generally deserved, to her confident persuasion that, if the crime had really been committed, it was not by the hand of Jessie.

As Martha Maxwell, though charitable and kind-hearted towards her poor neighbours, had never before exhibited marks of such strong feeling concerning them, her father listened to her entreaties that he would immediately endeavour to make himself acquainted with all the circumstances of the ease, with a degree of interest almost equal to her own; and, after meditating for a while upon the best way of obtaining the desired information, he decided upon going himself to the workhouse and questioning Dempster as to the evidence which had led to the accusation.

Ready enough was Dempster, and his wife also, to enter upon a theme so well calculated to excite their eloquence; but it soon became evident to Captain Maxwell that they really knew very little more than the fact that a child had been born, and that the mother had returned to the house after the birth without it. That this of itself was suspicious could not possibly be denied, particularly when coupled with the fact of her having secretly left the workhouse before she went; but the acute captain instantly perceived that there being no proof whatever that the infant had been born alive, the condemning the mother to death, however strongly she might be suspected, was by no means likely to occur; and he was about to trace his steps homeward with such consolation for his daughter as this assurance was likely to bring when the apothecary made his appearance, and immediately entered upon the subject.

"Sad business this, Captain Maxwell! 'Tis rare to see one of these thorough bad ones manage so clumsily, take it all together, as this one has done. The case of the murder is as clear as a pikestaff."

"Indeed? Have you any proof, then, that the infant was born alive?" said the captain.

"You have hit the blot, sir—you have exactly hit the blot, as cleverly as the first lawyer in the land could have done," replied the doctor, making him a jocose bow; "and till within ten minutes I thought just as you do, that the girl would cheat the gibbet for that very point. But after you went down, Dempster," he continued, turning to the governor, "I got a capital good word out of her, which will settle that point to a nicety."

"I am happy to hear you say so, doctor," replied the conscientious governor, "for it is always an injury to honest folks when the guilty escape just punishment. And what might that word be, doctor, if I may be so bold as to ask?"

"Why, if the captain, and you too, Dempster, have a mind to go up-stairs along with me, I don't much question but what she'll bring it out again. It is often providential that sort of chance letting out of the truth; it is not the first time I have observed it. And duty is duty, you know, captain, whether it happens to be agreeable or not." The apothecary then led the way to the room in which Jessie was still struggling with a feverish agitation of nerves, which sometimes almost amounted to delirium, though, at other moments, she was perfectly in possession of her senses.

The apothecary approached her bed, but her eyes were closed, and he fancied that she had fallen asleep. "It is a wonder, isn't it, how she can sleep, so quiet and comfortable like?" said the governor of the workhouse.

But they were mistaken; Jessie was not sleeping, and, upon hearing the words of Dempster, she opened her eyes, and fixed them upon him.

"She is not so much asleep but what she can hear, at any rate," said the governor; "so now is as good a time as any, doctor, if you want to ask her a few more questions."

"Here's a gentleman come to see you, my girl," said the apothecary, putting forward Captain Maxwell; "perhaps, you know, he can tell you what you were asking me about just now."

"I don't know, sir," replied Jessie, languidly.

"Ay, that's the lay she is upon, sir," said Mr. Dempster, shaking his head. "You'll see now; I'll lay any wager you please that it will be that very same answer you'll get, and no other, ask her what you will. I have observed that sort of cunning in her more than once already."

Captain Maxwell, who had perceived a something in the expression of Jessie's eye which led him to think that she stood greatly in awe of Dempster, suddenly turned round to him, and said, "Is there any objection, Dick, to my asking the girl a question or two by herself?"

"None, as I can see, sir, I am sure," was the reply, "seeing, as you are a guardian, there is no manner of doubt but what you have got a right, if you like it."

"Certainly, certainly," quoth the doctor; and they both left the room accordingly.

"Now then, Jessie, don't be frightened at me," said the veteran, kindly, "but just tell me quietly every thing you can about your child. Where did you leave it, my poor girl, when you came back here?"

"It was not I that left it," replied Jessie, bursting into tears; "if I ever had a child—if it is not all a dream—a wild and horrid dream, it must have left me."

"No, Jessie, it was not a dream; though it is no great wonder if it seemed so to you, wandering about by yourself, as I dare say you were. But it was no dream, you have had a child. Can't you remember any thing about it? Can't you remember if you heard it cry?" demanded Captain Maxwell, with an air of friendly interest, well calculated to awaken confidence, and banish fear.

"Hear it cry? didn't I hear it cry?" repeated Jessie, starting up from the pillow with sudden animation. "Yes, sir, yes, I did hear it cry, I am sure of it; I remember it all! It was no dream! I did hear my baby cry! Oh, for the love of God, let me see it, let me have it!"

"But we do not know where to find it, Jessie," replied the captain, with all possible gentleness; "you must tell us where we ought to look for it. What did you do with it when you heard it cry?"

The instant that he asked this question the whole countenance of the girl changed. The animation, and the something of passionate tenderness, which her voice and look had expressed, were gone, and a blank unmeaning stare succeeded.

"You were ill then, Jessie, very ill, no doubt; but tell me the truth, Jessie, tell every thing you can remember about it," said Captain Maxwell, convinced in his own mind that the wretched girl had destroyed the infant in a fit of delirium.

She continued to stare at him with a sort of terrified uncertainty for a minute or two, and then replied, slowly and distinctly, "I can remember nothing about it."

Had the worthy Captain Maxwell received the cut of a sabre, sharp enough to sever his ear, it would have scarcely given him so acute a pang as did these words, and the manner in which they were pronounced. Had it been his daughter Martha instead of himself who had listened to them, it is possible that her singularly analytical ear might have caught the simplicity of truth in the accent which, to him, seemed only indicative of a resolute determination to say nothing more that could criminate herself. The notion of her having destroyed her child was strongly confirmed; but that of her having done so in a fit of insanity as completely removed. He felt averse to question her farther, convinced that, in all probability, every word he contrived to elicit would only increase his conviction of her guilt; he therefore, somewhat hastily, bade her adieu, and contented himself, when questioned by the apothecary and Dempster, by saying that he could really make nothing of her. He felt, indeed, that one moment of genuine feeling, caused perhaps by his friendly manner of questioning her, had led to an avowal which threatened to destroy best hope of safety. The impossibility of *proving* that the child had been born alive *migh*t save her, but this, her positive declaration, that she had heard it cry, must at once destroy. He, therefore, immediately took leave of the doctor and Mr. Dempster, perceiving they both seemed to deem it their duty to give a little more time to the examination of an affair upon which, not having an atom of evidence, there was so favourable an opportunity of exercising their acuteness. Nor did these estimable individuals separate till they had naturally made up their minds, very completely to their own satisfaction, that it was, in fact, one of the very clearest cases of child-murder that had ever been made out against the mother; for was it not undeniably clear, from William Reynolds' statement, that she must have made away with the infant herself, because of the particularly obvious fact, that there was nobody else to do it? One only observation was produced between them, however, which had any tendency towards common sense, and that, unfortunately, made decidedly against the unfortunate Jessie. After really attending to her with all his professional acumen on the alert, and also without having been in the slightest degree intoxicated, the apothecary gave it as his opinion that, notwithstanding a certain degree of weakness inevitable after the difficulties she had unquestionably encountered, the girl's condition was, by no means, such as to give any reason for supposing that she was likely to have given birth to a dead child.

This opinion, together with the narrative of William Reynolds and Mr. Dempster's notes, recording every thing that had been obtained from the girl herself, having been submitted to a neighbouring magistrate, he, without hesitation, issued a warrant for her apprehension, by virtue of which the unhappy Jessie was conveyed to the county gaol at the expiration of ten days after her return to the workhouse.

# XLV

*The news flies, and creates great sensation—Jessie is greatly puzzled to know what it all means—she desires to see a clergyman, and is visited by the chaplain of her prison—truth may sometimes appear to wear the garb of falsehood, and very honest men blunder when labouring to discover which is which*

IT WILL BE READILY BELIEVED that such an event as this took no great length of time before it was known to every individual in the neighbourhood. A story of misery and horror always flies rapidly; and in this case there were many circumstances which tended to make the dreadful history a theme of even more than the common interest which any similar event could have caused. The nearer neighbours all personally knew the young creature, so lately the loveliest model of youth and innocence that the eye could gaze on or the fancy create. Among these, whether rich or poor, the excitement and the emotion were far greater than the oldest among them could remember on any former occasion; while those more distant heard of it as a tragedy almost too terrible to be true in all its details, and with the charitable hope that there were circumstances not yet known which might explain what now seemed too dreadful to believe. This party were right as to there being unknown circumstances which might explain, but quite wrong as to their being less terrible than those which were first circulated.

When Jessie, after the time had elapsed which was deemed proper for a sufficient recovery of her strength, was made to understand that she was to be conveyed to the county gaol, under suspicion that she had murdered her child, the only terror produced by the words which she heard spoken to her arose from believing that she had lost her senses. This dreadful idea, indeed, did not then occur to her for the first time, nor had it been always quite without foundation. On the dreadful day that she had left the workhouse to seek Dalton, there had been moments in which she was far from being clearly certain of what she was doing or intending to do; and then again came intervals of a calmer, but yet more dreadful and suffering state of mind, in which the consciousness of this mental weakness came upon her, and seemed to threaten a future more horrible than any she had yet anticipated. It was *not*, however, during a moment of temporary delirium that she had suffered her child to be taken away, but one of perfect unconsciousness; this had fallen upon her immediately after its birth, and had lasted till the visit and subsequent aid administered by William Reynolds and his wife restored her faculties. Every word she had spoken then and afterwards was not only most strictly true, but no exertion of her memory could have enabled her to add one syllable to her statements which would have added light to it. Jessie knew nothing, had been conscious of nothing, but such intense suffering of body and mind as had made her at one moment hope for death, and at another that she was about to live a maniac.

Not all the apothecary's orders about keeping her quiet had availed to prevent continually repeated questionings from the Dempsters and one or two of their particular friends, who asked as a favour to be permitted to try their sagacity in finding out the truth. But the nearer these colloquies went to betraying to her the real nature of the situation in which she was placed, the stronger became the morbid idea which had got hold of her imagination respecting her own state of mind.

Again and again did the poor creature endeavour to try, by some test that she thought must convince her one way or the other, whether the dreaded malady was upon her or not. But the attempt was ever in vain; for all that seemed most real and most certain in all that passed around her could never for a moment stand examination, when at length she was left in silence and alone; but as she steadfastly endeavoured to recall every thing that had passed, the whole seemed so like the frenzied fancies of a fevered brain, that all her efforts were directed to the keeping herself as profoundly still as possible, in a desperate sort of hope that the misfortune which she pretty justly considered as the most fearful that could befall humanity might in her case, as in many others she had heard of, be only temporary.

But in all this, though there was nothing seriously to alarm her friends (if she had had any, poor wretch!) with fears for her reason, there was a degree of danger that not friends only, but any human being possessed of common humanity, would have watched with anguish. There was scarcely a word she uttered but had a strong tendency to prove that it was her object to attribute to insanity every thing she had said and done after quitting the workhouse; and this, joined to more than one burst of feeling, in which she repeated her conviction of having heard her child cry, constituted altogether almost as strong a case against her as the circumstances which had really occurred would admit. It was not till after she had been two days and nights in prison, and had been visited by the clergyman who acted as chaplain to the establishment, that the whole astounding truth reached her understanding. She had herself repeatedly asked to see a clergyman, "if there was one to be found," before this indulgence was granted her; but at length, under the idea that she made the request for the purpose of relieving her mind by making a full confession, the chaplain was requested to attend her. He was an excellent man, gentle in temper, but firm in judgment, and with so deep a sense of the real duties of his mission, that while he sought to smooth the tremendous step that divides the fitful hopes and fears of life from the unchangeable continuity of eternity, by opening the blessed page of promised mercy, he shrank not from the more painful task of exhibiting in their true colours the crimes that required such repentance as might suffice to win it.

"Young woman, here is Mr. Green, the clergyman, come to visit you," said a gaoler, opening the door of the room in which she was confined to await her trial; and an old man entered whose aspect gave her perhaps a stronger feeling of satisfaction than she could at that moment have experienced from any other cause whatever.

"I understand that you have asked to see me?" said the good man, advancing.

"Yes, I have, sir," replied Jessie; "but the seeing you is almost more comfort than I dared hope for."

"I am glad that you wished to see me, my poor girl," he replied, "and I am glad that I was able to come. Is it that I should pray with you that you made the request?"

"No, sir, it was not for that," replied Jessie, with her usual simple truthfulness, "though, it would be a great and precious favour if you would do so."

"Wherefore was it then that you wished to see me?" demanded Mr. Green. "I have no power to serve you in any other way."

"I do not ask you to serve me, sir, by taking me out of prison or any thing of that kind," returned Jessie; "I could not be here if it was not the will of God, and therefore it must be right and best, in some way or other, that here I should be. What I want of you, sir, is quite in another way."

The heart of Mr. Green sank within him. He felt persuaded that the young creature before him was no hardened reprobate, let her crime be what it might, and he feared that he had been summoned to hear her confess what might doom her to immediate and ignominious death. But it was possible she might find comfort from it, and he prepared himself for the task that was before him.

"You probably wish, then," said he, "to relieve your burdened mind by confessing the crime for which you have been brought here?"

"It is not quite that, sir, either," said Jessie, shaking her head "but it is about it, too. If you will have the great kindness, sir, I want you to tell me what it is I have done."

"That question can hardly be put honestly," said Mr. Green, with some severity, and feeling disappointed at what seemed like premeditated artifice in one whom he had felt greatly disposed to believe free at least from that fault, whatever else she might have to answer for. "You must surely know but too well," he continued, "that you are placed here because you are suspected of having murdered your newly born infant."

Jessie started, and changed colour.

"I have heard them repeat these same words again, and again, and again, but never till now did I hear them from a clergyman, that is from one that I dare not disbelieve or suspect of wicked, cruel jesting. And do you, sir, think that I have murdered a baby—any baby in the wide world, to say nothing about my own?"

"Young woman, I know not what to think," replied Mr. Green. "I am far from wishing to entrap you into making confession of any thing which circumstances were not likely to divulge upon your trial without any assistance from you; but you must be aware that the facts which are already perfectly well known and established, without requiring the aid of any confession to confirm them, suffice to make it appear highly probable, to say the very least, that your child has been made away with, and by your hands."

"Then I suppose it is true!" said Jessie, turning as pale as death, while her working features expressed the deepest mental agony. "For a moment," she added, "it was but for one short moment, but during that one short moment I did hear the cry of a little child. Of that I am certain, perfectly certain, for the memory of it is unlike the memory of other wild thoughts, that I now believe were all madness. Yes! *I did hear my infant cry!* But what came after, what became of me, or what I did, or what I said, I know no more than that poor babe itself."

"But you think that when William Reynolds found you in the shed there was no baby with you? What do you suppose had become of it?" demanded Mr. Green.

"Oh! that is very strange!" cried Jessie, pressing her hand to her forehead, and endeavouring to recall all that had happened to her. "I never saw any body, I never heard any body, nor do I believe that any body ever came near me, till Mrs. Reynolds did, with her husband."

"But did they find the child with you?" said Mr. Green, solemnly.

Jessie paused for a moment, as if thinking what she should reply, and then said, "I really don't know, sir, but I think not. I do not believe that I was in any way out of my senses after they came to me, or at any rate after I knew of their coming, for I seem to remember every thing quietly and distinctly from that time almost to this; and I have no recollection about the child in all that time, except, indeed, now and then hearing people talk about it at the workhouse, as you do now."

"Then what is your last recollection respecting your baby?" said Mr. Green.

Jessie again pressed her forehead with her hand, as if at a loss what to answer, and it was not till after a minute or two that she replied, "The hearing it cry, sir!"

Her features were strongly agitated as she pronounced these words, and, as if conscious of this, she hid her face with her hands, and wept bitterly. Mr. Green looked at her earnestly, and sighed, good man! from the very bottom of his heart; but Jessie was spared the agony of perceiving that he truly believed her to have been wilfully guilty of the horrible crime laid to her charge, for such an idea never occurred to her as a thing possible. After another short interval of silence, Mr. Green renewed the painful conversation by saying, "Whatever the verdict of a jury may be in this case, my poor girl, it is impossible to deny that appearances are very strongly against you. The fact of your having heard the child cry, which, to do you justice, you have never attempted to conceal, and the difficulty of believing that any other than yourself could think it worth their while to make away with it—for who but yourself could find benefit or profit of any kind from the deed?—all this, I am sorry to confess, makes a very strong case against you, and all I can say to comfort you is, that we are taught to believe the mercy of Heaven unbounded, and that, if you bring your heart into a state of true and humble repentance for whatever evil you have done, you may hope that the punishment awarded for it shall end here. Shall I pray with you that this last, best hope of sinners upon earth may be yours?"

"God bless you, sir, for your goodness!" returned Jessie, with tearful eyes and clasped hands, speaking more plainly than any words could have done her grateful feelings. "I have, indeed, been a sinner," she continued, "and thankful will I be if punishment here and the repenting with a contrite heart may gain for me the mercy of my Saviour."

The minister drew forth a book, which he reverently opened; but while he was in the very act of kneeling down Jessie suddenly exclaimed, "Amongst all the things that I have done in my madness, why may I not have crawled with my babe to some safe place, and left it there? Oh! if I could but see it!—oh! If I could but for one single instant see its dear eyes and kiss its little lips I think I could die happy then, even by the hand of the executioner!"

Jessie would now again have been more fairly judged if Martha Maxwell's ear had criticised her words instead of the less delicate organ of Mr. Green. It was impossible that any one could listen to her with a more honest and earnest wish of ascertaining the truth of what she stated than the truly worthy clergyman; but this very honesty, by an unhappy fatality, was in the present instance most strangely against her. The good man felt that there was so much to soften the heart and warp the judgment in the youth, the beauty, and the suffering of this singular prisoner, that he dared not trust himself to judge according to the impression her words at first produced, but set himself scrupulously and conscientiously to examine into the probabilities of the vague and varying statements she put before him. It now appeared clearly evident to him that her purpose in all she said was to establish a belief that she had been insane; and this circumstance was itself so probable, that had he not unfortunately fancied he could discover a decided purpose to make it apparent in all she said, it was the conclusion that he would himself have most readily and naturally come to. As it was, however, the belief gained upon him, not only that she had destroyed her child, but that, although she might have been excited to the horrid deed by suffering and fever, there was no apparent probability of her having been at any moment so completely deranged as to be unconscious of what she was doing.

Again he sighed deeply as he felt himself driven to think so harshly of one so young, and replied, gravely, "No, young woman, I cannot think it at all probable that you conveyed the child to a place of safety. Do you ask the question because you remember that you did take it out of the shed where you were found?"

"I remember nothing!" replied Jessie, wringing her hands; "but if I have indeed destroyed it during that dreadful time, whether I am guilty about it or not, it is better that I should die too, for why,—oh! why should I live? Be pleased to pray with me, sir," she added gently, and with an air of more self-possession and composure than she had yet shewn.

He did pray with her, good man! with all the fervent piety of a true Christian, and, if he blundered in his judgment concerning her, he was not the less earnest in his petitions to the God of mercy that she might be forgiven, and supported by the humble hope of such forgiveness through the tremendous scenes which awaited her.

# XLVI

*Sundry adventures which befell Silly Sally, who proves that the parish authorities were quite right in not considering her a safe nurse—Mr. Frederic Dalton visits the donkey-shed, and leaves it again in great haste—after which, though contrary to his usual habits, he takes a dram, and then returns home to breakfast*

GREAT WAS THE DISAPPOINTMENT OF Silly Sally on returning to the shed to find her friend Jessie gone, and for many minutes she stood gazing on the spot where she had left her in the most disconsolate manner imaginable. At length some sort of theory on the subject suggested itself to her unsettled brain, from whence arose a notion that Jessie did not find the shed comfortable, and that she had conveyed herself away to better quarters. Nor did her reasonings on the subject stop here; Sally knew of another place, a sort of Dutch barn, with sweet hay in it, wherein a sick body might lie down to sleep like a cow in clover: it was a good step off, however, and Sally was well-nigh weary of carrying the baby on one arm, while she had so many other commodities to take care of with the other. But no sooner had the idea entered her head that it was possible Jessie might have gone to this barn than her intention of following her thither became so firmly fixed, that nothing short of personal restraint would have prevented her doing it. But, as I have said, she was tired, and, having turned the matter over in her mind according to her half-witted fashion, she came to the determination of dividing her burdens. Her first notion was that she would carry the baby with her, and leave her can of gruel and the rest of her treasures safely stowed in the shed till she could return for them. But a feeling of instinctive kindness towards her friend Jessie caused her to change the order of her arrangement, for Jessie she thought must be very hungry, and, with a broad grin of delight at the thought of taking her such a good meal, she decided upon leaving the baby comfortably packed in a bundle of fern in a corner of the shed, where she thought it would be sure to sleep quietly till she came back to fetch it. Having completed her nursery arrangements, therefore, very much to her own satisfaction, she left the little one, who was, in fact, profoundly asleep, and set off with her provender to the hay barn.

It may be remembered, that Mr. Frederic Dalton, after leaving Lawyer Lewis, had lingered in the neighbourhood of his dwelling, in order to ascertain whether Jessie would, in truth, fulfil her threat of going to him. This he achieved very satisfactorily, and, having done so, was about to return home, when the idea occurred to him that it might be as well to make Mr. Lewis a second visit after Jessie should have left him, in order to ascertain what impression she might have made on that gentleman's mind by the tale she had, doubtless, told. Mr. Frederic Dalton, therefore, again ensconced himself where, unseen, he might command a view of the lawyer's door. Jessie's visit was not a long one, and, sooner than he had hoped for, his watch was ended by seeing her pass out from it and regain the highroad. But, as the young gentleman would have preferred most things to the chance of a second interview with her himself, he decided upon remaining within the ambush he had chosen till all danger of her catching sight of him should be over. He watched her, therefore, as she slowly and with difficulty made her way to the entrance of the green lane, down which she subsequently turned, and, after following her with his eye till he had seen her enter the donkey-shed, he quitted his retreat and again presented himself before the lawyer.

"Well, Lewis, what was it the creature said to you?" demanded the young squire, boldly. "I should like to know if she made up the same story to you that she did to me."

"Faith, Dalton, I did not give her any opportunity to romance much with me. Her object evidently was to swear a child to some one or other, but she did not get so far as to name you, squire, or any body else, for I had no inclination, as you will readily believe, to become a party in any way in an attempt to evade an act of parliament. If this sort of ex-legal swearing, as I may call it, were once permitted to get head, one of the most admirable laws that ever was framed would lose nine-tenths of its usefulness. If I had let this girl, for instance, go on, it is likely enough that she might, upon second thoughts, have named Lord Pemberton instead of you, for these swearing young ladies often display a very noble spirit of ambition. Never certainly did any legislature do a wiser thing than thus preventing the very lowest and vilest of the people from having the power of fixing a child and a stigma upon any body they chose, no matter who. And, to be sure, there can't be a finer instance of the mischief of such a power than this very case. I flatter myself, however, that I have settled the young lady's notions of law in this matter, and that she will not for the future present any more subjects to the nation upon any such old-fashioned speculations as it is quite plain in this case she has been deliberately acting upon."

The young squire, delighted with the acute discernment and right views of his legal friend, cordially shook his hand and departed, flattering himself that, despite Miss Martha Maxwell and her secret adviser, he should have no more trouble from this tiresome affair, which, as he boasted to himself, was the only one of the sort that he had ever managed imprudently. When he retired to his room at night, however, it struck him, as he sat in his favourite arm-chair gazing at the fire, that if Jessie had been seized with such a contumacious fit about the workhouse, and had absconded from it with a view to remaining out of doors, and taking her chance of getting the helps she needed from the charity of her neighbours, it might eventually give rise to a degree of gossip that he should greatly dislike. He well knew that Jessie had been personally known and highly esteemed by precisely the set of people from whom he most wished to conceal the adventure; and the idea once awakened soon grew into so threatening a form of danger, that, greatly as he hated the idea of seeing her, he determined to seek an interview with her on the morrow, and either to coax or enforce a return to the only abode likely to keep her effectually from all intercourse with her former friends. He went to sleep with this resolution firmly fixed upon his mind, nor did any of his waking thoughts cause him to change it. If his suspicions were correct as to her remaining out of the workhouse, no place with which he was acquainted seemed more likely to be selected by the poor girl for a night's shelter than the shed on the waste, into which he had seen her enter; and to this spot he determined to go while it was still too early for there to be much danger of his meeting any acquaintance by the way. On reaching the shed he found—certainly rather to his satisfaction than otherwise—that Jessie was not there; and flattering himself that she must have returned to the workhouse, after having rested herself there on the preceding day, he prepared to quit the building; but ere he had passed through its ever open door the cry of an infant reached him from the most distant corner of the shed. He started, and turned back. Three steps brought him to the place where Silly Sally had deposited her forsaken charge, and where, for the half-hour which had elapsed since she left it, it had lain sleeping, but now awoke to startle its guilty father with its wail.

In an instant the thought suggested itself to Frederic Dalton that Jessie had abandoned her child, with the certainty that a few hours of such abandonment would cause its wished-for death, and his heart leaped with mingled agitation and joy as he thought that he should he thus saved from all future danger of discovery or inconvenience. With a sudden movement he turned away, in order to retreat as speedily as possible from the spot of earth whereon he would the least wish to be found; but, as he did so, the infant's piercing cry again smote his ear, and the wretch paused to curse it, as he remembered the probability that it might live till noonday brought wanderers, either for pleasure or for business, through the lane, who might, and must discover its existence, if it repeated such cries as it was then uttering. "Confound her idiot folly!" he exclaimed; "if she had common sense enough to determine that it should perish, why could she not silence this confounded cry?" He had turned as he muttered these words, and was again standing over the spot where the child lay. Again it uttered a sharp piercing cry. He raised his booted foot, and made a movement as in sudden rage, and the piercing cry was heard no more.

Frederic Dalton stood alone in the dark shed, trembling in every limb. He was perfectly aware of the horror that had been perpetrated, yet, with a strangely vehement attempt at self-delusion, he blended the word ACCIDENT with his muttered curses. He knew that there was no human ear to listen to him; did he hope to deceive the omnipresent Witness that inhabits space?—or did he indeed flatter himself that he could thus still the fluttering of his distempered heart? Frederic Dalton's short life had been perhaps stained with as much vice as the circumstances of his position could well permit; yet all that had gone before seemed but as wanton mirth and reckless jollity compared to his present state:—

> "Not poppy, nor mandragora,
> Nor all the drowsy syrups in the world,
> Shall ever medicine him to that sweet sleep
> Which he owned yesterday!"

His head reeled, and he supported himself for a moment against the wall of the building. And then came a panic fit of terror lest some eye should see him pass out from the scene of his crime. To conceal all traces of it was his next thought. Trembling, loathing, shuddering, he stooped down and raised the murdered babe in his arms. The slightest sound, the slightest breath would have thrown him prostrate, so completely had all strength abandoned him. Yet still his brain was working busily, and self-preservation was as wide awake as if his nerves had been of iron. "I cannot annihilate—I can only conceal it," was the thought that pressed upon him. "But these rags shall not identify the hateful tell-tale:" and then, with horrible deliberation, he drew a knife from his pocket, and disencumbered the body, almost by a single stroke, of the habiliments which Sally had so sedulously wrapped around it. The fragments he rolled tight and close together, and deposited them in his pocket, to be consumed in the privacy of his own room. The whole operation did not perhaps occupy two minutes, but this was long enough to permit one of the most ordinary and everyday traits of his character to come to his succour. Frederic Dalton was as artfully cunning as he was boldly vicious, and even in that moment of horror he remembered that, should any one enter, he had only to display a proper degree of astonishment and indignation at the crime that had been committed, in order to prevent the possibility that the most improbable of

all possible suspicions should attach to *him*. But nobody came, nor did the slightest sound disturb him; he therefore not only secreted the garments, but disposed of the body of the murdered babe with a facility that made him thank Heaven (the wretch) that matters were no worse. In the back wall of the shed was a small square opening, covered by a rude shutter that was fastened by a wooden button. Through this aperture William Reynolds was in the habit of throwing whatever litter was too rotten for his precious donkey either to lie upon or to eat. The little building being erected on the very edge of a wide ditch, the opposite side of which was so thickly planted with bushes as to make even their leafless boughs a screen sufficient to prevent any danger of his being overlooked, he scrupled not to let the baby drop from his hand into the mass of rubbish beneath. A few handfuls of the fern that had been collected by Sally were hastily, yet carefully dropped after it, and effectually concealed it from any superficial observation. This done, the pale man stepped hastily out into the lane; and not Cain, when he turned from his brother's bloody lair, moved forward with a fleeter step than did Frederic Dalton as he walked down the well-known Green Lane of Deepbrook. But it was not towards the highroad that he turned his steps. Did he feel that his lips were colourless, and that his eyes seemed so starting from their sockets as to make him look as if he could not close his eyelids over them? I know not; but certain it is, that at that terrible moment he would rather have met a roaring lion, and trusted to his power of climbing a tree for safety, than have encountered the gaze of the dullest carter that ever drove a team along the turnpike-road. The lane opened at the other end upon the village-common, on the borders of which stood an alehouse, "licensed to deal in spirituous liquors," and here, for the first time in his life, Frederic Dalton entered.

"Watson!" he cried, as the rustic landlord bowed low before him, "if you have got a drop of good brandy in the house, do give me a glass of it. I have been hunting a badger till I have got thoroughly chilled."

"Your honour does look pale, sure enough," returned the man, bustling to procure with the least possible delay the greatly needed dram. "Margaret!" he added, calling to his wife, "see and set a chair for the young squire close up to the fire. 'Tis likely enough he has got a chill this sharp morning."

The woman hastened to obey his command, saying, as she passed her apron over the seat, "Your honour would do well, maybe, to get it a little hotted with boiling water and ginger, for you do look terrible bad, and that's the truth."

"No, no, not any water, if you please, Mrs. Watson," said the shaking man, tossing off the contents of the glass; "but you may double the dose, if you please."

The potent draught did its work quickly, and the villain felt his failing spirits revive. "What's to pay, landlord?" he cried, with frightful gaiety; and turning to the woman, as he drew forth his purse, he added, "I look better now, Mrs. Watson—don't I?"

"Oh! yes, your honour; a deal better, no doubt about it. But still I be afeard that madam won't fancy that you be quite well either for somehow you do not altogether look like yourself."

"It's nothing but the cold," he replied, suddenly changing colour, and becoming as violently red as he had before been pale. "Good morning—good morning: it must be near ten o'clock, I'm afraid; and I must hurry home to breakfast."

And so he did, reaching the manor-house only a few minutes after the family had sat down to the morning meal. What with the brandy, the walk, and his own efforts to regain an aspect of tolerable composure, he had so far succeeded that his appearance excited no observation, excepting from his father, who said,—"You look heated, Frederic; what have you been about this morning? I am sure you have been walking a good round pace; and yet, you see, you are somewhat behind time."

"I started a badger, sir," replied the young man, as nearly in his usual tone as he could contrive; but he was evidently out of breath, which naturally accounted for his speaking rather thick. "And now, ma'am, you must give me leave," he added, addressing his mother, "to run up-stairs and wash my hands. Scrambling over hedges and ditches is dirty work."

Before he returned to the breakfast-room, every vestige of his murdered infant's garments had been converted into ashes; and the consciousness that such a witness existed no longer did much towards restoring the tone of his nerves. No further notice was taken of his adventure, and he sat down to breakfast with what appetite he could.

# XLVII

*More of Silly Sally's adventures—she gets into bad company and is robbed—takes fright in finding that she has lost her nursling, and seeks shelter in the workhouse—the thief gets credit for her honesty, and Jessie Phillips is proved to have committed murder beyond the possibility of doubt*

IT WAS LUCKY FOR SILLY Sally that the impressions made upon her mind by passing events were more like the short-lived shadows left by the fleeting fancies of a busy imagination than the enduring results of actual misfortunes and disappointments. Her gay spirits, and her kindly hopes, had been sadly checked, on returning to the shed, by finding her friend Jessie gone: but less than three minutes had sufficed to reconcile her to the necessity of trudging forth again to look for her elsewhere; and proud was she, and grandly independent, in her own estimation, of all control, when she made up a bed for the baby, and followed the new fancy that had taken possession of her. Again, for a minute or so, she was disappointed and chagrined at finding no Jessie in the hay-barn; but the vexation was speedily forgotten in the exceeding pleasure with which she contemplated the comfortable aspect of the sweet-scented retreat; and she rolled herself with such snugness into a corner where numberless recent cuttings of the hay-binder offered rare choice of mattress and pillow, that ere many minutes her troubles and her pleasures were alike forgotten in a sound sleep. The nap she took was a long one, for she had walked far, and slept little during the preceding night; but she paid for her luxurious repose by the loss of all her newly acquired treasures. For Sally was not the only houseless wanderer who had discovered that it was possible to lodge well in a hay-barn, and while she was snoring away in measureless, though unconscious content, a tenant of the previous night returned to it, for the purpose of re-possessing herself of a hidden hoard of broken victuals which she had collected at the kitchen-doors of half the gentry of Deepbrook, and concealed amidst the hay, while seeking to make equal profit from the other half. This woman, though a mere tramper, of the least reputable description, knew the parish of Deepbrook almost as well as if she had belonged to it, for in none of her regular beats did she come upon a village where so many good dinners were given, and, consequently, where so many relics were bestowed upon the sturdiest and best practised beggars afterwards. A very miscellaneous progeny called her mother; for, if it had ever happened to her to find herself unprovided with a baby, young enough to give the finish of helpless innocence to her constantly repeated histories of starvation, she would, by no means, have scrupled either to beg, borrow, or steal one, properly selected to suit her purposes. On the present occasion she carried one young enough to permit her, adding the plea of great suffering and weakness, on her own part, to all the other claims, upon the "kind gentlefolks' charity," which she so well knew how to bring forward.

On entering the barn, the heavy snoring of Silly Sally, who always slept with her mouth wide open, immediately attracted the woman to the corner where she lay, and where, close beside her feet, she had deposited the tin can which the farmer's wife had lent her to convey the gruel to the mother of the baby she carried. Wandering Winny, as this professional beggar-woman was called throughout more than one county, knew Silly Sally the moment she looked down at her, and conceiving, after the meditation of a moment, that the particularly convenient-looking tin can at her feet had been intrusted to her care, for some errand which she was thought capable of performing, it struck her that the very best thing to he done under the circumstances was to appropriate it to her own use, as being so very peculiarly well adapted to the purpose of carrying the fragments in which she traded.

The thought was no sooner conceived than executed, and perceiving, on removing the can, the little tidy packet which the womanly charity of Mrs. Smith had intrusted to Sally for the use of the "baby's mother," she possessed herself of that also, quieting her conscience as she trudged away by reflecting that nobody would think of greatly scolding an idiot girl, if she did give the things, by mistake, to the wrong body.

Wandering Winny was far enough beyond the reach of any search that Sally was likely to make after her long before the poor idiot had awakened from her comfortable sleep; and, so thoroughly had her senses been steeped in the deep oblivion, that when she awoke, and endeavoured to recall what she had been about, she only remembered clearly that she had got the thing she loved best in the world, namely, a darling baby to look after; and then, when she cast her half-speculating eyes around to see for something she was almost quite sure she had set down beside her when she went to sleep, she readily made up her mind to believe that she was mistaken, and that she had "left it all in t'other place along with baby." In this persuasion she set off again for the well-known shed, and, being now unencumbered with luggage of any kind, strode sturdily across the fields she had to traverse, and reached the spot she was making for without wasting a moment.

But, alas! the heedless nurse came all too late! Her helpless charge was no longer there. No longer was it numbered among the dwellers upon earth.

And now the grief and dismay of Silly Sally were of a different quality from any that had followed from her former disappointments, for fear of reproof was mingled with them. It has before been stated that the love and tenderness of the idiot girl for young children were such as often to make her services very acceptable, when no better could be had, and might have ensured her a constant maintenance, without being indebted to the parish for it, had not the infirmity of her intellect repeatedly shewn itself in some such capricious desertion as the present; upon which occasions a good deal of personal severity of discipline had been used in the hope of correcting it. But every effort of the kind had proved in vain, and the parish authorities, being at length convinced that Sally was decidedly an idiot, though a very harmless one, she had been placed in the work house as her permanent home, but with the sort of tacit license to come and to go, which has been already described. Her most powerful emotion, therefore, at not finding the baby where she had left it, was terror, lest she should be beaten for her negligence; and down she sat on the spot where she had left it, and wept bitterly. But ere long a sort of instinctive cunning changed the course of her thoughts, and instead of staying there to be beaten by Jessie, or by any body else, out of the workhouse, she determined to take shelter in it, remembering that nobody had ever set her to watch a baby there, and, consequently, that she had never got cuffed for neglecting it. So to the workhouse again she bent her steps, the affront of having her ears boxed by the matron being quite forgotten, and with as much conceited satisfaction at her own cleverness, as the most accomplished *intriguante* ever enjoyed.

This return brought her to the workhouse just about twenty-four hours after she had left it, and though such an escapade would have subjected any other inmate to expulsion, and the necessity of a new order for re-admission before he or she could have been again received, neither her being absent before, nor present now, seemed to produce observation from any "body," it having long ago been decided, on all hands, that the less notice they took of her queer, but harmless ways, and the less trouble they gave themselves about her, the better. Sally, moreover, was much too cunning to utter a single word relative to the adventures which had befallen her during her absence, the fear of chastisement being to the full as strong within her weak brain as it could possibly be where there was more power to reason upon it. Of Jessie's return she knew nothing, for the name of Jessie was connected with her fear; and she, therefore, never mentioned it, nor was there any chance that the poor idiot, whose loud unmeaning laugh was, perhaps, the most distressing feature of her calamity, would be admitted to that part of the building in which Jessie was placed till her removal to prison, as it was a standing order that it should be kept quiet, and "no persons admitted to it except on business."

The foregoing retrospect was necessary for the purpose of shewing in what light the removal of the child of Jessie Phillips was likely to appear at the trial. At one moment, indeed, there appeared to be an excellent chance that the truth, at least as far as it concerned poor Jessie herself, would be made manifest, for it happened that Wandering Winny, after enjoying, for several days, the great comfort of carrying her savoury fragments about in Mrs. Smithson's tin can, determined, that before she quitted the neighbourhood for the season (for Winny's visits at most of her favourite haunts were annual), she would make a call at the ever open door of Farmer Smithson. Her having a new-born babe would, she well knew, be a strong additional claim upon the motherly dame's charity, and sanguine in the hope of at least one good meal, with help to furnish out more than one, which should follow after, she made her way to the open porch which sheltered the kitchen-door.

"Mother!" exclaimed one of the elder girls, who was leaning in an attitude of idleness against the door-post, while her fingers, with unceasing activity, plied the knitting needles with which she was fabricating a stout stocking for her father. "Mother!" she exclaimed, "see here, if there is not Wandering Winny come again to visit us? Why, it is months and months since she was here before, and she's got a braw new baby this time. May she sit down in the porch, mother, and have a morsel to eat?"

"Yes, she may, girl," was the hospitable reply; and, trusting the entertainment of the familiar beggar to the care of her young daughter, Mrs. Smithson continued the neat plaiting of a cap-border, which was at that moment under her ironing box. But, in the next moment, her daughter's voice reached her again from the porch, at least the word "Mother!" was again ejaculated from thence; but no other word was added to it till the girl who spoke was close to her side, and then she said,—"Winny has got the can that you lent to Silly Sally t'other day."

"Has she?" said Mrs. Smithson, "then I'll come out to her in half a minute, as soon as ever I have finished this border."

"It was for her, doubtless, that Silly Sally came begging, and now the poor creatur's come to bring back the can, I suppose, and return thanks for the gruel."

Mary Smithson skipped back again to her guest in the porch, and while the *border* was completed, said, "Silly Sally then gave you the can to bring back to mother yourself, did she? Mother will come out and speak to you in a minute."

Wandering Winny was a sharp-witted woman in her way, and having, thus inadvertently, stumbled upon the real owners of her stolen can, she at once resolved to put a good face upon the matter and return it, by which she should not only get out of the scrape, but, doubtless, propitiate the further kindness of her hostess, by such a convincing proof of her honesty.

"Yes, indeed," she replied, "it is just for that as I have come all this way round; but I couldn't do no less, seeing that it was sent almost full of such beautiful gruel. Though poor Sally is an idiot, she has a kind heart."

"And this is the baby, then, that Sally brought out here, and washed and dressed so cleverly before the fire, poor wench!" said Mrs. Smithson, as she joined the group. "Yes, I see," she added, examining the remnant of an old shawl which was wrapped round the baby that lay sleeping in Winny's lap; "I sent this, because she said the mother was so badly off. And did she give you the bits of flannel, too?"

"Yes, indeed, did she," replied the lucky thief, confirming her statement by displaying the articles mentioned, which, together with the shawl, had made part of the bundle she had found lying beside the can at Sally's feet.

"Poor Sally!" exclaimed Mrs. Smithson, pleased at this trait of good faith and benevolence in her old acquaintance. "What a pity 'tis that the poor creature isn't a little more steady in her mind, for she is as good-hearted a girl as ever lived! And so she made you understand, Winny, did she, where you were to bring the can, too?"

"Oh! yes, she did, missis, indeed," replied the woman, with a grateful smile; "and a long step I have had out of my way to do her bidding."

This hint was not thrown away, and, after having rested and refreshed herself very effectually, the wandering beggar set off again, directing her steps to a distant part of another county, and, to do her justice quite unconscious of all the fearful misery she left behind, and to which the tale she had just told so essentially contributed.

It was three days after the departure of this woman from the neighbourhood before Mrs. Smithson heard that a girl from the workhouse had been sent to the county gaol under suspicion of having murdered her child; and when she did hear it there was no link whatever to connect in her mind the idea of the baby she had seen in the arms of the idiot girl with that of the unhappy creature thus accused. On the contrary, indeed, if by any chance inquiry had been made of her respecting the babe who had been permitted to pass the night with Silly Sally under the shelter of her roof, she would have been quite ready to swear, and that too with a conscience most perfectly void of offence, that the same babe had again been brought to her house, and that she had seen it alive and well several days after the time at which Jessie was accused of having destroyed her infant.

Silly Sally, meanwhile, still remained perfectly unconscious of Jessie's return to the workhouse, for, till the time that she was doomed to he in a condition to be removed in the prison, she had never left the remote room of the edifice appropriated to females in her situation. It never happened at any time that the idiot girl obtained much information through the medium of conversation, as the loud laugh with which she usually answered what was said to her brought any such communication very speedily to a close. But since her return from her last *escapade,* her fear of being questioned about the baby she had left, and then chastised for leaving it, kept her much more out of the way of talking than usual, till by degrees she began to forget all about it, and then she returned to her former habits, and might again be seen watching for an opportunity of slipping through the door, in order to take her usual scamper in the fields. It so happened that the removal of Jessie took place during one of these absences, and the fact that an event had occurred which gave her fellow-paupers something more than usually interesting to talk about only rendered it more unlikely than usual that any one should address a word to her; for it was only when there was nothing else to be said or done that the customary words, "Well, then, Silly Sally, what have you got to say for yourself?" were addressed to her.

Like all other wonders, either in town or country, in a workhouse or out of it, the committal of Jessie Phillips had given way before some other topic which, though perhaps of less interest, possessed the always unrivalled charm of novelty to recommend it; and probably her name might hardly again have been heard of, till its interest had been renewed by the approach of her trial, had not all gossipings upon the subject been again rendered "as good as new" by the discovery of the infant's body amidst the heap of rubbish upon which it had been thrown. This discovery was made, as might have been expected, by the owner of the shed, when employed in removing the accumulation of litter deposited in the ditch behind the building to a heap of manure at no great distance, which, in his little way, was a considerable source of profit to him. His horror at finding the body was considerably greater than his surprise; for so certain did it seem that the unnatural mother must, after committing the horrid deed, have concealed it near the spot where she lay, that he had again and again examined every corner of the shed, and by the help of more than one curious neighbour, as anxious to make the expected discovery as himself, had removed every atom of litter from its floor, throwing it, as the work proceeded, through the accustomed aperture, and thereby rendering the discovery of what they sought more difficult. Nay, even when one of the men thus employed bethought him that it was possible the body might have been thrown exactly on the spot where it actually lay, the quantity of rubbish with which it was covered sufficed to defeat his imperfect search for it.

When at length, however, William Reynolds made the discovery, though more than a fortnight had elapsed since the time of its having been thrown there, it was still in a condition to undergo the examination of a coroner's inquest, which was immediately summoned, and then two medical gentlemen, who were desired to attend, declared that, beyond all possibility of doubt, the infant had been born alive, thus confirming the unhappy mother's often-repeated declaration that she had heard it cry.

This discovery of the infant's body, together with the inquest, which declared both that it had lived, and that its death had been caused by violence, not only renewed the interest originally occasioned by the event, but rendered it much greater than ever. For now every part of the tragedy was brought clearly to light before their eyes. Who was there in the whole parish who did not visit the spot where it had occurred? Who was there that did not feel, while examining the premises, and in looking through the square shutter, so easily opened by means of its slight fastening, that the deed was not only done there by the monster-mother, but that it might have been done, even by one in her condition, with perfect facility? Unhappy Jessie! Not a single link in the chain of evidence appeared to be wanting. William Reynolds had found her in the shed. For her to deny the birth of her child was impossible; but she did deny that she knew any thing about it. She confessed that she had heard it cry, but uniformly continued to declare that she knew not whether it had been removed from the shed, or whether she had left it there when conveyed back to the workhouse by William Reynolds. In short, it was scarcely possible to imagine a case in which every thing tended to prove the guilt of the accused more satisfactorily; it would really have seemed to all who heard it a something like insanity to entertain a single doubt upon the subject.

# XLVIII

*The case of Jessie Phillips ably and acutely discussed and argued—the result of which is the clear conviction to every reasonable mind that she was guilty of all the crimes laid to her charge*

MR. LAWYER LEWIS WAS NOT the last man in Deepbrook to discover that, from evidence incontrovertible, the once well-esteemed Jessie Phillips was in a fair way of being brought in "guilty" of the murder of her bastard child by a jury of her countrymen. Neither did it take him long to ascertain that the audacious girl who had come to him to find out how she might bully the young squire into giving her money, by threatening to swear her child to him, in defiance of the law, was no other than the same identical Jessie Phillips, who now stood in such imminent peril of being hanged.

"I won't deny, Mr. Rimmington," said he, on happening to meet that gentleman in the reading-room,—"I won't deny that I do feel a little proud of my own sagacity on that occasion. I saw at once that there was something desperately bad about the hussy. And yet every body says that she is an uncommon pretty girl, too. But there was such a swaggering sort of defiance in her manner of declaring, as in fact she positively did, that she snapped her fingers at the law, and could just swear any man she pleased was the father, that I saw in the twinkling of an eye what sort of a customer I had got."

"I cannot pretend to judge of what her conduct and manner might have been when she came to you, Lewis," replied Mr. Rimmington, "for the very simple reason that I did not witness it; but I have known her almost from a child, and I certainly never saw in her any indication whatever of the sort of character you describe. On the contrary, indeed,

I have always believed her to be a particularly well-behaved and modest girl."

"Yes, till she met with a sweet-heart, my dear sir," replied Mr. Lewis, "I have no doubt whatever that her modesty and discretion were exemplary. But, unless you deny altogether the notorious fact of her being an unmarried mother, I presume that you will not continue to believe that your original opinion of her was correct?"

"I dare not deny your inference, I suppose," replied Mr. Rimmington, with a gentle smile, "for fear you should cast a stone at my morality; and yet, I cannot but think that there was a time, and at no very distant date, too, when Jessie Phillips was a very good girl. But, as the law now denies us the old-fashioned mode of finding out who her child's father is, we are unable to say to what degree of temptation she may have been exposed."

"You are always carping at some provision or other of our admirable law, my dear Rimmington," replied the lawyer, shaking his head: "but I must say I think this is about the very worst opportunity you could possibly have found for objecting to the non-swearing system, for it is as clear as that the sun is in heaven that this admirable Jessie of yours had made up her mind, when she came to me, both to say and to swear as downright a lie as ever was told about the paternity of her brat. Perhaps you do not know that she threatened Frederic Dalton with it. True, upon my life. She met young Dalton in broad daylight, and openly threatened to scandalise his family and friends by declaring that HE was the father, if he did not instantly give her money to hold her tongue."

"If this be so," replied Mr. Rimmington, quickly, "I should be apt to suppose that Mr. Frederic Dalton really was the father."

"Then, my dear sir, notwithstanding the pure and excellent motives which, I am quite sure, actuate every thing you say and do, I must take the liberty of saying that you would not only suppose what is false, but, by avowing such supposition, you would be robbing the country of one of the greatest benefits to be derived from the new poor-law, namely, the protection it offers against the vile insinuations and audacious claims of the worst, lowest, and most degraded part of the population."

"But what if my supposition should be correct, Lewis?" said Mr. Rimmington, fixing his gentle blue eye upon the lively and acute features of the lawyer.

"You are putting a case that I happen to know does not exist, my good friend," replied Mr. Lewis, with rather a sarcastic smile. "Your pretty client, Rimmington, made a terrible blunder in her dates, which would have overthrown her statement at once, if nothing else had done it. But I know that is a sort of incidental proof which men of my profession are more apt to attend to than men of yours. Every man knows his own trade best, my good friend, you may depend upon that. We are taught, you know, from the moment we first sit down before a desk, that we must take nothing for granted; that proof—proof—proof, must be looked for north, east, west, and south; and this gives us all such a habit of sifting whatever evidence comes before us, that from the merest lies we often find the way to elicit truth."

"It may be so," replied Mr. Rimmington, meekly, "and it may therefore be better, and more for the earthly interest of mankind, that the judgment of lawyers should be taken on all matters of fact than the judgment of priests; nevertheless, Lewis, I cannot give up my speculations, founded, I confess, much more upon general principles than upon particular facts; nor can I cease to think that, however low this unhappy girl may have fallen now, the time has been, and, as I said before, at no great distance, when she was, in truth, as pure, as innocent as I believed her to be."

"But at any rate, my dear sir, you must allow that the crime of which she now stands accused, and of which such a string of circumstantial evidence proves her guilty, as it is quite impossible, I conceive, that any jury can resist,—you must allow that in common justice this ought to go far towards making you doubt your preconceived notions of her peculiar virtue and purity. Can you deny this?" demanded Mr. Lewis, with earnestness.

"No, I certainly cannot," replied the worthy clergyman, mournfully shaking his head; "and yet what I have heretofore seen, and, I may say, known of the girl, cannot be so completely wiped away, as not to make me fancy it possible, only possible, Lewis, that with all your acuteness you may be mistaken."

"Pray say nothing about my acuteness, Mr. Rimmington," said the lawyer, looking considerably provoked; "I do beseech you, sir, to ground your opinions in this matter neither upon my acuteness, nor your own, but wholly, solely, and *strictly* upon FACTS."

"I, of course, presume that we all *intend* to do so, my good friend," replied Mr. Rimmington; "the only difficulty lies in finding out what the facts are."

"Exactly so," returned the lawyer briskly, "and there as I have said before, I really do think that I have a better chance than you. Besides, to speak plainly to you, Rimmington, I very much doubt if you have examined into this business in any way that can enable you fairly to judge of the facts of the case. Here is a girl who, though very decently brought up, misconducts herself most abominably at the very time when all her friends and acquaintance—all the ladies, young and old, that used to employ her, believed her to be staying at home to take care of her sick mother. And what is the next fact? Why, as soon as her mother dies, she sets off for the workhouse, which I think we can all pretty well guess would not have been the case if the father of her child had been the man she has now been threatening. And what comes next? Why the child is murdered, and the clearest possible evidence proves that it was the mother who committed the act; and yet, in the teeth of all this, you declare yourself still persuaded that Jessie Phillips is a very good sort of girl, and I dare say you think in your heart that it is a great pity that the cruel new law prevents her giving the validity of her oath to the accusation with which she had the audacity to threaten young Dalton."

"Did she tell you, Lewis, that Frederic Dalton was the father of her child?" inquired the clergyman.

"No, faith, Rimmington; not she. She soon perceived, I suspect that I was not sitting up in my office for the purpose of receiving young ladies' swearings, in defiance of the law. No, no, she never pronounced any gentleman's name to me, though she gave me very clearly to understand that she had such a scheme in her head, because she wanted money. She was frank enough on that point, I must confess. But I would not have said what I have done, my good friend, if I had not happened to know from the very best authority that she had positively waylaid young

Dalton, and threatened, if he did not give her money directly, that she would 'swear the child to him!' It is perfectly incredible how difficult it is to get out of their heads the notion that not all the law in the land can prevent this sort of damsel from picking and choosing a papa for her precious offspring amongst all the lords of creation, from the prince to the peasant. This is one of the instances, amidst a million others, of the incalculable benefit of the clause which renders this abomination impossible. You may rely upon it, my dear Rimmington, that but for this the peace and happiness of the excellent family at the manor-house would have been shaken to the very centre. A girl who will first have a child in this style, and then murder it, would not be likely to take fright at a false oath. You have too much of the milk of human kindness, my excellent friend, not to tremble at any thing, and every thing, that you think sounds like harshness to the poor; but I do trust, Rimmington, that you will let this girl's conduct open your eyes to the general benefit to society which this clause, so unjustly complained of, is likely to produce. If it does not, I am fain to confess that I do not expect any thing will, for I really think it almost impossible to imagine a case in which the obvious tendency of the new legislation on this point can be more manifest."

How strongly Mr. Rimmington's "foregone conclusions" might still be working in his breast, so as to render the admirable reasoning of the attorney of none effect, it is impossible to say, because he made no attempt whatever to reply to it. And rash indeed and utterly useless would it have been to do so, for Mr. Lewis not only declared himself perfectly well acquainted with all the facts of the case, and with the cleverly organised law which bore upon them, but drew such undeniable inferences with respect to the miserable prisoner's character, from the facts thus satisfactorily established, that, as he truly said, it would require a very bold pleader to make light of them. Mr. Rimmington was not a bold pleader, and though he might still have doubts, that seemed rather the offspring of instinct than reason, he was too conscientious to deny that the case against Jessie Phillips was a very strong one.

Notwithstanding the witty wisdom wrapped up in the often-quoted "Save me from my friends!" there may be occasions when a thorough-going ally, warmed with a tolerably strong dash of party spirit, and inspired with an intention of being really useful at a pinch, may do much towards turning popular feeling into whatever channel may best suit his *protégée*, particularly if the said ally be as glib a talker as Mr. Lewis. So glibly indeed, so ably, so reasonably, did he talk, that he ended by convincing himself most completely of the truth of every word he uttered; and, as Mr. Lewis was by no means a very dishonest man, this was really essential, for it soon became evident to himself, as well as to almost every body else in the village, that all his more than ordinary activity of gossip in this affair arose from a feeling of justice and duty, and he was listened to with more than ordinary respect accordingly. Yet, after all, it was only an accident, of which the lawyer himself knew nothing, which rendered his busy exertions beneficial to young Dalton, instead of being very greatly the reverse. So well sustained had been the caution with which the unhappy Jessie and her infamous lover had concealed their connexion, that no gossip whatever had joined their names together in the sort of chit-chat which travels from house to house through such a sociable village as Deepbrook, till Mr. Lewis himself set it in action after the miserable girl had been sent to prison. Ably, therefore, as his ex-parte statement had been made, it might perhaps have been better still for the young squire to have left the subject alone altogether, except for the strong suspicion of Ellen, and the something more than suspicion of Martha Maxwell and her friend Henry Mortimer. But on these the effect of his statements and his inferences was every thing that Frederic Dalton himself could desire. Dreadful had been the emotion of Ellen when she first heard that Jessie Phillips had given birth to a child, and sent to prison on suspicion of having murdered it; for in her heart she believed that her brother was the father of that child. And when the same news reached Martha Maxwell the horror inspired by the girl's crime was mixed with feelings of almost equal horror against her seducer. But strange, yet inevitable, was the effect upon her mind, as well as upon that of Ellen, which the reasoning of Mr. Lewis produced. What authority had they for believing that Frederic Dalton was guilty save that of Jessie herself? None whatever. No village gossip confirmed it; no known coincidence of any kind rendered it probable. And how much had the subsequent conduct of Jessie tended to throw doubt on her own statement! Ellen well remembered that there was a strange boldness, or rather an inexplicable assumption of dignity and confidence in the manners of the girl, during their last meeting at the manor-house, which had always puzzled her to account for. Even presuming that the connexion which the unhappy Jessie had now (according to Mr. Lewis's statement) declared, it could in no justifiable manner explain her speaking of her seducer to his sister, and of calling him "dear Frederic," in her presence. Infinitely more did it resemble the audacity attributed to her by the lawyer than the timid demeanour of an unhappy girl in the position relative to Frederic which she now proclaimed. Ellen so strongly felt the improbability that any young girl could have thus appeared before her, and have avowed her love as she had done, in that startling phrase, "dear Frederic," that despite all her former partiality to the favoured sempstress, and her low opinion of her brother's character, she could not conceal from herself, that the undeniable worthlessness of Jessie once established, it was more likely that she should have conducted herself at the manor-house in the daring manner she had done, for the purpose of turning to profitable account the caress witnessed at Lady Mary's, than that she should have endeavoured to establish the belief that Frederic was her lover from any other motive.

In the breast of Martha other feelings were at work, but all productive of the same result. The statement of Jessie's having murdered her child, and, all the damning proofs that confirmed it, created a degree of horror at the hypocrisy of the being who could so completely have deceived her, that, if possible, exceeded that produced by the crime itself. From the instant that Miss Maxwell became convinced (in common with all others who listened to the clear and unbroken narrative of the evidence) that Jessie Phillips had murdered her infant, she felt persuaded that every statement which the young monster had made to her was as false as was the seeming tender softness of her character. Mr. Lewis's statement also, that the girl had openly declared to him *her* determination of obtaining money in some way or other from the man she threatened to designate as the father, so contrary to the noble feeling she had affected when relating to her how she had rejected the pecuniary aid he had offered, served to rivet the persuasion of her falsehood so firmly that nothing could shake it. And thus it happened, that when Ellen and Martha met together to talk over this horrible occurrence, and to compare notes upon all that had passed between either of them and the unhappy heroine of it, they both with the purest sincerity of young and virtuous hearts and the most logical inferences which their clear and really acute young heads were capable of drawing from all the evidence before them—they both at once came to the conclusion that Frederic Dalton had only been thus fixed upon because he was the richest young man in the neighbourhood, and had been unlucky enough to salute the abandoned girl before the eyes of his sister—while of Jessie herself they only thought as of a wretch whose very name it would henceforth be a horror and a degradation to mention.

# XLIX

*A flash of light partially breaks through the obscurity occasioned by law and logic, but its illumination reaches not far—Mr. Frederic Dalton shews a little weakness for a moment, but his strength of mind returns to him with redoubled vigour*

ALL THIS VILLAGE EXAMINATION OF the event, and the pretty general uniformity of opinion to which it had led, took place in the interval between Jessie's removal to prison and the discovery of the infant's body by William Reynolds. This new occurrence again roused all the feelings of the country against the unnatural mother, and every conversation that followed upon it was made up of observations tending to demonstrate the peculiar facilities afforded by the premises for the perpetration of the crime, and the hardened atrocity of the young mother in so deliberately committing it. It happened that Mr. Mortimer, the amiable assistant poor-law commissioner, had been absent for several weeks in the most distant part of his district, and, on making a morning call at the house of Mr. Dalton on his return, naturally enough spoke of the tragedy which had been acted in the village during his absence. He had been shewn into the morning sitting-room, where he found no one but Ellen and Miss Maxwell, and, while he was expressing his horror at what he had just learned, Frederic Dalton, who had been informed of his arrival, entered the room. After the usual friendly greetings had been exchanged between them, Mr. Mortimer returned to the subject that Dalton's entrance had interrupted, and said, "A horrible story, Dalton, is it not, this about Jessie Phillips and her murdered child?"

"Horrible indeed!" replied young Dalton, who had heard it too frequently reverted to any longer to shrink from the subject. He had, indeed, suffered no slight martyrdom while schooling himself into this apparent calmness, *but he had done it*; and now added, without any quiver of the lip or even dropping his eyelids, "The whole history from beginning to end is one of unparalleled atrocity."

"It is indeed!" rejoined Mr. Mortimer, adding, as he turned to wards the young ladies, "Of course you have heard the news of this morning concerning this horrible event?"

"No, really," replied Miss Maxwell eagerly; "it is many days now since the subject ceased to be the especial topic of discussion throughout the parish. We have all turned from vice to virtue, from contemplating deserved misery to anticipating equally deserved happiness." And Martha made her words intelligible by casting a smiling glance upon the blushing Ellen, whose nuptials had recently been fixed for an early day by the repentant Duke himself.

"But, despite this very delightful and most welcome theme," replied Mr. Mortimer, bowing to the bride elect, "a circumstance has occurred this morning which seems to have revived that which stands in such tremendous contrast to it."

Ellen, whose eyes had naturally fixed themselves on the carpet, on hearing the words of her friend, now raised them again with a look of deep interest, as Mr. Mortimer answered Miss Maxwell, and as she did so her glance caught the countenance of her brother, who stood, leaning on the back of a chair, immediately opposite to her. He was ghastly pale, and his features, though fixed by a desperate effort into the regidity of stone, expressed a degree of agony which made his sister tremble from head to foot, she knew not why. At this moment, Lord Pemberton suddenly entered the room, having used his privilege, as an elected member of the family, to pass through the open door of the hall without ceremony. His eyes, as usual, sought out Ellen among the group assembled, and he immediately walked up to her; but, passing close by Frederic in his way, he laid his hand upon his shoulder as he advanced, and said, gravely, "Dalton, the child's body is found!"

Ellen's eye was still upon her brother, for not even the entrance of Pemberton had enabled her to remove it; and so dreadful was the livid hue of his complexion, so frightful the terror that glared in his distended eyes as these words were spoken, that, losing all command of herself before the horrible idea which seemed to pierce through her brain, she uttered a shrill scream and fell fainting from a chair. Lord Pemberton in an instant threw himself on the ground beside her, and, raising her head, supported it on his shoulder, while Mr. Mortimer, having first vehemently rung the bell, threw open a window near her, sedulously removing the sofa that impeded the current of air from reaching her. Neither of the gentlemen had for an instant turned their eyes towards young Dalton. Of this happy chance he was at once aware, notwithstanding the agony still thrilling through his frame, and, while yet looking the very epitome of guilty terror, he rushed from the room, calling aloud for "Water! water!" The open door of the hall was before him as he quitted the parlour, and, without pausing an instant to think or to see whether he were observed, he darted through it, and was presently sheltered from every eye by the thick plantations of the shrubbery. Here, as the trees closed round him, he stood still panting for breath as if he had been running for a mile, and trembling as if in sympathy with every leaf of the evergreens that the chill wind shook as it blew past him.

But this sensation of mortal terror did not long endure. He suddenly remembered that it was impossible Pemberton, the adoring lover, the affianced husband of his sister, could have uttered the words which had so unmanned him had they indeed inferred any personal reference to him. "Fool that I am!" he exclaimed, wiping away the cold drops that hung upon his forehead, "scared by a breath as harmless and unmeaning as that which waves yon laurel bough!" Yet still his knees smote each other as he stood, and gladly did he avail himself of the support of a bench hard by, where, thrown at his length, and strengthened by the cold wind that fanned the curls on his uncovered head, he reasoned himself into tolerable composure by dwelling upon the blessed chance of Ellen's fainting, which not only had fastened every eye upon herself while he was probably betraying a portion of the horror produced by Lord Pemberton's words, but had furnished him with so fair an excuse for suddenly leaving the room as to render it utterly impossible that any disagreeable remark could be made upon it. Frederic Dalton, in short, had received only a passing touch of alarm; it was sharp at the moment, but was soon lost, almost to memory, amidst the innumerable self-gratulations which followed upon finding that the discovery, which had for a moment so startled him, was considered on all sides as having only completed the chain of proof against Jessie. "And rightly is she punished!" he exclaimed in secret, and with most self-approving sincerity. "She has got into this scrape wholly and solely in consequence of her own wrong-headed obstinacy, and I really cannot immolate myself to save her from it. I should be sacrificing the interests of poor Ellen, and, in fact, destroying my whole family, if I suffered my former ill-placed partiality to her, ungrateful as she has proved herself, to influence my conduct now. It is her egregious folly and violence of character alone that has brought her to her present condition, and I really have no power to help her. God knows what I might not have done for her had she followed the course I set down for her; but, as it is, she must take the consequences of her own fault, let them be what they may."

These comfortable thoughts sufficed so completely to restore his self-possession, that, when the family at the manor-house assembled to dinner, he made one of them. Perhaps he was not sorry to find that his sister Ellen was not sufficiently recovered to be among them; it would be better, perhaps, not to have to talk to her about her fainting, though he was far from believing that any new-born suspicion had occasioned it. It would be saying too much did I assert that no idea of the kind had occurred to him; but, though it certainly had suggested itself as just possible, the alarm it brought was speedily stifled by two considerations, both comfortably strong in his favour. The first was, that he thought Pemberton's ghostly words might have been quite sufficient to produce the effect without any reference to him. And, by the second, he felt still more strongly assured that, even if any such suspicion existed, Ellen had just now too much at stake to venture upon exposing her whole family to infamy for the mere pleasure of denouncing him.

But was Frederic Dalton quite correct in believing that, if in truth Ellen's eye had rested upon him during that terrible moment, no other had? Where was the keen glance of the Martha Maxwell? There was outward truce between them, for so had Henry Mortimer desired his fair friend to let it be when he last left Deepbrook for London; but well did young Dalton know that she both scorned and hated him, and rather would he, under such circumstances, have stood the gaze of a dozen other eyes for an hour than the glance of hers for a moment. But, in fact, he had no idea that she had been in the room. On his first entering to pay his compliments to Mr. Mortimer, he had been too much shaken by that gentleman's immediate reference to the subject he least liked to look very freely about him; and, though he had rallied well, the arrival of Lord Pemberton, and the palsying effect of the words with which he had entered, had left the guilty man no leisure to discover the figure of Martha, who was sitting apart at a window, the curtain of which concealed her sufficiently to prevent his being aware that she was in the apartment. From behind that curtain, however, she *had* seen him. She had marked the almost livid paleness which had chased the youthful blood from his cheek when Mr. Mortimer announced that there was further news respecting Jessie Phillips, and plainer still, if need were, did she discern the agony which his countenance expressed as Lord Pemberton pronounced the words, "Dalton, the child's body is found!" In an instant all her powers of observation were on the stretch, and, even in the short interval which followed before he was out of sight, material enough appeared to rouse a terrible suspicion in her mind, which till that hour had never, in the very remotest degree, suggested itself. Ere Frederic Dalton's husky voice calling for "Water! water!" had ceased to vibrate on her ear, she felt in her very soul convinced that it was he who had destroyed the child of Jessie Phillips!

# L

*Ellen Dalton shews herself less strong-minded than her brother—Martha Maxwell is a good deal puzzled as to what she could, and what she ought to do, but at length takes a very wise resolution, and acts upon it*

WHETHER THE LESS RAPID, THE more timid, and the greatly more gentle spirit of Ellen had immediately arrived at the same conclusion may be doubted; but at any rate the horrible suspicion of it which flashed upon her was not only strong enough to produce the temporary suspension of all her faculties, but also to render her recovery of them a moment of great agony. When this recovery took place, she was lying upon her bed, and her mother and two of her sisters, Henrietta and Caroline, were standing round her. The first instant of recollection brought a vague and indistinct idea of crime to her mind, with which the image of her brother was mingled, and she started up with such a fearful expression of terror in her eyes, that her mother believed her to be still under the influence of some violent fit, the nature of which she did not understand. Inexpressibly alarmed, she rushed out of the room, more rapidly than she had moved for the last twenty years, to call for assistance. Ellen meanwhile watched her terrified countenance and hurried exit, and, grasping the hand of Henrietta, exclaimed, "Where is she gone? What is it I have said? Whom is she going to call?" and then, as her recollections became more distinct, she added, with an eager anxiety that seemed to amount to agony, "Oh! for mercy's sake, Henrietta, do not let her tell any body!—it is not proved yet. Let it not be my doing! Oh! call her back! call her back!"

"Lie down, my dearest Ellen!" replied Henrietta, fully as much alarmed as her mother, but with a vague idea that it was no passing fit, but positive madness, which had fallen upon her beloved sister. "Try, dearest, to compose yourself," she said, "you will be better presently. But your health depends upon your keeping quiet, Ellen." And the poor girl's hand, which Ellen still held, trembled so violently, under the influence of this frightful idea, that Ellen became still more dreadfully agitated, from the belief that she had unconsciously uttered all that she had observed—all that she had suspected.

"Tell me what I have said, Henrietta!" she exclaimed, while her pale lips trembled with emotion. "Remember that I have not been in my senses. It will be very wicked if any body takes advantage of what I may have spoken when I was delirious."

"You have spoken nothing, dearest Ellen!" said Caroline, soothingly, "believe me you have not; do not let any such idle idea torment you."

"Is that true, Henrietta?" demanded the poor sufferer, with sudden calmness, "or does dear Caroline only say it to comfort and quiet me?"

"It is perfectly true, my dearest Ellen!" replied Henrietta, earnestly. "I think that you must have fallen asleep while we thought you were still fainting, and that you have had some frightful dream. Believe me, dearest, nothing in the world has happened, or we must have heard of it, you know, as well as you. And even of your dreams, dear love, you have said nothing, so lie down quietly and sleep again, and all these feverish fancies will have vanished when you wake next."

Ellen fixed her eyes earnestly on the face of her sister, and immediately became convinced that she was not deceiving her. "Thank God!" she murmured with a heavy sigh. "Perhaps it is as you say, Henrietta. So now leave me, dear girls, both of you, and tell poor dear mamma that I am much better, and quite composed, and trying to go to sleep again. Oh! you are right, dear girls, nothing will do me so much good as quiet. Go now, dear children, go, both of you, and do not let any body come to me for the next three or four hours."

Ellen now spoke with so much seeming composure that the comforted girls obeyed her, and gave so favourable an account of her to Mrs. Dalton, that the good lady, who with all her indolence had energy to be as fond a mother as ever lived, consented to her being left, upon condition that Henrietta and Caroline should go by turns into the little dressing-room appropriated to the dear invalid, and, creeping over the carpet on tiptoe, should listen at the door which opened close to her bed, in order to ascertain that she rested tranquilly. And this was done, and so carefully, as not to disturb the object of their care, who still remained perfectly still, and, as her tender watchers flattered themselves, fast asleep.

But never had sleep been farther from the eyes of Ellen Dalton than during those silent hours. It required but a very few minutes after she was left alone completely to restore her to the most perfect recollection of all that had passed, and long and deeply did she ruminate upon it. Nor was it only the condition into which the words of Lord Pemberton had thrown her brother that occupied her mind; again and again she went over every circumstance relative to Jessie Phillips which had ever come to her knowledge, either by observation or report; and much, ah! very much, which when recently canvassed between herself and Martha Maxwell had appeared in one light, now shewed itself with terrible distinctness in another. Ellen now felt astonished that she could ever have permitted the result of so many years of familiar observation of Jessie's character to be effaced from her mind by any chain of unproved circumstances whatever. And then a pang, such as a poisoned dagger might have given, shot through her heart as she remembered the result of still more constant and familiar observation on her brother. But who can describe the horror of the inference derived from these different trains of thought? Her father, so pure from stain through every period of his existence, so gentle in nature, so firm in principle!—if the dark suspicions of her heart proved true, could her father hear of it and live? Her wretched mother, too, who, in truth, had yet to learn what sorrow and suffering meant, how would her proud maternal head be humbled to the dust! And her young sisters, so fair, so bright, so pure in heart and innocent in thought, where could they all, all find darkness deep enough to hide them? Then came the image of Pemberton, and one burning thought sufficed to picture palpably before her all the misery that was to come, compared to which all the lingering sufferings she had endured for years appeared but like the memory of tranquil contentment. A groan passed her lips as she thus thought of her affianced husband, and, the sound proving but too plainly that she no longer slept, the door from the dressing-room opened, and Henrietta approached the bed.

"Are you in pain, my dearest Ellen?" she said, gently taking her sister's hand. "If so, we must immediately send for Mr. Johnson."

"No, no, not in pain; I do assure you I am not in pain," eagerly replied Ellen, who at that moment dreaded nothing so much as the being exposed to the questionings and remarks of any one.

"Well, then," said Henrietta, kindly, "if neither in pain nor asleep, you will, I well know, be glad to see your dear friend Martha, and here she is, and here she has been for the last hour, I believe, watching for your eyes to open, that she might speak to you."

Martha Maxwell approached the bed as these words were said, and, bending forward, kissed the cold, damp forehead of poor Ellen. Of all the world, perhaps, excepting only her wretched brother himself, Ellen Dalton would at that moment have least desired to see her friend Martha. From all others she felt that it might be possible to conceal the dark thoughts that were poisoning the life-blood at her heart, but from Martha Maxwell she but too well knew this could not be. She doubted not, she never had doubted for an instant, that her keen friend had marked the effect of Lord Pemberton's words upon her brother, and now she was come to tell her so! Oh! doubtless she was come to tell her to prepare for the holy exchange from false witness and base calumny to justice and to truth! The heart of poor Ellen seemed to die within her as she felt the lips of Martha on her brow; it seemed to her that this kiss was the type and symbol of the union about to be formed between them, for the purpose of proclaiming to all the world that the son of her father was a murderer and a felon!

Nor was Ellen far wrong in her conjectures. Martha had, indeed, seen the face of Frederic at the moment when his startled soul, on hearing what to him had seemed an accusation, had looked out through his eyes, and cried GUILTY, with a truth of evidence which stamped itself upon her heart and understanding in characters not easily to be effaced. She waited but to know that her poor friend had given symptoms of recovered life, and then returned home to take counsel with herself how this terrible suspicion, this more than suspicion, should be acted upon. It is hardly necessary to say, that not for an instant did Martha Maxwell hesitate as to the righteousness and the necessity of taking immediate measures to prevent the innocent from being mistaken for the guilty; but she felt that the business was a thorny one. Whom was she to apply to for assistance? Henry Mortimer, who was the only person, besides herself and Ellen, possessed of any previous knowledge concerning facts, was in London, and the frankly avowed friendship which united them had not as yet ripened into a correspondence by letters. To addressing herself, in the first instance, to her father, which was the course she would greatly have preferred, there was one great objection, namely, that it would oblige her to repeat to him, not only all she had learned in confidence from Ellen respecting her brother, but also all the disagreeable circumstances which had subsequently arisen in consequence of the steps she had herself so unadvisedly taken in order to punish the young man's double dealing. It was not so much because she shrunk from confessing a frolic to her father, which she felt very disagreeably certain he would disapprove, that she wished to avoid appealing to him for assistance, but she feared that, by irritating his personal feelings against young Dalton, she might lead him to appear and perhaps to be a less disinterested agent and adviser than she would wish to employ. In this dilemma she at length, however, determined to appeal to Ellen for permission to communicate to her father all the particulars which she had communicated to her respecting the scene at Lady Mary Wayland's, as well as that which followed at the manor-house; and this, she thought, might suffice, together with Jessie's story to herself, and such a description as she felt fully able to give of the effect produced by the words of Lord Pemberton, to rouse the interest of her father on the subject, without making him in any degree an interested party in the business.

Had the temperament of Martha been a little less vehement, a little less prone to act on the impulse of the moment, her very sincere affection for Ellen Dalton might have led her to pause a little ere she thus determined to appeal to her for permission to expose what had so very obvious a tendency to inculpate her brother as either perpetrator or accomplice in one of the most horrible crimes of which human nature can be guilty. But, dismayed by the conviction which had now burst upon her of the probable innocence of Jessie, and the (to her) certain culpability of Frederic, she could see no object before her of sufficient importance to check the eager zeal with which she burned to vindicate the innocence of one whose interests she had solemnly promised to defend, yet against whom she had listened to fabricated or blundering reports, till she too had joined the deluded crowd in proclaiming a conviction that she was guilty. This first great object had so completely taken possession of her, that it never entered into her head to doubt the certainty of Ellen's participation in the same object. Often before had she lamented that her admirable friend had so worthless a brother; and there was nothing new or strange in this to check her in the coarse she was about to pursue. Accordingly, she made her way to the bedside of Ellen, no thought mixing itself with her ultimate object save somewhat of doubt and anxiety lest her friend should not have sufficiently recovered from the shock she had received to be able to converse with her.

But there was something in the manner with which the unhappy Ellen shuddered and closed her eyes, the moment she perceived her, that betrayed a feeling easily understood, though in no degree anticipated; and then, though not before, the tremendous position in which her friend was placed appeared to Martha Maxwell in all its real horror. Her heart smote her for having so permitted the absorption of all feelings into one as to have made her thus unmindful of her who so well deserved her tenderest sympathy, and she hastened to relieve the poor sufferer from the dread of such an interview as she had herself certainly projected by saying, "I am rejoiced that she has slept so quietly, Henrietta; but remember, she must still be kept very quiet. Do not let any one talk to her." And then, bending again over the pallid brow, she once more kissed it and withdrew. But as she gently resigned the hand she had taken on approaching the bed, she felt a gentle pressure from poor Ellen's fingers, which drew unwonted tears to her eyes, as she remembered how little she had deserved this mark of tenderness from her.

But pity for Ellen, though now a strong feeling in the mind of Martha, was not long predominant. Her homeward walk was slow and lingering, and not either her fearless spirit nor the usual prompt decision of her character could prevent her heart from sinking as she meditated on all the difficulties of the task which was before her. Unluckily for Martha, at least she persuaded herself that she thought so, the manner of Henry

Mortimer towards her had undergone a somewhat sudden change during the few last hours that they had passed together before he last left Deepbrook for London. The word "love" had neither then nor at any other time passed them; but when they were about to part the easy tone, sometimes of sportive intimacy and sometimes of rational discussion, which alternately marked their intercourse, seemed to have vanished. Henry Mortimer had looked grave, nay, almost sad, as his eye met hers; and, though he once and again attempted to rally and to converse with her and with others in his usual tone, it was in vain; Henry Mortimer had every ordinary symptom of being in love without feeling at liberty to confess "the soft impeachment" to the fair one who had stolen into his heart. Nevertheless, at the very last moment, when the evening party at his father's house, which preceded his departure, broke up, he did venture to whisper, while assisting the adjustment of the boa and the shawl, "Martha Maxwell must not forget me." Nay, the final shake of the hand concluded with so gentle yet firm a pressure, that it was quite impossible the young lady could have gone to sleep that night without confessing, in strict confidence, to her own heart that she did think Henry Mortimer was a little in love with her.

Such being the position of affairs between them, she felt a very strong repugnance to addressing him by letter. If her suspicion, or, in plainer English, if her hope were well founded, it was still evident that for some reason or other it was not his wish or intention to avow himself her lover at the present moment; and how could she, under such circumstances, endure the idea of attempting to lead him into a correspondence? She could not, she would not do this. But to whom, then, could she apply? Many a slow and uneven step was taken before the question was answered, but at length a bright idea struck her. The excellent Mr. Rimmington would be in every way an unexceptionable confidant, adviser, and assistant, and to him she felt she could address herself, not only without danger or fear of any kind, but with an infinitely greater freedom from every species of restraint than must, in common prudence, have accompanied the statement of what had passed to her father. Great, indeed, was the relief to poor Martha which this very wise determination brought with it; and though the nature of the business and the part she felt called upon to take in it could not but shake the accustomed firmness of her character, she braved all the singularity of walking alone on the following morning to the venerable clergyman's house, and, with a steadier voice than most young ladies, under her circumstances, could have commanded, desired to be shewn into his study.

# LI

*Martha Maxwell relates all she knows of Jessie's history to Mr. Rimmington; but they do not agree as to the inferences which ought to be drawn therefrom—the young lady, as in Duty bound, gives up her opinion and adopts that of the clergyman*

Mr. Rimmington was sitting alone beside a good fire, with a miniature library-table snugly placed before him, and volumes of various weight (in more senses than one) ranged in all directions within easy reach. His surprise at seeing Miss Maxwell enter was considerable, but not sufficient to prevent his giving her a very kind and encouraging welcome.

"You will not think I should thus break in upon you," she began, "unless I had something more than commonly important to communicate. Can you, my dear Mr. Rimmington, bestow half-an-hour upon me, and promise that it shall not be interrupted?"

"Undoubtedly I will," he replied, at the same time ringing the bell, in order to inform his servant that no other person was to be admitted. "I trust," he continued, as soon as they were again alone, "that you have no painful tidings to communicate?"

She shook her head, and said, "Painful enough! Terrible, oh! too terrible in every way; but it is nothing that relates to my own family."

"And yet you are pale, my dear Miss Maxwell," he replied, "and you tremble as if some fearful personal danger threatened you. What can you have to tell me, my dear child?"

Martha took breath for a moment ere she answered him, and then, in a voice resolutely slow and distinct, she related all the circumstances which led to the visit in which she had first obtained the confidence of Jessie Phillips. For an instant her voice faltered when she had to confess that there was a time when she believed that Frederic Dalton was attached to her, and that the belief had given her pleasure. But, that one moment over, she pursued her story to the end, admirably well avoiding every unnecessary word, yet touching luminously and distinctly on every point that could tend to make her auditor as well acquainted with the circumstances which had come to her knowledge as she was herself; nor did she pause till she reached the commitment of Jessie to the county gaol for the supposed murder of her child, and then she stopped, seemingly as if her narrative was concluded, but in truth only to take breath and courage to utter the tremendous sequel.

"I understand you, my dear child," said Mr. Rimmington, mournfully; "I guess but too plainly what it is you mean to infer. You believe that Frederic Dalton is the father of this murdered infant?"

Martha bent her head affirmatively.

"Nor can I, after hearing your statement," he continued, "feel any doubt that you are right. But this fact, my dear Martha, however well established, cannot now assist the wretched girl who, if she be indeed guilty of the horrid act of which she stands accused, will assuredly pay her life as the penalty of her crime; although, indeed, it may be, as I suspect you think, that this crime has been wholly occasioned by the brutal neglect of the father, upon whose protection the law denied her any claim."

Martha Maxwell had told a long story, and had told it well, yet she had not succeeded in eliciting the suspicion which she had intended her narrative should excite against the man whom she was about to accuse of the horrible atrocity of murdering his own child. She would have given her right hand if any gleam of the frightful light which had burst upon her could have reached her companion without her having to endure the horror of announcing, in direct words, the suspicion she came there on purpose to communicate. A deadly sickness seemed to seize upon her heart, and she became as white as a sheet.

Mr. Rimmington, whose eye was fixed upon her, started from his seat to support her, for he thought she was fainting and would fall; but poor Martha was not subject to the weakness which, at that moment at least, would have seemed a blessing to her.

"No, no, I am not fainting, Mr. Rimmington," she said, shaking her head mournfully; "but I have that to say which, though truth and justice force it from me, it is inexpressibly painful to speak."

Her dark eyes, painfully pregnant with meaning, were raised to his face as he stood before her; his hand was laid, with paternal gentleness, upon her shoulder, and, as he gazed upon her agitated features, a strange spasm seemed to pass across his own.

"Gracious Heaven! Is it possible?" he exclaimed. "God forbid! God forbid, child, that you should be right! What proofs have you? Heaven have mercy upon his father!—upon Ellen!—upon all! Oh! wide, wide-spreading will be the misery if this horrible suggestion prove true! Martha Maxwell," he added, with great solemnity, but with accents which trembled with emotion, "you are treading upon fearful ground. You hate and execrate this worthless boy. No wonder, child, no wonder; he deserves it all. But, for Heaven's sake, beware that ill opinion does not beget false judgment!"

"Mr. Rimmington," replied the pale and trembling girl, "I pass no judgment. Thank God, I have not that task to fulfil! But would you deem it right and righteous in me, believing in my soul, as I most firmly do, that another is guilty of the crime for which Jessie Phillips is accused,—would you deem it righteous that I should bury such belief in my heart, in order to spare myself what I now suffer and all that I know I must suffer?"

"Martha Maxwell," said the clergyman, almost sternly, "what are your proofs?"

"I have none, sir, none whatever," she replied, in an accent that seemed to indicate that it was a comfort and relief to say so.

"Have you mentioned your suspicions to any other but myself?" he demanded, eagerly.

"No, Mr. Rimmington, I have not," she replied.

"Literally and positively to no one?" said he.

"To no one!" rejoined Martha, with emphasis.

"Most truly do I rejoice to hear you say so, Miss Maxwell," he replied; "and let me earnestly entreat you to retain this silence unbroken. You have been, doubtless, agitated and excited by the thoughts and recollections which must have naturally crowded upon you in consequence of your former intercourse with the unfortunate girl who, justly or unjustly, stands accused of murdering her child. But, if you can succeed in calming your spirits sufficiently to give your excellent judgment fair play, I think that you will feel, as I do, the very doubtful justice of exonerating one against whom there are many proofs, because your previous knowledge leads you to think her incapable of the crime, in order to throw suspicion of it upon another without any proofs to support it, because you conceive that he might be capable of the atrocity."

Martha said nothing in reply, but almost involuntarily shook her head, as not assenting to a proposition which, however, she ventured not to contradict.

"Let me ask you one question more, Martha," resumed Mr. Rimmington. "Do you think that any other person shares your suspicion?"

Martha paused for a moment ere she replied, and then said, "I hardly know how to answer you, Mr. Riminington. I have no right to say 'YES,' and yet I should be scarcely honest did I answer 'NO.'"

"I think that in this you need not fear to trust me," returned Mr. Rimmington; "for I have just given proof, both to you and to my own heart, that I am not likely to suffer any slight evidence to lead my thoughts in the direction yours have taken. For I too, dear Martha, in the very teeth of circumstantial evidence of most terrible strength and coherence, have ventured to express to Mr. Lewis my doubts as to the possibility that Jessie Phillips can be guilty of this fearful crime. Yet, notwithstanding this obstinate doubt, as I may truly call it, you perceive that I am by no means disposed to throw the crime upon another, because I am not fully convinced of her being guilty of it. Scruple not, therefore, my dear child, to answer my question. Your doing so may explain to me how and why it has taken possession of your mind."

"You ask me," said Martha, "if I think that any other person shares my suspicion?"

"I do," replied Mr. Rimmington; "and fear not, my dear, that I should place more reliance upon your statement than you seem inclined to give it yourself."

"I think, sir," replied Martha, slowly, and almost in a whisper, "I think that my poor friend, Ellen Dalton, does."

"God forbid!" exclaimed the good man, hastily, while tears started to his eyes. "Do not make me believe this, Miss Maxwell! Do not let me think that one I so lately saw radiant with well-deserved happiness is now so infinitely wretched!"

"You cannot mourn for it more than I do, Mr. Rimmington; but the knowledge—the suspicion, I mean—which now wrings her heart came not from me," said Martha, feeling at the bottom of her own aching heart that she was neither so cruel nor so unjust as the amiable rector seemed to think her. "I have already detained you long," she added, "but I will beseech you to give me five minutes more, and then you will know all I know, and gladly will I afterwards listen to your judgment upon it instead of my own. Yesterday morning, Mr. Rimmington, I was sitting alone with Ellen Dalton, and we were sadly enough comparing notes upon the unhappy condition of Jessie Phillips, and the terribly convincing strength of the case that had been made out against her, when Mr. Mortimer entered. Ellen desired the servant to let her father know that Mr. Mortimer had called, and in the next moment Frederic came into the room, his father being out. Mr. Mortimer spoke of the horrible event which had occurred during his absence, in which conversation Frederic Dalton joined with a degree of calmness which, knowing what I know, was equally astonishing and disgusting to me. But, after this had lasted a little while Mr. Mortimer suddenly exclaimed, 'Of course you have heard the news of this morning?' I quickly answered, 'No;' adding, that of late our thoughts had been engaged on happier themes, alluding to poor Ellen's marriage. Ellen's eyes at that moment were fixed on her brother, and so were mine. He turned deadly pale; but, ere Mr. Mortimer could satisfy the curiosity he had raised, Lord Pemberton entered hastily, and his first words were, laying his hand on the shoulder of Frederic as he spoke, 'Dalton, the child's body has been found!' Mr. Rimmington," pursued Martha, "I have no words powerful enough to convey to you the horror, the dismay expressed by the countenance of Frederic Dalton as this statement reached him. I saw guilt in every feature."

"Stay, Martha Maxwell, stay," replied Mr. Rimmington, while a slight frown contracted his brow, "might you not have seen a natural horror upon the face of the man whom you have taught me to believe was the wretched girl's paramour, upon hearing of this fresh proof of guilt against her?"

"If I did so misread it, sir," replied Martha, after a pause, "his sister Ellen must have blundered equally, for, though we have not talked together since, I am not left in doubt as to the impression it made upon her; she fell fainting from her chair, Mr. Rimmington, as she gazed on the tell-tale features of her brother."

"And is this all, my dear Martha?" exclaimed Mr. Rimmington, eagerly; and again leaving his chair he approached her, and took her hand affectionately in his.

"All, sir!" replied Martha; "yes," she added, after the interval of a minute, "I have now told you every thing."

"Then let me implore you, my dear child, as you would save yourself from repentance, and your poor friend Ellen from misery, never repeat to any one a single syllable of the suspicion you have revealed to me. I have long thought ill of Frederic Dalton, and, on the other hand, I have long thought well of Jessie Phillips. In these opinions, dear Martha, we have thought alike. But, oh! beware the danger of suffering any pre-conceived opinion to lead you to point out to the execration of his fellow-men an individual against whom no shadow of suspicion lies, excepting that he changed colour on hearing that the wretched girl whom he had seduced to destruction stood in greater peril of conviction than he thought for. You probably know that the most favourable feature in the case has hitherto been the want of any proof that the child was born alive, save her own wandering statement that she heard it cry. But now this proof is found, and the fate of the miserable mother may be considered as certain; can you then wonder that Frederic Dalton, wretch as you think him, should tremble, and turn pale at hearing it?"

Martha was staggered, and willingly, most willingly did she welcome the possibility that she might have been mistaken. She had come to Mr. Rimmington in the firm belief that she was called upon to do an act of terrible justice, though the doing it involved the necessity of destroying the happiness of one she dearly loved; and the hearing the deeply respected voice of her reverend friend declare that this fancied duty was a chimera, raised by her imagination, and that by pursuing it she would be most unjustly condemning to the incurable purgatory of injurious surmises an individual who certainly *might* be innocent of the crime her fancy had laid to his charge, she felt ready to kneel at his feet in a paroxysm of gratitude and joy. Touched by this implicit reliance on his judgment, Mr. Rimmington kindly urged her to remain with him a few minutes longer, that they might, as he said, calmly discuss together the grounds whereon rested the opinion in which they now so happily agreed; and the conversation which followed between these two highly intelligent and perfectly honest human beings might serve as "physic" to the pomp and majesty with which human reason is wont to invest itself when passing judgment upon facts established upon "circumstantial evidence."

"Independent," said Mr. Rimmington, "of the unbroken chain of proofs which we possess against the mother, you should observe, my dear Miss Maxwell, that it is impossible to find the shadow of a motive for Dalton's commiting the act. Assuming, even, that he was the father, of which, as the girl's oath on the subject cannot be taken, he well knows there can be no legal evidence whatever—but, even assuming this from our own ex-parte knowledge of facts, there exists no reason whatever for his thus conquering every common feeling of our nature for the purpose of relieving the girl he had used so cruelly from the burden of maintaining her child. For HIS child, you will observe, in the eye of the law, it could never be; and he could therefore have no motive of any kind to spur him to so horrible an act, save a species of consideration for her, at once the most improbable and inadequate. Nevertheless, though I cannot impute to him the madness of putting in jeopardy his young and happy existence for an object which might have been effectually attained (if he really cared any thing about it) by his privately disbursing a very trifling sum in the way of settlement—although I cannot suspect him of this, I can conceive it extremely probable that the suddenly hearing that the only proof had been found which was wanting for the certain condemnation of the unhappy girl might have produced the effect you witnessed. What renders this the more probable is, that I have heard many persons say, and so, I doubt not, has Frederic Dalton also, that a very strong hope of acquittal lay in this difficulty of proving that the child ever lived. Can we then wonder that the sudden announcement of the loss of this hope should have produced the emotion you witnessed? And must not the young man be infinitely more depraved than you have ever conceived him to be were it otherwise?"

"Thank Heaven! which put it into my head to come to you, Mr. Rimmington!" exclaimed Martha. "The perfect conviction which your arguments bring makes me wonder at the extraordinary sort of delusion which led me to see every thing so differently before."

"Will you let me explain this, dear Martha," said Mr. Rimmington, with a gentle smile; "and will you promise not to be angry with me if I am very saucy?"

"Say what you will, my dear sir," answered Martha, returning the smile; "it is quite impossible that I should be angry with you."

"Well, then," he rejoined, "I will tell you how I explain the matter that puzzles you. Do you recollect the eagerness with which you set to work the moment you discovered the ill conduct of Frederic Dalton in order to punish his delinquency and avenge the wrongs both of yourself and poor Jessie?"

"I do, indeed," replied Martha, colouring; "and I think too that I understand your inference."

"I dare say you do, my dear," said Mr. Rimmington, laughingly; "and I dare say, also, that for the future you will endeavour to rein in a little that warm heart and eager temper of yours. Always give yourself time to think, my dear Martha, and I will venture to promise that you will never again blunder as you did then, and as you have done to-day."

"Thank you, a thousand times," said Martha, rising to depart, and feeling happy and grateful in no common degree for having enjoyed the inestimable advantage of listening to so much worth and wisdom. A cordial shake of the hand was then exchanged between them, and the good clergyman watched her depart with a sensation of the purest and most sincere benevolence as he thought of the good he had been able to do by removing from her mind a cloud of error which had threatened equally to destroy her own peace and that of every member of the Dalton family. How little did either of them think, as they thus parted with such comfortable feelings of mutual esteem and approval, that the result of their long conference was that most lamentable and most common of human blunders, the acquittal of guilt and the condemnation of innocence!

# LII

*A night of woe and dread to one sheltered and cherished in her father's house, and surrounded by care and love—the same night passed less miserably by Jessie in her prison—the Reverend Mr. Green does not understand Jessie at all better than the Reverend Mr. Rimmington*

Poor Ellen passed a very restless and feverish night, falling into uneasy sleep at intervals, but remaining awake for hours, in miserably uncertain meditation upon what she could, and what she ought to do. Martha Maxwell, while possessed with the same irresistible and almost instinctive conviction which had seized upon herself and her unhappy friend at the very same instant, namely, that Jessie was innocent of the crime laid to her charge, had fancied her own position one of the greatest difficulty and most distressing embarrassment. But what was it when compared with that of Ellen? Father, mother, sisters,—to say nothing of the kindred criminal himself—must all be sacrificed! Their future lives must be poisoned by undying shame and never-to-be-forgotten misery; their country made too full of ignominy to hold them, and their honourable name converted into a stigma and disgrace! Unhappy Ellen! Must all this be? and must she be the agent to effect it? Can it be wondered at if her intellect trembled under the weight of such meditations? Of Pemberton she dared not think at all; she shrunk from every idea connected with him as from misery too great to bear; and, if her stubborn fancy would persist in bringing his beloved image before her, she struggled to escape from it with a degree of agony that it is impossible to describe.

Poor soul! She felt, oh! how keenly, that the whole history of their past loves, the nature of the obstacles which had opposed it, and of the generous feelings which at last had removed those obstacles, seemed all prepared expressly to aggravate the misery of her present situation. The burning blush of shame kindled on her innocent cheek as she thought of the appalling disgrace that threatened his name by having suffered her own to be joined with it; and she thought too, till the paleness of death succeeded to that blush, of all the deep repentance with which the proud duke would look back and shudder at the mad consent which his son's matchless constancy had wrung from him! At one tremendous moment she fancied that she had determined *not* to take upon herself the frightful task of denouncing her guilty brother, repeating to herself, with delirious vehemence and rapidity, "It would be a sin! a sin! a sin!" Yet even then she mixed no thought of guarding her own happiness with this shuddering avoidance of directing the sword of justice against her wretched brother. Thankfully, most thankfully, would she have welcomed the permission of Heaven to close her eyes in immediate death, but no relief from her misery, save this, ever suggested itself for a moment. Her most definite and her most earnest wish was for the light of day, that she might at once write to Lord Pemberton her last farewell, and so draw an impenetrable veil of separation between them for ever. Nor did she ever, for a single instant of that dreadful night, falter in her purpose, though once, for a short interval of shrinking tenderness, she thought, while thus dividing herself from him for ever, she might still avoid the agony of revealing the dreadful cause of her doing so. But even this feeble consolation did not remain with her long, for the idea of avoiding the avowal of any thing that might lead to save the innocent, from suffering for the guilty again presented itself before her in all its true deformity; and the pale image of Jessie, about to suffer death upon the gallows for a crime she had not committed, took such fearful hold upon her imagination as to force a shriek from her lips that woke the watchers in her dressing-room.

The terrified Henrietta was instantly at her side, and her soothingly affectionate voice implored the dear sufferer to compose herself, and to tell her what uneasy dream it was which had caused her to cry out so painfully.

"Open your eyes, my darling Ellen," said she, bending down to wipe the moisture of terror from her brow; "open your eyes, my Ellen, and convince yourself how very safe you are, in your own quiet room, with nothing to frighten or hurt you, and your own Henrietta at your side."

For a moment or two it was a great relief for Ellen to hold her sister by the hand, to feel that she was indeed close to her, and to listen to her gentle words; but even this consolation, sweet as it was, soon seemed to be a restraint to her, for again she most earnestly assured her that, if left in perfect stillness, she thought she might be able to get to sleep again; and Henrietta once more left her to her terrible but desired solitude.

Nevertheless, the watchful entrance of Henrietta had been beneficial to her suffering patient, for, when the nerves are greatly agitated, it is often useful to affect calmness when we have it not; and so it was with Ellen. Instead of the vehement anguish to which she had given way when she uttered the cry that had brought her sister to her side, a sort of subdued and patient sadness followed her departure, which enabled her to meditate more calmly, if not more happily. She saw no more visionary shapes before her eyes; and her imagination ceased to torture her with representing scenes to come, in which all that was most terrible in possibility was already before her; but instead of this her memory went back to what had already passed, and changed the sufferings of half-dreaming delirium to the sober certainty of waking sorrow.

And then she distinctly remembered the manner in which she had received the visit of poor Martha, and all the feelings of horror and repugnance with which she had marked the painful expression of her eye, all the averseness which she had felt, and doubtless shewn, to any lengthened or confidential communication with her, and all the cold ingratitude with which she had received the sympathy she had come to offer.

"Alas!" thought the unhappy Ellen, as her mind gradually settled itself into the belief that all she most dreaded must of necessity overtake her; "alas! how idle, how childish, how very weak is this wish to avoid a true and faithful friend, merely because she is already in possession of the facts which I so well know must speedily be published to all the world! Poor, dear Martha! there was pity in her eye, oh! very tender pity, as well as the dreadful consciousness of all that had been, and all that must be! And yet, equally foolish and ungrateful, I turned away to avoid seeing her! My poor Martha! I sent her home again, with a heart still more painfully burdened than she brought, for she came to offer her pity, and I refused to receive it. I turned from the only being who could understand and pity me." And the tears which poor Ellen shed in penitence for this softened the tone of her mind, and in some sort relieved her. "She shall come to me again to-morrow," thought she, "and may God then give me strength to endure with firmness the listening to all that must follow! O Martha, what is there you can say to me which I have not said to my own aching heart already?"

And what was the condition of the wretched pauper girl? How were the long and lonely hours of the prison day and the prison night passed by her?

"Sweet are the uses of adversity."

Had the gentle-hearted but erring Jessie never tasted the bitter cup of disappointment; had she never known the anguish of discovering that the passionate, the devoted, the all-absorbing love which had led her to the entire sacrifice of herself, and to the abandonment of all that was most precious on earth and in heaven, had been felt for a villain, a base, selfish, hard, and treacherous villain, instead of being an offering, as she had fondly flattered herself, to the virtues of the best and noblest of the human race; had she never known this bitter agony, she would not now have laid her young head so unrepiningly on her prison pillow, nor have fallen asleep so peacefully, after having breathed a hopeful prayer to God for his merciful forgiveness in heaven, and for a speedy death on earth. Infinitely, oh! infinitely less bitter, less heart-breaking, were the night thoughts of Jessie in her prison, than those of Ellen in her father's house, and on her bed of down. She had prostrated her heart in deepest penitence before the throne of God, and had, in all singleness and sincerity of spirit, blessed the mercy which had sent her such chastisement for her faults in this world, as had taught her to bend in lowliness of heart and penitence of soul before the only tribunal that an immortal being has reasonable cause to fear. And yet she had at length become fully aware of the nature of the accusation recorded against her, and of the fearful penalty she must pay if she could not disprove it. She felt, too, with the most perfect and settled conviction, that such disproving was utterly and entirely out of her power. But, instead of adding to her sufferings, this unwavering conviction very greatly lessened them, for it spared her all the feverish throbbings of uncertainty, and that sickening vibration between hope and fear which is calculated to produce a species of suffering infinitely more hard to bear than the most violent crisis that ever tried the strength of human nerves. All such uncertainty was spared to Jessie. She had learned from the gaoler, with an emotion of positive joy, that her trial was to take place almost immediately, as the spring assizes for that year were particularly early, for she considered this portion of the punishment which her fault had entailed upon her as merely a necessary ceremony which must precede her death. Hope from it she had none, positively and literally, none, the very idea that any such chance could exist never entered her head for moment.

Jessie Phillips had, in fact, very deliberately passed judgment against herself already; for by degrees she had learned clearly and distinctly to understand all that had been, and all that was to be alleged against her, as well as all the well-connected chain of circumstantial evidence which so strongly confirmed every part of the accusation. She had gone over every part of this chain carefully and calmly, and had become perfectly convinced that no honest jury could fail to deliver it as their opinion that her murdered child had received its death from her. When told by Mr. Green (for that excellent man had made her repeated visits) that the body of the strangled infant had been found outside the shed, and immediately under the shutter which opened just above the spot where she had herself been found, she manifested more agitation than she had betrayed for many days past, and the sorrowing clergyman was more than ever confirmed in his belief that she had indeed been herself the destroyer of her new-born babe. Gladly, very gladly would he have welcomed the belief, also, that this dreadful act had been perpetrated in a fit of unconsciousness or delirium; but, if it had been the object nearest poor Jessie's heart to convince him of the contrary, she could not have succeeded better, for every word and every movement tended to convince him that no such hallucination had fallen upon her. She had

changed colour repeatedly, and shuddered perceptibly as she listened to his accurate description of the precise manner in which the body had been found, and more than once she uttered a stifled groan. At one time she covered her eyes with her hand, and seemed for several minutes to be plunged in very earnest thought. And then she removed her hand, and looking sadly, but steadily, in the face of her venerable companion, she said,—

"If you please, sir, you must not ask me any more questions that may puzzle me, one way or another, about all this dreadful business, or any thing that has happened to me since I left the workhouse, or how any thing of it all came about; for all such questions only seem to set me upon hoping, and guessing, and trying to make out that every thing may have been quite different from what it really was. I do not feel any wish or desire to deceive you, sir, or any body else, about what is done and over. Not all the words in the world can alter it; no, nor could every drop of blood in my veins, if I could pour it out on the earth before you, wash out my sin. I have not always been able to recollect things so clear and plain as I seem to do now, and if I have said first one thing, and then another, this want of clearness was the cause of it. But now I have quite come to the truth about it in my own mind, and I will tell it to you all at once, if you wish to hear it; but, afterwards, if you please, sir, I would rather not talk any more about it, for it will do nobody any good, nor me neither, but quite the contrary. The dreadful repeating of all the particulars can not undo the deed I have done, nor can all the talk in the world do me the good that praying to God does. It won't be very long now, you know, sir, before it is all over and ended; and all the time left won't be too much to be spent in praying for God's mercy and forgiveness."

"I fear, indeed, that you say truly, my poor girl," Mr. Green replied; "nor will I trouble you to repeat any of the unhappy circumstances a second time, but I should be glad to hear them from you once, and that now, as you appear to have recovered sufficient composure of spirits, to tell me every thing distinctly."

"Yes, sir," said the pale girl, with that rigid look of steadfast fortitude which, perhaps, nothing but despair can give; "yes, sir, I am now perfectly composed, and quite ready to tell you all I know, for your great kindness well deserves that I should do every thing you desire, let it be painful or not. And this, sir, is what I now feel sure must be the truth. It must have been I myself, and no other, that did whatever was done to my poor baby; and it must have been I that put it through the opening, which was exactly above the place where I lay, for who else could have done it? I remember well, perfectly well, seeing that large shutter, and the loose button that fastened it, just at the dreadful moment that I was laying myself down; I remember well, too, all the thoughts that were working in my head at the time. They were all mixed up with the dreadful fear that I should be seen and known; and it was thought of this kind, be very sure of it, sir, which made me do the dreadful deed I have done. It seems very strange to myself, now, that I should ever have been able to do it; but isn't it stranger still that I should be able to talk of it all so quietly, sir? So it is not that, it is not the strangeness of it that ought to put any such sinful thoughts into my head as the denying it would be."

"It would indeed," said Mr. Green, "be a very grievous crime were you to falsify facts stated at so solemn a moment as this; but neither would I wish you, Jessie, to steel yourself into a hardened state of indifference. You have much to answer for, and your repentance should be meek and full of sorrow."

"Oh! sir," replied the poor girl, while the but recently banished tears gushed anew from her eyes, "it is not hardened indifference that supports my courage; but how can I think of all the goodness and mercy of God, as I read it told in this blessed book, and as I feel it in the dark night come in comfort to my heart—how can I think and feel so, and not rejoice at the remembrance of what is coming upon me? Is it not a great comfort, sir, that I shall not mind death in any shape, or in any way; for what is *that*, with the hope of God's mercy joined to it, compared to living on, and having such things as I have done to think upon?"

"Then you have made up your mind to confess the crime and plead guilty?" said Mr. Green, with an involuntary feeling of regret, as the last gleam of hope for the unhappy girl seemed to vanish and die away.

"I hope, sir, that nobody won't force me to say any more about it," replied Jessie, somewhat fretfully. "I don't know any more about it than they must all know the for, of course, they will all have heard the same account of every thing that I have heard myself, and I do it will be very like cruelty to torture a poor creature by forcing her to talk about her own madness."

"Then you still mean that I should understand that you were out of your senses when all this happened?" said Mr. Green, fixing his eyes upon her with a strong expression of suspicion.

"Certainly I do, sir," replied Jessie, in a tone of quiet decisiveness, which produced the most unpleasant effect on the nerves of her auditor.

"I had better leave you, young woman," he said, rising from the chair he had occupied near her. "I neither desire to entrap you into making any confession beyond what you might wish to do for the relief of your own mind, nor yet to encourage you in the idle notion that your declaring yourself to have been insane, when no evidence whatever exists to confirm such a statement, will avail to avert the sentence of the law upon the act which you have committed; neither do I like to sit and listen to your declarations that you are looking forward with satisfaction to the execution of a sentence which you are evidently hoping to avert by a statement which appears to me utterly false, notwithstanding my earnest wish to believe it true."

So saying, he left the room, and the poor prisoner watched him depart without reluctance, for she saw that he attributed to her motives of which she was perfectly innocent, and, moreover, that he did not consider temporary madness as any excuse, even in the eyes of God, for what had been done under its influence; which she could not but think was somewhat a harsh judgment in a clergyman, though it might, and doubtless must, be very legally right in a jury.

Yet, in truth, Jessie at this time cared wonderfully little what any one thought about her. She clung with a sort of passionate hope to the idea of speedy death as the only possible relief left for her misery, and the mercy of God was now the only mercy that she seemed capable of valuing. Her melancholy composure, which was, perhaps, not altogether unlike the steadiness of a wreck, when settling in the troubled sea previous to sinking, was more shaken by the next visitor, whose humanity induced him to pass through the gloomy gates of a prison to visit her, than it had been by any thing which had occurred since she had made up her mind to receive the sentence of death as the "end-all" of her frightful sufferings. For this visitor was Mr. Rimmington, the honoured pastor, whose image was connected and bound up with all the happiest recollections of her life. Her first sensations at beholding him, poor soul! were those of joy, positive joy, and gladness; and when he appeared at the door she made a hasty step towards him, as if she thought he were come with power to redeem her from the abyss of misery in which she was plunged, and to lead her back to the dear innocent happiness of former days. But, ere she reached him, the heightened colour had already faded from her cheek; the eager eye, which had been raised to meet his, sunk to the ground; and, had she not taken hold of a chair to support her, she would probably have fallen at his feet.

Mr. Rimmington had decided upon making this painful visit from feeling that one who had from birth been his parishioner, and who, till her terrible falling away, had created sentiments of respect, affection, and esteem, in all who knew her, had still some claim upon him, which it would be a dereliction of his sacred duty to neglect, even in the degraded state to which her conduct had reduced her. Perhaps, too, his recent conversation with Miss Maxwell might have left some little feeling of restlessness upon his mind; not, indeed, as to the propriety of the advice he had given her, but as to the feeling of severity with which he was conscious he had spoken of the unhappy creature who was, in all human probability, about to atone with her young life for all the evil she had done. He wondered not at the state of trembling weakness which seized upon the miserable culprit upon seeing one whom she had been wont to meet under such sadly different circumstances; and while his own kind heart ached for the sufferings he witnessed, though believing them so thoroughly deserved, he silently motioned her to sit down, in order that she might recover strength and composure to listen to him, before he attempted to speak to her. A very few moments sufficed for this, for Jessie had lost all the hopes and all the fears which could render the presence of any human being sufficiently important to agitate her long.

"It is not necessary that I should tell you, Jessie Phillips," said he, as soon as he perceived that she was in a condition to understand what he wished to say to her—"it cannot be necessary that I should tell you that I am most deeply grieved to see you here, for you must know it well without my saying it. But I have thought it my duty to visit you, in case there were any thing you might wish to say to one whom you must remember as a friend as long as you can remember any thing. And I would wish, also, if you can tell me that your mind is in a proper state for it, that we should pray together."

Not all poor Jessie's stoicism of despair could prevent tears from filling her eyes, and soon trickling down her cheeks, also, at this address, but

"She wiped them soon,"

and gently, but earnestly, thanked him for his kindness in coming to her.

"Indeed, my poor girl," he replied, "I mean it kindly, though I well know that this meeting must be very painful to both of us. And do not fancy, Jessie, that I am come here to entrap you with questions," added the good man, while his mild eye rested with scrutinising earnestness on a countenance which, much to his surprise, appeared to him, notwithstanding the striking and most melancholy change which had passed over it, to wear the same expression of guileless truth that it had always done. "But, though to entrap you, or to say or do any thing that a friendly and pitying heart would shrink from, be equally out of my intention and my power, I should wish to ask you one or two questions."

"And I, sir," replied Jessie, mournfully, "am ready to answer them, let them be what they may; for I must be still deeper sunk in sin and shame than I am before I can forget all your goodness, all your long kindness to my poor mother, all your condescending notice to my unworthy self. I will answer any thing that you will please to ask, though I know that it is not within the reach either of my words, or even yours, sir, to change the very least thing of all that has been and all that is."

"True, Jessie," he replied, again looking earnestly in her face, for there was something in her tone that he did not well understand. It could not fairly be called reckless, but there was something of resolute firmness, if not of hard indifference, in her manner, which puzzled him. But his eye did not assist his ear with any power to comprehend what was the real state of the young creature before him. Nor did this shew any want of acuteness on his part. The moral condition of Jessie was no common one. Guilty she was, and she knew it, and felt it well. Had the accusations brought against her been such only as she deserved, Mr. Rimmington would have had no difficulty in reading upon her countenance what was passing in her heart; but though herself listening to the accusation of having murdered her child, as to a fact respecting which the evidence was too strong to be doubted, there was no answering throb of remorse within. Misery, lamentation, and woe, followed the horrible conviction that this dismal deed was her own; but remorse cannot be engendered in the mind by the same process; and as Jessie had neither the wish nor the power to simulate what she did not feel, that line of deepest suffering which indicates *remorse* was wanting, amidst the multitude of sorrows that the strangely altered young features shewed so plainly. And this it was which puzzled him; for it was beyond his power to discover in what consisted the sort of incongruity of which he was conscious.

After having thus vainly examined her countenance for a moment, he said, "Of course, Jessie, as you will naturally suppose, I have heard many strange and terrible histories about you, for such, as you cannot doubt, are now on the lips of all men. The most important of these, such, I mean, as concern the fate of your infant, are confirmed by too strong a body of evidence to leave any possibility of doubt on the minds of any who have listened to it. Concerning this part of the unhappy business I mean not to question you, for no benefit of any kind could possibly arise from it. But there are other statements which have reached me, of the correctness of which I feel less certain. Not, indeed, that there is any thing left in doubt that can be considered of much importance, yet, nevertheless, I should like to know whether the circumstances stated are true or false. For instance, Jessie, I wish you to tell me plainly, and without reserve of any kind, whether it be true that you went to the manor-house, a few hours only before your child was born, for the purpose of obtaining money from Mr. Frederic Dalton?"

Jessie changed colour violently, first becoming suddenly red, and in the next moment frightfully pale.

"If the answering this question be painful to you, Jessie, do not reply at all," said Mr. Rimmington; "for, as I have already told you, it is not one of any real importance, or capable of affecting your situation in any way. And, believe me, I should be very unwilling to give you unnecessary pain."

"Yes, it is painful both to hear it and to answer it," replied the miserable girl, while her working features testified the truth of what she said; "but this is no reason why I should decline to answer it. One pang, more or less, matters but little. And indeed the pang would be worse still, did I refuse to answer. Yes, sir, I did go to the manor-house, not very long, I believe, before my child was born … Yet, no, sir, no, it was not to the manor-house—I went to watch for Frederic Dalton outside the gates of the stable-yard,—I did watch for him,—I did see him,—and I did ask him for money."

There was a sort of dogged resoluteness in the manner in which she pronounced these words that caused the good clergyman to sigh deeply; and he thought to himself, as he gazed on her young face, where ingenuousness still remained more intelligibly stamped than crime, that it took less time to corrupt the heart than to impress a record of that corruption on the countenance.

"And the young gentleman, I presume, refused to give you money, Jessie?" resumed Mr. Rimmington.

"He refused to give me what I demanded," replied Jessie, sternly.

"And after this interview with him you went, I think, to Mr. Lewis, did you not?" pursued Mr. Rimmington.

"Yes, sir, I did," replied Jessie, knitting her brows with an expression of mingled misery and anger.

"And with what object, Jessie, did you go to Mr. Lewis?" continued the inquirer.

"In the hope, sir, that I might be able to make the lawyer frighten Frederic Dalton into doing for me what I wanted him to do," replied Jessie, in the same unnaturally resolute tone.

"But how could you be so very ignorant as to suppose that Mr. Lewis either possessed the power, or was likely to feel any inclination, to do this? Surely, Jessie, you must have known that the law gave you no power whatever to compel Mr. Frederic Dalton to give you assistance, or to stigmatise him in any way as the father of your child; neither, as I should imagine, could you have had any hope that Mr. Lewis would interfere to obtain from him what could only have been bestowed as a free gift, and which had been already refused to your own supplications."

"Yes, sir, I did know that the law left me helpless," she replied. "Yes, I did know it; but I thought I might frighten him into doing what I wanted by threatening to expose him, and I thought the lawyer was the proper person to tell him what I meant to do. God help me! Perhaps I ought to have known better," she added, pressing her hand upon her forehead. " I think so now. But it was a friend who meant to be very kind to me that told me to do it. But this friend was only a poor body in the workhouse. I could look for no other. And this it was made me escape from the workhouse as I did. It was my only chance. At least I thought so; and I had a notion then that it was my duty to my child."

"Your duty, Jessie Phillips!—your duty to steal away from the shelter legally provided in the hope of frightening a young gentleman into giving you money?"

"Yes, sir, I did," replied Jessie, with the sternness of suspected truth; which sternness Mr. Rimmington, with a feeling of the most profound sorrow, set down, without any mixture of doubt or hesitation, as the surest testimony of hardened depravity. This confession, as well as the manner of it, appeared to him a perfectly conclusive proof that Mr. Lewis's statement was not only true, but perfectly free from exaggeration; nay, the original suspicion which he had imbibed from that gentleman, as to the probability that the young squire had only been selected, by this thoroughly depraved and most unhappy girl, because his circumstances were such as to make her fancy it would be worth her while to threaten him, returned upon him with very greatly strengthened force, although the statement and the pleadings of Miss Maxwell had for a moment shaken it. Again he believed that the accusation against young Dalton was utterly false and unfounded, and he shuddered to think how little fitted this every way depraved young creature was of being permitted to the privilege of prayer. He shook his head mournfully as he looked at her, and for a moment repented that he had proposed a solace, the healing nature of which she was so little likely to feel. "Yet does she not the more require it?" was whispered by the truly Christian spirit within him; and once again he asked, with lips which trembled with his own earnestness, if she thought she could bring her mind into a fitting state to ask for mercy from the only source whence she could hope to receive it.

"I hope so, sir;" replied Jessie, rising and preparing to kneel. There was a steady sedateness in the tone, which sounded to the ear of the good, but greatly mistaken clergyman like hardihood and obstinacy; under such circumstances, there seemed to be something like profanation in pronouncing the words he was about to utter; yet still he felt that he had no right to refuse her. But happy was it for poor Jessie Phillips that the Judge she was about to address had the power of reading her heart more correctly than good Mr. Rimmington, for he was far, indeed, poor man, from guessing the deep and humble piety of the heart-broken young penitent who knelt beside him.

# LIII

*Ellen writes a letter to her lover, and then receives a visit from her friend, Martha, in which that young lady does full justice to all Mr. Rimmington's reasonings— but this does not produce all the good effects she anticipated*

When Ellen, late in the morning, awoke from her heavy sleep, her head ached fearfully; and the sort of desperate necessity which she felt existed, of recalling clearly and distinctly all that had passed on the previous day, made it ache still more. Nevertheless, she assured her mother, and her tenderly watchful sisters, that she was better, and she spoke sincerely, for the feverish anxiety to act and to do—she knew not well what— seemed to her like returning strength. She insisted upon immediately getting up, and, when her careful nurses opposed her doing so, persisted in her purpose with a sort of vehement pertinacity in strange and alarming contrast with her usual gentle reasonableness. Nothing, in fact, but actual coercion would have sufficed in that hour of agony to prevent her executing the project she had formed. She had not, indeed, lost her reason, but rather seemed to possess more power than usual of bringing before her mind at one view all the circumstances of her own condition, and their bearing and effect upon those most dear to her. There was no confusion of intellect; all was terribly distinct and clear in the frightful picture thus spread before her, but every feature in it was gigantic, and every feeling, every faculty, seemed stretched and distended into supernatural strength and power, that she might gaze upon, and understand it all. When addressed, she turned to the speaker, and, after the interval of a moment, replied composedly, but as briefly as possible; and having finished dressing, in which Henrietta and Caroline assisted her, she spoke to them for the first time of her own accord, saying, in her usual tone of gentle affection,—"My dear girls, I am going to write to Pemberton, so you must let me be alone, dear loves, for I have a good deal to say to him."

"You shall not be interrupted, dearest Ellen," replied Henrietta, soothingly; "but you will take some breakfast, dear, before you begin? You will not refuse this, I hope, for it is long since you have taken any thing; and, though you have slept so late, you look sadly pale and exhausted."

"No," replied Ellen, "I will not refuse some tea; but you must let me have it here, and then I shall not lose time; and you must bring it yourself, Henrietta, for I know you will be kind enough not to hinder me by staying to talk, after you have set it down."

Henrietta promised to comply, and then both sisters, having impressed a loving kiss upon her forehead, left her in the solitude for which she was again intensely longing. The having decided upon writing to Lord Pemberton was a relief to her; it soothed her with the belief that she was about to perform an act of duty; and she eagerly opened her desk, drew forth her paper, and prepared herself for the task. But she laid down her pen the moment she had taken it up, murmuring to herself, as she did so, "No, no. They must not come in, poor children, and find me at it! I may not always be quite as much composed as I am now." And then with steadfast resolution, which wanted nothing but the reality of what it feigned to be in truth a mastery over anguish and despair, she settled her features into a sort of rigid tranquillity, and awaited Henrietta's return. The interval was not long, but it sufficed to bring back with renewed penitence the remembrance of the terrible moment when she had opened her eyes and seen the friendly Martha beside her! Again she recalled all the circumstances of this truly kind visit, and perfectly well remembered, not only the almost repulsive manner in which she had received her, but also the shrinking feeling of repugnance to all discussion which it had caused. "That was not right—that was not righteous," thought poor Ellen, with a pang of self-reproach. "Ought I to shun, and hate to look upon her, excellent as she is, because I suspect that she sees all with the same horrible clearness that I do? It was cowardly—it was ungrateful! and oh, how vain!" To feel persuaded that she had been wrong was quite sufficient to make her decide upon offering instant atonement; and, when Henrietta brought in the little tray she had prepared, Ellen said, with more of her usual manner than she had yet spoken,—

"I should very much like to see Martha Maxwell again, after I have written my letter. It was very kind of her to visit me as she did last night, but I felt ill, and did not receive her as I ought to have done. Will you send to her, Henrietta, and ask her to come to me?"

"Yes, Ellen," replied her delighted attendant, now fully convinced that the fears which had been excited by the fainting-fit of her darling sister were altogether unfounded. "If you will eat a good breakfast, and not make your head ache by writing too long a letter to his lordship, I will bring Martha to you, as soon as the said letter shall have been despatched."

This was answered by a smile, but truly "in such a sort" that it expressed more woe than any weeping could have done. But the gay and well-contented Henrietta marked it not, and left the heart-broken Ellen to the *happiness* of inditing an epistle to the beloved of her heart—to her noble, affianced husband!

Ellen watched the door as it closed behind her sister, and then, with desperate courage, addressed herself to her terrible task. For one moment ere her pen touched the paper, she doubted her power to perform the stern duty she had imposed upon herself. A rush of tender, gentle recollections came upon her mind, that for a little while deluged her cheeks with tears, and rendered her quite incapable of writing. Poor Ellen! her past sufferings and her past happiness were both equally against her. The first, by their lengthened pressure on her nerves, had weakened and almost subdued her spirits; while the last, by the fulness of its innocent and holy joy, had soothed them again in a state of such exquisite felicity as made her present misery fall upon her with overpowering weight. But all that was left of unblighted energy within her seemed to rally round her heart as she remembered the high and unblemished honour of the man she loved. His steadfast attachment to her had clouded his early happiness, but it had brought no touch of disgrace; for his proud mother and still prouder father had declared that his conduct throughout the whole period, even while marked by unyielding fidelity to her, had been equally characterised by unvarying truth to them; and should she now suffer the shame, the infamy, the horror that was about to fall on herself and her devoted family, to reach to him? She reasoned the point no farther; she passed over her own agony, and even his, under eternal separation, as something not sufficiently important to create a doubt as to what it might be best to do; and once more, seizing her pen, she rapidly wrote the following note:—

> "It is with pain, certainly with great pain, Lord Pemberton, that I set about performing a task which is, however, too important to be longer delayed. My sentiments and wishes respecting our projected union have undergone a change, which renders it my duty to tell you, at once and explicitly, that this union can never take place. It is, perhaps, doing you injustice to suppose that, after this undisguised disclosure of my sentiments, you should make any attempt to change them; nevertheless, I think it best to add, that my determination on the subject is unalterable; and also, that it is my earnest wish and desire that you should immediately communicate my decision to your father and mother. Though they cannot understand the motives and feelings which have led to it, I feel assured that they will assist you—should such assistance be necessary—in receiving and acting upon it as you ought to do.
>
> "I remain, my Lord,
>
> "Your very sincere well-wisher,
>
> "Ellen Dalton."

These lines were written by a hand trembling violently both from fever and emotion; but nevertheless they were perfectly legible. Not so was a postscript of a few words which followed, and through which the same unsteady pen had passed and repassed; they were, moreover, still farther obliterated by more than one tear which had fallen upon them. Among these, the word "*forget*" was the only one that could be deciphered. "He will be better off than I," murmured Ellen, as she sealed this terrible note. "Contempt and indignation will do more towards a cure than—than such thoughts as I shall carry to my grave."

Her task was ended, and the sealed note placed before her, when Henrietta reappeared.

"Come I too soon, Ellen?" said she. "No; I see that both you and your note are ready for me. And now, dear duchess, I may tell you that I have obeyed your grace's commands, and that Martha Maxwell waits your pleasure below. Shall I usher her to your presence?"

Ellen could not speak, but she bent her head as she placed the note in her sister's hand, and then turned away as if seeking something on the sofa beside her.

"Dear love!" said Henrietta, looking at her anxiously, "you are still dreadfully pale, my Ellen! I am afraid that I am too indulgent a nurse. I ought not to have encouraged your writing, and now, perhaps, I ought not to let Martha Maxwell come to you."

"Indeed you ought," replied Ellen, again attempting to smile, "for her visit will do me good. Only, dearest, I must make a bargain that I have but one companion at a time, for I know that renewed headache would be the punishment, were I to indulge too freely."

Thus reassured, Henrietta brought Martha Maxwell to the dressing-room, and the two friends were left together. With a sort of desperate effort to meet, to brave, and to endure all the painful feelings which she knew it was her destiny to feel, Ellen at once raised her eyes to the face of Martha, expecting to read both pity and horror there. But with a degree of astonishment, that almost amounted to dismay, she was greeted with a cheerful smile, which appeared so unnatural under the circumstances as almost to make her shudder.

"My dear, dear Ellen!" exclaimed Martha, affectionately pressing the burning hand of Ellen between both her own. "How well I know all you have suffered and all you suffer still! But courage, Ellen! I am here to bring you the blessed tidings that we have both been wrong—utterly, totally, altogether wrong, dear friend. For once, the lawyers, and the justices, and the constables, and all such blundering bodies, have been right; and you and I, notwithstanding our superior perspicacity, mistaken.

Your brother has all too much to answer for, but of this crowning horror he is guiltless."

"Martha!" said Ellen, solemnly, "have you been told by my family that my intellect has been disordered, and do you come in the hope of saving me from madness by saying this?"

"No, as I live!" replied Martha, eagerly. "No such statement has been made to me, no such idea has entered my head. What you saw yesterday I saw also; and I have not the slightest doubt that the inference drawn by each was the same. Neither of us need describe to the other what dreadful thoughts followed—what prophetic visions of future anguish for those dearly loved, and, more dreadful still, what awful consciousness of duties to be performed, the very thought of which was enough to turn our hearts to stone. All this is too deeply engraven on our memories to require our recalling it to each other. But in all this, Ellen, it has been purely our imaginations which have been at work; judgment has had nothing to do with it."

Ellen shook her head, and breathed a heavy sigh, that spoke clearly enough her doubt of Martha's authority for coming to the conclusion which she appeared to have adopted, but she uttered not a word in reply.

"Nay, hear me patiently," resumed Martha, perfectly well interpreting this silent answer. "My conduct, in the condition into which I fell after the scene here, needs not, I think, any apology; but, if it does, I must seek it, Ellen, in your kindness. The agony into which I was thrown by the aspect of your brother was dreadful. I did not faint, as you did, at the sight of it, and certainly I could not feel an equal degree of personal interest in the horrible discovery which I fancied I had made. But the idea that I was called upon, by every feeling of justice and of truth, to save the innocent by denouncing the guilty, was horrible. A confidant, a friend, an adviser, was absolutely necessary to me. I dared not disclose all I suspected to my father, because I dared not tell him all I knew, to account for the suspicion; for such a narrative would have made him take a degree of personal interest in my story that I should have been very sorry to excite, as it would have been likely to lead to more mischief still. In this dilemma, Ellen, I went to Mr. Rimmington. Do you blame me?"

"Oh! no, I cannot blame you," replied Ellen, speaking with difficulty, for her tongue was dry and parched, and the effort to articulate was painful. "Mr. Rimmington, then," she added, after a pause,—"Mr. Rimmington already knows it all?"

"He knows all we know, Ellen," replied Martha: "but this, he says, contains no proof whatever, nay, not the shadow of a probability, that our suspicions are well founded. He says, and, as I listened to him, I felt perfectly satisfied that he was right, that my narrative shewed the unhappy Jessie to have fallen too completely to justify, in any safe degree, our believing it impossible she should have committed the crime that seems so clearly to have been proved against her. He confesses that his own prejudices in her favour were so strong as to make him long resist the evidence which others found convincing, but that now he considered the commission of the act too clearly demonstrated to be hers to leave any reasonable ground for doubt upon the subject. As to the emotion manifested by your brother, he says,—and surely he is right,—that the suddenly learning that the last proof wanting had been supplied against the unhappy victim of his sinful love was quite sufficient to account for it."

Ellen said nothing in reply, but she looked wistfully in the face of her friend, as if to discover if she had more to tell—something more tangible on which to rest her feverish thoughts. And then, with equal earnestness of purpose and clearness of language, Martha gave her the purport of all Mr. Rimmington had said, and dwelt strongly on the doubtful nature of the justice which should denounce one against whom no shadow of proof lay, and that, too, for a deed for the commission of which it must be evident to common sense that he had no motive whatever.

While listening to Martha, Ellen had remained perfectly still; but now a slight movement of her head and a heavy sigh seemed to indicate that she did not consider the reasoning, which she would have given half her life to prove true, could be received as incontrovertible.

"Nay," resumed Martha, again interpreting aright the feelings of her auditor, "do not for a moment imagine that either Mr. Rimmington or I forget the guilty part indisputably performed by your brother in this dreadful drama; or that it was not bad enough to doom him to endless remorse, and his family, of which he is so little worthy, to feelings of sorrow, which Time, with its providential healing, may soften, but which can never be forgotten by any unhappy enough to have learned the facts. No, no, Ellen, Mr. Rimmington was equally far from doubting these facts (with which I made him fully acquainted) as from absolving the actors in them from the obloquy incurred. But the practical good sense with which he pointed out the comparative probabilities and improbabilities as to which of the two guilty ones perpetrated the last act of this terrible tragedy, was to me perfectly irresistible. Against the wretched girl there exists an unbroken chain of circumstantial evidence, every point of which leads obviously to the catastrophe, and all of which it would be difficult to comprehend without it. Her sudden and resolute escape from the workhouse—her bold and desperate consultation with Mr. Lewis as to the possibility of enforcing a maintenance for her child from its father—and, finally, all the circumstances of time and place, which lead almost as certainly to prove her the murderer of the infant as its mother. On the other hand, Ellen, what conceivable motive could have induced your brother to have committed such an act as this, while his very name, as father of the child, is made a mystery by act of parliament, and while the same act protects his purse more effectually still from any claim upon it whatever? It is likely enough that the poor girl might have been out of her mind when she committed the act, and the more so, because, as we well know, she had previously suffered quite enough to throw her into this condition: but neither you nor I, Ellen, can persuade ourselves that such was the case with your brother; and yet, without doing this, it is well-nigh impossible to persevere, after a little meditation, in believing that which, in our agony and agitation yesterday, we did certainly both believe."

As Martha proceeded thus with her specious but most honest fallacies, Ellen's mind was at work on a process which she had as little power as inclination to communicate to her friend. The experience of her whole life, as far as her brother was concerned, and the constant opportunities afforded, through the greater part of it, for observation of Jessie Phillips, had left such a mass of powerful impressions as to their respective characters on her mind as all the plausibility of Mr. Rimmington's reasoning, as well as all the probabilities suggested by the circumstances recorded, proved unable to remove. But, notwithstanding the deep and terrible conviction which still lay like a mass of lead upon her heart, and notwithstanding also the feverish agitation of spirits, so unlike her usual gentle equanimity, which almost made her unconscious of what she did, Ellen still felt that it was not her duty to persist in expressing the horrible doubts which she was herself doomed to endure; and, when Martha ceased to speak, she bent forward, and impressed a kiss upon her cheek, earnestly exclaiming,—

"God bless you, my dear Martha! You are very, very kind!"

"No, no, Ellen, that is not the right word," returned her friend, by no means satisfied by the effect her statement had produced. "I have shewn no kindness, but I have endeavoured to be reasonable and just."

"And I, too," replied poor Ellen, more struck by these temperate words than she would have been by any more purely argumentative, "all my wish is to be just and reasonable too. But unfortunately, I do not feel well, Martha. My head is not as it used to be. I want to be very, very quiet, my dear friend; and, if I could be for some few hours perfectly alone, perhaps I might cease to feel the terrible sensations I do now. Will you go, dearest Martha, and tell them all downstairs that I have nothing now the matter with me but headache, and that I shall be soon quite well, if left to myself a little?"

Martha, who truly believed that nothing but a little tranquil consideration was necessary to render the reasonings of Mr. Rimmington convincing, instantly prepared to leave her; and having arranged a pillow, and partially darkened the apartment, she only uttered the words, "I will," and stole gently out of the room.

# LIV

*The lovers are indulged with a private interview, which does not produce much pleasure—Martha Maxwell visits Jessie in prison*

PERHAPS AN HOUR HAD ELAPSED before the solitude so ardently desired by the unhappy Ellen was again interrupted; but, alas! the interval had produced no healing influence. It was in vain that she repeated to herself the sedative words, "just and reasonable," they only served to increase the confusion of her intellect, and helped to hasten and heighten the delirium which threatened her.

At length the door of her room again opened, and Henrietta entered. The light was not sufficient to afford her any opportunity of examining her sister's countenance; but, as Ellen was not lying down, she flattered herself that the headache of which she had complained was better, and, not having the remotest idea of the real condition of that poor head, she said, with all the gay abruptness which the certainty of bringing pleasant news would give, "Lord Pemberton has answered your note in person, dearest Ellen! Here he is! It is no good to scold him, he will come in."

And, in truth, before the last words were well spoken Lord Pemberton was in the room. The happy bridesmaid elect, remembering that only a few days now intervened before the one fixed for the wedding, felt that no etiquette rendered it necessary for her to interrupt by her presence the interview which her future brother-in-law appeared so eagerly to desire; and, in another moment, the lovers were alone.

It is needless to dwell upon the feelings with which Lord Pemberton had perused the note of Ellen; a few moments' thought convinced him that she must have heard something, either utterly false or totally misrepresented, concerning him or his family; probably, as he thought, in allusion to the strong aversion formerly expressed by his parents to the connexion; and this idea, once conceived, sufficed to console him with the belief that five minutes of conversation with his beloved would be sufficient to set every thing right. A less perfectly adoring lover might have felt some touch of anger, mixed with the alarm which her unintelligible letter had produced, but not so Lord Pemberton; he knew Ellen much too well to believe it possible that she could be guilty of any worse offence towards him than listening to reports, which a few words from him would teach her in a moment to despise as they deserved; and, it was, therefore, with much more of hope than of fear that he approached her. But the instant he took her hand, which was almost mechanically held out to him, a terror, more overpowering than any fear of misrepresentation could produce, seized upon him; her hand was dry and burning, and, as it lay clasped in his, instead of the soft tremor it had so often heretofore communicated to his own, a convulsive catching movement in every joint of it convinced him that she was suffering from a violent access of fever.

In reply to his eager questions respecting her health, for every other fear was instantly forgotten, she only said, "You had better go, you had much better go."

It was in vain that he conjured her in accents of the fondest love to tell him what had happened thus terribly to affect her; it was too late for explanation of any kind; his sudden entrance had completed the mischief that was going on, and Ellen was already in a strong paroxysm of frenzy. For one instant only she seemed to know and to feel who it was that sat beside her, for she turned round on the sofa to look at him, and, having gazed earnestly in his face for a moment, she parted the dark locks upon his forehead, and impressed upon it the first kiss he had ever received from her. Lord Pemberton had endured much suffering, but this first caress from the woman he adored caused him the sharpest pang of agony he had ever yet known. The manner of it could not be mistaken; Ellen had lost her senses, and was now, beyond the power of hope to conceal it, in a paroxysm of fever, which perhaps threatened her life as well as her reason.

As little time as possible was now lost before the best advice which the country afforded was called to her aid; but the revulsion, from unlooked-for and most perfect happiness to such a degree of misery and agitation as she had since endured, had thrown her into a condition which might well make those who loved her tremble.

Meanwhile, the "measureless content" of the ardent-minded Martha Maxwell, on receiving Mr. Rimmington's interpretation of young Dalton's conduct, did not long bear the wear and tear of the incessant meditation which she gave it. Though certainly rather prone on many points to take her own opinion in preference to that of other people, Martha had a genuine as well as habitual reverence for Mr. Rimmington, which gave to all he spoke a value and a power over her which she was always more inclined to yield to than resist, and, on the present occasion, the discovering that his judgment differed from her own relieved her from a degree of suffering on account of her friend Ellen, which she hailed with thankfulness, and clung to with a pertinacity of faith which was not shaken without causing her much misery. Shaken, however, it was, and by the simple and inevitable process of meditating upon the ground on which it rested.

It is needless to pass in review all the reasons, or all the recollections, which this process set to work in the mind of poor Martha; it is enough to say that it ended by making her look as pale as ashes, and sending her to the side of her indulgent father, with a petition that he would suffer her to visit Jessie Phillips in her prison. Such a request, of course, led to a little discussion, which was so well managed on the part of the anxious petitioner that it was immediately granted without the good captain's knowing more of the causes and feelings which led to it than the petitioner thought proper to disclose. To say truth, Captain Maxwell saw nothing very surprising in the request; he knew the unhappy prisoner as a well-esteemed *protégée* of his daughter, and marvelled not that her terrible situation should have excited thus strongly her interest and compassion. Neither did he greatly wonder at Martha's unusual silence during the two hours' drive to the county town, and his not interrupting it shewed far more sympathy than any thing he could have spoken. He appeared to think it perfectly natural, too, that Martha should deem it best for her to see the poor prisoner alone; and all the good man said when they parted at the door of the room in which she was confined was, "Remember, Martha, if there is money wanted about a lawyer, or any thing of that kind, I am ready to help."

Martha, whose swelling heart left her at that moment no power to speak, replied only by pressing his hand, and then the door was opened for her, and she entered. Jessie was sitting at a little table, on which lay an open Bible; but it seemed not when Martha entered that she was reading it, for her head, which was supported by her hand, while her elbow rested on the table, was raised as if in meditation upon something she had found therein. In an instant, however, the sadly altered eye of the unhappy girl was turned upon her unexpected visitor, and an exclamation of surprise and pleasure escaped her; but it was not now accompanied by the eager movement with which she had received Mr. Rimmington. Short as was the interval which had elapsed, she was greatly changed. Even then, she was far, far unlike the blooming beauty of Deepbrook; but now it was not merely the absence of bloom and joy that was perceptible—the leaden hue of death seemed settled on her eye, and her sunk features plainly shewed that there was no strength left to suffer greatly more. The greeting between these two young girls had something appalling in it. Both trembled as their hands clasped each other; but Jessie was supported by the stern fortitude which grows from the belief that no increase of suffering is possible; and Martha, by the feeling that she had set herself a task which it would be sin to shrink from. For an instant Jessie had stood up, but, quite unable to continue standing, had sunk again upon her seat, and Martha drew another close beside her. It was Jessie who spoke first.

"You know every thing," she said; "you know how it has all ended? Ah! Miss Maxwell, how could I ever dare to think that sin and shame like mine could fail of bringing its just punishment?"

"Yes, my poor Jessie, you have suffered!" replied Martha, almost choking with the emotion produced by the heart-breaking spectacle on which she gazed; "but I come here in the hope of hearing from yourself what might prove that the hand of man had no right to inflict more; I want you to open your heart to me, and tell me all."

"Most willingly will I," replied Jessie; adding, with a mournful shake of the head, "But that all is so very little."

"Little?" repeated Martha, looking puzzled. "However shortly told, Jessie, it must at least contain all that it is important for your friends to know."

"True; that is quite true, Miss Maxwell," returned Jessie. "If there is more to be known than I have power to tell, it is all plain and clear before the eyes of God, and that is all that really signifies now. But if you will question me I will answer you to the very best of my power."

"My questions," said Martha, looking at her earnestly, "will be in a very small compass; in fact, there is but one question to ask, Jessie, the answer to which is of any real importance."

"And what is that, Miss Maxwell?" returned the pale prisoner, looking as if she had scarcely strength to speak.

"Jessie!" rejoined Martha, mournfully, "you must surely know what this question is before I speak it. Are you guilty or not guilty?"

"Guilty, Miss Maxwell!" replied Jessie, shuddering. "So deeply, deeply, guilty, that it is needful for me to keep in perpetual remembrance this promise—this eternal, everlasting promise of forgiveness, in order to save myself from madness." Jessie laid her head on the open Bible as she said this, and, closing her eyes, seemed as if inwardly uttering a fervent prayer. Tears streamed from the eyes of Martha as she looked at her; but, though she felt a shrinking repugnance from urging the suffering penitent farther, she still did not feel satisfied by the comprehensive confession she had made, for, in spite of it, her doubts as to the possibility of Jessie's having committed the crime of which she was accused increased upon her; and, determined that no false delicacy on her own part should deprive the accused of any opportunity of asserting her innocence plainly, she laid her hand upon her shoulder, and said, solemnly,—

"Jessie, answer me distinctly. Was it by your hand that your infant died?"

"I have no power to answer that question distinctly, Miss Maxwell," replied Jessie, fixing her melancholy eyes on her companion, with a look that seemed to deprecate the effect her words were likely to produce. "I have no power to answer it distinctly," she repeated, "because I have myself no distinct certainty on the subject. Most surely," she continued, "I have not the very slightest recollection of having ever seen my babe, or held it in my arms. But I do remember, perfectly remember, the hearing it cry; and all that I remember more, till the man and woman, who took me back to the workhouse, came to the shed, was, that I felt a sort of deathlike sickness, as I have done once or twice before in my life when I have fainted away."

"And when the fisherman and his wife came to you the child was gone?" said Martha.

"I suppose so," returned Jessie. "I heard it not again; nor did I at the time they found me and brought me back to life, as they did by their care, retain any recollection of having ever heard it cry, or of having been conscious of its birth."

"But when you fully recovered yourself after returning to the workhouse, you did remember it?"

"Yes, I remembered to have heard it cry," said Jessie.

"And nothing more?" demanded Martha.

"NOTHING," replied Jessie, with emphasis.

"Then why is it that you have suffered more than one friend, who was disposed to believe you innocent,—why have you suffered such to leave you, Jessie, with the persuasion that you had murdered your child? Surely they could not have left you with such an idea if you had spoken to them as you have now spoken to me!"

"There was no difference," returned Jessie, calmly, "in what I said to them and what I have now said to you, Miss Maxwell, except what came from the difference of their questions. You asked me what I remembered, and I could safely tell you that I remembered nothing; but, when they told me that my child was murdered, and that nobody could have done the deed but myself, how could I help believing that I had done it?"

"Is it not possible, Jessie," said Martha, turning extremely pale as she spoke—"is it not possible that Frederic Dalton might have done this horrid act? Do we not know that he is a villain?"

"No, Miss Maxwell, no!" exclaimed Jessie, with a degree of vehemence that for an instant restored a beautiful carnation to her cheek. "Do not, I implore you, be led by any pity for me to be guilty of such terrible injustice. Frederic Dalton neither did, nor could have, destroyed a creature whom he never saw. Nor would he have done it, Miss Maxwell, had it been as completely in his power, as it was, in truth, completely out of it. Frederic Dalton had no courage to avow his love for me, and broke all his promises for want of it; but his was the tenderest, gentlest heart! I do suppose," she added, "that I behaved very ill to him, though I did not mean to do it. But he will forgive it all soon, as I do all he ever said or did that seemed wrong to me. Oh! never let me hear such a word again, Miss Maxwell; never let me think that I have brought such thoughts upon him!"

Martha, as she gazed on the again ghastly paleness of poor Jessie's sunken features, while she thus, as it were, fondly raised her dying voice in his behalf, almost unconsciously murmured, "the ruling passion strong in death!" and she felt that there was something so beautiful in this total forgetfulness of self, and of all her sufferings and her wrongs, while remembering only the fatal but devoted love which had once filled her young heart, that she involuntarily bent forward towards her unhappy companion, and kissed her forehead.

Jessie looked at her in return both with surprise and gratitude, and, after the silence of a moment, said, "I had almost determined, Miss Maxwell, never again to hint to any body who questioned me my own opinion about my baby's death, because every body who has heard me hint at it seemed to think it quite as a matter of course, and the most natural thing in the world that I should say it, but without believing, for a moment, that it was true. But your great kindness seems to open my heart anew, and I do not think I ought to die without removing from your mind the dreadful idea that one you had so greatly favoured could wilfully commit so horrible a crime."

Martha Maxwell drew closer to her, and her very soul seemed to look out at her eyes as she listened.

"Alas!" resumed poor Jessie, interpreting this eagerness into a hope of finding that she could clear herself satisfactorily of the deed; "alas! Miss Maxwell, I fear it is but too certain that my poor babe was murdered, and that none but I could, by possibility, have done it. All I wish to leave impressed on your kind heart, my dear young lady, is the fact, that it was done when my soul knew not what my body did. I suppose, Miss Maxwell, that when people suddenly go mad, and afterwards recover, they remember no more of what passed during their madness than if they had been in a swoon during the time. At any rate, I think *you* will believe me when I say that I did not."

"Oh! yes, I do believe you," replied Martha, eagerly. "But why, Jessie, with this entire unconsciousness of having committed the act, should you now persevere in saying that you believe you committed it?"

"First, Miss Maxwell," replied Jessie, composedly, "because common sense teaches me to see, that if something has been done which none but myself could have done, it must be I that did it; and, secondly, because I have found, even among the kindest and the best, that I have never stated the fact of my being thus unconscious of having done that, which it seems clear to every body I have done, without their manifesting plainly, whether they spoke it quite openly in words or not, that they did not believe me."

"Even if you are right in this, Jessie," replied Martha, "I cannot think that you are justified in not persevering in the plea of insanity. I really think you are committing a sin in permitting yourself to be thus easily driven from it."

"I will repeat what I have now said to you, dearest Miss Maxwell, to every one who may choose to listen to me, if you tell me that I ought to do so," returned Jessie, submissively—"even," she continued, "though I am certain that I should again hear the same observations that I have heard already, namely, that every one in my condition says exactly the same thing, and that the jury will not be at all likely to listen to any such worn-out story, and, therefore, that I had better *prepare* myself. And this, my dearest, dearest Miss Maxwell, appears to me, after all, the very best advice I can follow; and all my hours, both by day and night, except when sleep quite overpowers me, are spent to the very best of my poor power in following it. Nor do I think it can be a sin to feel that it is better for me that I should pay my life for the dreadful act I have done unconsciously than that I should live long years to think of it. Alas! Miss Maxwell, it is, perhaps, another sin to think how very dearly I should have loved this poor child of shame if I could have ever pressed it to my heart! Perhaps I might have loved it till I forgot the sin that gave it birth! Oh! mourn not for the last scene that awaits me. It is ghastly to the fancy, but think how short it is! How can the sudden loss of life, under any circumstances, be compared to what I have been enduring for months and months? Oh no, Miss Maxwell, it is not worth a thought; and few, indeed, are those I give to it. Only sometimes I wish that I had to endure something more dreadful still, so that I might feel more certain than I now dare to do that it may be considered as atonement for crimes committed with no madness but that of forbidden passion to excuse them."

It may be remembered that Martha Maxwell has been stated to have great aptitude in discerning the characters of those with whom she associated, and great acuteness in discerning the truth or the falsehood of the words she listened to. Her having so readily adopted the false reasonings of Mr. Rimmington was no proof to the contrary, but, in fact, rather the reverse, for it only shewed her faith in his pure sincerity and holiness of purpose, a faith which no minister ever more justly merited from his congregation, while her confidence in his more enlarged experience and worldly knowledge can scarcely be ascribed to any defect in her judgment. It was the effect of long-taught, and, on the whole, of well-placed reverence. But now her own peculiar faculty had fair play; she looked at Jessie Phillips, and she listened to her, during the whole of the scene above described, not only with intense interest, but with the most earnest and unbroken attention; and, when the unhappy girl ceased to speak, Martha Maxwell would have felt not the very slightest repugnance to pledging herself to take her place, upon condition that any single word the poor prisoner had uttered were untrue.

When Jessie ceased speaking, Martha rose, and, throwing her arms around her, pressed her to her heart with a fulness of pity and affection that could hardly have been greater had the repentant culprit been her sister. But, much too wise to express hopes which, however well founded in truth and justice, had so little else to support them, she said not a word of the eager purpose that fluttered at her heart, but, breathing a whispered blessing and farewell, hurried from the room, and was received by her father, who had passed the time during which the interview lasted in pacing, in quarterdeck step, before the door.

# LV

*Ellen Dalton demands an interview with Frederic—the physicians think it right to indulge her, and he is sent into her chamber alone*

MEANWHILE THE CONDITION OF ELLEN Dalton became every moment more critical. She lay for several hours after her interview with Lord Pemberton in a state of the most alarming insensibility, to which succeeded a tremendous access of fever, attended by delirium so violent, as might well appear to them to deserve the name of frenzy, though none seemed to have the strength to utter it. It is needless to describe the agonies of Lord Pemberton, or that of her really adoring parents and sisters; it was such as scarcely any circumstance could have increased, save their being made acquainted with the cause of it.

But this was a misery which they were spared. Not one of the anxious watchers round her bed had the slightest idea of the frightful belief which had taken possession of her mind; and many a muttered word and sentence was suffered to pass unheeded, which, if listened to, commented upon, and fully understood, would have multiplied their wretchedness a thousand-fold. Poor Martha alone, of all those permitted to approach her, knew how to interpret aright the agonising terror of her voice, as she murmured incessantly,—"Is it over?—which prevails?—oh! which?—the guilty or the innocent? Which has been brought to the dreadful ending? Is it over?—is there nobody that will tell me how it has ended?"

Often, indeed, there was so much of reason and coherence in these exclamations, that Martha, while enduring one species of suffering which her friends were spared, had more hope to comfort her than the rest. The wanderings of poor Ellen were those of delirium, irresistibly impelled to talk of that which filled the mind; but to Martha they suggested no idea of frenzy. Another proof that her harassed intellect was not disordered to the extent which her terrified family so naturally supposed was, that she never ceased to testify a feeling of satisfaction at the approach of Martha; and, though others thought this but a feverish fancy, for they hardly believed that she really knew her, Martha herself felt convinced that it arose from the consciousness that she alone was acquainted with the cause of all the suffering and of all the terror which shook her reason. Whatever the cause, however, her influence on the invalid could not be doubted. She was infinitely more tranquil when Martha stood beside her bed, holding her burning hand, than at any other time; and both her medical attendants, upon this fact being pointed out to them, agreed in declaring that it was desirable that the young lady should be as much with her as possible. To this arrangement Martha submitted, both by day and night, with the most unwearying and affectionate zeal.

But ere she gave herself up to this anxious and harassing task she held one long conversation with her father. In this conversation she brought him fully to adopt her opinion as to the fact of Jessie's temporary insanity at the time the babe was murdered; for, on this belief, Martha flattered herself she had at length brought her own mind to rest. It was undeniably true that this hypothesis cohered best with the established facts, and was, consequently, the most probable; for which reasons poor Martha felt that she had no right to reject it. And yet, despite her utmost efforts to avoid the absurdity of leaning towards an improbable and totally unproved theory, in preference to receiving one perfectly the reverse, she could not, with all these strenuous efforts to avoid it, help suffering from a flash of suspicion, which from time to time shot across her mind, pointing out Frederic Dalton as the culprit. Happily, however, for her peace, and for the preservation of that composure of mind which her position as a constant attendant upon Ellen rendered especially needful, there was one part of good Mr. Rimmington's advice which she held it her bounden duty to follow. She might not always be able to avoid recurring to her former thoughts concerning young Dalton, but she could at least obey the injunctions of one whom she could not doubt knew better than she did what was right to be done, as to letting the legal examinations take their course, without attempting to interrupt them by her conjectures, which she well knew were supported by nothing that could be received as legal evidence. She therefore confined all her efforts in behalf of Jessie to the engaging her father to write instantly to Henry Mortimer, commissioning him to secure immediately the best legal assistance on behalf of the prisoner; and, having learned that this was done, she gave herself wholly up to attending upon her poor friend. In this melancholy office (and melancholy indeed it was to watch one whom she had so lately seen in the enjoyment of the most perfect happiness thus prostrate both in mind and body) Martha had the additional anxiety of fearing, lest every wandering word which the poor patient uttered might throw her family into still greater misery than had yet been their portion, by making them aware that the horrible suspicions she continued to murmur concerning Frederic were not altogether the result of delirium. She was greatly assisted in her wish to prevent this by the unequivocal desire which Ellen ceased not to manifest for having her beside her, in preference even to her dear Henrietta; and the watchful medical attendants, though far enough from guessing the sanity of this preference, continued their injunctions that it should be yielded to, simply from the persuasion that every thing that soothed her was desirable. Martha soon perceived that the "fixed thought" which tortured her poor friend was the guilt she should incur by permitting an innocent person to be sacrificed in order to shield a guilty one. Every word she uttered during her incessant talking, both by lay and night, shewed this to Martha beyond the possibility of a doubt, though, to all others, her words conveyed only the idea of continued and increasing frenzy. "Do you think I will wed him at the price of blood?" she exclaimed one moment; "shall I see them strangle the innocent girl with my own eyes, and not prevent it?" she murmured at another. But Martha only felt that these phrases, and a hundred others of similar tendency, shewed infinitely more of reason than of madness.

During one night of painful restlessness on the part of the patient, and of irresistible weariness on that of Martha, the latter sunk at length into profound sleep, and, notwithstanding her habitual wakefulness, enjoyed the very necessary refreshment for a couple of hours. At the end of this time, however, she awoke, and, gently rising from the easy chair in which she had slept, she looked towards her patient, anxiously alarmed at the idea of seeing her as usual wide awake, and seeking in vain for her unfaithful nurse. But, equally to her delight and surprise, the eyes of Ellen were closed, and she was evidently sleeping, though starting from time to time with such violence as to shew that even so the harassed spirit was not at rest. Yet even this troubled sleep was hailed by Martha as a favourable symptom; and she replaced herself noiselessly in her chair, trusting that the nurse, whose snoring she heard from the neighbouring dressing-room, would remain in the same harmless state of repose till Ellen awoke. She herself felt no further inclination to sleep, and remained watching her poor friend with more of hope than she had felt for many days past. At length, however, the profound stillness of the still dark chamber was disturbed by a deep sigh, and, rising up to look at Ellen, Martha perceived that her eyes were wide open, and, that though for the first time lying profoundly still, she was no longer asleep.

"Martha," she said, in a gentle tone, that had nothing of wildness in it,—"Martha, dearest Martha, you are always near me!"

The extreme delight produced by this evident improvement did not prevent the cautious and skilful nurse from avoiding every thing that might excite agitation; she only answered by a silent pressure of the hand, and by offering to the parched lips of the sufferer the cooling beverage which stood ready beside her. But Ellen was not to be so silenced. The fever was greatly abated, and with it all the symptomatic irritation of nerves which had caused delirium. After the pause of a moment, she said, "Are we alone, Martha?"

"Yes, dearest," was the reply; "but you must keep yourself very, very quiet, my Ellen. I do not think that I must let you talk to me."

"I have not strength to talk much," she replied "I think I am weaker now than I have ever been: but you must listen to me, dear Martha, and you must do as I bid you, if you wish to preserve me in my senses. Martha, I MUST SEE FREDERIC."

It would be difficult to say whether terror of the consequences which such an interview was likely to produce, or comfort at the unmistakeably improved state of the invalid, predominated in the mind of Martha, as she listened to these words. How to answer them she knew not. Ellen was evidently too completely in possession of her senses to be trifled with, or satisfied by the vague promises which had hitherto sufficed to silence many a wild demand. But the permitting her to see Frederic seemed impossible. What dreadful effects might not such an interview produce?

"Answer me, Martha," resumed Ellen, faintly, yet firmly,—"answer me with all your own truthfulness. Will you so manage as to let me see my brother, and see him alone? If you will do this, all may yet be well; but, if you refuse, or if you fail to bring it about, I shall be forced to obtain the object I have in view by other means; and many will suffer what now I might be able to spare them. Will you promise me?"

Martha dared not refuse, for she could not doubt that the satisfying Ellen's mind at this moment was more critically important than any thing else, and she answered solemnly, "I will."

Ellen made an effort to embrace her, and, having received a tender caress in return, she settled herself upon her pillow, and almost instantly fell asleep again. So profound was this second sleep, that neither the entrance of her mother, sisters, nor nurse, disturbed it; and, for above three hours, she continued, to the inexpressible delight of many who seemed to hang upon her life as if their own depended on it, to enjoy this heaven-sent restorative. When the medical men arrived, their judgment fully confirmed all the delightful hopes to which this change in the symptoms had given birth; and then the trembling Martha communicated to them the request Ellen had made, and the promise she herself had given.

"She must not be disappointed," was the reply of Dr. H.; and Mr. Johnson quite agreed with him that any irritation of the kind should be most carefully avoided.

But poor Martha, though glad to receive their sanction, could not but feel that it was given in the dark, and that, possibly, it might have been withheld had they known as well as she did the degree of excitement which such an interview was likely to produce. No choice, however, was left her; and her best comfort under the circumstances arose from her believing, on reflection, that it was in truth better that Ellen should be indulged in her demand than contradicted.

"You will then," resumed Martha, "have the kindness before you go, gentlemen, to communicate Ellen's wish to the family, and, particularly to Mr. Frederic Dalton himself, who, without your authority positively expressed, might be likely, I think, to refuse what, perhaps, he might feel to be both imprudent and painful."

"He must not refuse his sister, I assure you," returned the physician; "a more favourable alteration has taken place than we could have dared to hope for, and nothing like contradiction must be hazarded."

It so chanced that the two medical gentlemen found Frederic Dalton and his father *tête-à-tête* in the library; and Dr. H., after heartily wishing the squire joy of the improved condition of his darling child, briefly stated her wish for an interview with her brother. The intelligence did not seem to produce an agreeable impression on either father or son, the former exclaiming, "I doubt very much, Dr. H., if her head is quite right yet;" while Frederic turned suddenly away, as if to leave the room, muttering something not quite audible about being sure that he should do more harm than good in a sick room. But the physician was too much in earnest to permit his patient's wishes to be lightly thwarted, and, quickly following the young man, he laid his hand on his shoulder, saying, "You must not go, Mr. Frederic, till you have seen your sister."

The rapid strides of Dr. H. had more than overtaken Frederic; he had passed him sufficiently to turn, and look him in the face as he spoke. Greatly was he startled at the livid paleness of the countenance he gazed upon; and it instantly occurred to him that the violent mental agitation which he had been watching in his patient had not been merely the result of fever. Beyond this, however, his powers of divination could not carry him; it might, perhaps, be some quarrel with the noble bridegroom elect; but, be this as it would, Dr. H. only became the more determined that the interview demanded should immediately take place, and he resolved that he would remain in the house till it was over, in order to watch the effect it might produce.

While these thoughts were passing through the mind of the physician, Frederic had turned abruptly from him towards the window, whence he appeared to be earnestly watching something in the grounds, while, in truth, he was strenuously exerting all the strength he possessed in labouring to recover his presence of mind sufficiently to hit upon so expedient which might save him from the threatened interview. What he feared from it, indeed, he would himself have found it difficult to explain; most certain it is, that no very exact idea of the truth had ever suggested itself to his imagination; and infinitely as he disliked and shrunk from the idea of seeing Ellen, whose former interference concerning Jessie was sufficiently in his memory to make him turn pale at the thought of an interview, he had no more idea of her suspecting the whole horrid truth than he had of her having been present in person when his foot rested on the neck of his child. Had it been otherwise, not all the pertinacious authority of the physician would have sufficed to drag him to the bed-side of his sister. As it was, however, the energy he had summoned to his aid supplied him with sufficient courage to say, upon the reiterated remonstrance of Dr. H., backed by something very like a command from his father, that, though he hated a sick room, he would go in for a moment if they thought it would be best.

The short interval allowed him for meditation on the subject had sufficed to convince him satisfactorily that the worst his detestable monitress could have to say to him must be some canting beseechment that he would provide for Jessie's accommodation in the prison, or, perhaps, engage a lawyer to defend her on the generally anticipated plea of insanity. Being thus persuaded that he was doomed to hear the dreaded name of Jessie from her lips, he was by no means displeased to find that this hateful interview was to have no witness; and he entered the room very nearly, as to aspect and demeanour, as he might have done had he been as perfectly innocent as he was deeply guilty. Two or three female figures glided out of the chamber as he entered it. He turned not his head to ascertain who they might be, but, stalking to the bottom of the bed, he said, in a tone of the most perfect indifference, "How do you do, Ellen? What is it that you want to say to me?"

"A very few words, Frederic," replied his sister, in a low, yet not unsteady voice; "but it is necessary that you should attend to them. I wish no one but yourself to hear me at this moment; force me not, therefore to speak louder than is necessary, but place yourself there!" and she pointed to the side of the bed.

Frederic obeyed, and prepared himself, for the bore of a sermon which was to follow by the consoling thought that Ellen had evidently not

John Leech

strength enough to say much. In this he was right; but it was not much that she wished to say.

"Frederic," she began, as soon as he had removed to the spot she had indicated, "it is not necessary that I should tell you by what means I have learned the truth respecting the murder of your child; it is enough to say that I have learned it. Sit down, Frederic, sit down. Oh! you are deadly pale. But remember that no one hears my words,—no one shall hear them if you obey me; if not—I do not wish to threaten you, poor trembling man,—but, remember that I will not die with the weight of innocent blood upon my soul."

Ellen paused for a moment to recover breath, while the wretched culprit beside her, having sunk into the chair that seemed to stand ready for him, buried his face upon his arm, which rested on the back of it.

"What you must do is this," resumed Ellen, her strength of purpose supplying for the moment the want of all other strength,—"you must instantly leave the country. No human being save myself must know either why you go or whither, and so there will be no danger of pursuit. But you must go for ever, Frederic, for the life of Jessie Phillips can only be saved by your leaving a declaration of the truth. Remember there is no choice left you but remaining here to be denounced as your child's murderer, or escaping by means, which I will undertake to furnish, into some far distant land, where, under a name not borne by your unhappy father, you may live to make your peace with God. You shall find a packet at my father's London bankers with money, and there let your declaration be left, addressed to Mr. Rimmington. Now leave me."

The last three words were scarcely audible, and it was therefore that Frederic Dalton found courage to raise his eyes and look upon his feeble accuser. Could he have trusted that glance, he might have carried away with him the delightful belief that the hated lips which had so resolutely threatened his life were closed for ever. Ellen had fainted, and nothing, save death itself, could look more death-like than she did, as he now fixed his vengeful eye upon her. His fears, however, instantly suggested the truth, yet still a feeling of hope was strong and active within him. Though Ellen, with such terrible exactness of what seemed almost super-human knowledge, had thus taxed him with a crime which he still could not believe had been witnessed by any human eye, he felt perfectly persuaded that she was still insane.

That she had been so for many days he well knew, and there was in all she had said to him too evident a departure from common sense and common prudence for him to believe her very perfectly in possession of her senses now. He therefore instantly determined to take no notice whatever of what had passed between them, fully persuaded that the fearful truth she had uttered was but the result of delirium, however closely her foregone conclusions might have led her to stumble upon the truth. He therefore passed immediately into the dressing-room, saying to the nurse, whom he found there, "My sister has fainted, Mrs. Bates; I will send up Dr. H., who, I believe, is yet in the house. I am sadly afraid that she is still in a more dangerous state than they think, for every word she has uttered to me was as mad as Bedlam."

# LVI

*Conscience becomes executioner as well as accuser—matters draw rapidly to a conclusion—change of measures may not always infer infirmity of purpose*

On returning to the library, Frederic Dalton found not only his father and Dr. H., but Miss Maxwell and two of his sisters. All eyes were turned towards him, but it was those of Martha only which gazed with astonishment at the air of self-possession and composure with which he entered. Of this astonishment, however, he saw nothing, for he looked only at Dr. H., and, immediately approaching him, said, "I am greatly afraid, Doctor, that my poor sister is much worse than you imagine. Her reason appears to be totally gone, and her weakness is so great, that, after speaking a few wild words to me, she fainted."

Miss Maxwell and her two young friends instantly prepared to leave the room for the purpose of learning how far this now unexpectedly bad report of their beloved patient was correct, but, as Martha passed young Dalton, she raised her eyes, perhaps involuntarily, to his face, and there was something in her glance that made him tremble from head to foot; yet he did not read it aright. Martha now firmly and entirely believed that Jessie's own hypothesis was the true one, and that she herself, poor soul! had, in a moment of insanity, committed the act of which she was accused. It was not therefore suspicion, but curiosity, which caused Martha thus searchingly to examine his countenance. She wished to see how he had borne the words which she was persuaded had been spoken to him by his sister, but anticipated not the terrified start with which her glance was received. Few were the words which had passed between the young squire and Martha Maxwell since the return of the *promise*; and both parties seemed to think it wisest to sink the past in oblivion. But

Frederic Dalton, conscious, perhaps, that he deserved the dislike (to use a very gentle word) of the fair Martha, doubted not that it was cordially bestowed upon him, and now fancied that the penetrating glance she fixed upon him betrayed her knowledge of the fearful communication to which he had been listening from his sister. The thought shot like a sudden spasm through his frame. It was then no chance-led guess of the delirious Ellen! The deed must have been seen. And who so likely to have witnessed it as Martha—Martha, whose known custom it was to wander alone through every meadow, copse, and lane, in the country,—Martha, who was likely enough to have sought her miserable favourite even there—there, where the deed was done? Might she not have watched his approach?—might she not have hid herself in the obscurity of that fatal shed, and seen the whole?

Rapid, miraculously rapid, is the action of thought; and before the door was closed behind the last of the trio who quitted the room, these thoughts, and many more, had not only passed through the brain of Frederic, but had left an impression on it which changed the whole state of his existence. All his brave and bullying hopes of passing unscathed through the perils which surrounded him vanished for ever. Nor could he have thought himself more certainly convicted had he listened to the terrible word "guilty" from the foreman of a jury.

Hardly conscious of what he was about, or whither he intended to go, the miserable young man walked towards the door by which the girls had passed out, but was stopped by the hand of the physician, which, though it touched him gently, caused him to start as violently as if it had been that of the policeman about to arrest him.

"Hollo! how nervous you are, young gentleman!" said Dr. H., looking at him as a physician does look when some such unaccountable symptom occurs. "If your alarm is for your sister," he continued, fixing a pair of keen grey eyes upon his pale face, "I really advise you to compose your spirits, for, take my word for it, Mr. Frederic, she is much more in her right senses than you are."

These words were certainly not intended to convey the meaning assigned to them by the conscience-stricken man to whom they were addressed. Perhaps the good doctor was a little piqued at hearing his judgment concerning the amendment of his patient disputed. But Frederic Dalton listened to his voice as to that of the accuser whose office it was to announce his guilt to the whole world.

Amidst the whirl of terrible thoughts that now rushed upon him, the most distinct was that which suggested the idea that he might instantly be seized upon and conveyed to prison; but, too thoroughly bewildered by terror to have any judgment left as to what might still be the best chance of avoiding the fate which he fancied was before him, he rushed out of the room and the house with no definite idea of whither he was to go, and only bent upon leaving the spot where he then stood and the eyes that were then gazing on him.

This rapid progress through the open air, however, seemed to refresh his strength and calm his nerves; and he recovered sufficient self-possession to remember that, even if the eye of Martha had indeed witnessed his crime, there was still safety for him in flight, and still a resource in the plan proposed and the promises held out, by Ellen. There were numerous night-coaches and day-coaches to London, one of which would, he well knew, pass along the "High Street" within an hour; but he dared not meet the eye of any human being at that moment, and the only decision which his in part recovered faculties enabled him to come to was, that he would seek shelter and concealment amidst the copses, which, at a point not far distant from his father's house, skirted the river, and there remain till the darkness of night might enable him to pass through the village unseen. A few minutes' rapid walking brought him to the spot he sought, and there was something like relief to his throbbing temples and beating heart in the profound stillness of the place. There was little at that season to attract any one thither, though, when the thick hazel bushes, whose boughs even now formed an effectual shelter, were hung with nuts, there was scarcely a youthful foot in the parish that did not find its way to the spot.

"Here, at least I may breathe, and I may think!" he exclaimed, as he threw himself at his length upon the ground,—"here, at least, I shall be safe from the hateful glance of Martha Maxwell's eye."

So great was the relief of finding himself thus securely alone, and beyond the reach of hearing or seeing either such words as Ellen's or such looks as Martha's, that a feeling of luxury mixed, as he stretched himself on the cold, fresh, pathless grass, with the agitation that still made his heart beat and his temples throb.

"They have not hunted me to death yet," he murmured, with a ghastly laugh; "the game is not yet up with me, most beauteous Martha! … Hideous, spiteful fiend, and fury as thou art, thou shall not conquer me! There is much more to do, my lovely duchess sister, and my most peerless promised wife, before you succeed in your amiable schemes against me. Leave a declaration that I am a murderer! Oh! pretty Ellen, wise as beautiful, but madder than either! It was Miss Martha, perhaps, that put this clever notion in your head … No, no, my dears," and again he laughed, as he raised his head to look around, and cheer himself with the conviction that he was quite alone, "it shall be another sort of declaration I will leave to console you both for my absence. I will take good care to make my will and pleasure known to all my dear relations! … Here stay I till night shall come to shelter me, and then, off and away, wherever will and whim may lead me. It shall go hard with me if I do not find some spot of earth where I may still enjoy myself, where all that makes life loved and death abhorred may be had freely, without control, without restraint, and with no Ellen, no Martha, and no turbulent Jessie either, to cross my sight and blast me!"

Again he pressed his burning forehead to the earth, and again felt the relief of its cold freshness.

"But they shall hear of me," he again muttered to the tall grass that waved around him,—"they shall hear that the moment they cease to pay the tax I mean to levy on the family coffers for my existence in a distant land and under a borrowed name,—that moment shall be the last of their tranquillity … Let them refuse to honour a draft of mine, and they shall have me amongst them in a form they will not greatly love to welcome! … No, charming ladies, Frederic Dalton is not conquered yet!"

But the star of Frederic Dalton, in which now and ever he had so greatly trusted, appeared to be no longer in the ascendant. Scarcely had his troubled thoughts reposed themselves for a moment upon these distant hopes than he was startled by the sound of a step close behind him, and springing on his feet he descried the well-known figure of Silly Sally. Of all the human beings that it was possible his eyes could fall upon, this was perhaps the one he would have taken the least trouble to shun, yet the sound of her step, and the sight of her eye, was a dreadful shock to him.

The poor idiot wore an aspect much less cheerful than ordinary, for she had recently, poor creature! been made to understand that something very horrible was going to befall her favourite, her dearly beloved Jessie Phillips, in consequence of her having lost her baby—a species of offence concerning which it was considerably more easy to awaken her fears than any other, punishment having so often fallen upon herself for the same thing. It would scarcely be correct, perhaps, to say that Sally was tormented by feelings of positive remorse, because she was conscious that it was not Jessie, but herself, who had lost the baby; for such a phrase would express a more reasonable and settled state of mind than could with truth be attributed to her; but certain it is that she was suffering and fretting under glimmerings of reason, productive of feelings as nearly approaching such remorse as it was possible for one in her condition to do.

On seeing young Dalton, she sprang forward with a bound which brought her close to him in an instant, and, laying her hand upon his arm, she looked wistfully up in his face, and said, "The young squire won't let Jessie be whipped? The young squire kisses poor Jessie, and loves poor Jessie, and he won't let any body get hold of her, and shake her, and whip her, and put her to stand in the corner, and lock her up in the dark hole?" Then, lowering her voice, and looking carefully round, she added, "It wasn't Jessie, you know, that put away the baby; … it wasn't nobody a bit like Jessie that did that bad and wicked trick, was it?"

But the idiot laugh which accompanied these words sounded not in the ears of Dalton like what it really was, the laugh of imbecility, but as the taunting gibe of an accuser, whose voice was the ordained signal for his execution. All hope, all judgments all power of thinking, at once forsook him, and, vehemently pushing aside the girl, he rushed madly forward to the steep bank, which, at that point, bordered the little river, and plunged headlong into the stream. It was precisely here, if any where, that the rapid little rivulet deserved its epithet of "deep," but this circumstance would scarcely have been sufficient to render this desperate act one of much danger had not the depth been rather that of a sudden hole than of any more gradual variation in the bed of the stream. But Frederic Dalton, in spite of his star, was a doomed man, and the something which mortals call chance was singularly either for or against him, at this moment—according as such a life, or such a death, may be deemed preferable—for had Silly Sally happened to stand a very little either on one side or the other of the precise spot she occupied, his course would have been a little different, and that little would have sufficed to have made his plunge into the stream one that could scarcely have perilled his life for a moment. But so it was not to be. Before the rapid current could get possession of him and bear him onward in comparative safety, he was sucked down into a hole of some twenty feet deep, and, from some cause or other, rose not again till long after life was extinct.

The exertions of Captain Maxwell in the cause of Jessie were not in vain. He had wisely addressed himself to young Mortimer, to select the advocate most likely to conduct a difficult cause with skill; and so interested did that young man feel in the result, that he accompanied his older legal friend to the town which was to be the scene of his professional exertions. Perhaps the letter of Captain Maxwell might have mentioned the fact, that he, with his wife and daughter, intended to pass the period of the assizes at the county town, as Martha was so deeply persuaded of Jessie's perfect innocence, of intention at least, that she had implored too earnestly for permission to see the unhappy prisoner every day for either father or mother to have power or inclination to refuse her. Whether this information had any influence on the movements of Mr. Henry Mortimer, it is impossible to say, but it is certain that the judge and his legal train had not been many hours in the town before Mortimer was seated with his Deepbrook friends, Captain and Mrs. Maxwell, and their eccentric little daughter, Martha.

The reader knows, though the gallant captain and his lady did not, that Martha had really very much which it was important she should say to him, quite independent of any little personal observations respecting their mutual sensations at meeting again. But there was no inclination on the part of either parent to be troublesome. They had both, for some time past, made up their minds, after lovingly comparing notes together, that young Mortimer and Martha were very rapidly falling in love; and, as they saw nothing in this that would render it necessary for them to break through their long-established rule, of letting their daughter have her own way in all things, the captain soon recollected that he had business to look after in the town, and his lady, that her best bonnet would infallibly be ruined if she any longer delayed to inquire into its condition, after the dusty drive it had endured. So Martha and the young lawyer once more found themselves *tête-à-tête*. It was, however, but for one short instant that Martha remembered this, for her heart was really and truly too full of Jessie to leave her at leisure to think either of Henry Mortimer or of herself; and, promptly and decisively chasing the feeling, which for a moment had brought a very pretty blush to her cheek, she entered upon the cause of their thus meeting with all the zeal of her most zealous spirit. Mortimer knew her much too well to mistake her purpose, and after one short glance, in which perhaps there might have been a slight mixture of "the tender passion," he entered with her, heart and soul, into a full discussion of their poor client's condition. Martha related to him, without scruple or reserve, all that she had seen, suspected, thought, and finally believed, respecting young Dalton. She described her visit to Mr. Rimmington, and accurately repeated the arguments which had persuaded her that the emotion betrayed by Frederic did not warrant the interpretation she had put upon it. But the most important part of her communication respected her various interviews with Jessie, and the impression left on her mind by the statement she had received from her. To all this her friend listened with deep attention, and, well knowing the truthfulness of the narrator, he very soon adopted her opinion, that Jessie's own interpretation was the right one, namely, that she had herself caused her infant's death in a paroxysm of unconscious delirium.

"Now then, Mr. Mortimer," she said, as soon as she perceived that he saw the matter rightly, "let us not waste a moment. See your legal friend; arrange for his admission to his client, and go to her with him. You are now fully acquainted with the purport of all she has said to me during more than one quiet and deliberate conversation. It may be that, while conversing with the individual on whose exertions her life depends, she may be less clear, less distinct, than she has been with me; if this be the case, your presence may be of great use to her."

Henry Mortimer again gave her one glance that seemed to have nothing to do with poor Jessie, and then left her, having given her an assurance, but little needed, that nothing he could do to serve her unhappy *protégée* should he left undone.

What Jessie most hoped, or what she most feared, as the hour of the trial approached, it would be difficult to tell; but she displayed in her outward demeanour a degree of tranquillity that astonished all who approached her. Had a skilful physician been among these, it is possible that he might have discerned more symptoms of struggling against suffering, both of body and mind, than were perceptible to more ignorant eyes; but there was no symptom that seemed to call for medical advice, and therefore no such observations were made. On the evening preceding the trial, she desired to receive the sacrament, and, having been indulged in this wish, retired to her bed with an air of gentle serenity, which, had any eye witnessed it, might have given room for much conjecture as to its source. Yet, had the question been put to her, Jessie would have given an answer equally ready and true—she had sinned, she had repented—and hope was strong within her that her repentance had been accepted, and that she was forgiven.

It is needless to attempt giving any detailed account of a trial, in which no point either of law or fact was brought forward to startle, alarm, or in any way stimulate the curiosity of the reader. From a very early stage of the business, every one in the court became convinced that it must end in acquittal, on the plea of temporary insanity. The delicate features of the prisoner were ghastly pale; but this was so natural, under the circumstances, that it scarcely added a single sigh to the interest which the painful position of one so young and lovely was sure to excite. At one moment only did any circumstance occur, during the trial, which appeared to shake the steadfast calmness of her demeanour and this was purely accidental, and in no way connected with the business that was going on. During the whole of the proceedings, a stillness and decorum the most perfect had reigned in the court; but, when the judge had finished his charge, which was exactly every thing wished for and expected by the audience, and the jury had retired to decide upon their verdict, the silence was no longer so profound; whispering voices were heard in different parts of the court, but every where so subdued by proper feeling as to require no official interference to check it. Two persons, standing together so near the dock where the prisoner was seated as to render even this decorous whisper audible to her, took this opportunity of exchanging a few observations on a rumour which had just reached the town, and which stated that the body of young Squire Dalton had been found drowned in the river at Deepbrook. On hearing these words, Jessie started so violently as to draw upon her a multitude of eyes; but, as the words which had caused her emotion had not been heard, save by herself and the person to whom they had been addressed, and as she immediately pushed back the chair, which had been humanely allowed her, so as to conceal her face from the crowd, it was supposed by all that the movement was produced by the uncontrollable anxiety of her position, during an interval probably the most anxious to which the nerves of a human being can be exposed.

The moment at which Jessie Phillips had thus learned the death of her destroyer was in truth almost the earliest at which it was possible it could have reached her, for, till a very few hours before, his absence from his father's house had scarcely been known to half-a-dozen individuals out of it.

On recovering from the faintness which had followed her too agitating interview with her brother, Ellen had inquired the hour; and this inquiry she repeated from time to time till a late period in the evening, and then she added another inquiry, "Is my brother at home?" Being answered in the negative, and moreover informed that, though expected at dinner, he had not appeared, she settled herself on her pillow in an attitude of repose, and soon after fell into the most tranquil sleep that had fallen upon her for many days. No connexion, however, was dreamed of by any one between this sleep and the absence of her brother, neither did the circumstance of his not returning home excite any alarm there. He had many acquaintance in different parts of the county, to whom he was in the habit of making occasional visits; and, though it was usually his practice to mention such excursions before he set out upon them, the not doing so in the present instance produced little observation, and was probably attributed by the whole family to the fear of being told, if he did so, that Ellen was too alarmingly ill for any of the family to leave home with propriety. Thus, till his body was accidentally found, on the morning of Jessie's trial, by a party of boys who were fishing, no anxiety of any kind concerning him had been felt by his family.

Jessie Phillips had endured an immensity of suffering, and with a degree of resolute courage that none, perhaps, but Martha could understand. To others it is likely enough that she might have appeared desperately unfeeling; but to Martha, who knew right well that every pang which wrung that young heart was welcomed as a portion of the penance, to the humble endurance of which she looked as one means of reconciling her penitent spirit to a justly offended God, this unmurmuring calmness of endurance had something of the sublimity of martyrdom.

When the observant eye of Martha perceived the movement by which the countenance she had been so anxiously watching became concealed from her, she actually trembled with impatience for the announcement of the decision, which would enable her to hasten to the poor captive, whose patient spirit seemed subdued at last. The interval, though in truth but short, seemed to her immeasurably long; but, at length, the jury re-entered their box, and the universally expected verdict, NOT GUILTY, was pronounced in an audible voice. A murmur of very intelligible satisfaction ran round the crowded court, but the eyes of Martha sought in vain to ascertain how her poor Jessie, now no longer a prisoner, received it. "Let us go to her," said she, addressing herself by a look to both her father and Henry Mortimer, who were standing at each side of her. Both seemed to feel her right to have this natural wish complied with immediately, and, with her father's arm to support her, and the tall figure of young Mortimer preceding her as a pioneer, she was led with little difficulty through the crowd to the spot where she so ardently desired to be. Rapid as had been their passage from the place they had occupied to that they sought, they were not the first to enter it. The door was already open, and several persons were crowding round the object of their care. But the faces of those who could have entered there but to wish the rescued prisoner joy of her acquittal wore not the look of rejoicing, nor was there any sound that spoke of hope and thankfulness. A few whispered syllables, meaning she knew not what, met the ear of Martha as she entered, and then, her eager approach seeming to give her a right to precedence, two or three persons moved aside, and Martha Maxwell beheld the face of Jessie, scarcely more pale than when she had looked upon it last, but rigid in the stillness of death.

The curtain must now drop over the name of Jessie Phillips. Too weak, too erring, to be remembered with respect, yet not so bad but that some may feel it a thing to wonder at that she, and the terribly tempted class of which she is the type, should seem so very decidedly to be selected by the Solons of our day as a sacrifice for all the sins of all their sex. Why one class of human beings should be sedulously protected by a special law from the consequences of their own voluntary indiscretions, it is not very easy to comprehend; but it is more difficult still to assign any satisfactory reason why another class should be in like manner selected as the subject of special law, for the express purpose of making them subject to all the pains and penalties, naturally consequent upon the faults committed by the protected class above mentioned.

Not being, however, of those who conceive that the best mode of making laws for the well-being of society is by setting every individual composing it to work upon their formation, I will not venture any protest against this seemingly one-sided justice, beyond the expression of a wish that the unhappy class, thus selected for victims, were not so very decidedly, and so very inevitably, the weakest, and in all ways the least protected portion of society. There is no chivalry in the selection, and, to the eyes of ignorance like mine, there is no justice.

But little remains to be said of the persons of this village drama. Ellen Dalton was spared with careful tenderness the horror of knowing her brother's last act. Having told her father that she had promised to forward him money upon his consenting to go abroad till the unfortunate affair of Jessie Phillips was in some degree forgotten, Mr. Dalton gladly confirmed her in the belief that he was gone. The sentence of "not guilty," pronounced in vain, upon the unhappy Jessie, though she had died unconscious of it, removed from the spirit of Ellen the endless weight which would have rested on it had the sentence, though equally in vain, been otherwise; and no sooner did she hear it than the most devout thankfulness took possession of her heart, that her conviction of her brother's guilt had never been breathed but in the accents of delirium, save to the faithful Martha, who happily succeeded in persuading her, at last, that the sentence pronounced by the jury was, in fact, the correct one, and that all the terrible agitation they had remarked in her brother arose, as it very naturally might, from his horror at believing that the unhappy object of his unhallowed love was to pay by the horrors of a public execution for the sin of both.

As Ellen recovered from her very nearly fatal illness, she began to look back to all that she quite, and all that she half remembered, with a sort of indefinite vagueness and uncertainty which induced her to believe that much, or perhaps all, of the tremendous sufferings she remembered were caused, if not wholly, at least in great part, by delirium; and this idea, together with the revived happiness which now again awaited her, soon restored the delicate roses to her cheek, and once more made the faithful Pemberton feel that he was the happiest of men. But no sooner did Dr. H. assure her family that she was sufficiently restored to health to endure the fatigue of travelling without danger than it was decided that she should leave Deepbrook, in the hope that change of air and scene would remove the languor which still hung about her. When this decision was communicated to the family at the Castle, whose continuance there had been prolonged for some weeks beyond their proposed stay by her illness, the Duchess sought a conference with Mr. Dalton, in which she avowed to him that, if he and Mrs. Dalton would consent to it, they should on their side greatly prefer having the marriage, to which they were now again looking forward almost as eagerly as Lord Pemberton himself, celebrated abroad, as the want of state and retinue, to which for a while longer it was necessary they should submit, would on such an occasion be nowhere felt so painfully as at Rochdale. To this, of course, no objection could be made by the Dalton family, and Ellen hailed the arrangement with thankfulness, for neither the luxury of returning health, nor the deep happiness of the again brilliant future which opened before her, could wholly obliterate the feelings of sadness and of sorrow which the fate of Jessie had left upon her mind, and which almost every object that met her eye at Deepbrook tended to perpetuate. It was, therefore, in the chapel of the British minister at Florence that the gentle Ellen Dalton became Marchioness of Pemberton; and, when she had been for some months the happy wife of the man who had endured so much for her, she was told by her father that her brother had been some time dead, though all ceremony of outward mourning had been postponed till she could be told of it without danger to her greatly shaken nerves. Ellen was deeply shocked, but the delay in communicating the intelligence had enabled her to receive it with more composure than if it had reached her earlier. But even then it shook her fearfully; and all around her felt that, if it were possible, she should for ever live in ignorance of the manner of his death. Nor did it ever reach her, for none would ever willingly have caused a pang to a being so gentle. But this tender caution was a far greater kindness than any who practised it were aware, for, had Ellen ever heard the truth as to this, her thoughts would naturally have recurred to all that now seemed sleeping in oblivion, and, the fearful catastrophe might again have led her darkly to guess at a truth which must have in some sort obscured the enjoyment of her virtues and happy existence.

That young Mortimer and Martha Maxwell in due time became and and wife, must be already too well known to the intelligent reader for it to be at all needful to say any more about it here. The young man became greatly distinguished in his profession but this was not to be achieved without such a degree of devotion to business, as made both his elegant aunt and sister consider him exceedingly avaricious and altogether *mauvais ton*, which opinion very greatly contributed to the happiness of our friend Martha, who might otherwise have had considerably more of their society than she would have found desirable. But it was only when he became a judge, that this feeling of something between pity and contempt for a man who positively insisted that it was more desirable for him to live in Montague Place than in Grosvenor Street was overcome, and by that time Miss Agatha was married to a quiet country clergyman in a distant county, and Miss Mortimer began to suffer from a disagreeable redness in her face, which rendered her a good deal less particular about such matters than she used to be.

As for our very amiable Assistant Poor Law Commissioner, he remained in superintendence of the district of which Deepbrook made a part but a short time; for, in consequence of increasing intimacy with several persons thoroughly well acquainted with the state of the poor around them, and with what might, and what might not be done for them with advantage, he not only became deeply interested in their welfare, but decided on several occasions where his judgment and arbitration were appealed to upon no principle whatever but that of doing the most good that the circumstances permitted. This was unfortunately on more occasions than one, reported at head-quarters, where it was, as a matter of course, considered as exceedingly unphilosophical, to say the best of it; and once, when it was very clearly evident that, by advancing the sum of two pounds five and sixpence, he had actually kept a family of seven persons from coming upon the parish at all, he had been officially declared, though with great civility, to have been altogether wrong. As his general conduct, however, was not such as exactly to justify dismissal, he was permitted to retain his appointment; but all objectionable consequences which might have resulted from this were very ably and effectually guarded against, by constantly setting his judgment aside, whenever it appeared to lean towards common sense, in preference to the principles of the bill, and by removing him from one place to another with more than usual rapidity which in a very satisfactory degree prevented the possibility of his being useful any where.

---

The story of Jessie Phillips would have wandered less widely from what was intended, when the first numbers were written, had not the author received, during the time it was in progress, such a multitude of communications urging various and contradictory modes of treating the subject, that she became fearful of dealing too closely with a theme which might be presented to the judgment under so great a variety of aspects. The result of the information which has been earnestly sought for by the author, and eagerly given by many, appears to be that a new poor-law, differing essentially from the old one, was absolutely necessary to save the country from the rapidly corroding process, which was eating like a canker into her strength, but that the remedy which has been applied lacks practical wisdom, and is deficient in legislative morality, inasmuch as expediency has on many points been very obviously preferred to what the Christian law teaches us to believe right. Nevertheless, it appears evident that much of the misery so justly complained of might yet be remedied were a patient and truly tolerant spirit at work in *all quarters* upon the subject.

The constantly increasing evils arising from the attempt to generalise regulations upon points so essentially requiring variety of modification, as well as the radical mischief; and obviously demoralising effect, of substituting central, in the place of local authority, are already so strongly felt that it were a sin to doubt their ultimate reform; and on a subject both of such enormous difficulty, and such stupendous importance, it is quite evident that patience is equally required in those who make the laws and in those for whom they are made.

# THE END